THE TRUTH ABOUT CINNAMON

THE TRUTH ABOUT CINNAMON

A Novel

Cheri Laser

iUniverse, Inc.
New York Lincoln Shanghai

The Truth About Cinnamon
A Novel

iUniverse, Inc.

For information address:
iUniverse, Inc.
2021 Pine Lake Road, Suite 100
Lincoln, NE 68512
www.iuniverse.com

ISBN: 0-595-29973-3 (Pbk)
ISBN: 0-595-66093-2 (Cloth)

Printed in the United States of America

This book is dedicated to my daughter, Melissa Lynne, and to the conviction that no matter what anyone says, anything is still possible if you have the courage to dream—and if you get enough sleep.

Contents

Acknowledgements

In the beginning, various renderings of the manuscript were read by Lin Colby (who suffered through more versions than anyone else), Jim and Gerry Keyes (my precious parents), Elaine Walton Horsley (who can read my mind), Melanie Fomby (an all-weather friend), Denise Pierce (whose artistry contributed to the cover), Bob Laser (who pointed out that I'd forgotten to write an ending), and Tina Moskow (an editor whose early belief in me helped sustain the effort). To all those wonderful people, thank you for your support and honesty.

Bringing up the rear, the manuscript's latest adaptation was read and critiqued by Lucy Stamilla and Diane Menditto. The final edit would never have been possible without them.

References to the following self-study courses are factual: (1) American Dressmaking Step by Step—*The Pictorial Review Company* © 1917, and *Vintage Sewing Electronics Reference Library* © 1998–2002; and (2) The Nu-Way Course in Fashionable Clothes Making—*The Fashion Institute, Inc.*, © 1926, and *Vintage Sewing Electronics Reference Library* © 1998–2002.

PROLOGUE

Honolulu, Hawaii—May 20, 1953

"Who'd you have to kill?" Teddy joked, laughing into his scotch as he gestured around the club's lavish dining room.

Greg lowered his voice, his mischievous grin suddenly replaced by thin, tight lips that scarcely moved when he spoke.

"Excuse me?"

"Well, you must admit this is sort of luxurious for an Army man."

"Okay, Ted. Let's clear the air so the rest of our visit isn't as unpleasant as our dinner's turning out to be."

"Forget it. I'm going back to my hotel."

"No you're not. Not until we've finished this conversation."

Teddy began to feel something he'd never experienced during the lifetime he'd spent with Greg—fear. Responding to an unfamiliar instinct, he signaled the waiter.

"Please, may I have a glass of water, and the check?"

"Is there a problem, sir?"

"He's fine," Greg answered abruptly. "Probably stayed up too late last night discovering island women. Right, Ted?"

As the waiter backed away from the table, Teddy's apprehension accelerated. Fortifying himself by downing the last of his drink, he stared into the pale blue shadows of his cousin's eyes.

"Greg, my trip here was meant as a surprise—a cheer-me-up for the suffering troop, a goodwill mission bearing messages and trinkets from the family. Instead, *I'm* the one who's been caught off-guard. We've all had visions of you crawling through muddy trenches, dodging Korean bullets, grenades, mines, eating Army rations or dead things."

"Army rations and dead things are the same, Ted."

"Sorry, but I'm not in the mood for your clowning around."

"Believe me, I'm not kidding."

"Damn it, Greg! Will you listen to me? We've been crazy with worry about you. And Cinnamon's the worst. Not a day passes without her calling each of us to see if we've heard from you, since *she* obviously hasn't. Neither has Victoria, incidentally, which has only added to our concern. I guess that dropping a short note to your mother and wife hasn't been on your list of priorities. But I can see now that you've been rather busy. So, what would you like me to tell them? That you arranged to have me picked me up at the airport in a very large private car? Or that you're wearing a new diamond watch? Or that the people working here in this club seem to know you so well that they were cooking our meals before we even got here? Just exactly how would you suggest I explain this sudden elevation of an enlisted man with less than two years of service?"

As Teddy completed his outburst, another round of drinks was delivered.

"Well?" he queried again.

"Ted, you know what?" Greg asked, leaning back into the high curve of their booth. "We should be celebrating, not fighting. Don't you understand? I've finally discovered a way to escape the grip of our family—of my dear mother and wife—and I was hoping to share my good fortune with *you*."

"What the hell are you talking about?"

"I'm trying to tell you. This is the way *out*! Risk free. Do as you're told. No questions. Deliver the packages. I'm only a driver, but that's not important. *Everyone* will get rich."

"Greg! We already *are* rich. We've never wanted for anything in our lives!"

"Speak for yourself. I'm offering you a chance at something bigger than we ever imagined. Remember when we were kids..."

"Being kids together has nothing to do with any of this," Teddy interrupted."

"Fine. Think it over tonight. I'll call you in the morning."

"My plane leaves at noon, and I don't need to think about it. Whatever you're mixed up in has made you completely nuts! No matter how far back we go, I'm not going to be a part of whatever this is."

"Forget it, then. Just means more for me."

Their waiter appeared with the check and quickly departed, clutching an envelope handed to him by Greg. After finishing their drinks, they shook their heads at one another, as if to shrug off their irritation. But they had no further conversation as they left the restaurant.

Newspaper articles would later cite dinner patrons who'd overheard the cousins quarrelling, but who also recalled them smiling and walking shoulder-to-shoulder out the door. The family took small consolation, however, in knowing that Greg and Teddy had repaired whatever differences they'd encountered. As the men approached their waiting limousine that evening, a savage explosion rocked the street, shredding the automobile, imploding the restaurant's front windows, and scattering debris over the entire block. Despite the horrific devastation and injury, the miracle was—according to news reports—that only two people had died.

This is your life, of which you speak.
These are the loves you sought to earn.
Write it down so they'll remember.
Write it down, that they might learn.

And thus, I will continue.
M.E.M.S.

JUXTAPOSITION

Chapter 1

Albany, New York—October 3, 1988

Megan and Phillip Cole had been settled in the first class section of the aircraft for almost ten minutes when a crowd of passengers from a delayed connecting flight jammed the aisle. As the new arrivals unceremoniously stuffed personal belongings into overhead compartments, a staccato clicking of seatbelts punctuated the commotion. Phillip reached across the armrest for his wife's hand, and only then did he notice that she'd forgotten to remove the hospital identification band from her wrist. Megan followed his eyes, but seemed unconcerned, assuming that most civilized people wouldn't be rude enough to ask for an explanation.

But Phillip wished she would cover it up. Innocuous as the bracelet appeared, it symbolized for him the nightmare his family had just survived, and he wanted all remaining traces to be gone. He knew Megan wasn't quite at that point yet, however, having been an unwitting heir to the legacy that started everything. He recalled the uneasy pit in his stomach when his wife first flew up to her grandmother's bedside a mere three months earlier, and he was irritated with himself for not paying closer attention. He should never have allowed the situation to become so unmanageable. But the clarity of hindsight served only to frustrate him, and he forced himself to refocus on the positive points. Megan's three-day confinement at the Albany Medical Center was mercifully over, and she did seem to be rational again, for the moment at least. Furthermore, they were on their way home. *Home.* Just the sound of the word felt like a hot bath and clean sheets to him as he leaned back against the headrest and closed his eyes.

Megan's window seat afforded a view of nothing in particular while they remained on the ground at Albany's airport. Incongruously, growth had been introduced very slowly into New York's capital city and the surrounding Upstate areas. Even the airport appeared to have been plucked from a 1950's movie where progress had not yet unveiled jetway technology. Black and white images of Humphrey Bogart and Ingrid Bergman on a rain swept tarmac were easily rekindled in this setting, as she watched people leave the glass doors of the terminal and walk across the asphalt in the open air to the wide steps pushed up against their plane. *This is like looking through a time capsule,* Megan thought, *but somehow appropriate, in light of where we've been lately.*

When their 727 ultimately taxied, rushed, lifted and banked south toward Atlanta, she watched autumn's brilliant red and gold panorama unfold below her. On the ground, the colorful shift in seasons appeared to be nearing its end. But from the air, the landscape's bouquet lingered in full splendor and, as she'd expected, the plane's leveling brought her grandmother's estate into view. Even through dense clusters of trees, the compound was easily recognized. Complementing the historic Victorian house was lush terrain marked by a pond and fountain in front, and by three red barns originally built by her great-grandfather on the property in the 1920's. The largest of these weathered structures formed a triangle with the main residence and the guest cottage, and the sight of it awakened a series of uncomfortable images for her. Yet she felt a surprising serenity, almost as if nothing had happened there. Grateful to have been allowed this vista, she pressed her forehead against the window and peered straight down until the last edges of the estate disappeared beneath the plane.

"There! You see! That wasn't so bad," she said, turning to face her husband. "No reason for you to worry anymore, honey. In a couple of hours, we'll be home with our daughter, our dog and four tons of unraked leaves on the lawn. Normal—everything *normal.* On Monday I'll go back to work, and we can pick up our lives right where we left off. Well, fairly close, anyway."

"Just remember, Megan," Phillip's voice was soothing but firm, "we agreed to move slowly. These past three months have been pretty brutal, and you need to stay in one place for awhile."

How could it be that July was only three months ago? *July 11th—when Kenny first called me. I don't even feel like the same* <u>*person*</u> *I was then! I guess that's not surprising, though. In a sense, I've lived through another lifetime since that day.*

"I *will* need to come back fairly regularly, you know." Her reply wasn't at all what Phillip wanted to hear. "And I hope we can spend some of our vacations here, too," she persisted. "Oh, don't look at me cross-eyed, for heaven's sake. I'm not a lunatic, no matter what they told you. And besides, everything does belong to me now. There are just certain times of the year—especially fall and Christmas—when Fox Run is the most magical spot in the world. Let's not lose any of that. It's so important to salvage the good parts—for us, for Kristin, and especially for Gram."

"Okay," he yielded in a whisper, pressing an index finger against his left eyebrow to slow an annoying twitch.

Sensing that their conversation needed to be suspended for the moment, he began a mindless review of the in-flight magazine. Relieved at his withdrawal, Megan nudged her seat into a recline, closed her eyes and reflected upon her grandmother's tape-recorded voice.

"...I was born Margaret Elizabeth McClinty on January 26, 1906, in Albany, New York to Jonathon and Mary Mae McClinty..."

She tried to recall how Cinnamon had explained the plan to her. *Megan, dear, I've been thinking this through for more than thirty years...I know what I want to tell you, and I know exactly how I want to do it...All the words are carefully arranged in my mind...*

But how much had been embellished—or fabricated—by the matriarch's theatrics? Phillip kept asking her that question, yet somehow an answer wasn't important any more. The story that started as Cinnamon's on that July morning had become Megan's, exaggerations and all. The ancestors she never knew were now imbedded in her mind and soul as deeply as the blood that connected them to her. Despite her grandmother's penchant for drama, Cinnamon had gone to great lengths to put the rich heritage, and the truth, in Megan's hands. At the end of the day, as Megan had discovered, most of the drama had sadly turned out to be very real.

Realizing that her heart rate was accelerating, she kept her eyes closed and began the deep breathing the doctors had shown her in the hospital.

"Panic attacks can be controlled," they'd told her, "but you have to learn how to recognize the signals before they take hold of you."

It wasn't a panic attack. I don't know why they wouldn't listen to me. I'll be just fine as soon as we're home. Of course, it is true that part of me will never leave this old place—not anymore, now that I know everything.

Albany, New York—July 9, 1988

A sleek, black limousine, windows darkened and fog lights cutting through the mist, snaked through the quiet Upstate New York neighborhood. The street was trimmed on each side with white frame houses that had seen half a century of untamed winters. Those homes in need of a fresh coat of paint had, for the most part, just received it, and the front yards were as manicured as they could get. Gutters were clean. Potholes from last year's snow had been filled, and by all appearances, annual repairs and maintenance were on schedule.

Only a few cars seemed to be enroute anywhere on this Saturday morning, although an infinite line was parked against both curbs, significantly narrowing the already marginal two-lane road. Steady rain had been falling for three days accompanied by gale-force winds, and now the dripping air helped the extra-large vehicle appear less conspicuous than it would have been otherwise.

The scene was dreary in this village just outside Albany as the limo continued to a stop sign. Then, with one right-hand turn, the sedate residential strip exploded into five lanes of freeway traffic for the short ride downtown. Maneuvering with surprising grace, the automobile took the third exit, veered around several cars waiting at a traffic light, turned right and came to a stop at the corner of Broadway and State Streets. Slipping the car into neutral in front of Smith's R & R Pharmacy & Video, the driver issued an order to the man seated beside him.

"She wants six boxes of blank tapes, but make sure they're for audio—not video. Why we had to come all the way down to this place for 'em, I got no idea. She says to tell 'em it's her out here in the car, and there's not supposed to be any charge for the tapes, either. Go on, now. Holler if there's a problem."

The tiny old woman who'd issued those orders was barely noticeable in the rear seat. Staring at the gaudy neon sign, her large brown eyes with bright hazel specks still shimmered with mischief at the age of 82.

R & R Pharmacy and Video! What the hell is <u>*that*</u> *supposed to mean? Actually, it's pretty damn innovative,* she considered, *taking part of an old drug store and fixing up a bunch of shelves for videotapes! How in the world did Jarrett think of it? He never seemed that clever. Maybe it wasn't his idea. I wonder if he's dead and someone just forgot to tell me.*

The front seat passenger emerged from the store within minutes carrying a large satchel. He nodded affirmatively to the chauffeur, who turned off the engine, put the keys in his pocket and joined the other man behind the open trunk lid.

Curious passersby detoured around the limousine, casually trying to see through the windows, their movements catching the lady's attention and making her smile. *These nice people need to know there's no one famous in here, so they can be on their way. Well, as long as I'm down here, a stretch would feel good. And besides, I want to see that view again.*

"Barnes," she announced through the speakerphone when her chauffeur returned to the wheel, "I'd like to get out and walk for a bit."

"Mrs. Stafford, that's not a good idea. Your doctor wasn't happy about us takin' this ride in the first place. We promised him we'd only be gone an hour and that you'd stay in the car."

"Oh, hogwash! Is my doctor assuming responsibility for your salary now? I could have sworn that the last twenty years of pay and bonuses were a result of your employment with *me*."

"Yes, Mrs. Stafford, but..."

"But nothing! Come help me out of this car. I want to walk to the corner, and I want to walk there now!"

With a strapping man supporting her on either arm, the woman hobbled to the intersection of Broadway and State where she stopped and let her vision hike up the boulevard's sharp grade toward the Capitol building. As usual, the cityscape was breathtaking. State Street ascended for nearly a mile above her, the pavement leveling out briefly at each of the four intersections crossed before reaching the crest. Sitting on top of the hill and rising five stories was a massive stone structure reminiscent of a medieval French chateau. A cascade of steps half the height of the building seemed to pour out of the entrance. Construction of the old woman's favorite building began before the turn of the century and ultimately consumed twenty-five years, plus a full generation of workers who hauled granite blocks, marble, onyx and other materials up the incline. Now, more than nine decades later, the Albany Capitol remained one of the largest and most architecturally acclaimed in the country.

This view from the bottom of State Street inspired in her the same awe she'd experienced as a child, although she had not anticipated today's sadness. Most of the original buildings on either side of the roadway had been demolished and rebuilt since her recollections began in the early 1900's. Still, there were a number of familiar, surviving establishments. Several restaurants remained, and of course, there was Smith's R & R Pharmacy and Video. Overlooking the humor in Jarrett's commercial experiment, she began to cry. But her tears went unnoticed as they fell with the rain over the soft curves of her cheeks.

"All right, gentlemen. Let's go."

"Thank the Lord," mumbled Barnes.

"As my grandchildren tell me, dear fellow, you really need to lighten up! Where's the fun in life if you can't take a few chances?"

The limousine exited downtown via an alternate course. Barnes felt an urgent need to conclude this outing, and he guided the car back to the highway where he took the quickest route home. As he did so, Mrs. Stafford watched Albany's jagged skyline disappear through the rear window. Carefully planned though today may have been, she wondered if having the tapes delivered to the house might not have been a better idea. Her beloved city was so different than the one she remembered. But more disturbing to her than the changes she'd observed today were those that she knew she'd never live to see.

How very complex we are. We don't want to say good-bye, but we're forever complaining about this and that while we're here.

Barnes navigated south down the main road of the village, past the many homes once owned by friends of her family. Beyond the miniature post office, the antique store and the ice cream shop, the car skimmed by several country blocks, then turned into a private driveway bordered by a pond on the right and a chain of evergreens on the left. A stately white Victorian house was centered in the twenty-five acres of land.

When the car had come to a stop under the columned portico, the front passenger unloaded the tapes from the trunk while Barnes opened the rear door and held out his hand for the silver-haired matron.

"Thank you very much," she said, as if in response to a question, "but I'd like to sit here a bit longer. Please tell Heidi to brew some tea, and please ask David to join me."

"Mrs. Stafford, with all due respect, you can't stay out here. You need to go inside and rest. I'm afraid I'll have to be firm about this."

"You have many admirable qualities, Barnes, but you couldn't be firm about the damn time of day. Now, let me say this once more. I'm staying in the car until I'm good and ready to do otherwise. I want my tea, and I want David. Have I made myself clear?"

"Yes, Mrs. Stafford. Quite."

Settling back against the leather cushions, she waited while her instructions were being followed.

Why didn't I come up with this inspiration before? I really haven't left myself very much time. Maybe David can give me some suggestions to speed things along. First I need to get Megan up here. She's the most logical choice, and I know I can trust her to do what must be done, no matter how objectionable my directions will appear to her in the beginning.

Resting inside the limousine's cocoon, she was welcoming an untroubled sense of balance when, without warning, her chest felt as if it were being crushed. An unrelenting pressure was suddenly squeezing the air out of her body, and blades were violently stabbing at the remnants of her strength. She tried to fight back against the invisible assailant, but her frantic attempts to grasp the door handle were thwarted by surges of pain pumping through her arms and fingers, rendering her immobile.

Dear God, I can't breathe!

Drifting into a velvet darkness, she didn't see Heidi approaching the car. Nor did she hear the silver tray crash to the ground, scattering broken pieces of her china tea service across the asphalt. Oblivious to the chaotic activity erupting around her and to the anxious voices shouting commands, she was rushed by ambulance to the Albany Medical Center. David then placed an emergency call to Kenneth, just like he always did. Even in the absence of her personal direction, the pattern unfolded automatically. Everyone knew what to do. A decade of rehearsals had obviously been worth the effort, and she would have been pleased with the continuity.

July 11, 1988

The weather in Atlanta, Georgia had moved well beyond uncomfortable. Rain had been hammering the city for more than a week, and even at this early-morning hour, the merciless humidity was oppressive as indoor lights switched on throughout the upscale neighborhood. Steam was rising from the brick terrace and cement driveway, creating an eerie mist around the immense Greek Revival residence, nearly obscuring from view the four columns on the front of the house and the wide, freshly decorated veranda. Wrapped in hazy shadows, the home built by Megan and Phillip Cole had just survived eight months of construction and was settling into its place of honor surrounded by a thick expanse of hardwoods and pines. Despite the recent completion and faint remnants of hard-hats and porta-potties, images of a plantation emerging unscathed from the Civil War were not hard to visualize in the filmy air.

Having awakened just before dawn, Megan emerged from the kitchen's side door dressed in what used to be a sweatsuit before she cut off the arms at the elbows and the legs just above the knees—an alteration technique she'd learned from her sixteen-year-old daughter. Sprinting between her feet and leaping across a freshly planted flowerbed was a peach-colored blur about the size of a large pot roast. Phillip had insisted on naming the dog Buck, claiming an attachment to the animal in Jack London's Call of the Wild. Megan had initially voiced her objection, thinking the name *Buck* was ridiculous for a pet that would, at full maturity, weigh no more than eight pounds. But she'd learned how to choose her battles after nearly twenty years of marriage.

While the dog nosed around, she sipped her coffee and strolled leisurely toward the gazebo, savoring the solitude. As a young girl, she'd envisioned this setting in a dream—a magic, secret island on top of a hill belonging exclusively to her. Translating the dream into reality had not been simple, although none of those tedious details lingered in the stillness. In fact, most of life's frustrations seemed easier to handle in this house, perhaps because she and Phillip felt so triumphant after earning their way here. No one, not even her grandmother, with whom she shared her headstrong Irish temperament, had expected her to attain such heights. *Many* people had been derailed by underestimating Megan, or by predicting only modest professional achievements for her, because they didn't understand the power of her imagination. If she could first envision an objective in her Technicolor mind, she would figure out a way to make the event materialize, whether or not anyone *else* believed it could happen. Although she did miss an occasional target, none was a significant milestone, and her flourishing career in administrative management silenced most of her skeptics.

Disguised as the assistant to someone important, she and her new Bachelor of Science Business Degree had originally been housed in a basement cubicle. Now, almost twenty years later, she carried full operational and fiscal responsibility for a department of more than one hundred employees supplying what was referred to as *bread-and-butter support* throughout every segment of the company. Her people were computer operators and programmers, private assistants to upper management, and office technology specialists who handled everything from document creation to complex spread sheets and electronic mail distribution. She'd been on the leading edge of helping decentralize data processing to allow the functional areas more independent control over their costs and productivity. To the chagrin of her naysayers, her innovations were projected to save the company hundreds of thousands of dollars over the next two years. While she knew that deals and money would somehow find a way to flow with or without her organization, she also understood that higher volumes of both elements flowed faster and more efficiently because she and the members of her team were in place. Her superiors knew this, as well, and she was amply compensated for her contributions.

Megan Elizabeth Cole had, indeed, reached many of her professional goals. But since the move into their new home, her workday had grown shorter. Rather than leaving the office several hours after dark on more evenings than not, she now found herself heading toward the parking lot by 6:00. For the first time in her adult life, she'd begun to tire of slaying dragons. The battles had grown tougher and the stakes higher, especially since corporate allegiance as a concept had edged closer to extinction. The older and more seasoned she became—and the more pressure she felt to penetrate the glass ceiling—the less energy she found in reserve.

The only female in her classification when she was first hired after college, she'd watched as her male counterparts all defected over the years. A considerable number of them were either in top positions at other companies now, or successfully self-employed. She, on the other hand, was the sole survivor of her entering class at Strategic Data. She'd spent the *first* five years of her career making the seemingly obvious point that adding the roles of wife and new mother to a woman's professional agenda would not necessarily be fatal to any project assigned to her. She'd been fortunate that no unforeseen interventions had proven her wrong. What's more, once the men began finding more fertile business pastures in every new Classifieds section, her own position in the company became more solidified, due in no small part to her loyalty. Nonetheless, she'd forfeited a great deal of competitive mileage along the way, not to mention the aggravation she'd learned to digest.

In those early years, though, there wasn't any spare time to analyze issues of inequity or gender imbalance. Her choices about work and the subsequent crush of her daily schedule had been dictated by economic need. Later, once her family's finances had stabilized, she was too busy and having too much fun to feel oppressed. Now she found herself among a handful of females in her company still left in the race, and upper management was suddenly encouraging her to accept the vice president's position soon to be vacated. The attention was flattering, but she almost felt as if she were being patronized—or worse, that no other candidates were interested in the job. After cautiously reviewing the offer with Phillip, she had politely declined. Instead of eliminating her from whatever list her superiors were using, however, her refusal only appeared to further tantalize them. Enhanced compensation and bonus incentives had been added to the lure, and she'd been given another sixty days to reconsider.

Why couldn't this have happened to me when I was craving all that responsibility and power, she wondered, noticing Kristin's bedroom light turn on upstairs. "Time to go, Buck," she announced in a tone that brought the peach ball leaping across the flower bed once again, his tummy grazing a few blossoms beyond recovery. "Let's get today started. I'll meet you back here tonight."

The old woman had not yet opened her eyes but couldn't miss the unmistakable scent of fresh Irish linens swirling around her. Someone had lifted her window slightly higher than normal, allowing Albany's Northeaster winds to whip around the bedroom unimpeded, urging her to awaken.

"Where *is* everyone anyway?" she wondered aloud. "And what time is it?"

As the strength of consciousness began to take hold and the room came into focus, she saw her lace runner from the bureau lying on the floor, apparently blown there along with drifts of papers from her writing desk. Reaching for the bell on her nightstand, she heard the jarring pitch of three passionate male voices coming from downstairs. Easily identifying each of them, she elected to eavesdrop rather than ring for assistance.

"What the hell is she *doing* here? Who made the decision to bring her home, and on whose authority?"

The angry voice belonged to Kenneth Stafford, a handsome young man in his thirties who had just been ushered into the house by a blast of wind. He was completely disheveled and looked as if he'd used an eggbeater to brush his hair. With his blue silk tie upended over his right shoulder, he paced back and forth in front of the white marble fireplace as he awaited some sort of response from the two elderly gentlemen who were watching him.

Seated on a weathered brown velvet loveseat opposite the fireplace, his uniform somehow crisp despite the heat, Barnes Osgood was one of those gentlemen. At sixty years old, Mrs. Stafford's driver looked almost boyish, his cap poised in his lap, even though he knew he was in a great deal of trouble. His companion in crime was David McClinty, a vintage character in his late eighties, who perched precariously on the arm of a wing chair to the right of Barnes. Dressed in a dark blue, three-piece suit with a heavy gold watch chain draped over the vest's fourth button, his face was sagging and his neck had thinned so much that his starched white shirt collar appeared several sizes too big. But David's translucent blue eyes and square jaw prevailed as dim reminders of his youthful good looks, in the midst of the shrinking, wrinkled rest of him. Sitting quietly, he gripped his knees to keep his massive hands from trembling.

"Well? Do either of you plan to answer me?" Kenneth asked. "Or have you both suddenly lost your hearing along with your minds? *Who* decided to bring her home?"

"You need to calm down, Ken," David responded in a raspy voice. "I might have fifty years on you, but I swear I'll outlive you if you can't learn to control your temper! And if you must know, *I'm* the one who arranged to have her discharged. Waking up two mornings inside that hospital would have killed her!"

"Oh, I see, David. We're suddenly concerned about her longevity, are we? Well, what was that little stroll up State Street? Don't tell me. Let me guess. She was just warming up for her aerobics class! For God's sake, gentlemen," he shouted, pacing again, "the woman is eighty-two years old. And maybe—just *maybe*—she'll make it to her next birthday *if* she has constant bed rest and *if* she's living in a peaceful, quiet atmosphere. But no! We have to take her for a limousine ride through the city where, by the way, it seemed like a good idea to go for a little walk in mid-day traffic. And then, after her heart nearly gave in to the odds, we checked her out of the hospital one day later because we thought that if she woke up there too often it would kill her. Do you have any idea how absurd that sounds?"

"With all due respect, Kenneth, sir," Barnes interrupted, "Mr. McClinty here didn't have anythin' to do with the drive downtown. Mrs. Stafford said she felt like takin' a ride 'cause she hadn't had fresh air in weeks. Said she wanted to see how the city looked these days. She also needed to pick up that bunch of tapes she'd been talkin' about. So we called Dr. Coomey, and he said we could go as long as someone went with us. I took the new fellow who's been helpin' me out 'round here. Everythin' was fine 'till she said she wanted to walk. I tried to tell her not to, but you know how she can be. We only went to the corner so she could see the Capitol."

"In a raging downpour, of course," Kenneth replied, his voice more restrained as he sat down on top of the coffee table in front of the old men.

"Yes, sir," Barnes answered sheepishly, his eyes fixed on the faded Oriental rug beneath his feet.

"Look," Kenneth continued. "I realize how much you both love her. I love her, too, in case you haven't noticed. Hell. I even love *you* guys! But we all agreed a long time ago that, with Aunt Claudine traveling to God-knows-where, and with Megan in Georgia, I'm the one officially responsible for Gram's care. The objective is to avoid any further catastrophes, admittedly a challenge when it comes to her. But you need to call *me* in the future before any decisions are made about her—not Doctor Coomey. I'm sure he has good intentions, and forgive me if this sounds harsh. But a physician in his nineties is apt to make a few errors in judgment!"

"He's only an advisor these days," David said weakly. "She has a team of specialists looking after her."

"Yes. I'm aware of that. But Coomey seems to be the one consulted on things like your little excursion, and look what happened."

"That could have hit her anywhere," Barnes chimed in. "She was being watched over by folks who care about her. It's not like she was assaulted."

"I'm sorry," Kenneth responded, ignoring the chauffeur's plea, "but I think I'm going to move her someplace where emergency facilities are close at hand. I promise she'll be comfortable."

"She'd rather be dead," David whispered.

Just then the hollow clang of an old school bell sounded from a room off the top landing. The three men remained frozen for an instant, eyes locked together, before Kenneth rushed upstairs. While Barnes waited anxiously in the parlor, David followed behind Kenneth, hugging the mahogany banister for support as he was passed by a flurry of white that he recognized as the nurse. Then he heard his favorite familiar voice coming from the floor above him, *complaining as usual,* he thought to himself.

"Just look how things have been tossed all around this place!" she was saying. "And how did the damn window get open so far to begin with?

David continued to slowly ascend the staircase, struggling to make his way to her. *Thank you for letting me keep her a little bit longer.* After reaching the top step, he pulled a handkerchief from his pocket and carefully blotted any evidence of emotion from his face before entering her room.

"Hello, Mr. Cole. How good to see you! Will you be lunching alone today?"

"No, Clifford. A gentleman will join me shortly—a Mr. Leandro. He and I have never met, so I'll appreciate your assistance when he arrives."

"Will he be wearing a red carnation, sir?"

The maitre d's repressed wit was evident in his eyes and was not wasted upon Phillip Cole, a respected patron of the Atlanta Brigade Towne and Country Club.

"Perhaps," Phillip responded playfully. "But if not a carnation, he might have a rose clenched between his teeth. He *will* ask for me, though, which should give us both a reasonable clue to his identity."

"Of course. I'll remain on guard. Meanwhile, will your bay window table be suitable?"

"Yes. That'll be fine."

"Very good. I can seat you right away."

Clifford-the-maitre d' sashayed ahead, his tuxedo encasing him in formality. Phillip followed with long, measured strides as he canvassed the room. Once seated, he ordered a scotch on the rocks and leaned back in his chair.

Membership in this club, with its richly paneled decor and four-star dining facilities, provided him enormous gratification and a choice environment for both professional and social occasions. Celebrating his fifty-first birthday here one month earlier, he and a dozen of his associates toasted the blessings of this restrictive enclave—a rare and steadfast bastion of masculine sovereignty. His wife Megan did not share his appreciation, however, and spoke with open contempt about the exclusivity of Brigade's all-male membership. She was appalled at such blatant chauvinism and threatened to fuel a civil liberties campaign against the organization. But fortunately, her career left little time for her to follow through with such threats.

For twenty years since their wedding in 1968, Phillip had observed his baby-boomer wife, who was now forty-two, as she passed through a series of annoying phases, along with her friends from the Woodstock generation. He believed he'd been very tolerant while she'd balanced herself on the periphery of feminism, continually flirting with radical concepts yet keeping her distance from militants and protest signs. All the same, his alliance with this club had inspired more than a few arguments between the two of them. Although Megan had, from the beginning, been granted full access to the facilities, she'd refused to take advantage of them unless permitted to purchase a membership in her own name. This was, of course, impossible, as Phillip had tediously reiterated. Her stubborn attachment to the issue confounded him, along with her insistence on conducting her own business luncheons inside *diners* rather than within these classic surroundings.

But he did extend much credit to her—albeit privately—for periodically suspending her opinions and appearing at his side during club functions of importance to him. Despite her convictions, she'd never embarrassed him or let him down. He, in turn, allowed her to extort from him an occasional evening at some rock-a-billy establishment where the loud music inevitably gave him indigestion, if the food failed to do so.

Their practice of artful compromise was a hallmark of their marriage and was disrupted only once in a while by Megan's omnipotent family. Occasionally her work got in the way as well, leaving him home alone with their daughter more evenings than he would have preferred. But at least he and his wife were still together, unlike so many of their friends who'd given up the fight. On the verge of irritating himself with these unnecessary thoughts, he was relieved to see Clifford strutting across the dining room with a pinstriped man in tow. Sliding his chair back, Phillip rose to his full six-foot-three-inch height as the maitre d' and guest arrived at the table.

"How do you do, Mr. Leandro—and welcome."

"Thank you, Mr. Cole. This is a great pleasure indeed."

Phillip's vigorous appearance belied his age and was enhanced even further by his seemingly indestructible crop of Kennedy-esque hair. Mr. Miles Leandro was not as fortunate, having but a few smokey wisps left to smooth. Notwithstanding this contrast, Phillip suspected that he and his guest were not too many years apart.

Clifford dashed off to retrieve Phillip's overdue scotch, plus a brandy ordered by the newcomer, leaving the two businessmen to their rites of acquaintance. Predictable comments about Atlanta's thunderstorms and summer humidity, the lackluster performance of the city's professional sports teams, and favorable economic forecasts for the metropolitan area helped shape an amiable framework. Once their beverages had been delivered along with the day's menu selections, they raised their glasses in a friendly toast.

"You look very familiar to me, Mr. Cole. Have we met somewhere before?"

"First of all, please call me Phillip. I have enough trouble with my daughter's friends calling me *mister*. And no, I don't think we've met before. But at my age, I don't have the same confidence in my memory that I used to."

"Are you originally from Atlanta?"

"Actually, Miles, I spent most of my life in Excelsior, Minnesota. Took a summer job in Minneapolis after high school, and dated a few young ladies there, but didn't travel much outside the area while growing up. Even graduated from the University."

"Hmmm. I always thought Nordics were supposed to be some of the finest navigators in the world. How did you end up way down here?"

"Actually, the whole thing was a fluke. One of my fraternity brothers married a Southern Belle after we finished graduate school. I came to Atlanta for the wedding and flew home with a job offer in hand. The father of one of the bridesmaids was looking for a greenhorn with an eye for Finance. Guess I fit the bill, since I started working for him a week later and never left."

"And whatever happened to the bridesmaid?"

"Indeed," Phillip responded with a smirk, beginning to feel more comfortable with this man. "I do think her father had additional alliances in mind, but she and I developed independent interests shortly thereafter."

"Please excuse me for interrupting, Mr. Cole, but there's an urgent call for you."

Clifford handed Phillip the cordless phone then pranced away from the table and, with a theatrical wave of his arm, signaled his assistant for refills at the bay window table.

"Hello. This is Phillip Cole."

"Well, hello to you, too, Mr. Cole, you gorgeous hunk of a man! This is your wife, and I *do* hope I've caught you in a terrifically sensitive Club Moment where the global monetary balance could be swayed by the impending phone sex I'm about to force upon you."

"Megan! What a surprise! Are you at work?"

"Well, gee. Probably not. I don't think I've ever done this at work before. Have you?"

"No, and I'm afraid I'll have to call you later when *my meeting's over*, dear."

"Wonderful! My timing's perfect. Sorry I barged in. Actually, that's not even remotely true. When I found out where you were, I couldn't resist calling to annoy you. So, how am I doing?"

"Quite well," he answered, glancing uncomfortably at his guest. "And there will be ample time to discuss it further, I can assure you."

"Great. But first, what would you like for dinner tonight—meat, fish, poultry, vegetables, or some combination?"

"Excuse me?"

"Name your poison, darling."

"You decide," he said in a lowered clipped tone. "I need to go now."

"Tell you what. I have budget reports to finish—should be through by seven. How about if I pick Kristin up from her cheerleader tryouts and you stop off for

Chinese takeout. Just get our regular orders. We'll all be home by eight. Sound good?"

"Whatever. See you then."

"Hey, you! Put your clothes back on. I love you."

Miles lifted his eyes toward Phillip and grinned as he finished his drink.

"My apologies for the interruption," Phillip offered, placing the phone on the table and hoping the flush would soon drain from his cheeks. "So, where were we?"

"We were talking about bridesmaids, and about how you became a transplant. Actually, I'm one, too, you know," he added. "Spent most of my life in New York, but had a brief tour of Fort Benning when I was activated during Vietnam. Met Barbara on a weekend pass to Atlanta and married her before they shipped me off to Southeast Asia."

Clifford approached the table again and with the smooth, effortless movement of a pickpocket, lifted both menus without breaking his stride or saying a word. After a nod from Phillip, he walked directly to the kitchen and ordered two Specials, each including a large mixed salad with creamy dill dressing, grilled halibut steak, steamed broccoli in clarified butter, and a smothered baked potato. He also threw in a double basket of freshly baked bread on the house after ordering yet another round of drinks.

"What part of New York are you from, Miles?"

"Upstate. Just outside of Albany."

"You're kidding! That's my *wife's* hometown. Most of her family still lives up there."

"Seriously? I don't usually run into folks from that part of the country. Have they been there very long?"

"Since the first boat landed from Ireland. At least, that's the McClinty lore."

"McClinty. I've heard the name. Albany might be New York's state capital, but it's still a very small town where old Irish families are fixtures—much to the chagrin of old Italian families, and vice versa I'm sure."

"What a puzzle, don't you think? You'd figure that with something as significant as the Catholic Church in common, they'd find a way to embrace each other more readily."

"That, my friend, is a dialogue for those much braver than I. Holy wars—one of my favorite oxymorons—have seldom been explained in simple terms, much less calmly or rationally. Something akin to marriages," Miles added, the twinkle in his eyes still dominant. "By the way, how did you and your wife meet, if you were here and she was in Albany?"

"We both blame it on her employer," Phillip answered with a smile, before taking a sip of the fresh scotch and water just delivered by Clifford. "Strategic

Data's corporate offices are here in midtown, along with the company's training facilities. I was on contract with the company to conduct a series of finance seminars, one of which was designed for newly hired managers. Megan attended a three-day session and was hard to miss in the class since she was the only woman. I know I should be ashamed of myself, but I tricked her into giving me her phone number in Albany. A year later, the company transferred her to Atlanta. Then we were married, etcetera, etcetera."

"Nice story," Miles said. "Congratulations."

"Yes. Well, that's enough of *that*," Phillip replied, a little embarrassed that he was talking so much. "Our lunch will be here shortly, Miles, so speaking of finance, perhaps we should begin discussing how my firm might be of assistance to you."

Glenda Avery was Strategic Data's senior receptionist, but that title did not begin to describe her superiority on the high-tech switchboard. Her skills commanded such inordinate respect that her co-workers playfully referred to her as The Processor. Manipulating the massive communications network as if it were an orchestra, she directed every link and controlled every connection. Each lighted button represented a call needing to be transferred somewhere inside the eight floors of Atlanta's corporate headquarters. There were five hundred potential choices. A control panel allowed her to make decisions—hold for *location determination*, transfer to *secretary*, transfer to *message* or *word processing center*, transfer to *security*, transfer to *president*, signal *security*, and more. On average, thirty buttons were routinely illuminated at any given moment, and a key measurement of customer satisfaction was intercepting the lights before they flashed three times.

Her dark hair pulled into a ponytail and tied with a silk scarf coordinated with her outfits, Glenda looked like she'd been plucked from the 1950s. But she was clearly a contemporary master of her trade. Her long claret-colored nails strummed the computer console in a stream of motion, her headset framing her face as her professionalism rose above the crises that changed in complexity from one minute to the next. She loved the challenge behind every light, and she deftly siphoned any anxiety from the faceless voices giving life to the electronics and metal surrounding her.

Strategic Data recognized Glenda's intrinsic value and rewarded her with a paycheck she'd have a hard time duplicating anywhere else. But what she cherished most was her reputation inside the company—something she'd built by herself, for herself, in a job no one else wanted. Today had not been out of the ordinary for her thus far. Everyone's call was a priority. Everyone had a *major* problem. But when she heard the gravity in the bold, husky voice announcing an emergency for Megan Cole, Glenda believed the man.

"One moment, please."—HOLD FOR LOCATION DETERMINATION—

"Janice, where's Megan?"

"Sorry, Glenda. She's in the Boardroom."

"The Boardroom? She didn't tell me there was any big meeting this afternoon."

"I don't think she knew. From what I can tell, *nobody* did. Whatever's going on came up after lunch. Now the room is full, and I have orders not to interrupt."

"Sounds intriguing, but I have a fellow on the line with an emergency call for Megan. Believe me, the guy's serious."

"You'd better be right, or you owe me a drink at Homer's."

"Trust me, Janice. If I ever get one wrong, I'll treat you for a month. But at the moment, I have work to do."—CALLER ON LINE—"Yes, sir. Sorry to keep you holding. Ms. Cole is in a meeting, but she should be with you shortly. I'm going to transfer you now to the Executive Offices. If you run into any problems, or if no one picks up in a minute, just press zero on your touch-tone pad, and then ask for Glenda."

Ushered into a private room a few moments later, Megan focused nervously on the telephone at the far end of the empty conference table. She'd never received an emergency call at work before, and the potential reasons were listing themselves in her head while she walked the length of the room, as the door closed behind her.

"This is Megan Cole. May I help you?"

"Hi, Meg."

"*Kenny*? What in the world? Are you okay?"

"Yes, I'm fine. I hate to tell you this, but I've already put it off as long as possible. It's Gram again."

"Kenneth James Stafford!" she exclaimed, following a pause mixed with more relief than anger. "I thought we made a deal after that last fiasco. As I recall, we agreed to talk rationally about any summons she might issue *before* we panic and rearrange our schedules. Good grief! I simply don't have time for this."

"I know you're frustrated, but quiet down and listen for a minute. I wouldn't have called if I hadn't already checked things out. This is your favorite cousin, remember? Your buddy? Your pal? And believe it or not, some of the rest of us have careers, too. Honey, she went for a joy-ride with Barnes, and we nearly lost her. Long story, but her heart gave out completely for a couple of critical minutes. Now she's really bad—although, naturally, she refuses to go back to the hospital. Looks like M-A-S-H inside the house at Fox Run. And she wants a special audience, *immediately*, with you—you lucky devil. So, I've made a reservation for you on the 5:30 flight tonight. Gets in about 8:00. Barnes and I will pick you up at the airport."

"I beg your pardon? Kenny, you can't be serious. Is this a joke?"

"No, Meg. I promise it's not."

"Well, for your information, the meeting you interrupted involves a major corporate reorganization being announced as we speak—while I am out of the room, by the way, on this idiotic phone call. You and Gram are both nuts if you think I'm going to hop on a plane like I used to do. Her timing is way off on this one, and so is yours. But tell her I'll call her tonight. I'm sure she'll understand. Besides, she's probably just depressed because her phony attempts to get us all up there for a party haven't worked for over a year."

Knowing her better than she thought he did, he was calculated in his silence.

"Oh, Kenny," she continued after several hushed seconds, "I don't mean to be so crotchety with you. You've done more than your share of Gram-sitting. But frankly, I don't believe her anymore. You know I'd be there in a second if I thought something was really happening to her."

"You have to trust me." He tried not to dwell on the odds of her buying that line. "And I agree with you. It seemed like another ploy to me too, at first. But I'm watching the situation up-close-and-personal, so please do me a favor and call Dr. Coomey. After you've spoken with him, you can make whatever decision feels best to you. If it's the wrong one, I'll absorb the total cost of my medical expenses after facing our grandmother with the news of your defection."

"And what about my mother?" Megan asked, ignoring the image he was trying to paint. "Has Gram asked that she be there, too?"

"As a matter of fact, I *am* supposed to find her. But her itinerary is a bit—well, it's a little difficult to pin down. I'm doing my best, though. Got any suggestions?"

Megan's mood sobered even further at the thought of her mother's rather indelicate escapades since becoming a widow, and of her subsequent estrangement from Gram, which had kept her whereabouts a moving target for the last six years.

"No. No suggestions. Forgive me for being such a brat. Rounding up my mother shouldn't be one of your problems."

"Megan, you've always been a brat. It doesn't bother me any more. And besides, finding Aunt Claudine is more important to me than your personality flaws. But now I need to know your answer."

"What was the question again?"

"Can I count on you?"

"Oh, all right. I'll call Dr. Coomey. If he's convincing enough, I'll try and work in a trip up there early next week. Okay?"

"Well, that's an improvement, Meg, but not exactly what I had in mind. You see, I need you here tonight, not next week."

Phillip hung up the phone in disgust. An intercom buzz from his secretary and a knock on the door were ignored until they eventually went away. Those closest to him in his business were obviously more sensitive than the members of his wife's family, all of whom seemed happiest when they were trespassing upon the inner sanctum of his life.

Megan had just called after speaking with her cousin Kenneth, one of her more tolerable relatives who owned a prosperous chain of dry cleaning stores in the Albany area. Based on Ken's report, Cinnamon was gravely ill—again. Cinnamon, the supreme conspirator, was *always* pretending to be ill, and now the entire family was being convened yet again. As usual, Cinnamon wanted to see Phillip's wife more than anyone else. Megan was the only female of the three grandchildren, but she was also Cinnamon's namesake—*the carrier of her torch*, he thought cynically, baffled that the old woman still knew how to make everyone dance so readily. He'd assumed that no one took these bogus emergencies seriously anymore. But after calling other members of the family to sound them out, he'd learned that they were all going to Albany despite their skepticism.

"Always a great party," they'd said, and, "You never know! Wouldn't want to be counted absent when the time actually comes."

There'd been so many final events, so many curtain calls. Granted, Cinnamon *had* suffered various maladies off and on, but her condition had never been life threatening. Eventually the family caught on, but not until after several alarming occasions, over a ten-year period, when the lonely matriarch used predictions of her impending death to assemble family reunions. Upon arriving to pay their last respects, everyone—her daughter, grandchildren, cousins, and friends of them all—was greeted with champagne, elaborate displays of food, and a party atmosphere in concert with Cinnamon's melodramatic spirit. She simply wanted to see the people who were special to her, and she knew that she, alone, had the power to bring them home. But this time, the pattern seemed to be breaking up. Her power remained intact, but her tenacious hold on life appeared to be slipping away.

"It's all so sad," Megan sighed to Phillip over the telephone. "Can you imagine how lonely *David* must feel? How will he ever manage without her?"

"Maybe he won't have to face it just yet, honey. Remember, no matter what Kenny said, you won't know how real this is until you get there."

"You don't mind if I go?"

"Of course not," he lied.

Besides, his feelings were irrelevant. Cinnamon's influence had been so compelling for so long that *his* power was secondary. He did take comfort, though, in his practiced ability to handle these disruptions. What unsettled him was the difficulty his wife would have if something *did* happen to her grandmother. Coping with the loss of that woman's presence in Megan's life had never been a topic for discussion. *She's nowhere near ready for this*, he thought, as a sixth sense whispered the possibility that *none* of them were ready.

After speaking with Phillip, Megan spent the next ninety minutes delegating tasks to her management team and leaving messages for other associates who would need to know of her schedule change. Her abrupt decision to take personal time off, and her reluctance to estimate how long she'd be gone, would most likely haunt her when she returned, particularly at such a critical corporate juncture. But as her mind blocked out everything except her grandmother, she recoiled at the prospect of denying this latest request from Albany, regardless of the consequences. *Worst case, you could always find another job, if you had to*, she thought. Yes, a strange chemistry was clearly at work here, although she'd have to think about it later. At the moment, she had a plane to catch.

Phillip watched his wife disappear around the curve of the jetway three hours later, while Kristin reassuringly stretched her arm across his back and pulled him close to her.

"We'll be okay, Dad. You and I know how to deal with this. We've been through it a hundred times."

"Right," he responded as the plane taxied away from the terminal. "Come on. Let's go home."

At 9:35 P.M. on July 11, 1988, his best friend landed in Albany. He would discover before very long that he should have been there with her.

Megan poured a glass of Chardonnay from the limousine's wine cooler, and Kenneth mixed a bourbon and soda for the thirty-minute ride from the airport to their grandmother's estate. Although the automobile was luxuriously appointed with custom leather couches, a wet bar, television, stereo and backgammon board, the interior was stifling.

"Kenny, I thought you were going to quit smoking."

"Damn it, Megan. Don't start with your speeches. I'm really not in the mood for it."

"Well, I'm not either! I've just flown a thousand miles. I'm exhausted, and I can't even *find* you through the smoke in here. Would it be terribly inconvenient for you to at least crack a window?"

Within seconds, the air had cleared.

"Thank you. And I didn't mean to sound so dictatorial. I just worry about you."

"I know, Meg. Sorry I flew off the handle, too."

"So," she said, switching to more neutral ground, "are Justine and Tania at the house with Gram?"

"Nope. You probably won't see them until Tania gets home from summer camp tomorrow. Big track-and-field events for her, and she's her team's best hope for a gold medal in the standing broad jump."

"What fun! Maybe I can get out there to watch her. Tell Justine I'll call her in the morning to set it up."

"Frankly, Meg, I wouldn't plan on going *anywhere*. I'm afraid your calendar's already full."

"Okay. No more games. You need to level with me right now about what's going on."

"Well, if you insist, your best source of information—for the first part, anyway—is Barnes. Pick up the speakerphone and ask him to lower the window. He's expecting you."

After listening to the chauffeur's description of the trip to downtown Albany, and to the details surrounding Cinnamon's subsequent cardiac arrest, Megan questioned her cousin further.

"Why the great rush to get me up here? She's obviously stable, otherwise she'd still be in the hospital, no matter how much she protested."

"Even though she's holding her own, we do have a problem. She's convinced she's nearly out of time, and she's hell-bent on using every last ounce of energy to create some kind of record about our family history. She claims telling this particular story is the most important thing she's ever done."

"Well," Megan interjected, trying to sound relaxed, "it seems to me we've heard *that* a few hundred times before. Remember when we were kids? Perched on top of her skyscraper featherbed, huddled underneath those puffy quilts of hers, we were sitting ducks for the spells she used to weave around us."

Looking out the limousine's windows, watching the street lamps whiz by, they dipped into their private recollections, selecting favored classics and longing briefly for the innocence of those memories. Here, in the middle of their lives, they felt a deep appreciation for the drama of their grandmother's personality and her legendary genius for telling a story.

"Why would *this* one be any different than all the others?" she asked after several minutes of silence.

"I don't know, Meg," Kenneth answered as the limousine turned into the estate's driveway. "All I can tell you is that the whole thing just *feels* different for some reason."

"'Scuse me," Barnes interrupted, opening the door on her side after bringing the car to a stop beneath the columned portico. "I'll just go ahead and take your bags upstairs."

"No, not yet. Please leave everything in the car until I check things out," Megan instructed, winking at him as she squeezed his arm.

"We've missed you so much," the chauffeur said over his shoulder, as he walked around back to the kitchen door.

Kenneth stayed outside to have a cigarette while Megan went up the porch steps and through the front entrance. As soon as she crossed the threshold, a rush of familiar sights and smells enveloped her and began to lower her blood pressure, as only Fox Run could do. To her right in the dimly lit foyer was the bottom of a curved Victorian staircase and the arched entry into the parlor. To her left was the dining room, bordered along the outer wall by a butler's passage leading back to the kitchen. Straight ahead of her, a narrow corridor provided access to the formal living room on the right through double pocket doors beneath the staircase, and to a windowless oak-paneled library across the hall. At the far end of the corridor, a swinging door led to the kitchen, beyond which was tucked a two-room apartment now occupied by a housekeeper named Heidi.

Breathing deeply of McClinty air, Megan moved into the parlor and switched on a lamp. Then she returned to the foyer and noticed a figure seated at the dining room table. One candle glowing atop the sideboard cast a wavering outline of the person against the wall. Looking closer, she discovered that the shadow was David's.

"Megan! I wasn't…I…I'm so happy you're here."

"I'm sorry," she said, walking around the table. "I didn't mean to startle you. Are you okay?"

"Yes. I'm doing pretty well. Heidi made me some tea that she says will help me sleep. How are *you* doing? You must be tired after your trip."

She hugged him gently, kissed him on the forehead, and then took the chair beside him.

My God! He looks so old, and so small.

"Well, I am kind of bushed," she answered him at length, "although I'm not expecting to get much rest tonight. So, how's Gram doing?"

"She's not—not too peppy." His mind appeared to drift. One moment he was with her, the next he was not. "She's sure looking forward to seeing you, though. Maybe she'll be herself again after she's visited with you and the family. She doesn't want to talk to *me* very much. Told me to get lost this afternoon."

"Oh, David, you know how she can be when she doesn't feel well, and we're all so worn out that none of us is thinking clearly. Even Kenny and I've been irritating each other since he picked me up at the airport."

"Kenny's here?"

"Yes. He'll be in shortly. Now please do me a favor and lie down for awhile. I need to say hi to Gram, but I'll come back down shortly to look in on you."

"No need to bother. I'm fine. Heidi's always nosing around. Checking me for signs of life seems to be her main job."

He chuckled and poured himself more tea as Megan headed upstairs. Within minutes, she heard Kenneth bumping his way through the front door and dropping her luggage in a clamorous heap.

"If you're trying to get someone's attention with all that racket," she overheard David say to him, "you need to know that I'm the only one here, and I don't give a damn."

"Hey, buddy," Kenneth announced as he entered the dining room and placed his hands on the old man's folded shoulders, "you look like you could use some shuteye. Let's see if Heidi's fixed your sofa for you yet. Or would you rather go back over to the cottage?"

"No. I want to stay here tonight. And don't waste your energy. I know for sure that Heidi's fixed the sofa for me. She's been trying to get me into it for the past two hours."

"Guess you must still be pretty irresistible, you old fox," Kenneth kidded.

"What? What did you say?" David asked, looking confused.

"Never mind. It was nothing. Come on now. I'll bring your tea."

"All right. Might as well be awake in *that* room as in this one. At least I won't be bothered if all of you think I'm sleeping. It's so good to see Megan, isn't it?"

"If you say so. Did she go upstairs?"

"Yup. Went to see your grandmother. Cinnamon's very sick, you know."

"Yes, David, I know."

Kenneth guided him down the corridor and into the living room where Heidi had opened the queen-size sofabed and prepared thick layers of soft linens and blankets. Sitting on the edge of the mattress, David slipped off his shoes, then leaned back against the mounds of pillows as he pulled the covers up to his chin over his fully clothed body.

"Would you like me to get your pajamas?"

"No, Ken, I would not! And I'm perfectly capable of making my own decisions. I'm not senile, you know!"

"Of course you're not. I'll go get your tea."

"I don't want any more."

"Whatever. We love you."

Kenneth left the door ajar behind him and headed directly across the hall to the large, well-stocked bar in the library. There he discovered Barnes sitting behind the counter, sipping on a whiskey and looking quite embarrassed.

"Oh! Uh, hello, sir. Umm, they were out o' coffee in the kitchen, you see," he volunteered. "But Heidi's makin' some more, and she said it'd be okay for me to wait in here."

"Good!" Kenneth acknowledged supportively, much to the chauffeur's relief. "Sounds like an acceptable plan to me. You seen the Jack Daniels anywhere? I think it's going to be another one of those nights."

Upstairs Megan found her grandmother sleeping. *Dear Lord, please give me more courage than I feel at this moment.* Cinnamon's normally robust frame was skeletal, her face pale and gaunt, and her long unbraided silver hair spread in tangles across the pillow. A flicker of memory produced an image of a much younger Gram—one with gorgeous red hair and vivid colors living in her skin. *I'm not sure I'm ready for this.*

Slipping out of her business suit and high heels, she pulled on a favorite robe from the closet before nestling into the plump chaise lounge, which had been moved since her last visit and was now parallel to the foot of the bed. After covering herself with an afghan that she'd watched Gram knit in the midst of a long-ago childhood summer, a deep and rejuvenating slumber began its therapeutic work upon her.

Meanwhile, Cinnamon watched her granddaughter through sneaky eyes and was pleased with the resourcefulness she was still able to muster. Knowing that Megan was safely tucked in only a few feet away, the old woman enjoyed her first solid night's rest in months.

The following morning after the two of them shared a light breakfast together, Cinnamon asked Megan to close the bedroom door and load a tape in the recorder.

"Why me, Gram? Why am I the one you've singled out for this?"

"Because, my dear, you are the best choice. When we're finished, you'll understand."

Megan sat down on the bed beside her grandmother, cradling a brittle hand in her own. Then their eyes connected for a moment, without the need for words, before Cinnamon continued.

"Do you remember all the stories I used to tell you when you were little?"

"Oddly enough, Kenny and I were talking about that on the way here from the airport last night. We both have many wonderful memories of our once-upon-a-time's with you."

"Well, I can assure you that you don't even know what a real story is yet. You are finally about to learn, though. On my desk over there is a McClinty Family Chart, which Heidi helped me outline for this occasion. Please bring it here."

Megan readily located the diagram and was swept with a mixture of wonder and gallows humor. This was the first time she'd seen her entire family mapped out on a single sheet of paper. Repressing any comments about the maze of names in front of her, she stared at the page for a few moments longer while collecting her composure.

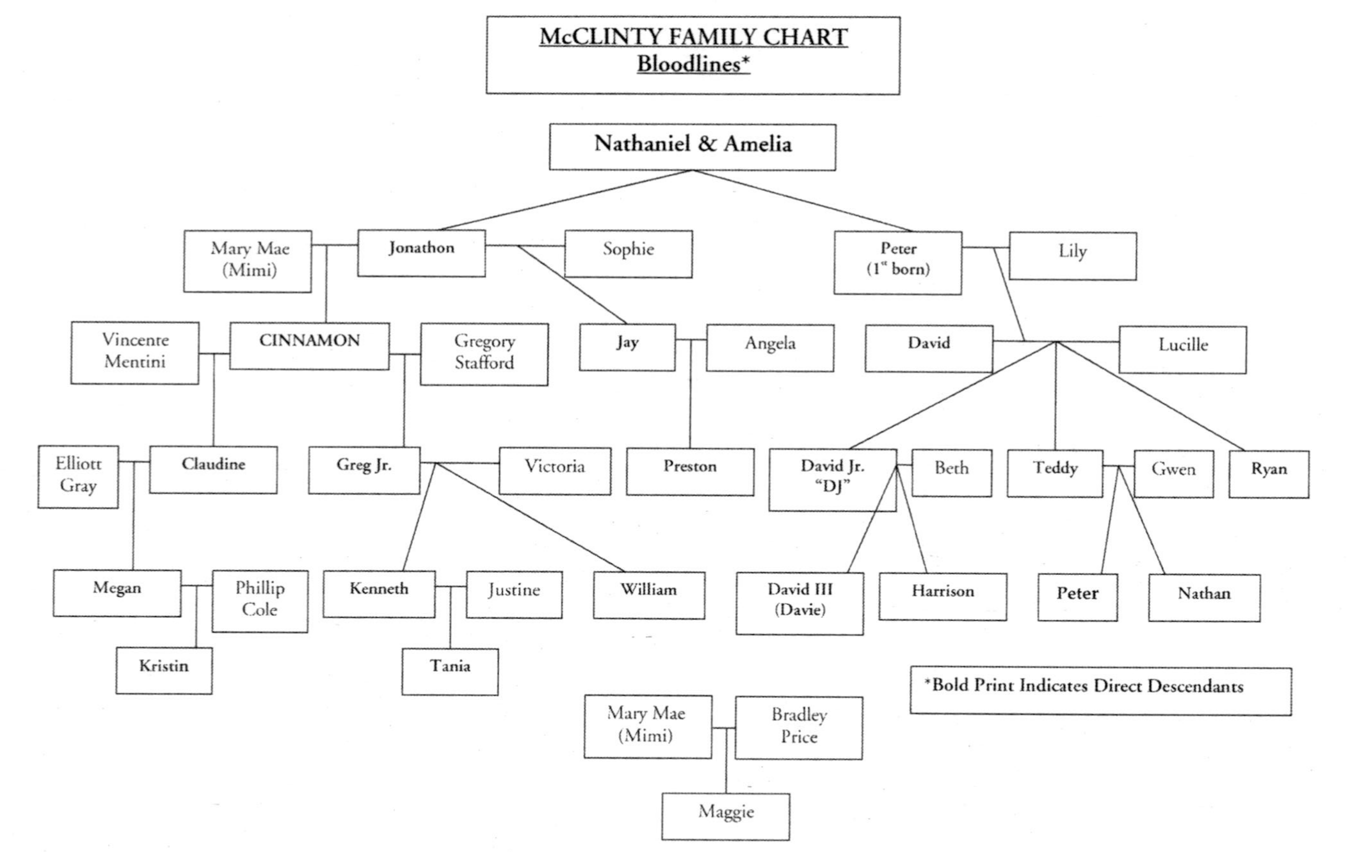
McCLINTY FAMILY CHART
Bloodlines*
Nathaniel & Amelia
Mary Mae (Mimi)
Jonathon
Sophie
Peter (1st born)
Lily
Vincente Mentini
CINNAMON
Gregory Stafford
Jay
Angela
David
Lucille
Elliott Gray
Claudine
Greg Jr.
Victoria
Preston
David Jr. "DJ"
Beth
Teddy
Gwen
Ryan
Megan
Phillip Cole
Kenneth
Justine
William
David III (Davie)
Harrison
Peter
Nathan
Kristin
Tania
*Bold Print Indicates Direct Descendants
Mary Mae (Mimi)
Bradley Price
Maggie

"Okay, Gram. What am I supposed to do with this—this *montage*?"

"Hang on to it. Things aren't always what they seem, my dear. Remember that. Now, reach over on the bureau and grab that dictionary—please."

Following orders, she began to question how long this would be entertaining.

"Okay," Cinnamon continued, "open it up and read out loud the definition of the word *ordinary*."

> **Or•di•nar•y (or'dn-er'e) adj. 1. Of common or everyday occurrence; customary; usual. 2. According to an established order; normal. 3. Common in rank or degree; average; commonplace.**

Megan had barely finished reading when her grandmother produced a crumpled sheet of paper from behind her pillow.

"Now, listen," she announced with pride. "I wrote *this* definition myself!"

Ordinary. Such is the baseline of all human life—the place where everyone starts. Accidents of birth bring an infant into the merits and shortcomings of a family, or group, or town. Genetic contributions and twists provide individual ingredients and complications. From that point on, however, each person moves under his or her own power, back and forth, above and below the baseline of ordinary, eventually arriving at a mark on someone's statistical graph. That mark coldly represents the value of a person's entire existence, and the final position is what gets all the attention. But a person's ending doesn't always correlate with where he or she has been. A life that began as ordinary might have circulated through times of grandeur, or poverty, or perhaps a respectable, unremarkable point in between. The only thing we know for sure about endings is that a unique story lies behind every journey just completed—and there's certainly nothing ***ordinary*** *about that!*

Folding her hands and resting them on her chest, Cinnamon squeezed out a smug grin while awaiting her granddaughter's praise.

"Gram, that was *lovely*!" Megan responded on cue. "I never knew you were a writer!"

"Oh, heavens, child, we do have such a long way to go."

Indeed they did, but their journey was destined to carry them much further than either of them could have imagined on that warm, tranquil July morning.

"So, let's begin, dear. Please turn on the recorder. At last, the time has arrived! I've been thinking this through for more than thirty years. I know what I want to tell you, and I know exactly how I want to do it. Please be patient with me. All the words are carefully arranged in my mind. Do you promise not to ask a lot of questions?"

"Gram, when have you ever known me to ask any questions?"

"How charming."

Smiling at her granddaughter, she began speaking into the microphone.

"I was born Margaret Elizabeth McClinty on January 26, 1906 in Albany, New York to Jonathon and Mary Mae McClinty..."

AMELIA

Chapter 2

Turn-of-the-20th-century Albany was a community defined by sharp contrasts of darkness and light. On January 26, 1906, most of the light was economic, driven in large measure by the railroads and the lumber industry. But the brightest source of energy feeding and nurturing the city's monetary and familial soul was the Hudson River. Running north and south along Albany's eastern edge, the waterway enabled the world to pass through this town daily, giving and receiving products and passengers while leaving a greater abundance of prosperity in the wake of every ship. On one or more occasion each spring, the Hudson would overflow its banks and cause pandemonium on Broadway Street, the level, bustling artery traversing downtown in a roughly parallel line with the river. But the port's heartbeat and the city's rhythm scarcely wavered during these swells; and until the Sacandaga Dam was built around 1930, the growth of many a child was marked by families frolicking together in the foot-high currents drifting through town between March and May. Even the floods had a bright side in New York State's capital.

No doubt the citizenry would have preferred to see such images of light featured more predominantly in area-wide publications, or in the memories of departing visitors. Positive press had not been Albany's strong suit, however—not since the early 1800s when the seemingly inescapable dark side of the city began cohabiting with the economic cornucopia. Rampant gambling, prostitution and lewd drunken behavior competed with widespread political corruption for headlines in the local newspapers. By January 26, 1906, elected power co-mingled with the underworld causing the rule of law to be enforced on a less than consistent basis. At the same time, the invitation to "*Bring me your tired, your hungry, your poor...*" extended far beyond New York Harbor one hundred fifty miles due south, beckoning those in search of a dream to leave the metropolis and head north to the capital. There will most likely never be an accurate accounting of the multitudes sucked into the dismal vortex awaiting them as Albany's downtown streets became bloated with tired, poor people who had migrated to the call, only to find themselves trapped in an unyielding search for opportunity and hope.

Meanwhile, the uptown population of decent, honest, hard-working citizens, rooted in urban soil since Albany's 1686 Charter, watched as their home town's reputation continued to worsen. Most people believed there was nothing they could do to stop the decline. But a few with power tried to make some small difference, and Nathaniel McClinty was very active in that effort. His roots in the area didn't extend back nearly as far as the Charter, but his dedication to the Albany community could not have been more fervent if he'd been among the founding fathers.

The American McClinty line originated with Nathaniel and Amelia, who emigrated from Ireland in 1875 when they were both eighteen. A defiant departure from their homeland had not been in their original plans. They had simply wished to marry, save their money and then sail west to the promise of America. After professing their love for one another since early childhood, and after openly sharing their dream of sailing across the Atlantic, they had not anticipated the frenzy triggered by their clear intention to follow through with their lifelong objective.

"We've completed our schooling," Nathaniel had answered after being showered with a barrage of protests against the couple's plans. "We've done everything you've asked of us, and now we're ready to begin our life together."

"No, son, you certainly are not!" Amelia's father had countered, regretting his dismissal of his wife's earlier warnings about the determination of their headstrong daughter. "You've just been seventeen for a few short months, and Amelia's birthday is still two weeks away. You are both *children*. But even if your ages weren't an issue, Nathaniel, you only have a laborer's job at the mill. This scarcely provides you with the means to support *yourself*, much less a wife and any wee ones who might come along. Where in God's name is your common sense, my boy?"

"With all due respect, sir, I am not a laborer. My work involves the business economics, and I've also been studying all aspects of the mill's operations."

"And what are your wages, if I may inquire?"

"They are sufficient, sir."

Nathaniel's parents were as distressed as Amelia's, each family having just the one child. But as astonished as they were at the girl's defiance, they were even less prepared for their son's persuasive skills. Within a month, Father McRaney from their village parish had become convinced that America was a fitting and inspiring plan for the couple. He had concluded further that the youngsters' grasp on their life's direction was far more considered than that of the adults, and he agreed to marry them.

Two nuns from the small convent of teachers that had instructed both children throughout their lives organized the small impromptu ceremony. Flowers and music were in great abundance. The convent choir sang Ave Maria. Nathaniel and Amelia's closest friends served as witnesses. While the tiny chapel was rich with love and blessings, however, not a single member of either family was in attendance. The breach caused by this brutal rejection—and it was viewed as such by all parties—would not be reconciled, despite Father McRaney's efforts at arbitration. He tried to warn them all about the dangers of unbending pride, but to no avail. They would eventually come to discover on their own what an unfortunate mistake they were making by not embracing each other.

One year later, having saved enough money for their voyage, Nathaniel and Amelia McClinty sailed for America. In April of 1876, six months after their emotional passage into New York Harbor, they followed rumors and their own instincts about the abundant opportunity awaiting them 150 miles north. When they arrived in Albany, they rented a bleak room in a downtown hotel, furnished with only a bed, a table, two chairs and a tattered sofa. A week later, Nathaniel secured a position as an accountant for Corbett Lumber Company, one of forty-six firms running lucrative businesses in the rich Upstate lumber district. Within another few short months, he and Amelia had settled comfortably into the small guest cottage behind Mr. Corbett's Madison Avenue home.

"We simply cannot permit you and your beautiful bride to remain in that sordid place any longer," Mr. Corbett had proclaimed unexpectedly when Nathaniel arrived for work one morning. "Someday you'll find yourself in a position to help clean things up in that hell hole downtown, and I urge you to do so whenever that time arrives. But you weren't here while the sorry lot—myself included—let the situation deteriorate, and you and Amelia should not be forced to endure the ugliness."

In March of 1877, Nathaniel was promoted to Financial Overseer for Corbett's Lumber, thereby assuming primary responsibility for managing and safeguarding the firm's revenues and profits. One year later, on June 8, 1878, Amelia gave birth to their first son, Peter. Thus, the third Christmas in their new world had not yet been celebrated before their dreams surpassed even their most extravagant expectations. But they both felt a similar void as they knelt in thanksgiving at the Cathedral's altar during Communion when Peter was two weeks old. Fearful of complaining in the wake of their many blessings, they spoke quietly and privately that afternoon about Ireland.

"I miss them all so much, Nathaniel. I always have. But since Peter's birth, I can't stop thinking of them—and of your family, too. Part of the joy I know I should be feeling is somehow being held in reserve until they can all be with us. Am I making any sense? Do you understand?"

"Yes, I am with you in everything you say," he answered, turning away from her to hide the tears she'd already seen sliding down his cheeks. "But what shall we do? It's been so long. Perhaps *too* long."

"Very simply, my love, as with each step we have taken since our hearts bonded as children, we must begin."

Late that evening, after nursing Peter to sleep and then looking in on her slumbering husband, Amelia brewed a pot of tea, lit a small oil lamp, and sat down at the kitchen table in her nightgown. She'd arranged a collection of writing papers and pen quills in front of her, hoping to create soft, artistic letters that would enhance her plaintive message. After awhile, however, she stopped trying to paint the moment with fabricated curves and angles. Without further thought, she pulled paper and pen toward her and began to write in earnest.

June 25, 1878

Dearest Mama and Papa—

Proper words attempt to elude me after four years without any form of communication exchanged between us. The Virgin Mary teaches much about forgiveness, and now I wish that her lessons had reached my soul before our ship sailed away from you. You did break my heart when you refused to bless my marriage while God Himself sanctified the union. Nonetheless, I'm certain that I broke your hearts as well. For this, I want you to know how truly sorry both Nathaniel and I are, and how deeply we miss you.

Sadness is difficult to tolerate on this glorious day because, you see, we have created a child. His name is Peter, and he is your firstborn grandson. We have not yet determined which of you he favors since he is only two weeks old. But the faint reddish tint atop his head indicates a clear connection. By the time he is christened, the resemblance should be more distinct. Perhaps you could be here to see for yourselves.

Aside from asking for your forgiveness, a primary reason for this letter is to request the honor of your attendance at Peter's baptism. We are naturally sending a similar request to Nathaniel's family. No date has been specified yet, and none will be set until we have heard from all of you.

Nathaniel is performing quite well in his job as financial overseer for Corbett Lumber Company. He has also become a favorite of the owner himself, although my husband is far too humble to admit this. We live in a small cottage behind the Corbett residence, but Mrs. Corbett has assured me that ample room is available in the main house for you and Nathaniel's family during your visit.

We have been saving a portion of Nathaniel's wages and could help you with the purchase of your voyage, if that would ease your decision. The journey, although lengthy, could be completed very soon if arrangements were made shortly after your receipt of this letter.

We await your response with anxious hearts, and we pray that the same need for recovery has touched you as it has us. I do love you both very much, and you are going to be so proud of your little grandson.

Always,
Amelia

Nine weeks passed before replies from both families were received in the same package, along with a thin white box measuring about ten inches square.

August 13, 1878

Dear Nathaniel—

Your mother has not stopped crying since Amelia's letter arrived. I cannot tell whether her heart aches more for the son she lost or for the grandson she will never see. As for myself, my heart stopped beating four years ago when you went away.

We are relieved, nonetheless, to know that you and Amelia are safe and that you have work to keep you busy. Still, we cannot help but wonder why you felt you had to leave your home and your family behind in order to find what you already had in full measure here. This we will never understand until our dying breath.

We are well, however, and admittedly we are even better after hearing from you. So that you may proceed with your child's baptism forthwith, we will not be coming to America for that or for any other purpose. If you wish to see us, we will be precisely where you left us.

Your Father and Mother

****

August 14, 1878

My Little Amelia—

Your sainted mother passed away last year. I had no way of notifying you. If she had only been able to cling to her faith and wait with me for your letter—but that was not to be. After so long, even I began to lose hope that we would ever hear from you again. Now I pray each day that our Lord will take me soon as well. My life has always been viewed through your mother's eyes, and thus I will remain blinded from all true meaning until I am able to see her on the other side.

At least I have the peace of knowing that you are alive and happy. Perhaps I was wrong in trying to hold you here. Perhaps you and Nathaniel are blessed, as your mother and I were. I pray this is true, because I could never wish a greater gift for you. I also pray that your new son—my only grandchild—and any other children who might follow him will never abandon you.

You spoke of forgiveness in your letter. We all share the burden of your leaving Ireland under such distress. We should have been more supportive, and we should have been with you to help you sanctify your marriage. I am very sorry for that. But the silence you sent us over the past four years—that is your sin alone, and one I have been unable to forgive. I will continue to pray that before I am reunited with your mother, I will have found my way to the recovery you referenced. This I will do, not for you, but for her, so that in passing the resolution on to her, she may finally be able to rest in peace.

I love you, my wee one, despite everything. Have a good life filled with the joy of your family. In the end, there is nothing greater or more important. Learn that lesson well, if you have not already. Regards to Nathaniel.

Forever—
Your Papa

Tied to a corner of the accompanying box was a sealed note. Nathaniel had to open it for his wife, who could not speak or move after learning of her mother's death.

Amelia—

As a postscript, I have decided to include this christening gown. Your mother made it while we were waiting for the letter that never came from you. Despite her broken heart, she always loved you. She prayed that you would be happy and have many children, and she often spoke to me of her dream—to watch her grandchildren baptized, one after one, in the gown crafted with such love by her own hand. My original intention was to withhold this gift from you, having it buried with me instead. My vengeful thoughts about writing that final note to you led me to the confessional yesterday.

Your mother is apparently managing my behavior once again, and I fear that if I do not forward her grandchildren's christening gown to you, I will ultimately face her anger and disappointment when I see her. This gesture, therefore, is not as much for you as for me—and for your mother who never deserved that broken heart.

Papa
August 15, 1878

Arrangements were nearly complete for Amelia's emergency trip to Ireland when word arrived of her father's death and burial. She would not be comforted. Wrapping herself in guilt, she also withdrew from her infant son, leaving him in the empathetic arms of Mrs. Corbett and her housekeeper.

Nathaniel used his work as a shield against the lamentable visions of families left behind by callous, selfish children. Denying himself the opportunity to nurture his own spirit, much less that of his wife, he found himself repeating the same self-absorbed behavior that pushed him to leave his homeland in the first place. At length, following more than a month of self-deprecation, he brought his wife to the rectory and together they confessed to Father Flanigan what they both viewed as their greatest sin. An immigrant himself, the priest was able to inspire healing over time, even to the point of corresponding with Nathaniel's parents, urging them to visit, and reminding the entire family of the importance their faith placed upon forgiveness. He neglected to mention, however, his penchant for orchestrating miracles.

By the time Peter was two years old, the senior McClintys had been persuaded to leave their home in Ireland and were living on a small farm south of Albany proper, in the village of Slingerlands, where their son and daughter-in-law provided for their every need. Such indulgence was largely out of love, but partially as a means of washing the guilt from their souls. On May 4, 1881, a second son was born to Nathaniel and Amelia. They named him Jonathon Allister McClinty in honor of Amelia's father Jonathon and Nathaniel's mother Maria Allister.

Three years later, after Mr. Corbett became too ill to remain active in his business, he and his wife decided to relocate to Boston where her family could help care for him. Having no children of their own, they invited Nathaniel and Amelia to leave the cottage and move into the main house for a nominal rental fee. At the same time, Nathaniel was also made General Operations Manager for Corbett Lumber and was given a twenty-percent ownership block in the company.

Jonathon and Peter McClinty thus became native sons of Albany. They paddled their share of small boats down the city's flooded streets each spring, and spent most of their summers on their grandparents' farm a few miles away. They attended school and worshipped with their family at the Cathedral of the Immaculate Conception where, along with an entire generation of Albany's Catholic children, they heard Father Flanigan sprinkle catechism with realism, sensitivity and historical grace.

The brothers also grew up in a home filled with broadminded conversations, a consummate work ethic, a sense of humor, and an unwavering, unconditional love from their parents. Yet, despite the evenhanded balance of their upbringing, the boys became increasingly boorish with respect to the deteriorating human conditions in the center of town. A favorite prank involved hopping on a trolley with their friends and riding down to the neighborhood surrounding the capitol building. There they would disobey all orders and sneak into the alleyways off State Street. The closer they got to Broadway, the more graphic their view of the poor, wretched people in the merciless grip of a man-made plague—and the more daring they became with their ridicule of what they were seeing.

"How can you let yourselves *live* like this?" they would shout at a group of ragtag men, who were huddled around a small fire beneath the railroad trestle. "If you had any dignity, you'd secure a job and rent a room the way *decent* people do!"

In sharp contrast to these mean-spirited words and activities, the McClinty brothers found themselves listening to their father's infinite stream of patriotic parables delivered each night after the evening meal. His sermons always concluded with a moral illustration requiring their attention, since they knew a summary of the week's lessons would be discussed during Sunday afternoon supper. Given the boys' clandestine curiosities and illicit ventures downtown, these family dialogues grew increasingly uncomfortable for them.

"What may look like a graveyard or a refuse area to you," Nathaniel would pontificate, "just might be someone's home. Be careful where you step lest you walk on the face of your fellow man. Our founding fathers did not envision the abuse of power we see around here, or this blind tolerance of perversion. But we are here to help, not to judge. Your civic responsibilities will always include setting a proper example, my sons, in your business dealings, your community activities and your personal affairs. The best of Albany must be heralded and enhanced by your generation. The worst, God willing, will expire on its own. Meanwhile, aside from your allegiance to the Church, the only other thing you must never compromise—*never*—is your family. Your expectations for the future should include these commitments and a reminder that your blessings must neither be taken for granted nor abused. Your riches must also be shared with those less fortunate. Follow these guidelines, keeping your family clearly in sight as you move forward, and your lives will be full and rewarding."

Eventually, maturity and their guilty consciences brought an end to the brothers' excursions downtown. Throughout the balance of their boyhoods, at least in the presence of their parents, they regularly made the declarations of philanthropic intent that Nathaniel and Amelia wanted to hear from them. Peter and Jonathon had all the acceptable words memorized.

By 1884, the rhythm of McClinty life was strong and steady. Nathaniel and Amelia became United States citizens and, after careful planning, were able to purchase the main house on Madison Avenue while they continued to lease the cottage to couples needing a start. Control of Corbett Lumber shifted to Nathaniel and, as the business expanded, the name was changed to McClinty

Mill. Only a few difficult moments interfered with their well-ordered, prosperous existence, the worst of which included the funerals of Nathaniel's parents, who died within a month of one another in 1891 when grandsons Peter and Jonathon were ages thirteen and ten.

Nathaniel had initially considered selling their farm after his parents' death, but he discovered too many memories inside and could not let the place go. Instead, he hired a tenant farmer to maintain the house and the twenty-five surrounding acres of rich land and forests on the edge of what would eventually become New Scotland Avenue. After learning from his new tenant of the prolific and beautiful red fox who made the farmland their home, Nathaniel named the property Fox Run. Subsequently, he prohibited any hunting of the animals on the grounds, and then commissioned a plaque to be engraved and mounted on a stone marker behind the house.

FOX RUN

May this land and its rich native family
live forever in harmony with what I pray will be
the honor, humility, and self-respect of my heirs.

Nathaniel McClinty
May 11, 1893

One might have thought this wasn't asking too much.

As Jonathon and Peter grew into men, people who knew them had difficulty believing that both had been reared in the same household, by the same parents, presented with the same lessons, and washed with equal amounts of love. Jonathon reached adulthood with a reputation for consistency and dependability, while Peter was known as the drifter who focused purely upon his own agenda, disregarding the wishes of his family as irrelevant to his life. But decades would pass before their differences wrought any serious consequences—or before anyone would question the accuracy of those early comparisons between the brothers.

Meanwhile, setting a proper example had been the keystone of Jonathon's development, and by the time he'd graduated from Harvard in 1903, he rarely made even the most minor decisions without first considering the impact and consequences upon his family and associates. The shock of his father Nathaniel's sudden death, however, only one year after Jonathon had completed his studies at the university, had immobilized him. Thus, none of his reflexes were operating correctly when he went to Boston for a short rest two months following the funeral, and returned a few weeks later with a wife on his arm.

"Jonathon!" Amelia had beseeched him in the cushy privacy of her study, "Who *is* she? And what possessed you to do such a thing? I would have expected this from your brother, but not from you—and when your father is barely in his grave and Peter has just gone away again! How can I bear it? Blessed Virgin Mary, how can this be?"

I don't know, Jonathon was thinking, *but it's done now*. "Mother, please sit down. I'm sorry I've upset you, and perhaps I should have handled this differently. Nonetheless, there is good reason for my choice. Please, sit."

Only Nathaniel had exercised greater command over Amelia. Not even Peter, her firstborn, had ever possessed any power to control her. But Peter had been a renegade since birth, repeatedly embarrassing the family with his unwillingness to conform. His latest and most lengthy escapade had taken him to the far side of the country where California was in the grip of a gold rush. His searing farewell in 1896, shortly after his eighteenth birthday, left the job of McClinty standard bearer and Harvard graduate to Jonathon, three years his junior.

When Peter returned from California in 1904 to help bury his father, the trip home was his first since those angry days. His demeanor poised with the benefit of age, he'd talked softly with his younger brother about regret and unspoken apologies. But Jonathon made little effort to mask his own deaf ear. He no longer knew nor cared about Peter, the sibling icon who had abdicated his role as mentor, companion, and best friend. Their mother was limp with grief, and many of their father's affairs urgently needed tending. Jonathon had modestly groomed himself for this eventuality, but had never once allowed himself to imagine that the change might occur so soon. Now, as far as he was concerned, Peter could cling to his cowardice if he chose, or he could make some amends by shouldering part of the burden. Either way, he'd have to handle his pitiful remorse alone.

But Peter was not alone. Accompanying him on this solemn visit was his wife Lily and their five-year-old boy, David, both of whom had been known to the family only through letters. Amelia's spirits were wondrously lifted upon the long-awaited meeting of her daughter-in-law and grandson, and slowly the two newcomers began to replenish some of the joy her husband had unintentionally ripped away from her when he died.

Little David was such a vision to her, a remarkable recreation of her beloved McClinty men, from his lucid blue eyes, his thick black hair and the square lines of his jaw. His presence illuminated every room for her, despite the toddler's mess and clutter, and she was surprised to feel a deepening attachment for Lily as well.

Together they strengthened Amelia's will; and the prospect of living as a widow for whatever time she had left no longer felt insufferable.

Yet inexplicably, as if he enjoyed contaminating his family's happiness, Peter's wanderlust would not be tamed. In another act of defiance, he recoiled at the idea of sharing even the smallest responsibility for running the McClinty Mill or for reinforcing the family's foundation left so badly weakened by his father's death. He and his brother had inherited equally, but his aversion to life in Albany would absolutely not be abated. Fearful of blending fresh anger with old, he announced to his mother that he was returning immediately to California where he promised he would wisely invest his portion of Jonathon's estate. She begged him to stay, or at the very least to leave Lily and David with her while he resettled his affairs. Even when faced with his brother's personal entreaties on their mother's behalf, however, Peter remained unmoved. Then, as quickly as they'd appeared, he and his beautiful family were gone, leaving behind an even greater void than the one they'd so recently filled.

"This is my final punishment, isn't it, Lord?" Amelia sighed in the darkness of her room the night they left. "Bearing a son who feels nothing as he rips his love from my arms is how I must finish paying for what I did so long ago to my own parents, and to Nathaniel's. Do as you must with me, dear God. I understand, and I will not complain. But you cannot stop me from having a broken heart."

In the shadows of Peter's retreat, the full weight and focus of the McClinty lumber and paper businesses had shifted to Jonathon. His conduct had always been unimpeachable, and yet he now stood before his lonely, emotionally bruised mother only moments after introducing a stranger to her whom he referred to as his wife. Attempting to charm his way around Amelia's questions regarding his judgment, he launched into his rehearsed explanation after Mimi judiciously left the room.

"She is not a stranger, Mother. I've already known her for three years. You remember George Emerson, don't you?"

"Yes. Vaguely."

"Well, we were classmates all through school, and he's her brother. She's been teaching this past term and has continued to live with her aunt and uncle, which is where she was when I first met her. George and I went over there for dinner one night."

"I see. And in between your first dinner with her three years ago and your subsequent marriage to her, there wasn't a single opportunity for you to mention the girl's very existence to your own mother?"

"Actually," *dear Lord, please don't be too far away*, "I did tell Dad about her once. But I'd only spent a few occasions with her at that point. I knew how much you wanted me to finish college, and I didn't want to worry you."

"Ah! You felt it best to wait until immediately after your father's death when I would be much stronger and more prepared."

"No. I didn't plan that."

"Finally, the truth."

"Mother, what I mean is that I'd spoken with her about marriage, but we'd both agreed not to discuss it seriously until I graduated and brought her home to meet you. I wasn't sure how you would respond, and I was hoping to choose the moment carefully. I just…I never…never thought we'd lose Dad."

The sound of his own words derailed his composure. Amelia moved predictably across the room and sat down beside him, pressing her hands around his.

"Go on, Jonathon. I'm listening."

"I know, and I can't believe I've handled this so miserably."

"It's all right. I simply need to understand the secrecy. Why didn't you bring her home and marry her here? Is there something…something *wrong* with her?"

He smiled at the delicacy of her inquiry.

"No, Mother. There's nothing *wrong* with her. She's quick, intelligent, Irish, Catholic, and really very lovely as well."

"Yes, that much is clear. So, why were you ashamed to let us know about her? And *where* were you married, by the way? In which parish? Who was the officiating priest?"

Oh, God, he thought in desperation, *if you help me through this interrogation, I give you my word that this will be the last consciously irresponsible act I'll ever commit.* His declaration was undoubtedly sincere at the time.

"I wasn't ashamed, Mother. You see, George and Mimi lost their parents when they were children. Their mother's sister took them in and raised them. George doesn't seem to have any difficulty explaining his circumstances when the need arises. But Mimi is terribly sensitive about not having her own father and mother, and for some reason she was frightened of meeting you. She believed you would not approve of her."

"Where on earth would she have come up with *that* idea?"

"I'm afraid that *I* might have been the reason."

"Jonathon, whatever do you mean?"

"Perhaps I spoke too often of my parents—too highly, and with too much pride. Perhaps I was boasting in an effort to win her affection. It's difficult for me to recall exactly what I said, but she tells me she'd decided not to accept my proposal because she was convinced you would never truly welcome her into the family."

"Oh dear heaven! That poor child. And with all she's endured! What happened to change her mind?"

"*My* father died," he whispered, trying to focus on the outline of his mother's face. "And then we were married by a judge."

She wasn't sure how long she'd been holding her boy, but when their eyes touched, she had no further need to question his motives. *Occasionally, people must do things without knowing why*, she thought. *Did he say married by a judge?*

"I believe we are neglecting a very important someone," Amelia continued, "a beautiful young lady named Mimi, who just happens to be my new daughter-in-law. Shouldn't we bring her back into the room for a celebrational toast? Nathaniel would want nothing less. And Jonathon, do you think the two of you might humor this old woman and submit yourselves to a second ceremony here, in the Cathedral, where we could show you off to the family, and to a short list of friends. Such a moment might help lift our hearts from all the sadness surrounding your father's passing, *not to mention saving you from damnation.* No, never mind. Don't answer me now. We'll talk about it again tomorrow."

On a crisp December afternoon in 1904, Jonathon McClinty and Mary Mae Emerson McClinty were married in a second ceremony, this time in the Cathedral of the Immaculate Conception before the eyes of God, family and friends. Peter forwarded his regrets, claiming that he and Lily simply could not manage another cross-country journey so soon after the last one. While the explanation seemed reasonable to most people, neither Jonathon nor his mother believed the message to be sincere. Amelia openly expressed her sorrow surrounding her eldest child's self-estrangement. But Jonathon wore a face of indifference, pretending not to care, even though his cutting words spoke otherwise.

If no one else took umbrage at the strained atmosphere at the reception, Mimi certainly did. She hadn't anticipated sharing this bright moment with the ghost of a brother-in-law not yet dead, and she kept waiting for her husband to diffuse the situation. But his preoccupation with Peter rendered Jonathon insensitive to Mimi's wishes and well beyond her emotional reach. Nonetheless, she moved graciously through each orchestrated movement, through each toast and dance, refusing to allow the many whispers of concern in her mind to undermine her day—or to warn her.

Believing that the time had arrived to begin establishing his own branch of traditions, in January of 1905 Jonathon purchased a three-story red brick house on Madison Avenue, just two blocks away from the home where he and Peter had been raised. The formal living room on the main floor of the new residence provided elegant settings for entertaining, and the soft, nurturing corners of the parlor across the hall offered solace during complicated moments. Private rooms upstairs on the second floor afforded privacy and space perfect for the growth of new love and the addition of family.

Amelia agreed that their original home down the street, which she'd shared with Nathaniel for twenty-one years, should be leased to a family in need, just as Mr. and Mrs. Corbett had done for them so long ago. She, in turn, moved into her own suite of rooms in Jonathon's new house, in what had formerly been servants' quarters on the third floor. Thereafter, the two Mrs. McClinty's, who were separated in age by nearly two generations, became devoted companions. Their shared affection for Jonathon gave them a common purpose, and their respect for one another enriched them both. The only element missing for Mimi in her new life was the classroom and her contact with children.

"Please, Jonathon, if I could only begin teaching again, our world together would be fulfilled from end to end."

"On the contrary, my love. Your world might be complete, while mine would become subject to your schedule. I saw how little free time you had in Boston, but I was not yet prepared to offer you the security of this marriage. Now that I *have*—and now that you've accepted—there's no further need for you to generate an income of your own."

"But it's not the income, darling. I want desperately to stay active and to do something meaningful. I want to be an interesting person—for *you*—and I long to be around children again."

"Then organize a reading club, or fix up this new house of ours in any way you like, or begin having your own children. Excuse me, *our* own children," he added with a grin. "What I'm trying to tell you in my clumsy way is that you are free to do anything you wish, as long as you do not seek employment outside of this house. Surely you can't take exception with that, my dear."

"But, Jonathon..."

"Please, Mimi. Let's not discuss this further. Excuse me now while I finish my work. I'll see you and Mother at dinner."

Having been dismissed, she withdrew into the fire-stoked warmth of the parlor across the hall. Moments later she was joined by Amelia.

"Forgive me, dear, but I couldn't help overhearing. Come. Sit down."

"What have I done wrong?"

"Nothing, child. My son simply finds himself in control now, and while he grows accustomed to his new role, we must learn to be patient with him."

"Yes, I understand. But he never listens to my perspective. My feelings are either overlooked completely, or they're dismissed without fair consideration. I respect his position and his wishes, but I do not want to see my spirit disappear inside of his."

"Nor do I, and together we shall see that it does not. I give you my solemn oath that as long as I am living, your place as Jonathon's wife will be distinctly defined. You may not be teaching in the classroom, but I can assure you that your life will be a happy one, and one with a purpose of your own choosing. Now tell me, where would you like to begin?"

They began with the house, and Mimi was quick to replace her classroom lesson plans with interior design blueprints for transforming the massive residence.

"What effect do you have in mind?" Amelia had asked the next afternoon over tea.

"I'd like to create a family refuge where real people live, a place where anyone of any station might feel comfortable. And I'd like to have a library, large and warm, filled with plump chairs and foot blankets, beautiful reading tables, and plenty of lamps. There must be a children's corner, too. Perhaps one day I might even offer a tutoring program," she mused, "something to benefit our community. I also want to fill each room with art. Not dreadfully expensive pieces, of course, just tailored to our needs and our preferences."

Spellbound by the vibrant colors of her daughter-in-law's imagination, Amelia had difficulty resisting the joyous possibilities. Yet she knew enough to be cautious.

"Your visions give new life to this old woman, Mimi, but you must certainly realize that original construction and works of art will be quite costly, even with the best of luck and the most inventive agreements."

"When secured through normal channels, that would certainly be true. But not if we are clever and find the skills we need locally."

"A novel thought, indeed," Amelia said, having no idea where this was going. "Please tell me more."

"Well, as I see it," Mimi continued, delighted that this woman was actually listening to her, "we have the opportunity—and the *power*—to invite people who truly need the money. We could put their talents to work for us in our home. All parties would end up with more than they had in the beginning. In fact, the artists would most likely be the greatest winners."

"And just precisely where would this little pot of people be found?"

"Based on what I've heard since I joined this family, many of them will be downtown. Oh, for heaven's sake, don't look so appalled! How often have you listened to your son, and to your husband before him, speak of the need to transform things down there? This might, in fact, be a small beginning toward that end.

"Let's assume, for the sake of debate," Amelia answered, playing along, "that such an idea were even remotely possible. How would we get the word out? And how would we make the selections? In fact, *where* would we make them? We certainly cannot have any of those people coming *here* to make application."

"On the face of it, my darling mother-in-law, that hardly sounds representative of our altruistic intentions, nor does it ring even a tone of Nathaniel's historic lessons. I do realize, however, that discretion is clearly advisable. We wouldn't want to do anything foolish. Let me think about this overnight. Let's *both* think about it, and then discuss it again tomorrow."

That evening after Jonathon had fallen asleep, Mimi stole out of their bedroom and downstairs to the kitchen where she composed a letter to the *Times Union* editor-in-chief.

February 2, 1905

Dear Sir—

This letter is to notify you of several employment opportunities. We are offering above-market prices for quality art and handmade crafts to become part of a personal residence. We will be in search of paintings, needlework, glasswork, pottery, weaving, cabinetry, and so forth. A total of eight or ten artists and carpenters will be selected, and we prefer those with both talent and personal need from the downtown neighborhoods. Samples of their workmanship will be carefully reviewed prior to selection. Professional experience is not required, but a reputable character is imperative.

Please, sir, I seek your assistance in this endeavor, and I request that you keep my identity private, as I am preparing (in concert with the senior Mrs. McClinty) a surprise for my husband. We would be deeply grateful if you could arrange for a proper and safe location for us to meet the candidates and preview their work, and then print that location in the advertisement you prepare. We would like to begin this process swiftly, thus your confidential reply to me by messenger (mid-day, any day this week, except Sunday) will be eagerly awaited.

Respectfully yours,
Mrs. Jonathon A. McClinty

"May the good Lord help us," Amelia exclaimed the following morning after Jonathon left for the mill.

Then she smiled and gleefully helped Mimi seal and address the letter. Later, once the postman had taken delivery, the two women went into Jonathon's study and shared a shot of brandy between them in their tea.

A conspiratorial messenger arrived with the editor's response after an agonizing four-day wait.

Dear Mrs. McClinty—

A light will soon be shining in the lives of a few now in darkness, and hope will be revived for countless more. You and the senior Mrs. McClinty are to be commended for your generosity. Included is a draft of the proposed advertisement for your review and approval. Another messenger will return at the same time tomorrow for your reply.

Sincerely,
Bradley C. Price
Editor-in-Chief

<u>LOCAL ARTISANS</u>: OPPORTUNITY! UPTOWN FAMILY SEARCHING FOR UNKNOWN TALENT OF HIGH CHARACTER. NEED ORIGINAL PAINTINGS, NEEDLEWORK, GLASSWORK, POTTERY, WOVEN GOODS, CARPENTRY AND MORE. UP TO 10 ARTISTS WILL BE SELECTED. SAMPLES OF COMPLETED WORKS WILL BE REVIEWED FEBRUARY 18, BEGINNING AT NOON, AT THE *TIMES UNION* OFFICES. ONLY CLEAN, NEATLY DRESSED ARTISTS WITH PRODUCTS IN HAND WILL BE ADMITTED. GOOD LUCK!

"Shall we tell Jonathon?"

"No, Amelia. Not yet."

The ladies were to arrive by mid-morning at the *Times Union* building on February 18 to avoid any crowds that might begin gathering before noon. But they left the house even earlier than planned due to the eight inches of fresh snow that fell over night. After riding the trolley east on Madison to South Pearl, they walked cautiously over snow banks and unshoveled sidewalks for three blocks in the newspaper's direction. With two blocks left to go, they could see the line of people already pressed like a shivering ribbon up against the building and extending around the corner at the intersection of Pearl and Beaver Streets.

"Dear Lord! I had no idea!"

"Nor did I, Mimi. I do pray that we're not causing more harm than good."

Linking their arms, they trudged as anonymously as possible past the masses of hopefuls and through the *Times Union* front door. Bradley C. Price and his teeming room full of energetic reporters met them inside with warm rounds of introduction that helped the women relax.

"Ladies, I'm so very sorry," Mr. Price said, helping them off with their coats and scarves. "The response to your advertisement was much greater than any of us anticipated. I hope no one bothered you on your way in."

"No. There was no trouble whatsoever, sir," Mimi answered. "I'm only shaken by the fact that so many are in need of this work. As you know, we have funds for ten people at most. And," she continued in a near whisper, "your reporters *are* aware, aren't they, that this venture is not to be publicized?"

"Yes, of course. They understand that your identities are confidential, but the thrill of such a story-in-the-making is hard to suppress. Please don't be concerned." His attempts at assurance were unconvincing. "You and your mother-in-law will not be compromised."

"We are placing our trust in you and your staff, Mr. Price," Mimi continued. "But once again, I 'm troubled by the fact that so many have come here today. And why, if I may ask, does your staff have such a keen interest in our little project?"

"Mrs. McClinty," he answered, looking back and forth between the two women, "what you may perceive as a *little project* is actually, in troublesome times like these, a potential way out of a nightmare for a few of these people. Everyone who has shown up this morning is fully aware of this opportunity's competitive nature, and I'd be willing to wager that the majority will be at the top of their form."

Mimi took a moment to study this man. At first glance, he looked like a disheveled, disoriented beat reporter. But a more careful inspection revealed a well-groomed, finely suited gentleman in the midst of a highly frenzied moment. His lanky body moved athletically from one side of the room to the other, and when he turned his face away from her, she tried to remember the color of his eyes. She thought they were brown, but she had difficulty recalling as she attempted, with some embarrassment, to disengage her thoughts from *him* in general. When he looked at her again—or more accurately, straight through her—all she could see were shamrocks. His eyes were hazel, and his thick black eyebrows and lashes etched a striking contrast against his freckled complexion and full head of blonde hair. Watching Mr. Price dart around the office, she felt herself blushing at the fact that she was no longer concentrating on his eyes or any other part of his face.

"What was your question?" he asked, his essence scarcely a foot away from hers.

"She was wondering—or more precisely, *we* were wondering—what will happen to those people we do not select." Amelia hadn't missed a single nuance of this exchange and instinctively grabbed the reigns of conversation. Mr. Price felt the transfer of control and directed his response toward her instead of Mimi.

"Better things await those standing outside, madam, than any of them could have hoped for, prior to your project. Regardless of your selections, your idea has re-awakened the enthusiasm—the passion—inside all of them. You don't see them every day like we do down here. But you need to believe me when I tell you that they are dressed in their Sunday best for you. A large percentage of them will be carried for a long time by the inspiration they feel this morning. Right now, though, if you are both ready, I suggest we begin letting them in for their reviews."

The women were stunned by the disparities between their Madison world and the one they came to see. Allowed to enter the *Times Union* building in groups of ten, the hopefuls huddled by the news desks, happy to be inside. Their lips and fingers stiffened by the wind chill, they each stepped forward when their names were called. Men and women of ages difficult to determine were well-padded with clothing, the outer layers appearing clean and pressed, with yarn unraveling at the edges. While there could be no certainty, an observer would suspect that, given the condition of their other attire, their shoes and boots might very well have holes in their soles. Yet, without exception, every individual who stood before them held a quality, classic, breathtaking piece of work in hand.

Mimi was promptly overtaken by the improbability of eliminating even a single one of these poor people until, after the procession had been curbed by her indecisiveness, Amelia guided her to the back of the newsroom.

"My dear, I know what you are thinking because I share your dilemma. But we simply must go forward with our plan. We owe everyone our time and consideration. More importantly, we owe them our decisions. Whoever is not chosen may be disappointed, but the rules were made quite clear. Our word must prevail. And who can tell? Perhaps we'll start a new trend that will benefit the others. Or perhaps, once the Madison house is completed, we might host a reception for our neighbors and friends where we could introduce our artists and promote our means of finding others like them. That way, anyone here today who is really serious will have another opportunity to secure work."

"Yes! Oh, Amelia, how perfect! The value and purpose would then go far beyond our personal plans for today."

By mid-afternoon, the choices had been made. Three brothers were commissioned to paint oils for the front hallway, the parlor and the dining room. Two elderly gentlemen who worked as partners were engaged to create Tiffany-style lamps for two of those rooms, and discussion was also underway about their constructing pieces of stained glass for several windows throughout the house. Three women were chosen for the needlework projects; and finally, there was

Mimi's favorite—a widowed man, who could not have been much older than twenty, with his toddler son clinging to his trousers. Caressed beneath a blanket in the young father's arms was a three-story Victorian dollhouse complete with furniture and two generations of a fictitious family. Every floorboard, shingle, table leg and tiny human representative had been designed, carved and built by Emanuel Smith. This, Mimi decided, was the carpenter she wanted for her library, and she suggested that he might bring his young son Jarrett along with him once his work began.

"Perhaps," she had considered aloud, "I could help your boy with his school tasks while you are working."

After dismissing the other contenders, Bradley Price congratulated those who'd been selected. He then recorded their names and the most probable place they could be reached to arrange their first meetings at the Madison house. Once the jubilant group of winners left the newspaper's office, he turned toward Mimi and Amelia, watching them as they secured their fur bonnets and muffs.

"Ladies, I want to extend my offer of full responsibility for any of these people, in the event we discover them to be something less than they've represented themselves to be. At your convenience, I will personally escort them, one at a time, to your home so they can learn more about the details of their commitments and the specifics of your requirements. My assistant and I will provide the security for those visits."

"Nonsense!" Mimi interjected. "Oh my, please forgive my abruptness," she added, noting the fallen look on his face. "Your offer is certainly generous, and naturally we accept any assistance you so kindly wish to provide. What I meant to say was that I think our first meeting at the house should be something on a larger scale, perhaps a luncheon or a tea, where all of our craftsmen can attend together."

Mr. Price and Amelia both stared at her in disbelief.

"We will be in touch with you in a day or two once we've finalized our plans," she persisted, taking her mother-in-law's hand and pulling her toward the door. "Thank you so very much again, sir, for your efforts on our behalf. We'll be forever grateful, and we're terribly excited about working with you. But we really must dash now. We're far later than we expected we'd be."

The frigid walk to the trolley, and the not much warmer ride up Madison Avenue, inhibited their desire for further conversation. Once home, they were swept immediately into the motions of lighting up the house, rebuilding the fire and preparing dinner, all with the intent of looking as if they'd been there all day. By the time everything was in order, they were too exhausted to discuss the afternoon's events. Ultimately, Jonathon was so late that he found his wife and mother asleep in their rooms while his lukewarm meal limply awaited him on the stove.

During the next forty-eight hours, Mimi and Amelia entertained themselves by debating their methodology and the covert undertones that would be required for the initial stages of their project. But the necessity of actually launching the endeavor soon gained priority. In a polite override of Mr. Price's reservations, a luncheon was scheduled for the nine artisans on March 15.

"With the greatest of respect, ladies," he'd proffered with caution, "you realize, of course, that we've managed to create for ourselves a rather substantial unknown quantity—full of risks, I might add—with this group of...of *folks*. Perhaps you might reconsider my original suggestion about greeting them one-on-one, and with a little less fanfare than the plan you've just presented to me. After all, we do want to minimize the potential for this secret of yours escalating into..."

"My dear Mr. Price," Mimi interrupted, "your concern for our welfare is always such a comfort. And your insistence on being present whenever we meet with our new craftsmen has brought you ever closer to our hearts. But I feel assured that no harm will come to us, or to *anyone* for that matter, as a result of this project. With your guidance and our instincts, I believe we have chosen well. And besides, we must periodically let our trust in God, and in human nature, run free. Wouldn't you agree?"

One more time, Amelia and Mr. Price found themselves muted by her persuasive charms, and if any misgivings lingered, none were ever given voice.

Jonathon left for the office an hour later than normal on the morning of March 15.

"So, Mimi, when can I expect the ladies from your luncheon to have departed this afternoon? I wouldn't want to walk into the midst of a hen-pecking session."

His forced laugh was almost as annoying as his patronizing attitude toward her of late. But she pretended not to notice as she playfully kissed him on the cheek and helped him button his coat.

"Actually," she answered, hoping her tone sounded customary, "we have so much catching up to do that I expect we'll be occupied most of the day. If you'll just arrive home in time for dinner as usual, we should have everything back to normal."

"Very well," he said stiffly, tramping down the snow-crunchy steps and across the yard.

"Good-bye, darling," she shouted, leaning over the porch railing and waving to him as he boarded the trolley. "See you tonight."

Shortly before 11:30 that morning, another trolley unloaded ten people one block away from the Madison house. Nine of them briskly made their way toward the McClinty residence, their enthusiastic stride marginally contained by Bradley Price, number ten. He was in the lead, looking dapper in an ankle-length black wool topcoat, a matching fedora, and a gray and white striped muffler tossed casually around his neck.

"Take it easy, my friends," he admonished gently, walking backwards as he held out his hands to slow them down. "We certainly wouldn't want our two Mrs. McClintys to think they'd engaged a stampede, would we? Remember, civility and manners are a priority for each of you. This is your opportunity to uplift your lives. Don't do anything you'll regret. Today is a happy occasion, and we all want it to stay that way."

Heeding his advice, they at least pretended to be under control by the time they assembled on the McClinty front porch. Moments after Mr. Price rang the bell, the door flew open and the two beaming hostesses welcomed their guests inside the entry hall where a quiet man and woman dressed in gray uniforms collected the layers of coats, hats and scarves.

"Please," Mimi said, gesturing toward the parlor, "go in and make yourselves comfortable. We've prepared a few things to nibble on before lunch, and Drake will be in shortly to take your beverage requests. Once everyone has something to drink, we'll tour the house so you can see the rooms you've agreed to transform. Then we'll move into the dining room where we'll enjoy Irene's marvelous meal and get to know each other. How does that sound?"

Bradley Price was standing between Mimi and Amelia, and the two women suddenly noticed that he was the only one other than themselves who appeared to be breathing. The remaining nine people looked as if they were paralyzed. Huddled in a tight cluster, they stared unblinking at the three in charge, never lifting a foot to leave the front hall. Leaning behind Mr. Price, who desperately needed to laugh, Mimi whispered to Amelia.

"Good grief! They're completely terrified. Use your magic to calm them while I go find Drake."

Within five minutes, Amelia had seduced them into a zombie-like march into the parlor, and Mimi had altered Drake's priority from hanging up coats to returning with her to take drink requests. His military stance did little to relax the mood, however, as the artists remained bunched together in a frozen pack. At length, Amelia began to speak.

"All right, ladies and gentlemen, we see that you are uncomfortable, and we understand. But we don't *want* you to feel this way. You are here as our guests, and we are about to entrust the rooms of our home into your care. Please, have a seat, have a bite to eat, and let Drake know your drink preferences. We can provide almost anything you'd like. Naturally, we have tea and coffee, lemonade and a fruit punch. But we also have a variety of spirits as well—brandy, port, whiskey blends and such. Don't be shy. We want you to feel welcome, and before you begin sharing your creative gifts with us, we wish to serve you with *our* gift of this afternoon. Now, Drake will be happy to take your requests."

Fifteen or twenty seconds of silence followed.

"I'll have a brandy straight up, thank you. With a bit of lemon, if you have any, sir."

Joseph Magglio, the eldest of the three brothers engaged to create oil paintings, stood well over six feet tall and weighed 240 compressed pounds. After making the first move to lighten the moment, he edged away from the others and deliberately walked across the room to a burgundy velvet sofa where he sat down. On a small table in front of him was a plate of miniature ham sandwiches, each one about the size of a half-dollar. Reaching out with his right hand, he used two of his stocky fingers to pick up one of the tiny appetizers. Rather than putting the whole thing in his mouth, he gently took a small bite off one corner, holding his left hand underneath his chin to catch any crumbs.

Watching him convert himself into a caricature, his two brothers and his other companions could not contain themselves. Breaking into laughter, they all appeared to relax as they jockeyed to find a place to sit down. Several minutes later, Bradley Price was in the front hall, allegedly blowing his nose. Amelia and Mimi were passing out handkerchiefs. Joseph Magglio was finishing his seventh sandwich, and Drake was still standing at attention awaiting beverage requests.

"If it's not a lot of trouble," said a female voice, "I'd love to have a lemonade."

That statement should not have been particularly funny, but it was to these people.

"I'm sorry, madam, "Drake queried over the fresh outburst of conviviality, "would you care for a sprig of mint with that?"

"A what?" the woman asked, forgetting about the handkerchief and wiping her eyes on her sleeve.

"Yes, she would," said a second lady. "And so would I. A sprig of mint, that is, sounds lovely with a glass of lemonade, for me as well,"

"I'd prefer a little spot of port, if that wouldn't be too much trouble," added a third woman.

There was a thankful buzz throughout the room, and the three ladies engaged to craft afghans, needlepoint covers, and quilts seemed quite pleased with themselves. Friends since their teens, Marjorie McClure and Ethel Prinibar met during the tenth grade in their Brooklyn public school. Anne Delicampo, two years older and the daughter of Italian immigrants, had a full-time job at the bakery where Marjorie and Ethel worked on weekends until they graduated. The following summer, Anne persuaded her two friends to move north with her where, according to Anne's parents, the rest of the American dream was supposed to be located.

Only by God's grace had they survived with their dignity in tact, always clinging to some mythical promise. Anne's idealistic attitude never wavered, though, and while this fact did not keep Marjorie and Ethel from grumbling mercilessly, it did keep them from aborting their stay in Albany. Today on Madison Avenue, they both claimed to have been zealous believers all along.

"All right," Matthew Magglio bellowed in a voice that sounded the same even when he was trying to whisper. "My brother Anthony and I would like some ale. Sir. *Please*," he added, in a raised octave after catching Joseph's glare.

"Ale we have in plentiful supply," Drake responded. "Would you prefer dark or light?"

"Light."

"Dark."

All of the Magglio brothers had thus been accommodated.

"I say, my good man, the two of *us* would surely appreciate an Irish whiskey."

Pepper Shanahan was surprised to feel so at ease in the McClinty home. Now in his early thirties, he had arrived in Boston from Ireland just three years ago. Quickly frustrated by that harbor city's congestion and clogged economic opportunities, he had chosen to follow the Rumored Light westward to Albany. After spending his first rainy night in the promised utopia, however, where he'd scrunched up against a brick building along with half a dozen derelicts, he'd seriously questioned the wisdom of his decision. At sunrise, his doubt deepened when he discovered Geoffrey Mapleton unconscious in the street only a few yards away. The man was well dressed, clean-shaven and nearly dead. Pepper Shanahan soon learned that Mr. Mapleton was a native of Albany whose stained glass studio had been demolished by thieves. Completed works had been stolen. Projects in process had been smashed, and the artist at work had been beaten then dragged to the street where Pepper found and befriended him.

What little money Pepper brought with him from Boston was subsequently used, after Geoffrey's recovery, to help rebuild the shop's inventory of materials. In the process, Geoffrey taught his craft to Pepper who, much to the amazement of both men, had a natural artistic gift. Together since then, the two men had fed each other's malnourished souls, tossed back more Irish whiskey than they cared to remember, and slept in the guarded trust and mutual consideration of their friendship. Pepper was clearly the more optimistic of the two, but then, as Geoffrey often reminded him, he was not the one who'd been left to die in the middle of South Pearl Street. On this fine occasion in the magnificent Madison House, *both* men were jubilant. They could not stop toasting their good fortune at securing this contract to deliver stained glass lamps and perhaps a window or two.

"Yes, sir," Drake answered with a grin, "the McClinty household has a plentiful supply of Irish whiskey."

"And would there be any wine?"

Emanuel Smith was a small man compared to the rest, even compared to the women. According to Bradley Price, he was in his early twenties, but he looked far younger. Mimi had been enchanted with him and his son Jarrett from their first meeting downtown when she selected him to build her library.

"Indeed, sir," Drake replied after seeing Amelia's supportive nod. "The wine cellar has many options for you. I'll bring up a selection."

Having returned from the hallway where he'd been attempting to stifle his own amusement at this entertaining scenario, Bradley Price stood uncomfortably close to Mimi. Stepping back from him, she unobtrusively touched the sleeve of his suit jacket before speaking.

"You've been so kind, helping us find these wonderful people and then bringing them here today. Please relax along with the rest of us."

"Yes. All right," he said, those eyes of his lifting her face upward as if through some magnetic pull. "I suppose remarkable events give us license to bend the rules a bit, and a little brandy does sound delightful."

Within an hour, the tour of the house was complete and everyone had finished nursing their drinks. Taking their places at the mahogany dining room table, they were served Irene's much-heralded menu of roasted game hens, wild rice dressing, buttered green beans, hot-from-the-oven biscuits, and a fresh mixed-fruit salad. Amelia and Mimi did not understand yet that the food on one artist's plate was more than the group's normal combined intake for an evening meal, and this was only *lunch*. But the guests recognized the women's innocence and refrained from saying anything. Instead, they held each bite in their mouths for as long as possible, chewing slowly and hoping to memorize every flavor and aroma.

While Amelia and Mimi suspected that most McClinty family members and friends would have looked upon their odd assortment of guests with considerable disdain, the two hostesses were proud of their new project. They also found themselves forging unexpected attachments, as they listened to nine stories of wrong roads, bad luck, bad decisions, and missed chances. The thought of returning some value to these broken lives touched them both as they basked in the mutual respect shared by everyone seated together.

Consequently, as Irene and Drake were serving dessert, none of them could have been prepared for Jonathon's sudden and dramatic appearance beneath the arched dining room entrance. Stretched in a wide stance and draped in his heavy brown fur coat, he looked and sounded like a rabid animal. His eyes were fixed directly on Mimi, glowing red from fury, and when she stared back at him she saw less of her husband than a figure out of Dante.

"What the *hell* is going on in here?" His commanding voice reverberated against the twelve-foot ceilings, immobilizing everyone at the table, while their forks were still balancing food in mid-air. "Who in God's name *are* these people? And why have you allowed them into our home?"

The ensuing silence echoed in every corner, as the artists and Mr. Price, stunned by the contrast between this scene and the past several hours, awaited instructions. Carefully swallowing the bite of chocolate pie she'd been holding in her mouth, an obviously embarrassed Mimi struggled to find the words—*any* words—to answer him. Amelia had less difficulty, however, and was the first to speak.

"Jonathon," she said firmly, suppressing a surge of anger toward her son, "I think we should discuss this in the parlor."

"Mother, with all due respect, I was talking to my wife."

"Maybe so. But whatever questions you might have can just as easily be addressed to me. Our luncheon today has been a cooperative effort."

"Luncheon?" His face twisted in disgust. "An entertaining definition, to say the least. Mimi," he continued, deferring only slightly to Amelia's power, "please follow me into the parlor—*now*. You will excuse us, Mother," he added, as if there were not ten other people in the room.

When they had gone, Amelia rose from her chair, pressing her fingers against the table's edge for balance as she searched for a way to calm her guests.

"My, oh, my! What a dreadfully unfortunate way for our lovely afternoon to end."

"Does this mean we won't be keeping our new jobs, ma'am?" Joseph Magglio was on his feet, his left hand gripping his right, as if to restrain himself.

"No, Mr. Magglio, it certainly does not. Your new jobs are secure. And please accept my profound apology for Mr. McClinty's conduct. He's really a very kind and gracious man, as I'm certain you will learn once you've begun your projects."

She could tell that no one believed her, and her efforts to relieve the tension were not working. She was also distracted with worry about Mimi, and she felt her strength beginning to evaporate along with her self-control. Without warning, a row of tears slipped down each of her cheeks. The truth was, she realized, that Jonathon had humiliated her, and the possibility that he could do this to her had never crossed her mind. For the first time, she was thankful Nathaniel had not been here to witness their son's behavior. *Whatever could have taken hold of him?*

"Mrs. McClinty," Bradley Price consoled, easing her back down into her chair, "we have all had the most wonderful day. Your hospitality has been overwhelming, and absolutely nothing could diminish the warmth we've felt here in your home. I do think it prudent, though, that my friends and I begin our ride back downtown.

Perhaps you and your daughter-in-law could contact me later this week regarding the manner in which you'd like us to proceed."

"Yes, Mr. Price, that does sound wise. Thank you."

Ringing the small bell next to her coffee cup, she summoned Drake and Irene from wherever they'd been hiding.

"Please help our guests with their coats. They must be going now."

"Yes, Mrs. McClinty."

Spinning around, they rushed off to retrieve the odd assortment of garments collected earlier. Amelia remained seated as she accepted handshakes and expressions of gratitude from each of her new employees.

"If you don't mind," she told them, "I'll let Drake and Irene show you out. Please don't think me rude, but I…"

"We understand, mum," Pepper Shanahan assured her. "Believe me, we do."

Bradley Price ushered his nine charges through the corridor and out to the front porch. Just as he, too, was ready to leave, the heavy pocket doors separating the parlor from the hallway slid open. Jonathon was planted there, his arms stoically folded across his chest as he stared at the stranger he now knew to be the *Times Union*'s editor-in-chief. Neither man spoke, but when Mr. Price glanced over Jonathon's shoulder and saw Mimi curled up on the sofa, her hands quivering and covering her face, he was grateful that his own mother's lessons about holding one's tongue and temper had taken solid root.

"Good day, sir," Bradley said with all the civility he could rally.

Not until he arrived back at his office did he become aware of the pounding ache in his jaws from the force of his clenched teeth. While he was copy-editing later that afternoon, he could not shake the visions of Jonathon's fierce expression and his beautiful wife cowering in the background. Bradley didn't understand yet that his indignation accounted for only a small part of what he was feeling, and he could not have imagined how much worse things were going to get before his future would be set free.

Chapter 3

After tapping without a reply for several minutes, Heidi slowly turned the bedroom doorknob and coughed to announce her presence.

"Please forgive me for interrupting, but it's almost one o'clock and way past Mrs. Stafford's lunchtime."

"I'm sorry, Heidi," Megan responded, pressing the STOP button on the recorder. "I can't believe we didn't hear you! Come in."

"Don't I have a vote?" Cinnamon protested.

"No, I'm afraid not, Gram. You need to eat, and I need to stretch my legs."

"Actually, I fixed a plate for you, too," Heidi announced, proudly rolling in a cart stacked with lunch for two.

"You're very thoughtful, and I do appreciate it. But frankly, I need a break more than I need to eat. Maybe you could leave the tray up here for me, in case I feel like nibbling later."

"Sure, Miss Megan. I'll be happy to fix you up."

"Thanks. Now, Gram, you should give it a rest for a while. I'll either be downstairs or in the yard. Call me when you're ready."

"Well, it won't take me long—half an hour at the most—and I have no extra time for a rest!"

Heidi was bustling around Cinnamon, fluffing her pillows, setting up the bed tray and arranging the food service as if she were in a fine restaurant. Then she began chatting about some television show from the night before while she straightened papers on the desk and generally behaved as if no one else was in the room. Noting that her grandmother appeared perfectly content, Megan hastened her way downstairs and outside. The early afternoon sun was high and warm, tempered by the soft breeze that lifted her long hair off her neck. Meandering toward the pond in the front yard, she felt a refreshing spray from the fountain, which rose ten feet high in the water's center. *We are so fortunate,* she thought, *to have this place in our family—in our lives.*

Sitting down on one of the stone benches dotting the property, she took a rare moment to study Fox Run. The estate included the main house, guest cottage, three barns, and a half-dozen outbuildings, all encircled by thick concentrations of maples, oaks and pines that extended for twenty-five acres around the sides and back of the compound. White fencing along the roadway and a matching hinged gate at the driveway's entrance served as a visual connection binding it all together. Ethereal clusters of deer, hyperactive families of rabbits, and lumbering, rotund raccoons were among the wildlife that regularly ventured beyond the protection of the woods. Tailored lawns, flowerbeds and vegetable gardens were vulnerable prey for these creatures, but no effort was ever made to inhibit the invasions. Somehow, the recurring thrill of spotting two or three deer grazing yards away from the front porch was worth any munched and trampled petunias left in their stead.

"Hey, Meg, are you out on parole?"

The breeze conveyed Kenneth's voice, and it took her a few seconds to spot him walking briskly toward her from the cottage.

"I don't know about parole. Visitation might be a better word."

"Maybe this will help," he said, arriving at the bench and handing her a tumbler filled nearly to the top with a clear liquid as he sat down beside her.

"What's this?"

"Chardonnay. Why?"

"Well, it wouldn't have been my first guess," she answered, trying not to laugh.

"Want me to take it back?"

"No, but I might need a doggy bag. So, what have you been up to this morning?" she asked, taking a sip of wine and finding the dry bite a welcome surprise.

"Playing Scrabble with David since first light, and watching for signs of life from Gram's window for the past two hours."

"I thought Tania's track and field competition was today."

"It is."

"Why aren't you there cheering her on?"

"Well, Justine's on duty since I drew the Fox Run straw. How's everything going upstairs? Is the story over yet?"

"Not even close. Our Margaret Elizabeth McClinty hasn't been born yet. She's only been talking about our great and great-great grandparents."

"Oh *great*," he cheered, ignoring her grimace. "And how long did it take you to fall asleep?"

"Frankly, it's been rather interesting. Of course, she could be making most of it up, but she's managed to produce a few letters that go back more than a hundred years to support what she's saying."

"What *is* she saying?"

"I don't know yet."

"I see—and Who has just stolen third base."

"What?"

"Oh please tell me she didn't just say that!"

"What?"

"Stop it, Meg! And don't say 'what' again, please."

"Why?"

Kenneth was lying on the grass looking up at her, having performed an Abbott and Costello roll off the bench.

"You're supposed to be out of practice."

"Never underestimate me, Kenny."

"Ah-hah! That's right. I remember now. So, where were we?"

"We were talking about Gram."

"Yes, and you were saying…"

"She hasn't mentioned much about the Nathaniel and Amelia saga that we haven't heard before, in one form or another, except for the letters. But there's obviously a lot more to come. She must have a hundred blank tapes up there. One thing *is* sort of surprising, though."

"What's that?"

"To your knowledge, has she ever made even one negative comment about her father?"

"No, not that I can recall. Why?"

"Because Jonathon is sounding like sort of jerk, to put it mildly. Maybe part of Gram's mission is to straighten out misconceptions that have developed, or that she's created, over the years. And maybe she's finally going to tell us what really happened, I mean, with *your* dad and everything. Do you think that's part of what this is all about?"

"First of all, it was Dad and *Teddy*—and maybe what she's trying to do is re-write history on her death bed. Megan, I love Gram, and I don't mean to be rude. But I don't trust her motives any more than I do her promise to stick with the facts."

"Maybe you should be sitting upstairs with me—you know, sort of like a reality monitor?"

"Thanks, but no, thanks. I like the arrangement the way it is. Besides, some-one has to entertain David. I'll just leave it up to you to share what she tells you, so we can crosscheck information against what we're sure is factual."

"Why are you so suspicious?"

"Always have been. Don't know why. But I'm not the only one. William is too."

"Seriously? Did he get that way by himself? Or did you plant the seeds?"

"Maybe I did in the beginning. But my little brother's a big boy now, and he's been keeping his own mind ever since he moved to Buffalo."

"Much as I love William, don't tempt me with that lead-in."

"I won't. Mind if I smoke?"

"Yes."

"Meg, we're in the great outdoors. Lots of air, lots of civil rights," he said, lighting up.

"Let's assume, for discussion purposes," Megan continued, repressing her urge to lecture him again, "that Gram *has* been hiding something, or, *perhaps*, that she's not always rowing with two oars."

"And *new* data will be arriving shortly."

"I can do this without you, Kenny."

"Sorry. Okay. Gram is a wacko."

"Still, she seems serious about supporting her story with documentation."

"Easy so far because, according to you, she hasn't even been born yet."

"Correct. But at least she's introduced a *few* items."

"Besides a couple of letters, though, what has she offered you other than third-hand memories?"

"Not much, I guess. But I vote that we be patient—give her the benefit of the doubt, because..."

"Because *what*?" Kenny asked, noting the changed expression on her face. "What just popped into that head of yours?"

"Want to help me see if we can find something?" she asked, smiling at her cousin's handsome face as she took another sip of wine.

Without waiting for him to answer, she grabbed his arm with one hand. Holding her tumbler in the other, she began leading him toward the back of the main house.

"Somewhere in there," she told him, gesturing toward an area that covered about an acre, "there's supposed to be a plaque. I think she said it was mounted on a stone marker."

"Oh? What kind of plaque? What does it say? And why do we care?"

"If it *is* there, it would mean that she's at least reasonably clear-headed—so far."

"Interesting supposition, Meg. But I don't think you want to go stomping around in all that ivy. Things *live* in there—*scary* things."

"Look, Kenny," she said, pointing to a rise in the blanket of green between the cottage and the field behind the large barn. "I never noticed that before."

"Me neither. What if it's Jimmy Hoffa?"

"Stop it. Would you be a sweetheart and go check it out?"

"Moi? I don't think so, Meg. But thanks for asking."

"Please?" she begged shamelessly, lifting a pair of garden gloves off the back steps. "I promise not to ask another thing of you."

"Until when?"

"Until later."

"That's what I thought. Oh, what the hell. Hand me that stick." After pulling his socks up over his pant legs, he slipped on the gloves and waded into the ivy. "You're lucky you're not criminally ugly, Megan," he called over his shoulder. "Just enough to make people feel sorry for you."

As he moved closer to the rise, pausing occasionally to see what he might have just stepped on and jab whatever it was with the stick, Megan felt her pulse throbbing at her temples. *This really isn't such a big deal. Why in the world am I so excited?* But after he reached his target, she watched as he began to rip and separate the layers of ivy.

"Well I'll *be*!" she heard him shout.

"Why? What is it?" she yelled back.

Their words floated in and out to each other on the brisk wind.

"It's a plaque all right, Meg. I can't believe it, but it's definitely here. Is this the one she told you about?"

"I don't know. What does it say?"

"It says," he continued, looking down to see the writing, then turning to face her as he repeated the words, "*FOX RUN—May this land and its rich native family live forever in harmony with what I pray will be the honor, humility and self-respect of my heirs.* It's signed or etched, or whatever you call it, by none other than Nathaniel McClinty on May 11, 1893."

"Amazing," she whispered to herself. "Yes," she answered as loud as possible. "She told me about it."

"That does it, then," he muttered, high-stepping back toward her. "I'm going to call someone and have all this ivy cleared away. Eighteen-ninety-three! Can you imagine? That thing is almost a hundred years old, and we never even knew it was here. And the guy was our great-great-grandfather! Sort of gives me chills."

"Me, too. But I have a feeling this is only the beginning."

"Well, next time it's *your* turn to traipse through the bugs and snakes."

"Okay, and thanks for volunteering to go first," she said, putting her arms around his neck and pecking him lightly on his cheek. "Guess I'd better get back upstairs, though. Gram said she only wanted to break for half an hour, so I'm already in trouble."

"I don't think so. Otherwise, she would have said something. She's been watching us for the past twenty minutes."

"You're kidding!" Megan glanced across the back yard at the second floor window and saw that it was open. "She must have been listening to everything we were saying."

"Right." Kenneth's focus drifted as he thought about whether their grandmother might have overheard anything that would get him in trouble with her later on.

"Don't worry," Megan said as if reading his mind. "Your wisecracks weren't R-rated, for a change. But now I really *do* need to get going. The saga awaits. I'll see you the next time we come up for air."

"I'll be waiting. Hope there's another plaque or something when you surface. I think I could start to enjoy this game."

Recovery was slow from the artists' introductory day at the Madison house. Jonathon's anger, he had explained later, was the result of Mimi intentionally misleading him. He'd been suspicious about her luncheon story and had planned in advance to drop in unannounced. But in the aftermath of his outburst, he'd begun to wish that he'd asked a few questions first. His wife and mother, he realized, had been operating with admirable, if misguided, intentions. Once they'd explained their scheme to him, he was sorry he'd overreacted. While he never actually apologized, he brought flowers home every evening during the following week. On Friday, he presented both women with gold heart-shaped lockets on long chains. Each locket was engraved on the front with a large ***M*** and had places on the inside for two tiny photographs. On the back, in barely discernible lettering, was the simple inscription, *Mea Culpa.*

"He does seem to be trying."

"I know, Amelia, but I must be honest with you. Something broke that afternoon—something deep inside my love for him, something that used to make forgiveness easy. I can't fully explain the change. I can only tell you that I fear he and I will never be quite the same again."

"Of course you will, my dear. One day I'll share with you a long and tragic story about forgiveness, which will give you a fresh perspective on this situation. Meanwhile, you must trust me and believe that as long as I'm here, you will be safe, and you will be happy. *We* will be happy—all of us. You'll see!"

Shortly thereafter, in early April of 1905, the Madison house projects were officially underway. Jonathon had agreed to the contract for each item, conditioned on the premise that the workers would not be around whenever he was home.

"If the two of you wish to interact with them, I won't stop you, and I'll eagerly await their finished products. But I would rather not be exposed to those people any more than necessary. I'll see that you both have a complete agenda of my time so you can create their schedules."

"Your father must be horrified after watching from heaven as this disgraceful attitude has risen up in you!" Amelia's impassioned assault managed to quiet him momentarily. "God forgive me," she continued, "but you seem more like your brother Peter than you do yourself. What has come over you?"

"Mother, you witnessed nearly all of Dad's directives while Peter and I were growing up, and I challenge you to recall even one instance when he suggested that the proper way to make a difference is to bring inside our own home the very element we abhor and wish to change. He always told me to perform good works and use the gift of my financial resources to help the less fortunate. But he told me to do it *down there.* Forgive me if my methods are unpolished or if I seem unduly insensitive to the many individuals I'm being asked to absorb. I'm not very good at this yet, I suppose. Nonetheless, if you and Mimi insist on pursuing this experiment of yours, you'll simply have to do it on my terms. I trust I've made myself clear."

For awhile thereafter, life in the McClinty household assumed a split personality, bustling and alive with activities for six or seven hours each day, then quiet and sedate whenever Jonathon was home. But the small family unit was adapting, and by late April, Mimi's enthusiasm about her artists and their work had buoyed her spirits, defusing somewhat her worries about the fraying fabric of her marriage. After all, she concluded, she should have been more prepared for the complexities of a union with a man like Jonathon. Perhaps the tension and misunderstandings between the two of them were more her own doing than she'd been willing to admit. Vowing to curb her maverick inclinations, she adopted a more conciliatory tone around her husband, occasionally feeling as if she might choke on the words she was aching to speak, but holding her tongue nevertheless.

If Jonathon noticed his wife's conspicuous attempts to please him, he made no mention of them. He did discover, however, that she was once again receptive to his nighttime advances, whispering her soft declarations of love at the height of his passion and leaving him limp with satisfaction. She, on the other hand, would have preferred to read a book, which she often did after he retreated to the large guest room to sleep, insisting he woke up feeling more rested there.

"As always, Amelia, you were right." Mimi had prepared a pot of tea, which the two women were sharing amidst the steamy comfort of the kitchen early one spring morning. "We *will* be happy—*all* of us. Just think," she added, gazing out the back window across the lawn, "we're already into May, and before long, everything will be blooming. And Pepper and Geoffrey ought to have our lamps finished soon, so we'll be blooming *inside* as well."

"You, my dear, are always in bloom," Amelia said, playfully patronizing the young lady she'd grown to love so much. "You look a bit pale, though. Are you feeling all right?"

"Actually, I've been a bit queasy off and on now for the past few weeks. Nothing awful. Just tired and a bit out of sorts. Mostly in the mornings."

Staring at each other, both of them recognized the truth at the same moment.

"Amelia, I think I'm going to be ill."

"Not to worry, child. I'll be right behind you."

Realizing that she should be ashamed of herself, Amelia simply could not stop smiling as she dampened a towel in the kitchen sink and followed Mimi down the hall.

One consequence of our country's early puritanical history was that a woman's pregnancy was an indelicacy and was to be hidden from view, even when packaged inside a wholly consecrated marriage. Never mind that thousands of babies were born each day and that the process of conception was certainly no secret. Still, despite the miraculous nature of the event, once a baby's development became noticeable, any mother-to-be with a remote inkling of social convention would not permit herself to be seen in public. This practice was theoretically rooted in the male population's profound respect for women "in such a condition" and an almost pathological concern for their safety. Clearly, the concept that a woman who was *with child* might have a vaguely productive moment was completely absurd. While later generations of both sexes would have difficulty believing that the majority of American women ever complied with such constraints, prenatal confinement was once, indeed, an accepted practice.

For many women, especially those who found themselves creating large families, their child-bearing years were marked by extended periods of loneliness and an incongruous sense of loss. As new life was being formed, their marriages were being redefined and restructured. Where there had once been an effort to balance the needs of both partners, the introduction of children left the husband's world largely unaffected while the wife's body, daily routine, responsibilities, sphere of influence, and self-esteem were grossly altered—generally in a negative direction.

But these issues were still more than half a century away from open discussion and reform when Mimi's pregnancy was confirmed. Thus, she had no reason to question her circumstances, nor was she able to fully appreciate her life as compared to others with the same *affliction*, because there was definitely *not* any loneliness in the Madison house. Too many beautiful crafts were taking shape, and people were constantly dashing in and out. In those rare moments when absolutely nothing was happening, she always had Amelia.

Naturally, no one noticed Mimi's physical changes for several months. The three Magglio brothers seemed particularly immune, arriving each morning by 10:00, Monday through Friday, unless Jonathon planned to be home, and then departing by 3:00 in the afternoon. Their respective oil canvases, set up on easels in their assigned rooms, were left in place, enabling the artists to capture the permanent and shifting elements of light in each area. Jonathon had objected to this arrangement at first, complaining about the obstacle course of paraphernalia in his way.

"Why can't they paint at home?" he'd asked. "Surely, if they are as talented as you say, they can just as easily visualize a boat or whatever they're drawing, in their own studio."

Mimi elected first to remind her husband that true artists need to define their settings on *their* terms. She then decided not to tell him that the Magglio brothers had neither studio nor home, at least none of their own. Two generations of the Magglio family had struggled against a ne'er-do-well, scruffy Italian image belying their self-educated, well-read, artistic heritage. Sadly, the brothers and a younger sister Velita had been orphaned. But the Albany court system had been able to divert the children from State homes in a quiet response to the dozens of relatives—many of whom the boys had never heard of—who flocked to their adoptive rescue. Before any proceedings were final, however, Joseph turned eighteen and persuaded the court to place his two younger brothers in his care. Velita went to live in New York City with an aunt and uncle where she attended school in a convent.

Knowing his sister was protected, Joseph focused on the rearing of his brothers while he unloaded freighters in the harbor during the day and perfected his art at night. In the beginning, the one room they could afford was sufficient. As the boys entered their puberty years, however, Joseph not only recognized the need to find an apartment with more space and privacy for them, but also the necessity of reigning in their rebellious spirits. Having sold his first two paintings, he leased a four-room flat above a shop on Lark Street. There he began redirecting his brothers' adolescent distractions by introducing them to his craft. Much to his relief, they both demonstrated encouraging skill, and more significantly, they also began sharing his interest. Within a year, he was finding buyers for their work as well as his own.

Remaining devoutly unmarried, Joseph had loved only once. Her name had been Veronica, and she'd been seventeen at the time, a year behind him in school. But after his parents died, the responsibility for his brothers began to dominate his priorities. Veronica claimed to understand, although she'd moved to Boston when she finished high school and married someone else within the year. Convinced his heart would never open to another woman, Joseph committed himself to his family, establishing a firm control over his brothers. Using paints, brushes and canvas as tools of instruction for more than just art, he taught Matthew and Anthony about beauty, respect, and the permanence of one's word.

When the boys began developing an interest in the opposite sex, any girl introduced to life in the small Lark Street apartment could not help but see the power structure at work. Daunting as this should have been, Matthew and Anthony were more charming than Joseph was intimidating. When they were nineteen and twenty-one, respectively, they had each fallen in love with young women who were happy to take on the responsibility of nurturing this captivating family of men. In June of 1900, at a small private service inside the Cathedral's chapel, Joseph stood up for both of his brothers when they married their brides in a double ceremony.

"May you forever conserve energy, resources, canvas, oils, and wine," he toasted, "and may you have much happiness and many babies under God's watch."

Now, almost five years later, the four-room Magglio apartment was home to the three brothers, two wives, and Matthew's two daughters, ages three months and one-and-a-half years.

It could be worse, I suppose, Joseph mused. *If things had worked out differently, I'd have my own woman and little tykes as well.*

"Joseph! Joseph!" Matthew's whisper aroused his older brother from his faraway thoughts one afternoon at the Madison house.

"What, for God's sake? And why aren't you at work? Do you know what would happen if Mr. McClinty came home and found you wasting time?"

"I *have* been at work. Walk down and see for yourself. But this can't wait. Have you noticed anything different about our Miss Mimi?"

Joseph's look of exasperation was all too familiar and included an unspoken directive to stop gossiping.

"All right, then," Matthew grumbled, heading back to his station. "But you just take a good look the next time she comes around. I'm telling you, Joseph. Twice I watched my Helena change when a baby was beginning inside her. The look is like no other, and Miss Mimi is wearing *her* look like a fine new dress."

That evening, in the tightly clustered cocoon of the Magglio apartment, Joseph made a declaration, which would one day be remembered as nothing short of prophetic.

"A lovely pair of Irish women has hired us. They are wealthy, but they are offering us an opportunity that no one else has been willing to give. Now it seems that Miss Mimi might be having, as *they* call it, a wee one. Irish as this child may be, our family will bring it inside our hearts because I have seen the father first-hand, and my soul is heavy with what I believe awaits that baby. We will complete our paintings as our contract indicates. But when our business is finished, we will not abandon those women. God is letting me know that we'll be needed later, so there will be no discussion on this matter."

The subsequent seasons of 1905 each left a notable signature upon those who lived and worked in the Madison house, and on the house, as well. Because Mimi's pregnancy was common knowledge by August, plans for a nursery were already being discussed. A corner bedroom on the second floor had been chosen for its spaciousness and for the six tall sash windows along the two outer walls, which welcomed soft indirect light all day. At first with curiosity, and then with imagination, the Madison artists carved out time on their own inside the room, studying the contours, the shadings, the sounds.

Anne Delicampo was the first to approach Amelia on a Monday in early October with the idea she'd conceived along with Marjorie and Ellen. Following the colorful illustrations in her favorite children's storybook, Anne had drawn sketches for a knitted baby blanket, a needlepoint footstool with a matching chair cushion, a braided rug, and a cluster of embroidered pillows. Every design was infused with such intricacy that it appeared three-dimensional—the fantasy rabbits, chickens, bears, princes and princesses coming so alive with animated spirit that they seemed to be in motion.

"Do you think she'll like them, Miss Amelia?" the three zealous women asked in a unified whisper during the mid-morning rest period mandated by both Mrs. McClintys, once Anne had introduced the concept.

"My dear ladies, Mimi would be delirious over such beautiful gifts. But I fear you've committed yourselves to far more than necessary. Not only do you have your own work, but I believe you promised her that you'd begin taking a few courses at the university. Am I mistaken?"

"No, ma'am, you're not." Anne was never the one to be timid, and she proved to be a fitting spokesperson for the trio. "We did make that promise. Miss Mimi said we could wait, though, until Emanuel has finished the library, which he tells us won't be until November. Then she'll have a proper place to help us with our studies. By that time, we will have completed our new gifts. Naturally, our commissioned work for you will be done first."

"Well, I suppose if you ladies think you can manage all of this," Amelia said with a grin as she passed her hand over the sketches, "please go right ahead. And on behalf of my son and daughter-in-law, I thank you for your generosity and your desire to do this for our new baby. I would like to ask, though," she continued in a lowered voice, "that the four of us keep your gifts a secret. There's no need to create any additional sense of obligation on the part of our other artists."

Anne and her friends looked at one another then nodded weakly in agreement. Miss Amelia would obviously be discovering very soon that her latest request could not possibly be honored.

"Excuse me, ma'am." Joseph Magglio was whispering to her through the dining room's open French doors while she stood on the side porch early the next morning. "May I please speak with you?"

"Yes, of course. Is everything all right?" Amelia was whispering, too, for some reason.

"All of us could not be better. But I was hoping you might have time for me to show you something, whenever it's convenient."

"Right now would be fine. How can I help?"

She was taken completely off-guard by his response, as she watched him unfold the design he and his brothers had created for a continuous mural to be painted on the nursery walls.

"You see, Miss Amelia, our brushes will tell the story of a little angel sent to live in the Madison house. We'll paint a peace into that room with our pastels that will comfort the baby and soothe every caretaker. This will be our gift to the child—and to you."

Amazed at the gentle nature of this stout, rugged man, Amelia felt herself touched by his peace already.

"Will you have the time, though, Joseph? Your responsibilities for your own family are so overwhelming."

"We are all in agreement, Miss Amelia. Even our women."

"I see. Well, if *your* women have given their blessing, how could *I* possibly refuse?"

"Oh, thank you so very much," he said, clearly pleased but missing her jest. "If you wouldn't mind going along with us, we'd like to keep this a secret from Miss Mimi so we can surprise her."

"And just how do you propose we do that, Joseph? Won't it be rather difficult for you and your brothers to paint this masterpiece without her noticing?"

"We know you'll think of something, Miss Amelia. You always do. Now, if you'll excuse me," he added, rolling up his design, "I must get back to my work. I've been gone too long as it is."

Drake materialized only seconds later.

"May I get something for you, madam?"

"Yes, as a matter of fact, I think need a new appointment calendar. That was an attempt at humor, Drake," she added, noting the *how do I find one?* worry-lines on his brow. "Actually, some tea would be wonderful. Our fall is so pleasant this year, and since I have much to think about, I'd like to do it out here on the porch for a little while. After all, snow will be covering everything before we know it."

"I believe you're right. Other than your tea, will there be anything else?"

"Not at the moment, thank you."

Keeping the ladies' projects from Mimi is going to be manageable, she reflected, seating herself on a concrete porch bench, *but the Magglio mural would be impossible to hide, unless…*

"Pardon me, Miss Amelia, am I intruding?"

Pepper Shanahan stood in front of her, his arms straight down at his sides.

"Hello, Mr. Shanahan," she purred. "How nice to see you! And would I be correct in assuming that you have something you'd like to show me?"

So grateful was he for the painless admittance that, in his enthusiasm, he skipped right over any reply and went directly into his proposal.

"These first designs are mine, one for a stained glass ceiling fixture, or perhaps a floor lamp. The others are from Geoffrey for matching table lamps, maybe for the baby's dresser and end table, or wherever Miss Mimi would like to put them, of course. Marjorie loaned us a storybook filled with illustrations that we've used for patterns. If you think these gifts are appropriate, and if we have your approval, we'd ask that you keep our plans secret so we can make this a surprise."

Drake deftly slid in and out of the conversation, pouring tea for Amelia, then leaving condiments and a half dozen empty cups for any other unexpected guests. Beneath the stack of napkins on the tray was a small black leather book, the front embossed in gold with the word APPOINTMENTS.

Where in the world did he find that? Amelia wondered. "Secret plans," she said, lifting the steaming china cup in a toast to Pepper. "What a unique proposition."

Having been visited that day by all of the other artists, she waited for Emanuel Smith to approach her. But he never did. Finally, once the foyer clock had chimed three, Amelia decided to take the offensive. She knew that Mimi would be occupied with her tutoring of little Jarrett in the parlor. So, for the first time in many weeks, she pushed open the heavy doors leading from the main hall into the library-in-progress.

Stunned by her first close-up view of the intense detail imbedded in Emanuel's towering cabinets and solid tables, Amelia found herself unable to speak.

"Miss Amelia! Hello there!" Emanuel's voice was coming from ceiling-height. Balanced on top of a twelve-foot ladder, he was sanding the upper shelves. "I'm sorry. If I'd known you'd be popping in, I would have cleaned up my mess."

"Nonsense, Emanuel. You have your work to do, and I have no desire to interrupt you. I simply wanted to see how you were getting along and to find out if there's anything else you need," she said, talking to him from the base of the ladder. "Your work, by the way, is magnificent."

"Thank you," he answered softly, looking down at her. "I'm happy that you're pleased."

"How could I *not* be? You've surpassed all of my expectations, and now I understand what an amazing gift we were given when we found you."

"No, ma'am," he said, wiping his forehead on the sleeve of his shirt. "*I'm* the lucky one. Actually, both Jarrett and I are. The day you and Miss Mimi showed up was when the sun started rising for us again each morning."

"Well, we could probably toss our mutual admiration around until that sun sets, Emanuel. But I think it best that I quit bothering you. I'm afraid you're going to fall, and I'm getting dizzy just looking up at you."

"Don't you be worrying yourself about me. I'm closer to God up here," he said smiling.

"Yes, I can see that. Please let us know, though, if we can do anything for you, down here on earth."

I certainly hope he doesn't hear about the other plans for baby gifts, she thought as she closed the tall double doors behind her. *He has his hands quite full enough creating a library for us that the City of Albany may try to acquire once they find out about it. I wonder if Mimi has any idea what's happening inside that room.*

"Amelia." Her daughter-in-law's voice was right behind her. "Forgive me for not visiting with you earlier, but I wasn't feeling very well this morning, and Jarrett needed extra help with his reading lessons. Now that we have a moment," she continued, linking her arm in her mother-in-law's, "what delicious scuttlebutt have you overheard today that we can share together?"

"Well, my dear, I doubt that I've heard a single thing of interest. In fact, for a Tuesday, it's been rather dull around here."

Early one November afternoon a few weeks later, a messenger arrived at the Madison House with a letter addressed to Mimi and Amelia.

Dear Ladies—

Forgive me for not contacting you sooner. I had planned to arrange a visit last month, but my schedule became unexpectedly full. Besides, I trusted that you would let me know if you were having any difficulties with your new employees. Also, I cannot tell a lie. Each of them has been stopping by on occasion, either en route to Madison or on their way home, to update me on their progress. My instincts tell me that sometimes I'm privy to the exact truth, and other times I'm hearing either an exaggerated account or an underrated synopsis.

Since every person speaks of you both with such a high level of praise, however, I have not worried too much about the discrepancies. I have been thinking of you, though, and I'm now about to be extremely brash by asking to be invited whenever your artists unveil their final works. Realizing that I've merely served as an intermediary, I know I should not be feeling such a part of what is taking place out there. Nonetheless, I do. If I am overstepping my bounds, please tell me.

Wishing you both a joyous conclusion to your original plans, I will respectfully await your reply.

Regards,
Bradley C. Price

Having read the mail after awakening from her late-day rest, Mimi waddled in her nightgown and bare feet as fast as she could down the hallway toward the kitchen.

"How could we possibly have been so insensitive?" she moaned to Amelia, who trailed behind her daughter-in-law as she pushed through the swinging door and sat down at the cutting table.

Irene looked up from her dinner preparations and awaited a signal from Amelia. The pregnancy frequently brought Mimi to the kitchen, and during the past few months Irene had seen and heard more than she cared to know about a variety of topics—most of them related to bodily functions. But she'd learned in the process to take her cues from Amelia and then go about her business as if nothing unusual were taking place. This time, as she watched Mimi wildly waving a letter in the air, she worried that she might have to leave the room.

Relax, Amelia's eyes told her. *Just pretend like we're not here.*

"I can't believe we've ignored him so shamefully!" Mimi lamented.

Six months into her pregnancy, her tummy rested on her thighs as she sat on the kitchen bench. Her cheeks were puffy and flushed, yet somehow complimenting the shaggy round bun piled loosely on top of her head.

What a mess she is, Amelia thought with a blend of amusement and concern.

"You're right, dear. We'll send him a letter of apology tomorrow, and in the process we'll assure him that the finale would neither be complete nor proper without his presence. Now sit there and relax while I fix you some warm milk."

Keeping all the nursery secrets straight became a little easier once the holidays approached, partially because the paint fumes made Mimi nauseous and thus forced her to remain a safe distance from the baby's room-to-be. But Jonathon's escalating impatience with the decorating projects also required Amelia to tighten the reigns on her artists and to abandon her flexibility regarding deadlines. This ultimately proved helpful, as well, as the secrets became harder to contain.

"We simply must have everything completed by the first week in December," she announced in an uncharacteristically stern voice during a meeting arranged over breakfast two weeks before Thanksgiving. "We've grown very fond of all of you and will miss seeing you here every day, but your projects now need to reach their conclusions. Snowy months will be here before we know it, and we want to pay all of you in full so that you and your families might celebrate the end of this wonderful year. We, on the other hand, have to make ready for a new baby due in January. As you're all aware, Mimi tires very quickly now and is *supposed* to have bed rest most of each day."

Amelia thought this would strike a chord of laughter, because those present had rarely even seen Mimi sit down. But realizing how seriously everyone was taking this baby, she continued in a more moderate tone.

"She's also going to require a peaceful and *finished* place to live during the final months. I know all of you will do everything within your power to meet this deadline for her, and for me, and for Mr. McClinty, as well. He's looking forward to reclaiming his house."

"And to the arrival of his baby, we hope."

She tried to ignore the deep Italian voice, muffled slightly by a napkin, as she passed another basket of muffins around the dining room table. She knew a line had been crossed with that comment, but chose not to do anything about it, other than cast a cautionary glance toward Joseph. Even then, she could not help but smile, as she watched him lift his china coffee cup by the handle with his oversized right thumb and forefinger. After blowing gently on the steam, he took a sip and leaned back in his chair, still holding the cup while resting his wide arms on the ledge created by the intersection of his chest and belly.

For the first time, Amelia felt a little melancholy. *I will miss this. We are not going to have an easy time restructuring life within these walls once these dear people have gone.*

By eight o'clock on Friday morning, December 14, 1905, Drake and Irene were preparing to serve a full breakfast for the artists after the projects were unveiled. Even Jonathon committed to be there, but then at the last moment—only half an hour prior to everyone's arrival—he'd informed his wife and mother that he preferred to go to the mill.

"I don't really know your artists, and I'm afraid they're not easily relaxed when I'm around. Besides, I have some problems to iron out with the latest shipment to Philadelphia."

"But don't you want to be with us when we see everything for the first time?" A very bloated Mimi could not believe he was leaving. "They've been working on these projects for us since April!"

"You say that as if I didn't know. Perhaps you've forgotten that I've wanted them out of here for the past eight months! So, don't you worry, darling. When I come back this evening, you and Mother can give me a tour. Then we'll celebrate together, just the three of us. Have I made myself clear?"

After he left, the women readily agreed that they would all be much happier throughout this much-anticipated morning with their friends now that Jonathon would *not* be joining them.

Anne, Marjorie and Ellen were the first to arrive, missing Jonathon by only a few minutes. Irene and Drake met them at the front door.

"We've put both Mrs. McClintys in the kitchen," Drake volunteered. "They're warm and reasonably comfortable, and they're not supposed to peek."

"That's the plan anyway," Irene added. "But they're so excited that they might not be very trustworthy."

"We'd better hurry, then," Anne announced. "Marjorie, why don't you take the things for the dining room and parlor? You know where they go and how to arrange them. Ellen and I will be up in the nursery when you're finished."

Drake was still putting the ladies' coats in the closet when footsteps and voices were heard on the front porch. Irene opened the door and greeted the three Magglio brothers, each holding a large narrow rectangular package wrapped in brown paper. Two additional packages, even larger than the others, rested against the porch wall.

"Please come in, gentlemen." Drake was beside Irene, offering his assistance. "The tools you requested, Mr. Magglio, are on the terrace outside the dining room."

"Thank you," Joseph answered, then directed his attention to Matthew and Anthony. "Double-check your measurements with each other before you hang them. We don't want them off by even a fraction. I'll be up in the nursery."

"I can't remember this much excitement since I was a little girl," Irene said, helping Drake with the coats after the brothers left the foyer. "It's truly remarkable that we've managed to keep all of this from Miss Mimi. All we need now are the Irishmen and Mr. Smith."

"They're already here," Drake announced. "I let them in before dawn so they could carry everything upstairs while our ladies still slept."

"Oh, my," Irene sighed, her eyes widening with delight. "So you've seen it?"

"Yes, and it's astonishing."

The door chimed again just as Anthony began hammering his nails over the living room fireplace.

"I thought everyone was here," Irene mumbled, cautiously opening the door. "Why, Mr. Price, how good to see you! Do come in."

Drake collected the editor's stylish coat, hat, scarf and gloves, while Irene led him into the parlor.

"Please make yourself comfortable, sir," she said. "We have quite a bit of last-minute activity going on, and our ladies have been relegated to the kitchen temporarily. We should only need to wait a short while longer, though. Can we bring you something?"

"Yes, as a matter of fact, some of that coffee I'm smelling would be perfect."

Drake's wife and sister had been enlisted to help with breakfast preparations and to keep Amelia and Mimi contained in the kitchen. By the time Irene returned there to get coffee for Mr. Price, the room was filled with delicious, steamy aromas, light-hearted chatter and a sense of expectation one could almost touch.

Mimi was seated in a large wooden rocker brought in from the porch, her swollen feet and ankles propped up on an empty, overturned flower box. Her pale blue woolen tent dress wrapped her in a soft simplicity, the fabric covering her legs and then draping on the floor beneath the rocker. Pulled loosely over her shoulders was a white shawl she'd crocheted the week before, which complimented the thirty-inch strand of tiny pearls cascading down from her neck then up and over her tummy. Pearl stud earrings completed the look, as she readjusted one of the silver combs holding her hair on top of her head.

"Irene," she asked, clapping her hands together in an almost childlike fashion, "who was that at the door?"

"Just about everyone who's supposed to be here, Miss Mimi," the housekeeper responded, not exactly certain how much she should say.

"Let's go, then!"

"Not so fast, dear." Amelia was helping Drake's wife remove the ham from the oven. "I believe our artists are finishing a few final details. Our whereabouts are quite well-known, however, and we will be summoned when it's time."

"I'm not sure how much longer I can wait. This is starting to feel like torture."

"Here," Amelia said, recognizing the early symptoms of a Mimi-mood. "Have a muffin and some milk."

As hoped, the food diverted her attention, and the last few minutes of waiting passed in relative quiet.

"Excuse me," Drake said, peering around the kitchen door a short while later.

"Is it time?"

"Yes, Miss Amelia. Everything is ready."

Mimi rather ungracefully disengaged herself from the rocking chair and flower box and pushed herself to her feet with Drake's assistance.

"Thank you," she said, smiling at him as she tucked a long strand of loose hair behind her ear. "I think I can manage on my own now."

While Drake, his family, and Irene stayed behind to complete breakfast preparations, Mimi and Amelia made their way down the hall to the foyer where their artists and Mr. Price greeted them with a round of applause.

Choked with an unforeseen rush of sentiment, neither woman was able to speak for a moment. Not surprisingly, Mimi was the first.

"Hello, everyone. And Mr. Price! How very good to see you as well. We're so happy you could join us. You've most likely noticed a few changes since your last visit."

"Not really, Mrs. McClinty," he responded, gazing shamelessly at his very round, ruddy-cheeked hostess. "Everything appears to be just as lovely as it was before, if not more so."

"Yes, indeed," Amelia added, watching the group look back and forth between Mr. Price and Mimi, unable to ignore the chemistry passing between them. "Both my daughter-in-law and I want to thank all of you for arriving so early this morning and for your kind applause a moment ago. However, we are the ones applauding you. Your talents and efforts have brought us to this most exciting day, and we are deeply grateful for the way each of you has enriched our lives. Now, how would you like to proceed?"

Mr. Price stepped forward.

"I've been asked to act as master of ceremonies, guiding us from room to room, and then introducing the artists who will point out their projects and comment on any special aspects of their creations."

"This must be the first stop," Mimi interrupted, touching the tall lamp on the foyer sideboard.

"Yes, you're way ahead of me," Mr. Price continued, wondering how long he could maintain control of the tour. "Pepper and Geoffrey, would you like to tell us about your work?"

Both men moved to the front of the group, but Pepper did all the talking.

"This lamp base is brass, and the glass pieces in the shade are from a broken window at the Cathedral. We saw some workmen replacing it, and Father said we could have the old one. We had to cut the pieces real small because of all the cracks, and we ended up with a bit more than we thought we would, which you'll see in a minute someplace else. First, though, the beaded trim hanging down from the shade came from a fellow we met on the docks. He was a trader who earns his living traveling across the sea from England, back and forth, buying and selling whatever he can find. Geoffrey had just finished making a tabletop, and this fellow wanted it. So we traded for a bag of beads, which we knew would help us complete about six lamps. The thing is, we had a jeweler friend of ours examine them, and they're not just beads. They're Austrian crystals. So," he concluded with a huge grin, "either Geoffrey's tabletop was worth a lot more than we thought, or our trader friend was new on the job."

Following an undercurrent of good-humored support, everyone stepped up to see the crystals more closely, taking their time to admire the lamp's intricacies. After several minutes, Mr. Price came up with a better idea.

"May I have your attention, please? Our hostesses have assured me that there will be plenty of opportunity after breakfast to study each of your contributions. Because we have so much to see, let's move quickly through the tour, and then enjoy our meal together. We'll come back and revisit everything later."

Noting the room full of nodding heads, Pepper continued by introducing two sidelight panels constructed from the same Cathedral glass.

"These will be installed on either side of the front door, offering privacy as well as beauty. Then, later on in the tour, we have a few surprises."

"Oh how delightful," Mimi cooed, bobbing up and down in one large wave of movement.

"Joseph, would you and your brothers like to be next?"

"Yes, sir, Mr. Price. We would." He remained where he was standing, in the back of the group, his arms folded across his chest. "Our project was to create oil paintings for the living room, parlor and dining room. As a theme, we chose the seasons we've spent working in this house, and we chose the house, itself, as the subject. Please. Come see for yourselves. In the parlor we have *Spring*, which is the time of year we began our job here. Across the hall in the living room, we have *Summer*."

Mimi and Amelia could not believe what they were seeing. Hanging over the fireplace in each room was a canvas of color that moved from inside to outdoors. The parlor view had been sketched looking through one of the front windows across the porch and onto the lawn. Hanging baskets of wisteria and beds of tulips brought spring to life inside the oils. The living room painting had been viewed through the side window, capturing the deep full-summer greens of oaks and maples, and the crimson expanse of rose bushes at their peak of summer bloom.

"While we're here," Anne Delicampo interjected, "this might be a good time to draw your attention to the needlepoint footstools made by Marjorie and Ellen. They also have the spring and summer themes and contain the same flowers and colors that Matthew and Anthony used in their paintings. Also the yellow afghan folded on the wing chair over there in the parlor is one that I knitted. Later on when you have a chance to open it up, you'll see that I embroidered a replica of the wisteria basket hanging on the front porch."

Suddenly everyone's focus shifted from the afghan to the sound of sobbing coming from the living room. Mimi was drooping in an overstuffed armchair, her hands squeezed together in her lap.

"My dear child, are you all right?" Amelia asked.

"Shall I send for the doctor?" Joseph's face was tight with concern.

"No, no, please," Mimi insisted through her stuffy sinuses. "I'm fine. *Really*," she added, blowing her nose on a handkerchief handed to her by Mr. Price. "I'm just a bit overwhelmed by all of this. It's not only the beautiful things you've made, but the priceless love you've brought into this house by being here—by being yourselves and letting us get to know you."

She barely finished her sentence before she began weeping again. Someone handed her another handkerchief and a glass of water, and then Amelia spoke.

"All right. I think we need to readjust our schedule."

"No, Amelia. Honestly, I'm fine."

"Yes, of course you are. We can all see that. But we still have a great deal to preview, and I'm afraid you'll never make it if you don't eat something first."

"I tend to agree," Mr. Price chipped in supportively. "Is there anything else we need to show in this part of this house?"

"Just one." Joseph's voice could be heard coming from the front hall. "This is a surprise, something my brothers and I added on our own. We worked with the colors used by Pepper and Geoffrey in their lamp and sidelights, and we've called it *Madison in Fall.*"

Mimi had stopped crying and, with Amelia and Mr. Price on either side of her, was slowly making her way to the foyer. There, propped on top of the sideboard, was a painting of the house as it looked from the street out front, the contours of brick, porch railings and columns all captured in minute detail. Even the new stained-glass sidelights had been painted.

Now *Amelia* was weeping.

"I swear to heaven, this household sees more crying time than any I've ever witnessed in my life," Ellen whispered to Emanuel, who'd been watching in silence. "It's like they're all hooked together on some long, invisible chain. One yank is all it takes to get the whole family going. Happy, sad, funny, disgusting—doesn't seem to matter. Eventually, regardless of how they begin, they always end up crying."

"I think it's part of why they're special."

"I guess you're right, Emanuel. But at this rate, how will they ever get through the rest of the tour—particularly *your* part. When they take their first look at that library, we'll be mopping up all around them."

"I'm just praying that the first thing to happen in that new room is not the birth of Miss Mimi's child."

"Very amusing, Emanuel."

"Believe me, I wasn't trying to be funny."

As Amelia had suggested, delaying the rest of the tour in order to have breakfast proved to be the perfect tonic. Seated on Anne and Marjorie's twelve new needlepoint chair cushions, the artists, hostesses and Bradley Price reigned in their emotions as they ate and talked throughout the next hour.

The first challenge had been working their way through the initial sighting of Joseph's surprise portraits—one of Mimi and one of Amelia—mounted on the walls at opposite ends of the dining room. Other than Matthew and Anthony, nobody had known these were coming, and there was not a dry eye until well after the fresh fruit was served. Joseph had indeed exceeded his own expectations through his ethereal oil visions of the two women who had changed all of their lives. Canvas-to-canvas, across the room from each other, their faces were strong, yet soft—one still dripping with youthful beauty, one aging with extraordinary grace. Their eyes, different blends of Irish green, saw not just each other, but everyone in the room, everyone they met, with the same clarity and absence of bias. Joseph loved these women beyond his powers of verbal expression, and by painting their portraits, he had, in a quietly selfish way, hoped to somehow preserve that love beyond the inevitable ending of this bittersweet day.

Amelia was seated at the table's far end, her own portrait on the wall behind her. Mimi was at the other, also framed by her painted image. Mr. Price was in the chair to Amelia's left, having been guided there by Amelia herself. The artists had then taken the remaining places at random, except for Emanuel Smith, who'd been assigned to the chair on Mimi's right. His job was to prepare her, through light conversation, for her first glimpse of the library. He was also supposed to lay the preliminary groundwork for her introduction to the nursery. But he had not anticipated the mild panic, which had begun to make his feet throb. *I do believe I need some help with this assignment.*

After the eggs and ham had been consumed, while Irene was pouring coffee, Emanuel excused himself from the table and found pen and paper in the parlor desk. When his note was finished, he asked Drake to quietly slip it to Amelia.

> ***Please, Miss Amelia, after we show her the library, we need to tell her about the nursery before going upstairs. I'm afraid that if she's allowed to see it before she's properly prepared, she might become ill, or worse, have her baby too soon—for example, this morning. On my own, I doubt that I'm handling the situation the way we had planned, so I thank you for any assistance you might provide.***
>
> *Emanuel*

She looked up and smiled at the small nervous man sitting next to her daughter-in-law. *What a dear person,* she thought. *He doesn't even realize that I have not seen the nursery myself. His warning may unknowingly do more good for my heart than for Mimi's birthing schedule. And it does help to have some hints. Surprises, I suppose, are not always the best of ideas.*

"May I have your attention again please," Amelia announced, clinking spoon against glass and rising to her feet. "Before we proceed to the library and then on to our final room…Yes, Mimi," she inserted, watching the round body try to sit up straight at the other end of the table, "there *is* one room you do not know about yet, and there will be no questions at this time."

The guests looked from Amelia to Mimi and back again, smiling and understanding.

"As I was saying, before we proceed, I have a few remarks that simply cannot wait any longer. It's been nine months, almost to the day, since we as a unique group shared our first meal together in this dining room. You have not only become our friends, but we feel as if you've become part of our family. Just because your projects are finished now, we don't want you to disappear from our lives. All of you will forever be welcome here, and we hope you'll come visit us often after the baby is born."

Everyone glanced in Mimi's direction as she blotted her eyes with her napkin.

"I'm sorry," she said, trying to clear her nose. "It's as if someone walked away and left the faucet running on my face."

"Don't you fret, dear," Amelia continued. "We *all* feel a little bit sad today, but there are so many *happy* things to celebrate, in spite of our mixed emotions, not the least of which are the many works of art that these good people are leaving with us—lovely things that will remind us of them every time we see and use them. All right," she said, walking to the china cabinet and opening the center drawer, "here we have the *most* fun!" In her hands, she held nine envelopes, each bearing an artist's name. "In addition to the amounts we agreed upon so many months ago, we have included a holiday bonus for each of you, so that you and your families can do something extra for yourselves. We wish we could give you more, and as the years pass, we hope to employ you again. We will also be spreading the word about you and your many talents. Now, let's finish our tour, shall we? Then we'll visit awhile longer before calling it a day."

What the artists did not know as they folded their napkins and pushed back their chairs was that the holiday bonus doubled the amounts they were expecting. Making such a significant contribution to so many Christmases caused Mimi to weep again each time she thought about it, forcing her to dab continually at her eyes as she joined the group gathering in the hallway outside the library. Emanuel stood beside her, his hand on the doorknob, as Bradley Price made his brief introduction.

"All right," he said. "We've waited long enough. Emanuel, please do the honors."

With a turn of the knob, Emanuel pushed open the double doors revealing a high, narrow room full of polished mahogany and gleaming brass—and more stained glass. Straight ahead was a tall window at the far end of the room facing the door, and on both side walls were Emanuel's floor-to-ceiling shelves. Leaning against the right-hand side was a library ladder crafted with engineering detail that enabled a reader to safely reach a book catalogued nearly twelve feet off the floor.

Perpendicular to the far window was a double-sided desk—a place where Amelia and Mimi could both work and visit with one another—the top of the burgundy leather freshly oiled and smelling rich, as were the two matching high-backed leather swivel chairs. On the window end of the desk was one more lamp from Pepper and Geoffrey, this creation measuring a yard in height with a wider base and shade than the others, but with the same Cathedral glass. Coordinated lamps with oil wicks rested in the middle of each of three round mahogany reading tables that had been placed throughout the room, providing additional seating for nine. A sofa upholstered in burgundy floral chintz was centered across the narrow width of the library, facing the desk and positioned about five feet from the room's entrance. Flanking the sofa were two end tables, with a tea table positioned in front—all pieces the product of Emanuel's amazing craftsmanship.

No one spoke when Mimi entered the room. She moved slowly, brushing her fingertips across the tables, the desk, the shelf edges, and she seemed to float along the wood flooring despite the fact that she felt as if she weighed a ton. Standing near the window, she turned toward the group, her eyes and face dry for the first time in two hours.

"Thank you—*all* of you. I had no idea when we first met you last winter that you would bless us so generously. As Amelia said earlier, you will always be welcome here because we love you and because so much of the house now comes from you. Emanuel, all I can say to you is that I hope my family and I can do this room justice. I pray that our children and others will learn in here and laugh in here—and that grown-ups will, too. I give you my word that your work will be honored, and your beautiful shelves will be filled with books and mementos that enrich and commemorate this family. Beyond that, I am speechless."

The others had filtered into the library as she was talking and were touching, admiring and examining everything at nose-length.

"Frankly," Joseph declared, his voice needing no further amplification, "I think we *all* did a damn fine job!"

Then the room erupted in an enthusiastic round of applause, the most animated coming from Amelia and Mimi.

"But we still have one special place left to see," Anne reminded them.

At that point, everyone turned in unison to look at Mimi. Seeing their expectant faces, she made a guess.

"Is it…the nursery?" she asked in a near-whisper. "Have you done something extra for my baby?"

"*Yes*! Yes we *did*!" they began shouting. "Come on. We can't wait to show you!"

"Oh my God, I don't believe this," she exclaimed as they guided her carefully up the stairs.

Gathered again around a doorknob, the group looked at Mr. Price.

"No," he said, "I'm not the right one to introduce this room."

"All right," Joseph volunteered, addressing his remarks directly to Mimi and Amelia. "In the rest of the house, we each had our own projects. Sometimes we worked as a team to make sure our colors and themes were blending, and sometimes we conspired to surprise you with a few products you weren't expecting. But most of the time, we worked alone on our individual assignments. In *this* room, however, we're all in here together, and we have been from the beginning. What's more important, though, is the fact that we'll *always* be in here, watching over both of you and this baby."

With that, he opened the door and stood back, allowing Mimi and Amelia to enter what felt like an illusion. The Magglio mural covered all four walls and, through the use of hushed pastels and whites, told the story of an angel's journey from heaven to its birth in the Madison house. Anne's white lace curtains draped the six windows, three on the far wall and three on the outer side wall.

Centered with the headboard against the left wall was Emanuel's carefully guarded secret—a cherry wood crib crowned with Marjorie's white crocheted canopy. Ellen's white satin quilt and matching pillow created a cloud-like puff cover for the mattress. In the corner where the windows met was a wide oak rocking chair, and beside it was a brass floor lamp topped with Geoffrey's stained glass shade. Pepper's companion table lamp was on the mirrored dresser to the right of the door, and a yellow and white striped loveseat was positioned in front of the three side windows. Finally, covering all but the outward edges of the plank flooring, was a hand-braided rug in blues, yellows and pinks, which all nine artists helped construct after being instructed by Anne and Marjorie.

Neither Mimi nor Amelia could find a single remaining word to speak. Seated beside each other on the loveseat, all they could do was hold hands, as tears of gratitude streamed down both of their faces.

"There they go again," Ellen whispered to Emanuel. "They are *so* predictable."

Ultimately, Bradley Price broke the silence.

"I cannot imagine any child having a more perfect room in which to begin life. You are all magnificent artists and individuals, and I feel honored to have come to know you so well. Furthermore, I sincerely hope that our association continues to develop. But, since the time is growing late—already past noon—I suggest we move back downstairs and begin working toward our good-byes."

"Please don't use the word good-bye." Mimi sounded weak. "We truly want you to visit often, especially after the baby's born. And then, of course, you must all attend the christening. We'll let you know the details through Mr. Price."

"Oh how grand! Another party!" Amelia exclaimed, pushing the maudlin moment aside. "Right now, though, what I really want to do is take another look at all of the glorious things you've made for us."

Nearly two more hours passed before the reviews had been completed and the guests had exchanged their watery farewells. Mr. Price was the only one who lingered—much longer than he should have, he realized, after noticing how tired Mimi had become.

"Forgive me for overstaying my welcome, ladies."

"That would not be possible, Mr. Price," Mimi responded graciously, but without her customary flirtation. "Were it not for you and your kind assistance, we would have none of these new friends, none of these memories and none of these beautiful things. I'm numb from all that has happened. When I'm feeling better, I will write to you, thanking you more properly for your contributions."

"And please come by to see us sometime," Amelia added a bit hypocritically. "We wouldn't want to lose touch." *Partially true,* she thought. *He has served, and most likely will continue to serve, a valuable function for this family. Nonetheless, something tells me that our lives will become more complicated because of him.* "See you soon." *No need to be rude. He's been very kind.*

Expecting that a return visit would be long in coming, Bradley Price said good-bye and boarded the trolley heading back downtown. Despite his efforts to concentrate on news stories and deadlines, the further he got from the Madison house, the more dispirited he became.

Mimi fell asleep on the new loveseat in the nursery only minutes after Mr. Price left. Amelia napped in her third-floor room, intending only to rest for a short while. When both women were still sleeping at 5:00, however, Irene thought it best to wake them.

"Miss Amelia," she whispered, gently touching her employer's shoulder, "I'm sorry to bother you, but it's quite late."

"What? Oh, Irene. What time is it?"

"It's after five, and I thought you'd want some notice before Mr. McClinty arrives home."

"Dear heaven! I can't believe I slept so long. Is Mimi up?"

"No. I waited so you could wake her yourself."

"Yes, thank you."

"Dinner is almost ready. I re-heated the ham and made a cheese and potato side dish. There's also plenty of bread left over from breakfast, or lunch, or whatever that was."

"It was a miracle, Irene. *That's* what it was—and you, my dear, are a blessing. I'll be down in a minute to help."

Rising slowly, she stretched and breathed deeply. *What a day this has been. What a magnificent day!* By the time she reached the nursery, Mimi had awakened as well, and she was standing over the crib, with the satin quilt in her hands.

"None of it seems real to me yet, Amelia. How *could* it be real? Just look at this room!"

"Yes, and this was our *bonus.* There's so much more, in nearly every corner of this house."

"None of which I've fully seen or appreciated yet. This morning was completely overpowering. After living with those wonderful people in our lives all these many months, how could I have been so unprepared?"

"I'm partially to blame for that, dear. I thought it would be fun to surprise you. Never did I think of the effect it might have on your nerves. Please forgive me."

"Don't be silly, Amelia. I'll cling to this as one of the most amazing days of my life."

"Good. But now we need to tidy up a bit for Jonathon. Irene is taking care of dinner, and you might want to wash your face. Perhaps," she added playfully, "you could also take a look at your hair."

"I must be a sight."

"An appropriate description. See you downstairs."

By the time Jonathon arrived home a little before eight that night, Mimi could hardly keep her eyes open. As soon as she heard his voice, though, she pretended enthusiasm and joined Amelia to greet him in the foyer.

"Darling, I'm so glad you're here. We've had *such* a day, and I can't wait to show you…"

"*My* day has been rather gruesome, Mary Mae," he interrupted, using her formal name as he touched her forehead with his rough lips. "You look well, Mother," he added, planting a frozen kiss on Amelia's cheek, then hanging his hat and coat on the hall tree.

"Irene has dinner ready," Mimi announced, "but your mother and I thought you might want to see some of the more special things first. You can't even imagine all the splendid gifts we received."

"As I recall," he responded, his gruff tone assaulting the women, "we paid handsomely for those *gifts*, as you call them. And frankly, I'm not at all hungry. We had a very late lunch because of the problems at the mill. I had hoped the two of you would have eaten already."

"But we wanted to wait for you, Jonathon. Mimi and I have been looking forward to sharing this evening with you, perhaps more than you realized."

"Yes. Perhaps. Forgive me, Mother, but I think you'll find that I'll be a better audience tomorrow. I told everyone that I won't be at the mill until after noon. We'll talk in the morning, and then you can tell me about your day. Right now, however, I'm going to bed."

Too tired to respond much less retaliate, the women watched him climb the stairs.

"Are you coming up soon, Mary Mae?"

"Yes," she answered, forcing an obligatory reply. Then turning to Amelia, she asked in a quiet voice, "What has happened to him? He stood right here and didn't even notice Pepper's lamp or Joseph's painting only inches away. How could he not see—or care? What have I done to push him away like this?"

"You have done nothing, my child," she said, linking her daughter-in-law's right arm in her left. "Lord knows you've been carrying his baby for eight months. I cannot explain his behavior at the moment, but I will speak with him tomorrow and see what I can learn. At the very least, he'll know by the time I'm finished that I find his treatment of you a disgrace. Now, my dear, you need to eat something."

"No. It's too late, and I seem to have lost my appetite anyway. Besides, I ate enough at lunch to easily last until morning. Right now I simply want to sleep."

"Very well, then. You run along. I'll have Irene put dinner up. Sweet dreams, and just remember the beauty of what we shared here today. No one can take any of those memories away from us."

"Thank you, Amelia. I love you."

There never was a tour. Jonathon discovered the artistic creations one at a time on his own, with the exception of the nursery and the library, which were difficult to overlook since Amelia had flung all the doors and windows wide open to draw his attention. His indifferent response to both rooms was infuriating, but no information was gleaned about his strange behavior. Amelia spoke her mind as promised, and while he seemed momentarily humbled in front of her, he offered neither explanation nor apology.

Mimi listened over the next few weeks as Amelia tried to make her feel better about herself, conjecturing that Jonathon might be feeling foolish, or perhaps even envious. After all, the women had done a remarkable job of selecting the artists and following the projects through to completion. Jonathon, on the other hand, had been uncooperative and unpleasant from the beginning.

"He might possibly be feeling like an idiot," Amelia said.

"I hope so," Mimi confessed. "It would be nice to know he's feeling *something* about this house and family."

Snow was still falling when Mimi awakened on Friday, January 25, 1906. A series of storms had been dumping layer upon white layer throughout the Albany area since Tuesday, and even the stalwart trolley cars were having difficulty navigating their routes. But none of this troubled Mimi because she had no plans to leave the house. In fact, she'd be lucky, she thought, to successfully work her way down to the kitchen.

Giving herself a once-over in the mirror while brushing the tangles from her hair, she didn't know whether to laugh or cry.

Good Lord! I am enormous! Of course, this hideous warehouse of a nightgown doesn't help the view very much. After breakfast, I think I'll change into the most slimming frock I can find and then do something productive, like reorganize the attic. Doesn't really matter what I look like anyway, as long as my baby and I feel all right. Amelia, Drake and Irene are the only people I see anymore. Maybe I won't change clothes at all before I start the attic. What difference would it make?

Pulling a heavy brown shawl tightly around her shoulders, she padded slowly downstairs in her sheepskin slippers and was greeted heartily as she pushed open the kitchen door.

"Good morning, my beautiful child," Amelia said, as Irene and Drake each took one of Mimi's arm and escorted her to the now familiar wooden rocking chair and plant box footstool.

"Here's your tea, dear," Amelia said, automatically adding cream to the brim without asking.

Not really wanting any cream, but unwilling to complain, Mimi accepted the tea as offered.

"As usual," she sighed, "you have all managed to make this kitchen smell and feel magical on a dreadfully cold morning like this."

"Can't even see outside," Drake commented. "Thick icescapes have formed on all the windows except on the east side of the house."

"Yes, I was looking at them earlier," Mimi said. "They are spectacular, don't you think? Each one so different, and yet how can that be when you think of the millions of glass panes they etch? And can any of you imagine who I was thinking about as I investigated every single one at each window on my way downstairs?"

Mimi asked the question while she downed a corn muffin in one bite. None of them replied as they gaped at her gorging cheeks.

"Joseph and his brothers, of course," she continued, oblivious to their stares and uncharacteristically talking with her mouth full. "What a painting *that* would make! Winter. It's the only season we don't have on canvas from them, you realize. Could I please have another muffin, and maybe some juice? We have *Spring* in the parlor, *Summer* in the living room, and *Fall* in the foyer. I suppose they left out *Winter* because—well, I have no idea why they left it out. Do you? Irene, would it be a great deal of trouble for you to fix one of your famous sandwiches from last night's roast? After I eat, I'd like to bundle up and take a little walk before I clean out the attic. Anyone want to go with me?"

Mother of God, Amelia prayed, watching her precious daughter-in-law sprawled unceremoniously between the rocker and the flower box, inserting food into her mouth with both hands.

"Drake," she said, speaking in as calm and lilting a tone as possible, "could you please help me move a few things around in the parlor while Mimi finishes her breakfast?"

"I think she's eating lunch and dinner, too," he added so only Amelia could hear. "Yes, ma'am. Lead the way."

Once they were inside the parlor, she pulled the pocket doors shut behind her.

"Drake, we're going to have a baby."

"I beg your pardon, Mrs. McClinty!"

He looked so aghast that she wished she had time to drag this out a bit for her own amusement. But she did not.

"No. You misunderstand, for some ungodly reason. What I'm trying to tell you is that Mimi will be having *her* baby today."

Now he was speechless.

"Please tell me you can hear me, Drake," she joked, grinning as she took his hands. "This is supposed to be a wonderful occasion!"

"I know, and it is indeed. But what makes you think it's going to happen today?"

"Trust me. Part of it has to do with her plans for cleaning the attic. The day Peter was born, I polished our furniture—what little we had then—and scrubbed all the floors. That cottage was never as clean, before or after. But mostly, it's just a sixth sense. And frankly, Drake, after that vision we left out there in the kitchen, do *you* honestly think there's much time left to go?"

"Forgive me," he said, "but I hope not. So, what are we to do now? More specifically, what am *I* to do?"

"First, I will ring the operator so she can begin her search for our doctor. Your job, my friend, will be to find Jonathon. We can try to reach the mill using our telephone machine, but I've attempted to do that before without success. You might have to take the trolley and go to his office to personally retrieve him. Irene and I will be fine here, in the interim."

Unexpectedly, Irene was knocking on the parlor door.

"Excuse me, Miss Amelia. May I come in?"

"Of course," she said, sliding the doors open. "What is it?"

"I don't really know for sure. But Miss Mimi tried to get up, and we both heard little popping sounds. Then water came pouring out of her. Sorry, Drake," she added, noting the flush spreading across his neck and cheeks. "She says she's not in any pain, but she's sitting back in the rocker and wants another sandwich. What should I do?"

"Give her the sandwich and then help her upstairs to bed. Make her comfortable and keep her still, if possible. I'll gather extra blankets, pillows, towels and sheets. Drake, I believe you have your instructions. Please don't be concerned, though. Babies are born every day."

"Not *this* baby, Miss Amelia."

"No, but everything will be all right, and later on we'll celebrate. Now, go find my son."

Thus, Margaret Elizabeth McClinty came to be born on Saturday, January 26, 1906, just after one o'clock in the morning at the Madison house. Amelia was called upon to serve as a midwife since the snowstorm delayed the doctor's arrival until Mimi had been in hard labor for several hours. Drake did not arrive back at the house with Jonathon until late in the evening. By the time the baby was born, Amelia had to awaken her son, who'd nodded off in the guest room.

"Mimi has just finished delivering a beautiful new daughter for you, my dear."

"How nice, Mother," he said in a groggy voice. "Thank God *that's* over." Then he pulled the quilt up around his shoulders. "Tell her I'll see her and the baby in the morning," he added just before he rolled over and went back to sleep.

CHAPTER 4

"Gram, whatever happened to all the things the artists made?"

The two women had agreed to take another break, and Megan was walking around the bedroom, stretching and shaking her arms and legs in an effort to get the circulation moving again.

"The pieces went every which way, I'm afraid. Help me with these pillows, would you please? They've somehow become one enormous lump."

"What does *every which way* mean?" Megan asked, obliging her grandmother but not wanting to lose the thread of conversation.

"It means *scattered*, to-and-fro, here-and-there."

"I *know* the definition, Gram. But what *happened* to them? Were the things given away to somebody? Or sold?"

"Good grief. Why does it matter?"

"Well, don't you care? Didn't that stuff have a special meaning to you?"

"My dear, I'm afraid that for a rather extended period in my life, I was preoccupied with only myself—difficult as that may be for you to believe, looking at me now." Her frisky self-appraisal tickled them both. "Nonetheless, the decorations in one McClinty house or another clearly did not merit my concern. That was really more my mother's passion."

"But when did you last see everything?" Megan pressed, leaning against the side of the bed. "Surely it hasn't *all* disappeared!"

"No, it probably hasn't. I think Mother kept some of it for awhile after she left, and I recall seeing a few things just before the New York City move. Then, of course, there were the things that I..."

"What do you mean *she left*? Where did she go? And *what* New York City move?" A frustrated edge appeared in Cinnamon's voice.

"Look, Megan, you need to pick a subject and stick to it, or I'm going to become irritable. We've been doing quite well up here for these many hours. What time is it anyway?"

"Almost three o'clock."

"Gracious me! And there's so much more to tell. You must humor me, my dear, despite your impatience. And please try not to skip ahead. You'll have more questions than answers by the time we're through anyway, but I'll share all that I know—just maybe not in the sequence you think sounds reasonable. Perhaps it would be helpful if you took a few notes, to keep track. And there *is* a place you might want to check for the artwork—in town. I'll tell you about it later. Meanwhile, I'd like to freshen up a bit. I could also use some lemonade. You probably need something to drink, too."

"Probably," Megan confirmed, eyeing her empty Chardonnay tumbler.

"Then let's get to it, my child. We have no extra time to waste. Help me out of this bed, please. And go tell Heidi that I'd like to see her about plans for dinner. Maybe you could brush my hair later on, too."

"Sure, Gram. But I'd also like to find Kenny. I promised him I'd check in periodically to see how he's doing with David."

"David! Oh that man! I can't believe he's still here."

"Gram, he's lived in the guest cottage for twenty years."

"Precisely. Ouch, Megan. Be careful, will you! I don't need any broken bones."

"Sorry. So, how much longer did you say this story's going to take?"

"Not much if you let me die on the way to the bathroom," she answered, trying her best to sound cranky as the two of them slowly made their way across the hall.

Cinnamon received her nickname shortly after sunrise on the day she was born. Jonathon had been in the bedroom with Mimi and the baby since Amelia awakened him, his sudden attentiveness and apparent desire to help with even the most menial tasks taking his wife and mother by surprise.

"Really, Jonathon," Amelia coaxed after the doctor had gone, "Irene and I can manage now. Little Margaret Elizabeth won't be doing much but eating and sleeping—and if we can keep things quiet, the same can be said for Mimi. So, if you have work to do, your conscience can be clear."

Perhaps he mistook her comments and impish smile as a subtle form of chastisement, or perhaps he was feeling a heavier burden of guilt over his recent negligence than anyone suspected. For whatever reason, he insisted upon remaining close at hand, running up and down the stairs as required, refreshing the cold compresses on his wife's forehead and neck, and stopping every few minutes to stare at the tiny creature inside the bassinet.

"Jonathon, darling." Mimi's voice was weak as the day's first light became visible, but her words called him to attention as if a trumpet were blasting inside the room. "Would you mind opening the curtains? I love watching the early sun work its way through the window frost."

"Yes, of course. You should really be resting, though. Mother will have a conniption if she comes in and thinks I'm disturbing you."

"Oh, nonsense. Besides, as the new father in the house, I suppose you have a few rights." Her smile was as tenuous as her voice, but color was starting to fill her cheeks once again.

"A new father," he repeated. "I can scarcely believe it's true. It all seems to have happened so quickly."

Amelia, who had just returned with hot tea, considered telling her son that the transition might not have been so abrupt if he'd spent a little more time with his wife during her pregnancy. *I'd best keep such unkind words to myself,* she thought, *at least for the moment. This is the side of him I've been missing, and insulting him would not be wise.*

"Would you like to hold your new daughter?"

"Hold her? No, Mother, I don't think so. Maybe when she's older."

"I see. Perhaps when she's nine or ten? On the contrary, I think this would be a very good time. Go sit over there by the window."

"Mother, I said…"

"Yes, I heard you. And *I* said to sit by the window."

Mimi watched in delight as the scene unfolded and as she realized that, for the first time in more than thirty hours, she was not in any pain.

Amelia scooped the bundle of blankets from the bassinet, kissed the delicate cheek of her granddaughter nestled inside, then walked across the room and gently laid the child in Jonathon's large, hesitant arms.

"There," she said, pulling the blanket back to fully reveal the baby's face. "This is your very own daughter—forever—Miss Margaret Elizabeth McClinty.

He was almost comical, his arms bent at the elbows, completely rigid, his spine straight and locked, as if any form of movement would cause the child to evaporate. But after a few minutes of motionless staring, he began to relax, shifting his weight toward the back of his chair and moving the baby into the curve of his left arm so he could touch her with the tip of his right index finger. Cautiously, he moved that finger across the baby's cheeks, her arms, her ears, and her mouth.

"She is so beautiful that she doesn't seem real. But I thought she'd be heavier."

"Quite heavy enough, though, as she made her way out to us," Mimi added, feeling a welcome lift to her spirit.

"Yes, I suppose that's true," he said, giving the graphic concept more consideration than he wished. "Miss Margaret Elizabeth McClinty." The pitch of his voice rose involuntarily as the baby found his finger and started sucking. "Oh, no! What should I do?" he asked Amelia, who began laughing despite her efforts to maintain a poker face.

"As a beginning, I suggest removing your finger."

"Why did she do that?"

"Because that's the one thing she does very well," Amelia answered, taking more pleasure in these moments than she'd imagined possible. "And she's probably hungry."

He offered no comment, but having the sucking sensation fresh in his mind, he looked over at Mimi and smiled at her, sending inside that one glance a message of love and respect, for which she'd been yearning.

"Margaret Elizabeth," he said, peering back down at his daughter. "Such a long and formal name for a little thing like you."

Just at that moment, the sun began reflecting through the frost patterns on the window behind him, sending prisms of light darting throughout the room and across his baby's face.

"Look at her hair!" he exclaimed, amazed at first to discover that she had any at all. "It's the same color as yours used to be, Mother," he added, his voice growing meditative as his finger grazed the reddish brown peach fuzz. "Spicy. Isn't that how folks used to describe it? What do you think?" he asked the baby, talking to her as if they were alone in the room. "Should we call you Spicy? Spicy McClinty. No," he continued, looking up at his wife and mother with a broad smile. "Sounds like a meat packer."

"Or a gangster," Mimi giggled.

Angels in heaven, Amelia prayed, *I thank you for the miracle of this child and for whatever joyous changes her birth is creating in my son.*

"How about Red?" He was on a mission. "Actually, it's not really red. It's more like the color of rust."

"Or Cinnamon," Amelia hinted.

"*Cinnamon.* Yes," he said, confidently shifting the baby in his lap so she was facing her mother and grandmother. "What do you think, Mimi?"

"I think it's perfect," she answered, pushing herself up so she could get a better view, "if it makes you happy."

"Cinnamon," Amelia echoed, noticing the baby's face moving into a pre-wail scrunch, "may need to excuse herself from all this attention so she can have a bite to eat."

"Of course," Jonathon said, reluctantly letting his mother take the baby from his lap and transfer her to Mimi's.

"You know that you're welcome to stay while I feed her, if you'd like."

This option had not occurred to him, and he briefly considered accepting until he'd taken a moment to visualize what would be involved.

"Yes, darling, I suppose my schooling in babies needs to continue along that vein, but I believe I've reached my saturation point for now."

"I understand." Suddenly feeling tired again, she was relieved to know that the demonstration would be temporarily postponed.

"And the good news," Amelia chimed in, "is that we will have no shortage of feeding circumstances in the foreseeable future."

The three of them joked and kissed and hugged one another as if such behavior were routine. Then Amelia went downstairs and began consulting with Irene regarding dinner. Mimi brought Cinnamon softly to her breast, and Jonathon—exhausted—closed himself in the parlor for an extended nap.

Roses on Valentine's Day were further symbols of Jonathon's transformation. There were twenty of them—one for their first full year of marriage, and nineteen for the days since Cinnamon's birth.

The diamond heart pendant was a premium. Hanging from a platinum chain, the heart was engraved along the edges on the back with the declaration, "*I Love You, from Jonathon.*" She could not remember when he last spoke those words out loud to her, but she had learned to accept whatever sentiments came her way—and during the past three weeks, she had been showered with devotion.

"He's going to spoil me, Amelia."

"As well he should. Didn't I tell you that everything would be all right?"

"Yes, and I hope you'll forgive me for having doubts."

"It's no wonder that you did, dear. I was beginning to have them myself. For a time, I scarcely recognized my own son. But the good Lord has prevailed, answering my prayers and bringing at least one of my boys back home."

"Speaking of Peter, which we were, in a way," Mimi interjected, "I wonder if they received your letter about the baby. Surely, at least Lily will respond, don't you think? She sounds like such a lovely person and someone who thinks very highly of you. From what you've told me, I can't imagine her ignoring the news."

"Whatever makes you think we were speaking of Peter?"

"Bringing one of your boys home. That's what you said, and I *know* you."

"Yes, I suppose you do, my dear. And I agree. Not hearing from Lily has been a surprise. As we've learned, though, people change and behave unpredictably. No telling what has truly been happening out there in California over the past two years. Lily's birthday and Christmas notes to us are dreadfully lacking in news. Peter occasionally condescends to add a postscript, and someone—probably Lily again—makes certain that David sends a drawing or some other message over his little name."

"How old is he now?"

"He turned seven last November." Her voice trailed off as she stared ahead, trying to recall the details of her grandson's face.

"You miss them terribly, don't you?"

"Yes, I do," Amelia whispered.

"I'm sorry. Please forgive me for being so insensitive. I should never have brought them up, but you and I have not really discussed that whole situation. I simply didn't realize how deeply they had hurt you."

"It wasn't *they*, Mimi. It was *he*. Peter. And he alone must bear that particular burden. I've done my best to forgive him and to avoid dwelling on what cannot be reversed. The reason you never understood is simply that I never told you. But all of those old emotions have grown easier to overlook since you came into our world—and now, of course, we have the baby. *And*," she said quickly, seeing that her daughter-in-law was on the verge of probing the subject further, "I've talked about it quite enough for one day. I'd much rather discuss the christening. Shall we create the invitation list this afternoon?"

Recognizing that she would be powerless to redirect this conversation, Mimi decided to pursue the issue of Peter and his family at another time. She also decided to correspond with Lily herself. Amelia's broken heart needed some attention, and the only people with sufficient influence to affect any healing all lived in San Francisco, California.

"Why, yes, Amelia. Working on the christening list sounds like a perfect afternoon project. And none too soon, either, with the day only three weeks away."

"I do hope your brother George will attend as promised. I'm looking forward to meeting him."

"I think Jonathon's anxious to see him as well. Me, too. All of us haven't been together since our wedding. The *first* one, that is, in Boston." Mimi's smile was wide, her love for this woman staggering. "Not the real one, of course, which you arranged for us here in Albany. And while we're talking about it," she added, trifling a bit with Amelia, "I've always wanted to ask you something."

"Yes?"

"Did you think I was pregnant when Jonathon brought me home to you? Is that why the second wedding in the Church became such a priority?"

"Nothing of the sort ever crossed my mind," Amelia answered far too quickly, cocking her head and pretending to listen for noises upstairs. "Isn't that your baby, dear? Ready for lunch, no doubt. Why don't you bring her down to the parlor? I'll have Irene fix us a tray of sandwiches, and we can begin making our plans for Margaret Elizabeth's baptism."

Mimi would often think about that afternoon in years to come, remembering the security and balance in every corner of her household, the warmth of the parlor fire as lists were made for shopping and chores, and the suckling baby whose tiny hands were both wrapped around one of her fingers. When future circumstances would lead her into dreadful times, she would sit in the old rocker, close her eyes and reach back for the aroma of Irene's ham roasting in the kitchen, and for the memory of finely-etched lines of lacy frost on the windows, which she could touch in her mind and which would forever remind her of Amelia.

Jonathon and Mary Mae McClinty
Invite you to the baptism of their daughter

MARGARET ELIZABETH

Saturday, March 10, 1906
Ten O'clock in the Morning
Cathedral of the Immaculate Conception
Corner of Madison and Eagle Streets
Albany, New York

Reception immediately thereafter in the Assembly Hall

With Jonathon's agreement, a separate note was also included inside the invitations to family members, a few of Jonathon's business associates, a handful of special friends and neighbors, the Madison artists, and Mr. Bradley Price.

Jonathon & Mimi McClinty
Invite you to attend a private party in their home
Celebrating the birth and baptism of their daughter,
Margaret Elizabeth

Saturday, March 10, 1906
Two o'clock in the Afternoon

643 Madison Avenue
Albany, New York

RSVP

Amelia hastened down the staircase after hearing Mimi's cry, only to find her daughter-in-law sprawled on the parlor floor surrounded by invitations ready to be addressed and mailed.

"What has happened? Did you fall?"

"No! I threw myself down here after realizing how stupid I am."

Relieved, and a little amused at the scene in front of her, Amelia sat down on the floor as well.

"What are you talking about, my dear?"

"It's quite simple. We cannot put a single one of these invitations in the post."

"I see. And why would that be?"

"Because we cannot have this baptism. At least not yet."

Sitting three feet away from each other, both women waited for the other to speak. At length, as she had done periodically since the baby was born, Mimi began talking at the precise moment when she began crying, her sentences thus becoming difficult to understand. But Amelia had become practiced at picking up key words, and she now listened intently, occasionally dabbing drips from Mimi's nose with the handkerchief she'd learned to keep hidden in her sleeve.

"Oh, Amelia, we have no christening gown, and there's no time to make one. And worse—so much worse—we have no *godparents*. And we have no *friends*, so who could we even ask? If Jonathon knows a soul, he's never told me. And all *I've* been thinking about is the party. So add selfishness to stupidity. This is supposed to be a holy occasion, a sacrament of the Church. And I've been worrying about what everyone will eat and what I will wear now that I'm so fat from the baby—ugly, along with stupid and selfish. Jonathon will be furious, and I..."

Amelia stopped her from continuing by scooting next to her. Then, when she wrapped her arms around the young woman's shoulders, she felt Mimi's chest heaving rapidly, as the wet face nuzzled against her neck.

"There, there. Just take a moment to calm down. Here. Blow your nose on this. You are such a worrier. My goodness, you really do win the prize. Now, that's better."

"I'm having a bit of a fit, aren't I?" Mimi asked, sitting up again and brushing a few stray lengths of hair off her face.

"A small one, but I doubt that the asylum will come to fetch you any time soon," Amelia replied, glad to see a smile coming back her way.

"Thank God Jonathon isn't home," Mimi added, blowing and sniffling with alternate breaths.

"Yes, I'm afraid I'll have to agree with you there."

"But what are we going to do?"

"Relax, my dear. The gown and godparents have been on my list all along, but I'd planned to discuss them after the invitations were out of the way—unless, you brought them up first, which I believe I can safely say you have."

The humor of their circumstances struck both women simultaneously, as they sat unceremoniously on the floor—and when they began laughing together, all traces of tension disappeared.

"Let's focus on one issue at time," Amelia began, resituating herself on the sofa. "First, we'll start with the godparents. Have you thought about asking your brother George, since we know that he'll be here?"

"What a grand idea! He'd be so proud! And surely Jonathon won't object. He'll wonder why I haven't mentioned it before, though—just one more example of my..."

"Stop! No more conversation using the words stupid, selfish, or, what was the other one?"

"Ugly."

"Right. Or ugly. Now, we need to find ourselves a godmother."

"Perhaps I could ask my Aunt Ethel. Remember, George said in his last letter that she might be coming. Since Uncle Martin isn't feeling well enough to travel, this could be the ideal solution. How do you think Jonathon will feel?"

He'll feel the way I instruct him to feel, Amelia mused. "I'm certain he'll agree with your suggestions, dear. After all, how could he find fault with such considered choices?"

"I suppose he cannot, although the term *considered choice* might be stretching the truth, don't you think?"

"Not in the least," she replied, standing up and smoothing the folds of her dress before heading out of the room.

"You're not leaving, are you? We still have to talk about..."

"I'll be right back. Just going to see Irene about some tea."

When Amelia returned, she was carrying a box measuring three feet in length, a foot wide and five or six inches deep.

"Here. This should resolve your final issue."

Suspecting what it might be, Mimi ignored the steaming tea Irene had poured moments earlier and removed the blue satin ribbons securing the box. Inside, beneath layers of parchment paper and resting atop a thin cotton cushion was a white Irish linen baby gown nearly as long as the box. The delicate neckline, sleeves and hem were trimmed with dime-sized rounds that had been crocheted with silk thread and then fastened together with small white lace rosebuds. There were no other adornments, and the graceful simplicity was spectacular.

"You're not going to start crying, are you?" Amelia asked, prepared with two fresh handkerchiefs.

"No," Mimi said through her tears.

"I didn't think so."

"Was this Jonathon's?"

"Yes. And Peter's before that. It needs a little mending. When Jonathon wore it, the hem caught on the edge of the baptismal font. Thankfully, Nathaniel spotted the problem before too much damage was done. We will need to do some repair work, however."

"I don't think I've ever seen anything so exquisite. Where did you find it?"

Without a word, Amelia went briefly into the hall and returned holding a small, yellowed envelope.

"Open it," she directed softly. "There's a note inside for you to read."

Amelia—

As a postscript, I have decided to include this christening gown. Your mother made it while we were waiting for the letter that never came from you. Despite her broken heart, she always loved you. She prayed that you would be happy and have many children, and she often spoke to me of her dream—to watch her grandchildren baptized, one after one, in the gown crafted with such love by her own hand. My original intention was to withhold this gift from you, having it buried with me instead. My vengeful thoughts about writing that final note to you led me to the confessional yesterday.

Your mother is apparently managing my behavior once again, and I fear that if I do not forward her grandchildren's christening gown to you, I will ultimately face her anger and disappointment when I see her. This gesture, therefore, is not as much for you as for me—and for your mother who never deserved that broken heart.

Papa
August 15, 1878

Mimi was weeping again.

"This is horrible! What happened?"

"Do you remember when Jonathon made that humiliating scene at our artist's first luncheon? I told you then that I had a story to share with you about forgiveness. Apparently, this is the time."

If Cinnamon had not awakened for her feeding nearly two hours later, the women would have remained in the parlor, locked in the safety and unconditional love found in each other's company until night had fallen. Nothing gave them greater pleasure, they'd discovered, than spending their time together. After their remarkable day of revelations, they did not drift far from that emotional fulcrum, appreciating the balance while they participated as full partners in all of their undertakings. Since they approached every new morning as a blank slate awaiting their creativity, there was always an adventure to share and something new to learn. As the weeks passed, they drew more and more contentment from one another, filling the empty places that, for different reasons, their husbands had created. But they didn't know this equilibrium was about to shift, because the fulcrum they believed they'd anchored so firmly was about to break.

In the interest of time, every invitation was hand-delivered by courier, the largest single batch going to the Madison artists in care of Mr. Price. Amelia and Mimi had expected to wait a week or more before hearing from anyone, but responses began arriving via messenger, mail, telegraph, and a few by telephone, within twenty-four hours.

"This is astonishing!" Mimi kept the small cradle rocking with her right foot as she slid the letter opener through the seals of note after note. "We'll need to reorganize our plans for food. The menu, as it stands, will never accommodate this many guests."

"Fortunately, we're not facing the opposite problem," Amelia answered, pulling the parlor draperies open. "We would all be feeling terribly glum if no one wanted to come."

"I suppose that's true, but there's already so much to be done that I can't imagine how we'll bring everything together."

"My dear, I'm surprised at you. With all the miracles we've managed to orchestrate since you married my son, you and I are an indomitable team."

"You're right, as usual. How foolish of me to spend even an instant of worry," she said, reminded of the security she felt in the presence of this woman. Then she stopped rocking the cradle and opening envelopes, and simply smiled. "Whatever would I do without you, Amelia?"

"I shudder to think, and I'll start praying about it immediately. For now, however, I'm going to check on Irene's progress with the christening dress. She said she'd have it mended this morning, so we'll have plenty of time to spot clean and press it to perfection."

"I hope she's being gentle. After all, it's been more than twenty-five years since it covered Jonathon's little body."

"And nearly *thirty* since Peter wore it. There's a comforting continuity in all of this that I had not anticipated, and that Nathaniel would also have appreciated. I find myself thinking about him a great deal these days, for some reason—missing him all over again. Well, enough drivel," she said, concluding the conversation and heading down the hall toward the kitchen.

"Re-working the menu will be next when I've finished updating the guest list," Mimi called after her. Just then the front door chimed. "I'll answer it," she said, moving into the hall and peering through the stained glass sidelight to see a messenger standing on the porch. "More responses," she mumbled to herself.

"Delivery for Mr. Jonathon McClinty," the young man announced.

"He's not here at the moment, but I'm his wife and will accept it for him."

"I'm supposed to get a signature, ma'am."

"Very well. I'll be happy to oblige."

"I'm supposed to get *his* signature, ma'am."

"Sadly for you, mine will have to do," Mimi answered, annoyed at his impertinence and quickly writing her name on the receipt he held out to her.

"Here," he said, rudely shoving a letter-sized white envelope into her hand before spinning around and riding away on his bicycle without a goodbye.

How very odd, she thought, turning the piece over so she could see the address.

For Personal & Private Delivery To
Mr. Jonathon McClinty
643 Madison Avenue

Noting the hint of perfume wafting up from the paper, her first inclination was to rush down the hall and share the entire experience with Amelia. But some dark misgiving, which she chose not face, sent her upstairs instead where she placed the letter on top of the bureau in the guest room. Jonathon would see it there and would certainly explain to her later the mystery behind its arrival.

"Who was at the door?" Amelia asked, returning to the parlor.

"Just another messenger with more mail."

"Honestly, this becomes more and more exciting by the minute, doesn't it?"

"Indeed it does. Now let's talk about this menu."

By Saturday, March 10, a northeastern spring was a month or more away, and yet the sun pretended otherwise as the clear air warmed to nearly sixty degrees. The occasion would have been framed by perfection even without the weather's cooperation, but as the McClinty and Emerson families gathered in the Cathedral at nine that morning, the promise of a new season had become infectious.

A young Father Garretty officiated at the baptismal Mass, and while Amelia had begun to accept his arrival at the church, she was still not certain if she liked him. This was none of *his* doing, but rather a result of her lingering sadness about Father Flanigan. She had not been able to mute the vivid memories of the kind priest who had not only baptized both of her boys, but who had served as mentor, teacher and confessor to them throughout their schooling and Catechism classes. He had also been with the family through their joyous moments, one of the greatest of which was bringing Nathaniel's parents to Albany from Ireland. He had escorted them through difficult times, as well, burying Nathaniel's mother first, then his father, and then Nathaniel himself. Finally, almost a year ago, Father Flanigan died after a short illness, leaving behind a legacy that would have been impossible for even the hardiest saint to follow.

While the Monsignor at the Cathedral held the highest supervisory position, the priests who served along with him had the principal day-to-day contact with adult parishioners and children attending the Immaculate Conception School. Amelia watched now as Father Garretty held her granddaughter, and she felt a little ashamed about not having been more helpful to him. He'd been struggling to establish himself as a pastor within a community still grieving over his predecessor. Most church members, like Amelia, had not been very subtle about their resistance to him. Nonetheless, he had performed the marriage ceremony for Jonathon and Mimi, and now he was baptizing their child.

He's no longer a stranger to us, Amelia thought, wiping her eyes in a futile attempt to curb the stream. *And I've been so unfair to him. I really must apologize.*

"This has to be the most beautiful child I have ever seen!" another guest exclaimed during the reception in the Parish Hall. "And just look at that hair! You must be very proud."

"Yes, we are," Mimi answered for what seemed like the thousandth time. "And thank you so much. We're delighted you could be here." Then turning to George and Aunt Ethel, she whispered, "I'm not sure what I would have done if you two hadn't come. Other than our artists, I scarcely know a single face in this crowd."

"Everyone certainly seems to know *you*, though," George replied.

"And the two of us, as well," Aunt Ethel added. "We're feeling a bit famous the way people are fussing over us."

"That's because godparents are very, very special," Mimi declared, peering into the bassinet beside her to check on her sleeping child. "I can't believe how well she's behaving!"

"Or how she can possibly nap through all of this," George added.

"At least she should be well-rested for the party later on," she said, checking her wristwatch with a start. "Oh my goodness! It's after twelve. We really need to be heading home soon."

"If you can pry Jonathon and Amelia free from their admirers," Mimi's brother commented good-naturedly. "Just look at them over there."

"Yes, I know. They're having such fun seeing all of their old friends during a happy occasion for a change. I think this particular collection of people has not been assembled since Nathaniel died. Still, I need to remind my husband of the time. Would you two keep an eye on the baby for a minute?"

Many of the guests were already at the house when the family finally arrived. But Irene and Drake had been prepared for this eventuality and were acting as able hosts, serving drinks, passing hors d'oeuvres, and conducting well-rehearsed tours of the Madison original works of art, which had been widely discussed at the reception.

The artists were indulging themselves in this newfound notoriety, having been among the early arrivals after the baptismal service. Each of them looked polished and professional in their new suits of clothes, compliments of Bradley Price and, as they became more clearly associated with their artistic creations, a number of guests began discussing their own needs for paintings, stained glass, woodcrafts or needlework. The Magglio brothers and Emanuel Smith had commitments for new projects before the afternoon was over, and the promise of additional work was rich for the Anne Delicampo team, as well as for Pepper and Geoffrey.

Watching them all move about with such comfort and grace, Mimi cornered Amelia in the front hall.

"Remember that first day when we had to ply them with spirits before they would even speak?"

"I do, indeed. In fact, Drake mentioned the contrast to me only a short while ago. It's quite remarkable how they all feel so natural here now."

"And I'm thrilled that they seem to be acquiring more work as a result of what they've done for us."

"Just as we'd hoped, my dear. Do you realize that more than a year has gone by since our trip downtown to the newspaper when we first met everyone?"

"Speaking of the newspaper," Mimi interjected, abruptly changing the subject, "where do you suppose Mr. Price could be? I know I saw him at the church."

"Oh, I nearly forgot. He delivered his regrets after the service. Apparently, there's a deadline to be met this afternoon, and he's unable to get away. He did say he'd schedule a time to stop by, however. I think he may have a little something for the baby."

"I see."

Drake then approached the two women.

"Excuse me, ladies." His voice was lowered as if he were about to tell a secret. "Have you been in the library lately?"

After indicating they had not, he led them down the hall, looking one way and then another, as if he feared being followed.

"Your guests have all been putting things in here. I thought you would like to know." Piled high on Emanuel's round tables were colorful gifts of all sizes and shapes, some tied with ribbons, others decorated with small toys. "I especially thought you'd want to see *that* one," he added, pointing to a corner by the double desk.

"Dear God in heaven!" Mimi gasped. "It's the doll house!"

The hand-carved house complete with all its furnishings and people—the one Emanuel brought to the *Times Union* interview as an example of his work—was adorned with a immense pink bow and an open-faced card hanging from a piece of yarn tied to the chimney.

From Emanuel and Jarrett Smith
To Miss Margaret Elizabeth McClinty
March 10, 1906
Because you live in our hearts,
our little house now belongs with you.

"How can we possibly take this from him, Amelia?"

"On the contrary, dear. We aren't taking anything. He is *giving*, and I suspect that gestures of this sort will be going back and forth between us for a long while to come."

The house had quieted by early evening when Mimi joined her brother and aunt in the parlor.

"I'm in need of a snooze before Cinnamon wakes for her next feeding. But you've just arrived and now you're already leaving in the morning. It's been far too short a visit. Couldn't you stay a bit longer?"

"I'm afraid not," Ethel replied. "Your Uncle Martin worries me to death when I'm there with him, so you might imagine how I feel being so far away."

"We are both very pleased to find my little sister so happy, though," George said, patting Mimi's arm, "and we won't be quite as worried about you now."

"You're such a sweetheart, and I really should be telling you that more often," she said, an Irish lilt tripping through her voice.

"Please do, and why not tell me—*us*—face-to-face in Boston sometime?"

"Yes, I'd like that. Perhaps when the baby is a little older, Amelia could make the trip with me. I doubt we'd ever get Jonathon away from the mill long enough to join us, however."

"He does seem to be quite busy with activities away from home."

"He's much better about that since the baby arrived, Aunt Ethel," Mimi defended, "and I could not be more content."

"So it would seem."

"Fortunately you have Amelia," George added.

"You have no idea. She's my ally and my dearest friend, and I do believe she'll end up being the finest grandmother on earth."

"Is someone talking about me behind my back?"

Amelia entered the room carrying a large pot of tea. She was followed by Drake, who balanced a tray full of cups, saucers, spoons, creamers and sugar, and by Irene, who carried a large basket of rolls, butter and jam.

"We'll be having a late dinner tonight because of the party, so I thought this would tide us over. Are you still planning a nap, Mimi?"

"I was, Amelia, but I'm feeling much better after sitting down."

"I still think it would be wise to close your eyes for awhile. That baby will be up half the night. Besides, Jonathon's working on some invoices or something in the library, so this would give me the opportunity I've been waiting for to visit with your lovely family."

"Oh all right. You're in charge."

"Finally, the truth," Amelia laughed, dismissing Mimi with a lighthearted wave.

While the positive changes inside the Madison house had been welcomed, they were short-lived. Soon after the baptism, Jonathon once again began to distance himself from his family and his new child, for reasons neither Amelia nor Mimi could explain. They both presented a strong front, however, and did their best to move through their responsibilities without appearing too concerned.

By lunchtime on Wednesday, April 18, 1906, they had returned from their morning walk in Washington Park across the street. Amelia had suggested this addition to their daily routine when the weather began to warm consistently. She thought it might help them shake their minds free of the tension that always seemed to be lingering inside the house these days. The outings also enabled Mimi to become more acquainted with neighbors emerging from the winter confinement of their own houses. Her favorite new friends were the Prestons, who lived only two blocks away, next door to the original Corbett home, which Amelia still owned and leased. Louise and Robert Preston were married a year before Jonathon and Mimi, and they had a daughter named Angela, a baby girl two months older than Cinnamon.

Louise was a robust woman with a loud, jolly laugh, and yet she was extraordinarily shy. She and her husband were originally from Rochester and had moved to Albany the previous winter after his election to the State House of Representatives resulted in his staying away from home for too many lengthy intervals. Her subsequent pregnancy was confirmed shortly after their relocation to Madison Avenue, and she had been isolated ever since, which is why Mimi and Amelia had only met her recently.

"Let's invite Louise and the baby over for lunch next week," Amelia suggested, locking the carriage brake before leaving it on the front porch. "We've been visiting with her for weeks now in the park, and I think she would be a great friend for you."

"That's a wonderful idea! And who knows? Cinnamon and Angela might turn out to be friends too."

They had no idea.

Around half past three that same afternoon, the front chime rang. Drake had gone home for the day, and everyone else was sleeping, so Irene peered through the sidelight. She was surprised to see Bradley Price standing on the front porch, and she opened the door without hesitation.

"Hello, Irene. Please forgive me for calling unannounced, but we've had news over the wireless and I need to speak with Mrs. McClinty—Amelia, that is."

He looked terribly grim, and even in the crisp afternoon air, beads of perspiration were popping out across his forehead and above his upper lip.

"Both the misses are resting, sir, while the baby sleeps. I'm sorry you've come all this way. You're welcome to wait, or perhaps there's a message you'd like to leave for them."

"How much longer before they awaken?"

"I'm not certain. That's generally up to the baby."

"Yes, of course. I think I'll wait, then."

"Please make yourself comfortable in the parlor. Would you like some tea?"

"No, thank you."

"There's also some brandy on the server."

"Frankly, that does sound like a better option."

"Help yourself, then. I'll be in the kitchen if you need anything else."

After pouring a large shot into one of the snifters on the tray, he took a deep sip, letting the spirit bite, then burn, then warm and calm him. He'd been studying the array of family mementos on the fireplace mantle for only a few minutes when he heard Mimi's voice in the hallway.

"Irene, was that someone ringing our bell?"

"Yes, ma'am. It was Mr. Price from the newspaper. He's waiting for you in the parlor."

A moment later she appeared in the doorway, her sable hair free from its customary bun and spilling over her shoulders. A pink, floor-length house gown with long sleeves and a high collar covered her body, and a white crocheted shawl was demurely wrapped around her back and arms. Instead of shoes, she appeared to be wearing beige woolen stockings, which stretched upward to some unknown point beneath the gown. On her cheeks was the natural blush of having just awakened, and in her arms, wrapped in a yellow knitted blanket, was her new baby.

God help me get quickly beyond the delivery of this news, he thought, *and then out the door.*

"Mr. Price, how good to see you. Have we forgotten an appointment?"

Clearly she was not expecting company, but she graciously welcomed him, hoping he would overlook her dreadful appearance.

"No, I'm afraid I've come on my own without notice. Please forgive the intrusion, but telegraphs have been arriving since late morning with news that I thought you should know. Miss Amelia, in particular, should be informed."

"She's still sleeping, but if you'd like to tell me, I'll see that she receives the message right away."

He sat down on the sofa, placed his brandy on the table in front of him and dropped his head into his hands.

"I'm sorry. I'm really not sure what to do, or what to say. Maybe I should not have come."

Recognizing his distress and suddenly feeling alarmed, she excused herself for a minute.

"I'll be right back. Irene can watch Cinnamon while we talk."

"What's wrong, Mr. Price?" she asked upon her return, facing him as she sat in Amelia's favorite chair.

Reaching inside his jacket pocket, he produced a folded sheet of paper and handed it to her.

"This came by telegraph earlier today," he said. "It's probably the best way to begin."

From the Publisher of The Daily News
San Francisco, Wednesday, April 18, 1906

KILLER EARTHQUAKE STRUCK CITY AT 5:13 A.M.

City left in ruins. Loss of life enormous. Exact numbers of dead and injured unknown. Hundreds already at Mechanics' Pavilion which is being used as a morgue and hospital.

Fires rage through downtown and neighborhoods causing further destruction and impairing rescue. More temblors continue to strike.

Newspaper offices demolished. Relocating operations to Oakland for issues beginning tomorrow. Updates will follow whenever possible.

Mimi laid the paper in her lap, her face now void of color, her eyes clouded.

"My brother-in-law," she whispered, "his wife, their young son—they all live there."

"I know. That's why I came. I wanted to tell you before we print the news. Our front page will be covered with the story this evening."

"Amelia will be frantic. How can we find out if Peter and his family are all right?"

"From what I've been able to learn, we may have to wait several days. Apparently, the city is in complete chaos, and until the fires are controlled, there won't be any way of getting reliable information."

"Dear God! This is unimaginable!"

"Well, good afternoon, Mr. Price." Amelia's cheerful voice was entering the room far too soon. "To what might we owe the pleasure of your visit?" she continued, expecting that a baby gift was in the offing. When no one replied, she sat down on the sofa. "For heaven's sake! Why do you both look so ghastly?"

"I'm afraid," Mimi began, coughing lightly to buy herself a few extra seconds, "that something horrible has happened."

After studying their faces for a moment, Amelia repositioned herself against the sofa cushion and gripped her hands tightly together.

"It's Jonathon, isn't it? There's been an accident at the mill."

"No. Jonathon's quite fine, I think. Here," she said, handing the teletype across the coffee table. "Mr. Price brought this to help us understand."

Just at that moment, Jonathon burst through the front door. Seeing the trio in the parlor, he seemed unconcerned about the presence of Mr. Price and focused his attention instead on his mother.

"Have you heard the news?"

"Not yet," Amelia answered. "But that's obviously the direction you're all heading. Please, Jonathon, come in here and join us."

Amelia's guarded emotions were deceptive, and they belied the terror she could not hold at bay. After reading the telegraph, she remained precariously reasonable, fighting against her instincts, denying her visions of a young family crushed beneath some building or burned beyond recognition, and struggling to salvage a trace of hope. But she couldn't bring herself to talk about it. Instead, she insisted that Jonathon ride with her to the *Times Union* office later that first afternoon and again the next morning. On both occasions, he continued on to the mill, after leaving his mother to wait for some word amidst the commotion and disorder of the news room. Mr. Price was kind enough to escort her home, and by the time he did so on the second day, evidence of her withdrawal had begun to appear.

"Mrs. McClinty, may I speak with you privately about your mother-in-law?" he asked Mimi in a lowered voice after Irene helped Amelia upstairs.

"Yes, of course," she answered, leading him into the parlor and gesturing for him to sit down. "But first I must insist that you begin calling me by my first name. Under the circumstances, I believe we can safely dispense with our customary formalities."

"Very well," he replied, feeling uncomfortable with the request, but complying nonetheless.

"Now, what is it about Amelia? I'm sure she's been underfoot at your office, but she's just trying to do something constructive with her worry. Is she causing a disruption?"

"On the contrary. That's why I'm concerned. Almost by the hour, she seems to become more dazed, even disoriented, and unwilling to move around. And she isn't talking at all, which, from my limited experience with her, is hardly typical. If I hadn't insisted on bringing her home, I believe she'd still be sitting in my chair."

"Actually, I noticed similar behavior last night. I'd almost prefer that she were hysterical. At least we'd be able to see what she's feeling. But she's such a strong woman, always in control. Perhaps this is just her way of managing the nightmare."

"Perhaps. Is there anything I can do for you?"

"Bring us good news, Mr. Price. *Bradley.*"

"The very moment I hear. Messages containing the names and descriptions of your relatives have been sent to every receiving location we can raise in the San Francisco area."

"I cannot thank you enough. Meanwhile, I'll see that Amelia stays home tomorrow, regardless of her wishes. I'm certain that Jonathon will support this."

"I believe that's wise. Now I must be going."

"Good bye, and please be careful, Bradley."

Why on earth did I say that? she wondered after he left, watching him through the living room window as he walked down the sidewalk toward the trolley stop.

The fires in San Francisco ultimately burned for five days. Amelia refused to eat anything after the first two and had to be maneuvered into sipping even the smallest amounts of fluids. The doctor made a house call on the *fourth* day and suggested her condition looked like a mild level of shock, or perhaps a temporary emotional paralysis. He was also concerned that she was becoming dehydrated. But he offered no other explanation for her lack of responsiveness. He did give her an injection, however, which everyone who'd been taking care of her agreed had only worsened her condition.

"Jonathon, couldn't you please stay home just this once?" Mimi begged her husband early on the sixth day, as he was preparing to leave again. "I'm nearly sick with worry over your mother, and I think it might be affecting my milk. I'm not sure the baby's getting enough nourishment. She's been so fussy and sleeping so irregularly—probably missing her grandmother's magic touch. I'm exhausted, and you've hardly been home at all since this calamity began. Couldn't you rearrange things so you could be here to help me today?"

"I understand what you're going through," he said, putting his arms around her and patronizingly patting her on the shoulder the way he used to do before the baby was born. "But Drake and Irene have both agreed to stay around the clock, so there's really no constructive service for me to perform. Besides, staying busy at the mill helps me keep my mind clear. I promise to be home for dinner, and Mr. Price has instructions to send a messenger to me as soon as any information comes in. So, darling, I suggest you use the freedom of my absence as an opportunity to get some rest yourself."

"Very well," she answered reluctantly, dismayed that he didn't consider consoling his wife to be a *constructive service.* "But please try to come home early."

As was her custom, she waved to him from the front porch while he boarded the trolley. Then she went back inside and headed down the hall toward the kitchen. *The freedom of his absence? What a very odd choice of words.*

When Jonathon had not returned by six o'clock, Irene prepared a tray for Mimi, who had been with Amelia in her room for hours.

"Here you go, Miss Mimi. I hope it's still hot."

"I'm sure it's fine. Now you and Drake need to go ahead and eat as well. And when the baby wakes, I think I'd like to move the bassinet up here. We McClinty women need to stick together. Right, Amelia?"

But Amelia did not answer, nor did she open her eyes.

"I don't know what to do about you!" Mimi exclaimed, pretending to be angry after Irene left the room. "Here we are in the midst of the very worst time in our life, and you have chosen this moment to take a holiday! It's not fair, and when this is all over, you and I need to have a chat. There will be a new agreement between us, because I have no intention of going through even one more catastrophe without your assistance. Do you hear me?" she added, dropping her voice to a hush.

The sound of the front door chime froze her in place. She waited for either Drake or Irene to see who was there, and then for the voice that she both dreaded and longed to hear at the same time.

"Good evening, Mr. Price," she heard Drake say, his tone subdued. "Come inside, and please wait in there."

Then Irene appeared at the bedroom door to summon Mimi.

"Tell him I'll be down in a minute. And kindly offer him some brandy."

Her heart was pounding with such force that she thought Amelia must surely be able to hear in whatever peaceful spot she'd taken refuge. Wishing she could go there, too, she pushed herself up from the chair, walked over to the bed and leaned down to kiss her mother-in-law's cheek. The familiar softness and warmth beneath her lips was comforting, even in the silence.

"I love you, and I'll be right back. Feel free to help yourself to my dinner."

When she got downstairs, the look on Bradley's face was hard to decipher. He was situated exactly where he'd been before, on the parlor sofa with a brandy snifter in one hand and a teletype in the other. As she entered the room, he stood up and smiled weakly.

"Please be seated," she said to him, easing herself into her customary armchair. "Shall I read what you're holding in your hand, or do you have something to say first? Is the news good or bad?"

"Reading would be best. There's a little of both."

Mimi took the paper from him and saw immediately that the sender was Lily!

"Oh my God! They're *alive*!"

San Francisco, Tuesday, April 24, 1906

Receiver: Mrs. Amelia McClinty, c/o Times Union, Albany, New York

Your messenger found us with friends across the Bay. David is fine. Completely unharmed. My right leg is broken, but not as badly as my heart. With deepest regret I must tell you that my beloved Peter—and yours—has died—killed trying to help people downtown in the beginning—buried yesterday in an Oakland cemetery. Will wire later with details and more about our plans. He was a good man who loved you and Jonathon very much. He didn't know how to tell you. I should have done it for him.

Sender: Mrs. Lily McClinty

Mimi could hardly breathe, much less see. With every blink of her eyes, another rush of tears fell down her face, grazing her chest and dropping on the evil piece of paper in her hand. Bradley Price was a blurry figure who remained respectfully motionless as this first wave of information cut through her. She did not know how much time had passed before she was finally able to speak.

"We need to find Jonathon," she said, her voice remarkably steady at first. "He has to be told before his mother finds out, assuming she can even hear us, of course."

Mr. Price stared at her for a moment with a puzzled expression on his face.

"But I believe your husband already *has* been told. I sent a messenger to the mill four or five hours ago, and I'd hoped he would be here by the time I arrived."

"*What*? *No*!" she demanded, her composure giving way to her physical exhaustion and the cumulative pressure of the past six days. "How could he *do* this to me?" She was crying and bending over in her chair, her voice growing louder with every word. "How could he leave me with this? How could he expect me to be the one who has to tell Amelia that Peter is dead? Where *is* he? And why isn't he here with *me*? Why can't he *ever* be here with me?"

Bradley Price could no longer restrain himself. He walked over to her, pulled her up from the chair, and took her in his arms, holding onto her with a gentle strength as she heaved in pain. Feeling her pliant body begin to shake, he was about to ease her back down on the cushion when Irene's shrill outcry from the third floor hallway filled the house.

"Help me! Help me! Somebody! Oh my God!"

Racing up the stairs in response, they found Amelia motionless on her back, her hands clutching her gown at her chest.

"She's dead! She's dead!" Irene kept wailing.

"Don't be ridiculous," Mimi scolded, her strength returning as she grabbed the crazed woman in an attempt to calm her while Bradley checked for a pulse. Without delay after finding none, he lifted Amelia's head and let it tilt backwards over his arm in an attempt to get air into her mouth. But there was no sound of her breathing and no sign of her heart beating in her chest. At length, Bradley looked up at Mimi, his eyes speaking the unspeakable.

"No," Mimi whispered. "Please take her to her room and keep trying. *Shake* her! *Make* her breathe!"

Bradley and Drake gently lifted Amelia and placed her on the bed where her ashen color and flaccid skin became evident in the soft light from the window. No one moved or spoke for an icy slice of time while Bradley again checked for a pulse.

"There's nothing."

"I don't believe you. This is impossible! She was just fine. Check her again!"

Mr. Price obliged, as did Drake, for what seemed an interminable amount of time. Then both men pushed themselves up from the bed and stepped back. Tears fell quietly down Bradley's cheeks, while Drake wept openly. Irene stood between the men, shaking her head back and forth in denial, her face completely dry.

"Don't stop!" Mimi ordered. "There must be something we can do. How can there be nothing? Please, Bradley, look once more. She just *has* to be breathing!"

He obliged, then stepped back again. More than thirty minutes had past since Irene first called them upstairs.

"I'm so sorry, Mimi. I…I don't know what to say."

He searched for the right words and movements to ease the moment. But he wasn't finding them, and he wasn't certain how to proceed or how bold he should be.

Fighting against the horrific vision of sudden, unimaginable death that was stretched out in front of her, Mimi's voice could scarcely be heard.

"How could this have happened? I just left her when you arrived. I feel so helpless, as if there's some action we should be taking. Or perhaps this is a frightening dream. Surely, this woman who completed my life cannot be lying there in front of us, gone. How can this be?"

"Please. Sit down," Bradley entreated, pulling a chair up behind her, "and allow me to assist in any way. I, too, feel powerless, and I want to help you. My

God," he sighed, looking down at the old woman who had so endeared herself to him, "she's been under such a terrible strain this past week."

"Yes. The strain." Mimi's voice was nearly diminished, and the others in the room had to lean forward to make out what she was saying. "I think her heart must have simply broken over Peter one last and final time. Somehow, she must have heard that you were here, Bradley, and she must have been listening to us. As deeply as she loved life, she didn't have the power to survive the news, and I must have been expressing my dismay far too loudly, after reading Lily's telegram. The shock was too sudden for her. That's the only explanation I can envision. Forgive me," she said, her tone rebounding slightly, as she turned to face the three of them, "but if all of you wouldn't mind, I'd like to be left by myself with her."

Replacing the unused wet cloth on the wash basin in the corner, Irene hesitated and then allowed Drake and Bradley to escort her downstairs without further word. Once alone in the room, Mimi felt a wave of panic begin to rise, but she managed to quiet her thoughts momentarily, her voice remaining steady, as she sat down on the bed next to Amelia.

"This has to be a very bad idea," she announced, lifting her mother-in-law's limp hand and cupping it between her own. "You weren't given permission to go away. You never asked, and therefore you cannot be gone from this house. You promised things would be all right as long as you were here. We never discussed how it would be if you *weren't*. You taught me so many things, but you never mentioned *this*. What will I do without you? Oh dear God, *please* make her open her eyes. Don't take her. *Please*."

Stretching out on the bed and edging as close as she could get, she burrowed her face into that special spot on Amelia's neck, clinging to the last touch, the last fragrance, the last few minutes of this woman's warmth and essence, as only Mimi had come to know them. Expecting to feel those sheltering arms fold around her, she did not move. Waiting for that heart to begin beating, she placed the palm of her hand on Amelia's chest. Hoping to hear that bright voice poking fun at her, Mimi made no sound. But the only heart beating was her own. Those arms would not comfort her again, and that melodic voice would never sing through another room.

"No, Amelia! No! *No*!" Her cry was deep and guttural as she pressed herself tightly against the inert body, holding on as if she were going to fall. "Why did you leave? I would have helped you. I promise. We could have talked like we always do, and…"

As she collapsed beneath the crushing loss of this woman, the agonizing convulsions of her grief reverberated throughout the house, begging for release—begging for this not to be true. Time as she'd known it came to an end in those few moments, and the cataclysmic passage tore at her soul. There was no light, no air—just a shell next to her that used to be Amelia. Her head pounded with a lonely rage that would not be stilled as she continued to embrace the inert body for nearly thirty minutes. Then, as if by feather touch, the pain of transition began to fade away. She lay still, emotionally shattered, and gradually loosened her grip on her beloved mother-in-law. There was a distinct chill surrounding her as if to signal disappearance, or evaporation, but she also felt an infusion of strength and empowerment that helped lift her to a sitting position.

"All right," she murmured, her face red and swollen, her throat raw. "I suppose if you're serious about this, I have no choice but to proceed without you."

After pulling the quilt up over Amelia to her neck, she cupped the woman's face in her hands and spoke directly to her, having no doubt that she was being heard.

"You'd better know what you're doing," she sighed, "and you'd better figure out a creative way to teach me how to cook."

Dry-eyed, steady, and resigned to the inevitable, she then joined Drake, Irene and Bradley Price downstairs where she found them mopping their faces and drinking brandy in the library. Irene was attempting to interest a squirming Cinnamon in a bottle of breast milk as she entered the room.

"Here, let me take her," Mimi said softly, scooping her baby into her arms. "We need to make some arrangements," she continued, looking at the men.

"I've already asked the operator to put a call through to your doctor," Bradley replied, "and I'm sure he's sending an ambulance."

"But we also need to contact Father Garretty. Amelia has to have the Last Rites administered, and I can't remember how much time we have to do that."

"Miss Mimi," Drake said sheepishly, "I hope you're not angry, but we also took the liberty of asking the operator to call the Rectory."

Clinging to fine threads of self-control, she wished someone could take over *all* the decisions, so she could be free to fall apart.

"I'm sorry," she said, sitting down in the chair on Amelia's side of the double desk. "I'm not very good at any of this, and I suppose we're all waiting for some leader to step forward and provide guidance for us. But the truth is that we no longer *have* a leader, and we'll all need to work very hard together for awhile as we move from one day to the next. Discovering how to find any joy while living without her will be no small challenge, will it?"

"No," the three others answered in a ragged chorus.

"As a start," Mimi continued, her voice sounding eerily like Amelia's, "I suggest we move into the parlor and make ourselves presentable for the officials when they arrive. I'm certain they will have questions and things for us to do. And Irene, prudence might also suggest that we replace the brandy with some fresh coffee."

"Yes, ma'am. Right away. And if you want to go back upstairs to be with Miss Amelia again, I'll tend to the baby for you."

"Thank you. That's very kind, but it won't be necessary. Amelia isn't up there anymore."

Jonathon came home a little after nine that night looking for his mother, only to learn he would never see her again.

"They just took her away about an hour ago," Mimi told him.

"But what happened to her? How can this be?" he asked, pacing from room to room with no pattern or direction.

"We aren't certain, but she probably overheard my reaction to *this*," she answered, handing him the telegraph. Rather than waiting with him in the library while he read the transmission, however, she rejoined her group in the parlor. They had all stayed with her, not wishing to leave her alone until Jonathon returned.

"Wouldn't you prefer to be with your husband?" Bradley Price asked when she reentered the room, knowing as soon as the words were out of his mouth that he'd overstepped his bounds.

"He'll survive," she said coldly, not seeming to mind. "Thanks to your messenger, Bradley, my husband has known of his brother's death for the better part of today. He might have considered the devasting impact of such news on his mother and come home right away. Since he did not, he will most likely want some time alone to reflect upon how his behavior might have affected the outcome."

Feeling uneasy with this frozen scenario, Mr. Price made certain he was no longer needed that evening and politely excused himself.

"I will contact you tomorrow if you'd like, Mimi, to further assist with the arrangements and whatever obituary you wish to have written."

"That will be fine. By morning, I'm sure I'll be ready."

Drake and Irene then took their leave as well, retiring to their respective sleeping cots, which they had graciously been using since the crisis began. A limp, despondent Jonathon appeared a short while later, finding Mimi alone in the parlor. She knew he needed sympathy and comfort, and she admitted to herself that he probably deserved a little of each. But wicked as her reaction may have been, no sign of emotion was forthcoming from her as the two of them wandered in prophetically separate directions throughout the hollow reality of a Madison house empty of Amelia.

The funeral for Amelia McClinty was a reflection of her life—strong, bold, beautiful and humble. In attendance at the Cathedral were more than two hundred people who loved her—and at Mimi's urging, Father Garretty told the story from Cinnamon's baptism, which he'd shared with the family only the night before.

"She came to me with an apology. She said she was embarrassed because she loved my predecessor so much that she'd had great difficulty endorsing me. She rambled a bit and then told me that she felt terrible about being so *uncharitable*, as she put it. And then she immediately invited me to a party."

He watched as a soft mixture of laughter and smiles spread across the seated congregation.

"Yes," he continued, "I believe that was the moment I really began to know her. In fact, she proceeded to give me a list of several functions that she had planned, and as she started describing in detail the decorative themes and the menus she'd be serving, I felt her embrace me. As all of us here today came to understand, parties were her favorite ways to give her love to us, and Amelia McClinty delivered that love in abundance. Everyone who knew her was considerably richer for the experience, and her unique light will be deeply, deeply missed."

The words on her headstone were taken from a small sheet of stationery that Mimi discovered in one of Amelia's bureau drawers the morning after she died.

My prayer and greatest wish is that not only will I be granted the power to forgive all things, but that the same power will be given to those I love.

Appreciating how profoundly Amelia believed in those words, her daughter-in-law fought hard over Jonathon's objections to secure the epitaph. But the ultimate irony lay far ahead, as Mimi would struggle and fail to find her own way to that same conviction. Falling prey to the future, her inability to grasp Amelia's lessons would prove far more destructive than the throbbing loneliness born in April of 1906.

CINNAMON

Chapter 5

"Where are we going?" David asked, peering through the limousine's rear window as they turned left out of Fox Run's driveway.

Kenneth, who was beside him, looked across at Megan on the opposite seat.

"Fair question, my friend. How would you like to answer that, Meg?"

"Out—for dinner."

"Why?" the old man asked again. "There's plenty to eat at the house, and I'd rather not leave right now. What if something happens while we're away?"

Kenneth shot a glance at his cousin that said *I told you this wasn't a good idea.*

"Look," he continued, leaning around in front of David's face, "we'll only be gone a little while—probably less time than it'll take for Heidi to follow all of Gram's orders. And the phone number in this car is posted all over the main house, in case we're needed. We can also check in from the restaurant."

"No!" David demanded. "Take me home." Raising his voice even louder, he leaned forward and knocked on the window behind Barnes. "Turn this damn car around. We're going back to Fox Run." Looking first at Kenneth, then at Megan, he added, "Sorry. I might not be as strong as I used to be, but I'm still a hell of a lot older than you are—and I don't take orders from you. Heidi can fix us something to eat and bring it over to the cottage. We can talk there."

The lack of response, particularly from Megan, prompted him further.

"Well, talking *is* the reason for my captivity, right? Or would the word *grilling* be a more accurate description? You just want to pump me for information. How much has she told you already?"

The hint of mischief in his eyes eased the tension slightly.

"Okay, you're right." Megan replied, feeling herself sway as the limo made a lazy U-turn. "We *would* like to discuss some of this with you, and she's been telling me about Amelia, who I never knew was so…"

"Good grief! At this rate, she'll still be yakking after we're all dead," he said, gently ramming his elbow into Kenneth's side.

"Actually," Megan continued, relieved to see him lighten up, "that's why I thought you might be of some help, maybe fill in a few blanks, so I can discreetly direct her toward the Reader's Digest rendition."

"Don't waste your energy, Megan. She's been working on this far too long for her to make any changes. And *I'm* not going to be your source, no matter what tricks you try to play."

Shaking his head in mild exasperation, the old man turned toward Kenneth in a silent plea for assistance.

"Well, don't look at me, David. I'm trapped just like you—only *I* do what Megan tells me."

Heidi microwaved an assortment of finger foods, which she'd been cooking and freezing for days in anticipation of such a circumstance. After arranging a buffet on the round oak dining table, she left David, Megan and Kenneth in the cozy confines of the guest cottage.

"Shall I call you when Mrs. Stafford wakes up from her nap?"

"Yes, Heidi. Thanks."

"We'll be lucky if we have ten minutes," David advised with an attitude. "I can't believe she nodded off at all."

"We'd better get right to it, then." Megan sat down on a footstool in front of David, who had nestled into the sofa cushions.

"And what am *I* supposed to be doing during this process?" Kenneth asked, piling meatballs on a small plate.

"You, my boy, are my witness, so Megan doesn't get me in trouble," David chuckled.

"Got it," Kenneth responded from an armchair, popping a meatball into his mouth and stretching his legs out on the square coffee table that centered their conversation.

"Just exactly where is her story going?" Megan pressed, her focus unbroken by the men's bantering.

David paused, looking back and forth at each of them.

"I can't tell you that. She's the one who will take you there. But you say she's been talking about Amelia?"

"Yes, right up to her death. That's when I stopped her. She seemed to be upsetting herself."

"The part about Amelia always upsets her. Makes her think about her mother. What a sad story *that* was! Instead of dimming, some of those memories have grown more painful over the years, and dwelling on Amelia dredges up all sorts of stuff."

"Can't you help shorten some of this, David? Tell us *something*? Anything?"

"Anything? Well, okay. How's *this*? Bet she didn't tell you that finding out about the annulment could *not* have come at a worse time. I remember her..."

"Annulment? *What* annulment?" Kenneth asked as he sat up.

"Jonathon and Mimi's, of course." David watched the two cousins stare at him.

"Obviously, she hasn't mentioned it," he said, shaking his head again. "Should have figured. Well, let's see. I was about ten when it happened, but I hadn't moved from San Francisco to Albany yet. Later, after I got here, I learned that when Amelia died, the Madison place was almost an extension of her tomb. Those two women had been so devoted to each other that life without Amelia was hard to figure out. I heard, though, that Mimi eventually made a valiant attempt to pick up the pieces. But she never gave herself enough credit for holding things together, and neither did Jonathon, so the story goes. Naturally, there were lots of rumors and innuendos floating around in those days, and I don't think anyone in the grapevine knew the truth about what was really going on inside that house."

David continued his revelations with the shocking statement that no one was sure at the time whether Sophie was the cause or the result of the difficulties in the McClinty marriage.

"All they could see was the fact that two years after Amelia died, Sophie was Jonathon's leading lady, and Mimi had moved with Cinnamon into the cottage behind the old Corbett place. Jonathon had maintained ownership of that property when Amelia originally moved into the Madison house, and he continued renting to a string of tenants all that time. But for some reason, he'd left the cottage empty. In hindsight, the obvious questions raised by that setup were apparently never vocalized by anyone who mattered, even after he'd sprung the annulment trap. He also never seemed to consider how an annulment might one day affect your grandmother, even though the Church's position is that it technically has no affect on a child's legitimacy."

David removed a handkerchief from his back pocket, blew his nose, and drank half a glass of water before continuing summarily, noting that neither member of his audience was attempting to interrupt him.

"This family has consciously avoided any discussion of that moment in McClinty history. But on the few occasions over the years when people who actually lived through the period would let their guard down, they admitted that Jonathon's treatment of Mimi was damn shameful. I guess no one had the courage, though, to confront him. In fact, I never heard the whole story until after he died. When she told me about it, she tried to pretend that she wasn't hurt—that her sadness was mostly for her mother. But I could tell otherwise. At any rate, I'm sure she's planning on giving you all the gruesome details and connecting the dots for you. So, that about wraps it up for me."

Watching Megan and Kenneth continue to stare at him wide-eyed, with the proverbial *deer in headlights* look on their faces, he could not resist.

"What's the matter with you guys? I thought you wanted to *talk*."

Megan was the first to find her voice.

"Why haven't we ever heard that Jonathon was such a son-of-a-bitch?"

"I don't know," David replied. "Maybe because he was so complicated. He was considered a great man in the community, you know. The impact of his economic contributions can still be seen in many parts of town, and his marriage to Sophie turned out to be long and strong. Frankly, even though he was my uncle, he also filled in as a father figure for me, beginning when I was twelve. He was very good to me, and most people spoke of him with admiration. And don't forget, your grandmother worshipped him—until she learned about what happened to her mother. Even then, secretly, I don't think that changed the way she felt about her father."

"Well, I'm having a hard time getting past the vision of Mimi and Gram being pushed out of one door," Megan said, "while Sophie was coming in through another. I never realized that her arrival in the family was so..."

"Distasteful?" Kenneth asked, feeling the need to make a contribution.

"That's one way of putting it, I guess. Now I have even more questions than I had before we started this conversation. And what, for example, ever happened to all the artwork created for Mimi and Amelia? Apparently, Jonathon never gave a flip about any of it."

"Are you talking about all that stuff made by those homeless people?"

"They weren't homeless, David."

"Yes, Megan, they were, no matter what folklore she's been laying on you. I met them myself. Most of them disappeared into the masses downtown after the Madison project—except the Magglios, of course. Actually, now that I'm thinking about it, I believe Vincente's family was given several of those art pieces when Jonathon and Sophie moved to Fox Run."

"Vincente? What does my grandfather have to do with the Magglios?"

"Ken," David said, shifting his focus, "why doesn't she know about this connection? Or have you also been left out of the loop all of these years?"

"I guess I have, because I don't even understand the question, or have the slightest idea what you're talking about. What *is* a Magglio anyway?"

David broke out laughing.

"What's so funny?"

"Your grandmother. She's sure going to have her hands full trying to lay this whole thing out on a straight line. But she's on her own, because I'm through talking."

"Oh no you don't! Not before you finish explaining the relationship between Vincente and the Magglios."

After staging a theatrical rearrangement of the sofa cushions—and recognizing that Megan was not going to release him unless he completed this train of thought—David folded his arms across his chest and fixed his eyes squarely on hers.

"All right, but this is the last thing I'm going to say. You'll have to hear the rest from her. Your grandfather Vincente was Velita's boy, and Velita was Joseph Magglio's sister. She lived with her husband and children in New York City, in Little Italy, I think—and when Mimi and Brad Price decided to get out of Albany, Velita befriended them at Joseph's request. That's when Cinnamon and Vincente met. Well, that wasn't actually the *first* time, but anyway, the rest, as they say, is history. Now I've said enough. So, Ken, how about a game of Scrabble?"

"Actually, I could really use a drink first after listening to this. Then, sure! I'd love to play, and leave you in the dust."

"Dream on, my boy, if it boosts your confidence."

"I guess this means our meeting's over?" Megan queried, observing the two men ignore her as the subject changed without notice. "Great," she answered to herself, "I'll go get my own information."

"Careful what you wish for," the old man whispered.

Megan and Kenneth helped David stand up, and then the three of them slowly made their way along the path between the cottage and the main house, just as they had done so often throughout their lives. In the days ahead, they would take this walk again, but the ground would not feel this solid for a long time to come.

At least a half-dozen lamps were turned on, giving Cinnamon's room the look of midday despite the fading sunset seen through the tall west windows.

"Where the hell have you been, Megan?"

"Ah, I see that your nap and dinner have done wonders for your disposition."

"Stop sassing and push the button on that recorder. We're running out of time."

"Not so fast, Gram. I have a few questions." Megan retrieved the McClinty Family Chart from the bureau and studied the line of descendants from Nathaniel and Amelia. "Is the annulment the reason Mimi's on the bottom of this page, and that her box is a dotted line instead of solid?"

"*What*?" Rows of tight wrinkles pulled across Cinnamon's forehead and between her eyebrows as she paused for a moment. "Oh, I see what's going on here. That incorrigible man! He has no business talking to you about this. He should be shot, and I'm going to do just that," she huffed, throwing off the covers as she unsuccessfully tried to move her legs to the edge of the bed.

"Relax, Gram. Kenny and I harassed him. Actually, I was the one who needled him for information. But he finally refused to tell us anything else. He said the story was yours alone, and he was very protective of your right to control the way you do this."

"Really?" Cinnamon asked, a coquettish look replacing her anger. "Where is he now?"

"He's with Kenny down in the parlor. They're playing Scrabble."

"Maybe when we're through, he could come upstairs and visit with me. Now, what were you asking?"

"I'm sure he'd like that very much," Megan replied, uneasily noting her grandmother's abrupt mood shifts. "So, I was wondering about the annulment?"

"Ah, yes," she said, settling back into the layers of pillows and pulling the sheet up over her chest. "The end of my parents' marriage. Next to Greg's death, and then later, the…" She stopped in mid-sentence, glancing furtively at Megan who was arranging herself on the chaise, and who didn't seem to notice the hesitation. "Yes, the annulment was very nearly the most evil thing ever to happen in my life. Naturally, though, no one bothered to tell me about it, as usual—not that my knowing would have made the slightest difference."

July 12, 1907
2:30 in the afternoon

By this time tomorrow, Cinnamon and I will be living in view of this grand Madison home rather than within these walls. Jonathon has been sending men from the mill to help us move our things into the cottage. Although the houses are separated by only two blocks, the lives broken from one place to another might as well be marked by miles. How tragic that the fabric of a family should be shredded in such a manner. Perhaps one day he will look back upon this lamentable failure the same way I do, acknowledging this as the loss that dismembered our future. Then again, grasping the full measure of something lost requires, first, a belief that something existed. I must have been alone in that faith from the beginning.

Waiting for anger to rise up from within me, or perhaps rage outwardly against the awful events that have transpired since shortly after Amelia left us, all I am able to feel instead is a sadness so thick and deep that my body is bent from the weight. I haven't the faintest idea how I will move on from here, but I have been presented with no alternative, so move on I must.

Mimi rested her pen across the open pages of her journal, and then relaxed her head and shoulders against the high back of her library desk chair. Looking around the room, her sadness widened as she recalled promising Emanuel Smith that her family and friends would forever learn and laugh amidst his honored craftsmanship. Jonathon did agree to let her take this desk to the cottage, along with her chair and Amelia's. But the rest of the library pieces would be left in what she was certain would become a hollow remnant of what should have been.

"Promises," she whispered aloud. "They do seem to be at the root of our difficulties." Her eyes came to focus on one of the round reading tables to her left where, neatly positioned in the center was an unfolded, handwritten letter. On top of the letter was the diamond heart pendant and chain that Jonathon had given her for Valentine's Day after Cinnamon was born. Engraved on the back of the heart were the words, "I love you, from Jonathon."

"So much for promises."

Her voice became more than a whisper as she recalled the letter's delivery that afternoon more than a year earlier while she and Amelia were preparing for the baby's baptism. After signing the receipt, a wave of suspicion had rushed over her, carried by the hint of perfume rising from the letter's seal. If she had pursued her instincts when Amelia was still alive, would the outcome have been altered? Most likely not, because Jonathon's domineering manner only grew more daunting with the addition of a woman named Sophie.

How would Amelia have reacted to the fact that the diamond heart was first a gift from Jonathon to this new woman, who had apparently suffered an attack of conscience shortly thereafter and returned the heart to him while also withdrawing from the relationship? Finding himself in a bit of a bind at home, due to his vow-breaking distraction, Jonathon subsequently made good use of his purchase and gave the heart to Mimi after their daughter's birth. Omitting Sophie's name from the engraving had been a fortuitous oversight.

However, Sophie's love for Jonathon would not be quieted despite the risks, and she wrote to tell him of her desperate need for him, as well as her regret about returning the pendant. Her letter had passed through Mimi's hands on that remembered afternoon. Several months following Amelia's death, while gripped by a fit of frustration when Jonathon did not arrive home yet one more night for dinner, Mimi found the opened letter during a childish raid of her husband's bureau. She would never forget the shock of seeing another woman's love pour out so blatantly on those perfumed pages toward the man she'd married—the father of her baby girl. At the same time, there had been an almost wicked sense of relief at the implied explanation for his negligent behavior.

"Sometimes the answers aren't the ones we wish to hear," she'd said through her tears, as if speaking to Amelia, "and yet *some* answers are preferable to *no* answers at all, I suppose." Later that night, after the new reality had taken effect, she'd refolded the clothes in Jonathon's bureau and slipped the letter back in as close as possible to his hiding place.

Thereafter, she never confronted him about her discovery, but she did cease her efforts to engage him. Her retreat from him led to an odd relaxation in the tension between them, resulting in a stiff civility that allowed them to maintain appearances. Nonetheless, when the year of mourning for Amelia was over, Jonathon approached Mimi with his confessions of unspecified unhappiness. He respected her as his wife, he'd said, and he had the deepest affection for Cinnamon. He suggested, however, that life for all of them might require restructuring without his mother's presence, and he offered to help Mimi secure a teaching position if she would relocate to the cottage down the street—taking Cinnamon with her, of course. He would provide for all of their needs and would see his child as frequently as possible throughout the week.

"Perhaps a bit of separation will help us heal."

She thought those had been his words, and in the recollection, she could not imagine how she'd escaped that moment without throwing something at him or otherwise acting out her rage. Still, she did not reveal to him her knowledge of Sophie. She never cried, begged, or spoke of injustice. Nor did she attempt to share with him the unbearable anguish at the other end of betrayal or within the fragile binding of a broken heart. Even had she been warned, she could not have prepared herself for the unrelenting sense of loss and humiliation that greeted her each morning and shadowed her throughout each day. She tried not to imagine Jonathon's arms around Sophie, or to dwell on his unbelievable absence of guilt, not to mention Sophie's confident takeover of Mimi's life. Disappointment about the future seemed to wrap around every activity, and Mimi found herself catching her breath whenever her thoughts touched upon her aborted dreams. She was least prepared for the physical aching deep within her body, or the throbbing pulse at her temples as she felt the desecrated love for her husband unravel throughout her soul.

Rather than trying to communicate any of this to Jonathon, she chose to focus instead on the place where she would live—much as she had done with Amelia in the early days at the Madison house—and she began preparing the cottage for her arrival with Cinnamon. She would take with her the nursery furniture, the Delicampo-inspired rug, plus Geoffrey and Pepper's lamps from that same room. Tragically, she could not remove the Magglio mural from the walls. Wondering how the artists must have looked as they devoted countless hours of their personal time to the painting, she tried to soothe herself with notions of inviting Joseph, his brothers and their families to the cottage for a long-overdue dinner, where she would attempt an explanation of her change in circumstances. Certain that she would have their support, she also understood the wrath she would most likely need to pacify.

Additional furniture en route to the cottage included the parlor sofa and chairs, two more lamps made by Pepper and Geoffrey, the footstools from Marjorie and Ellen, Anne's afghan, the library desk and chairs, and the old rocker from the kitchen. Sadly, everything else would remain in the Madison house, even the Summer, Spring and Fall oil paintings. Nevertheless, Jonathon could not separate her from the memories, and when he arrived home from the mill that night, the letter and pendant would wait to greet him. He had been such a fool to leave Sophie's missive in his bureau all this time. Now, on her last night in what she had naively believed was her home, she wanted him to face his lies, and to feel discomfited, if nothing else. She wasn't going to leave without his participation in at least a small measure of this disgrace.

Hearing the workmen's voices as they maneuvered the nursery furniture down the stairs, she knew they would be coming for the desk and chairs before long. Leaning forward, she lifted her pen with her right hand and slowly moved the palm of her left hand back and forth across the desktop's smooth surface. The cool remnants of the oil she'd used as a cleaning polish made the leather feel like a soft piece of fabric against her skin, the sensation somehow having a mild sedative effect upon her. Looking at the empty chair facing her, she pictured Amelia's spirit sitting there, serious and equally sad, but determined to see Mimi come through this with dignity. Once again, she began to write.

My marriage has been over for a long while. In truth, I am not convinced now that there ever was a marriage, other than the union's obvious technicalities. Romantic love was the first element to disappear, and ultimately the least important. Trust was the last holdout, the consummate pillar. Once that had been shattered into pitiful grains of dust, answers appeared to questions yet unasked—and by then, there was nowhere for either of us to go but away.

Placing the journal and pen in her skirt pocket, she walked out of the library and into the parlor, where she poured herself a glass of sherry. Then, with her glass in one hand and the bottle in the other, she wandered slowly from room to room, reliving the laughter, embracing the visions, and saying goodbye, unaware of the prophetic nature of what she had just written.

Unlike her mother, Cinnamon's attitude toward the Madison house was formed from the outside looking in. She had no recollection of living there, and did not associate the residence with family experiences for many years. Instead, she knew her home to be the cottage behind her father's *other* big house two blocks down the street, a house her mother always called The Corbett Place. Cinnamon used to watch through her bedroom window in the cottage as people came and went through The Corbett Place with great frequency, and she recalled imagining on each occasion how grand that house must be on the inside. But she would be almost four years old before she would see for herself.

Next door to the cottage lived a little towheaded girl two months older than Cinnamon. Her name was Angela Preston, and her mother Louise had once been a confidante of Mimi's. But something came between the women that Cinnamon wouldn't understand for a long time, and thereafter her mother and Louise rarely spoke. Angela and Cinnamon were still allowed their own friendship, however, which began to solidify when they were old enough to play unattended in the yard between the cottage and The Corbett Place. About this same time, Mimi began to gradually pull herself back from the darkness she'd entered after leaving the Madison memories behind her. Actually, Bradley Price was the one responsible for pulling her back.

He appeared six weeks after she'd been tossed from Jonathon's web, when the pall of depression was making her feel as if she and Cinnamon had already been displaced for an eternity. She'd been successfully managing the routine of daily survival in the cottage by holding herself accountable to the timetable of child-rearing duties. She did the best she could with her baby, just sixteen months old when they first moved into the cottage, making certain there were healthy meals, naps and regular bedtimes. But she couldn't remember eating anything herself, or sleeping, or feeling. Her body and mind responded exclusively to the cues and needs of her child, this routine serving unpredictably to salvage her sanity. During this period, she was living a life still married by law but alone in reality, and every day was running into the next, absent of any clear purpose or plan for the future. Then one fall afternoon in 1907, she answered the front door chime and saw Bradley Price standing on the cottage porch, smiling at her, with a large pumpkin balanced between his right arm and hip.

"Hello, Mimi," he said, as if they'd just seen each other the day before, "Please forgive me for stopping by unannounced, but I thought you might be willing to help me make a pie."

Amused and far happier to see him than she thought she should be, she laughed aloud.

"My dear Mr. Price, if that is the sole purpose of your visit…"

"Bradley," he interrupted.

"Yes, of course. *Bradley*," she continued, dropping her eyes slightly, then lifting them to meet his. "I fear you will be greatly disappointed, since the art of baking—and meal preparations in general—were lessons left undone when Amelia went away. Please do come inside, though. I'm so very delighted to see you, and the least I can do is offer you some tea."

"I think it highly doubtful that you could ever be disappointing, Mimi," he said, easing past her and through the doorway in an unspoken acceptance of her invitation. "Perhaps we could work together to convert this ungainly pumpkin into something delicious. I admit the task appears intimidating, but other people manage all the time. Surely, between the two of us, we can figure it out."

"Actually, I believe that creating the pastry shell is the most challenging element," she added, unable to stop smiling as she led him into the small parlor where the familiar furnishings were comforting to him. "But surely there is a more direct path to your pie than traveling all the way out here. Whatever possessed you to come up with such a notion?"

Following her gesture to be seated on the sofa, he placed the pumpkin on the floor by his feet and looked up at her with those insightful shamrock eyes.

"I must confess, Mimi, that the pie, while of immense importance, is not the primary reason why I'm here."

"Oh?" She pretended surprise at the obvious, and leaned back, half sitting on the end of her library desk, refreshed by the brightness about his face, not to mention the humorous sight of the pumpkin beside his leg. "Shall I make our tea while you gather your thoughts?"

"No. I mean, yes, I'd love some tea. But first, please let me speak. I hope you don't think me too forward when I say that I needed to come here to learn for myself how you're getting along. Joe Magglio has stopped by the newspaper office a few times to tell me he's visited you, but he's been quite guarded about any details. Frankly, he's the one who suggested I make the trip, although I realize now that I should have written to you first with the request."

"Nonsense, Bradley," she said, making no attempt to push back against the magnetic pull she felt with him in the room. "You're so very thoughtful, and I'm thrilled with your surprise visit. In view of your kindnesses and everything we shared the day Amelia died, I am the one who should have written to you after my relocation. Please forgive me for being so remiss. I can only imagine what people must be saying about this change in my circumstances. The silence of private happenings can so easily be misunderstood."

"That's why I needed to talk with you, Mimi, even if I'm stepping beyond the boundaries of my place. I have been very concerned about you, and no matter how I've tried to put the stories together, I've had great difficulty understanding why you made the decision to move out of the safety and security of your previous home—and your marriage—into this place by yourself. Of course, it's none of my business, and I do not expect you to answer. I simply wanted to make certain you were all right."

"What did you say?" she asked, certain she'd heard him incorrectly.

Even without her words, her face would have told him everything he needed to know.

"That's not actually what happened, is it?"

"Bradley, I know you mean well, but this is a very personal issue—and I'm suddenly uncomfortable with your probing."

"And I'm uncomfortable addressing you this way. But Mimi, someone needs to let you know that this is apparently a private matter to you alone. While avoiding specifics, Jonathon has been openly attributing your change in residence to *your* decision to leave. He claims to have been disillusioned by *your* behavior, and he's telling people the only explanation he can come up with is that you simply needed time away from the Madison house to recover from Amelia."

"You have actually heard this from him directly?" she asked, pressing her palms against the desktop behind her to support her loss of equilibrium.

"No, not from him expressly. But the same story has come from a number of valued sources who have been with him at various events during the last month. As a journalist, I know that after one party speaks openly about a conflict with another, there is usually an opposition put forth, and I've been searching for someone who could tell me how you've been presenting your own view of events. What I've learned, however, is that you have apparently been saying nothing."

Rising to her feet, she knotted her hands in a double fist against her chest as she listened to him, wondering if there could possibly be any more layers to Jonathon's cunning betrayal. Finding her voice, albeit a whisper, she moved slowly toward this man she believed she could trust.

"You are right, Bradley. I have not said anything to anyone, laboring like a fool under the impression that Jonathon hadn't either. Since I have evidently misinterpreted many aspects of my association with him, however, I feel suddenly free of any obligation to confer further respect upon his position. Talking with you will be a great relief. I hear Cinnamon in her crib, though. If you'll be kind enough to carry your pumpkin into the kitchen and wait for me there, I'll join you shortly with my daughter. Then I'll feed her while we have our tea and search Amelia's recipe files for the secret to making a pumpkin pie. Somewhere during this process—if you have the time to stay, that is—I will be delighted to…how did you put it?…present to you my view of events leading me out of the Madison house."

"I have no other plans for this afternoon," he said, hesitating only a moment as his concern for propriety swiftly exited his thoughts, "and I would be honored to stay for awhile."

Noting the uncharacteristic look of steel in Mimi's eyes, he picked up the pumpkin from the floor, then followed her out of the parlor and, inextricably, into her life.

They began as friends, with an undeniable attraction drawing them closer at each meeting. From the onset, Bradley had felt immeasurable respect for both Mimi and Amelia, admiring not only their strength and intelligence, but their wit and endearing appreciation for one another. Having been present at Amelia's death, he believed an exclusive bond had been formed with Mimi, but there had never been an opportunity to discuss his feelings until what subsequently became known as The Pumpkin Afternoon. From that point forward, their conversations were unrestricted, and their mutual affection was not only impossible to overlook, but even more difficult to suppress.

Nonetheless, after hearing Mimi talk about her husband's philandering, Bradley was intent on salvaging whatever might be left of her reputation in the face of Jonathon's clear attempts to rewrite facts about his own behavior. He began petitioning educators on Mimi's behalf whenever a teaching position came up in conversation at the civic meetings he covered for the newspaper, since Jonathon's own pledge to help her reenter her profession had obviously been another empty ploy. But he soon met with the McClinty's far-reaching influence when every introduction of Mimi's name was greeted with a *you-must-be-joking* response from even the most judicious administrators in search of applicants. Undaunted, he continued to appeal on her behalf, regardless of the dim prospects.

Also, despite his mounting fondness for her, Bradley insisted that the two of them avoid situations where they would be alone, or where they might further fuel idle gossip. Unfortunately, he had no family to share with her. He and his parents had taken an ocean voyage back to Ireland one Christmas when Bradley was still in college. But his mother, who'd been unhappy in America, did not wish to return to New York. Unwilling to leave his wife, Bradley's father remained in

Ireland with her. They assured their son—their only child—that they would sail to see him in the United States for periodic visits, and they encouraged him to pursue his ambitions, which were making them enormously proud. Despite his reservations, he had agreed to this arrangement. But sadly, he returned to Ireland twice over the next three years to bury each of his parents. Now, as a substitute for family, he organized dinners, or picnics, or river outings with friends like Joseph Magglio, his brothers, and *their* families, all of whom had become steadfast protectors of Mimi and her child as their lives intersected once again.

Joseph had made significant advances since he first met the McClinty women. He had saved enough money to lease the shop beneath his Lark Street flat, and he and his brothers had relocated their studio from their apartment into the new space. This gave them room to display their budding collection of canvases, which had begun selling with surprising regularity. As a result of their recent successes, the three men were trying to secure permission from their landlord to install Anthony's newly painted sign out front, thereby designating the establishment as ***Magglio Originals***. But the landlord was asking for additional rent just for the sign. This impasse did not interfere with activities inside the shop, however, where most of the initial Madison artists had begun consolidating their talents.

Pepper and Geoffrey were the two unaccounted for, missing now for nearly a year. When Bradley first heard they were in trouble, he sought them out with offers of assistance after discovering that their store had been empty of merchandise for some time. The post-christening good fortune experienced by the other artists had somehow bypassed the men and their stained glass products. When Bradley last saw them, he was disappointed that their pride prevented them from accepting his help. He also observed that they'd become far too dependent on Irish whiskey, which had always been their weakness anyway and was most likely contributing to the decline in requests for their services. The next time Bradley tried to locate them, they were nowhere to be found—and thereafter, he was never able to track them down.

Joseph pretended empathy, but in truth he had little patience for those who squandered opportunity. In his opinion, Pepper and Geoffrey created their own difficulties out of what should have been their life's most positive twist of luck. In contrast, Joseph's idea for his own business had taken root shortly after Cinnamon's christening introduced the Magglio brothers and their talents to the McClinty neighbors and associates. Three orders had been placed that very day—one for an oil portrait and two for watercolor scenes. Anne's collaborative projects with Ellen and Marjorie also won favor, inspiring Joseph to consolidate the projects under a single protective enterprise. Each of the craftsmen worked independently, but whenever specific orders for any one of them were lean, they did not stop their individual productions. Instead, their goal was to establish an inventory, and the shop on Lark Street served as storage and retail space for the entire troupe. Joseph helped organize consignment sales and managed the business finances while Matthew and Anthony, who had matured into the better artists, produced most of the new paintings.

Moving the studio downstairs into the shop created welcome living space in the apartment for the family, space which was particularly appreciated by Anthony and Matthew's wives and Matthew's two small daughters. Once they had rearranged the rooms, dedicating one as the children's bedroom, they celebrated by inviting Bradley to an Italian feast in the flat's new dining area, where the girls had previously slept. Bradley readily accepted, and then seized the opportunity to ask if he could open the invitation to Mimi and Cinnamon as well, knowing the Magglio flat would be a safe environment for him to nurture his budding affection.

Joseph could not stop slapping Bradley on the back.

"Excellent, sir! Eccellente! Yes, we will all open our arms to that dear woman and her little girl. Good job, sir! Excellent!"

"Careful now, Joe. Mimi needs our help in sheltering her from evil eyes and sharp tongues. Jonathon is a clever and powerful man, and his motives are not yet clear to me. But until he plays his hand, we must do what we can to see that Mimi is as happy as possible and has all the support she needs with Cinnamon. Aside from that, there will be nothing to congratulate. Not yet. Understood?"

"Yes, sir," Joseph answered, his wide brow narrowing into furrows as dark visions of Jonathon's appearance in the Madison dining room crossed his mind. "I understand completely, and you can count on all of us."

That first Saturday dinner visit began with Joseph and Anthony taking the trolley north on Madison to the cottage where they met Mimi and Cinnamon and then rode with them back downtown to Lark Street. After much discussion, the choice of Joseph and his brother as escorts had seemed the least conspicuous option. Bradley would then wait to greet them at the Magglio flat.

A late October sun still held a hint of warmth, redirected only slightly by the breeze that brushed another wave of leaves from the tree branches with every swipe. A portion of Mimi's sable hair was pulled back on the sides and anchored near the crown of her head with a pair of Amelia's matching silver combs. The rest spilled over her shoulders and below her neck, resting in rich contrast on the pink gingham dress she'd selected to wear. The fabric covered the full length of her arms, which were further wrapped in a white wool shawl, and the skirt's hem flirted with the tops of her black lace-up shoes. But her collar was loose and open at her throat, revealing a pearl drop necklace that slid and rolled against her fair freckled skin. Mimi was truly joyful about this outing, and the flecks of green in her large brown eyes seemed to wink in the sun's reflection.

Cinnamon, whose second birthday was only three months away, was sitting upright in her carriage, bundled in a coordinated caramel-colored set of coat and leggings. The fine reddish curls of her hair were pressed tightly around the rim of her face by the edges of her matching hat, and her eyes, which were exact replicas of her mother's, were curious and unafraid. A few pedestrians and passengers aboard the trolley leaned in to coo at her or to address Mimi about her extraordinarily lovely child. But most of the stares were condescending, applying judgments to the odd assortment of ages, gender and station, as she and Cinnamon were unmistakably accompanied by two men of questionable character.

In the eye of the beholder came to mind, and Mimi felt a rush of self-consciousness followed by an urge to explain the actual circumstances to everyone watching. She also wondered if the people recognized her and, if so, whether they might have heard or believed Jonathon's fictional stories about her. Attempting to divert her thoughts, she began thinking about her ride downtown with Amelia to the *Times Union* offices on a frozen day that now seemed a full lifetime behind her. Sinking into those memories, she felt her shoulders begin to relax. Then Joseph took her hand in his and leaned down close to her cheek.

"We'll be getting off in the next block," he whispered.

Instantly, the passengers, who could not possibly have heard what he'd said, began talking among themselves, glaring at the entourage and leaving Mimi feeling as if all the air had suddenly been sucked out of the trolley. When the doors opened after the car had jerked to a stop, Anthony lifted Cinnamon's carriage down the steps, and Joseph supported Mimi's arm as they followed. After the car pulled away from them on the tracks, Mimi glanced up at Joseph, the rosy happiness on her face having been replaced with a flush of panic. He did not say anything, but boldly attempted to calm and reassure her by putting his arm around her. Then Anthony pushed Cinnamon's carriage, and the four of them silently walked the three blocks to the Lark Street flat.

Joseph's need to protect this woman was almost eclipsed by his anger at her predicament. Over time, only his fear of losing her respect would prevent him from seeking a physical confrontation with Jonathon, the man who had so shamefully dishonored his lovely friend. As he guided Mimi to his apartment that afternoon, he grew fearful about the road her life was taking, and he recognized how harsh the journey was going to be for her, and for her little daughter, in this heartless town. Their paths would be even more difficult if she would eventually be traveling with Bradley Price, an outcome Joseph hoped to personally orchestrate. Thinking about her future, the seed of an idea began to take life in his mind at that moment.

That dinner in October of 1907 would be the first among a multitude of such gatherings with this new family of friends. Mimi was not only welcomed by the Magglio women—Olivia who was Anthony's wife, and Helena who was Matthew's—but the affection they shared with her would soon expand to fill much of the emptiness left by Amelia. Throughout the next three seasons, Mimi would travel regularly and comfortably from the cottage to Lark Street, where she learned to cook, sew, and help with the shop inventory, and where Cinnamon came to be friends with Matthew's three-year-old daughter Christina and her two-year-old sister Rebecca. After Joseph hired Emanuel Smith to build shelves and a retail counter in the new shop, the playgroup would also be enhanced by frequent visits from Jarrett Smith, who was now four.

Cinnamon's preliminary social skills were etched in the company of these children. She began her association with them as a shy toddler who had, until then, experienced little contact with anyone other than her mother, Jonathon, and Bradley. Before long, however, she had clearly established herself as the director of whatever activities might be under development, frequently leading Christina and Rebecca in a forced march toward the production of a picture dictated by Cinnamon or the acting out of some game from her imagination. The sisters would occasionally resist the control exerted by this visitor in their home, but the three little girls genuinely enjoyed being in one another's company. Eventually they fashioned a system of give and take that seemed to work well for all of them, most of the time.

Jarrett, on the other hand, presented a greater challenge. As the oldest in the group, and the only boy, he made all of the natural, culturally expected attempts to assert his dominance over the girls, but he turned out to be fairly malleable when they ignored his orders and began, instead, to dress him up and tell him what to do as if he were one of their dolls. Frankly, he was content when they were together, and he soon began adapting to whatever roles seemed to make them happy, contesting their ideas only occasionally when he wanted to work on his own drawing, or when he was tired of wearing that huge purple hat they kept dragging out from the closet.

This extended support network of people shared meals several times a week, and if Mimi was present, chances are that Bradley was there as well. Somehow, when in the downtown neighborhood, there was less concern about what others were saying or thinking than there was on upper Madison Avenue. So they openly walked around the block many evenings when the weather was calm, and they celebrated on the Lark Street sidewalk with everyone present, including Emanuel and Jarrett, when Joseph and his brothers finally hung the **Magglio Originals** sign above the shop door. Even the landlord stopped by to add his best wishes that night.

There were also times when Mimi entertained the entourage at her cottage, testing her new cooking skills and treating Olivia and Helena to a rare meal that they had not been required to prepare themselves. These uptown visits afforded the Magglio children an opportunity to play outside on the grass, in the large yard shared between the cottage and the Corbett Place, and the adults eventually developed an eagerness about these outings as well. Initially, they'd been uncomfortable, feeling as if their trips to Madison were intrusions where they did not belong. But after the first cottage occasion, they had a discussion with Bradley, explaining to him that their visit left them guarded and uneasy about being seen by the neighbors. He empathized, but reminded them of their original dreams and the promise of America, suggesting that, on the next trip, they might try to use their creative powers of observation to begin building a collective list of things they'd like to achieve themselves.

"Some of what you'll see in that part of town would be worth the effort," he said to them. "Others, if you look closely, are not as rewarding as you might think. Most importantly, though, you should never consider anything out of your reach, especially as you look at your children's future and how you can help them."

They took his advice thereafter and began to unwind, slowly acquiring a taste for the Madison atmosphere where even the air seemed easier to breathe. Mimi loved having them visit her, and after Bradley told her about their anxieties, she often reminded them that they carried their enviable artistic talents and human qualities with them wherever they went, regardless of the neighborhood.

"No matter how people might present themselves," she would say, "we should not envy them or set our sights on emulating them. They could be pretending about everything we see in them. Our dreams should be built on our *own* passions and what feels right in *our* hearts."

At every turn of their experiences, they found joy and humor in each other's company. They worked together to overcome any lingering sense of inadequacy as events at the cottage became as frequent as those on Lark Street, leaving scarcely a day when they weren't traveling to one place or the other. One of the few times Mimi found herself on her own with her daughter anymore was at Mass in the cathedral every Sunday. One such morning in April of 1908, Father Garretty approached her as she was leaving the church to make sure she knew about the memorial Mass for Amelia, which was planned for the following

Thursday, on the second anniversary of her death. Mimi behaved as if she were fully aware of the arrangement, but asked him to confirm the time in hopes of deflecting his attention from what must surely have been a look of surprise on her face.

"Two-o'clock, next Thursday afternoon," he said. "I felt confident that you'd been told, but I wanted to make certain."

"Yes, Father. Thank you for your kindness, as always. We will see you there."

Later that afternoon in the Magglio's Lark Street flat, Mimi's mood was less conciliatory.

"How could Jonathon have been so cruel as to leave me out of this?" The rhetorical question went unanswered by any of the troubled faces looking back at her.

"Here," Olivia said, placing a hot cup of tea in front of her. "This will help calm you down."

"But I don't want to calm down. I want to throw a fit. Amelia would certainly be doing precisely that if she were here. Whatever has possessed Jonathon? Why would he make the decision to do this? Amelia was part of my soul, and I have not done one single thing to cause him to behave this way toward me."

"No, Miss Mimi, you have not." Joseph was using all of his energy to keep himself seated. "Please forgive me if I'm being too outspoken, but he has been hateful since I first set eyes on him. I don't care what others say about him, I do not believe there's a decent or honest drop of blood in his body."

"Perhaps you're right," Bradley interjected, a faint smile forming on his lips. "In this particular instance, however, his well-rehearsed deceit may have outwitted him. He obviously wished to avoid having Mimi at the service, for some reason we have not yet uncovered. But he clearly did not count on Father Garretty's compassion."

"He's damn incapable of any kindness or sympathy." Joseph was leaning forward in his chair, his hands clasped so tightly together that the tips of his fingers were red from lack of circulation. "How the hell could he anticipate anyone *else* showing compassion?"

"Joseph, your language, please," Olivia scolded softly, completely comfortable about addressing her brother-in-law in this manner since he didn't have a wife of his own to keep him in line.

"There isn't any other way to talk about that man," he stated in a half-apologetic tone.

"I agree," Bradley said. "But there might be something we can do to show him that Mimi is no longer at his mercy. In the process, maybe we can learn what he's up to."

Inside the tiny, warm Magglio kitchen, Mimi watched and listened as her six dear friends conspired. She was unspeakably grateful for all of them, and as she sipped the tea Olivia kept refilling, she finally did feel herself beginning to relax.

On April 23, 1908, they gathered together in front of the cathedral one half hour ahead of the service, as agreed. Everyone looked fashionable in the same clothes they'd worn to Cinnamon's christening, since those were their finest church-worthy outfits. Emanuel and Jarrett were the first to arrive, and they sat on the stone steps watching the Magglios walk up the street from the trolley stop. Joseph lumbered ahead of his group, consumed with intent and seemingly oblivious to his family behind him. Matthew was next, carrying Rebecca, while Helena held Christina's hand, tugging at the resistant toddler. Anthony and Olivia were linked arm-in-arm behind them, secretly thankful at this moment that God had not yet blessed them with children. Shortly after the Magglio family had joined Emanuel and his son, Bradley sprinted around the corner, apparently concerned that he was late. Joseph then pointed to the trolley stop where Mimi was disembarking with Cinnamon. Still out of breath, Bradley went to greet them and ushered them the rest of the way back to the others.

Once fully assembled, they entered the cathedral, moving in a somber procession down the center aisle to the front pew on the left. The overcast light outside was barely filtering through the heavy stained glass windows, which somehow seemed appropriate on this occasion. Anthony and Olivia genuflected and entered the pew first, followed by Matthew, Helena and the girls. Emanuel and Jarrett were next, then Mimi and Cinnamon, and finally Bradley, who was seated on the aisle. There was not an inch of empty space across the entire length of the pew.

Several minutes passed. They were each in their own prayerful worlds, vaguely aware of people filling pews behind them, when a rising wave of whispers began rolling through the sanctuary. Mimi had been kneeling, her head resting on her folded hands, her thoughts and spirit with Amelia, when she looked up and to her right in response to the sound. Bradley had turned to look as well. So had Joseph, and all of them were astonished when they realized that the buzz was obviously related to Jonathon's arrival at the pew directly across the aisle from them. After he genuflected and crossed himself, he eased in and sat down beside a diminutive blonde woman, who wore a gray felt hat, with a spray of black netting falling over her eyes. Cinnamon was the next to spot the new arrivals.

"Papa!" she squealed, bounding across Bradley's legs and onto the floor.

Jonathon reached out and lifted his daughter into his lap, as he looked first at Mimi, then at Bradley, then at the row of friends. After shaking his head in a disdainful show of recognition, he held Cinnamon for a few more minutes, then spoke something in her ear and put her back down on her feet. She looked up at him with disappointment, but obediently walked across the aisle without a word.

Bradley was tempted to embrace the child on his own lap, but passed her to Mimi instead, who buried her face in Cinnamon's hair, wishing she could disappear altogether. Once the Mass began, the only sounds she could hear were her own prayers asking Amelia to forgive her for being so distracted. Occasionally, she became aware of the music, or the choir, or Bradley beside her, or her daughter who had fallen asleep against her breast. She did not recall hearing a word of Father Garretty's homily, however, although she did respond to the Eucharistic bells, and she did go forward to the altar for Communion, leaving Cinnamon with Emanuel, who was not Catholic and remained seated. Throughout this process, she felt too embarrassed to look at anyone. When she returned to the pew, she knelt again in prayer, trying to calm her racing heart and squeezing her hands to stop them from shaking.

At length, she lifted her head as the rest of the congregation continued to move in a single line toward the altar. Only then did she see the empty pew across the aisle. *They must have walked out after receiving Communion.* She thought she was thinking to herself again, but she was actually murmuring out loud.

Bradley leaned in toward her.

"Yes, they did, Mimi."

As she spoke back to him in a hush, she found herself not caring who might be watching.

"I should have left well enough alone and stayed away today. How could I have been such a fool?"

Feeling her discomfort as if it were his own, Bradley was also a little ashamed to be taking such pleasure in this intimate dialogue. Pressing his arm against hers, he lowered his head, his lips coming within an inch of her face. His need to speak to her was accommodated by an insulation of privacy offered by the series of thundering hymns rising from the massive pipe organ.

"The better question, my dear, is how he thought he could bring her here to his mother's service without any repercussions. This public appearance was hardly supportive of the tales he's been telling."

"But he didn't expect me to attend," she whispered in return. "And besides, how must this look? Here I am, accompanied by you—*all* of you."

"Mimi, *he* is the one who should be worried about how things look. You have every right to be at this service. In fact, your absence would have been the inconsistency. And you should not feel uncomfortable that you're here with your friends who care about you, and who've been trying to assist you through your difficult time. One might wonder, though, how *she* has been assisting *him*," he continued, pleased with the way this was progressing. "How is *that* suggested image one that befits a man in his position? I suspect that, since they no longer appear to be in the cathedral, his actions might not have been so carefully considered as he originally thought."

Everyone in the congregation seated behind them must have noticed the way she turned and looked into his eyes, his lips still a breath away from hers. They could scarcely have missed the way he looked back at her, either. Their friends were also aware of the exchange, having followed Mimi's reactions since Jonathon's arrival. As time would pass, they would all reminisce about that occasion every April. Joseph became particularly entertaining through the years, his theatrical accounts of homicidal urges during Amelia's memorial Mass growing more dramatic, and further from the facts, with every telling.

The most significant insight for Mimi on that day, however, was simple and unscripted. Somewhere along the way, at some blurry point between the cottage, the trolley, and the Lark Street apartment, she had fallen profoundly in love with Bradley Price.

CHAPTER 6

Two weeks after Amelia's memorial service, an envelope of legal papers arrived at the cottage by courier. Mimi could not bring herself to believe what she was reading until, after a half-dozen passes through the scrolled lettering, the key points began highlighting themselves.

On this date, the sixth of May in the year nineteen hundred and eight...Marriage...covenant by which Jonathon McClinty and Mary Mae McClinty sought to establish between themselves a partnership of the whole life, which is by its nature ordered toward the good of the spouses and the procreation and education of offspring. This covenant between baptized persons has been raised by Christ the Lord to the dignity of a sacrament...

...a fervent review has determined that these essential elements have not been present from the beginning...This marriage was therefore not a sacramental covenant...

...Declaration of Nullity has been granted...lawfully entered into the records of The Cathedral of the Immaculate Conception...City of Albany...State of New York...

...Further, said Declaration of Nullity does not affect in any manner the legitimacy of the single offspring, Margaret Elizabeth McClinty...

Jonathon A. McClinty

Jonathon A. McClinty Mary Mae McClinty

Mimi realized that she was sitting on the parlor floor. She prayed that Cinnamon would not awaken because she didn't think her legs would carry her into her daughter's room. Bradley was the first person she thought of, the one she realized she needed, and the only friend with whom she could bare such distress. But he had taken the ferry across the Hudson to the city of Troy to cover a story for the *Times Union*, and he was not planning to return until the following day.

"Amelia," she spoke aloud, her lips moist from the tears she made no attempt to wipe from her face, "if this weren't so horrifying, I would mention that a very twisted sense of humor appears to be at work here. But since I'm clearly in the midst of something dreadful, I'm asking that you and God work closely together to help me survive the night in front of me. Even with all the surprises that have befallen me thus far, I could never have foreseen Jonathon using his authority to make me completely disappear from the record of his life, and with the blessing of the Church no less."

She did survive the night, although the half-empty sherry bottle and overturned glass on the kitchen table the next morning explained why she had little recall of exactly how she'd managed. But Cinnamon was fine and still sleeping in her crib when Mimi awakened shortly after dawn. Her subconscious had apparently been working on a response overnight, and her thinking was remarkably clear as she began heating water for tea. A few minutes later, she carried her cup into the parlor, removed her journal from the drawer on her side of the library desk, then sat down and released her thoughts onto the paper.

May 7, 1908
A Thursday morning—the sun has just come up.

Yesterday, Jonathon organized the delivery of papers to me, the signing of which will make the statement that our marriage never existed. His precise words were that "the sacramental elements were missing from the beginning." This heresy, of course, is an extension of the lie named Sophie. But through his power as a man and as a McClinty, he is presenting me as the reason for the missing elements referenced.

I 'm beginning to believe that Jonathon's brother Peter may not have been the uncaring renegade he's been painted to be. In truth, Peter could possibly have been the only person who understood that his brother's character was the one flawed. Despite his regret about leaving Amelia behind, I now think that Peter's only chance for survival was to move far afield of Jonathon's reach. He must have known his brother would eventually destroy him if he remained close to home, but he also knew that his mother would never accept such a possibility. So he fled to the country's furthest side where he could build a life free of Jonathon's interference. If only I had been so wise!

Tomorrow I will speak with Father Garretty at the cathedral. I need to understand from him directly how all of this will affect my relationship with the

Church. I'd also like him to arrange a meeting between Jonathon and me so the man can explain in my presence precisely which of the missing elements in me he has found so sacramentally in place with Sophie. I want to hear from his own lips the explanation he will give to Cinnamon one day when she learns that her father used all of his might to erase her parents' marriage from history. The papers say that her legitimacy will not be in question, but he can be the one to tell her!

My Lord in heaven knows all too well that I'm imperfect and weak, but neither my daughter nor I merit such hatred. I ask forgiveness for the retribution I seek in this moment, and I pray for strength to overcome my bitterness about Jonathon and Sophie's apparent bliss. God, give me guidance as I wonder where to go from here. Will I ever feel whole or beautiful? Will anyone ever want me again?

Bradley's concern for Mimi's suffering was nearly impossible for him to contain, and he loathed Jonathon's tactics and disregard for Cinnamon. If he understood this correctly, however, his prayers might just have been answered. Following a respectable period of time, he could gradually begin to court Mimi in public, without sullying her name or his professional status with the newspaper. Further, she would eventually be free to marry again in the Catholic Church, assuming, of course, that she might ever consider another union. Given her current state of mind, that would certainly take some convincing. Nevertheless, he was pleased to see her mood brightened the following day when she returned from her meeting at the rectory. Father Garretty had reassured her about her standing in the Church, although he had not been as positive about her suggested meeting with Jonathon. He was rather adamant, in fact, and said that her life might move more readily toward peace if she did not confront him.

"You haven't sinned, Mimi. You know that. I know that, and most importantly, God knows. Jonathon's methods aside, he has, in my opinion, offered you more of a life this way. His mother is most likely in agreement—may the Lord forgive me for saying so—as she watches us from her place in heaven. You will always remain part of this parish, and I will continue ministering to you and your family without regard to any of this. Now, go home and feel at liberty to find happiness and love again, and try not to burrow in the past. Too often, while we're looking over our shoulder at what might have been, we walk right by the open door to what could be."

Although Mimi did not immediately set out to follow Father Garretty's advice, Bradley wasted no time in devising and implementing his plan to capitalize on what he viewed as an extraordinarily positive turn of events. Initially, he stayed within the familiar routine of group activities at either the cottage or Lark Street, recognizing that Mimi's comfort level was stable in those circumstances. But as the months added distance between their lives and the annulment, he began to create opportunities for them to begin building a history of experiences together, outside their customary circle of companions.

At first his ideas centered on short excursions in the countryside south of Albany. He and Mimi would take the Madison trolley to the northern-most station where they would transfer to a horse-drawn carriage arranged by some well-connected politician or civic patron. There was no shortage of people who wished to assist Bradley with his courtship, although the allies universally requested anonymity. Despite their personal aversion to Jonathon's treatment of Mimi, they could not afford to alienate him.

Thus, the picnics and conversations amidst the scenic hills and farmlands surrounding Albany became common occurrences that were slowly beginning to work the desired magic on Mimi's heart. Satisfied that Cinnamon would be in the nurturing hands of the Magglios, she welcomed with increasing anticipation these occasions alone with Bradley. He was cautious about not exposing her to situations involving anyone who might know Jonathon, or who could have been biased by him, which took some doing considering the breadth of the man's influence. Consequently, these early courtship experiences may have been romantic, but they were also isolating and gradually began disconnecting them from the mainstream of their city. But they didn't care, as they embraced the freedom to love one another.

By the fall of 1908, Bradley was ready to take the relationship to the next level. During his periodic trips to Troy, New York, just across the Hudson River from Albany, he had grown familiar with the Troy Savings Bank Concert Hall. Originally opened in 1875, the hall was actually situated on top of the bank. At the time, Troy was a major industrial center famous for iron products such as stoves and horseshoes, as well as meatpacking and the manufacturing of shirt collars and cuffs. Historians would write that, after the Civil War, the Troy Savings Bank was left with a surplus of money unclaimed by dead or missing depositors, and the bank officers decided to give the money back to the community by constructing a concert hall on top of a new bank building.

Experts subsequently speculated that the hall's shoebox shape, 60-foot high vaulted ceiling, and the irregular reflective surface of the wooden seats and floors all contributed to the remarkable acoustics. This exceptional quality was not widely known until 1890 when a massive pipe organ was installed, which magnified the sound projection. Patrons then began to notice as far away as New York City, favorably comparing the hall to those in Vienna and Amsterdam.

As editor-in-chief of The *Times Union*, Bradley's presence was frequently required at these concerts and their associated society dinners and receptions. His familiarity with the location, as well as the ferry options to and from, made the hall a clear choice as the centerpiece of his next move with Mimi. Two months in advance, he targeted a November performance of Beethoven's "Coriolan" Overture, Liszt's Piano Concerto No. 2, and Brahms' Second Symphony, asking her to reserve the entire day of Saturday, November 21 for a surprise of unspecified proportions.

Once he'd tipped his hand to Joseph Magglio, the plan became increasingly elaborate and included a shopping trip to New York City, which would be coordinated by Mrs. Velita Magglio Mentini. After their parents died, Joseph, Anthony and Matthew had seen their sister far too infrequently once Velita had been sent to live with relatives in the City. Any opportunity for a reunion was therefore welcomed, and this particular production was no exception.

The purpose of the trip was to find a dress appropriate for Mimi to wear on November 21, although she was the only one who did not know where she'd be going that day.

There were undoubtedly shops in Albany that would have been perfectly suitable, but what fun was *that*? Instead, the entire Magglio family, including the children, joined Mimi, Bradley and Cinnamon for the train ride from Albany to Manhattan where they were greeted at Grand Central Terminal by Velita, her husband Alberto Mentini, and their son Vincente, who was four years old at the time.

The Mentini's earned their living in the garment trade. Velita, whose talent as a seamstress had enabled her to work since she was thirteen, was now a respected dressmaker in an exclusive tailor shop catering to the Vanderbilts and other members of New York's aristocracy. Alberto was a tailor's assistant in the same shop, and between the two of them, they had access to dozens of defective garments received from women who worked as seamstresses doing ready-made piecework in their homes. Other seamstresses employed inside the tailor shop were often assigned the task of repairing defects on returned dresses, but occasionally Velita was asked to completely reconstruct a new garment from fresh cuts. In those cases, the rejected but otherwise finished gowns were relegated to a rack in the back of the shop where a collection of such articles was gathering. After learning of Mimi's story from his brother-in-law, Alberto approached his employer and was given permission to select six of the rejected dresses in what he and Velita believed to be Mimi's size. The garments were then transported to the Mentini apartment for review upon the visitors' arrival from Albany.

The trip turned out to be a three-day stay on the crowded but energized lower east side where Mimi and Cinnamon were openly welcomed. As the family and new friends gathered around the long table occupying most of the apartment's main living space, they laughed while sharing stories, wine and recipes. When the nights were exhausted, they slept on a variety of sofas and floors in the Mentini household and flats belonging to three of their neighbors. Bradley was taken to an apartment on the floor above, while Mimi and Cinnamon were given Alberto and Velita's bed, despite Mimi's protests.

The camaraderie and unity of the building's residents was striking, especially in view of their obvious struggles to support themselves. Bound by their heritage and various dramatic tales of their voyages across the Atlantic Ocean, this community of Italian immigrants was united in purpose as Mimi had never before witnessed. Many of them had labored to learn English, and though they were far from fluent, they were amazingly successful in communicating their opinions to her, as well as some of the secrets behind their ambrosian meals. In turn, she asked them to teach her a few Italian words and phrases they thought would be helpful to her, a task in which they all took great delight.

"Una signora bella che proviene dall'Irlanda e desidera imparare come parlare italiano! Ciò potrebbe soltanto essere idea del dio."

"What did she say?" Mimi asked Velita when the round buxom neighbor who'd just spoken remained standing a foot away, with a colossal smile on her face.

"She says you are very lovely, and she apparently forgives you for being Irish."

In this setting, Mimi was reminded of Nathaniel and Amelia's respect for the American dream. For the first time, she began to understand their passion, as well as the risks they'd taken when they'd journeyed north to Albany in pursuit of their ideals. She also marveled at the way Joseph's extended family accepted her, and she realized that she hadn't felt this sense of community since Amelia died. Drawn to the generous open arms of these amazing people, she felt very much at home. Even the children blended together as if fashioned from the same cloth, including the fair, red-haired Cinnamon playfully embedded in the cluster of her olive-skinned Mediterranean contemporaries.

As things would turn out, the search for Mimi's dress became secondary to the friendships and relationships being forged. Nevertheless, the selection process began taking priority as the visit was drawing to a close. Two of the six dresses did not fit at all. A third was an unflattering shade of red, and a fourth was deemed entirely too dull. Velita, Olivia and Helena stuffed and pinned Mimi into the two remaining gowns, after which she modeled and twirled for her enthusiastic fans.

At length, everyone reached agreement on the choice, a design inspired by a French Belle Epoch ball gown. Even Alberto and Velita had difficulty spotting the defects that had relegated the creation to the rejection rack. On the contrary, when wrapped around Mimi, the dress not only appeared perfect but seemed to have been made exclusively with her in mind. Luscious cream-colored China silk and silk satin fell softly around her body, the sleeves ending at her elbows and the skirt dusting the tops of her shoes. The scooped line of the bodice was not quite off-shoulder and was trimmed with creamy silk ribbons and pale pink, gold and green floral appliqués that rested against her fair skin. Falling from the bodice line all the way around was a gathered ruffle of soft net lace in the same cream hue that spilled over her shoulders, bust line, and upper back. Along the bottom edge, the ruffle was trimmed with more silk satin ribbon. The same net lace and trim finished the sleeves at her elbows and the hem of her skirt. Around her waist was a wide satin sash fastened at the back with additional pink, gold and green floral appliqués and loops of ribbon. From the sash, the dress fell in soft shiny folds that hinted at her shapely form and moved in sinuous waves around her as she walked.

The room was silent with admiration as she stood before them, and no one was more taken with her stunning appearance than Bradley Price. Joseph saw the look on his friend's face and was about to say something irreverent to break the stillness when one of the women from the apartment next door spoke first.

"Dove porterete il vestito, il mio caro?"

"She wants to know where you'll be wearing the dress," Velita volunteered.

"I don't know. I mean, non so. Nessuno mi diranno," Mimi answered, feeling quite pleased with herself as she looked first at the neighbor, then at Joseph and Bradley. "I'm told this is to remain a surprise, and I cannot persuade a single soul here to break the bond of secrecy. How do I say *that* one, Velita?"

"L'occasione è una sorpresa per la signora e non può fare chiunque dirle il segreto," Velita translated to the neighbor, whose eyes brightened at the news. "Nor will you succeed in your efforts to make us tell you, despite your charm," Velita continued, turning again to Mimi. "All right, everyone," she said, facing her friends. "I believe the time has come to remove our lady from this gown so we can finish preparing dinner. Our dear family returns to Albany tomorrow, and we need to secure the dress for travel while making certain everyone has plenty of rest for their journey. Grazie per la compartecipazione del questo con noi. Li vedremo alla mattina."

The crowd began dispersing while kissing each other's cheeks and delivering animated commentary on the vision of Mimi in that dress. As Velita suggested, the group assembled again the next morning with more of the same, waving and wishing *buona fortuna* as the Albany visitors walked with their hosts to the trolley, none of them having the vaguest idea how foretelling this visit had actually been.

Mimi and Cinnamon arrived at Lark Street early on the morning of November 21, 1908, only to be swept up in the air of anticipation filling the flat. Joseph was the first to greet them since he'd spent nearly an hour watching for them through the shop window.

"Helena is prepared to take care of Cinnamon and the other children throughout the day," he said, lifting Mimi's daughter in his arms and walking ahead up the stairs. "Olivia has everything arranged to help you with your hair and other grooming tasks, although Helena insists that she'll have time to help as well. We also expect that you'll want to sleep awhile this afternoon before Bradley arrives. He said he'd be here to call for you at five."

"Dear heaven," Mimi chuckled as a flurry of hands assisted with the removal of her coat, hat and gloves. "I realize that this tightly held secret is giving all of you great pleasure. But I believe I can say with confidence that this event is merely a courting gesture, and that you, my friends, might be a slight bit over-indulgent."

Joseph, Olivia and Helena all stopped moving for a moment, fully informed as they were on the night's actual agenda.

"Right," Joseph said, suppressing a grin and hoping for quick additional words from his sisters-in-law.

"Perhaps we're just a little impatient to see the full picture of you in your new dress," Olivia responded. "Helena and I have been protecting it, as promised, since our return from New York, and every day we've come to admire it more. I suppose we've been carried away with expectation. I'll make some tea to settle us. Joseph, why don't you go check on your brothers in the shop?"

"Yes, a good thought," Joseph said. Occasionally he was annoyed by Olivia's brashness, but today he was grateful for her control. "Come tell us if you need anything. Otherwise, we will join you for lunch."

By four o'clock, Mimi was rested, dressed, accessorized, and filled with butterflies unlike any she'd experienced since her childhood. The fact that the Magglio family and a few invited neighbors had gathered in the parlor to view her as if she were a museum piece would have made her feel uncomfortable if she didn't love them so much. Besides, she'd seen her own reflection in the full-length oval mirror and silently conceded that she was thrilled with everyone's efforts on her behalf. Her long-ago worry about never feeling beautiful again had given way to this moment, for which she would be forever grateful.

Olivia had done a masterful job on her hair. Sweeping the dark, rich tresses back from her face, she wrapped and wove the thick lengths into a soft mound at the crown of her head, securing the design with wide pearl combs Helena had worn when she married Matthew. A few fine wisps and curls remained free next to her cheeks and at the nape of her neck, highlighting the off-white velvet choker, which had been a gift from Olivia. The dress itself seemed more striking, if possible, than Mimi remembered—the creamy satin and silk lace flowing as extensions of her every movement and skimming the tops of her new ivory button shoes.

Had there been any question about the fashion success, none would have remained after Bradley's first sighting of her. He was bewitched by the full bloom of her loveliness, and only Joseph's exuberant back-slapping kept him from stammering.

"I have never seen a woman more alluring," Bradley said, taking her hand in his and slowly raising it to his lips as their friends watched and clapped with approval.

"Thank you. You look quite dashing yourself," she said, reviewing his formal black suiting, charcoal topcoat and hat. "We do make quite the pair this evening, don't we?"

"Yes, indeed!" Joseph exclaimed. "I feel like someone's father."

"Hopefully not mine," Bradley replied, playfully grazing Joseph's chin with his fist.

Caught up in the high spirit, the group gathered in a semi-circle around the couple, everyone talking and laughing at once. Then Bradley raised his voice above the commotion and asked Mimi if anyone had told her yet where they were going.

"No! They've been unmerciful in their secrecy. But I have so thoroughly enjoyed every moment of preparation that we could stay right here tonight and I wouldn't mind."

"And deny the world a view of you? Impossible!" Bradley could not stop smiling. "We are going to the symphony," he announced proudly.

"Oh, my!" she gasped. "To the Troy Concert Hall you've been telling me about?"

"One and the same, my dear. Now we really must be leaving. We wouldn't want to miss the ferry."

She pulled on her elbow-length white gloves and the black velvet cape that Alberto and Velita had shipped as a surprise. Then she linked her arm in Bradley's while they walked down the stairs, with the entire household trailing behind. Outside, a horse-drawn carriage and driver awaited them, and as they rode off, the Magglios, their children, the neighbors, and Cinnamon waved behind them, as if they were watching a fairytale come to life.

Mimi still felt suspended in a fantasy when they reached the dock. Dozens of other men and women in their finery were en route to the same destination, and as she disembarked from the carriage she was entirely unaware of the admiring looks coming from every direction. Bradley missed nothing, however. He was buoyed by the crowd's subtle validation of his fine taste in companions, and he congratulated himself on the perfection of his plan.

Having secured a table off to one side in the ferry's sheltered cabin, he sat down across from Mimi and removed his gloves. Feeling the vessel beginning to move, he reached for her hands.

"Would you mind removing your gloves as well, my dear? We'll have some time before we reach the other side, and I want to feel your warmth while I tell you something important."

"What about all of these people?" she responded, trying not to let anyone else hear her.

"*What* people?"

The impish look on his face chased away any reluctance as she removed her gloves and folded them on the tabletop. Bradley's eyes locked on hers, and he realized that the rest was going to happen much faster than he'd anticipated. But he didn't care. Taking her left hand in his, he touched the fourth finger.

"Did you know a legend tells us that, on this hand, the path to our hearts runs in a direct line from *this* finger?"

"No, Bradley, I wasn't aware of that," she answered, suspecting his words were a prelude to one of his funny stories, but suddenly open to wherever he wanted to take her.

"Yes, it's true, and that's why this is the place so long associated with symbols of love."

From out of nowhere a pear-shaped diamond ring appeared, which Bradley pushed onto the finger he held so gently.

"Mimi, will you honor me by saying that you'll become my wife?"

For a moment she could hear no sound, as though a space had been created just for the two of them where only they remained. Her breathing was quick and shallow while her heart swelled with devotion for this man. Then the sound rushed back in, and she thought she heard applause. But he was the only person she could see, this kind and generous soul with the shamrock eyes who had lifted her out of the darkness. Was it really possible that he loved her this much?

Mimi remembered answering yes to his proposal, and then she became lost in the rest of the evening. In the coming days, Bradley would help her reconstruct glimpses of their sumptuous meal before the concert, and then the extraordinary symphonic experience followed by another ferry ride back to Albany. But her own memories of that night were made up of feelings rather than sights—soothing, sensuous, intoxicating feelings born of magic. No other gift in her lifetime would come close to matching November 21, 1908. In retrospect, had Bradley known, he might not have set the standard so high.

Bradley and Mimi Price were married by Father Garretty in March of 1909, during a simple Mass where Mimi wore a plain white, long-sleeved silk blouse and a straight, floor-length grey wool skirt. The Magglios were there, of course, along with Emanuel, Jarrett, Anne, Ellen and Marjorie. Alberto and Velita also surprised everyone by taking the train to Albany with their son Vincente. Bradley had suggested a larger wedding to include Mimi's brother George, her aunt and uncle from Boston, and an assortment of local acquaintances. But although Mimi understood she was free to marry openly—just as Jonathon and Sophie had done in a lavish ceremony the previous summer—she preferred to keep things small and quiet.

Bradley's love brought her respectability and a life where she was revered by her husband, and for this she said daily prayers of gratitude. But close behind the bounty of this relationship was a bitterness from which she could not break free, despite Father's cautions. The thought of celebrating her new marriage on too grand a scale somehow made the line between this new life and her last one more prominent. She could hear Amelia's voice urging her to forget and immerse herself in the joy of her fresh beginning. Absolution had been such a staple of Amelia's character, and the example was one Mimi knew she should follow. For a very long time, those who were watching understood that she tried.

After the wedding, Bradley moved into the cottage with his new wife and Cinnamon, and life took up a comfortable tempo that still included regular visits to Lark Street. Then in October of that same year, Joseph noticed a familiar round shape beginning to replace Mimi's trim figure. The news was soon confirmed. A child was on the way and was scheduled to arrive in late winter. Sequestered at home again after she began to show, she was fighting the threat of gloom when Bradley arrived from work one evening and teased her by dangling a large key in front of her face.

"What is that supposed to be?"

"Well," he said, giddy once more with yet another surprise, "since we're going to need additional room, I thought we should have a new house."

"What? Bradley, whatever are you talking about? We don't need a new house—and besides, where would we find one if we did?"

"I have the answer, but first you must promise not to be angry with me."

"My dearest," she said, touching his cheek, "I promise."

"Wonderful!" he exclaimed, thrusting his arms outward and pivoting in a circle. "Because I bought the Corbett Place from Jonathon! In fact, I bought the cottage, too! Hallelujah! Now the tenants can stay here, and we'll be there—and all is right with the world, at last!"

She was certain she'd misunderstood, but he made no attempt to rephrase his triumphant statement. Instead, he continued.

"I can tell by the way you're looking at me that you're thinking about being angry, despite your pledge. But please hear me out."

She had no choice because she was unable to speak.

"Think about it," he said, his exhilaration fully unleashed. "That rogue got away with deceit and infidelity, with his name and reputation virtually untouched, while you were left to struggle in your innocence. But most observers around here have a sense for what really happened, and putting you and Cinnamon in this cottage is the one overt move he made that didn't settle very well. Now that he has Sophie with him in the Madison house, I thought he might like to know what people have been saying about him. So I went to see him, and I took the liberty of offering my suggestion about what he could do to repair some of the damage. *Sell the Corbett Place to me*, I said to him. I even brought a deposit with me to demonstrate good faith. Oddly enough, he was remarkably agreeable."

Mimi looked at her husband, whose smile filled his face, and she was suddenly reminded of the Pumpkin Afternoon when he stood at the door with that awful thing under his arm, ridiculously declaring that he wanted to make a pie. All he had really hoped to do was save her from Jonathon, and from herself. Now, with the same motive in mind, he had clearly been at work behind the scenes and had somehow managed to wrest control of the prized property from Jonathon's grasp. The Corbett Place was where Nathaniel and Amelia had lived, where Jonathon and Peter had been raised, where the history that had become *hers* was conceived. Would that same house now truly be the one where she would live as well? Suddenly, she found the whole scenario hilarious, and she threw her arms around Bradley, her laughter reverberating throughout the cottage.

"May I assume," he whispered, his face nuzzled in her neck, "that this means you're not going to be angry?"

Over the next few weeks, with the Magglios' assistance, the Price family exchanged residences with the tenants in the big house, who were grateful not to have been displaced entirely. Mimi remained excited, but once the transfer was complete she worried that her new home was too large. Coming from the cottage, they scarcely had enough furniture to fill even a handful of the spacious rooms. But over the next month as her pregnancy expanded, she was certain she sensed Amelia's presence while wandering through each section of the house. As she listened for the familiar voice, fresh decorative plans began to formulate in her mind.

"All right, Amelia," she said one day while having tea alone in the kitchen. "You've been very clever, weaving your spell through Bradley and miraculously getting us into this place. Now that I'm here, I expect you to remain a good ghost and help me make things livable around here. And by the way, I don't think I ever thanked you for Olivia and Helena. I knew you'd come up with a way to teach me how to cook. Besides that, they've become such dear friends. Of course, it took both of them, their husbands, plus Joseph, to replace you. But then, no one could ever really replace you. So, what design would you recommend for *this* parlor?"

In addition to several pieces of new furniture crafted by Emanuel, a number of other selections were made from the shop's inventory for the new house. Originally, the artists wanted to donate the items, but Bradley insisted on paying them their asking prices, as if he were any other customer. Slowly, The Corbett Place became The Price Place, and Mimi earnestly fought to let go of her emotional demons.

Cinnamon, on the other hand, had acquired a temper. Her behavior had become particularly challenging since the birth of Jonathon and Sophie's son, Jay, almost a year earlier. She'd always looked forward to her visits with her father several times each week, her chubby three-year-old legs anxiously running ahead of whomever was walking her to the Madison house. Upon her return, she would characteristically chatter about her experiences, bombarding Mimi with a litany of details. Once Jay arrived, however, Cinnamon had to be carried to Jonathon's house, often kicking and creating a scene during the two-block walk. When she returned, she would curl up on the sofa and remain silent until she fell asleep. Both Bradley and Mimi doted on her and arranged for her to be with other children whenever possible, hoping to reassure her that she was loved and expecting this phase would pass quickly.

They met with disappointment on both levels and were totally unprepared for the child's violent reaction when, in preparation for Mimi and Bradley's baby, the original nursery furniture was moved out of Cinnamon's room and into another room down the hall. Not even the introduction of her new grownup bed and matching dresser would calm her. Eventually, she fell asleep on the parlor rug that first night and did not awaken even when Bradley carried her to bed. Over the next few weeks, she seemed to mellow in the wake of all the attention suddenly pouring over her and in the celebration of her fourth birthday on January 26. This came as a considerable to relief to Mimi, who'd ballooned in her final stage of pregnancy and was confined to her bed. Left in the care of Bradley and the Magglios most of the time, Cinnamon appeared to have gained control over her attitude, and everyone was grateful to see her finally adapting to the abrupt changes in her young life.

On the morning of Valentine's Day in 1910, nearly a week past her due date, Maggie Marie Price was born to an exhausted Mimi and a euphoric Bradley, whose back was beginning to bruise from Joseph's slapping. Cigars and brandy were shared on Lark Street that evening and for several nights thereafter. Cinnamon stayed at Aunt Oly's, as she'd come to call the Magglio flat—much to Olivia's delight—for ten days until Mimi came home from the hospital, with Bradley joining them regularly for dinner. These unlikely companions, he realized, had long ago moved from the realm of friendship into that of a treasure. He could not imagine for a moment how Mimi would have survived the loss of Amelia, and then Jonathon, without their support. He also knew for certain that Mimi would not have become his wife without Joseph and his incomparable family.

Snow was falling on Thursday, February 24, 1910, when Bradley arranged through a patron of the newspaper for an enclosed motorcar to drive him, Mimi and Maggie Marie from the hospital to their home. While in the car, he had his first private opportunity for a close-up review of his new daughter.

"Would you like to hold her?" Mimi asked, noting his curiosity

"Yes, I would very much," he answered, as he confidently lifted the baby from her hands and nestled her into the curve of his arm. Her hair was dark and fuzzy, and so were her eyebrows. Her skin looked and felt like cotton, her fingers the size of Cinnamon's doll.

"Fortunately, she has her mother's features," he said, turning toward Mimi, who'd just flashed back to January of 1906 when Jonathon first held Cinnamon. *What a contrast*, she thought.

"I'm sorry, darling. What did you say?"

"I said thank God she looks like *you*," he answered, almost childlike as he rejoiced in this new life. "Her eyes are so sleepy, though, I can't tell what color they are."

Mimi reached up and touched his hair, lifting a strand off his forehead and admiring his handsome face.

"They are as they should be, my love—the color of shamrocks. And you, along with this perfect creation, have given me back the joy of Valentine's Day."

When the motorcar arrived in front of the Price home, the entire Magglio family watched with Cinnamon through the front window as the doors opened.

"Here they come with your surprise," Joseph said, bouncing the child up and down in his arms. "They can hardly wait to see you!"

When she saw her mother walk through the front door, she slipped from Joseph's grasp, hands outstretched, and ran to Mimi, who was giving a bundle of something to Helena. While everyone else gathered around the bundle, Mimi leaned down, pulled Cinnamon's face toward her and kissed first her forehead, then both cheeks.

"How's my beautiful little girl? I heard you've been very good, and I'm so proud of you. Mommy can't pick you up right now, though, so let's walk into the parlor and sit down. We have someone we'd like you to meet. Bradley," she said over her shoulder as she took her daughter's hand, "please bring everyone in here."

With Cinnamon snuggled happily on the sofa next to her mother after such a long separation, the group gathered around them. Then Helena placed the bundle in Mimi's lap and pulled the blanket open.

"See! This is your new baby sister. Her name is Maggie Marie, and she has come to live with us. Isn't she wonderful?"

Cinnamon looked at Mimi, then at Bradley, the Magglio adults, and finally at their children. Glancing down again at the intruder in her mother's arms, she slipped off the sofa and walked without a word to her room where she quietly, but deliberately, closed the door.

The adults left behind were troubled and a bit disappointed by her reaction, although they decided to leave her alone. Later she came out to eat because she was offered cake, but she refused to go near the baby. When the guests had departed, however, and Bradley was helping Mimi get into bed, Cinnamon edged next to the bassinet and peered over the side. Maggie was on her back, awake and focused intently on the dollop of red hair that had suddenly appeared in her line of vision. Their eyes met for the first time and remained fixed for several seconds. Then Cinnamon pulled herself up so the baby could see her entire face. Checking to make sure no one was watching her, she looked down at Maggie and whispered, "Go away."

In that moment, a journey began for both of them, from which there would be no escape, and for which there would be no mercy.

CHAPTER 7

Megan didn't know where she was at first when she opened her eyes, until she recognized the chaise on which she'd rolled up like a potato bug. Pushing herself over on her back, she slowly stretched out her legs and arms, amazed that her blood was still circulating. Staring up at the slow circles being made by the ceiling fan directly above, her mind gradually came into focus, reminding her whose room this was and why she was here.

"Oh, my God!" she said, sitting bolt upright at the foot of her grandmother's bed where, when she turned her head, she met with the old woman's face looking back at her.

"Good morning, my dear. Don't worry. You didn't miss anything."

"Excuse me?"

"As soon as I saw you nodding off last night, I stopped the recorder. Frankly, I was sleepy, too, and I might not have made myself clear if we'd kept going."

"No offense, Gram, but you haven't made yourself clear since I got here."

"Yes, I can understand how you might feel that way. So I've decided we need a little break. I've already asked Heidi to wake Kenneth. He ended up sleeping in the library last night. Must have been one hell of a Scrabble game! At any rate, I'm actually feeling pretty good and thought I'd do some paperwork for a couple of hours. After you get cleaned up, I'd like you and Ken to run an errand in town for me. We can restart the recording again when you return."

"What kind of paperwork could you possibly have to do up here? And what time is it anyway?"

"None of your business—and it's five-thirty."

"In the morning? You can't be serious."

"I know how long it takes you to get ready, and I figured you'd want plenty of notice."

"Gram, as I tell Kristin, you're lucky you're so cute. The difference is that you're also certifiable."

"Well, everyone has to be something."

"I rest my case. What day is it anyway? I need to call Phillip. He thinks this whole family is daffy, you know."

"Oh, I meant to tell you. Heidi said he called when you were over at the guest cottage last night with Ken and David. Sorry. I forgot."

"Right. That's just great."

"There wasn't anything urgent. He was making sure you're okay, that's all. He did ask you to call him as soon as you get a minute, though. He's such a nice boy."

"He's fifty-one years old, Gram."

"He's still a boy to me. And today is Wednesday, July 13."

"Thanks," Megan said, swinging her legs off the chaise and slipping her feet into her sandals. "I'll call my husband after I have my coffee and shower. Even he doesn't get up this early."

Kenneth was shuffling around the kitchen in a pair of David's slippers, which were two sizes too big for him, as Heidi opened the oven door and stuck a toothpick in the coffee cake to see if it was done. Through the breakfast nook's bay window, Megan could see pink and yellow edges of the sunrise creeping up over the trees behind a still sleeping Fox Run.

"Good morning, everybody."

"Hello, Miss Megan."

"Hey, you." Kenneth was shadowing Heidi as if he were waiting for a crumb to drop. "Bet my torture was worse than yours last night."

"Bet not. Why didn't you go home?"

"I talked to Justine, and she didn't want me driving. By the time I got David to the cottage and into bed, I decided she was right. He won both of our games, you know."

"You're kidding. How long has it been since you let him beat you?"

"That's the scary part. I didn't *let* him, and he'll probably make sure his conquest is in the newspaper tomorrow."

"Well, good for him! So, I understand that you and I are supposed to run some errands for Gram this morning?"

"That's what I'm told, Meg."

"What is it that she wants us to do?"

"I'm under orders not to share that answer with you," he said, rolling his eyes. "She wants it to be a surprise."

"Good Lord. What is it with her and surprises? I've been listening to them all night."

"Coffee's ready," Heidi interrupted, "and the cake will be out in just a minute."

"Terrific!" Kenneth squeezed the maid's shoulders and then sat down at the crescent shaped breakfast table, which had been designed to fit in the bend of the bay window and was finished on top with tiny yellow ceramic tiles. "Let's talk about something else. By the way, Meg, I found your mother. She was in Boston, and when she heard what was going on, she dropped everything. Didn't even complain or question the sincerity of Gram's condition. Said she'll be here this morning and will stay at the Albion Inn."

Megan hadn't seen her mother for more than a year, and only a handful of times since her father's death in 1982. Elliott Gray's abrupt passing had not only disorientated the family, but made Megan feel as if she'd lost both of her parents when the one died. Elliott had been Claudine's anchor for thirty-seven years, and Megan had grown to understand and respect their relationship, although she clearly recognized that her Mom's top priority was her husband rather than her daughter. Still, this never became an issue because Elliott, who viewed Claudine as his partner, looked upon his daughter as the jewel of his life. He helped her with her math, showed up at every school event that was important to her, taught her how to drive, and told her she was beautiful even during her gawky stages. He frequently visited her at college, proudly celebrated her graduation, and after she married Phillip, he never missed an opportunity for a family get-together. When Kristin was born—his first and only grandchild—he admittedly made a pest of himself.

Because Claudine apparently fell more in love with her husband every year, wherever he went, so did she. As a result, Megan had both parents nearby much of the time, an arrangement she'd never fully appreciated. After Elliott Gray's heart suddenly stopped beating in the spring of 1982, Megan moved around in a fog of disbelief and denial through the wake, Mass and burial service, reaching for her mother, who was there beside her but distant and unresponsive. No one could even remember seeing Claudine cry at the funeral. Phillip speculated later that something must have snapped in her with Elliott's last breath, propelling her into a carefree, flashy lifestyle that seemed to offer her a refuge. Within six months of his death, she'd booked passage on a worldwide cruise, and since then she'd never stayed in one place—or with any man—for very long.

"I just don't understand her at all," Cinnamon would complain. "Why won't she tell me where she's going anymore? She's my daughter and only living child, for God's sake. Elliott always used to be so good about keeping us informed."

Megan was confused as well, and deeply hurt. Her grief over her father's death was prolonged and intensified because she needed her mother, and she was consumed by the fact that, evidently, Claudine didn't give a damn. Walls went up and estrangement moved in, allowing only a few clipped words between the two of them over the next three years, until Cinnamon's spurious deathbed reunions became regular occurrences. Forced to communicate with her mother during these events, Megan had begun to soften and to consider that Claudine's life experiences could very possibly have left her ill-prepared to nurture her daughter while in the midst of her own grief. Growing up as Margaret Elizabeth McClinty's daughter must have been unconventional, to say the least, and Megan now suspected that her grandmother's story would ultimately shed light on some of those details. *Maybe there's hope for reconciliation*, she thought, *eventually, at least. What was it that Amelia kept saying about forgiveness*?

"So, Kenny, did Mom say she wants to see me?"

"Of course she did. I thought we might run over to the Inn while we're out. Okay with you?"

"Sure. I guess that would be fine."

By 8:30 that morning, Megan had showered and felt revitalized. Dressed in a pair of black jeans and a sea blue silk blouse with elbow-length sleeves and a mandarin collar, she kissed her grandmother goodbye then sprinted down the stairs and outside to meet Kenneth. He was leaning against the passenger side of his white pickup truck, finishing a cigarette, as she bounced toward him, her long hair loose and springing with fresh curls.

"I must say, girl, that you still wash up real nice."

"Thanks. And I like you better without the mountain man look. Where'd you get the razor and clean clothes?"

"After Gram came home from the hospital last week, Justine brought a bag out here for me. Now I feel like I live here. Any guess about how much longer she's going to hang on with this?"

Megan shot him an admonishing glance.

"Sorry. I didn't mean it *that* way. She actually looked pretty healthy when I saw her earlier."

"I have no predictions about time, Kenny, and I really don't want to think about it for awhile. Frankly, I feel sort of strange, like I'm in another world. A change of scenery is going to be very welcome. Where's David, by the way?"

"It's Barnes' turn to watch him."

"Are you sure they'll be all right?"

"Trust me. They're fine."

"Okay, then. Let's get out of here. What's our first stop?"

"Actually, it's a place David thought you might want to see—downtown. Then we'll head over to the Inn after that."

"What about Gram's errand?"

"Remember, I'm not supposed to tell."

"Right. Whatever. Just drive."

They rode in silence for the first few minutes, except for the pounding bass coming from her favorite country music station, which he'd tuned in on the radio for her pleasure. She appreciated his thoughtful gesture, although the rock concert volume was a little overpowering. Sometimes she wished they didn't live so far apart. Sharing their children and occasions unrelated to their grandmother's periodic dramas would be so rewarding. Kenneth was one of the most genuine human beings she knew, and among her best friends, whether family or not. But they were always teasing each other, and she couldn't recall the last time she took a serious moment to tell him how she felt. She needed to make a point of doing that before she went home—not right now, though.

"Where are we going again?" she asked, after he'd navigated several miles up New Scotland Road.

"As I said, someplace David thought you might want to see."

"What sort of place?"

"Megan, I have no idea. I just do what I'm told around here these days."

He looked straight ahead at the road, and she could tell that he was suddenly not in a joking mood.

"I'm sorry. I bet you feel like you've been left out in the dark, and this hasn't been fair at all. When we get back to Fox Run, I'll talk to Gram. You should really be up in her room with me, too."

"Thanks, but that's not necessary. As I told you, she made it pretty clear that my job is taking care of David. But I *would* like to be clued in a little bit more about what's going on. Remember? Like we talked about yesterday?"

"Okay. I can do that for you. In fact, if I talk fast, I could probably summarize a lot of things before we get wherever it is that we're going."

He smiled at her and turned off the radio as she began. Over the next ten miles, she highlighted key people and events, beginning with Amelia and ending with Maggie's birth.

"I feel like a soap opera digest. Naturally, I'm leaving out Gram's theatrics, but when this is all over, I'm sure she would encourage you to listen to the tapes so you can get the full effect. By then, who knows what other fascinating revelations will be recorded."

"I can't wait. Actually, I sort of like your high-mileage version. Good job. How is it possible that we've lived our whole lives in this family and have never heard about most of those people?"

"Because nobody's been talking. We've become a collection of separate duets and trios—or singles like Mom—who live walled off from each other. We rarely even talk about the present, much less the past, or God forbid, our *feelings*. And we value our privacy so highly that we unintentionally add more secrets to the pile with every passing event. Maybe that's why Gram started organizing her bogus curtain call jamborees. At least she could count on all of us being pushed together for a few days each year. Even though we caught on to her game, we still showed up. Of course, now that she's really sick, there's no party. Figures."

"Right. Leave it to her."

They drove beneath the Thruway overpass, curved along New Scotland Avenue by the Albany Medical Center, and came to a stoplight across from Washington Park.

"Look, Kenny. This is Madison Avenue."

"That would be correct. How did you know?" he chided, peering up at the huge street sign mounted over the center of the road.

"Seriously, which way was Jonathon's house from here?"

"That much I can tell you. It's to our left, five or six blocks up, beyond the end of the park. Somebody turned it into a suite of doctor's offices, just like other people have done with so many of these old houses. Too bad. The street's not the same since it became commercial. By the way, since you're suddenly into this stuff, were you aware that after Jonathon and Sophie moved to Fox Run, *David* lived in the Madison house for many years? He and Lucille had all three boys there, and after Lucille died, he refused to leave. Even when the boys grew up and went out on their own, he stayed there by himself for a long time."

"I guess I did know that, but I never gave much thought to it. Funny how this trip is changing my perspective."

"So it seems. But now we're headed *downtown*," he said, making a right-hand turn. "Where did you say Bradley kept taking Mimi to visit Joe Magglio and his family?"

"Lark Street. Why?"

He reached into his shirt pocket and pulled out a small folded piece of yellow paper, which he handed to her.

"That's the address David gave me."

She opened the note and read *227 Lark Street between 2nd and 3rd*.

"What? That's where we're going? Oh my God! Somebody still lives there?"

Megan felt her pulse throbbing in her temples, and she realized she was sitting on her hands, a reflexive behavior since childhood when she felt insecure.

"Looks like we're about to find out."

Kenneth drove another mile then turned left off Madison onto Lark Street, which created the southeastern border of the park serving Albany much like Central Park served New York City. The deep summer green of grasses and trees had already enticed both residents and visitors outside on this early morning, as did the freshly stocked fish in the clear-water lake, a long narrow body extending over more than half the park's length.

"Wish we had time for a picnic," he said, sounding completely serious.

"How can you even think about food?"

"'Cause I'm hungry, and you're a little over the top on this one, in my opinion. What can you possibly expect to find down here after seventy or eighty years? The place might not even be there anymore."

"Then why did he give us an address?"

By the time the park was behind them, narrow red brick row houses lined the street on both sides. Their construction in the late 1800's had placed them flush with each other as if they were all connected, with the ground level spaces designed for, and still occupied by, small retail shops, eating establishments, liquor stores, pawn shops, and an occasional empty storefront. There were a few visible indications of the renaissance taking place, which was theoretically bringing young professionals into the neighborhood to renovate the structures. But for the most part, a gritty tenement feeling still hugged the area.

After maneuvering around a sharp jog in the pavement, Kenneth slowed down as he approached 1st Street, squinting his eyes to see the house numbers.

"It's going to be on the left-hand side," he said.

"One more street up. If you see a parking space, just pull over."

He found a spot big enough for the truck on the corner of Lark and 2nd. Megan jumped down from the cab, locked and closed the passenger door, then crossed the street with Kenneth, her arms folded in a defensive position. She was walking slowly, hoping to forestall the probable disappointment, when, instead, she saw the tiny store about a third of the way up the block on the left. No lights were on inside. Nothing was in the small dusty display window, and a two-foot long banner hanging on the inside of the glass panel door said CLOSED. Yet mounted on a crossbar extending above the door and window was a metal sign with brass lettering, long blackened from weather bearing down over three-quarters of a century, but distinctly announcing ***Magglio Originals***.

Although the air temperature was climbing toward 80 degrees, Megan was hit by an uncomfortable chill.

"Are you all right?" Kenneth asked, putting his arms around her.

"I think so. I just need a minute to breathe. This is so amazing that it's almost spooky."

"I'm with you on that one, girl. Look. There's a coffee shop up there on the corner. Let's go mingle with the locals for a few minutes. Maybe one of them can tell us something."

The waitress was too young to remember anything earlier than the Beatles and too scatterbrained to have paid attention anyway. But a couple of scruffy old men sitting in the back had overheard the questions. They came forward as if heading for the door, then stopped and stood beside Kenneth and Megan's table.

"They don't open up that shop very much any more," said the one with the least amount of stubble on his face, as both men stared at Megan. "Even when they do, nobody comes to buy anything. Not sure why they're keepin' the place. You in the market?"

"No," Kenneth responded, redirecting their attention toward him. "Actually, we're doing some family research on the original tenants. Would you like to sit and join us? We'd love to buy you a cup of coffee, if you have a minute to talk."

"Sure, why not," the first man said, glancing at the other. "Nothin' much else to do."

They both pulled out their chairs and sat down, emitting that unique musty odor of age and tobacco worn by old men who don't shave or change clothes very often and who are living the last part of their lives on front porches or in dark rooms. The four of them sat in silence, their eyes pivoting from one face to another, while the waitress poured coffee. Then she dropped a stack of menus in the center of the table and walked away.

"My name is Megan Cole, and this is my cousin Ken Stafford."

"I'm Richard. He's Dominick. You from around here?"

"Our family is. Ken still lives here. I'm in Atlanta now."

"A Georgia peach," Richard said smiling, revealing more missing teeth than not and then taking a slurp of his coffee. "What brings you to *this* neighborhood?"

"Well," Megan continued, feeling more stable and very relieved that Kenneth was with her, "our grandmother might have visited that shop many times when she was a little girl, with her mother. Do you happen to know who owns it now, or who comes back to open it up?"

"Young kids," Dominick said, speaking for the first time, "about your age. I think the girl's a Magglio. The fellow is her husband."

"Do they live in town? And would you know their name?"

"Aren't they from Clifton Park or someplace up there?" Dominick asked, looking at Richard.

"Think so. Don't know the name, though. But folks on the street always see 'em when they come by. We could tell 'em you're lookin' for 'em next time."

"That would be great." Kenneth opened his wallet and removed a business card imprinted with the address and phone number of his main dry cleaning store. "Silver Linings is the name of the place where I work, so they could call me there. Or," he added, turning the business card over, "got a pen, Meg? Thanks. This is another place where they could leave a message," he said, as he wrote the phone number for Fox Run along with his and Megan's first names.

"We really appreciate your passing this along," she said, surprising herself by not being concerned about his giving out the information. "And it's been such a pleasure talking with you."

"Sure has." Kenneth placed a $20 bill on the table. "You fellows relax and finish your coffee, then pay the tab and keep the change."

"You're very kind," Richard said softly. "Hope you find what you're lookin' for."

"Thank you. We do, too," Kenneth answered, just to close out the conversation.

Megan pushed back from the table and stood up, with her cousin supporting her. As they walked toward the door, Dominick's voice came from behind.

"You know, miss, when I was a boy, I used to see a little girl every so often playin' with other kids in front of that shop. I remember her 'cause she stood out in the crowd with red hair just like yours. Not sure if that was your grandma, but you're the only other woman I ever saw with hair like that. Don't know if that helps."

"Yes," Megan answered, looking back at the old men and suddenly filled with enormous admiration for Mimi and Amelia's altruistic efforts. "It helps very much. Thank you for telling us."

She and Kenneth walked arm-in-arm toward the shop on the way back to the truck, then they slowed down and stopped to peer in the grimy window with their hands cupped around their eyes. The place appeared to be completely empty.

"Kenny, I just have to find these people."

"I know, and we'll do it together. Right now, though, we need to get over to the Inn. Your mother's waiting for us, and then of course, there's your surprise."

Immediately upon entering the Albion Inn's lobby, they could hear the melodies of a live jazz combo coming from the vast, sky-lit courtyard one fourth the size of a football field. The room had been host to dozens of McClinty weddings and graduation parties over the years, and to all of Cinnamon's deathbed reunions. Kenneth was clearly headed in the music's direction, and Megan began feeling suspicious when she heard the clinking of silverware against china amidst the buzz of spirited voices. But she grabbed his arm and came to a stop, looking up at him with her hands on her hips, after hearing the unmistakable chord of her mother's laughter rising above the rest.

"Surprise!" he said sheepishly, shrugging his shoulders.

"Is this what I *think* it is?"

"Yes, ma'am. Afraid so."

"This wasn't supposed to happen anymore, Kenny. What was Gram thinking? And how could you possibly have cooperated with her?"

"Hey, I'm innocent! I didn't even know about it until David told me last night. The two of them are very practiced conspirators."

"Well, on top of everything else, I'm certainly not in any mood for a party."

"Oh, let it go for a little while, Meg. I told Gram we'd be back by 2:00, so I'm sure you can handle this for a couple of hours. Besides, you have to give her credit. I never thought she'd be able to pull another one of these off. Actually, I think it's sort of hilarious."

"That's a great word," she said, softening her voice and her stance. "I guess it's hard to be upset in the face of *hilarious*. Okay. But you absolutely *must* promise to leave when I'm ready."

"Scout's honor."

As they entered the courtyard through open double doors, arms went up all over the room waving hello in a relaxed, familiar welcome. They both waved back as they acclimated themselves to the elaborate setting. Six buffet tables were draped in layers and levels of pastel linens. Three of the tables were filled with banquet-sized platters of jumbo shrimp, shelled baby lobster tails, sliced chicken, prime rib, hot vegetable dishes, and an array of accouterments. Two more tables were lined with a variety of salad bowls and pasta dishes, and the sixth table held a seemingly endless selection of cakes, pies and sinful cream-filled pastries. A large semi-circular bar and a coffee counter, attended by two men and a woman all dressed in tuxedos, ran parallel to the fourth wall. In the middle of the room, beneath a resplendent brass and crystal chandelier, a tiered fountain drizzled champagne into a pyramid of flutes.

Spread across the courtyard were twenty round dining tables, each covered in coordinated pastel linen cloths and set with china and silver flatware for a party of six. In the center of every table was a three-foot tall glass vase full of pink, white and lavender flowers that spilled over the glass edges in thick explosions of color, with glossy vines draping halfway down the vase stems. Circled around the base of each floral arrangement was a ring of crystal votives, the candles lit and flickering, casting a soft, intimate glow across the cavernous piazza. From the left corner of the room, nearest the double doors, the five members of a jazz ensemble played their music, which was lively but pleasantly conducive to conversation.

"Boy, Meg, she's sure got this down to a science."

"And we're like sheep to the slaughter. Well, at least one of today's objectives has been accomplished. I see my mother over there, entertaining some guy who's probably her date. Since I'm sure your first stop will be the bar, would you please get a glass of champagne for me on your way back? Meanwhile, I'll let Mom know we're here."

"My pleasure. Fortification is on the way."

"Megan, dear!" Claudine said, after turning around in response to the touch on her shoulder. "You look absolutely gorgeous!" she added, exchanging cheek-to-cheek air kisses with her daughter.

"You look good, too, Mom," Megan lied. Her mother's appearance was almost anorexic, her thick makeup unsuccessfully attempting to hide lines and circles that were shockingly new since their last meeting. "Kenny tells me that you were in Boston. So what have you been up to?"

"Real estate. Can you believe it? After last year's cruise, I spent some time with friends on the Cape, and that's when I was bitten by the bug. I actually took all the courses, exams, and everything, and then got my license. I've had some nice commissions and lots of fun. That's how I met Lyle. Oh, my. Pardon me for being so rude. Megan, this is Lyle Mathis. Lyle, this is my daughter, Megan. Isn't she beautiful?"

"Indeed she is, and I'm delighted to finally meet you."

He took her hand in his and leaned down to kiss her fingers, his thick head of lacquered hair looking as if it might fall forward in one stiff piece. The word *hilarious* crossed her mind again, and she was worried she wouldn't be able to keep a straight face much longer when Kenneth thankfully arrived with her champagne.

"Hello, Aunt Claudine," he said, putting both of his arms around her. Then he stepped back to look at her. "It's been a long time, and you look so…tan. Been doing lots of traveling?"

"Not since last year, actually. I was just telling Megan that Lyle inspired me to do something productive, and now I'm selling real estate."

"That's terrific. And you must be Lyle," he said, turning toward Claudine's friend and extending his hand. "I'm Ken Stafford, and I admire your courage for coming to this shindig. We're all a little nuts, in case you haven't figured that out yet."

"On the contrary. I find you all very charming."

"Well, that's super." Kenneth took a long sip of his drink, trying to think of something patronizing to say back. But Lyle spoke first.

"How do you fit into the family tree?"

"Ah, yes, the old tree." Kenneth was absently chewing on a piece of ice. "Interesting visual. As a matter of fact, my Aunt Claudine here, who, as you know, is Megan's mother, is also my dad's sister. *Half* sister, really. And Aunt Claudine's mother is our grandmother," he continued, gesturing toward Megan and then back to himself. "Our Gram is the feisty old woman who keeps throwing these soirees, and that about sums it up."

"By the way, Megan," Claudine interjected, her smile fading momentarily, "how *is* your grandmother?"

"She's pretty weak, Mom, at least physically. But you know how she can be, and this morning the mischief was back in her eyes. Now," she said, glancing around at the courtyard festivities, "I know why."

"So tell me, Ken," Lyle went on, doggedly pursuing his own list of questions, "which one of these gentlemen is your father?"

He was unprepared for the speechless faces staring back at him. After several seconds that seemed interminable to the newcomer, Kenneth answered him.

"Actually, my dad's not with us anymore. He died during the Korean War when my brother and I were little kids."

"Please forgive me," Lyle said, clearly embarrassed and dropping his effusive mannerisms. "I had no idea," he added, sending a reproachful glance in Claudine's direction.

"I apologize, Lyle," she said, the pluck missing from her voice. "My mother never really recovered from my brother's death, even after all these years. When she calls us together for these parties, I always feel it's safer not to talk about that sad time in our lives. I didn't intentionally leave Greg out of the briefing I gave you."

Searching for a way to divert focus from their shared discomfort, Kenneth was relieved when he spotted William entering the courtyard with Justine.

"Speaking of brothers, Lyle, that's mine headed our way. And that fine woman with him is my wife!" Megan rushed ahead to embrace the two of them.

Scarcely a year separated the birthdays of Kenneth and William Stafford. While they were extremely fond of one another, William, who was now thirty-five, was his brother's antithesis. Kenneth was svelte and athletic. William was just plain round—the boundaries of his face, his body, his fingers, his haircut—everything was round. Megan couldn't remember a thin William, even as a boy, and judging from the layered plates of food and dessert balanced on his arms, his image was not apt to change in the near future. He remained a bachelor, to no one's surprise, supporting himself on his lean earnings as a social worker for the State of New York. Unlike his enterprising older brother, William's academic record at the Albany campus of the State University—and his subsequent professional history—had been unremarkable. Five years earlier, he'd chosen to settle in Buffalo, claiming to enjoy the city cloaked in snow for nearly half of every year, and insisting that his interest in lifting the human spirit would find ample sources of fulfillment there.

The greater truth, Megan suspected, was that William had elected to reinvent himself in a place without ties, far enough away to avoid comparison with his more dynamic sibling. A weak parallel crossed her mind as she thought about Jonathon and Peter, the key difference being the love and respect that William and Kenneth had for one another, and the freedom they gave each other to become their own men, without judgment, knowing they could always count on one another. Losing their father when they were so young had probably forged this relationship even more than their minimal age difference would have done anyway. Watching the uninhibited affection and good-natured ribbing between the two brothers, Megan thought further of the odious familial journey required to get from a place like the one William and Kenneth occupied to the pathological point where Jonathon and Peter's relationship ended. *How tragic that the fabric of a family should be shredded in such a manner.* What a loss for all of them. *Then again, grasping the full measure of something lost requires, first, a belief that something existed…*

"Hell-o-o-o in there!" Kenneth was waving his hand in front of her face.

"I'm so sorry," she said, shaking her head and wondering how long she'd been drifting. "I guess I must be more tired than I thought."

"Are you sure you're all right?" The sound of Justine's voice shut down the reverberation of Cinnamon's story, at least for the moment. "Why don't we sit and relax for a few minutes so you can get off your feet, and *we* can catch up? Kenny, I think a glass of ginger ale or something else without alcohol would be better for her than champagne right now. Would you be a dear and go get some please? I'll have one, too."

He was incapable of turning her down. His wife completed him, and the two of them functioned together like the gears of a fine Swiss timepiece. They had started out as platonic sidekicks while they were college freshman, becoming soul mates by their junior year. In spite of her diminutive stature—just barely five feet and weighing a hundred pounds on a fat day—she was the center around which he pivoted. But she also had her own goals, pursuing a career in property management when they graduated, and for five years after they were married, until Tania Kaye Stafford was born. Then Justine's priorities shifted to her family, without a thought or a glance backward. Subsequently, she also made the decision, with Kenneth's agreement, not to have any more children, choosing instead to walk away from her thriving career and dedicate her time to her husband and the development of the one perfect progeny with whom they'd been blessed.

Justine and Megan had lived vicariously through one another for years, seeking in each other those aspects of their lives that had given way to other preferences. Megan was nourished by details of Justine's domestic symmetry, and Justine was invigorated by Megan's tales of corporate complexities. While their visits together were far too infrequent, their pleasure at seeing one another never faded.

"Two ginger ales on the rocks," Kenneth announced, placing their glasses in front of them atop napkins imprinted with the words **MCCLINTY FAMILY GATHERING, JULY 13, 1988**. "Sorry it took so long. David was locked in a conversation with DJ and wouldn't listen to Barnes, who was trying to take him home. I had to intervene."

Megan looked up at her cousin with surprise, then turned her head and scanned the room, spotting her mother and Lyle at the bar, but not David.

"He's here? Where?"

"He *was* here, Meg, but he finally agreed with Barnes that he'd had enough. He said he'd see you later."

"But what was he doing here in the first place? He didn't even want to go out for dinner last night."

"I think DJ's being in town had something to do with it."

DJ was David's oldest and only surviving son. The nickname was given to David McClinty Junior shortly after his birth when the family grew weary of their constant need to clarify which *David* was being referenced in conversation. He was born in 1924 a few months before Claudine, and two years before David's middle son Ryan. Teddy was the third boy, and his surprise arrival in 1931 brought another in the series of McClinty tragedies that had never piqued Megan's curiosity until this trip. Now she decided she needed to start making a list of her questions. She did remember hearing her mother tell stories, however, about how she'd been squired around as a little girl by DJ, who was captivated by his bold female cousin—the only girl in his life except his mother. Of course, that was before their friendship was beaten into silence by the much-hushed family siege in 1953 during the Korean War, after which two of David's boys were dead, in addition to Cinnamon's son Greg and her sister Maggie.

"You know," Megan said softly, looking at Justine across the table and then up at Kenneth who stood next to her, "whenever I think about this family's troubles during the 50's, I always zero in on *Gram's* loss. I'm ashamed to admit that I've never really spent much time thinking about what David must have gone through, and how painful things must have been for him all those years. He's always hidden his feelings behind his sense of humor, not letting on how he must have been hurting."

"No offense, Meg," Kenneth said, pulling a chair between his wife and cousin and sitting down. "And I'm not saying this to make you feel guilty. But he's given out *plenty* of clues and signals, which you would have seen if you'd been around more."

"Ken," Justine admonished, "that's not fair."

"I *said* I wasn't trying to make her feel guilty. It's just that I've been so close to him, and I've picked up lots of tidbits from him over the years, which touch on that whole era."

Megan wasn't totally immune to his insults, but she was more focused on this glimmer of new information than she was on her bruised feelings.

"You never mentioned anything about his tidbits, even when we were talking about him earlier. I thought you wanted to share. What did he tell you?"

Tempted to answer her with sarcasm, he saw his wife shoot him a reproving look in anticipation, and he opted for a more serious reply.

"I can't remember exactly how we got into it, but in a conversation a long time ago, he told me he felt such a strong connection to William and me because our dad was killed with Teddy. That accident would have been awful enough, but apparently Gram laid some sort of guilt trip on David, as if Teddy's visit to Hawaii had somehow caused the whole thing. He acted like he wanted to say more, although he didn't open up about it very often after that. But sometimes I just knew he wanted to let something out. He did make it clear that life wasn't very pleasant for him for many years after Dad and Teddy died, especially while Gram was in her hibernation period. He said she wouldn't even allow him in her house, and I guess he was a real mess as a result. You've got to give him credit, though. He never gave up trying to see her."

Megan was engrossed in her cousin's words as she began to realize the scope of what she *didn't* know.

"Obviously, they patched up their differences," she said, "thank goodness for both of them—and for *us*. Do you know what finally made them reconcile?"

"Nope. But DJ's right over there. I'm sure he could tell you."

"Maybe I'll ask him later," she replied, looking at her watch. "Frankly, I think I'd like to get back to Fox Run right now. Something tells me that Gram has a long afternoon in store for me, and I'm starting to get a little saturated. Besides, some of these answers might be waiting for me there. Would you mind, Justine?"

"You shouldn't even need to ask, Meg, and I'm sure I'll see you tomorrow."

"Of course. How long is everyone planning to stay?"

"I think about two or three days," Justine said, looking over at Kenneth for verification.

"Right. That's my understanding. Two or three days, per Gram's normal agenda at these things. Not everyone's here yet, though. Some are coming in later tonight and others tomorrow morning—Preston, for one."

"Preston's actually coming this time?" Justine asked just as Megan was about to pose the same question.

Cinnamon's nephew, and the only child of Jay and Angela, had rarely shown up for the mock mourning parties after the family caught on to the old woman's scheme.

"That's what he said when I talked to him last night," Kenneth replied. "He'll drive over from Boston in the morning."

"Well, it will be great to see him again," Megan acknowledged. "Preston has always been one of my heroes. But not as much as *you*," she added quickly, turning to Kenneth with a smile. Then she stood up and hoisted the strap of her pocketbook over her shoulder. "Are you coming with me, Kenny, or am I taking your truck?"

"Go ahead," Justine said, answering the question for her husband. "After I pick Tania up from camp in a couple of hours, I'll bring her here to the Inn with me, so you'll know where to find us. Meanwhile, Megan, if you need anything at Fox Run, just leave a message for me in my room. I can be out there in a flash."

"Thank you so much, and I might take you up on the offer. For now, though, would you just say hi to anyone I haven't seen yet, and let them know I'll show up again as soon as I can? Also, please encourage my mom to come visit Gram, if you get the chance. I think it's important for the two of them to connect."

"Of course. I'll do what I can. Now you guys need to get going."

The truck was pulling into Fox Run's driveway when she remembered.

"Oh my God! I never called Phillip! I can't believe I forgot to return his message."

"I'm sure he understands, Meg. He knows what happens to you when you're in this place."

"That's what I'm afraid of. He's apt to be on the next plane if he doesn't hear from me pretty soon. Would you be a sweetheart and let Gram know we're home? Tell her I'll be up in a minute."

"Oh, sure. Send *me* into the lion's den first."

"It'll build your character—make you a better man. Anyway, I think she'd appreciate the time with you. Maybe this is your chance to ask her about joining me for the rest of this."

"No, thanks. I'll go say hi, but I think we should leave the arrangement the way it is."

"Whatever. It's up to you. I'll be on the phone in the library, assuming—please, God—that Phillip is home. See you in a little while."

Once inside the library, she pulled the heavy pocket doors closed then sat down on the leather wing chair beside the telephone table and dialed her home in Atlanta. Phillip answered on the third ring.

"Hi, honey. I love you."

"Well, hello. I love you, too," he said flatly, unable to disguise his annoyance. "Didn't you get my message last night?"

"Yes, I did, but not until this morning. I know I should have called you right away, but the day sort of ran away with me before I realized what time it was. I'm sorry."

"You're forgiven. But please try to check in with us more often. *Anyway*, how's your grandmother?"

"Truthfully, I'm not sure. When I first got here, I thought the worst. She really looked dreadful. But this morning she seemed to be much better. So maybe this will pass like all the other times."

"I hope so, Meg. Kristin and I are thinking about you, and we miss you. When are you coming home?"

"I can't quite answer that yet. She's got me involved in a bit of a project—something she's apparently been planning for years. This is going to sound ridiculous, but she's recording her autobiography on tape, with me as her witness."

There was no response from him.

"Are you still there?"

"Yes," he answered after prolonging the pause. "I think I'll withhold any editorial comments."

"I know what you're thinking, but I do need to stay until she's finished—and right now I can't predict how much longer she's planning to take. Probably only another day or two, I imagine. Of course, on top of everything else, she's managed to organize a family gathering. Mother's even here, and Ken says that the whole gang will arrive by tomorrow."

"You can't be serious. I thought all of you agreed not to fall for that any more."

"*So much for promises.*" The words almost felt like they belonged to someone else. "Would you and Kristin like to fly up and join us for a couple of days? Everyone would love to see you—especially Gram—and I'm sure this thing will be wrapped up by the weekend. Besides, I miss you, too," she concluded, realizing that she actually did.

"No, Megan, I do not want to come up there. I know your grandmother encourages the situation, but frankly I find the scene quite morbid, with everyone flying in and circling around her like vultures."

"That's an awful thing to say, Phillip."

"Well, the fact that your mother's in town is a case in point. With all due respect to Claudine, she's hardly been attentive to Cinnamon—or to you, for that matter—except for these tasteless occasions."

"I can't believe you're being so judgmental, and..."

"Please Megan, let's not argue. I'm sorry. I didn't mean to upset you. It's just that I love you, and I guess I'm a little suspicious about things going on up there. But do whatever you need to do, and then come home as soon as you can. By the way, Jerry Rogers called from your office yesterday. He asked if you could phone him, and he gave me his home number."

Struck by the realization that she hadn't spent a moment thinking about her work since she left Atlanta, she was surprised to feel a sense of intrusion even now.

"Did he say what he wanted? Is something wrong?"

"I have no idea. He just asked me to deliver the message, but he did sound like he hoped to hear from you sooner than later."

"Okay. Thanks, honey—and one more time, I love you, too. Please don't be mad at me, or at Gram."

"You know better than that. I'm worried about you, that's all."

"Give Kristin a hug and kiss for me. Tell her I'll be back in a couple of days, probably."

"We won't put the bread in the oven yet. Say hi to Ken."

She waited to hear the dial tone before placing the receiver in the cradle. Then she remained still, staring at the telephone. Jerry Rogers, head of the Research Division, was one of her counterparts. They'd been colleagues since he was brought in from another corporation five years ago to replace a retiring senior manager. His controversial selection from *the outside*, over the heads of several career company men, resulted in a cool reception for him and a few difficult weeks at the beginning of his tenure. Acutely sensitive to his position based on her own career struggle with some of those same individuals, she'd befriended him early on, bolstering him with the best support from her organization and making sure he was connected to other managers she knew he could trust. He'd never forgotten her bold gesture, and the two of them had been watching each other's backs ever since.

Alone in Fox Run's library, she wasn't in the mood for any work-related conversations, and if this had been anyone else, she would have let him wait. But believing that Jerry would not be reaching out with something frivolous, and uncertain when she would next have an opportunity, she picked up the phone again. Dialing his direct office extension to bypass Glenda's switchboard, she hoped to get his voice recorder so she could just leave a short message.

"Jerry Rogers here."

"Well, hi there. This is Megan. I wasn't expecting you to be in, but I'm happy you are," she added parenthetically, realizing that he probably knew she didn't mean it. "I just finished talking with Phillip, and he told me you called."

"Hi! Good to hear your voice. How's your grandmother?"

"She's not terrific, but better than I expected. Thanks for asking. So, what's up?"

"Hold on. Let me close my door." His words were a clear signal that this wasn't going to be good news.

"Okay, Megan. First of all, I feel awful about bothering you during a family emergency, but things are moving pretty fast around here, and I just couldn't let you be blindsided by this."

"What is it, Jerry? What's happened?"

"Well, as you heard in the meeting before you left, the Board mandated a restructuring. But we didn't know the full scope until that afternoon when we received the cutback recommendations for each department. Not a single area is escaping the hatchet, but some are being hit worse than others. It's damn depressing wherever you look."

"Good Lord, Jerry. I had no idea this would be so drastic, or so quick! How bad is the damage in my group?"

"There's still a little room for negotiation, but the first pass has you at a minimum fifty percent reduction."

Stunned, she tried to translate that percentage into the faces of those in her organization—real people with goals and families and mortgages—and she could not begin to imagine how she would make those heart-wrenching decisions. Her professional life, especially as a manager, had been all about building something positive for her employees, herself, and the company. She believed in enabling an environment where people looked forward to their arrival at work in the morning, and where they left at the end of each day feeling as if they'd made a personal contribution to something meaningful. She wasn't always successful, even with herself. But the consistency of her efforts resulted in an enviable level of morale among those who reported to her. The fact that she hadn't seen this coming left her feeling exposed and ineffective, with an unfamiliar sense that she'd left the gate unguarded.

"Jerry, how could I have been so unprepared for this?"

"Don't make this a personal thing, Meg. *No one* was ready. My department's being cut almost as much as yours, and all of us on the management team have been directed to finalize our lists for approval so we can give people notice by the end of the month. There will be a fairly respectable severance package, if it makes you feel any better."

"That's a noble gesture, but no, it doesn't make me feel better at all. I need a little time to take this in."

"Unfortunately, you're not going to have that luxury. Any idea when you're coming home?"

"No."

"Believe me. I understand the pressure this puts you under. But you'll need to be here by next week to work on your list. Otherwise, somebody else will do it for you. I'm not sure if this adds any incentive, but Glenda's position is considered surplus at the moment."

"What? They must be nuts! We could never replace her."

"Actually, they apparently think we could hire three people for less money and not lose any value. That's why you need to be here to defend things yourself."

"Oh brother. What a mess! Well, I'll touch base with you again tomorrow. Hopefully, I'll have a better feel for things up here by then. Meanwhile, Jerry, I really appreciate your call and your friendship. Thank you for being so concerned about me—and take care of yourself."

"You, too, lady. I'll do my best to protect your interests. Keep your chin up."

Megan replaced the phone and limply dangled her arms over the sides of the chair as she tilted her head back and stared at the ceiling. How had her life become so complicated and filled with so many questions in the span of a few days? The greater quandary might be how she'd allowed other people and circumstances to take control away from her. Suddenly her meticulously managed life was filled with a new array of conflicting priorities that could not possibly be blended or aligned.

Shaking herself free from the moment, she stood up, walked across the room and pulled the pocket doors open. Hearing Kenneth's voice still filtering down from Cinnamon's bedroom, she was pleased that the two of them had carved out these few minutes together. She was also grateful for the clarity and simplicity of her relationship with her cousin. *He is one thing I don't have to worry about,* she thought—a *small slice of comfort* amidst the mushrooming swarm of twists and tangles, mysterious personalities and clandestine histories, her mother, her husband, her daughter, her work, and her grandmother who might be dying, or not. Furthermore, this mixture was layered with geographical distances that would soon force choices upon her.

"Hey, Meg," Kenneth said once she'd reached the top of the stairs and entered Cinnamon's room. "We were about to dispatch the cavalry. Everything all right?"

He was seated on the bed, holding their grandmother's hands, and the light around his face told her all she needed to know about the value he'd just received from time spent in this room.

"Phillip and Kristin are fine, but there's some stuff going on at work that will be challenging. That's why I took so long. Sorry."

"Not to worry, my dear." Cinnamon was almost chirping as she reached up and patted her grandson's cheeks. "We've had the nicest visit."

"Yes, we have. But it's time for me to go check on David. Barnes is probably ready to strangle him by now."

After kissing his grandmother on the forehead, he gave his cousin a one-arm squeeze around her shoulders then left the room, closing the door behind him.

"Okay, Gram, where were we?" she sighed, a solemn tone evident in her voice.

"First, come close so I can see you. My heavens. Look at those worry lines all over your pretty face. Have I done that to you?"

"Don't be silly, Gram. I just have some things I need to work out. I'll be fine. Really."

"Of course you will, and it's very important that you are. I'm counting on you—more than you realize. Now, why don't you make yourself comfortable again while I get this contraption going one more time?"

Megan obeyed, settling on the chaise lounge at the foot of Cinnamon's bed. She sat upright with her legs folded against her chest, her chin resting on her knees and the afghan wrapped around her bare feet. The view of her grandmother from this vantage point was one of an old woman almost playful in her enthusiasm for the project at hand. Then their kindred eyes met, and as a smiling Margaret Elizabeth McClinty Stafford pressed the **RECORD** button, Megan was surprised by an almost balsamic sense of relief as every priority except this one melted away.

Chapter 8

Cinnamon wasn't certain how old she'd been when she finally understood that Jonathon was her father, but she did remember the discovery as being confusing. Until that moment, she'd looked upon him as a kind, affectionate man she called Papa, who seemed to like her very much and who invited her to visit him in his home every week. Whenever she was in his house, she had the freedom to move around at will, to hide and to explore what seemed to her like an infinite number of nooks and secret compartments, all of which fed her sprouting imagination. She felt comfortable there, as she did at Aunt Oly's downtown, and she counted with anticipation the days she had to complete each week before someone would pick her up and walk the two blocks with her.

Unexpectedly, understanding that Jonathon was her father interrupted the easy flow of her life, replacing the rhythm with questions such as why she and her mother lived down the street with Bradley, and why her father lived with another woman named Sophie. While she was still trying to sort this out, the questions gave way to feelings without names when babies began arriving in both households. Her subsequent sullen attitude seemed to irritate the grownups around her, but she didn't care about her bad behavior, which seemed to irritate everyone even more. Had she not been able to escape into her fantasies with Angela, Jarrett and the Magglio girls, she would have been left without a single happy place to be.

Later on, when she had a family of her own, she would look back on that time with amusement, often longing for the purity of those traumas. Further, as the mounting complexities of her adult life evolved into a thorny imbroglio, she would review those early years in an effort to find the pivotal moments where her fate had been defined. Clearly, there was a wide selection from which to choose. But most of those were byproducts of the main event when David arrived to live with Jonathon just before Christmas in 1910.

Her introduction to him came slightly more than a month before her fifth birthday, and his arrival was gift enough for that season of holidays. Well ahead of the historic day, Jonathon had explained to her that the boy would most likely be very sad. Both of his parents had gone to heaven—actually, those were *Sophie's* words—and since Jonathon was the only family left for him, David was traveling all the way from California to come live in the Madison house. A map was unrolled on the dining room table to trace for her the length of his journey, which didn't seem so far to her as she stood on a chair and studied the colorful piece of paper.

Irene and Drake, who had remained in Jonathon's employ after Mimi moved out, allowed Cinnamon to help in the preparation of David's bedroom—the space she did not realize had been her own nursery at one time. She'd always been fascinated with the vibrant images of clouds and flowers and angels drawn across the four walls of that room, and she was disillusioned when she saw two men on ladders covering up the beautiful scenes with brushes dipped in white paint. But she wasn't nearly as upset as Irene, who sat on the kitchen bench unable to stop crying.

"I'm just sorry that those angels had to go back to heaven."

Irene blotted her face with a towel as she responded to Cinnamon's concern.

"Are they going to be with David's mommy and daddy?"

"Yes, I suppose they are," she said, lifting the child into her lap.

While Cinnamon's small hands swept more tears from the maid's cheeks, her innocent queries continued.

"Will David be sad like you? Papa said he was."

"I don't know, little one," she answered, blowing her nose into a handkerchief she'd removed from her pocket. "He's only a boy, but I hear he's very brave."

"How many years is he?"

"He's twelve, sweetheart," which did not sound like a boy to Cinnamon.

"That's old, Iree. Will he play with me? Will Papa still play with me, too? Mommy says they will be busy."

Irene wasn't certain how to respond. Her allegiance to Mimi had survived the cataclysm five years ago but had been suppressed in favor of continued employment. Her aversion to Jonathon, however, had never softened. She thought she might feel better about him after he remarried, since Sophie surprised everyone and proved herself to be a likeable woman who treated the household personnel with respect. But the man's character seemed irredeemable, and his steely exterior never appeared to yield, even after Jay was born. Today he had given further example of his willful nature by following through with his decision to paint over the nursery mural. Months earlier, before they even knew that David was coming, Sophie had voiced her objection to this desecration. Recognizing the exceptional artwork, she'd pleaded with her husband to let her use the magical room for Jay. But he had recoiled at the thought and insisted that their son use the bedroom next to theirs instead.

"What will you do with an empty nursery, then?" she'd asked, "One stripped of all its fairytales?"

"We'll see. The proper use will become clear, and I don't want you to speak of it again."

Several weeks thereafter, word arrived from San Francisco that Lily had been stricken with a virulent case of influenza and had died. An attorney wired Jonathon that his nephew David was staying with neighbors until the boy's travel to Albany could be arranged. Lily's last will and testament transferred guardianship of her son to Jonathon, who initially did not receive the news well. He was unaccustomed to the interference of others, particularly the widow of his deceased brother, a man who had abandoned the family and forsaken his own heritage. Furthermore, his life was quite full enough with Sophie, newly born Jay, and Cinnamon down the street, who visited more frequently than he'd planned. But the more he analyzed the situation, the more he saw some potential good.

Aside from the fact that he appeared to have little choice in the matter, he imagined that David—who, after all, should not be held accountable for his father's cowardice—might be old enough already to begin making a contribution to the McClinty enterprise. Jay would not be useful in the business for many years. But David could begin apprenticing in short order, and having a young man around to assist with the household management could prove refreshing as well. In the back of his mind, Jonathon was also besieged with thoughts of Amelia, who might be willing to forgive him for any transgressions she'd witnessed from her celestial vantage point, if he graciously assumed this responsibility. The decisive moment of acceptance, however, followed the delivery of a subsequent wire from the San Francisco attorney. One section, in particular, stood out.

> **...aggregate estate of Peter and Lily McClinty in total funds of seventy-eight thousand dollars, established in trust for their sole living issue, David McClinty, until he reaches the age of twenty-five or until he marries, whichever event comes first...Trustee of said estate named as Jonathon Allister McClinty...**

Jonathon was both shocked and curious about how his brother could have amassed such wealth, and how Lily could have preserved the money during four years of struggle after the earthquake and fire. At least he *assumed* she'd been struggling, although he felt somewhat uncomfortable with the fact that he had made not a single attempt to contact her all this time. He imagined that she might have grappled with considerable misgivings about entrusting her son and resources to her absentee brother-in-law, but conditions had apparently left her with no other options. At any rate, he found the entire development to be immensely intriguing, and he began to anticipate his nephew's arrival with unexpected enthusiasm. Sophie was also supportive, although an opposing opinion on her part would have carried no weight whatsoever. With only a few weeks' notice, plans had been readied, and now David was traveling cross-country by rail to Albany, escorted by the attorney.

When he arrived, his freshly painted room would await him, and he would have to uncover the mural's story—and the complexities of this family—on his own. Irene prayed for him as she held Cinnamon on her lap, hoping that he was a strong boy and that he'd inherited Amelia's iron will along with her compassion. If he was at all like his grandmother, he might have a chance.

"Yes, Cinnamon," she said, rocking back and forth slowly as she pressed the child close to her chest. "I'm sure David will play with you, and I know he'll grow to love you very much. But you'll have to inquire yourself about any time your Papa might have available for you."

David certainly did not *look* sad the day he arrived at the Madison house and turned her into a parasitic gnome. Drake had walked down the street that morning to pick her up, and the two of them had only been back in the house for an hour when the front door flew open and the light sauntered in. He was much taller than she'd expected, almost the same height as Jonathon. When he saw her in the entryway, he stooped down so his whole body was at her level, and he definitely did not look like a young boy. There was something else, too—something that drew her in, that soothed her and put her completely at ease.

"Hello," he said, extending his hands toward hers. "You must be Cinnamon. I've heard wonderful things about you, and I'm so happy to finally meet you. I'm David."

He was handsome, in a peculiar sort of way, the lines of his cheeks and jaw angled sharply, his abundant coal-black hair slicked back on the sides and top, with the edges curling up along the nape of his neck. His face was lightly browned from the sun, his open coat and shirt collar revealing the natural, fairer version of his skin on his upper chest, complete with freckles. But his eyes were the features that transfixed her, seeing past all pretenses, and reaching in as if to eavesdrop on her thoughts. The large azure circles were deeply set in shadows, and were lined all around with densely dark lashes that seemed to punctuate his sentences with their movement. Completely absorbed by him, she placed her tiny hands in his huge outstretched palms and studied, for the first time, the image of this person who would still be smiling at her three-quarters of a century later.

"Hello. My Papa said you were sad. But I wish you wouldn't be. I could draw pictures with you and make you feel better."

"Why, thank you," he said, standing up as he lifted her off the floor and into his arms. "I would love to draw pictures with you, and I'm already feeling better. Coming here to live has made the sadness go away."

Nestled without reservation against him, she clasped her little wrists behind his neck and clung fiercely to this unforeseen prize, saying not another word.

"Yes, indeed," Jonathon intervened, "and a fine welcome this is. But I think we should give David time to get in the door, for heaven's sake. Irene, please take Cinnamon into the kitchen for some milk while I show the boy his room and the rest of his new home. Sophie," he continued, turning to his wife, "our young man is finally here. Is Jay awake?"

Jonathon's failure to make any proper introductions was remedied by Sophie as she graciously embraced David and welcomed the attorney, who stood in obvious discomfort just inside the threshold.

"No, our son is still sleeping," she responded to her husband while helping Drake collect coats, scarves and hats, "although I expect he'll be up and under foot before long."

Cinnamon did not appreciate being removed from the scene or the conversation she could hear unfolding behind her as Irene took her hand and guided her down the hall. Yet she was content in the implied promise that *David* would *never* leave, and for the first time in many months, she knew precisely where she wanted to be—right here, in her father's house.

"Iree, why does Papa call him a boy? Jarrett is the one who's a boy. But David is *not*—and he's *mine*."

In the beginning, Cinnamon and David's perceptions of one another were colored by the nearly eight-year difference in their ages. He found her to be exceptionally precocious and entertaining, and he assumed—at least he hoped—that she would become attractive at some point. For the moment, however, she was a continuous source of amusement. Her blaze of hair always seemed to be unleashed, and she had inevitably spilled a portion of her most recent meal on her dress, with remnants of the same menu encrusted on her face. When she engaged him in play, he saw his role as that of a teacher to her, patiently helping her with finger painting techniques or word pronunciation in books she pretended to read to impress him, such as Jonathon's encyclopedia of common medicinal treatments, which she rolled out of the library in her doll buggy. He found himself to be an unforeseen student, however, where the game of checkers was concerned. She'd taken him off-guard with the remarkably skilled strategies she claimed to have learned at some place called Aunt Oly's house, an overheard piece of information that caused Jonathon to clear his throat in disgust.

She, on the other hand, considered David to be a trophy she had won, and her requests to visit the Madison house grew more and more frequent throughout that first holiday season and well into January. Mimi, who'd become increasingly frustrated with Cinnamon's inability to absorb Maggie's presence, began welcoming the added number of peaceful afternoons absent of her eldest daughter's sulky temperament. Besides, David seemed to be a fine young man. He often stayed for tea when he walked down to accompany Cinnamon, and he always inquired about Amelia, the grandmother he'd met only once when he was about five years old himself, and who'd left an enduring impression upon him.

Mimi was eager for such conversations, and she not only shared her memories with him, but also as much of Amelia's tangible legacy as she'd been permitted to bring with her—a few letters, items of clothing, hair adornments, and the christening gown. Charming him with her story of the Madison art projects, she detailed the specifics of those items she'd left behind in Jonathon's house, in the event David was interested in searching them out. Then she told him about her friendship with the Magglios and her belief that Amelia would be pleased with the extended family that she and Bradley had created downtown on Lark Street.

"Is Lark Street, by any chance, the same place as Aunt Oly's?"

"Yes, it is," she said with a smile. "Why do you ask?"

"Cinnamon has mentioned it on occasion, with great affection, although Uncle Jonathon doesn't seem to share her enthusiasm. Why is that?"

Mimi was very careful not to let her feelings about Jonathon creep into her discourse, although she was often tempted. With every conversation, she also wanted to ask David about his parents, particularly Peter, in hopes of learning whether or not her speculation about her former brother-in-law was accurate. Further, she longed to inquire about life in Jonathon's house, since David was so forthcoming that she knew he would answer her questions honestly. But she kept all of these curiosities to herself, waiting for him to initiate dialogue on the subjects, which he never did. Instead, when she eventually felt the comment suitable, she encouraged him to have Jonathon show him those items relative to Amelia, which she was certain must be scattered throughout the house, or perhaps up in the attic by now.

"Frankly," he confided, "I'm more comfortable discussing things relative to my grandmother when I'm here with you. Any time Amelia's name comes up at home, the talk inevitably leads to references about one event or another that included you as well—and Sophie generally ends up weeping."

That divulgence was as close as Mimi would ever come to having her many questions answered.

Cinnamon had no patience for these tête-à-têtes and would begin tugging on David's arm, insisting that the time had come to leave shortly after he sat down. But by April of 1911, at the end of that first winter, she was yearning to have any time at all with him, even if crowded by her mother. Whenever he wasn't in school, he was with his uncle at the mill where he would complete his homework and observe operations under the tutelage of Jonathon's senior foreman. David was energized by this exposure. His inclusion in the business as well as in the family provided him with a comfortable sense of permanence. He was also feeling quite mature and preferred spending his time with the adults he was meeting rather than the little girl down the block.

While waiting for this imbalance to correct itself, Cinnamon reached out to Angela. They had already bonded by experiencing together the changing body shapes of Sophie first, then Mimi a year later—episodes that were a spellbinding prelude to the appearance of babies. The two girls had peered around corners in both houses to witness gigantic round stomachs and swollen ankles rendering the two women frightfully unattractive, not to mention crippled. They also watched as the ladies cried secretly in their lonely captivity, although this was difficult to understand at the time. Confused and wishing to help, Cinnamon and Angela persistently made themselves available, but they might as well have been invisible. Neither Sophie nor Mimi chose to explain what was making them look and feel so miserable, and they repeatedly sent the girls off to another room or outside by themselves.

Once the new babies arrived, the women no longer looked as if they were ill. But the atmosphere in each house became far noisier, leaving the adults with headaches and even less interest in the older children. After David's entry on the scene, however, his apparent affection for both babies persuaded Angela—and subsequently Cinnamon—to reconsider their approach and at least investigate the reasons why he found them so appealing. Without warning, the girls found themselves holding the smelly, squirmy bundles that all too quickly grew into crawling and then wobbling sources of irritation that would not be gone. Once they were imprisoned in this snare, they watched in disbelief as David abandoned them and gravitated again to the preferred gatherings of Jonathon and his grownup associates, frequently leaving the girls on their own in the company of Cinnamon's little half-sister or brother.

Crushed by this trickery, but fearing his disfavor and unwilling to believe that he meant any harm, the girls maintained appearances, feigning pleasure with one baby or another. Angela eventually took this one step further and became completely annoying by declaring a *genuine* interest in them—and in Jay, most particularly. Three years younger than Angela, the boy had already grown nearly as tall as Cinnamon's best friend, and his ability to express himself was considered remarkable.

Regardless of anyone's opinions about the purity of Jonathon's character, no one—not even Mimi—could find fault in his talents as a father. Notwithstanding his remote relationship with Cinnamon, he devoted admirable effort to incubating her social and verbal skills, although he ascribed to himself much of the credit for similar efforts rightly belonging to Mimi. With Jay, however, Jonathon's self-acclaim was merited. Perhaps as a tribute to Amelia—perhaps out of guilt—Jay's intellectual stimulation became a priority from the moment he and Sophie brought the child home from the hospital. Even the household staff was instructed to read to the baby at every possible interval between feedings and sleeping, and any conversations containing baby talk were explicitly prohibited. Well ahead of many 20th century child psychologists, Jonathon's theory was clear.

"The boy will attempt to emulate whatever he hears you say. But his most difficult challenge will be to comprehend the correct way to speak about the object you're attempting to name for him, or the point you're trying to make. Frankly, despite his recent arrival on this earth, if you are directing his attention to a *blanket* and calling it a *banky*, I suspect he will be wondering why you're being so absurd. Never assume that he doesn't know what you're talking about. He simply hasn't learned how to *say* everything yet, and I'm convinced he will rise to any level of expectation we set for him, if we are diligent and consistent in our teaching."

Jay did, indeed, respond to this group effort, which was prescribed by Jonathon in methodically detailed lessons and exercises that were tenderly enforced under Sophie's guidance. By the time the boy was three, he was speaking in impressive sentences, with a vocabulary well above the norm for children born years ahead of him. This ability to communicate, plus the fact that he was tall and husky for his age, created a much older image, belying the active toddler inside his proud frame.

Angela didn't understand or care about such accomplishments or contrasts. All she knew was that she wanted to be around him. He was both fun and funny, and even though she remembered the day he came home as a baby, he had abruptly grown up before her eyes. Now that she was five, she was certain that they must almost be the same age already. *Eventually*, she would tell Cinnamon, *he will be the oldest.*

Cinnamon countered her friend's snowballing requests to involve Jay in every activity by maneuvering through Aunt Oly to widen their playgroup with another boy, just to even things out. Jarrett Smith was escorted up to Madison several times a week, usually by Anthony and Olivia whenever Emanuel was working in the Lark Street shop. Jarrett had proven himself to be the most pliable selection, and together the four childhood companions conspired to trap fireflies in jars, chase stray cats up trees, and on rainy days compete for best drawing, a game with which Jarrett was all too familiar. Cinnamon also showed them how to play checkers, intentionally leaving out key points of instruction and thus ensuring her consistent winning streak.

Sometimes Christina and Rebecca Magglio would come to visit along with Jarrett. But Rebecca, who was almost six, now, had something wrong with her legs and couldn't run. If inclement weather required the theme to be calm and indoors, the six children interacted quite nicely. But when the action was lively and outside, Christina wouldn't leave her little sister alone. Over time, the Magglio girls stopped coming, and Cinnamon only saw them when she went downtown.

Periodically, her favorite day would arrive when David would usher her, Angela, Jay and Jarrett to Washington Park, directly across the street from Bradley and Mimi's house on Madison Avenue. Plans would usually include a picnic lunch packed tightly inside a large wicker basket by Irene and Sophie and then spread out by David on the quilt he would unfold on the grass. After they ate, and sometimes before, there would be an exhausting game of catch or hide and seek, followed by a long period of stillness when the children would stretch out on the blanket and listen to David's dramatic stories about his life in the far-away place called San Francisco. Most of his tales were elaborate fabrications, which he embellished to the delighted squeals of his audience. But every now and then, he would talk about the earthquake and fire, his customary theatrical delivery giving way to a soft, melancholy voice. Cinnamon came to recognize this mood of his as the one her Papa had described before David arrived. When she would see his face grow tense and his focus drift skyward, she would know his thoughts had traveled back in time. Pulling herself up off the quilt, she would walk to where he was sitting and wrap her arms around his neck.

"Don't be sad," she would whisper. "Please don't be sad any more."

When this alliance of children was first formed, Maggie was only thirteen months old and too young, Mimi believed, to participate with the others unless they were inside under her watchful eye. But by David's second summer in Albany, Maggie could be seen peering out at the familiar group playing and picnicking in the park on the opposite side of the street.

"Look," David said one Saturday, directing everyone's attention to Maggie's face framed between the white lace curtain panels on Brad and Mimi's front window. "I'm guessing your little sister would like to come out with us, Cinn—and I'll wager that your mommy would let her."

"No!" Cinnamon announced defiantly. "I don't want her. She's too little, and she gets in trouble."

"But I'll take care of her. Come on," he urged, "let's go talk to Mimi."

"Stop!" Cinnamon screamed. "No! Stop, I said!"

She had thrown herself down on the ground, and was lying on her back, furiously kicking her legs, while her screaming continued. Picnickers nearby were turning to look at the hysterics, propelling David to scoop her up in his arms and begin gently patting her on the back.

"All right—all right. That's enough," he soothed, noticing that the onlookers had returned to their own affairs. "We'll have Maggie join us another time. Calm down now, Cinn. I've got you."

Feeling herself sway as he moved with her, she realized that she had just learned something very valuable about the strength and extraordinary power of her will, although not in so many words. While this lesson would be called upon frequently throughout her lifetime, she would sadly be well into adulthood before that power was used wisely, or for any good whatsoever.

David was still holding on to her tightly when she saw over his shoulder that Maggie's face remained fixed in the window across the street. Cinnamon stared back at her sister, willing with all her might that she would disappear. After a few seconds, the lace curtains fluttered closed, and then Maggie's face was gone. Up until that moment, destiny might have been altered. But now the course was set.

Bradley came home early one afternoon in September of 1912. The house was quiet, and he discovered by wandering around that Maggie was asleep in her crib, and his wife was napping on the parlor sofa. Cinnamon, he assumed, must be at Jonathon's, per usual. After removing his shoes, he silently made his way to the kitchen for a drink of water where he saw the unwashed sherry glass in the sink, signaling that all was not right. Later that evening after Cinnamon returned home and dinner was over, he helped the girls get ready for bed and tucked them in. Then he sat with Mimi on the front porch swing, his arm around her shoulders as he controlled the swing's slow motion by pressing his foot against the plank flooring. A few crickets were still clinging to their warm weather routines, and the metric sound of their chirping was a comfort.

"You cannot hide your heart from me," he said at length "I know you're troubled. Please tell me what happened today."

She looked up at him and smiled, then leaned her head back against the curve of his arm.

"You amaze me with your intuition, my sweet Bradley, and I am so lucky to have you. With all the blessings we've been given, I shouldn't complain about a thing. But since you ask, I can tell you that Louise Preston was very cruel. I've been trying for a long time now to reestablish my friendship with her. After all, Cinnamon and Angela are constantly together, and when Amelia was still with us, Louise and I appreciated each other's company so much. Then I must admit that, with all the awful Jonathon business, I did avoid speaking with her for awhile. I was never unkind or mean, though. I simply didn't know what to say to her while things were so unsettled, and frankly, I was embarrassed about my personal circumstances. Now that a normal routine has returned, I thought it a waste of potential to be next door to one another and never have contact. So, I made some cookies, and then Maggie and I went over to see her this morning."

"She didn't like your cookies?"

"No, silly. She didn't like *me*."

"Well, that hardly sounds possible. Are you sure you didn't misunderstand her?"

"Yes, I'm quite positive. She never let us past her front stoop, saying she appreciated my gesture but would prefer my staying away. Her husband's position in the legislature, she said, prevented her from being loose with her friendships. She actually used the word *loose*, and when I asked her what she meant by that, she said she'd rather not be too specific, but she needed to confine her relationships to those within her own circle."

"And what circle would *that* be?"

"Obviously one that excludes me. She did make a point, however, of assuring me that Angela's association with Cinnamon was perfectly fine with her. In fact, she said she's happy that the girls are such good chums. Then she had the nerve to thank me for the cookies and actually took the plate from my hands. I must have been looking at her in shock because she asked me if there was anything else. When I didn't answer her, she closed the door and just left Maggie and me standing there."

Bradley could feel the blood rushing to his face as one thought filled his mind. Jonathon was somehow behind this. He imagined Mimi might have been thinking the same thing.

"What did you do then?"

"I came home, of course. I cried as well, and I confess I had some sherry after putting Maggie down for her nap. Poor little thing. She didn't like my tears, but she was most upset about the cookies being gone. I'll probably never see that plate again, either. I still can't believe Louise could have behaved in such a manner. Can you?"

He was clearly unnerved by the story, but he didn't want to tell her that he wasn't surprised. He'd been running into similar situations himself for some time now. The references or comments had been subtle at first, coming from men he didn't know very well. Lately, however, the uncomfortable occurrences had become more frequent and more pronounced, involving people who were close to him. For years he'd been a trusted member of Albany's journalistic community, and he was frequently tipped about political stories and far-reaching scandals, enabling his reporters and *The Times Union* to break headlines ahead of other publications. Known for honoring his word, even when others weren't returning the favor, his editing genius led young reporters, and their veteran counterparts as well, to regularly seek his help.

But sometime during his first year of marriage to Mimi, Bradley began noticing an erosion in all of these associations. More and more frequently, he found himself discovering, after the fact, that he had not been included in dinners or meetings, to which he would previously have been invited. He also encountered increasing objections from his reporters regarding his daily schedule of their story assignments, and he observed a marked decline in the number of journalists seeking his guidance or editorial expertise. His professional efforts had always been rewarded with respect, but more importantly with a belief that at the end of each day his contributions were somehow making a constructive difference in the community. Now he felt as if obstacles were being thrown in the path of every project, and his support network had grown distressingly thin. He also wondered if his deliberate efforts to keep his early courtship of Mimi separate from the rest of his life were now working against him. If his friends and associates had come to know her then, perhaps the effect of Jonathon's fictional stories about her would have been easier to discount.

Of course, he had not mentioned these concerns to his wife, or to anyone, for that matter. Tonight, as he continued pressing the porch swing in motion with his foot against the floor, he experienced an advancing sense of alarm. Stroking Mimi's head, which she was now resting in his lap, he was happy to see her eyes closed. Hopefully, her bruised feelings would mend quickly. She certainly had done nothing to merit such treatment, and she had sadly become far too familiar with such seedy aspects of human nature during the past six years. On this particular evening, he began to believe that he had not spent nearly enough time trying to protect her.

Jonathon and his cronies are trying to push us out of Albany, he thought. *Perhaps the moment has come for me to start saving them the trouble.*

Five days later, Mimi learned that her husband would be traveling to Manhattan for some sort of week-long editor's conference.

"Joseph will be riding down on the train with me," Bradley told her, "so he can spend time with Velita. He said you and the girls are welcome to stay at Lark Street while we're gone."

"That's very thoughtful," she answered, "but we'll be all right here. This will give me a perfect opportunity to begin working on Cinnamon's First Communion dress. I actually came up with the design myself, and Olivia helped me with the preliminary outline for the pattern pieces. So there will be plenty for me to do. Besides, Cinnamon is at Jonathon's so often these days, and Maggie is never any trouble, always content to play or paint by herself. By the way, have you noticed, dear, that your little daughter has the markings of a budding artist?"

"Yes, I have," he said, realizing that he had not noticed at all, but promising himself that he *would* just as soon as his new plan had been implemented.

The morning after Bradley left, Mimi approached her sewing project with the best of intentions. First she measured key parts of her fidgety and uncooperative daughter, then began the intricate translation of those measurements into the pattern dimensions, which she first sketched on pieces of cardboard then traced onto thin paper spread out on the parlor floor. Several hours after nightfall, however, when her girls were both asleep, she found herself being pulled into a murky place where she'd been before, where her thoughts were too heavy to think about, and where any desire for productivity had been terminated. Undulating back and forth in the old rocking chair, which was chipped and sagging after use through two pregnancies and babies, she kept refilling her sherry glass from the bottle on the table beside her. A small dim lamp on her desk across the room offered the only light, and it pitched against the ceiling and wall an eerie silhouette that rose and fell in cadence with the slow tempo of the rocker.

Her eyes were half open, not focusing on anything in that space, but rather on a scene deeply imbedded in her memory. She and this chair were in the Madison house kitchen. The month was February, the year 1906, and Cinnamon was a suckling baby whose tiny hands were both wrapped around one of Mimi's fingers.

The aroma of Irene's ham roasting in the oven and the glow of burning wood through the stove grate tugged at her senses while she studied the fine lines of lacy frost outside the windows above the sink. Drake had just carried a fresh bin of split logs in from the porch, and the room's steamy warmth wrapped her in balance and safety. Mundane conversations about chores to be done and shopping lists to be made encircled her and kept her from feeling lonely. Amelia was there. Life was secure, and she had no knowledge yet of rejection or the scourge of being told by the man she'd married that she wasn't good enough for him anymore.

"Where did that go?" she whispered, returning to the present moment and adding more sherry to her glass. "Why can't I recapture that feeling of being safe in my new life? Will I ever be able to forget? Will I ever be able to trust that such an ending can't happen again?"

After taking another drink, she lowered the glass into her lap and closed her eyes. She could not have known that, in the place toward which she was descending—a place further down than the one after Jonathon—there would be no one to listen or to answer any of her questions. Finally, in the blackness that would eventually claim her, not even Amelia would be able to reach her.

When Cinnamon first realized what moving to New York City meant, she was inconsolable. She was not supposed to have been told yet, since preparations on both ends of the move were expected to take six months or more. But after evidently overhearing a conversation between her mother and Bradley, she had rushed to Jonathon for clarification. Whatever words the man had said to his daughter were not chosen very carefully and had left her in such turmoil that she clung to furniture legs and banister spindles in an effort to keep herself from being taken home that night.

Bradley and Mimi were angry that he'd had spoken out of turn. Once their decision to move had become final, they'd labored over how they were going to inform Cinnamon of their plan. Of course, Mimi wasn't aware that that she'd been kept in the dark, herself, until a week before word leaked to the child. Bradley meant no harm by this secrecy. His theory had been that the relocation needed to look like a natural evolution stemming from his work, rather than a defeated retreat from Albany that could potentially give Jonathon a sense of conquest. Accordingly, after his initial trip to the City with Joseph, he'd carefully orchestrated his first dialogue with Mimi, telling her that he'd been approached during the New York assembly of journalists about an available position as a senior editor with *The New York World.*

"This is merely an opportunity, dear, not a fait accompli. I explained to them that such an uprooting might not be something you'd wish to entertain. Nonetheless, I did want you to be aware of the possibility."

"How very intriguing," she'd said after only a few moments, much to his relief. "I hope you realize, darling, that I will happily go with you anywhere you wish, so you needn't be concerned about my feelings as you evaluate this important choice. Frankly, although a move of such magnitude seems intimidating on the surface, there might be a great deal to be said for new scenery."

Her quick reaction fortified his conviction that he was doing the right thing, although sustaining the ruse was key to his plan's successful execution. She mustn't know that there had actually been no conference in Manhattan, or that *he* had been the one who'd initiated contact with *The New York World* editors, or, most importantly, that his employment had already been secured. In fact, his new political column would begin running the following month, at which point he would terminate his association with the *Times Union* and begin spending two out of every four weeks in Manhattan until the move was complete.

There had also been no appropriate occasion yet for her to learn that Joseph and his brother-in-law Alberto had secured a large two-bedroom flat in the building next door to the Mentini's apartment. The space would not be available for several months, which Bradley found fortunate. He wanted time to give this element of his plan a little more thought. Regardless of Mimi's expressed support, he wasn't certain how readily she would adapt to the change in status from her spacious home on upper Madison Avenue to an apartment in the crowded working-class Italian community on Manhattan's lower east side. On the other hand, he believed that same community was going to offer her a life where she felt included and appreciated, and he prayed this would have more value to her than her personal surroundings. Joseph assured him that Velita and Alberto were preparing the neighbors for Mimi's arrival, and Bradley could only hope that the welcome would not let him down.

While all of these arrangements were being consummated, Mimi thought the move was still in the conversational stage.

"If we were ever to make such a change in circumstances," she'd begun with some concern in her voice, "how would you propose we explain things to Cinnamon? She spends almost as much time at Jonathon's as she does here, and she's grown quite dependant upon Angela's company, not to mention David's. We would be taking her away from everything she knows, assuming of course that her father doesn't engage Albany's legal community to prevent me from leaving with her."

Bradley strove to maintain a steady tone as he began delivering his rehearsed response.

"Should we ever arrive at a decision of such importance, we would create images of a great adventure for her—images of fun and opportunity that would help dispel any fear she might have of leaving Albany. In fact, those images could prove useful for you and me, as well," he said with a smile. "As for Jonathon, I'm afraid he forfeited any right to custodial decisions about Cinnamon when he decided an annulment was a proper solution to his difficulties. I'm also quite certain that arrangements could easily be made for Angela or David, or anyone else who cares, to visit us in Manhattan. Since the trains run in both directions, Cinnamon could readily travel up here as well. Furthermore, I'm convinced that Maggie would adapt nicely to the changes, too. She'd probably look upon the entire process with her customary curiosity. So you see, my love, there's nothing we couldn't overcome."

"Yes, of course. I hadn't considered Maggie." Mimi's focus shifted toward the kaleidoscope of autumn colors on display outside the parlor window. "But she never seems to object to *anything* we do. Well, then," she added, turning back to Bradley, "I suppose we'll simply wait now to see if the New York position materializes for you. There will be plenty of time to ponder alternatives once we have that piece of information. Did they give you any idea when you would hear from them?"

Afraid she might see that he was being less than truthful, he averted her eyes and moved toward the window, pretending interest in that same fall panorama.

"They said they'd wire me very shortly. What an invigorating time of year, don't you think? Come. Let's take Maggie for a walk in the park before Cinnamon gets home. We can address this issue in more depth at another time—assuming, of course, that there's ever a need to do so."

Mimi was surprised at the speed with which the job offer was made and accepted. She had scarcely processed the news when Bradley suddenly shed his old position at the *Times Union* and took over his new one in New York. Her head was also spinning with the many associated decisions being made so quickly, and without her involvement. But Bradley was uncharacteristically evasive when she questioned him, assuring her that they would have ample time for long talks when the pace of activity slowed down.

"I'm taking care of everything for us in the City," he told her as he prepared for his first trip, which would keep him away for more than two weeks, "and I've finalized all the arrangements for the sale of our house."

The one thing they *had* agreed upon was the impracticality of trying to maintain the Corbett Place in any capacity once they were no longer in Albany. In an unnecessarily charitable gesture, they'd given Jonathon the opportunity to repurchase the property, but he'd immediately declined the offer. There was no shortage of politicians and businessmen, however, who wished to move their families and their social standing to upper Madison. Once the property was advertised, Bradley was taken off-guard when securing the preferred buyer and consummating the sale took less than three months. Wishing to avoid the massive transfer of their belongings in the dead of a northeastern winter, he insisted that provisions be written into the purchase contract that enabled him to retain occupancy for Mimi and the children until spring arrived the following March.

In the interim, those long months seemed a brief episode to Bradley, who was unpredictably rejuvenated by the challenges of his new job. He had arrived with an intellectual grasp of New York's unique magnetic energy. But once immersed in the City's core, he discovered a pulse more vibrant than he'd imagined was possible. By 1913, only Tokyo and London were larger than New York on a global scale. Yet those cities did not have the beacon of light beckoning legions of immigrants to risk everything they knew and possessed for the hope and opportunity of an American dream. Bradley could not envision any profession, other than journalism, that would give him equal access to every stratum of class and neighborhood, where hope was sometimes fulfilled and other times obliterated. From the southern tip of lower Manhattan to the northern end on the Harlem River and extending outward to the other four boroughs, he became addicted to the stories. Without his family close by, he lost himself in this new work, and the days and weeks were swiftly consumed.

Back in Albany, however, the same period seemed an infinite torment to Mimi. Anyone associated with Jonathon withdrew from the Price family, making it clear that few were saddened to learn the family was leaving town. Alone with just the Magglios to help her, Mimi steeled herself through the cleaning, the organizing and the packing, all of these activities intermingled with recurrent battles to keep Cinnamon from running away from home. Jonathon had given his dissertation on the perils of moving to New York City to his young daughter only a week prior to Bradley's departure, and the child had been completely unmanageable ever since.

"Please, Sophie," Mimi implored, after curbing her pride one morning and walking up to the Madison house. "I'm so very concerned about Cinnamon, and I'm begging you to ask Jonathon for his assistance. If he could help quiet her fears about this move, and reassure her that he will bring her up here for regular visits, I believe she will calm down. She's only a little girl, and she's deeply distressed, believing that she'll never see any of you again. Although I'd love for her to be excited at the prospects ahead, I would be relieved, at this point, to know that she's not terror stricken. Whatever personal issues you and I might have, let's please set them aside for *her* well-being."

Sophie had been astonished to see Mimi standing on the front porch, and was utterly unprepared for this speech. Opening the door only a few inches wide, just far enough so they could hear one another, the thought of inviting her husband's former wife inside never crossed her mind. Instead, she'd responded with a harsh edge to her voice.

"Your message is well-taken, although, if I may be blunt, your daughter's feelings were apparently not considered when you made the decision to uproot your lives. Nevertheless, I will tell Jonathon what you've said. Beyond that, I can promise you nothing."

Jonathon did not give the courtesy of a reply, and Mimi wasn't convinced that Sophie ever passed her message along to him. But Irene knew about her visit—and the housekeeper, whose conflicting loyalties never ceased to distress her, made a point of mentioning it to David. A week later, he stopped by the Corbett Place, and Mimi invited him inside for tea. Rain had been falling since noon, and the dark sky made the hour seem much later than the three o'clock chime would suggest. She lit several candles on the dining table where they'd grown accustomed to talking, and when he took his usual chair, she thought for an instant that she felt Amelia hovering. But she couldn't hold onto those moments very long any more.

"I'm sorry about your problems with Cinn," he said, sipping his tea as the steam rose up in front of his face. "I will double my efforts to help her find some fun in this move of yours."

"Thank you, David. You'll never know how grateful I am for your willingness to try. She has been turned upside down by the changes."

"Or so she would have you believe." He smiled at her, the blue in his eyes seeming to twinkle. "Your daughter might be feeling some genuine degree of distress about leaving Albany. But the current dramatization, in my opinion, is more theatrical than anything else. She's learned how to act her way into, or out of, whatever she wants, and she assumes I'm not aware of what she's doing. But she's easy to see through, once you know what she's up to. Consequently, I have faith that she will weather this event with far less suffering that she would have you *think* she's experiencing. Yesterday, I overheard her telling Jay and Angela that she wanted them to come see her in her new house, in Mannyhat, she called it."

David laughed at the recollection and pulled Mimi in with him. He was fourteen now, charming and secure, surely a perfect blend of Peter and Lily, and blessed with his grandmother's compassion. *He will need all of those strengths to survive prolonged exposure to his uncle,* Mimi thought.

"I can't tell you how much better you've made me feel," she said, "and I hope you know that you have an open invitation to visit us as well."

"Yes, thank you. But I pledge to write even if I can't see you for awhile. I've made a pact with Cinnamon about exchanging letters one for one, and I told her to watch how quickly the months will pass. Before long, I'll be leaving Albany myself, you realize, to attend the university—hopefully in just two or three more years, if I continue to accelerate my studies. Remarkably, it's been that long already since I came from California, so the same amount of time will disappear again before we know what's happened."

He was right. She could not believe the years had dissolved so quickly. Naturally, he *would* be attending university, but she was amused that he addressed this next phase of his life as if it were arriving tomorrow.

"How marvelous for you, David. Amelia would be so very proud of you. Have you considered the schools you might want to explore?"

"There's only one choice, Mimi—Harvard, where Uncle Jonathon graduated."

Ascending those long-forgotten memories, she thought back to a time of youth and joy, to love in the full hope of innocence, when she was fulfilled in her new teaching position in Boston, and Jonathon was her brother's handsome college friend brought home for dinner to meet her. She saw only clear roads and fair weather ahead of her then, much like David was seeing now. Every question was simple, with the promise of a simple answer to follow, and hopeful tomorrows were taken for granted.

"When your plans get closer," she said, reeling herself into the present as she poured more tea in both cups, "please do write to me. My brother George still lives in Boston, along with my aunt and uncle and a few friends from my childhood. I grew up there, you know, and your Uncle Jonathon and I met and married there."

He looked at her and seemed to be a much older man.

"No one told me. Yes, I'll be diligent about keeping you informed, and I would like very much to meet your family someday."

"Good. Well, there will be plenty of time for that. Meanwhile, thank you again for offering to help with my little girl. I'll never forget you for it."

Thereafter, David regularly ushered Cinnamon from one house to another throughout the holidays and winter that followed, as the date for the New York move remained suspended, and as the child's disposition slowly improved. Jay and Angela occupied her time when they weren't all in school, giving her an excuse to stay at her father's house more frequently. Mimi chose not to fight this trend. In return, she was rewarded with a reasonably even-tempered daughter while the seemingly endless wait continued.

Bradley traveled home for a week over Christmastime. But after that he only came back for a few short days during the next two months. Then, in late February, he returned to help Joseph and his brothers transport the heavy household crates to the rail yard for shipment to the new apartment in Manhattan. Startled to see his wife's buttery skin looking like chalk and a lethargy replacing her normally vibrant nature, he began to worry that his noble plan to improve their circumstances had, instead, been ill-conceived. Moreover, he realized that he'd allowed himself to become so distracted by the change in jobs and the allure of his temporary single life that he'd all but abandoned Mimi during what had to be a very difficult time for her.

"I won't be leaving again until we all leave together," he told her when they were quiet in bed one night after he'd been home for several days. "Please forgive me for expecting you to manage all of this without me."

"Sweet dreams," she said, the back of her body curved into the front of his.

He wondered for a moment why that was all she'd said in response to his apology. Surely she meant to give him a more supportive reply that would help minimize his guilt. Before he could worry very long, however, a narcotic-like sleep overtook him. Beneath the rise and fall of his deep breathing, he did not feel her slip out of his arms, nor did he hear her in the kitchen opening the cupboard where she now hid the sherry bottle and her special glass.

On Friday, March 28, 1913, the trolley stopped alongside the cemetery covering acres of landscaped ground about two miles from the cathedral. Mimi stepped down and waited for the car to pull away. After she secured the top button on her coat and fastened her scarf around her neck, she walked up the grassy hill to the spot she'd visited so many times over the past seven years. Today's sun still traveled its low winter arc, delivering less warmth than one would think from looking out a window at the bright, clear day. She was glad she'd decided against wearing her shawl, and pulled the bottom of her coat snugly around her legs as she sat down to face the headstone. Classic early birds, who dared to trust in the apparent appearance of spring, hopped along the green and brown patches of ground and jumped on top of grave markers nearby. Their trilling and the flutter of their wings were the only sounds, and Mimi seemed to be the only living person in the cemetery. Looking at the granite marker rising from the earth like a biblical tablet, she slowly moved her fingers across Amelia's name etched in the stone, and began speaking in a quiet voice.

"We're leaving Albany tomorrow, although I'm certain you're well aware of this. Frankly, I'm a little frightened, despite my insistence with Cinnamon that there is not a single thing to fear. All indications are that this is the appropriate move for us to make, and I must say that I've never seen Bradley happier with his work. His professional opportunity will, in turn, lead all of us to a grand new world filled with promise for the children, which I know you will appreciate. So, I can't imagine why I have even an ounce of apprehension. And who could have ever guessed that Joseph and his family would come to play such a major role in plotting our life's direction? I confess that his influence has taken me by surprise, but then my assessment of people has fallen far short of reality before. Still, I promised myself that today I would not give voice to any of those mistakes in judgment. Thankfully, I'm now blessed with two precious girls and a husband who loves me. That must be the happy place my thoughts return whenever I feel as if I'm sinking—a sensation I've been experiencing rather frequently of late. By the way, I'm so sorry we had to sell your old house. You and Nathaniel still had a presence there, you know. Yes, of *course* you know. Anyway, there was no sense in our keeping the place when we'll be so far away. Again, I do hope the decision was a good one, and that you understand."

Her need to speak ended and she sat in silence for nearly half an hour, her concentration drifting across the expanse of green and graves toward Albany's jagged skyline of steeples, spires, domes, brick building tops and chimneys. She had never taken time to study this view before, and despite the bitter taste in her mouth, she conceded that the city was essentially quite beautiful, in design if not character. But none of this would be her concern any longer. Reluctantly pulling herself to her feet, she brushed the crushed leaves and thawing dirt from her coat. Then she leaned down and kissed the top of the headstone.

"I love you, Amelia."

Tears began filling her eyes as she turned to walk away, when something made her look over her shoulder. Blinking to clear her vision, she felt the streams fall down her cheeks as the inscription came into focus.

MY PRAYER AND GREATEST WISH IS THAT NOT ONLY WILL I BE GRANTED THE POWER TO FORGIVE ALL THINGS, BUT THAT THE SAME POWER WILL BE GIVEN TO THOSE I LOVE.

AMELIA ELIZABETH MCCLINTY
FEBRUARY 2, 1857—APRIL 23, 1906

"Not as easy as it sounds, Amelia," she said, turning again to walk toward the street as she noticed the trolley making its way in her direction. "But thanks for the reminder."

On the ride home, she passed by the cathedral, then the trolley stop where she and Amelia first embarked on their walk to the *Times Union* offices. After a few more blocks, the car crossed Lark Street and proceeded up Madison Avenue. Behind her lay the axis of a town that once belonged to her, until she was no longer useful, along with the resting place of the most authentic woman she would know in her lifetime. She considered the breadth of those contrasts and wondered where, on that spectrum of darkness and light, her own existence would fall by the time she returned again to visit both places. As fate would ultimately dictate, she would never find her way back to either one.

Albany's Union Station was buzzing the next morning with energized passengers and those wishing them bon voyage. But the most boisterous assembly moved in a tight, animated cluster around the Price family. They walked the station platform in unison to the ninth car on the train, as directed by the conductor who had reviewed their tickets.

Bradley carried Maggie with one arm and gripped Mimi around her shoulders with his other. He could still feel her shaking, just as she'd been doing when he found her alone in the parlor shortly before dawn. He'd believed ardently in the soundness of this move. But now, when the time had past for reversal and when his wife's anxiety was so palpable, he found himself disquieted about what might happen to them if he turned out to be wrong.

Walking immediately behind him was a chorus line of four, with David serving as the anchor. Cinnamon and Angela were on either side of him, holding his hands. Jay was next to Angela, his arm looped through hers. The children were all talking at once, but not listening to or answering each other, as their voices rode the brisk wind slicing through the open boarding area. David was quiet, more sober about this departure than he'd expected to be.

"Will you help us make a package of letters and pictures every afternoon to send to Cinnamon?" Jay and Angela had asked him the day before. "We think we won't miss her so much that way."

Missing Cinnamon had not previously occurred to him. Now that it had, the children's request gave him something to anticipate as he glanced down at the little head of red curls and felt her squeezing his hand harder with every step.

Joseph walked heavily to Bradley's right, wrestling with the mélange of emotions that began to overtake him last night. For weeks his mind and muscle had been occupied with the move's logistics, the packing, crating, moving and shipping. Infused in this activity was contentment in knowing that his friends would soon be under the vigilant eyes of his sister Velita and her husband, never again to be made a target of Jonathon McClinty's malevolence. In the midst of all the preparations, he had not stopped to envision his life absent of those same friends, or a Lark Street without their presence and laughter. As he surveyed the curtained passenger windows above him, he decided that he and his brothers would need to begin discussing, in short order, their arrangements for a Manhattan visit.

Behind David and his three charges, Matthew held Rebecca, his arms forming a chair for her fragile legs. Helena was next to him, with Christina and Jarrett Smith each clutching one of her hands. Anthony and Olivia were moving up alongside of them while the final group, which included Anne, Marjorie, Ellen and Emanuel, scurried forward and hugged the edges of their party the rest of the way to the ninth car. There they handed the small bags they'd been carrying to the porter who greeted them. As he transferred the luggage up the steps and into the passenger compartment, the improbable collection of friends and family closed in around Brad and Mimi. Cinnamon could scarcely see light through all the bodies towering above her. But her hand was still tightly encircled by David's, and that was all that mattered to her. She would hold on until they pulled her away, and then she would cling to his promise to write every day.

"Before you can count the years," he'd told her yesterday, "you'll be all grown up and free to come back here to live, if you want to. We'll be waiting for you. In the meantime, we'll see you in the summers and on vacations. Your Papa told me to make sure you know that." Jonathon hadn't said any such thing, but David hoped the words would help her board the train without need for restraints.

Eventually, everyone in the group realized the impossibility of each person kissing and hugging every other person in the time allotted. Bradley, with Maggie still in his arms, turned to face them.

"Thank you all," he said, his voice catching. "We will miss you, but you must travel to see us as soon as we're settled. We should not let too much time pass before that happens either."

"Yes," Mimi added, watching their images blur as her tears began to rise again. "We love you very much, and I cannot bear to think...Oh, my. Please forgive me. The words won't...Cinnamon, come now. It's time to go."

Reaching out toward her daughter, she prayed this was not going to be excessively dramatic. Recognizing that the moment had come, David leaned down to kiss Cinnamon's cheek, as he pried her fingers from his hand one by one.

"Go on, Cinn. Remember what I said. I'll always be here."

Then, before she knew what had happened, she found herself on the train. Through the window, she could see David huddled with the others. The only person missing for her today was her Papa. She'd expected him to be there with Sophie, but when David arrived alone with Jay, there wasn't time for disappointment. Now she was thinking about him and wishing she'd been able to say goodbye.

As her mother and Bradley began removing their coats and organizing their belongings around two of the wide, upholstered passenger chairs, Maggie was demonstrating uncharacteristic merriment, darting in and out of the aisle and bobbing up and down to the point of exasperation. Having no patience for this, Cinnamon claimed the chair behind her mother's by the window and began waving at the crowd on the platform below. She noticed that most of them were crying, especially Aunt Oly. But Angela and Jay were holding hands, and they looked quite happy, actually, which was rather irritating. She couldn't tell about David, although he waved back at her, and then blew her a kiss. As she blew one to him in return, she felt a thud next to her.

"Thank you, Maggie," Mimi said, kneeling on her seat in front of them and peering over the top of her chair. "You need to stay there beside your sister. We have a long ride ahead, but the train has a lovely dining car where we can have lunch in a little while. Cinnamon," she continued, handing her eldest daughter a large pink cotton satchel with white looping handles of braided rope, "this is your play bag. Why don't you help Maggie draw some pictures?"

Then Mimi turned around, her head disappearing behind the back of her chair, as Cinnamon glanced over at her little sister.

"Here," she declared, passing the bag to Maggie. "I don't feel like drawing. You can do it by yourself."

In that instant, the train lurched and began crawling forward along the tracks. Cinnamon quickly faced the window again, her nose and hands pressed against the pane. Everyone kept waving at her except David and Joseph, who were jogging along the platform trying to keep up with the rail car. The train moved a little faster, then they ran faster, too—then the train, then they. As the locomotive picked up speed, the men's pace became slower and slower, until they finally stopped running. Even though she pushed the side of her face against the glass to keep them in sight, they grew smaller and smaller, still waving at her—and then they were gone.

Trying to grip the window with her small fingers, her breathing came in short bursts that stuck in her throat as her tears spilled out in a rush. For more than a minute, her palms and cheek remained flattened against the wet window, while she hoped no one would see or hear her if she didn't move. David had told her to be brave, just as *he'd* been when he traveled from California. But as the train sped away from the only place she'd ever known—and the people who made her happy—she did not want to be brave. She wanted to play with her friends, and then have David hold her and bring her home. But none of those magical things was going to happen anymore, and the crushing reality of that moment was nearly unbearable.

Once the train station disappeared into the skyline being left behind, she slowly peeled her face off the window and leaned her head back against the attached chair pillow. After wiping her eyes on the sleeve of her sweater, she kept them closed and rocked with the train's movement for what seemed to her like a very long time. When she opened them again, the view outside the window had been transformed from a cityscape into a spray of early spring colors across the countryside south of Albany. Feeling a little less sad, she noticed to her left that Maggie had unbuttoned the play bag and, on a sketchpad, had begun to pencil an amazingly realistic interpretation of the station they'd just departed.

"Oh, my!" she exclaimed before she could stop herself. Bending forward for a closer look, she thought about her own pictures, which had always been the best, but which were nothing like *this* one. "I didn't know you could draw like that, Maggie."

Lifting the pencil off her paper, Cinnamon's little sister angled her head up and squeezed her eyes into a piercing stare.

"Why do *you* care?"

In the row ahead of them, Mimi pulled the curtain closed across the window.

"I'll open it again when Albany is far, far behind us," she said to her husband. "That way we can look upon the fresh sunlight coming in as the point marking our new beginning. How do you feel about *that* thought, my love?"

God help me, he mused, *if she opens the curtain and it happens to be raining.* Of course, as usual, he didn't want her to know what he was really thinking, or that his sense of foreboding would not be stilled. With a hand on either side of her face, he brought her toward him and softly kissed her forehead.

"I think that will be the perfect way to signal our start—just perfect, Mimi."

What else could he say? There wasn't any possibility of turning back now.

Chapter 9

In and out of happy.
In and out of sad.
'Round and 'round the trouble tree.
In and out of bad.

In and out of love me.
Trying not to need.
In and out of daydreams.
Nearly out of creed.

Touching, holding, letting.
Tossing as I sleep.
Singing, then forgetting.
Can the hills all be this steep?

In and out of wisdom.
Reaching to be free.
Quiet moves a season
In and out of me.

Margaret Elizabeth McClinty
Saturday, May 1, 1921

Cinnamon's interest in poetry began as a curious exploration shortly after her arrival eight years earlier at the Broome Street apartment, between Mulberry and Mott Streets, on Manhattan's lower east side. Shortly thereafter, her casual interest escalated into a means of escape. Looking back, the elaborate preparations and story-building in advance of their leaving Albany had turned out to be pure chicanery, and she had come to realize that her initial reaction to her new home was probably the first thing she'd ever shared in common with her mother. *How could Bradley have done this to them*?

In January of 1898, the five independent boroughs of Manhattan, Staten Island, Brooklyn, the Bronx, and Queens were consolidated into one unified city referred to as Greater New York. With a combined population of 3.5 million residents, the new city was the world's second largest after London. Some hailed this unification as having an historical significance equal to that of Rome's founding. Others expressed deep regret at the colossal outcome. But none could deny the magnitude of America's entry onto the world stage.

Between 1900 and 1910, the City's population increased again by nearly fifty percent, primarily due to an inundation of immigrants from Eastern and Southern Europe. In 1902 alone, half a million foreigners landed at Ellis Island. By 1910, most of New York's residents were either new arrivals or first-generation Americans, the greatest number of which settled on the lower east side of Manhattan, as they'd been doing since the earliest colonization of what was originally known as New Amsterdam in the 1600's.

This population explosion at the beginning of the 20th century led to the development of neighborhoods filled with low-cost housing for the tens of thousands numbered among the poor and the working class. Buildings up to nine stories or more in height were stacked against each other like books on a shelf, lining the streets which were so narrow that windows on one side of the road faced almost directly into windows on the opposite side. From the second floors on up, the buildings housed a mixture of apartments and flats configured for large or multiple families. Space at ground level, block after block, was used for food markets, woodworking and tailor shops, bakeries, delicatessens, butcher shops, restaurants, and any other enterprise born of someone's imagination. Most of the products being sold were actually displayed and exchanged on the streets and sidewalks in front of the shops. Teeming crowds of vendors and customers mingled every day except Sunday amidst stacks of wood furniture, displays filled with needlework and other handmade crafts, clothing on rows of racks, bins of fruits and vegetables, clusters of café tables and umbrellas, all open for business from early morning until dark, regardless of weather, unless seasonal conditions became intolerable.

Attached to the full height and width of every building facing the streets was a maze of fire escapes that zigzagged across the brick and stone frontages like a wire grid. Necessary for the safety of residents, these labyrinths of outdoor stairways and landings became the seats of neighborhood subcultures where families and friends met and socialized on hot sultry nights many floors above the sidewalks, and where people frequently stored items such as kitchen provisions, house plants and flower pots filled with herbs. Sounds of voices talking, laughing, arguing, crying or singing wafted skyward in the evenings, up and down the fronts of the buildings, where people were accustomed to hearing and seeing their neighbors' lives unfold on a community stage with a great view, on a landing or through a window across the street—or perhaps above or below their own.

One thirty-block-square section embedded in this picture was bounded by Houston Street on the north, Canal Street on the south, and Broadway and Mulberry Streets to the west and east, respectively. Italian immigrants first settled this area in the 1850's and quickly divided into subgroups of Genoans, Calabrians, Sicilians and Neapolitans. People in these new neighborhoods would lean out of their tenement windows or sit on their fire escapes and watch their children play in the midst of the bustle and commerce on the streets below. Melanzane and pommi d'oro were stacked on the sidewalks, where vendors known as fruttivendoli would peddle their goods, along with the other proprietors. Goats and rabbits hung in butcher shop windows, while the pungent scent of Provolone and soppresatta drifted through the air.

Everyone spoke in loud voices and rapid sentences. Young women labored in the sidewalk shops, or in the factories, or they became seamstresses for the proliferating fashion industry. When they married, they cared for their husbands and children, working to supplement their meager household incomes whenever they were able. The older women tended to their sizeable extended families, cooking throughout a major portion of every day and growing plump from decades of pasta. Young men also worked in the factories, or on the waterfront, or they found jobs in the fashion industry—usually as a tailor's assistant, but sometimes as a designer if they were courageous enough to expose their creative talents. When *they* married, nothing about their lives changed, except that their beautiful young wives were pregnant much of the time, and their small apartment homes became crowded with children. Older men huddled together discussing business—which could have many definitions, some of which caused them to lower their voices—and then they gathered to share their women's Herculean meals, subsequently growing plump along with them. Children of all ages ran freely and unafraid on their neighborhood blocks, playing in the spray of fire hydrants, growing in the rituals of their Church, and unaware that a pulsing, prosperous world existed outside the perimeter of their impoverished community. In that other world, a few blocks away, right around the corner, a future of dreams and hope awaited those children. That future, which could be theirs if they would just reach out to find it, was being purchased daily by the extensive sacrifices of their parents and grandparents, who crowded around them in a noisy, predictable, nurturing existence.

From the wide and peaceful road called Madison Avenue in Albany—from the clean, spacious and very private home on its own grassy lot across from Washington Park—the Price family came to live in a two-bedroom flat on Broome Street, just off Mulberry, the Main Street of Little Italy, on March 29, 1913. Their home was a third-floor walkup, and they considered themselves fortunate because their building had eight stories. Bradley never intended these surroundings to be permanent, but rather a short transition while he made a name for himself in his new job. Eight years later, however, they were still there.

Notwithstanding this setting, their circumstances weren't entirely grim. They'd been welcomed into the Genoan community without question and with enormous affection, almost as if there weren't a fair or freckled feature about them. The fact that Bradley had chosen to put down roots with his family on Broome Street, despite his obvious education and prestigious job, was impressive enough. But whenever he wasn't working, he made himself available to help his new friends in their businesses or with maintenance in their apartments. This endeared him early-on to any skeptics who might have been suspicious of him and allowed him to build trust and acceptance for himself, as well as for Mimi and the children. Their quick immersion into the parish church activities further secured their welcome.

Although Mimi was somewhat familiar with her new environment due to the trip from Albany prior to Bradley's marriage proposal, her memories were primarily of the people and their warmth. Thankfully, that element had not appeared to change, although what she remembered as a charming cultural venue was viewed far differently once she actually lived there. Finding a peaceful moment in the crowds that never seemed to dissipate was one of her most challenging adjustments, but not as troubling as her daughters and their ability to blend in with the other children.

Cinnamon actually chose the easiest path by striking up an early friendship with Vincente, who was two years her senior. Velita's son had many friends and was respected by both his peers and the adults. Beside him, the girl with the red hair was spared much of the possible harassment that concerned Mimi, and the newcomer quickly moved from being a curiosity to an accepted member of Vincente's circle.

Maggie, on the other hand, preferred being alone, occupying her free time with her artwork. Her sketches were maturing with remarkable speed, and her talent proved astonishing for one so young and tiny. She convinced Bradley to buy an easel for her, enabling her to expand her creativity through watercolors. Within a year of her arrival, her paintings were hanging in apartments up and down Broome Street. Because she frequently stayed with the Mentini's next door when Bradley and Mimi were out, she eventually found herself enjoying the company and friendship of Vincente's twin sisters, Rosa and Maria, who were six months younger. They were almost as quiet as she was, and they shared her preference for indoor activities as opposed to the noisy, rough-and-tumble games the other children played outside in the middle of the road. They were also mesmerized by the magic Maggie performed with a brush and canvas, and they persuaded her to teach them her secrets. She eagerly accepted this undertaking and never expressed the slightest frustration when she discovered that Rosa and Maria had not one artistic bone in their combined bodies.

Once the many social rudiments of the move appeared to be under control, Mimi engaged her own energy by enhancing their new living quarters.

"Here we go again, Amelia," she murmured one morning that first summer when she was by herself in the apartment.

After brewing a pot of tea, she filled her cup and sipped slowly as she sat on her side of the library desk, surveying the main living area. The reality of this petite flat, which Bradley had once described as a spacious, two-bedroom apartment, had come as the biggest surprise of the entire move. Material comforts and grand residences had never been among her personal goals. Nonetheless, she'd been fortunate enough to stumble into both, and had, over time, become used to their advantages. As a result, she not only viewed Broome Street as a step down in the beginning, but as a plunge off a precipice. However, her sense of well-being and peace of mind were so dramatically improved amidst her new community of friends that her attitude soon shifted to one of gratitude—and her attention turned to spinning her legendary flair for interior design on yet another home.

A sizeable portion of their belongings and furniture, including the nursery pieces and other items no longer serving a practical purpose, had been left with the Magglios in the back of their shop. Even so, there would not be enough space for the items they did bring, and her challenge was to decide what they should keep. First she pushed her library desk perpendicular to the large window in the front room, which overlooked the street. Then she centered the desk between the room's two side walls, putting her chair and Amelia's in their rightful places, facing each other across the desk. Next she used this arrangement as the focal point around which she had Alberto and Bradley position several of the more functional pieces built by Emanuel when they moved into The Corbett Place. The double armoire in rich mahogany was placed against the shorter side wall next to the kitchen and was used to store linens as well as most of her dishes. The ceiling-high expanse of bookcases, in the same wood and measuring twelve feet wide, was on the wall opposite the armoire. Emanuel had modeled each section of shelves after the Madison library, enclosing more than half with carved beveled glass doors. Mimi now had them filled with everything from her collection of literary classics and Bradley's journalism reference books, to pots and pans that wouldn't fit elsewhere, to the children's toys. Somehow, clutter and extraneous items of all sorts seemed far less intrusive and unsightly when placed inside those bookcases.

The parlor sofa was in the middle of the floor facing the desk and window, with the ottoman and old rocking chair on either side. The three pieces created a semi-circle that rounded out a comfortable conversation area. One of Geoffrey's lamps was on the desk and another on an end table between the sofa and rocker. Behind the sofa, in the corner nearest the apartment door, stood the round dining table also built by Emanuel for The Corbett Place. Finally, a woven tapestry rug in varying shades of browns and autumn reds covered the room's wood floors almost wall-to-wall. She'd found the rug in a small downtown shop shortly after she departed the Madison house for the cottage. As Alberto and Bradley positioned it for her on Broome Street, she considered how perfectly the carpet had blended with three homes so different from one another in both size and opulence—not too unlike her own blending, she mused. Once she finished with the front room, she applied similar treatments to the two bedrooms, and then, with Bradley's concurrence, gave the remaining furniture to their neighbors on a first-come-first-serve basis. Velita and Alberto had the prime choices, which included a china cabinet that would free up their small kitchen cupboards and enable them to transfer supplies inside from the fire escape.

Mimi's innovative use of balance, color and paint had become a well-honed craft, and within a month, the Broome Street Place was not only cozy and inviting, but the talk of the block as well. Women began approaching her whenever she was out in the community, whether in the butcher shop or at church, asking if she would help them spruce up their apartments. Gratified by the validation and excited about having something useful to do outside of her family responsibilities, she enthusiastically embarked on one project after another. While she was weaving her techniques up one side of Broome Street and down the other, she also used her teaching skills to bring English to those neighbors who wished to learn. In turn, they helped her attain greater fluency in Italian, to the never-ending pleasure of all who heard her speak their language with her Irish lilt.

One night toward the end of that first year, while Bradley lay asleep beside her, she reviewed the rewarding activities of her new life and realized that she'd begun to recapture part of the symmetry she thought she'd never find again. Slipping from beneath the covers, she pulled on her robe and shawl, then tiptoed out of the bedroom, closing the door behind her. Stopping at the other door in the hallway, she listened for the sleeping sounds of her daughters before continuing into the living room where she lit Emanuel's lamp on the desk. Moving so quietly that she could scarcely hear her own motions, she opened the bottom door of the armoire, reached way into the back, and removed the bottle of sherry and her special glass. *Just a little to celebrate*, she thought, as she filled the glass to the rim.

Anxious for his family to understand the uniquely energized city outside their neighborhood's boundaries—especially since they would be moving in that direction *someday*—Bradley used every available opportunity to expose them to the excitement and opportunity within their reach. He loved taking them on the subway, which began operating in 1904 from City Hall downtown all the way north to 145th Street, traveling the entire distance in 26 minutes. A favorite place to go—sometimes with the added company of Vincente, his parents, and other friends who'd been invited—was the newly completed main branch of the New York Public Library, which filled the entire block at 5th Avenue and 42nd Street. The library stood on the site formerly occupied by the immense Croton Reservoir, the smaller of two reservoirs built as part of New York's first water system. A series of underground conduits brought water from the Croton River in northern Westchester County, and then distributed the water to the City's faucets. After being torn down to make room for the library, which opened in 1911, the reservoir's function was replaced with a tunnel constructed in 1917, and the entire site immediately became an attraction for residents and visitors alike.

Inside the library's vast rooms, Bradley's family and friends would wander with intrigue, the heels of their shoes clicking against the marble floors as those sounds reverberated throughout the respectful silence and low whispers of patrons clustered in every corner. Irresistible smells of books and bindings would seduce them into spending the afternoon reading at one of the wide solid tables that looked like something Emanuel might have built. No one ever turned down a trip to the library, and when the children were older, they frequently made their way back to 42nd and 5th on their own to study their school lessons, or to read a book they couldn't afford to buy.

At other times, Bradley would escort his charges further north to Central Park where they would amble through the green and trees that reminded them of Washington Park in Albany, or where they would picnic by The Lake in warm weather, ice skating there in the winter using hand-me-down skates Bradley managed to find someplace. Often while they were in the neighborhood, they would walk the streets on the West and the East sides of the park, listening to Bradley's plans about moving to *this* grand place or *that* one—*someday*.

"Imagine if we lived *there*," he would say to Mimi, his arm linked in hers as they passed yet another impressive building.

"Yes, my dear, I can see it now," she would answer, never wishing to discourage him, always hoping, but believing in the possibility less and less every time they returned to Broome Street after such an excursion.

Sensing his wife's doubt, Bradley began widening her exposure to his dream by taking her into New York's night life one evening each month. Their routine generally included dinner at New York's largest restaurant, which was housed in the second incarnation of Madison Square Garden located at Madison Avenue and 26th Street. Dinner would then be followed by an adventure in movie-going, for which Bradley had developed a particular fascination. By 1910, New York's theaters were largely congregated in an area south of what would eventually become Times Square, and the collection of facilities could seat more than 150,000 people. Movies also contributed to the local economy through a burgeoning film production industry, well in advance of California becoming the preferred site. But in a movement contrary to the medium's enormous popularity, civic reformers and moral overseers were distraught about what they perceived to be the devil's imprint on a degenerating society—and they managed to engineer ordinances that prohibited anyone under the age of 16 from entering a theater without a parent. They also banned crime depiction on the screen while they had everyone's attention.

But Bradley's interest in this form of entertainment was undeterred by these conservative elements, and he was elated when the Regent Theater opened in 1913. The first of the great movie palaces, the Regent was built at 116th Street and 7th Avenue and elevated movie-going to a respectable option for the middle classes. The Strand Theater, which seated 4000, opened a year later. At these new movie houses, patrons could even enjoy a symphony orchestra, a ballet troupe, and opera selections, all before the feature film began. Never seeing himself as anything other than part of the middle class—*upper* middle class, actually, once he arrived where he was supposed to be—Bradley valued his access to such culture, and regularly included one theater or the other in his monthly evenings out with Mimi.

While these various day and nighttime jaunts were both admirable and appreciated, by the turn of 1921 even Bradley had grown impatient with his inertia about upgrading his family's surroundings. His steady employment and respectable income had enabled him to build a savings, and he was determined to keep his promise to Mimi about moving the family out of Broome Street.

Earnestly setting a plan in place, he pledged to follow through with their uptown relocation before winter descended. In his heart, however, now that his decision was being put in motion, he was surprised to feel reluctance about leaving. Not only did he have deep affection for the people, but his financial strength and local proximity enabled him to repay the Mentini's for their many kindnesses. He often helped them out with expenses when times were especially lean, or during the holidays when he wanted to ensure a bountiful assortment of packages under everyone's Christmas trees. He also loaned money to a number of other neighbors when their luck turned from bad to worse, and he almost felt guilty about walking away from them in order to improve his own circumstances.

Unbeknownst to him, Mimi had similar reservations, although she remained supportive of his commitment on their periodic walks through the streets bordering Central Park. But once she realized he was getting serious early in 1921, she persuaded him to at least wait until June or July before entering into any real estate pursuits.

"After all, Bradley dear, Cinnamon and Maggie still have several more months of school, and I'm fighting to keep Cinnamon focused on her studies as it is, with her summer trip to Albany scheduled to begin on the fourth of June. She receives a letter from Angela, Jay and David nearly every day in anticipation, and I've reached the point where I'm withholding the letters from her until she has completed her schoolwork. I'm afraid that if we begin heading in earnest toward our long-awaited new place to live, she will lose any remaining thread of concentration."

"Of course, Mimi, you're right, as always," he said, after hurriedly rearranging his thoughts. "Frankly, upon reflection, our plans will be far easier to pursue while she's away. I'll begin making inquiries about Upper East Side homes that might become available this summer, and Maggie can stay with Velita when we go exploring. Perhaps we'll have everything arranged by the time Cinnamon comes back in August."

"Well, that was far easier than I anticipated," she said, smiling and looking up into the shamrocks.

Squeezing her close to him, he smiled back at her and kissed her forehead.

"My love, you never give your persuasive charms the credit due. Now, let's enjoy the rest of our walk today. We'll have plenty of time for the dream to unfold in a few months."

Cinnamon awoke early, before anyone else in the apartment on Saturday, May 28, 1921, and climbed out onto the fire escape through the kitchen window holding a glass of milk in one hand and her satchel full of letters and journals in the other. She had discovered several years ago that private time was best stolen while her neighborhood still slept. Perched on the landing grid three floors above the sidewalk, she was usually the only one moving around at this hour, except for occasional factory workers riding their bicycles home from a late-night shift, or members of some other family who'd made the same private discovery and waved to her from a fire escape landing on the building across the street. On this particular morning, the sun edged up over the east end of her block, throwing just enough light over the roof for her to read by on her northern roost. Balancing her milk on the window sill, she pulled David's most recent letter from the satchel and read it again for the hundredth time.

May 12, 1921

Dear Cinn—

Please forgive me for not writing sooner. You were right to say that I seem to have slipped back into the neglectful correspondence habits I acquired while at Harvard. But I must tell you that my absence has been neither intentional nor personal. The fact is that Uncle Jonathon has been keeping me extremely busy at the mill. My responsibilities have increased substantially in the year since my graduation. (Can you even imagine that a year has passed already since all that pomp and circumstance?) And while I do enjoy my work, I sometimes grow frustrated that I have so little time to give back to you, and to the others.

Soon we will not have to be concerned with such distances, however, since you will be here for your summer visit in less than one short month. Jay and Angela claim to share the same level of excitement as mine about your arrival, but I doubt that could be true. You bring such light to my life through your letters—a light that pales when compared to what you bring in person. By the way, I don't think I've mentioned how impressed I am with the poetry you've been writing of late. You have a natural gift, and I do hope you pursue a course of study that will allow you to build and develop your substantial talent.

If I do not write to you often (or again) before you leave for Albany, please do not be angry with me. You know that I think of you every day, and that I love you very much. We will have plenty of time together before you can blink. Then we can leisurely catch up on our lives and discuss the many plans that everyone seems to be making. Meanwhile, work hard in the final weeks of school—and please give my best to your mother.

Always,
David

Resting the letter on her chest, she leaned against the red brick window sill and took a sip of milk. Below her, she could hear the shop doors opening and the voices of men who'd grown up together greeting good morning to each other at the beginning of yet another day. Despite all of her complaining about the crowded conditions and Bradley's delayed move to one of the northern neighborhoods—which she'd been hearing about for eight years—she realized that life on Broome Street had not really been so awful. People were nice to her, and she enjoyed her friends, although she missed Angela desperately. Vincente was fun, too, and she knew she was special to him because he was always around when he wasn't working, eagerly running any errand she asked of him. Even Maggie seemed easier to tolerate now that she was eleven and starting to grow up, although her paintings were usually in the way and very annoying. But all of this was, upon reflection, not so bad, and could easily be abided during the two years remaining until her high school graduation, after which she would move back to Albany on her own. At the rate Bradley was going, Cinnamon suspected that she would be long gone from Broome Street before his heralded relocation ever took place. Meanwhile, next Saturday—one precise week from this moment, in fact—she would be securing her luggage for the train ride that would take her home for vacation where she really belonged, and where her heart had always remained bound.

Bradley left for the offices of the *New York World—Telegram & Sun* later that same Saturday morning, excited about the Memorial Day parades and ceremonies that he and his colleagues would be covering throughout Manhattan and the other four boroughs. After World War I concluded with the Armistice of 1918, followed by the Treaty of Versailles in 1919, Memorial Day had become a major event across America, with some of the most elaborate celebrations being held in New York City. Ellis Island and the Statue of Liberty inspired passionate patriotic demonstrations, while the harbor and East River Waterfront provided a fitting stage for naval and other military displays.

Bradley felt a particular attachment to the holiday events because the war began just four months after he'd moved his family from Albany. Subsequently, his editorial work at his new job had addressed the Allies' progress over the four years of conflict, and then the aftermath and consequences during the three years since the war's end. His extensive knowledge of details, and of the human stories behind the lives lost, imbued Memorial Day with a profound purpose for him.

This year, the preeminent parade would take place in Manhattan on Monday, the route covering the island from City Hall downtown, up Broadway to Central

Park South, then right to 5th Avenue, turning north on 5th and traveling passed the luxurious mansions, before continuing to the park's upper end at East 110th Street. He had promised to ride the subway early Monday morning with Mimi, the girls and the Mentini family so they could find space at the best viewing position on 5th Avenue and East 65th. Because of his commitment to them, he'd arranged with his managing editor to cover parades on both weekend days, instead of on Monday. When he left the Broome Street apartment shortly after 7:00 that Saturday morning, Mimi and Maggie were still sleeping. But he said goodbye to Cinnamon and kissed her on the cheek as she was climbing back in through the fire escape window.

"Tell your mother that I expect to be home between 3:00 and 4:00. I'm assigned to a parade that's supposed to end with a ceremony at the main library around noon. Then I'll need a couple of hours to file my report and get ready for tomorrow's events. I'll be home as soon as I'm finished."

"All right. But remember that our street festival starts this afternoon. Mother plans to dazzle everyone with her interpretation of a few selections from Velita's recipes, and *I* have promised to help her with the cooking."

He stopped moving for a minute as he tried to visualize Cinnamon being at all useful in the kitchen, but he decided against any editorial comments that might hurt her feelings.

"Thanks for the reminder, Cinn. You have whetted my appetite in the most literal sense, and I'll race home as quickly as possible to enjoy the fruits of your labor."

Maggie had been playing next door with Maria and Rosa since mid-morning, and Cinnamon was surprised to discover how much fun she was still having with her mother four hours after they'd begun cooking. The two of them had started pressing tomatoes and garlic for the sauce while Maggie was still eating her breakfast, and they had not stopped working since Vincente left with Cinnamon's sister in tow at 9:00 A.M. Under Mimi's tutelage, her eldest daughter had finally learned how to carefully cut and then boil the strips of pasta, which had been prepared the day before and had been drying over night.

Most of the worries that weighed Mimi down were catalogued under Cinnamon's name, along with the lengthy list of skills her daughter must acquire in order to maneuver through the unavoidable responsibilities of womanhood. Thankfully, Velita had identified early-on the girl's aptitude for mastering a sewing machine's operation, in addition to her natural focus on detail and the patience for perfection when she set her mind to a project. Through Velita's steady instruction, enhanced further by Alberto's counsel on design and the constantly shifting seasons of style, Cinnamon was equipped by her early teens with above-average knowledge of fabrics, assembly expertise, and fashion terminology. As a result, her mother was grateful to know that her daughter would have little difficulty contributing to her eventual family's wardrobe and home decor, or to earning a wage if circumstances required. But regrettably, a similar interest was sorely lacking on the subject of cooking.

Mimi acknowledged that this deficiency was most likely inherited, recalling her own culinary ineptness prior to Amelia's death. That shortcoming had been more humorous than anything else at the time due to her comfortable economic circumstances. But Mimi believed that Cinnamon's limitations in the kitchen were far from funny. There could not be a more serious deficiency in an Italian woman—never mind that Cinnamon was *Irish*—than an inability to cook. In 1913 when they'd first arrived, her daughter's lineage might have been a valid excuse for such a problem in this neighborhood, but not any longer. Mimi doubted that anyone remembered or cared what country of origin actually ran through the girl's blood. She knew only that if Cinnamon wanted to marry well one day—or at *all*, for that matter—her aversion to the kitchen would have to be remedied. Thus the suggestion for today's activities spent together had been intended as a hopeful, albeit calculated, introduction to the craft of food preparation. Much to Mimi's delight, the day had turned out to be a full primer instead. Furthermore, her daughter seemed to be enjoying herself. She also learned quickly and appeared to take pride in her creations.

Sitting down at the small kitchen worktable, Cinnamon surveyed the variety of dishes in staggered stages of completion that were placed anywhere they could find an empty spot. Her smile was broad and refreshing.

"Look at all we've accomplished, Mother. Everyone will be so amazed to see what we've done. What shall we do next?"

"As soon as the pies are done, we'll start baking the lasagna. At the same time, we'll continue assembling the cheeses, and then we..."

Suddenly, their attention was drawn to a group of voices rumbling in the hallway outside their apartment door. They couldn't tell how many people were there, but they heard both men and women, some of whom sounded as if they were weeping. Others among the voices were pitched with emotion, and then one cried out loud, "Madre del dio, perchè questo è accaduto?"

Cinnamon had resisted the pressure to become fluent in Italian, but she recognized the words *Mother of God*—and the look of alarm on Mimi's face was chilling.

"What did she say, Mother? Who *is* that?"

"I don't *know* who it is," Mimi answered, wiping her hands on her apron. "But would you please open the door and find out?"

She walked across the tapestry rug, turned the knob and pulled the door toward her as her heart rate accelerated. Velita and Alberto were standing in the hallway surrounded by a dozen neighbors, men and women who'd been closest to Mimi and Bradley since the dress selection trip more than twelve years earlier. Velita and the other women had obviously been crying, but so had Alberto, which was particularly shocking. As the group moved in a single line through the doorway, Cinnamon and Mimi saw, at the same moment, Father Panito—their parish priest—entering the apartment behind everyone else.

"What's wrong?" Mimi asked, her face flushed and her hands gripping her apron. "Please. You are frightening me." Cinnamon could not remember ever seeing her mother afraid, and she felt numb as she watched and listened.

"Mimi," Father Panito began, moving to the front of the group, "sit with me." He put his arm around her and edged her gently to the sofa, where he eased her down beside him. "A merciful God is not always understood."

Velita began sobbing and Alberto held her close as one of the older women wailed, "No, non possiamo capire che il dio è merciful."

"Please, Father," Mimi implored, her eyes wide and glassy. "What has happened?"

"I'm so very sorry, my dear. It seems that earlier today Bradley was walking with a parade when he became ill and fell. Many people tried to help him, and…"

"Where is he?" she asked, jumping to her feet. "Have they taken him to a hospital? Alberto?" she continued, struggling to catch her breath. "Will you come with me to find him? I know he'll be looking for me."

Transferring his wife to the arms of a friend, Alberto moved to Mimi's side.

"My dearest," he began, embracing her and fighting to say the impossible, "we don't know how to tell you this, and I truly cannot believe it myself, but I'm afraid that Bradley did not survive what we've been told was a heart attack."

She looked up at him, her eyes searching for shamrocks, as her entire body began to tremble.

"You can't mean that he…" She could not bring herself to finish the whispered plea that was crushing every heart in the room.

"Oh, my precious, Mimi," he answered, pulling her close so he did not have to see her face. "It is so very sad. But yes, I have to tell you that Bradley has died."

Cinnamon felt as if all the air was being pressed out of her own lungs, while she watched her mother inhale Alberto's words and then expel a cry of anguish so wrenching and prolonged that she thought the echo would never leave her ears. At first no one moved or spoke as Mimi screamed, but when her body grew limp in Alberto's arms, with that haunting sound still coming out of her mouth, the room erupted into waves of grief. Cinnamon remained still as her young mind tried to process the enormity of what was happening in front of her. *Bradley has died...Bradley has died...*The sentence circled around and around in her head, searching for a place to stop, but unable to find one, because the vision would not come into focus.

Surrounded by flailing arms and soul-gutting calls to heaven, she continued watching as Mimi collapsed and grew silent. Several neighbors rushed out to find the physician who lived a block over. Velita and a few other women filled a bowl with water from the kitchen and carried it to the sofa where they began applying wet cloths to Mimi's face and wrists. Standing in the same spot she'd been occupying since the procession of people came through the door, Cinnamon felt starkly alone. No one thought to reach for her amidst the chaos. Isolated in the whirl of commotion, she was too frightened to cry, too stunned to speak or ask for help. In that moment, no one saw the young girl in her slip away, or the woman begin to emerge. *Bradley has died.* The words fell mutely from her lips. *Oh my God! What will happen to us now?*

What she did not understand—and would not for many years—was the irony that, on this day when she lost Bradley, she also lost something else equally as tragic. Just when she'd finally begun to know her mother and to enjoy the woman she'd never taken time to understand, the essence of Mimi had been extinguished with a cruel swipe. On the brink of rediscovering the peace for which she'd been searching, her mother had now been carried to the precipitous edge of nothingness, where she would hover, without Bradley and without purpose, for many years longer than mercy would have prescribed. In the interim, Cinnamon would grow up too quickly, without the counsel of the woman—or the love and protection of the man—she had not realized she needed so much. *Bradley has died.* The man whose presence could not be separated from a single one of her memories, almost as if *he'd* been her father, was gone.

While she would labor in the ensuing years to find her adult foothold without Bradley's familiar compass, mistakes would be made that would redirect fate's agenda for her. By the time she understood what had happened to her, she would have created quite a mess of things, and many more years would pass before a provident approach would bring her remaining tomorrows back into alignment. Occasionally, during those unsettled times, she would allow herself to conjecture how many wrong turns might have been averted if Bradley had not died, if he'd only lived long enough to move them away from Broome Street, and if she'd only been paying attention to him while he was still here.

But during the summer of 1921, she knew only that all the color had drained from her world. No one took her on excursions outside the neighborhood any more, and there was no trip to Albany in June. She did not see David, or her

Papa, or her own room in the Madison house. Instead, Joe Magglio and the Lark Street family came to Manhattan, where they stayed nearly two months adjusting to the shock of Bradley's loss and trying to help Mimi find her way back from her living tomb. Jonathon also arranged an extended visit for Jay and Angela, hoping they would bring comfort to Cinnamon that would help the healing process. Yet eventually, everyone had to return to their respective homes, leaving the dismembered Price family fragile and once again in the ever-watchful care of Velita and Alberto, who would now be asked to help save whatever life might be left, for Bradley's sake.

Before any of this unfolded, however—on that first night, on May 28, 1921—Velita and several of the neighbors helped Cinnamon clear away her mother's cooking projects, which were neither finished nor shared at a street festival that never happened. Working as if by rote with the women, she heard her little sister weeping in confusion in the next room as a blur of people lingered near Mimi on the sofa, changing the cold cloths on her head and kneeling in prayer on the carpet. Cinnamon's mind was stuck, unwilling to think beyond the moment. But she knew she was different than she'd been at dawn that morning out on the fire escape. She was somehow older now and able to distinguish a really bad thing from something silly like a letter that was too short, or too late. At length, as she dried the dishes, she thought about David and her Papa—men she believed she would see again, and touch, and hold—and in place of their faces was Bradley's, looking just as he did when he kissed her goodbye in the kitchen a few short hours ago, telling her how excited he would be to come home that afternoon. Without warning, her heart erupted in sadness and she dropped her head, her face covered in tears.

Velita saw her, held her, and then walked with her through the crowded apartment into the privacy of the room Cinnamon shared with Maggie. There the two of them sat in silence on the bed until Cinnamon fell asleep. Velita wondered what lessons the girl would take from a nightmare like this one, and she hoped that the legendary Irish spirit, of which Mimi had always spoken so zealously, truly did exist in abundance. Closing her eyes in the relative quiet, she could see Bradley's smile and the light on his face when he looked at Mimi. She could hear him laughing with Alberto while the men relaxed together after a long day at work. She thought of his patience when he helped Cinnamon write a school report, and she recalled how funny he looked when he posed as a model for Maggie. Trying to imagine all of their lives with that kind, gentle man ripped from those pictures, Velita shuddered and pulled the quilt up over her shoulders. Then she turned on her side, facing away from Cinnamon, as her own tears streamed onto the pillow. Just before she, too, welcomed a brief sleep, she crossed herself and whispered aloud a promise and prayer to the merciful God everyone kept insisting she trust.

"Alberto and I will do all in our power to carry on, to help Bradley's family survive this loss, to keep You in their hearts, and to remember the possibilities in life that he so proudly dreamed of bringing to them—*someday.* But I fear we'll need divine assistance with the children, especially with Cinnamon. So, please stay close to them, and to *all* of us. Also, I pray that you might send extra strength to Mimi, whose despair I cannot begin to imagine. Finally, dear Lord, take good care of our wonderful friend, who left us far too soon today and will be missed beyond words. You will not believe how much brighter heaven becomes now that he is there with you. Thank you. Amen."

November 26, 1921
Saturday Afternoon

Dearest David, Angela and Jay—

Thank you so much for the letters I receive almost every day from you. Without your correspondence, my life would be terribly grey.

Angela, in the three months since you and Jay left for Albany after your visit when Bradley died, there hasn't been much improvement in the circumstances here on Broome Street. Mother is the greatest concern to everyone, as she simply sits or sleeps most of the time. Occasionally, I see a bit of life spring forth. Once she even laughed out loud when Alberto was in the midst of a rather unkind imitation of the tailor at his shop. We were all quite hopeful that this was a sign of her recovery. But she retreated again into the place Velita refers to as Mother's netherworld, where she stays most of the time now—and where she is never out of Velita's sight. They've even prepared a special alcove for her in their front room, which is separated from the rest of the space by a tall, hand-painted privacy screen (very lovely, but a bit too bright for my taste) that Alberto says he traded for six custom-made dress shirts.

As a consequence of this new arrangement, Maggie and I either spend our nights at the Mentini's, or one of the neighbors watches over us in our own apartment. Maggie isn't happy with any of these changes, although she still works on her paintings (constantly), which are extraordinary, I must admit, despite the dreary colors she's been using of late. I don't think she likes me very much, and I cannot imagine why. I'm the only sister she has, after all, and I walk with her to and from school every day now. Furthermore, I never get in her way, even though we practically live on top of one another. I realize she lost her father. But we all lost him, and I'm trying to help her. She pulls away from me, though, when I reach for her hand, and she looks at me sometimes as if she were trying to make me disappear. Oh well, if she chooses to be hateful, then she'll find herself alone, which she claims is her wish anyway.

How was Thanksgiving in the Madison house? I'm sure the celebration was fabulous, just as it is every year. I do miss those times dreadfully. I was worried that the holiday would be grim down here, given all the sadness. Granted, there were moments when Bradley's absence was especially noticeable. All in all, though, we managed to celebrate with a respectable amount of joy, and Bradley must have been pleased to see us finally having a good time again. Alberto has not the first idea, however, how to handle a turkey, either in the preparation or the carving. Velita isn't any better at it, and Mother—who had a bit too much sherry on top of her other distances from us—wasn't exactly reachable to give them instructions. (By the way, there was a rather generous supply of spirits on hand throughout the neighborhood when Prohibition took effect last year. But since then, the bottles seem to be magically refilling themselves. Have you noticed the same thing happening up there?) Anyway, the whole turkey sequence was something of a disaster, although I found it to be the most comical thing I've seen in a long while.

Otherwise, I'm surviving from month to month, anxious already for my next summer visit up there with you. By the time I arrive, almost two years will have passed since I was last in Albany, and next June still seems an eternity away. But I know if I stay busy, it will be here in a blink. Please keep writing to me so I'm not left out of a single thing. I love all three of you very much!

Always,
Cinnamon

Repositioning herself at her mother's desk, Cinnamon wrote the complete letter two more times so all three recipients could have their own copy. Not wanting to make any mistakes, she had to start over twice when her pen skipped or when she inadvertently left out a word. But when she finished, she appreciated her need for perfection. Her letters and poetry were her own artistic expressions—the paper her canvas, the pen her paint. After she folded and slipped them one by one into separate envelopes, she wrote each name and address with a particular flair, dotting her i's with tiny hearts and looping the crosses of her t's. Alberto had promised to mail the letters for her, as he did with all her others, on his way to the tailor shop Monday morning.

Leaning back in her mother's chair, she looked across the desk at the other chair facing her, trying to picture her grandmother sitting there, as Mimi had so frequently described. But no image was forthcoming. Instead there was a knock at the door.

"Cinnamon, it's Vincente. I'm going to take the subway up to the library, and Ma said you could come with me—if you want to, that is."

She walked to the door, a little annoyed at having her quiet moment interrupted, but energized by the idea of going somewhere—anywhere—outside of the neighborhood. She hadn't been on the subway, or to the library, since Bradley died.

Pulling the door open, she was amused to see that Vincente looked and smelled as if he'd just come out of the bathtub. He was much taller than she was now, and he seemed to be growing broader in the shoulders every day. His dark eyes and complexion, and his thick jet black hair were enormously attractive, especially when he was well-groomed like this, and when the smells of the East River Waterfront had been soaped away. He'd become a good friend to her, and had been her salvation during that awful time after Bradley left. Lately, he seemed to be inventing even more creative ways to entertain her than he usually did.

"Why, yes, Vincente, I think that would be wonderful. Are we going to the library for any special reason, or just for fun?"

"Actually, Ma wants me to see if I can find a book for her on Victorian dress. But I felt like going out anyway, and I'm so very happy that you'll be coming with me."

He helped her with her coat. Then she pulled on her gloves, wrapped the scarf around her neck and put her knit hat in her pocket, in case her ears became chilly later on. Closing the apartment door behind her, she linked her arm in Vincente's and walked down the three flights of stairs with him, feeling quite grown up and uncharacteristically content.

Yes, she thought, as they began the five-block walk to the subway station, *having him around will certainly help the next year and a half pass more pleasantly, until I graduate and return to Albany, where I'm supposed to be.*

Chapter 10

March 25, 1922
Saturday Morning at 7:30

Dear Cinn,

The hour is very early, but I wanted to write before we get too busy. The most exciting thing has happened! We're moving! Yes, Papa decided that we should all live out at Fox Run now. Madison Avenue has become very crowded (and noisy) with everyone's new motorcars, and he says he wishes us to have the peace he remembers as a boy.

So, this weekend a lot of men from the mill will be here to put things in wagons for us and drive them to our new home. We won't be taking everything because David will continue living in the Madison house. Mama has been very happy with the plans and her new selections of furniture, dishes and such. She seems to be going or coming from shopping almost every day, and I've been busy with my school work—trying to earn better grades than you do, as I promised you I would. The rest of the time, I've been trying to cheer Angela up.

As soon as you can, please write to her. She's very upset about the move and the fact that I will be so far away. I keep telling her that, by motorcar, Fox Run is not even one hour from her. But she reminds me that one hour is a major change from a two-block walk. Mama has assured her that she will be able to visit whenever she wishes. Either David will drive her out, or her parents will bring her. She's already talking about coming every weekend, which would be fine with me, but I'm not sure about Papa's reaction. He told me he thinks I'm spending too much time with her. Of course, as usual, he doesn't understand. Only you know that I could not possibly spend too much time with her. There isn't enough time from here to eternity for that to happen.

Anyway, I need to say goodbye now and get ready to help with the day's activities. But I wanted you to be aware of the exciting changes going on up

here—and to know that when you come for your visit in June, you'll have a brand new beautiful room in our new (actually, it's quite old) house in the country. Won't that be wonderful?

All my love,
Jay

"No, this will certainly *not* be anywhere *near* wonderful," she said to Vincente, after reading Jay's letter aloud to him while they sat on her fire escape landing. "How could Papa—or especially David—conspire to make such a decision, without even consulting me? I truly cannot believe this is happening! They promised not to leave me out of a single thing!"

Jonathon had retained ownership of Fox Run, and had continued to employ the tenant farmer and his family to maintain the house and property, largely out of deference to his father's unwritten request. Nathaniel and Amelia had purchased the farm for Nathaniel's mother and father after persuading them to move from Ireland, and there the elderly couple lived the final happy decade of their lives. Jonathon carried warm memories with him about his monthly treks as a boy from Madison out to the country to see his grandparents. Their deaths a month apart from each other, when he was ten years old, left a hole in the magic of his childhood. But holding on to the farm had been his father Nathaniel's way of keeping them alive, and Jonathon was pleased that he'd resisted the tempting offers to sell, after Nathaniel and Amelia were also gone.

Now that his own children were getting older, Jonathon made a rather hurried decision to relocate to the country place ahead of Cinnamon's summer visit in 1922. The deed to the Madison house was transferred to David, enabling him to have a residence of his own in which to raise a family—and *soon*, Jonathon hoped. Sophie readily embraced this plan. Although she'd acclimated herself thirteen years earlier to what was clearly her husband's home, she'd been abiding for that entire time the indelible signs of Amelia and Mimi that confronted her in every room, regardless of the small changes she'd been permitted to make. This new expectation of applying her personal imprint on a house, free of any lingering ghosts, was exhilarating for her, and she immediately began organizing her ideas for Jonathon's review.

David, on the other hand, did not warm so quickly to the change when told that he would, in effect, become the new proprietor of the Madison house.

"With all due respect, sir," he began, while sipping brandy with his uncle in the warm confines of Emanuel's library, "what about Cinnamon and Jay? Shouldn't this place be rightfully theirs?"

"How noble of you to be concerned, my boy," Jonathon replied, the smoke from his cigar rising in front of his eyes and causing him to squint. "But you needn't worry about such things. Jay will ultimately inherit Fox Run, and Cinnamon's eventual husband—may God have mercy upon the unsuspecting man—will have the duty of providing a home for her. Even though you are not my son, we share deeply in McClinty blood, and you have more than earned your position in this family. Soon, I trust, you will be taking a wife of your own, and it is my wish that you build your life here in this house, where you belong, just as if you were one of my children. Now, let's toast your future and then discuss my thoughts about the timing and implementation of our residential transfers. Sophie will be calling us for dinner shortly."

Recognizing that resistance would be both futile and unwise, David leaned across the round reading table and clinked the side of his brandy snifter against Jonathon's.

"Thank you, uncle, for your generosity and your trust. Rest assured that this home will always remain guarded and appreciated."

Cinnamon's face flashed briefly through his mind as he suspected she would be less than thrilled with the development. Then his thoughts skipped to Lucille Bennett, the woman he could suddenly visualize being the one to call him for dinner.

Following David's graduation from Harvard two years earlier, he had not been making any noticeable effort—in his uncle's estimation, at least—to search for a suitable wife. Since this task was critical for a man of his nephew's stature and age, Jonathon had taken control of the matter. Notwithstanding David's self-conscious protests, dinner parties were organized at the Madison house with embarrassing regularity, each affair including among the guests an assortment of beautiful, eligible young women accompanied by their guardians.

Angela's mother and father were frequent attendees at these events, due to Mr. Preston's political connections. On more than one morning after such a party, Cinnamon's best friend overheard her parents discussing the odds of one girl winning out over another from the delicious choices available for David's marital selection. As time went on, Lucille Bennett's name surfaced more frequently than most. Angela chose to leave this information out of her letters to Cinnamon, however, knowing how possessive her friend was about David. But not until her visit to Manhattan after Bradley died did she realize that those tales of courtship over veal and baked potatoes would best be kept secret until the world ended, at the very earliest.

A few days before Jay and Angela were scheduled to return home in the summer of 1921, after spending a month amidst the mourning on Broome Street, the girls sat on the fire escape outside the Price apartment while Cinnamon shared a satchel full of her journals, poetry and letters. Angela, who was still treading gingerly around the family's grief, had agreed somewhat patronizingly to this review, overwhelmed at first by the size of the bulging bag. But after becoming privy to the private thoughts being revealed to her, she devoured line after line in disbelief.

"Margaret Elizabeth McClinty! How could you be so brash as to write these feelings down, much less mail them off to David? Whatever does he say to you in return, or does he respond to you at all?"

"Of course he responds to me, you silly thing, and he says he loves me beyond the expression of any words. Here. Read for yourself."

Angela took the letter being handed to her and read the passage that Cinnamon had marked with stars, in blue ink, along the outer margins.

"He says that he thinks of you every day, and that he loves you very much."

"Precisely."

"Cinn, I'm not sure that he means he *loves* you."

"Whatever else would he mean, Angela? He's always been there for me, as long as I can remember."

"Well, yes, but he's, um—so…*old*."

"Nonsense. Age is nothing. Look at you and Jay, for heaven's sake. And don't cock your head looking innocent at me. I know how you feel about my brother. *Everybody* knows, the way you goo at each other."

"As I recall, we were not talking about *me*. Besides, Jay and I are practically the same age, and we see each other every day. David, on the other hand, has already graduated from college, and he lives far away in Albany."

"A temporary situation. I'll be back there soon, the very moment I complete high school."

"But what if David gets married or something in the meantime?"

Angela blurted out the question, without thinking, before she could stop herself, and Cinnamon looked at her friend as if she were speaking Chinese.

"Married? Who on earth would he *marry*? That's the most ridiculous thing I've ever heard."

Having ventured well beyond her comfort level into this subject—and uncertain how she could possibly help repair this unfortunate misunderstanding—Angela decided to exit the issue.

"Actually, Cinn, I couldn't guess who he would marry, if he ever *will.* Maybe he'll become a priest," she could only hope. "And frankly, we shouldn't even be worrying about such things right now."

"I suppose you're right, although your priest idea is very funny. Anyway, Jay and Vincente will be back from the park soon with Maggie and the twins, and I promised Velita that we'd come help with dinner when they return. We can always go through the rest of these things tonight."

Much to Angela's relief, the satchel was not produced again, nor did the subject come up for the remainder of her Broome Street visit that troubled summer. During the trip back to Albany with Jay, she tried to find the words and courage to disclose her quandary to him, in need of his suggestions about how to handle his sister's hopeless infatuation. But every time she began a dialogue, the words became lodged in her throat. When they'd completed the five hour ride, she still had not been able to tell him. Then, after a few months, when Cinnamon's many letters each arrived without mention of the fire escape conversation or further questions about David's activities, Angela began to believe that the problem had blessedly gone away, without requiring her intervention after all.

On June 17, 1922, as Cinnamon's train pulled into Albany's Union Station, she saw her father waiting on the platform, trying to spot her through every window. But he appeared to be by himself, a supremely disheartening discovery. She'd been anticipating that everyone would be huddled in an anxious crowd, waiting to greet her when she arrived, so she was unprepared for this disappointment.

"Hello, my beautiful, grown up girl," Jonathon beamed, scooping her up in his arms before her feet had scarcely touched the ground. "I have missed you more than words can say. We *all* have."

"Hi, Papa," she said, hugging him back and feeling the warm infusion from his embrace. "I have missed you very much, as well."

When he pulled away to take a good look at her, she realized that she was far happier to see him than she'd expected to be. Having been gone so long, she'd almost forgotten how safe and important she felt in his presence.

"Where *is* everybody?"

"They're waiting for us at Fox Run," he said, hugging her close again and kissing her on the forehead. "They wanted to ride with me, but I convinced them that their welcome would be more fun, much louder and longer, out in the country than on this busy platform. I suspect that they are ready to burst by now. We've hardly been able to sleep, knowing your visit was so near."

Collecting her baggage from the porter, he carried a suitcase in each hand and walked alongside his daughter through the station lobby then outside to his motorcar parked on the street.

"Forgive me for staring at you, my sweet. I simply cannot believe how much you've grown and how lovely you've become. Of course, I realize that these two years have not been the easiest for you, but I wasn't prepared for the remarkable changes in you. You have weathered the hardships with a grace that reminds me of your Grandmother Amelia."

"Thank you, Papa. Oh my," she added, her attention diverting to the motorcar and the spacious seating visible as soon as he opened the door for her. "Is this yours?"

"Yes it is. We've had it for some time, but now that we live out in the country, the luxury has become more of a necessity."

"This is beautiful," she gushed, rubbing her hand across the leather cushion as he climbed in through the driver's side. "There aren't any motorcars on Broome Street. But we travel through the city without much difficulty, walking or taking the subway. This is wonderful, though. I love it."

Jonathon's eyes narrowed and the lines on his forehead became tight, as he tried to visualize the place where his daughter had been living and the dubious assembly of people he prayed had not caused her too much damage.

Margaret Elizabeth *Cinnamon* McClinty was introduced to Fox Run for the first time that Saturday afternoon when her father made a right turn off the main road, drove through the wide, open gate and headed straight up the long gravel driveway toward the line of people emerging from the side door. No matter which direction she looked, everything, everywhere, was green. Soaring pines and deciduous trees encircled the property, and more had seeded up close to the residence through the years, where their trunks had grown wide, their branches spread and linked together like a canopied ceiling over the house and lawn. A thick carpet of grass surrounded the pond, which was located to the right of the driveway and filled more than half the front yard. The water glittered and moved in the breezy sunshine and appeared to be a mirrored reflection of the sky above.

As the motorcar came to a stop under the covered portico in front of the bobbing, squealing crowd of family and friends, Cinnamon looked up at her father.

"Is this really where you live now, Papa?" she whispered.

"Yes, my dear," he answered, squeezing both of her hands between his, "and this is where you live, too, whenever you wish."

"I must tell you that I've been a bit angry with you for making this move without discussing it with me first, and I fully expected not to like it here at all. But I've never seen any place so magnificent."

"I had a feeling you'd forgive me."

Someone pulled the passenger door open, and a pair of arms reached around her from behind.

"Guess who!" announced the unmistakable voice.

"David," she said softly, allowing the arms to gently remove her backwards from the car. When her feet were on the ground, he spun her around, his hands still gripping her shoulders. Then he looked at her, and the gleeful expression on his face changed into a different sort of smile.

"Cinnamon. My God, I can't believe what I'm seeing. You've grown up so much, and you're so—so beautiful."

If no other event had taken place, if no other words had been spoken, she would have happily concluded a perfect visit in that moment. She did not see Angela standing on the other side of the motorcar, rolling her eyes.

During the balance of that summer, she became firmly committed to returning permanently to Fox Run in one year, following her graduation. Her father's new home was seductive in its beauty and simplicity, not to mention the endless space and peace. In the mornings, the touch of a warm gentle wind awakened her as it filtered through her window. After opening her eyes, she had to remind herself that she wasn't dreaming as she surveyed the French provincial four-poster bed with end tables on each side, the dressing vanity and oval mirror, armoire, chest of drawers, and a chaise lounge upholstered in a pale lavender chintz. Soft white folds of lace draped the window casings and fluttered gently in the same breeze that nudged her awake. Fresh and colorful flower arrangements—some in tall, willowy vases, some in short, rounded sculptures of petals—rested on every wood surface, imbuing a spray of provocative fragrances across the room. At the start of each day, she would pull herself up and lean against the headboard, breathing deeply and taking in all the details. *Mother would love this so much,* she found herself thinking, for some reason.

Her bedroom was the first one at the top of the curved staircase, enabling her to tiptoe down to the kitchen without the creaking floorboards in the rest of the upstairs hallway threatening to wake anyone else. A light shawl or sweater was all she needed over her nightgown as she began her bucolic morning routine. After picking up a piece of fruit on her way through the kitchen, she walked outdoors free from concerns about modesty, because as far as she could see in any direction, no one was looking back at her. Privacy was an unknown commodity on Broome Street, but a resource available in unlimited supply on these twenty-five acres of land. Sometimes, as she would meander through the early light toward the stone bench by the pond, she would see the heads of several deer fifty yards away turning to look at her. Then she would hear the swish of their legs against the tall grasses as they raced back into the woods, the soft sound standing out in the silence of her father's country air.

Sitting alone on the bench as the day brightened, she studied the curves and rounded corners of the sprawling Victorian house compared with the clean, sharp lines of the guest cottage and three red barns, which Jonathon had built during the past year. The two smaller barns had been placed further out, in the back of the property toward the edge of the woods. But the largest of the three structures, which was supposed to become a carriage house, according to her father, formed a triangle with the main residence and the guest cottage. The yard contained within the triangle was completely shaded by the mammoth trees that cooled the houses, as mild morning temperatures evolved into hot, sticky afternoons.

What a difference, she thought, *from the fire escapes and crowded sidewalks on Broome Street.* Dreading her return to Manhattan at the end of August, she took strength from Fox Run's timeless majesty, knowing that she would only have to wait a little while longer until this would be her home.

Meanwhile, in order to make the best of things, she needed to devise a plan that would secure more of David's time during the rest of this particular visit. He'd been extremely busy at the mill since her arrival, and the fact that he lived all the way in town on Madison Avenue meant that she saw him only occasionally during the week. Every now and then Jonathon brought him home for dinner between Monday and Friday. But the only time she could *count* on seeing him was on the weekends, when he would arrive on Saturday afternoon and stay until Monday morning.

His interests, she'd been dismayed to learn, were now centered mostly on his work. Even when he was at Fox Run, he seemed to prefer talking with Jonathon about one important thing or another rather than being with her. She remembered him going through a similar phase after he first came to Albany, when Jay and Maggie were babies, but she couldn't remember what she'd done to cure him—and she was frustrated without a plan. But periodically, when David was at the estate for the weekend, her mood would lighten at the sight of him emerging through the cottage door early on a Sunday morning, on his way to join her beside the pond. There he would lift her spirits, inquire about her hopes and dreams the way no one else ever did. He always listened to what she had to say and never told her that she was silly, or that she should be learning how to cook instead. He said he believed she could accomplish whatever she chose to do, and he continually encouraged her to pursue her writing.

"Who knows?" he'd asked, completely serious on one such morning in mid-August, when a light drizzle was doing nothing to interrupt their pondside conversation. "You seem to have been given a gift, and maybe you'll be another Elizabeth Barrett Browning."

"Thank you for your confidence, David, but I think your heart has inflated your expectations. Nonetheless, when I move back here next year, I'll have my whole collection of work with me, which I'll be anxious to show you."

"Yes, I'm sure we'll have time, Cinn. Meanwhile, keep writing. That's the beauty of your intended vocation. You can take your work with you wherever you go. I envy you that freedom."

But freedom to her wasn't *writing*—it was being *here*, living in moments like this one. Knowing that only two weeks remained until she would be leaving for Manhattan, she chose this opportunity to suggest a favor, since he seemed unusually receptive to whatever she had to say today. Not only was she in search of more time with him, but she was also looking for a way to keep a promise she'd made to Velita.

"Speaking of freedom, David, would you be willing to help me out with something—maybe this afternoon?"

"Like what?" he asked, recognizing the manipulative inflection in her voice.

"Like driving me downtown to see the Magglios."

Stretched out on his back on the grass, his hands behind his head, he looked up at her sitting on the bench and said nothing.

"Please? I promised Velita that I'd go see everyone on Lark Street and tell them firsthand how Mother's doing." When he still did not respond, she pressed on, adding a touch of aggravation to her tone. "If I could go by myself, I would. If we still lived on Madison, I could simply take the trolley and not bother anyone. In New York, I walk and take the subway all the time. But we're out here in the middle of nothing, and I am trapped, unable to go anywhere unless someone takes me, as if I were a child. You know how Papa feels about the Magglios, although I'll never understand why. So I cannot possibly ask *him*. But if you could suggest that we go for a day-ride, we wouldn't have to say *where* we're heading, and we would easily be back before supper. Please?"

Long before she understood the calculated power of silence, she remained quiet, staring down at him on the grass, her hands folded demurely in her lap.

"Oh, all right," he said, lifting himself to his feet and brushing the ground debris from his sleeves. "If your father ever finds out about this, though, I might be forced to return to California."

He was joking, but he was nearly right.

Joseph and his family were overjoyed to see Cinnamon, even with David as her escort. They knew he was Jonathon's nephew and business heir apparent, but they also remembered Mimi's kind words about him, which took preference for them at this happy reunion. The visitors were welcomed into the Lark Street apartment and then included in the Sunday afternoon meal, which was just being served when they arrived. Seated around the dining table that Cinnamon remembered as a child, they took turns telling stories. Christina, who was now seventeen, had decided that she wanted to become a teacher and was preparing to reenter school in the fall. Rebecca had learned to paint under the nurturing instruction of her father and two uncles, and although she'd completely lost the ability to walk, she was content and productive, carried downstairs every day to the shop where she helped customers and sold her own paintings with a respectable frequency. Anthony and Olivia still did not have any children of their own, but they never stopped trying while they shared in the raising of their two nieces and the management of the family business.

After the Albany updates were complete, time was suspended as the Magglios listened to sad descriptions about Mimi and her struggle to cope without Bradley. None of them had adjusted to the man's loss either, and they could only vaguely imagine the dark place where their beloved lady friend now lived. But their faces brightened with news of Maggie and the twins, and of Vincente, who had been the first member of their family to graduate high school the previous year. Sadly, the boy's accomplishment had been dwarfed by Bradley's death, but he had never complained—a fact Joseph noted while blotting his eyes with his napkin.

"He was so quiet about it while we were there last summer during that dreadful time, just taking care of his sisters and helping wherever he could. I'm afraid everyone forgot about him and his proud achievement. Did Velita and Alberto ever do anything for him after we left?"

"No, Joseph, they didn't," Cinnamon answered. "I guess taking care of Mother, and Maggie, and me too, has occupied all of their time. But Vincente hasn't said anything to me about it, and I don't think he was troubled or disappointed."

"Is he still working on the waterfront?"

"Yes, every day, and he's also designing garments at home, which Velita then cuts, sews and markets on the sidewalk racks for extra money. His ideas are really quite good, and he never seems to run out of new ones."

"Tell him that, one day, his uncles will reward him for his hard work, and let him know that we're very proud of him—*all* of us—his aunts and nieces, too."

David had moved from the table to the chair by the front window and was checking the time on his pocket watch.

"Cinn, I wish we could stay longer, but we do need to be leaving. I didn't realize how late it's become."

Everyone stood up reluctantly and began exchanging goodbyes.

"Thank you, sir, for your hospitality," David said, shaking Joseph's hand.

"You are very welcome, son. We're glad to finally meet you. Were you aware that we knew Miss Amelia?"

"Yes. Mimi told me all about you and the Madison house art projects. That seemed to be an exceptionally bright period for her and for my grandmother."

"It was for us, as well. Two finer women never graced the earth, except the ones in this house, of course," he added with a quick smile. "And they both spoke of you often, with great fondness. Mimi was so pleased when you moved back to Albany from California. Good God, we do miss her—and Bradley. My mind simply cannot accept that we won't see him again."

"I understand. But I think he and Mimi would be happy to know the rest of us came together for this visit, and that Cinn was the organizer."

Joseph nodded a warm agreement, attempting to reconcile the fact that this fine young man was any relation whatsoever to Jonathon.

"Take care of yourself, my boy, and of our young lady here."

As David drove the motorcar away from Lark Street, Cinnamon watched the old buildings grow small through the rear window. Memories rushed in with visions of trolley car rides with her mother, the cottage, Bradley, laughter, and Madison Avenue.

I'm too young, she thought, *for so much to have changed!*

Neither she nor David spoke for several miles, but as the edge of the sky faded from a pinkish grey to black, she turned to look at him.

"Do you think we're going to be in a great deal of trouble when we get home?"

"There's no doubt in my mind."

"I'm sorry."

"Don't worry, Cinn. We'll get through it. And even though I'll never say this to your father, I'm very glad we went there today."

"When I move back here next year, maybe we could go again."

"Maybe."

Their peaceful ride to Fox Run ended with the eruption of Jonathon's fiery temper. After discovering that the two of them weren't dead, he made David tell him where they'd been. Cinnamon was then sent to her room and could not hear the rest of her father's explosive reaction, especially when Jonathon ushered his nephew into the small library and closed the door. But her summer visit effectively came to a conclusion that night.

She did not see David again until she left Albany two weeks later. Her father, Sophie, Jay and Angela gathered on the platform to send her off. But David arrived late, running up to the family just as her train was starting to pull out of the station. Instead of kissing him goodbye, she could only wave to him through the window, watching him disappear down the track, just as he had when she was a little girl.

Saturday, August 26, 1922
Aboard another train taking me away from home

Hear ye, hear ye! This is not going to happen anymore!

After straining unsuccessfully to hold her tears at bay, she had removed her journal from one of her bags, hoping that, by writing, she might calm herself. Then, as the view outside changed from brick buildings, steeples, and factory stacks to the sloping hills and narrow roads of the countryside, she found herself wondering if these tracks ran anywhere near Fox Run. The scenery looked familiar, but she couldn't remember hearing the rumble or whistle of a train while she'd been here. Still, she almost felt as if she could reach through the window and touch the gentle boundaries of her father's estate.

I'm so tired of always watching everything I love fade in the distance behind me when I've been forced to leave, and when I'm perfectly happy to remain in one place. But this is the last time I'm going to watch people disappear as I'm driven away—the last time I want to see yet another home sink into the horizon. Next year I will begin a new life, with the freedom to come and go when <u>I</u> decide the time is right to do so. I will make my own decisions—<u>all</u> of them. Yes, things will be very, <u>very</u> different once I've assumed control over my own life. After that, nothing can go wrong. Then these infuriating tears will dry up and will be carried off in the wind like dust.

Eventually, the rhythmic clacking of the rails managed to calm her when her writing would not, and she fell asleep against the soft high back of the passenger chair.

"Please forgive me, Alberto, if I'm being impudent, but I would feel terribly uncomfortable attending any sort of graduation celebration next month that does not equally feature Vincente." Cinnamon was addressing him on the sofa of her apartment after asking him to come over, on the pretense of repairing a leak in the kitchen. "Your son was the first in your family—and one of the first in the entire neighborhood, I might add—to receive his diploma. But no one suggested any parties for *him*."

"If you'll recall, young lady, we had just lost Bradley."

"Of *course* I remember. How could I not? But two years have passed since then, and still there have been no congratulatory efforts from anyone on his behalf. How could you possibly imagine that I would welcome any form of festivity acknowledging *my* similar achievement, unless he is also recognized?"

Alberto studied Mimi's eldest daughter, realizing that he hadn't paid much attention to the fact that she was growing up. This was no longer a child speaking to him. Somehow, she'd become a woman, without giving notice, and although he wouldn't exactly call her beautiful, she had a striking presence that was more attractive the longer he looked at her. She was taller than most women he knew—nearly his own height, which, if he stood up straight, was close to six feet—and her legs and arms were long and graceful. She wasn't too thin, nor had she acquired the round look already carried by many girls her age. Instead, her shape was trim, and her firm curves were subtle but intriguing. He did notice, however, that her feet were quite huge, and he suddenly wondered where Velita had been finding shoes for her. But he lost his train of thought on her face. Her large, round brown eyes had the same specks of green as her mother's, and her fair freckled skin had taken on a soft, rosy sheen that almost had a velvet appearance. Finally, spilling over her shoulders were thick glossy curls of red hair that had evolved into a deep russet hue. Sitting perfectly still, her hands resting in her lap, she could have been a model for one of Maggie's paintings.

"Alberto?"

"Yes. Forgive me. What did you say?"

"I *said* that unless the party honors Vincente, too, I do not wish to have *any* party."

"All right. Velita and I will make the addition, and we will let everyone know, including my son. I hope he has no objection to this."

"He won't. I already mentioned that I was going to talk with you."

"Indeed. I must say that he is very lucky to have you, Cinn."

"Yes, well, his friendship has been very important to me, and I hope we can continue to help one another, even when I'm living in Albany again."

Alberto leaned back into the corner of the sofa and crossed his arms on his chest.

"When are you planning to do *that*?"

"Next month. My summer trip this year will actually be my journey home."

He could not believe she was referring to this decision as if it had already been made. He had certainly not been informed of any such thing.

"And when were you planning to share this fantasy with us?"

She was on her feet and had walked over to the desk.

"I've been discussing this with Velita for a year now. And it's not a fantasy."

"Oh? And what about Maggie and your mother? Have they also been included in your plans?"

"They belong here, with you. This is their home, and since I know Bradley left instructions in his will that placed you in charge of his savings, I don't have to worry about them."

"How did you find out about Bradley's savings?"

"I *listen*. The way everyone is crowded together in your apartment, no one can utter a word without being overheard."

He remained seated, looking at her as if that fact had never occurred to him.

"Please don't be angry with me, Alberto. I love you and Velita very much, and I will come back to visit all the time. I'll also help with Mother and Maggie in as many ways as possible. Maggie could even come stay with me at Fox Run for awhile, if that would make things easier. But *my* home is in Albany, with my Papa, and I'm old enough now to go there if I choose."

"And Vincente? Does *he* know you're leaving?"

"Yes, he does. I've talked with him about it more than anyone else."

"I see," he said, standing up and moving toward the door. "You seem to have worked everything out very nicely—for *yourself*. But please allow me to suggest the possibility that a few fine points might have escaped your consideration. I will leave you to discover any such oversights on your own, however. Meanwhile, as agreed, I will tell Velita to include our son in your high school celebration honors."

He turned the doorknob in his hand then looked back over his shoulder at her, noting that she didn't seem quite as confident as she had a moment earlier.

"We love you, too, my dear. Although this may seem of little importance to you right now, please remember that we will always be here should you ever need us, no matter where your life might take you."

She didn't how soon she'd find herself falling back on those words.

A total of seven students were going to be honored from the neighborhood at the graduation festival. The idea had been Vincente's, one he suggested to Cinnamon during a fire escape conversation following her exchange with

Alberto. Velita was sewing in her own flat that afternoon rather than at the tailor shop, keeping watch over Mimi while working on a gown that one of Alberto's clients needed for a wedding the following week. Vincente, who had worked through the night on the waterfront, had just awakened two hours earlier and had been waiting for Cinnamon to come home from school. She'd completed the last of her exams that morning, and when he saw her walking up the street, he brought his sisters over to the Price apartment to join her. Before long, Rosa and Maria were sitting on either side of Mimi's desk while Maggie made an initial sketch of them on her easel. Vincente climbed ahead of Cinnamon through the kitchen window and stepped out onto the iron landing. The late May weather was warm, but absent the smothering humidity that would come all too soon, making this a favored time of year for fire escape sitting.

"Here. Take my arm," he directed as she strained to save her modesty, pushing the folds of her dress down over her legs with one hand while accepting his help with the other. Then she leaned back into the kitchen to reach the two glasses of lemonade she'd placed on the edge of the counter.

"Thanks," he said, taking his glass and easing down beside her on one of the vegetable crates they used as chairs. "I heard about your *meeting* with my father. Ma told me."

"Really? What did she say?"

"Something about your being brash and rather disrespectful, but all on my behalf, which is the only thing that saved you."

"That's definitely the abridged version," she said, smiling at him and playfully pushing against his shoulder.

"What matters, Cinn, is that I appreciate your wish to include me in the party, and I've been thinking that you make a lot of sense. *Everyone* who graduates should be celebrated, and not just the two of *us*. There are at least a half dozen or more students in the neighborhood, from my class all the way up through yours, who received a diploma without a get-together. Why not feature them and their families, too? Maybe we could start a new tradition—something that people could plan on every year—something that might even inspire more of us to make graduating a priority. How do you feel about that?"

"What a grand idea!" she said, reflexively taking hold of his hand. "You are so thoughtful. What does your mother think?"

"I haven't mentioned it to her yet. Maybe we could tell her together."

Looking up at his strong handsome face, and into his eyes that were such a deep brown they were almost black, she realized how much she admired him. She felt at ease with him, and she trusted him, because his heart and intentions were as pure as they'd been when she arrived ten years ago. Yet he was stronger and more complex now, a study in contrasts with his rugged waterfront experience and his creative talent for apparel design, a skill he'd kept to himself when he was younger but now spoke of with open ambition.

"Imagine the power," he'd said, during one of their recent fire escape dialogues, "if wealthy, influential women from the uptown neighborhoods depended upon *me* for the designs that would make them look more beautiful and elegant than their contemporaries—or better yet, than their rivals."

He was the only person she knew, now that Bradley was gone, who had living dreams and who spoke about them with passion. Now for the first time, as she continued to look up at him, the thought crossed her mind that she was going to miss him when she was back in Albany. She would miss these conversations and the opportunity to watch him become someone important, which she was convinced he would do. But in less than a month, she would be leaving, no matter how she felt about him or anyone else.

"Yes, let's tell Velita together. The neighbors will be excited as well. Celebrating a group of graduations will be absolutely marvelous! What a wonderful idea of yours, and what a special memory for me to take with me to Albany! Oh, by the way, if you have time later this week, would you come with me when I visit Mr. Falzone's leather shop? I've been watching him work on a trunk that would be perfect for my trip. I'm hoping he'll barter with me, trading the trunk for the seamstress work he's been saying his wife needs to have done for the children. But you're so much better at dealing back and forth than I am. Would you help me?"

He paused and stared at her, as if he wanted to say something. Then he turned his face away from her, toward the fire escapes across the street.

"Of course, Cinn," he answered, with what almost sounded like a catch in his voice, "just let me know when you'd like to go."

The first annual Broome Street Graduation Festival filled the entire block in front of the Mentini and Price apartment buildings, with food and craft kiosks stocked by the personal efforts of cooks and artists across the neighborhood. Even Maggie had been persuaded to bring out part of her collection of watercolor canvases and charcoal sketches to offer for sale. On the west end of the block, on the corner of Broome and Mulberry, a platform had been erected for the seven graduates. Cinnamon, Vincente and five others of varying ages in between them, who weren't too self-conscious to participate, were introduced at noon. They were honored with framed, embroidered certificates that spelled out in red, white and blue yarn their names, their dates of graduation, and the words **Broome Street Graduation Festival, June 16, 1923**. The weather became more overcast as the day wore on. But no rain fell on the hundreds of jubilant people milling about, laughing, eating and openly celebrating American opportunity and their seven proud representatives in possession of their new high school diplomas.

Velita and Cinnamon alternately went upstairs throughout the day to sit with Mimi, who had refused to let anyone take her past the apartment door. At one point, when it was Cinnamon's turn, she was sitting in the kitchen, rolling another batch of cookies into little balls and then pressing them flat on a baking sheet. Looking up, she saw that her mother had come out from behind the privacy screen and was watching her.

"Hello, Mother," she said, as she usually did, talking mostly to herself and not expecting any response, since Mimi rarely spoke at all any more. "I'm preparing what surely must be my ten-thousandth round of cookies for the masses outside. Perhaps you'd like to help me."

"No. But thank you for asking. You're doing quite well on your own, I'm happy to see."

Cinnamon dropped the ball of dough in astonishment and immediately walked across the bare wood floor to Mimi's side.

"Mother! *Hello*!"

"Don't repeat yourself, dear, or you'll sound like an old woman."

"All right," she answered, not catching the humor as she tried to figure out how she was going to get Velita and Alberto up here to witness this. "Come. Let's sit on the sofa together. I'm so happy to see you—to *talk* with you, I mean."

"Then don't wait so long next time. Your hair seems different," she said, reaching up to lift the curls off her daughter's shoulder and smooth them down against her back, "and so lovely. You're old enough now that you could start wearing it up, wrapped softly and secured with Amelia's combs."

"Yes, I suppose I could," Cinnamon replied, peering out the window to see if she could spot Vincente. "Maybe you can show me how to do it. I'm afraid I've tried, but it either ends up tangled or falling off-center."

Mimi brought her hands to her mouth and began giggling like a child.

"Then let Bradley help you when he comes home. He'll straighten it out for you."

Turning from the window toward her beautiful, heartbreaking mother, who'd found her way out of captivity for such a brief moment and whose focus was now on the floor, Cinnamon was unable to stop the slow stream of tears rolling down her cheeks. The depths of this tragedy went far beyond the limits of what Father Panito's merciful God should allow, although the priest and everyone else kept assuring her that everything in life had some divine purpose, whether we could see it or not. But in the pathetic remnants of her mother, she could not detect the faintest flicker of any divine presence.

Thirty minutes later when Mimi was once again sleeping on her cot behind the screen, Amelia's granddaughter sat at the kitchen table rolling more cookie dough as if nothing had happened. She had also decided not to mention the incident to anyone. What difference did it make anyway? If there'd ever been a doubt, Cinnamon was now convinced that the woman in bed across the room would never miss her when she went back to Albany, no matter how guilty Alberto tried to make her feel.

After surveying the trunk, along with the other satchels and bags that Cinnamon was packing, Alberto set out to find someone with a motorcar who might be willing to help transport the girl to the train station in a few days. The tailor for whom he worked offered to speak with the shop's landlord, a wealthy young gentleman who owned a number of buildings in the fashion district and who drove to and from his uptown home in a large motorcar.

"He's very kind," the tailor told Alberto, "and he's always been generous with offers of assistance whenever he comes by. If he is open to this idea, his motorcar would easily accommodate your whole family, in addition to Cinnamon and her baggage."

Mr. Gregory Stafford was generous, indeed, and he caused quite a stir on Broome Street when he arrived on the morning of June 29, 1923, to escort people he'd never met to Grand Central Terminal. Neighbors gathered from blocks away to witness the departure, amazed at Alberto's resourcefulness and fascinated by the shiny black vehicle that looked terribly out of place parked next to the jumble of sidewalk racks and displays. Cinnamon's appearance in front of the apartment building reminded them, however, that this was a somber occasion. They were losing one of their own.

Over the years, they'd grown familiar with her summer absences, but this time they were told she would not be coming back, at least not to live. While they were happy that someone from the neighborhood had a chance at the opportunity they all spoke of with such reverence, they were saddened she had to go so far away to find it. Somehow, they'd come to believe she might stay with them, marry and bring more babies to Broome Street. Judging by the expression on Vincente's face, they had not been alone in their expectations, and they were all beginning to feel quite sad for him. But they would not discuss this now, not while they had an uptown stranger in their midst, one who was clearly enjoying the robust crowd's unity and camaraderie.

In Gregory Stafford's Upper East Side neighborhood, populated with decorum and restraint, a scene like this would never happen. He warmed easily to the informal atmosphere, and was delighted when he was introduced to the traveler causing all the commotion. She was an attractive young woman, with hair the color of autumn apples piled haphazardly on top of her head beneath a floppy grey hat. Furthermore, she turned out to be vastly amusing as she ended up sitting on top of her fresh leather trunk, which had to be placed on the floor in the back seat for lack of any other space. He imagined that this day had begun with her plans to look graceful and sophisticated in her grey-blue travel dress with the long skirt and ruffled sleeves. Now, with that same skirt spread unceremoniously over the trunk and her hat barely hanging by the pin, he suspected that her newly-minted maturity would be fully unraveled by the time they reached the station.

Alberto sat in the front of the motorcar, beside Mr. Stafford. Vincente, Velita, the twins and Maggie were scrunched together in the back, with their feet propped on the edges of the trunk. Satchels rested on all of their laps, and they could not have looked more uncomfortable. *There must have been a less chaotic way to accomplish this journey*, Cinnamon was thinking. But no one had given her any suggestions, *so how could they hold me responsible for the mess*? The only good part about this morning was this nice man's willingness to drive them. How they ever would have managed without a motorcar was something she cared not to consider. Of further relief were the women who'd volunteered to stay with Mimi while everyone was making the trek to midtown. Their presence in the apartment made the final quick kiss on her mother's cheek much easier for Cinnamon, and, as anticipated, Mimi wasn't really there to say goodbye anyway.

When Mr. Stafford started the engine and began slowly navigating the cobblestone pavement toward Mott Street, the neighbors all pulled together and began waving at the same time behind the car. When Cinnamon saw them through the back window, her breathing became shallow and her eyes began to sting. *This isn't supposed to happen when I'm going to Albany,* she thought, as Mr. Stafford turned left turn and the crowd disappeared, and as she caught the edge of Vincente staring at her from his place on the back seat.

She experienced those same feelings again at Grand Central Terminal, when she was watching the family on the platform through the window, as the last passengers and baggage were being loaded. Maggie, who at thirteen looked remarkably like their mother, was standing between Velita and Alberto and appeared to have tears on her face. If true, this was a puzzle. She could not imagine a single reason why Maggie would be sad to see her go. Rosa and Maria were preoccupied with the other people and activities on the platform, but intermittently turned to wave at her. Then there was Vincente, who stood apart from the others. His eyes were fixed on her face framed in the window, but oddly, he wasn't waving or in any way attempting to elicit a response from her. What she could not have known was that he was sketching every detail of her in his mind.

With a short jolt, the train began moving forward, and she was surprised by the unexpected familiarity of emotion rising inside of her. For once, no one was making her leave today. Besides, she was heading *toward* home, not away. So why was she sad? And where was the long-awaited gratification from making her own choices? Confused and annoyed with herself, she leaned back against the passenger seat and slipped into the memory of a train ride more than ten years earlier. Bradley and her mother had been in the row ahead, and Mimi had just handed her the pink cotton play bag—which she'd saved all this time, by the way, and which was packed in her trunk—to use with Maggie, who'd been sitting beside her. Turning now to look at the strangers across the aisle and at the empty seat to her left, she felt a tug in her chest. No one had explained to her that growing up required learning, as a first lesson, how to be alone.

Closing her eyes, she tried to fall asleep as she usually did after leaving a train station, but she could not. Eventually, she removed her journal from the largest of her satchels, but her words weren't coming either. While she watched hypnotically as the towns and countryside sped past her window, the hours slowly advanced and her thoughts gradually began shifting to the family waiting for her at Fox Run. Finally, by the time the train began nearing Albany, she was starting to believe again that her decision to leave Broome Street had been the right thing to do.

Chapter 11

The strongest of our heart's wishes rely upon the deepest of our mind's resolve—
and, sometimes, on a few cents for the subway.
August 12, 1923
M.E.M.

Pure bliss was the only way to describe the impact on her senses when she awoke in her own private, perfect bedroom on June 30, her first morning back at Fox Fun. The smells of muffins, bacon and coffee being prepared had found their way upstairs and had lured her out of the cocoon she'd made from her sheets and comforter.

First, she stretched her arms high and wide while still sitting on the bed, as if to embrace the moment. Then she got up and walked to the window. The early sky was overcast, and the tree branches sheltering the yard held the darkness captive, despite the hour. Directly across from her and facing the rear of the main house was the guest cottage, where she could see a lamp lit in the front room. The curtains were open, and a warm circle of light reached out onto the grass.

"This is the beginning," she spoke quietly, not a second thought remaining from the previous day, as she pulled her white quilted robe on over her blue pajamas. Then she pushed her feet inside the new yellow slippers crocheted by one of Velita's neighbors, noticing as she did the intricate variations of stitching and the double thickness of yarn, all of which must have taken days to complete. After brushing her hair and fastening the sides back with two white combs, she took a satisfied look at herself in the mirror then opened her door and bounced down the stairs.

Jonathon and Sophie were sitting at opposite ends of the extended dining room table, eating a mixture of fresh fruits arranged in white china bowls. Their view of each other was obscured by the two-foot high centerpiece made from flowers Irene had cut from the garden yesterday. During dinner conversations last night, members of the family kept peering underneath and around the arrangement to see the parties with whom they were speaking, with no one suggesting that the impediment be temporarily relocated to the sideboard. Jonathon and Sophie still did not seem to mind the obstruction, particularly since neither of them appeared the least bit interested in talking to one another, as they read quietly to themselves.

He was immersed in the *New York World*, which he began purchasing every morning at the Delmar Rail Station several months after moving to the country. The daily drive—a half hour round trip at dawn—had become something of a social event for him. By 1920, the annual production of U.S. automobiles approached two million vehicles. Motorcars became accessible commodities for forty percent of Americans, not only enabling them to drive to the commercial products and services they heard advertised on their new radios, but also to live further away from their jobs. As a consequence, a number of Jonathon's Albany Area Chamber of Commerce associates had moved their families south of the city limits around the same time he'd relocated to Fox Run. Those were the gentlemen with whom he met in the mornings at the Delmar station. They had collectively discovered a business advantage to reviewing the financial and editorial pages well ahead of their rivals and competitors. The newspaper, which was printed and loaded in New York City by midnight, was not distributed in downtown Albany until later in the day. But the train generally reached the Delmar station by 6:00 A.M. Barring a family illness or an emergency at the mill, Jonathon was always there to greet the arrival with his friends.

Aside from the fellowship the men experienced while waiting together, Jonathon looked forward to the fresh smell of ink as the bundles of newspapers tied with twine were dropped on the platform by the conductor, the thuds of paper on concrete signaling another round of printed secrets about to be revealed. Then, after the twine was cut, the gentlemen handed the conductor a nickel, picked up their copies from the stack and scattered off to their respective homes or places of business to learn details of major news events, economic trends, and various political happenings. Half of all American homes now had radios that delivered much of this same information. But nothing was quite as graphic, tantalizing and timely as the *New York World*, and Jonathon was intoxicated by the anticipation every morning. Normally, during the week, he would return to Fox Run and skim through his paper over a hurried breakfast. Then he would rush off to the mill, or to one of his many business meetings at or near the capitol building. But on a Saturday such as this one, when he didn't need to leave for town until much later, he luxuriated in reading every column, on every page, while lingering over his meal.

As Cinnamon reached the bottom of the staircase, she could hear his voice coming from behind the open paper, which was stretched across the front of his face.

"President Harding must believe he can distract us from his administration's vice and corruption by traipsing up and down the west coast to campaign for America's partnership with the League of Nations. Doesn't he think we'll find his position grossly hypocritical, in light of his strong stand against the League up to this point?"

He appeared to be speaking to himself, since Sophie wasn't answering him, and since he didn't seem to waiting for a response from her.

"Good morning, Papa," Cinnamon chirped, walking to the far end of the table where she surrounded his head and shoulders in a hug and a series of kisses. "How *dare* President Harding interfere with our morning? And Sophie," she added, circling back to the other end, "here's a kiss for you, too."

Resting the open newspaper on the table, Jonathon shifted in his chair.

"What a wonderful thing to have you home, at last. As I'm certain I told you a dozen times yesterday, I'm very proud of you, my dear, for completing your education, and for coming back to us."

"Thank you, Papa. I didn't think this time would ever arrive."

"Well, now that it has, I do hope you will quickly make your place here."

Whatever does he mean by that? she was thinking.

"Along those lines," he continued, "I trust that you will shed any of the unsuitable behaviors that might have accompanied you, and that you will not, for example, attempt to join us again in the dining room while still wearing your nightclothes."

"Jonathon," Sophie admonished, "is that really necessary on her first morning with us?"

"Yes," he answered, delivering the look that both women had seen before and that cautioned against further challenge. "She cannot be faulted for habits she's acquired in that Godforsaken place she's been living. But now that she's with us again, she needs to conduct herself appropriately."

Feeling hurt and a bit stunned at what she was hearing, she was also tempted to remind her father that, since she was standing right there in the room, he could speak directly to her and not through Sophie. But she chose the least hazardous response.

"I'm sorry. I was just so excited to come downstairs that I guess I wasn't thinking."

"Good. Then we'll see you shortly."

She watched as he lifted the newspaper in front of his face again, and as Sophie gave her an *I-can't-help-you* glance before returning her focus to the book she was reading. Unwilling to acknowledge the thoughts of Broome Street that suddenly rushed in on her, she spun around and walked out of the room. Then she turned left and went straight down the hall, through the kitchen's swinging door, to see Irene.

Drake and Irene had been in Jonathon's employ since he'd first purchased the Madison house more than eighteen years earlier, and they'd stayed on with him following Mimi's departure. While both of them were invited to continue their work after the move to Fox Run, Drake had respectfully declined. He'd explained to Jonathon that he preferred not to travel so far from his grandchildren, who were now growing up near his apartment on the other side of Washington Park. Happily, David had intervened, telling Drake that his services and loyalty were of great value, especially now that the Madison house was going to be David's sole responsibility. Without realizing what had happened, Drake found himself promoted to assistant in charge of household management, with responsibilities that included control of operational expenses. He was also given an increase in pay and an allowance to purchase suits of clothes more appropriate for his new position.

Irene was pleased with this good fortune for her long-time friend and coworker. They had been together for more McClinty parties and crises than she could count, and they would always be united in the silence they kept about those stories. But she had never married and had lived all this time at her family home in the village of Guilderland, the eastern edge of which was just two miles from Fox Run. For almost twenty years, she'd walked each morning to the local depot, where she caught the train that took her on a thirty-minute ride to Albany's southwestern line. There she would get off and walk two blocks to catch the trolley that eventually stopped right in front of the Madison house. The whole trip took an hour, and she had traveled the route faithfully every day of the week. Frequently, she would do it again on Saturdays or Sundays, whenever large functions required her assistance, because working for the McClintys never stopped being worth the effort.

When told about the family's relocation to Fox Run, Irene had been overjoyed. This was, she told her aging mother, the reward for all her sacrifices. Even in the worst of weather, she could walk to the new residence before she would have even boarded the train under the old routine. But greater news was forthcoming, if that was possible. Jonathon told her that, whenever schedules permitted, either he or David would drive her to and from her home in one of their motorcars. Occasionally she would also be reunited with Drake when David brought him to the estate to work an event with her, or to help with some sort of special project that would keep the men huddled in the guest cottage.

After Cinnamon learned of her father's decision to move to the country, the possibility never once crossed her mind that the new picture might not include Irene and Drake. When she made her first visit to the estate last year, the appearance of Irene's face and familiar welcome had provided a more important continuity than anyone realized. This kind woman had been there throughout all of Cinnamon's life, cooking great food and making tough times a little easier. No home of Jonathon McClinty would feel right without her quiet presence, and now, on what was supposed to be this first special day back home, Cinnamon headed straight for the kitchen. That's where she knew she'd find a predictable, unconditional and *normal* good morning, after being summarily dismissed by her father.

"Well, hello, young lady." Irene was dressed in a full body apron and held a spatula in her right hand. A stack of bacon was warming on the back of the stove, and another layer was cooking on the griddle. "Don't you look cozy and comfortable, and aren't those the prettiest yellow slippers I think I've ever seen?"

"Thanks," Cinnamon said, brushing her cheek against the housekeeper's. "I *am* comfortable, but apparently I'm also completely unsuitable for dining. Papa told me to get dressed, but I wanted to come in here first."

"I see," Irene said, as she stopped flipping the bacon and looked up at Mimi's eldest child. "Well, Mr. McClinty is nothing if not proper."

"Right, although I can't imagine that he's never allowed *Jay* to eat breakfast in *his* pajamas. What time does my brother usually wake up anyway?"

"I'm afraid you've already missed him. He left with David more than an hour ago."

"Where did they go?" she asked, her fresh and happy morning further diminished by this information.

"To the mill, I believe."

"But last night at dinner David didn't say anything about not being here today. There was such a celebration. Everyone was so excited, and they seemed so pleased about my being home. Now they're either upset with me, or they're gone."

"My dear," Irene answered, laying the spatula on the stove and motioning for Cinnamon to join her at the table in front of the bay window. "You must know that the whole family has been delirious about your impending arrival. But this trip does appear to be different from your other summer visits because, thank the Lord, you won't be returning to Manhattan anymore. I overheard your father discussing that point with Mrs. McClinty. He told her that this was not a vacation for you, but rather your introduction to your real life. I think that was the way he put it. He said everyone in the family needs to hold fast to their normal routines, enabling you to quickly settle in and make your place as a permanent resident. Yes, I'm sure those were his words. At any rate, Jay generally goes with David to the mill on Saturdays, so they are simply following Mr. McClinty's directive. You cannot think for one minute, however, that they don't want you home. Having you live here is all they've been talking about, for heaven's sake!"

Cinnamon was listening, her hands folded on the placemat.

"Irene, how many times," she asked, "have you offered this sort of comfort to me inside the kitchen of one McClinty house or another?"

"I couldn't say, my dear. A time or two, though."

"Yes, and *no one* is better than you!" Getting up, she touched the top of the housekeeper's head as she passed by her and moved toward the door. "Now I need to go put on a dress and start this day over from the beginning. I'll see you again shortly for some of that bacon, and for the muffin I know you're hiding in the oven. Thank you," she added, blowing a kiss across the room.

But even after putting herself together as quickly as possible, by the time she came back downstairs, she discovered that the dining room had been cleared away, except for one clean place setting looking very small on the far side of the massive table. Apparently, Jonathon had also gone to the mill, and Sophie had returned to her bedroom. Irene went through the motions of serving fruit, bacon and muffins, along with freshly squeezed orange juice and coffee, despite Cinnamon's insistence that she wasn't hungry any more. After eating a few bites as she sat there by herself, she pushed the rest of her food around on the plate for several minutes, then carried her dishes into the kitchen.

"I just saw Mrs. McClinty go into the parlor," Irene said, holding her tongue about how she was really feeling at this point and trying to offer something positive to the poor girl. "I suspect, based on past observations, that she'd also like some company. And I can bring tea and more muffins in a little while, if you'd like."

"Well, I suppose there's nothing else to do," Cinnamon responded with a sigh. "Sure glad I went to the trouble of being *dressed* appropriately, though."

Sophie's concentration was inside the covers of the same book she'd been reading at breakfast. Positioned in the center of the peach-colored velvet sofa, her frame was so diminutive that there would have been room for two other fairly large people on either side of her. Most of her yellow blonde hair was pulled up into a braided twist on top of her head. But a spray of fine, loose strands had come free and reflected like a halo around her face in the gray light coming through the parlor window directly behind her. The contrast between this woman and the statuesque, dark-haired beauty of her mother had never occurred to Cinnamon before, nor had the question about why her father would have preferred one over the other so many years ago.

"Hello, Sophie. Irene told me you were in here. I hope I'm not intruding."

"Nonsense, dear. I'm delighted to see you. Please, sit down and join me," she said, gesturing toward the brown leather wing chair to her right. "Also, let me apologize for your father's abrupt tone this morning. He means well, I hope you know."

"Yes, I do, and I appreciate his guidance," she replied patronizingly, as she nestled into the high back of the chair and tried to get a look at the cover of Sophie's book. "What are you reading?"

"Actually, it's a correspondence course. Now that the Better Homes Movement seems to have arrived in Albany in full force, your father is pressing me to become more involved."

"What, may I ask, is the Better Homes Movement?"

Placing the book in her lap, Sophie leaned her tiny shoulders and back into the downy sofa cushions.

"Surely you must have been told about this in your school, particularly in the advanced grades, and especially since you have completed your course of study."

Feeling dim-witted for the second time in as many hours, Cinnamon was tempted to get up and leave, until she realized there wasn't any place to go that was interesting, or populated.

"Perhaps the reference in my school was under some other title. What does the movement do? I'm sure I'll recognize the description."

"Yes, I suppose schools in *that* neighborhood might present things differently," Sophie continued, having no apparent idea how condescending she sounded. "It's really quite fascinating when you begin to understand the scope, although I still have much to learn. Your father says that, with the economy in such a thankful upturn, citizens will reap greater benefits the more actively they participate. The Better Homes Movement draws attention to home ownership and the inevitable maintenance and improvement of those houses, all of which require the purchase of consumer products and services. Home decoration is another part of this, too. Last fall, Albany held its first Better Homes Demonstration Week on State Street. You should have seen the crowds and the companies that were on hand to show and sell all manner of products for every type of residence you could imagine. Quite a few of the wives were actually paid to be demonstrators of sewing techniques and various other crafts. In something of a miracle, they had the full blessings of their husbands for this activity, since the national movement has such a high purpose—*a far-reaching economic impact,* to use your father's words. The second annual demonstration week is planned for this October, and I'm attempting to prepare myself."

"How intriguing," Cinnamon replied, her interest genuinely piqued by the concept, which her school had obviously decided was not a priority in a community where people bartered for life's necessities in rented apartments or tenement buildings. However, as she thought about her mother's efforts in the early Broome Street years to help improve the décor in several neighborhood apartments, she considered that this Better Homes Movement might, indeed, have some universal appeal.

"Which demonstrations did you participate in last year? And what are you planning this time?"

"I'm sorry to say," Sophie answered, looking rather pitiful—almost fearful—and lowering her voice as if not to be overheard, "that I wasn't very useful last year. I just wandered through the displays and did a fair amount of purchasing, telling myself I was at least making a patriotic contribution to the movement by spending your father's money. But the fact of the matter is that I don't know how to *do* anything. My life has always been filled with people doing things *for* me, which has been perfectly fine with your father all these years. Occasionally, he would refer to your grandmother's creative genius around the house, but I never took his comments to mean that I should be acquiring any similar skills myself. Then, out of the blue, he began placing in front of me tale after tale of wives with superior talents of one sort or another. One woman even knows how to make new cushions for her sofa, and another actually built a chest of drawers, if you can imagine that. Therefore, when he pointed out this correspondence course to me, which was advertised in *The Delineator* magazine last winter, I decided to give it a try."

"How exciting," Cinnamon declared, noting Sophie's clear absence of enthusiasm. "What's the name of the course?"

"The title is *American Dressmaking Step by Step©,*" she answered, holding the book up for Cinnamon to see. "My intention is not actually to make *dresses*, but the instructions are very specific about learning how to sew. Once I acquire that skill, I will be ready to take on various projects in this house, and I will also be ready to assist with some of the sewing demonstrations in October."

Not able to recall seeing a sewing machine anywhere in her father's home, other than her grandmother's old one in the Madison house attic, Cinnamon wondered how Sophie was planning to accomplish her mission.

"May I take a peek?"

"Of course," Sophie said with a look of expectation on her face. "I'll be interested to know what you think."

The book was astonishing. In the Table of Contents, fifteen chapters were introduced that listed 321 lessons teaching everything from basic terminology about fabrics and tools, to the specifics of body measurements, the study, selection and use of patterns, techniques and applications of eighteen different stitches, construction and assembly steps, finishing and ornamental work, and four separate chapters that focused on the beginning-to-end creation of more than fifty individual garments. Cinnamon was only guessing, but based upon her initial review of this book, she already knew how to do most of what was being covered in the lessons. Was it possible that all those hours spent under Velita's tutelage—not to mention the countless conversations with Alberto and Vincente on the subjects of fashion and dress design—could have equipped her with skills and knowledge that could actually help the American economy? She felt an unexpected need to rush the news to Broome Street, to hug them all, and to tell her mother, even if the words couldn't reach her. But there was only poor Sophie to talk to, sitting motionless and looking like a porcelain doll, as she waited patiently for a response.

"This is a remarkable course of study," Cinnamon said at length. "I'm almost speechless as I see how they've put this together. There doesn't seem to be a single area that they've overlooked."

"Do you know how to do any of the things they describe?" Sophie asked, a hopeful tone suddenly evident in her voice.

"Well, yes I do, as a matter of fact. How about you? Have you been practicing?"

Sophie paused, that fearful expression spreading across her face again.

"Not exactly, dear. You see, your father hasn't purchased a sewing machine for me yet. I *have* been doing my reading, though—religiously."

"Sophie, please forgive me if I'm being impertinent, but in order to learn the craft of sewing, you need to be *sewing*. *Reading* about it won't make any sense, unless you're performing each lesson as you go. When is Papa planning to bring a machine home for you?"

"I'm not sure. I reminded him several weeks ago, but..."

"This is ridiculous!" Cinnamon declared, standing in exasperation. "You need to speak *up* to him, Sophie. How does he expect you to acquire this new expertise? Through some divine endowment?"

"Cinnamon, don't be disrespectful!"

"Forgive me, but you can't read a book on dressmaking as if it were Pride and Prejudice. If you'd like, I'll help you with this. And unless David has thrown it away, Grandmother Amelia's sewing machine should still be in the Madison house somewhere. I'm sure he'd be happy to bring it to us."

The worry lines on Sophie's face began to relax.

"Oh, thank you," she said. "I would so appreciate any assistance you can give me. I hope you don't think me completely dense."

"On the contrary," Cinnamon replied, a bit calmer as she sat back down. "I admire your determination. So tell me, what would you like to make as your first project, once we get started?"

"Actually, I was thinking about new draperies for the parlor windows."

Realizing that the woman was absolutely serious, Cinnamon could not stop herself from laughing out loud.

"I'm so sorry. I don't mean to be glib, but something on a slightly smaller scale might be—well, shall we say *less complicated* as a beginning."

"All right. What would you suggest instead?"

"How about a hot pad?"

The two women entered the kitchen hand-in-hand.

"Hello, again, Irene. Sophie and I are embarking on a project together, and we need your help."

"How delightful! What sort of project?"

"She's going to learn how to sew. I'll tell you more about it later," Cinnamon added, observing the housekeeper raise her eyebrows. "But for now, would you have an old hot pad, and perhaps an apron, that you could live the rest of your life without?"

"Let's see," Irene answered, wiping her hands and moving toward a series of drawers in the pantry. "Yes, here we go," she said, handing one of each to Cinnamon. Both had obviously come in contact with fire more than once, and Irene answered the questions before they were asked. "When I first began working in this new kitchen, I'm afraid I had some difficulty understanding the stove's temperament."

"Oh. Well, I do hope this was the worst of it," Cinnamon kidded, sensing Irene's regret at having confessed her mishaps in front of Sophie. "At any rate, these are perfect. Thanks."

Next on the list were a hat pin and a pair of scissors, and once the items were collected, the women seated themselves again in the parlor where the explanations began. Using the scissors first, Cinnamon cut a stitch of thread along the hot pad's edge, and then she began lifting successive stitches from the fabric with the hat pin's point.

"Until we have a sewing machine and the proper tools, so we can proceed in an orderly manner through these lessons, you'll be able to learn a great deal about construction just by taking a garment—or, in this case, a hot pad—apart. You can pick up some of the terminology, too, if you reference these pictures as you go along. I know this to be true, Sophie," she said, smiling and playfully nudging her stepmother's arm, "because I've made *so* many mistakes that taking things apart and starting over has become my specialty. Look! As I lift these stitches out, you can see how the *inside* is put together."

"Yes! How interesting!"

"Far more interesting than just reading the book, don't you think?"

"I do, indeed. Perhaps some of this will make more sense now.

"Especially after you've also dismantled the apron. You'll actually be able to identify the individual pattern pieces and lay them out, similar to the pictures show here," she added, pointing to Lessons 9 through 12 in The Table of Contents.

"You are such a dear," Sophie said, bringing her stepdaughter into a long, grateful embrace. "I can't tell you how important this is to me, and how much brighter this dreary day has suddenly become."

With Sophie in the parlor feeling productive and challenged for the first time in God knows how long, Cinnamon went through the hallway and front door, initially intending to sit for a few minutes on the porch. But once outside, she was drawn to the silent splendor of Fox Run, and she walked around the house, past the guest cottage, then through the acre of tall grass beyond the two smaller barns. The rain, which had been threatening all morning, had been transformed into a thick mist that parted like a curtain against her face, making her feel part of the landscape's symmetry.

When she arrived at the point where the grass began giving way to pine straw and dirt, she turned and meandered along the invisible line separating the field from the woods. Glancing over at the house, cottage and barn, she became aware of how surreal they appeared from this distance, like a black and white still-life protruding from the fog. *A shift in perspective,* she thought, *and not just about structures.* The soothing silence and peace that she remembered from last summer had changed during the year into something else. *Lonely*, she thought. *And empty.* But she had not even been here for one full day yet. Surely these impressions would soften when everyone came home tonight, and when she had an opportunity to relax in their company. After all, this was her father's home—*her* home—and as Irene said, she wasn't on vacation any more. *She* was the one who would need to make the adjustment.

After hearing muffled sounds that she could not identify coming from the dark cavity of trees to her left, she cut across the grass again and walked up behind the large barn. The cottage was to her right, the rear of the main house directly in front of her, the lace curtains in her bedroom barely visible through the upstairs window. Deciding she wasn't ready yet to go back inside, she rounded the front of the barn and pulled the heavy, creaking door open just far enough for her to slip through.

No progress appeared to have been made since the previous summer on her father's plan to turn this structure into a carriage house. Arranged along the sides of the open space, on all four walls, were sweet-smelling bales of hay, four or five bales deep, stacked in various configurations that resembled giant stepping stools and toy building blocks. Hanging down in the center of the room was a ladder secured with stakes at the bottom, and some sort of grips at the top where it rested against the edge of a loft area twenty feet above her. The loft formed a high ceiling for most of the barn, except in the center, where the open space extended all the way up to the pitched roof. Six small windows, evenly spaced around the side and back walls below the loft, were letting in traces of the grey haze from outside, providing just enough light for her to see.

Inhaling the hypnotic scents blended of hay and wood, she walked past the ladder and sat down on a cluster of bales that formed a massive chair. As she pulled her legs up to her chest and leaned her head back against the straw, she imagined how deep her sleep would be in here during a rain storm, sheltered and dry, with water pounding down on top of the roof that towered over her. Visions of Broome Street flashed through her mind again, and she thought how unfair God was to give so much texture—so much space and privacy—to the members of one family, and yet crowd hundreds of other families on top of one another.

"*There* you are!"

The voice was so startling that she jumped to her feet, gripping the bodice of her dress with both hands as a pathetic squeak came out of her mouth.

"Sorry, Cinn," David added with a chuckle, edging his muscular body sideways through the opening in the door. "I didn't mean to scare you, but we've been looking all over for you."

At the sight of him, her heart rate began to slow with relief, and then accelerated again just because he was there. The next emotion, in a quick series of waves, was aggravation.

Really?" she asked, sitting back down on the hay. "When I left the house a little while ago, there wasn't *anyone* to miss me. Seems they all went other places today, on my first day home, without the courtesy of any notice."

"Oh, so *that's* the difficulty." His frame was silhouetted against the door light as he moved toward her. "We're a bit out of sorts, are we?" he asked, sitting down beside her and taking her hand in his.

"Disappointed, actually," she said, "although I'm sure that must sound quite childish. Please forgive me."

"All right. I do." His arm went around her shoulders, and he pulled her in close to him where she met with the familiar smell of his starched shirt. "Perhaps *I* will be forgiven," he continued, "when I tell you that Jay and I have a surprise for you."

Uneasy about letting her expectations rise again, she leaned away from him and tried to read his eyes in the dim light.

"Oh? And *what*, exactly, would that be?"

"*Who* would be a better question. The fact is, my dear, that we brought Angela home with us, to stay the entire week—for our July 4th celebration on Thursday and then until Sunday."

"Truly?" she squealed, jumping to her feet as he stood, too. "Oh, David, thank you! *Thank* you!"

Going up on her tiptoes, she threw her arms around his neck and felt him lift her off the ground, swinging her in that lazy sway she'd cherished since she was a girl. In that instant, while she nuzzled her face in the curve of his neck, all traces of exasperation and isolation slipped away.

"Come. Let's go inside now," he said, putting her down. "They'll begin to think I've disappeared as well. Also," he continued, guiding her through the door with his hand on her back, "sometime before the 4th, I'd like to spend a few more private minutes with you. There's something very important I want to tell you. But this isn't the right moment, with everyone waiting for us."

"Yes, of course," she said, taking hold of his hand again, and knowing for certain as she looked up at his strong, handsome face, that all of her dreams were about to come true at last. "I'll be ready whenever you are. By the way," she added, "before I forget to ask you in all of the excitement ahead of us, would you mind looking through your attic for Grandmother's sewing machine? I'm sure it's up there somewhere, along with a padded case full of threads and needles and other sewing tools I remember seeing."

"Sure. But I don't think I've ever run across a sewing machine. If it *is* there, it's probably in need of a good cleaning and lubrication, especially if Amelia was the last one to use it. What, may I ask, is prompting this? Some project that popped into your head during your solitary afternoon?"

"It's not for me, but for Sophie. She wants to learn how to sew and make new draperies for the parlor."

Turning toward her as they reached the kitchen door, his eyes danced and the corners of his mouth lifted upward.

"Please don't poke fun at this, David," she said, noting the irreverent twinkle, "I'm trying to be respectful of her ambition."

"Right," he said, throwing his head back and laughing out loud as he opened the door and followed her inside.

"And what evidence makes you believe he intends any such thing?" Angela asked in a whisper that night in Cinnamon's bedroom. The two young women sat on the floor talking, still unable to sleep at one o'clock in the morning.

"He practically told me as much right then and there."

"What were his precise words? E-ver-y syllable, please."

"Well, let's see. He said he needs to speak with me privately before the party on Thursday, because whatever he wishes to tell me, and to ask me, is something he plans to announce on the 4th. Actually, I might be paraphrasing a bit, but those words are close enough."

"But how can you be positive he'll say what you're imagining he'll say?"

"I *know* his intentions, Angela. I could see them and feel them in his eyes and touch."

"Honestly, Cinn, you've reached the point where you think and talk in poetry. Sometimes I worry that your creative heart isn't prepared for the flat reality of prose."

"And what in God's name is *that* supposed to mean? You're rather bold to critique my choice of words when yours are absolute gibberish."

Perhaps, Angela considered, but she couldn't bring herself to use the straightforward language necessary to bring her dearest friend out of the clouds—or to warn her of the impending disaster.

The next two days were filled with so much activity, conversation and humor that Cinnamon could not believe she'd been fretful for even a moment about the wisdom of her returning to Albany. In order to accommodate the unusually large crowd expected this year, elaborate preparations for the July 4th celebration were underway in every corner of the property. In addition to supervisors from the mill and their families, Jonathon had invited a score of his Chamber associates, along with their wives and children. Arrangements had been made for ten clowns and magicians—some playing both parts—to provide entertainment, and a platform was being erected between the house and the pond, from which patriotic speeches would be delivered. A five-piece musical ensemble had also been engaged and would use the platform as a stage for their medleys of American songs, including some of the new dance tunes being showcased on the Saturday night radio broadcasts.

Each family that was confirmed to attend was being asked to contribute a casserole or dessert to the banquet. But Irene had additional plans. She'd enlisted Drake, who'd arrived with David at the estate on Monday morning, to help her harvest three bushels of vegetables from the garden, including potatoes and corn, for the dishes *she* was preparing. She'd also begun baking cookies and pies on Sunday, placing the completed pastries inside the tin pie cupboard in the cellar to keep them fresh. An area about twelve feet in diameter had been cleared in the grass behind the large barn, and two workers from the mill had shoveled out a four-foot-deep pit in the dirt. On Wednesday afternoon, the pig intended for roasting would be delivered on ice, then seasoned, wrapped in burlap, and put in the pit's slow fire that same night. Large portions of Irene's vegetables would be bundled in smaller sacks, to be added on Thursday morning.

David's arrival on Monday, with his announced intention to remain at Fox Run throughout the week, answered prayers that Cinnamon had not yet offered. *This means we'll be together every single day! He's thought of everything!* Further adding to the joy of these circumstances was the sewing machine in his arms. Drake had oiled and tuned it at David's behest, after the two men located it in a dusty corner of the Madison attic. They'd also found the hat-box sized container she'd described, which held all manner of sewing notions, including every color of thread she thought could exist plus several packages of needles for hand-stitching and for the machine itself. Although she felt confident that she could figure out how each needle was supposed to be utilized, she was relieved to see the instruction book included in the box as well.

After David and Drake placed the equipment in her bedroom on a table she'd borrowed from one of the guest rooms down the hall, she spent an hour making sure she understood the machine's operation. This model wasn't nearly as modern as Velita's or those in Alberto's tailor shop. But she was rather impressed with her ability to readily understand the differences. Armed with a clean but worn bed sheet and blanket to use as fabric samples, she declared herself ready to teach her first sewing class, and then she invited Sophie upstairs to join her.

Thereafter, the women managed to carve out several hours together, during the first three days of that week, to focus on their shared endeavor. But by noon on Wednesday, they mutually agreed to postpone further lessons until the Fourth of July celebration was behind them.

"Besides," Sophie said as they tidied up their workspace, "we've covered so much information that I'd like to review the lessons on my own before we proceed any further. Perhaps, after all the festivities are over and our guests have gone, we could even move the sewing machine into the parlor so I can practice without bothering you here in your bedroom. I doubt your father would object, particularly since I'm doing this at his request. And thanks to you, I'm catching on to the course material must faster than I thought I would. So you don't need to fret over me as much."

Cinnamon recognized the reach for independence and respected Sophie's need to become self-sufficient.

"I think that's a good plan, and I'm happy we've made so much progress. Whenever you come to a new section requiring my assistance, though, I'll be close at hand."

She enjoyed the sense of accomplishment, knowing that Sophie appreciated her supportive instruction. She was also discovering that helping someone develop a useful skill was immensely rewarding. *This must be how Mother felt when she was teaching.* As the women walked downstairs together, Cinnamon wondered if there might be a way for her to earn a respectable income by expanding this role outside the family. But this idea would have to wait until tomorrow's party was over—after David's promise had been fulfilled—when she'd have an easier time concentrating.

Irene was cooking a large pot of fresh vegetable soup and two loaves of bread for an early dinner that same Wednesday. All the men were behind the barn seating the pig in the roasting pit, and Angela was out in the field with them. Jay had persuaded her to overcome her squeamishness and observe the procedure, and since Sophie wanted to help Irene in the kitchen, she suggested that Cinnamon go join her friend and brother. Imagining that the activities surrounding the pig pit would be far more interesting than cooking vegetable soup, she'd begun making her way across the yard when she saw David open the front door of the guest cottage.

"Cinn," he called out, running to meet her, "I've been hoping to see you."

He was wearing heavy brown boots and work pants splattered with mud. His pale green shirt was also filthy, with buttons open half way down his chest and sleeves rolled up to his elbows. The combination of stubble and soot on his face made his blue eyes stand out like beacons. *What a mess he is,* she thought, looking at his black hair blown in every direction. *But perfect still.*

"How are your lessons going with Sophie?"

"Frankly, she's doing quite well. I didn't realize how serious she is about this project. But if her determination is any measure, she might surprise us and make those parlor draperies after all."

"And her excellent teacher will share credit for that unimaginable feat."

She blushed at the compliment and then watched him remove a folded piece of stationery from his pants pocket."

"Here," he said, offering no explanation and extending his hand as if he were passing the butter. "I'm on my way back to the pit. Are you headed there, too?"

"No," she answered, lying to him as she took the paper without inquiry. "I mean, I *was* going to the pit, but I just remembered something I need to do."

"All right then. I'll see you later at dinner."

As he strode away from her, she made sure he wasn't watching her before she redirected herself to the barn door, which appeared to be open already. After confirming that no one else was inside, she sat down on the same bale she'd shared with him the previous Saturday. Then she unfolded the letter and tilted it up to catch the light seeping in through the windows.

Dear Cinn—

As I mentioned the other day, I would like to spend some time talking with you before the frenzy of tomorrow's party overtakes us. I had hoped to create an opportunity sooner than this, but the week's activities have run away with any other plans.

Therefore, if you would do me the pleasure, I would like to meet with you tonight, after everything has quieted down, perhaps around eight o'clock. The barn seems to be a favored spot for you, so let's rendezvous there.

I have much to tell you—much to share—and I'm anxious to be with you at this important moment. See you tonight.

Always,
David

Clutching the paper to her breast, she raised her head and looked up at the barn's roof beams high above her, whispering a prayer of thanks to what she now believed must, indeed, be a merciful God.

She could not believe that her father chose *this* evening, above all others, to engage the family in a hearty and lengthy after-dinner dialogue on President Harding's west coast tour. *How could there possibly be so much to say,* she thought, *about the merits and shortcomings of America's joining the League of Nations?* Adding further to the interminable gathering was Sophie's suggestion that they all share in a game of charades in the parlor, to which Jonathon uncharacteristically agreed.

Angela understood Cinnamon's impatience, having heard the news about David's invitation while the girls were changing clothes for dinner. Angela had not, however, been given the benefit of actually seeing the infamous note, a fact of no small concern to her. Nervous about the direction her friend's encounter could take, she was anxious for one of the two charade teams to win quickly so the rest of the night could soon be over. After an agonizing number of rounds, the women were victorious over the men, and good-nights were exchanged at last.

When everyone had dispersed to their respective sleeping quarters and the house lights had been extinguished, the girls sat silently in Cinnamon's darkened bedroom, without changing their clothes, until they heard no one else moving around. Then Cinnamon pulled her door open and gingerly descended the staircase. Stepping lightly on her tiptoes, she moved down the hall, through the kitchen and out the back entrance, breaking into a sprint for the barn as soon as her feet touched the grass.

David was waiting for her, and he'd brought with him two oil lamps that gave off so much light she was afraid someone might come to investigate. He appeared unconcerned, however, as he patted the bale of hay with his hand in a motion for her to sit beside him.

"Did you have a good time tonight?" he asked.

"Yes, I suppose, despite the endlessness of it all. And, by the way, *I* saw Jay peeking at your paper when you were trying for your seventh win."

"Must have been your imagination," he said, grinning. "In any case, you women proved your superiority, momentarily, which we men plan to nullify in the next game." Standing up, he put his hands in his pockets and walked a few paces away from her. "I realize it's late," he continued, lowering his voice, "but I'm glad we arranged this time together."

"Me, too. You can't imagine how much I…"

"Tomorrow," he interrupted, "a new chapter of my life will begin."

She watched him looking at the ground instead of at her, and suddenly she felt a peculiar twinge.

"Because you mean so very much to me," he went on, "I had to be certain that you knew before anyone else."

Of course, silly. I already know. But the feeling without a name was growing stronger.

"Tomorrow morning, I will tell your father…"

Yes.

"…and I will request that he announce during the party, after all the dull speeches are over…"

Good idea.

"…that I have asked Lucille Bennett to marry me, and that we plan to wed in September…She and her family…will be here, and…I…can't wait…for…you…to…meet her…"

While the sound hammered in her head as if she were inside a kettle drum, an unforeseen force siphoned all the oxygen out of the barn. At the same moment, that undefined feeling began screaming out its name—*humiliation.* Then came another—*imbecile.*

David kept on talking, although she had no idea what he was saying. Then he finally stopped pacing and turned to look at her as she sat on the hay, her heart exposed and vulnerable.

"Cinn, you're *crying*! What's wrong?"

"I…we…," she stammered, unsuccessfully groping for her voice.

He was now a wavy blur in the glow of his oil lamps, and she was worried that she wouldn't be able to move her arms and legs. But one fact was apparent. There was no way she could breathe or think, much less speak, until she was somewhere else. *I must get myself out of here! How can this be happening?*

"Please, Cinn. I thought this would make you happy."

Relieved to feel her legs supporting her as she put her feet down on the dirt, she walked to the foggy outline of his body, reached up and put her arms around his neck. The words were then pulled from someplace, somehow.

"Of course. I *am* happy—and I love you." After allowing herself to bury her wet face in the curve of his neck for a brief moment—one last time—she let go of him and moved toward the slice of darkness she hoped was the door opening. "Good night, David."

Her vision cleared slightly in the outside air, and she widened her stride in the direction of the pond, sensing that her composure and dignity were both nearing an end. Looking over her shoulder, she noted that he did not seem to be coming after her or calling for her to stop. He wasn't on his way to hold her or assure her that there'd been some awful misunderstanding. But why would he do *that*? Obviously, there *had* been a misunderstanding, although David had not the vaguest idea, because *she* was the only fool. *Oh my God!* Arriving at the stone bench, she sat down and bent over at her waist, her arms wrapped across her stomach. *Oh my God!* From a place lower and deeper than any she'd known could exist inside her, the soundless cries came out. There she stayed, folded in half, rocking up and down while her tears poured onto the ground, until there was nothing left.

At length, as the narcotic calm of spent sadness spread through her body, she sat up and observed that there were no more lights burning in either the barn or the guest cottage. While wiping her face and nose on the handkerchief she'd taken from her dress pocket, she became aware of noises that could be deer, or rabbits, or more sinister night animals moving in the field near the woods. A little frightened and wishing she could disappear altogether, she pulled herself up and reluctantly made her way back to the house. As she walked, she could tell she was changing again, much like what she'd experienced after hearing the news about Bradley. But this time, the feeling was accompanied by a decision, one she now realized had been in the making all along. In the few minutes it took her to cover the distance between the pond and the kitchen door, she'd become ready to do whatever was necessary. Almost as if a curtain had opened to let her pass through, she felt herself leaving all the frayed remnants of her childhood behind her.

Not caring if she made any noise or if anyone discovered her, she moved steadily up the stairs and into her room. She tried to be quiet, though, while changing her clothes, not wanting to awaken Angela. But the continuous need to blow her nose was difficult to muffle. Even so, her friend remained motionless as Cinnamon pulled on her nightgown, draped her dress over the chaise and eased into bed, facing outward and lying on her side. Bunching the comforter up around her shoulders, she was just starting to close her eyes when she felt Angela turn over and sit up behind her.

"What happened, Cinn?" The question came in a soft voice, with far more concern than curiosity. "Are you all right?"

Her first inclination was to say nothing in response. Her second was to fabricate an answer that would postpone the embarrassment she knew was inescapable, and imminent. But what was the use?

"The only way I could be all right, Angela," she said in a thick, gravelly voice, "is if I were stone-cold dead."

In the next few moments, the sudden sleep of exhaustion took hold, and Angela's next question, "Do you feel like talking about it?" was answered by the silence.

The Fourth of July at Fox Run was celebrated with all the planned food, music and entertainment—and the hoped for high spirits—despite the unfortunate onset of Cinnamon's influenza. She knew of no other way to survive the day and was grateful for Angela's unquestioning collaboration. When not being tended to by Irene or Sophie, she stayed in her bed, or sat by the window, listening and watching as the happy guests milled around the grounds. She could smell the pig roasting, but instead of feeling hungry, she felt nauseated. She heard people laughing, but instead of being energized, she wanted to sleep. She watched the band perform rousing patriotic melodies and foot-tapping sing-a-longs, but instead of feeling inspired, she cried. This was how the hours passed, until the moment when she heard her father's voice call everyone to attention. Throwing off the comforter, she pulled on her robe and moved again to the window, where, if she sat sideways, she had an unobstructed view beyond the barn and out toward the pond.

Jonathon stood on the platform with his back to her. The crowd, which looked even larger somehow from her second-floor vantage point, had gathered together and was slowly growing quiet. A large group clustered close to the stage, and the rest spread out on either side of the water. Angela stood next to her parents, directly in front, and she acknowledged seeing Cinnamon in the window by fluttering her fingers in a subtle wave. On Jonathon's right, David was unforgivably handsome in his grey pinstriped pants, with red suspenders stretched over his crisp white shirt. She didn't have a full view of his face, but his thick hair was smooth and shiny in the sunshine. Then, of course, Miss Lucille Bennett was on his left arm.

Apparently, David had asked Sophie earlier in the day if Lucille could come upstairs to meet the poor girl, who'd so sadly taken ill. But Cinnamon expressed concern about needlessly transferring her influenza to anyone else, and thankfully had been spared the close-up ordeal. From her window perch, she could see everything she needed to know. The woman was absolutely stunning. Her blonde hair was several shades lighter than Sophie's—more like bright beach sand than honey—and it fell nearly to her waist in thick bouncing curls. She'd pulled the sides back and tied them together with a purple ribbon that matched the trim on her modern dress. Cinnamon had seen advertisements for the airy designs, with hem lengths at the knees, in her father's daily newspaper. But she'd never been around anyone who actually *wore* them.

Studying the sleek, fashionable picture drawn by this woman, and by other ladies in the crowd who were also wearing the latest style, she was glad for her creative influenza. Any dress from her closet that she might have worn today, no matter how much time she would have spent putting herself together, would have left her feeling self-conscious and shamefully out-of-date. Then again, she didn't know how she could possibly have felt worse than she did when Jonathon opened his arms in David and Lucille's direction, or when the cheers and applause erupted, or when she watched the couple embrace. But the moment she saw David lean over and kiss Lucille on her cheek was when Cinnamon knew it was finally all over. There wasn't any need to observe further. Returning to her bed, she lay down with her robe still wrapped around her. Staring up at the ceiling, she felt her tears sliding backwards over her ears, as she considered what would be the least painful way to tell her father she was leaving Albany.

July 4, 1923—10:30 P.M.

Angela fell asleep in the middle of our conversation a few minutes ago, but I don't mind. If I could sleep, too, I would. Besides, she deserves the rest. She's the only reason I'm still breathing, after living through the nightmare that began twenty-four hours ago—the nightmare I can only pray will end eventually. For now, however, I must remind myself of the other people I know whose lives are in far greater distress than mine and who have far fewer options than I'm only now appreciating.

I must begin placing one foot in front of the other, in a deliberate movement up and out of this muddle. The first will be the most difficult—my conversation with Papa—which I will live through somehow, early next week. From there, I hope the steps will grow less painful the further away I get from this moment. The most important thing will be to find a place where I no longer have to watch events unfolding directly in front of my face.

Meanwhile, I'm oddly at peace with my own culpability. There's no need to expend energy making excuses for my folly or harboring ill will toward—well, toward anyone who might otherwise seem logical. This leaves me with a clear head added to my resolve, although I may need some time to untether the grip on my heart.

Before I conclude this entry, I want to record the verse that came to mind this afternoon. This will be the first time I've created something he'll never see—and it's also the last time I'll care. What a sad and unexpected juncture this has turned out to be.

There will be no more songs for me to write.
There cannot be a dawn beyond tonight.
The sun cannot rise
Without the light from your eyes.
You and I, and our love, are out of sight.
It's all gone.

The poems that were written have all died.
A lifetime of my tears has now been cried.
There isn't any way
To add an act to this play.
The curtain fell the last time that I tried.
It's all gone.

Gone the way of dreamers, trusting in desire.
Gone, the love and friendship that we forged in fire.
Where will I find the meaning to rebuild?
How can I raise the hope that has been stilled,
Now that you're gone?

Tomorrow I need to speed up Sophie's lessons. I don't want to disappoint her or leave her unprepared for the October Demonstration Week. She's been so worried about it.

Her explanation was that she felt ill-equipped to effectively assume her responsibilities at Fox Run, or to even understand what those responsibilities might be, *having been brought up in such a primitive environment as Broome Street.* She thought those particular words would help make her point clear to her father, but Jonathon was completely bewildered when she initially told him of her decision. He worried that he'd been too abrupt with her when she'd first arrived, remembering Sophie's words of chastisement. Then he considered the possibility that he'd neglected her and left her without direction. But after several weeks of thought and observation, he came to believe that she might be right.

Although he could not shake his long-held disdain for the place where her mother had raised her, he had to admit that she'd turned out to be a promising girl. Yet, she was still very young in so many ways. He convinced himself that living in relative isolation in the country at Fox Run would have offered few avenues for his headstrong daughter to explore and exhaust her willful nature. Much as he disliked the idea of her returning to Manhattan, he knew she'd be under close supervision with the Mentini's. Furthermore, *those people* did seem to be in the unlikely position to help her develop her interest in fashion, an industry he believed would become a major element of America's new economic expansion.

So, he agreed to let her return to Manhattan for a period of one year, a term Cinnamon accepted without debate, telling herself that one year would not come close to being long enough. Jonathon also agreed to let her be the one to make the announcement about this development, to both the Albany family and to the Mentini's. Explaining things to Angela turned out to be easy, of course, even though her dearest friend was going to be desperately missed. But their relationship was far stronger than this separation, and they would always have each other, no matter how much distance or time came between them. Jay required a bit more work, however, since he could not comprehend his sister's preference for Broome Street, having seen the neighborhood himself. He was so occupied with his studies and his work at the mill, however, that he'd scarcely spent a day with her since she came home anyway. Furthermore, he'd lived the greater portion of his life without his sister around, so news of her decision was assimilated and accepted with minimal trauma. Once resigned to the change, he did promise to visit her, though, whenever Angela made the trip as well.

Sophie and Irene were the most distraught—Sophie because she'd come to feel such an unexpected and enjoyable kinship with her stepdaughter, and Irene because she loved the girl as if she were her own child.

"But when you think about it," Irene said to Sophie on a late July morning, trying to be cheerful, "one year isn't really all that long. Then we can have a fresh homecoming once again."

David was the only person who didn't hear of the development directly from Cinnamon. Jay told him while they drove to the mill, on the first Saturday after Cinnamon broke the news to the others.

"She's doing *what*?" he'd asked, first in disbelief, then in utter confusion, especially in light of her conduct since the Fourth of July. But his attempts to engage her in a conversation on the matter met with one excuse after another, until he finally stopped trying. He was too busy with his work, and with social events involving Lucille, to be wasting time in search of an explanation for her behavior.

"If she wants to discuss this with me," he said to Sophie one Sunday afternoon, having been told yet again that Cinnamon wasn't feeling well, "she knows where she can find me." But no such discussion took place, at least not for a very long time.

By August 2, 1923, everyone had adjusted to the fact that she was returning to Broome Street—everyone, that is, except the people *on* Broome Street. She had not yet assembled the right set of words to explain her decision to Velita and Alberto. Assuming they would be pleased to have her back, and knowing that Alberto had used some of Bradley's money to keep the apartment, she felt confident that there would be a place for her to stay. But she wasn't sure how the Mentini's might have reconfigured their living arrangements after she left, although she would be happy to sleep anywhere they wanted to put her. She didn't know how to *say* this to them, though, since her return meant she'd made a horrible mistake by leaving Broome Street in the first place. So, she decided not to offer her explanation in any letter or wire, worried that they might be more comfortable telling her not to come back, if they didn't have to look her in the eye. Her only choice, therefore, was to surprise them.

A date for her departure had not been scheduled yet when, just after dawn on August 3, Jonathon returned from the Delmar train station with his newspaper. He was in a state of extreme agitation, and the sound of his voice awakened Cinnamon. Without regard for her attire, she pulled her robe over her nightgown and went downstairs to investigate. Her father had already gone into the parlor with Sophie and turned on the radio, which normally did not broadcast so early. But transmission was clearly coming through this morning.

While Jonathon adjusted the tuning, Cinnamon picked up the newspaper that he'd tossed on the dining room table across the hall. The front page banner headline declared **PRESIDENT HARDING DIES OF THROMBOSIS**. She'd never paid much attention to politics, and she'd participated with even less interest in discussions involving presidents. But having one *die* was terrifying. What was America supposed to do *now*? Still holding onto the newspaper, she joined her father and Sophie in the parlor, along with Jay and Irene. The radio signal wasn't very strong, but as the five of them gathered close to the cathedral shaped box, they understood what the broadcaster was saying, despite the static.

"...Harding had been on a trip, which he'd been referring to as his Voyage of Understanding, to bring to the people his advocacy of America's joining the League of Nations World Court. His travels since June had taken him up and down the west coast, and they'd concluded with speeches in Alaska last week. He and his entourage were beginning their return journey to Washington, and were on a stopover in San Francisco last night, when he collapsed. He did not survive this event and died from what is being described as a thrombosis. He was fifty-seven. According to the provisions in our Constitution, at 2:47 East Coast time this morning, on this tragic day of August 3, 1923, the transfer of power took place. In his rural Vermont home, Vice President Calvin Coolidge was sworn in by his father and became the 30th President of the United States. President Coolidge reportedly left a few hours later for Washington, where he will take office amidst a swirl of shock, grief, and mounting claims of government corruption. Arrangements for President Warren G. Harding's funeral have not been announced yet. We will return to the airwaves whenever additional news breaks..."

Warren Harding was a poker-playing president who'd been elected by a landslide in 1920. But with the increasing evidence of his subordinates' dishonesty, and the collapse of the war boom following World War I, a turn of events that subsequently led to wage cuts, unemployment, and strong urban resentment of Prohibition, Harding's popularity had eroded by midterm. The result was a rebuke of Republicans in the 1922 Congressional election. This sobering setback only seemed to inspire his leadership, however, and led to his *Voyage of Understanding*. Ironically, his inspiration had now proven fatal.

"No matter how controversial he may have been," Jonathon said, after the radio went silent, "the death of a sitting president is a dreadful loss, and an historic moment at the same time."

Then he stood up, took the newspaper from his daughter's hands, left the room, and walked out the front door. Moments later, he drove off in his motorcar without saying another word to his family, without considering that they might need his reassurance or comfort, and certainly without noticing their frightened faces watching him through the parlor window. As Cinnamon saw the car turn left out of Fox Run's driveway, she wondered how soon a ticket to Manhattan could be purchased.

When her train departed Albany the following week, on Saturday, August 11, Jonathon was the only person standing on the platform. He'd kissed her goodbye, but otherwise had been stiff and unemotional, and the train had barely begun moving when she saw him turn and walk away. For the first time in her life at such a moment, she didn't cry at the sight of the city disappearing behind her. Uncertain about what might be waiting ahead of her, she was surprisingly unafraid as the train picked up speed and the landscape began zipping past her window. How many times had this exact scene been reenacted over the years? But how different was she *this* time?

As a reward for her help with the sewing lessons, Sophie had taken her shopping for one of the modern dresses she'd been quietly coveting, and today she was traveling in sleek sophistication. The dress was cotton with a pale yellow hue. Trimmed with ivory lace around the hemline that fell just below her knees, the fabric complemented her new cream-colored stockings and two-inch heeled shoes. Green satin ribbon finished the scooped neckline and the bottom of her elbow-length sleeves. A cut of the same ribbon tied back the sides of her hair, the rest falling long and loose down her back, in a style similar to an unjustly beautiful woman she'd recently observed at Fox Run.

Unlike her previous trips, this time she carried only two satchels with her, one filled with fruit and sandwiches, the other containing her journal, a few personal items and this morning's newspaper. She'd arranged to ship everything else in her trunk, telling her father that she wanted to make things simple when Alberto picked her up in New York. The part about simplicity was true. But when she arrived at Grand Central Terminal, Alberto would not be meeting her, because no one knew she was coming. Instead, she planned to ride the subway home, carrying her two satchels, without depending on a single soul to help her get there. The feeling of independence was invigorating, and she smiled readily at the other rail passengers across from her and those walking down the aisle, all of whom smiled back with what felt like admiration. Settling into her seat with her new self-assurance, she was unaware that, in Albany, amidst the unseen tears being shed at her departure, Angela was finally gathering the courage to tell Jay about his sister's secret infatuation, in a well-intended effort to help him understand this change of plans more clearly.

A short walk from Grand Central Terminal took her to the elevated railroad, which she rode south toward Houston Street. Then she pulled the buzzer several blocks ahead of the normal neighborhood stop, deciding to go the rest of the way on foot. For all of the crowded conditions and economic struggles, there was something uplifting about the durability—the certainty—of these streets, of the sidewalk displays and kiosks, even the fire escapes. But what she had not anticipated was the recognition. By the time she was within three blocks of Broome Street, people began calling her name and approaching her, taking her face in their hands, spinning her around to admire her, and speaking the fast-paced Italian that she found so charming all of a sudden.

"Vada dicono a Velita ed a Alberto che sia un miracolo! La figlia bella del Mimi è venuto a casa!" exclaimed one very robust elderly woman. Although Cinnamon couldn't translate most of the words, she clearly heard reference to Velita and Alberto, and she began to understand that, by the time she reached Broome Street, the surprise could very well be over. She was correct. Walking south on Mott Street, she crossed Spring, and then Kenmare. With Broome Street next, she was midway through the block when she saw a crowd forming on the corner ahead. People were jumping up and down, waving to her and then gesturing to someone she couldn't see. The first person to come around the curve, hesitate, and then run toward her, was Velita. Her arms were extended as she approached, and Cinnamon slipped readily into her uninhibited embrace. Over Velita's shoulder, she could see Maggie holding Alberto's hand, and as they grew nearer, her little sister's smile was, unbelievably, almost as wide as his. Rosa and Maria raced up behind them, and they all wrapped themselves around Cinnamon and Velita, who were still clinging to each other. Then the six of them started laughing and talking all at once.

"What are you *doing* here?" Velita squealed. "Why didn't we know you were coming? Are you here a long time? Just *look* at you! You're so much older! But how can that be? It's been less than two months! And yet somehow you're more beautiful than ever! Alberto, can you believe this? Maggie! Your sister is home! Oh, please God, let Mimi be able to see this, too."

Alberto took her satchels, as Cinnamon began an introductory explanation over the shouts of neighbors who had poured from every doorway.

"I'll tell you everything later, but I made the decision myself. Nothing is wrong. In fact, I'm certain that everything is so very *right* now."

Velita's arm stayed around her shoulders as Maggie walked close beside her, examining the fabric of her dress.

"This is lovely, Cinn. Did you make it yourself?"

"No, Maggie, I didn't. But thank you for thinking I *could*. Actually, I might be able to figure out the pattern, though. Would you be interested?"

"I don't think so. Well, maybe."

Before anything else was said, they rounded the corner at Mott and Broome. A half block up, on the sidewalk in front of the Mentini apartment building, Vincente stood perfectly still, his arms hanging at his sides. He was watching her walk in his direction, as if he were seeing an apparition. Dressed in black pants and a thin, white short-sleeved shirt, he was simple and unadorned. His tall bronze body was lean and well-developed and far more striking than she remembered. But she wondered if she'd ever really *looked* at him, with all of her previous, senseless distractions. Standing directly in front of him, inches away, she was definitely looking at him now.

"Cinn, I can't believe this! What are you doing here?"

"We'll learn all about it later," Velita interjected, gently moving a neighbor aside so she could get to the door. "Besides, what does it matter *how* or *why*? She's home!"

"To stay?" he asked, searching Cinnamon's eyes and afraid to hope again.

"Yes—to stay," she answered him, starting to reach for his arm but bumped away by a crush of new bystanders who'd rushed across the street.

He wanted to touch her, to kiss her cheek, to tell her that his heart had only been partially beating since the day she left. But she was already being ushered upstairs. She did turn and look over her shoulder at him, though, sending a coy smile and a wink in his direction. When she had disappeared inside the building, he walked into the middle of the street, threw his arms out, his head back, and inhaled deeply of today's perfect air as he spun around in circles. Then he broke into a sprint toward St. Paul's, where he spent the next hour on his knees at the altar rail. Father Panito, who rarely saw this young man in church any more, noticed him while passing through the sanctuary and was worried that some further catastrophe had happened.

"Vincente, hello. Is everything all right? Your family? Mimi?"

"Father!" he exclaimed, standing, then genuflecting, then crossing himself, then genuflecting again, much to the priest's amusement, "I'm here to tell you that we could not be better. Cinnamon has come back to us—*today*—just *now*!"

With thoughts of Mimi and Bradley and the heartrending story of those children flashing through his mind, Father Panito noticed a light in the boy's eyes that he had not seen for many years.

"Jesus, Mary and Joseph! What wonderful news! Perhaps our merciful God has decided your family is finally due for a miracle."

"Amen, Father. And hallelujah, too! See you on Sunday!"

Vincente virtually slid down the aisle, out the church doors and home to the Price apartment, which is where he'd been staying. He wanted to change into the new suit Velita and Alberto made for him as a surprise after Cinnamon went away. He'd been saving the exquisitely tailored garment for an occasion worthy of the silk fabric, an occasion he'd only dared to imagine in his dreams, until now.

Chapter 12

Death's searing finality is stunning when witnessed. No wonder so many people who are left behind go completely batty afterwards. Right now I find it rather comforting to know that, should such madness ever decide to arrest me, chances are reasonably good that few of my relations would be able to tell the difference.

M.E.M.
December 18, 1923

Vincente was a fine husband, but he was an even better man—and to top off Cinnamon's stroke of luck, his intriguing contrasts became more appealing as he got older. The most visible side of his nature had enabled him to remain steadily employed on the East River Waterfront since he was in his teens. His physical strength was his first advantage while transferring cargo to and from ship after ship, although his lean, six-foot three-inch frame was misleading at first glimpse and belied the power in his arms and back. First impressions also found his sculptured appearance incompatible with the offensive smells and working conditions on the docks. But he was naively unaware that he looked at all out of place, applying himself to his job with self-assurance and a sense of solidarity with his fellow workers.

He was valued by his employer for many reasons, not the least of which was his willingness to try his hand at any task. He learned quickly, worked through the night without complaint, and sometimes into consecutive day shifts when needed. By the time he was seventeen, he was being paired with the younger boys, because he'd proven to be an effective and respected teacher, and because he was one of the few who'd managed to keep himself out of trouble. While Vincente was not always able to steer his apprentices away from harmful influences, his supervisors knew that his chances were better than most of their others choices.

The small but reliable income he produced was vital to his family, but the qualities they found most engaging in him were his sensitivity, his artistic gifts, and his fascination with the way fashion could transform a woman. Of course, he knew better than to share this aspect of his life with his fellow dockworkers. But he was blessed with parents, sisters, and eventually a wife, who shared and nurtured those interests. As a result, his relationships with his family were deep and fulfilling.

Cinnamon's discovery that this exceptional man was in love with her promptly led to a breakdown of all communications with her father. The finality of this parental estrangement might have been negotiable over time, if Mimi hadn't stepped out of her netherworld to intervene again. But she did. The problem began shortly after Cinnamon returned to Broome Street in 1923, in a letter she wrote to Jonathon, Sophie, Jay and Angela, telling them of her plans to marry to Vincente. She had not anticipated her father's fierce reaction, and certainly did not expect to see him at her front door. Yet, there he stood, having traveled to speak with her in person, fully believing that a face-to-face conversation would bring her to her senses. Once he arrived, however, his rage was only heightened by his first view of her actual living conditions. Thereafter, anything resembling a rational conversation never happened.

Cinnamon had been staying in her old apartment with Maggie since her return, and that's where she also planned to live with Vincente after they married. By Broome Street standards, the dwelling was an upscale place to live, due in large part to Mimi's lingering touches. The rooms were tasteful and inviting, but Jonathon could only see deprivation and hopelessness for his daughter, despite the valiant efforts of Vincente and his parents to reason with the man. When Cinnamon refused his demand to return with him to Albany, he stormed out of the neighborhood on foot, shouting to her over his shoulder that she'd seen the last of him and seemingly unintimidated by the silent, seething throng of neighbors that stalked him for three blocks.

Dismayed by the sight of her father walking away from her in such anger, she wrote letter after letter in an attempt to soften him, but without response. She did hear from Jay, who was thankfully not being prevented from communicating with her. But he wasn't the least bit encouraging.

"Frankly, Cinn," he wrote, "I'm not certain that the economic element is upsetting him as much as the—please forgive me—the *Italian* element. I understand how awful that sounds, and I hope you know that *I* certainly don't care. I would love you if you joined the circus and wed an elf. So would Angela and Mama. But Papa won't talk about it any more, even after we reminded him that you'll still be married in the Catholic Church. Please keep writing your letters to him, though, and we won't stop trying either."

There was a time when she could have enlisted David's help during a catastrophe such as this. He would surely have used his charm and his favored status with her father on her behalf, and then the crisis would have ended. Approaching him now was out of the question, however, with the sting of her embarrassment still fresh. Besides, he had just married Lucille and was clearly too busy and unconcerned to become involved. The fact that he was the only person from Albany who'd taken no initiative to correspond with her was too obvious to overlook. Even Irene had sent her a letter, enclosing five dollars along with her love and support, and a reminder not to mention the gesture to anyone.

On December 7, 1923, when Cinnamon married Vincente in a simple, candlelit ceremony, Saint Paul's was filled to capacity with her Broome Street friends and family. But no one from Albany was there. Still, she made the best of it. Even with all the acrimony, she believed that time would moderate her father's perspective and open his heart to her. But that was before Velita and Alberto sat talking early one evening, two days after the wedding. Vincente had moved out of his parents' flat and into the Price apartment with his bride. Maggie and the twins were sitting on the steps in the hallway outside the Mentini's apartment door, having a quiet conversation with several of their friends. Appreciating the rare moment alone, Velita motioned for her husband to come join her on the sofa. Within minutes, they found themselves reliving the ceremony and the reception, again.

"She did look so lovely," Velita said. "I'm sure she used to have dreams of a grand affair, maybe held someplace like the cathedral, where she could wear a fairytale gown. But when it all came together this week, she actually seemed content with the small things we were able to do for her. And even though her dress was simple, she carried it like a queen, don't you think?"

"Yes, I do, and she acted pleased about the ceremony, except for the short walk with me, as I escorted her down the aisle. I could feel her shaking a bit, and although she smiled at me with every ounce of love she could gather, it was obvious that *I* wasn't the one she wanted to see standing next to her in that moment."

"Please, God, forgive me for what I'm going to say." Velita's serenity had been disrupted by even this vague reference to Jonathon. "In my opinion, that man lost any remaining claim to his daughter, and to his place in heaven, with his shameful, hateful treatment of her. I know she missed him at her wedding, but he didn't deserve to be there, even if he *had* apologized and reconsidered his position."

She rose to her feet and began pacing back and forth in front of her husband, who remained seated and tried not let his own emotions escalate.

"How could he have said such horrible things that day, Alberto, particularly right in front of our faces? Words like that can only come from a blackened heart!"

"You mean his declaration that we're all filthy, uneducated, penniless tenement dwellers?"

"Well, that, too," she answered, smiling back at him, in spite of herself. "But I was actually thinking about what he said to Cinnamon regarding his views on the sacrament of marriage. Remember how he told her that her vows were supposed to be holy promises, and that she should say them to someone very carefully—to someone *worthy*—because the contract was not only with the man she was marrying, but with God as well? And then he had the gall to say that God could not possibly mean for her to enter into this eternal covenant with someone like Vincente? He didn't even *know* Vincente! Honestly, if I hadn't been so worried about upsetting Cinnamon even more than she already was, I would have pointed out that God might not appreciate his sanctimonious behavior, in light of his own disrespect for the covenant. He seems to have conveniently forgotten that he *divorced* Mimi. Furthermore, he remarried! So here's a man banned from the sacraments, who's passing judgment on his own daughter, as if he were some kind of saint. How hypocritical can one person *be*?"

"Velita, sit down by me." Alberto's voice was steady, in an effort to appease her. When she was next to him, he put his arm around her shoulders. "We have no control over Jonathon, what he says or what he does. But we have a beautiful new daughter-in-law, and a son who has loved her, I think, since he was a little boy. And we *do* have some control over their future, so I suggest we…"

They were startled by a rustling sound in the corner of the room, and they both turned around just as Mimi was walking out from behind the screen. Her sable hair, which fell loose down her arms and back, was now streaked with silver, and her robe was buttoned crooked, each button fastened one hole below where it was supposed to be. Her skin had a grey tone, and she was alarmingly thin. But in that instant, her brown eyes with the green sparkles were clear and focused.

"Mimi!" Velita said, standing up before Alberto did and holding out her hands. "We thought you were sleeping."

"It wasn't a divorce." Cinnamon's mother spoke in a voice as strong as if she used it every day.

"What?" Alberto asked, since he was the one in Mimi's line of vision.

"I *said*, it wasn't a *divorce*! Velita," she continued, shifting her attention to Vincente's mother, "where are my things?"

"Which things, Mimi?"

"My papers. My books and journals. I must show Cinnamon, before there's nothing left of me."

When the knock came at the door, Vincente was nestled with his new wife in the closest they would get to a honeymoon bed. They'd been left alone for the past two days, except for the intermittent interruptions when neighborhood women, who grinned at them and commented on Cinnamon's rosy cheeks, delivered meals to the apartment. Some of the children from the block also tossed pebbles up at the front window every now and then, a customary torment for newly married couples, who, the children had been told, were not supposed to be bothered for three full days and nights.

Somewhat awestruck by the private things they'd been experiencing together since their wedding feast ended, the newlyweds were amused at these benign disturbances. They had participated in similar shenanigans over the years, when others in the neighborhood had married, and now they appreciated the rite of mischief. They also found humor in the poorly disguised looks of curiosity on the old women's faces, as they placed bowls of pasta on the table and glanced around the apartment for signs of mating activity.

This new knock on the door at such a late hour was, they both thought, just another piece of the ritual. Instead, Alberto was waiting on the other side.

"I'm sorry to bother you, but we have a situation."

"What's wrong?" Vincente asked, insisting that his father come inside.

"It's Mimi. No, she's all right," he added quickly, noting Cinnamon's frightened expression. "But she's refusing to lie down again until she sees you, Cinn."

"Why? What happened?"

"Velita and I were talking, and—oh, I don't know. It's hard to retell. But she overheard us, and now she—well, she just wants to see you. Please get dressed and come over."

Without further explanation, he kissed Cinnamon on the cheek, squeezed his son's arm, and left.

When Cinnamon and Vincente reached the top of the stairs in the other apartment building, Maggie was still in the hall with the twins and their friends. Alberto had told them to stay there, out of the way.

"Is something wrong with Mother, Cinn?"

"No, I don't think so. Apparently, she just wants to talk with me. Well, don't ask *me*," she added more abruptly than she'd intended, after seeing the skepticism on her sister's face. "I don't understand it either."

When Cinnamon entered the room, Mimi was sitting on the sofa beside Velita, and the low table in front of them was covered with books and loose papers.

"Here I am, as summoned. What's the problem?"

"She asked me to get these things from the storage closet," Velita answered, sounding almost apologetic. "I'd actually forgotten that we were keeping the box for her. It's been so long. Joseph brought it down with him during one of his visits shortly after you moved here with Bradley. Come and sit." Velita stood up and motioned for Cinnamon to take her place. "She's been struggling to stay awake until you got here. Alberto, Vince and I will be next door with the Saverinos, if you need us." With that, she coaxed her husband and son out of the apartment and closed the door.

"Hello, my dear." Mimi's voice was weak, as she lifted an inch thick book with brown leather binding from the table. But there was a determination in her eyes that Cinnamon had not seen in a long while. "I know you love him, and for that reason, this is even more urgent."

"Yes, of course I love Vincente, but I…"

"I'm not talking about *him*. This is about your father."

"Mother, please, there's no…"

"Listen to me," she commanded sharply, startling her daughter. "I'm sorry. It's just that I…*you*…don't have everything."

Cinnamon could see her mother fighting to stay in the moment, as she opened the book in her lap and removed a folded piece of paper that had been hidden in the pages.

"It's all right to love your father, but don't grant that love any power over you. Don't let him—or *anyone*, but especially *him*—diminish you with his words. Don't let his view of you become your destiny."

"Mother, forgive me, but I'm missing your point."

"Well, forgiving is part of the point. After the words, you must find a way to let go. If you fail to do that, you will never be free. The words you hold prisoner will first diminish you and then consume you, becoming stronger than the good things you want to do and be. Are you paying attention?"

"I'm trying, but I'm afraid I don't…"

"Here," Mimi interrupted, placing the folded paper in Cinnamon's hand. "Read this first, then read these pages." She took the open book and turned it upside down on the table, to mark the place. "I want to rest."

"Let me help you."

"No. I can manage. You just sit and read. We'll talk when you're through." Then she walked slowly across the room and disappeared behind the screen.

Cinnamon waited in confusion, willing her mother not to fall, until the sounds of Mimi settling on the bed had stilled. Then she looked down at the paper, not at all anxious to go wherever this scenario seemed to be taking her, and unfolded what appeared to be a legal document. As she read the highlighted words, which had been underlined in blue ink, she nearly stopped breathing.

On this date, the sixth of May in the year nineteen hundred and eight...Marriage...covenant by which Jonathon McClinty and Mary Mae McClinty sought to establish between themselves a partnership of the whole life, which is by its nature ordered toward the good of the spouses and the procreation and education of offspring. This covenant between baptized persons has been raised by Christ the Lord to the dignity of a sacrament...

...a fervent review has determined that these essential elements have not been present from the beginning...This marriage was therefore not a sacramental covenant...

...Declaration of Nullity has been granted...lawfully entered into the records of The Cathedral of the Immaculate Conception...City of Albany...State of New York...

Further, said Declaration of Nullity does not affect in any manner the legitimacy of the single offspring, Margaret Elizabeth McClinty...

Jonathon A. McClinty *Mary Mae McClinty*

Jonathon A. McClinty Mary Mae McClinty

"*What*?"

She read the words over and over. Finding no greater comprehension in the tenth reading than she did in the first, she grabbed the book off the table, which turned out to be her mother's journal. Amazed at the similarity to her own, she hesitated, aware of the private line she was about to cross. But even if her mother hadn't given her permission to proceed, her need for sensible answers would have pushed her forward into the journal's pages anyway.

May 7, 1908

A Thursday morning—the sun has just come up.

Yesterday Jonathon organized the delivery of papers to me, the signing of which will make the statement that our marriage never existed. His precise words were that "the sacramental elements were missing from the beginning." This heresy, of course, is an extension of the lie named Sophie. But through his power

as a man and as a McClinty, he is presenting me as the reason for the missing elements referenced.

I'm beginning to believe that Jonathon's brother Peter may not have been the uncaring renegade he's been painted to be. In truth, Peter could possibly have been the only person who understood that his brother's character was the one flawed. Despite his regret about leaving Amelia behind, I now think that Peter's only chance for survival was to move far afield of Jonathon's reach. He must have known his brother would eventually destroy him if he remained close to home, but he also knew that his mother would never accept such a possibility. So he fled to the country's furthest side where he could build a life free of Jonathon's interference. If only I had been so wise!

Tomorrow I will speak with Father Garretty at the cathedral. I need to understand from him directly how all of this will affect my relationship with the Church. I'd also like him to arrange a meeting between Jonathon and me so the man can explain in my presence precisely which of the missing elements in me he has found so sacramentally in place with Sophie. I want to hear from his own lips the explanation he will give to Cinnamon one day when she learns that her father used all of his might to erase her parents' marriage from history. The papers say that her legitimacy will not be in question, but he can be the one to tell her!

My Lord in heaven knows all too well that I'm imperfect and weak, but neither my daughter nor I merit such hatred. I ask forgiveness for the retribution I seek in this moment, and I pray for strength to overcome my bitterness about Jonathon and Sophie's apparent bliss. God, give me guidance as I wonder where to go from here. Will I ever feel whole or beautiful? Will anyone ever want me again?

Cinnamon realized that she was grinding her teeth. *Don't let him diminish you.* Methodically refolding the document, she placed it back inside the journal and closed the covers, her thoughts shifting from herself to her mother. How *degrading* that must have been for her. How sickening to be tossed aside like yesterday's table scraps! How patient she was, too, living with a daughter who constantly gushed about her happy adventures at the Madison house and who pined for years about moving back to Albany. All that time, her mother never said a word about her father's unthinkable treatment of her. *Don't let him diminish you. The words you hold prisoner will…consume you.* How did she ever survive? Apparently she *hadn't* for very long, even with Bradley. And then she lost him, too—the man who'd adored her so unconditionally, but more importantly, who'd *valued* her. The crushing depth of that loss was now so clear, along with the shame of a selfish child. Tears began sliding down her face, as she wished she'd understood all of this before so much wasted time had past. Then she picked up the journal and walked over to the screen.

"Mother?"

But Mimi had fallen asleep. She was lying on her back, with the sheet pulled up to her chin. Her sable-silver hair was folded on top of her head, and the skin on her face followed the sinking places that had once been her round, peach-colored cheeks. Never wanting to be held by her mother more than she did in that moment, Cinnamon gently pushed the journal beneath the pillow, instead, then turned and left the apartment.

In the hallway, Velita sat on the steps with Maggie, Rosa and Maria. Their other friends had gone home, and Alberto was downstairs with Vincente, where the men waited together on the sidewalk.

"Are you all right?" Velita asked.

"Yes, although *my* state of mind hardly seems important. Mother fell asleep, which isn't surprising after all that. She's looking especially drawn, though. Maybe we should take her out in the fresh air more often, even if the weather is chilly. We can bundle her up."

"I'll mention it to Alberto. But perhaps she'll begin to feel better, now that she's told you."

"Told you what, Cinn?" Maggie was standing with her hands on her hips. "I'm getting very annoyed at all this secrecy. She's *my* mother, too, and I'm not a child anymore. You need to stop hiding things from me!"

"Yes, you're right," Cinnamon answered, walking past her sister and starting down the stairs. "Come over tomorrow afternoon, and we'll talk. Velita, I left the book with her, under her pillow, but the rest is still on the table. Although I didn't read anything else, I suspect it's probably more of the same, and I'm sure she'd want the box safely put away in storage again."

"I'll take care of it, dear."

"Cinn!" Maggie called after her.

"*Tomorrow*, I said."

Later that night, after sharing the story with Vincente, Cinnamon held onto her husband with a genuine appreciation for his companionship. Only now starting to see how lucky she'd become, she couldn't reconcile the unjust fate handed to Mimi, a woman who'd been so consistently virtuous. What sort of twisted destiny was that?

Almost as if he could sense her thoughts, Vincente closed his arms snugly around her, pressing her against him in their bed.

"Are you going to do anything about it, Cinn?"

"About what?"

"About your father, and what you learned tonight."

"Well, what *would* I do, Vincente? That was certainly one calamity *I* did not create, and I can't imagine any action I could take to improve the situation, at this point."

"But aren't you angry that you didn't know about it?"

"Strangely, I'm just extraordinarily sad—for my mother."

Four days later, mid-morning on December 13, 1923, Cinnamon was organizing her new sewing area on her grandmother's side of the library desk. She'd begun taking in piecework from Alberto's tailor shop, and was also acquiring a personal clientele from referrals that had developed over the last few months through a most unexpected source.

While she was still in Albany that previous summer, the shop's landlord, Mr. Gregory Stafford, had stopped by for one of his periodic business discussions with the tailor. After spotting Alberto in the office, Mr. Stafford had pulled him aside.

"How have you been, Mr. Mentini? And how's that lovely, traveling redhead?"

"We're all quite fine, thank you, and Cinnamon's doing well, too, as far as we know. She's busy establishing her new life in Albany, and we're all very proud of her."

"Excellent. Glad to hear it. I thoroughly enjoyed meeting her and your family, and I'm frankly delighted that our paths crossed again today. I've been intending to look you up. My mother has decided that she would benefit substantially from having a private seamstress, rather than having her garments made and altered within the shop's pool of workers. Would you, by any chance, know of a talented, dependable woman you might recommend?"

Naturally, Velita was the first name out of Alberto's mouth, and with little need for persuasion, she began taking Mrs. Stafford's orders shortly thereafter. The additional income was a godsend, but the workload, when added to her commitments at the tailor shop, soon escalated to the point where she was straining to manage everything by herself. Maggie and the twins were enlisted to help, but their combined lack of skill and interest resulted in work that had to be redone more often than not. Bone weary from working well into the nights, in addition to caring for her family and for Mimi, Velita was ecstatic when Cinnamon came back to Broome Street. She was even more thrilled when she learned about the dressmaking course Cinnamon had discovered through Sophie, and the inventive measures she'd taken to try her hand at teaching those skills.

Sharing the workload and money between the two women became an even more natural arrangement after Vincente and Cinnamon were married. But sharing a single sewing machine proved to be completely unworkable. Using a few dollars of Bradley's savings, Alberto ordered a brand new machine for his wife, expecting that she would give her old one to Cinnamon. But Velita had grown accustomed to the familiar operation, preferring to keep the original rather the new one. Thus, Alberto showed up at his son's apartment, with the early Christmas gift in his arms, three days after Mimi's annulment revelations. Thrilled with the surprise and the sense of independence accompanying the shiny new machine, Cinnamon began to organize what she dreamed could be a little shop of her own, right in her apartment.

The double-sided desk was so large that she could use Amelia's half for her sewing and the storage of her tools, with the opposite side remaining available for her writing and Vincente's design work. She'd already been using the dining table to cut fabric and pattern pieces, and the iron was constantly warming on the stove for pressing anyway. *Everything I need for my make-believe shop is right here, and it all fits perfectly!* Smiling at her active imagination, she arranged the last of her threads, notions, and reference books in the desk drawers. Then she sat in her grandmother's chair and surveyed the room where every detail, except her new sewing area, had been put in place by Mimi.

This is still very much my mother's house, she thought, feeling a little uncomfortable that she and Vincente had more space in this apartment than they could, in good conscience, justify by themselves. *Maybe he wouldn't mind if we move Mother back into the second bedroom, so she can have all of her things around her again.* There would be a place for Maggie to stay as well, and Vincente's parents and sisters could spread out in their own home again. She decided to discuss the idea with her husband that evening, and the plan filled her with a sense of balance as she thought about what task she should begin next. But footsteps outside the apartment and a faint rapping on the door shifted her attention. Before she could get up, the knob turned and Maggie entered.

"Velita asked me to come get you. It's Mother again."

"You can't be serious. What more could she possibly have to tell me?"

"I don't think this is about talking, Cinn. Something's wrong. Alberto went out to find the doctor."

Cinnamon immediately pushed herself out of the chair and lifted her wool cape off the door hook.

"Let's go."

"No."

"I beg your pardon, Maggie?"

"*You* go. I want to stay here. Please."

"What's gotten into you?"

"I…too many people are over there. You can tell me how she's doing later. Please, don't make me go."

In a hurry to leave, Cinnamon decided not to press her sister any further.

"All right. Vincente should be home before long anyway. Would you like me to send Rosa and Maria over?"

"No…thank you."

"Fine. I *will* send someone, though, to tell you what's happening, and to get you if we need you. Meanwhile, don't touch that sewing machine."

"Maggie said you wanted to see me."

Cinnamon spoke softly as she peered around the screen into the alcove. Velita stood up from where she'd been sitting on the bed. Her face was flushed and puffy, her eyes swollen.

"Your mother is…I think she's…"

She couldn't finish. Instead, she dropped her shoulders, her arms hanging loose at her sides, as she looked at Cinnamon with a helpless, haunting expression.

"Maggie also told me that you sent Alberto to get the doctor. Is that right?"

"Yes, I did, Cinn. But he's going first to find…"

She didn't hear the rest after Velita stepped aside and her mother came into view.

"Oh my God. What happened to her?"

What used to be Mimi's tall, graceful body now barely seemed to exist beneath the blankets, and her hands, which extended from her nightgown sleeves and rested outside the covers, bore nothing but bony fingers and skin. Spread across the pillow, her hair appeared to have been drained of all the sable, and the silver left behind was dull and dry. All that looked remotely familiar about her face were the long eyelashes, which still flirted with the tops of her cheekbones from her closed lids.

"What *is* this? How can this *be*? She didn't look *anything* like this yesterday!"

Velita stood behind Cinnamon and touched the tops of her shoulders when she sat down on the edge of the bed.

"That's the way it happens, sweetheart. I'm afraid she's leaving us."

"*No*! She's *not*! That's ridiculous. I was just thinking this morning that she should come back over and live with Vincente and me. I know she hasn't been well, but she was talking to me the other day, so I'm sure she can get better. Mother! Wake up! Please, *open your eyes*."

Cinnamon leaned forward and put her arms underneath Mimi's head and back, lifting what felt like a feather into her embrace. Her mother's breathing was labored and hollow from her open mouth, her neck needing support like an infant's.

"Mother," she said again, holding and rocking her, "I love you."

Suddenly the sounds of good-bye began rising in a tremble—the deep guttural sounds that cannot be described or forgotten—the final sounds as the body struggles to no avail against the soul's command to be set free. Clutched firmly inside her daughter's arms, chest-to-chest, cheek-to-cheek, Mimi's life slipped from this earth, her last breath soaring out of her lungs and tearing straight through to the center of Cinnamon's heart.

December 17, 1923
Just before midnight

We buried Mother today. Now she's resting right next to Bradley, and I hope, at last, that she is happy again. Perhaps Amelia is with her, too, and that vision gives me a little bit of peace. Otherwise, this season of holiday joy has become almost too sad for words.

She was so beautiful, so bright and funny, with such promise. But hers was a tragic path, where her beauty and humor and talent were all smothered by her inability to fight back against people and circumstances that worked, in her words, to diminish her. For all of her preaching about believing in things that could be, her belief in herself wasn't strong enough to save her, not so much from everyone else, but, in the end from her own demons.

As I write this entry, I'm struck by the thought that someday these words might be read by my own children—if I'm blessed with any—just as Mother's words eventually reached me. The sobering concept makes me wish for one thing above all others—that I will never become lost, and that I'll always be stronger than the tragedies I'm sure must be lying in wait for me. There is no sadder vision than that of my children reading someday, in my own hand, about their mother's hopeless, floundering life. Instead, may I write about the losses and crises with honesty, not diluting or denying the pain, and then, as Mother said, find a way to let go. For the benefit of my heirs, may the subsequent pages of my journals be filled with equal devotion to the recovery and pleasures that surely will follow any future adversities.

At tonight's writing, the pain of this particularly endless day is far from over. Maggie has pulled away from us and has hidden deep within herself. I pray that she is not infused with Mother's inclinations, and that she will begin painting again to help ease her remorse. I do believe she's tormented by the fact that she wasn't in the room with me when Mother died. But as usual, she won't talk to me, and I can't assist her unless she does. She is now staying with us in the second bedroom, however, and I hope the proximity will prove to be constructive.

Velita and Alberto seem to be suffering more than anyone, even though the Magglios came down from Albany and have been taking care of absolutely everything while they hover close by. But Velita won't let anyone touch Mother's alcove. Sometimes we find her just sitting in there on the bed, which she made fresh after they took Mother away, and which she fluffs and plumps each morning as if they might be bringing her home any minute. Joseph told me he will stay here until he convinces his sister that the screen should be removed. It needs to come down, he said, to let light back into the apartment, and into the family as well. He is such a good person.

Vincente is deeply fond of his three uncles, and he is clearly cut from their same cloth, with his artistic sensibilities wrapped so cleverly inside his rugged presence. I do wish we could all be together more often, for happy occasions, so he could benefit from their company. Besides, there's nothing better for a room full of women than a room full of kind men who love them. How fortunate I am to have been blessed with one of those men as my husband. He's been so dear throughout these past four days, and I think he misses Mother, too. I must remember that thought, the next time he's comforting me.

For now, I should try my best to sleep. Vincente is scheduled to work an early shift, beginning shortly after dawn, which will be here in a blink. While he's away, I want to sit with Joseph and listen to his rich (and immensely entertaining) stories about Mother and Bradley, and my grandmother. Somehow, hearing him talk about them seems to help, as much as anything can at this point. Then, later on I want to offer my support to the neighbors who've faithfully been preparing all of our meals this week, especially since the turkey they're going to attempt cooking in the morning was my idea.

M.E.M.

After Mimi died, the sewing area already established on the library desk became a refuge for Cinnamon, making it possible for her to stay busy making clothes for Maggie, herself, and for several of the neighbors, who had come to rely upon her. She was also helping Velita with the custom garments on order for Mrs. Stafford. Work for the uptown woman was steady, and Velita paid Cinnamon a percentage equal to the amount of work she performed per item, from a few cents for piecework to many dollars for a start-to-finish article of clothing. When her earnings per week became consistent, Vincente opened a savings account for his wife's money in the World Exchange Bank and usually made deposits for her on his way home from the waterfront after a night shift. She kept track of the balance in her journal and watched proudly as the number slowly increased from $10 to $12 to $18, and more over the first few months.

Pleased that she'd discovered a way to make a meaningful financial contribution to her family, she learned early in 1924 that her small, in-house business would also give her the means to make preparations for a baby. Her eighteenth birthday on January 26 marked one full week of illness that sent her reeling at the first smell of anything cooking, whether in her own apartment or in another nearby. Velita suspected, after a few days, that this was neither a case of influenza nor the result of eating bad food, and the pregnancy was finally confirmed in late February. While she was *incarcerated,* as Cinnamon described her state of being over the next seven months, she thought she would surely have gone mad had it not been for her sewing machine.

"Honestly, Vincente, I wish someone could explain to me why women who are expecting babies are shoved away behind closed doors, as if they were some sort of freaks. After all, it's not as if the process should come as any surprise to people. As far as I can tell, everyone we know has arrived on the earth in this same manner, and other than a bulky body, I am still the exact person I was before this happened to me. So why can't I go anywhere?"

"If the decision were mine, Cinn, I'd take you with me everyplace, all the time. I *like* the way you look with a baby in there. But since none of the other women wander around when they're in your condition, I'd prefer that you not be the first in the neighborhood to do so."

"All right. But I'm going to write a letter to the newspaper. Bradley always said that if you disagree with something, you should publicize your point. Nothing ever changes, if people simply complain all the time, without taking any corrective action."

"If that will make you feel better, I won't stop you," he said, continually amused at her spirit. "But don't be disappointed if all the pregnant women in New York aren't suddenly invited to lunch at City Hall."

By the time Claudine Marie Mentini was born on October 6, 1924, Cinnamon had written a dozen letters to the editor of Bradley's former newspaper, without receiving a single response. But she had not been dwelling on her discontent. Instead, she'd been sewing night and day, not only on her assignments from Velita, but on her nursery as well. Half of the small bedroom, where Maggie now slept with the baby, had been decorated with the original nursery furniture, which Joseph had been storing in his Albany shop. He and the other Magglios shipped the pieces to Broome Street as a surprise, an event that escalated into a neighborhood affair when Velita and several of her friends arranged for Cinnamon to be called across the street on a bogus mending assignment. They managed to keep her over there for several hours while the furniture was unloaded and set up in the bedroom.

When she was finally allowed to come back home, she could not believe what she was seeing. Even the nursery's original stained glass lamps were in place, and the white crocheted canopy had been hung over the cherry wood crib. Velita stood beaming, delighted with the beautiful scene and pleased to have discovered her knack for secrecy. After the cluster of neighbors finished applauding and blotting their damp faces, they all moved back into the living room to share in the opening of more baby gifts.

Cinnamon was still savoring the warmth and camaraderie when she awakened for her new daughter's dawn feeding the next morning. Unable to stop admiring the room full of lovely things for her child, her mood grew even more lighthearted. While nursing Claudine again after breakfast, she found herself alone in the apartment with her sister, and she began reminiscing.

"You have no idea how hysterical I was, Maggie, when Bradley moved that very same furniture out of *my* room in preparation for *your* birth. Now it seems that we've come full circle, doesn't it? The beautiful pieces are here for my new baby, who shares *your* room with you. Don't you think that's rather amusing?"

"I suppose," Maggie said, never lifting her eyes from the watercolor she was working on that captured impressive details of fire escape life across the street.

Despite her hope for a dialogue with her sister, Cinnamon didn't press the point. Maggie's creative drive had all but disappeared after Mimi's death, and no measure of encouragement from the family or neighbors had been able to reignite the spark. As a result, they'd all been surprised when the girl's artistic desire reappeared with the arrival of the furniture crate from Albany. Her inspiration didn't seem to come so much from the nursery pieces, but from the three-foot square, framed oil painting that had been included.

The scene on the painting depicted the inside of a parlor that reminded Cinnamon of the Madison house, with a view looking out a large window toward a yard filled with bare, leafless trees. The glow of coals and wood in the room's fireplace was so lifelike that one could almost feel the heat, and with a little imagination, the windblown snow outside the window felt cool to the touch. Centered and attached to the lower shelf of the painting's frame was a small brass plaque engraved with the single word Winter. But the most intriguing thing, aside from the artwork's inclusion with the nursery furniture in the first place, was the accompanying note sealed in an envelope.

November 1, 1924

Dear Vincente and Cinnamon—

Please accept this painting as a belated wedding gift. We will try to come up with one more appropriate for your baby, now that we know we have a little *girl*—our very own great-niece!

Meanwhile, we all felt the need to finish *this* canvas for you first. The snow of **Winter** is, for us, the purest of all seasonal gifts, requiring no planting or effort in preparation, and coming whenever it pleases, without regard for our convenience. This work is the fourth and final in the series. Amelia and Mimi live on in every stroke of our brushes.

We are fine here, but we miss you. Olivia, Helena, Christina and Rebecca asked us to send their deepest excitement, as well, about the news of your new daughter.

Love,
Joseph, Anthony and Matthew

"Velita, what does this mean?' Cinnamon had asked. "The fourth and final in *what* series? They make it sound like there are three other paintings somewhere."

"I have no idea, Cinn. Why don't you ask them in your next letter?"

"Yes, that's precisely what I'll do. I can't imagine why Joseph didn't explain. Someone really needs to start writing this sort of thing down, so people like us won't have to wonder in the future."

"I'm not sure that would always be wise, dear. But at the moment, a greater concern is this blouse for Mrs. Savarino."

Life on Broome Street over the next year and a half was blessedly uneventful, giving everyone time to adjust to their losses, while they all worked from dawn until dusk in search of the economic prosperity being hailed in the daily newspapers. While Alberto and Velita saw little improvement in their own circumstances, they were grateful for the relatively comfortable lives they'd been able to create for themselves and their family. They didn't stop believing, however, that they could still have a piece of the wealth they kept reading about, if they just worked hard enough—and if they were always on the lookout for unexpected opportunities.

Alberto first learned of the new correspondence program through an advertisement received at the tailor shop in April of 1926, and he placed an order for the full complement of lessons, with Cinnamon exclusively in mind. Several weeks later, when he brought the books home to her, she thought *The Nu-Way Course in Fashionable Clothes Making©1926* was merely an updated edition of Sophie's dressmaking course. As a result, she set the books aside, since her hands were already quite full enough with her family and her work. Claudine had begun walking before she was a year old and had been running willy-nilly around the apartment for the last six months. Maggie had been helping with the baby whenever she wasn't in school and did her best to keep the child under control. But Cinnamon's intervention was frequently required, which often took time away from important Stafford garments that always seemed to be needed within an impossible timeframe. She was also giving earnest effort to her cooking, although the hours had a way of disappearing, leading her more often than not to Velita's dining table for the evening meal, with her husband, sister, and baby daughter in tow.

Thus, when Alberto kept pushing her to take a look at the new correspondence course, she tried to be polite, but could not believe he actually thought she would have one free minute to learn another detail about sewing techniques. Growing impatient with her dismissal, he followed her back to her apartment one evening, after the family had eaten, and forced her to sit down on Mimi's side of the library desk. Then he drew her attention to Lessons 49 through 56, in the Table of Contents. Unable to escape the moment, she began reading the section titled *Introduction to the Dress Shop*—and the direction of her life was forever altered in that review, starting with the first paragraph of the *Foreword.*

"If you have any idea whatever of owning your own little dress shop some day, the pages that follow will offer you many valuable suggestions. Perhaps you are planning merely to convert one of the rooms in your home into the equivalent of a dress shop. Or you may be planning to have one of the prettiest shops on Main Street. In either case, you will find just the information you want in the following lessons."

That night when Vincente was at work and both Maggie and Claudine were asleep, she turned up the lamp on the library desk and sat down again in her mother's chair. There she stayed until several hours after midnight, when her eyes would no longer remain open, as she poured over the words the authors seemed to have written as if they knew who she was and where she lived.

"...There can certainly be nothing more satisfying, more to be desired, than an interesting, worth-while career and an income that makes one independent. Particularly is this true of the married woman who finds she has to stint and

economize when her taste demands certain luxuries. It is true also to the younger woman who feels within her the urge to engage in some profitable work that she will enjoy and will earn her a substantial income.

"To these women, the fashionable dress shop offers a splendid opportunity...Do not attempt to read the whole book through at one sitting—and then expect to open a shop that will be successful. Study the lessons just as you did the dressmaking lessons...

"Before anything else, you must know exactly how to approach your lessons and how every woman is the moulder [sic] of her own life, the master of her own destiny. If she wishes to step away from the commonplaces of life, into a broader and more congenial environment where she will meet more people and have greater opportunities for success, there should be no one to stand in her way. If she feels the desire for independence, if there are luxuries that are being denied her, she has every reason in the world to reach out and get them for herself.

"There was a time when women foolishly assured themselves that their only place was in the home. But that day has passed. Never before have there been so many women successfully engaged in business as there are today—women in all classes of life, from the busy housewife to the society woman—women who have found at last the happiness that independence and pleasant work bring. It is no longer necessary to long for a career, or an independent income—you can have it.

"Of course, the answer to your demand for a career, or a profession, is dressmaking. Perhaps you are not content just to make dresses for your friends and neighbors in your own home, dividing your time between your household duties and your clothesmaking. Perhaps your dream is to have a smart, fashionable dress shop with delightful creations on display, with a splendid patronage and a still more splendid income. Then you will be able to pay someone to do your housework; you will be able to employ people to do the details of the sewing and cutting. You will be the clever modiste—the creator of the styles, the designer of the modes, the owner of the shop!

"...Of paramount importance, of course, is the amount of capital that can be placed into the business...If the capital is limited, we suggest that for the time being the home be converted into a shop...Even one room will serve the purpose if necessary. But if one has sufficient capital to attempt taking a little shop and furnishing it correctly, then by all means that should be the choice.

"...You will want to know exactly how much capital you need, how to furnish the shop, how to get and keep customers. That is the purpose for which the following lessons are written...When computing the necessary amount of capital, first figure out carefully the number of garments that will have to be made to realize a certain profit. This profit must be sufficient to cover the overhead

expense—which means the expense of rent, light, heat, insurance, etc...Do not attempt to carry greater expense than your shop can stand. It is not wise to invest one's last penny...and it's very easy to lose everything if you haven't got a hundred or two hundred dollars when you need it at some critical point in your business.

"It is possible to start a dress shop on as little as $500, and more can be added to this regularly from the profits to increase the business. $1000 is a safer amount to have available, and with $2000 you can open an attractive dress shop indeed...We strongly advise you...start small and increase your business as you progress.

"Having determined the capital, it is now necessary to select both a location and a name for your business...You may use your own name, of course, calling your shop the 'Grace Frank Dress Shop,' or the 'Helen Roberts Dress Shop,'...but it is always better to have an odd, attractive name that will suggest the policy of the shop and give to it a certain distinction...

"In your choice of name, remember that dignity is important. Do not choose a name that is obviously 'made up,' obviously forced—like this name we recently saw: 'We Serv-U-Fine Shop.'...

"But even an excellent name won't bring you success if your location is wrong...The very best place for your dress shop is in that section of the city, or village, where stores cater to the needs of women. For instance, where there is a beauty shop, a large general store, a millinery shop, etc., you can be sure women come to the section during the day...provided it is not a 'market' section where the streets are untidy and unattractive...

"Very often you will find that by taking a shop on a side street, instead of on the avenue, you will save a great deal in the matter of rent. And often the side street location is almost as good a location...that leads on to the avenue..."

Despite the Introduction's cautionary remark against reading the remainder in its entirety, Cinnamon skimmed Lessons 50 through 56, simply because she couldn't stop herself. She had never felt such a passion for any idea, and the perfect fit of this one excited her more with every topic—Furnishings, the Reception and Fitting Rooms, Stationery, Business Cards, Customer Records, How to Get New Customers, Selecting Employees and Salespeople, Bookkeeping, Bank Accounts, Computing Overhead Expenses, Keeping Memorandums, Business Methods including greeting the customer, little services that count, the ethics of dressmaking, and Seasonal Changes addressing good and bad business seasons, suggestions for Christmas, maternity clothes, underwear, lingerie, and children's clothes.

"Every possible thing I need to know or do is right *here*," she exclaimed to Vincente, almost in disbelief. "I do not see how I can pass this up, especially since I've sort of been running a shop right here in this living room for the last two and a half years."

"I understand your enthusiasm, Cinn, and I agree that this seems to be a good match for your natural ability and recent experience. But we don't have $2000, or $1000, or even the minimum $500."

"No, *we* don't. However, the lesson on capital talks about the importance of finding and using *other people's* money. This would be a great investment for *someone*, particularly since the whole idea supports the Better Homes Movement so beautifully. According to the newspaper, people are putting their money into stocks and other gambles that are a far greater risk than a little dress shop. And with the economy growing stronger every day, there are few things more certain than a woman's need for nice clothing to wear. I'm convinced I could effectively present the merits of this to the right person. Could we talk with your father? Maybe he would have some suggestions."

Alberto had been waiting for Cinnamon to approach him, and in anticipation had already mentioned the idea to Mr. Gregory Stafford, who was deeply interested in helping this family. But Cinnamon didn't know any of this when she was informed that Mr. Stafford wanted to take a look at her business plan.

"At my *what*?

Vincente was even more amused by her reaction that he expected to be.

"I thought you said you knew how to present this idea."

"Well, yes, I do," she said. "I just didn't anticipate that anyone would want to see my plan so soon, and therefore, I haven't exactly written all of it, or more precisely, *any* of it yet."

Experiencing an energy level she had not realized was possible, she worked well into the night for nearly a week, as she prepared her detail. On Tuesday, May 4, 1926, Alberto and Vincente rode the subway with her to the brownstone Mr. Stafford shared with his mother on East 67th Street. Cinnamon had been there one time before with Velita, when she was delivering a garment, but the women never left the front parlor where Mrs. Stafford greeted and paid them. On *this* day, however, a nice man who reminded her of Drake led them up two flights of the home's narrow staircase and down a hallway to Mr. Stafford's office, which overlooked a beautiful garden.

"Good morning," he said to them, walking out from behind a desk even larger than Mimi's, with his hand extended. "I hope your ride here was uneventful."

"Yes it was, thank you, sir," Alberto answered, sensing the nervousness in his son and daughter-in-law, and hoping to God that Cinnamon was ready for this.

"Please sit down and make yourself at ease." They followed his direction and took their seats in the three chairs arranged in front of his desk. "Tea will be brought in shortly," he added, moving back behind his desk and sitting down to face them. "So, my dear, what do you have to show me?"

Cinnamon froze momentarily when he looked at her. But she had practiced this over and over with Vincente, and she wasn't going to let a little terror get in her way now. Removing her business plan from her pocketbook, she returned his look with every ounce of confidence in her body.

"I've prepared this proposal for your review, Mr. Stafford, which I would first like to explain in my own words. Then I'll be pleased to have you examine the detail I've written. Will that meet with your approval?"

Impressed with the leap of maturity in this young woman since he first met her three years earlier, he could also see the combination of talent, determination and self-discipline that were mandatory for an enterprise such as this to succeed. Aware of the strong support network available to her through her family and neighbors, he was sold before she spoke another word. But he found himself a trace smitten with her courage, and he let her finish presenting what she'd obviously labored hard to prepare.

"All right," he said, after she'd completed her explanation, and after a silence she was certain had lasted an hour while he studied her papers. "I'm comfortable with the full $2000, but in addition to a small rate of interest on the loan, I'd like to ask for ten percent of your first $1000 profit. Other than that, once the loan is repaid, you will have no further commitment to me. Would that be acceptable to you?"

Cinnamon assumed that she'd given him a relatively intelligent answer, although she honestly could not remember much of anything after hearing *I'm comfortable with the full $2000.* She was also fairly certain that Vincente and Alberto had engaged her in dialogue during their subway ride back to Broome Street. But she couldn't recall a single detail about the trip home, or a moment when her feet had touched the ground. She did have a hand-written document in her possession, however, which listed Mr. Stafford's terms for the loan. The agreement further stated that he was going to assign someone in his company to assist in the search for a proper location—*a shop of reasonable size and condition, with a current owner ready to sell.* Furthermore, he told her he was going to provide this additional service to her at no charge.

"Just write a summary of your activities for me each week until you've become established," he'd said, "and I'll let you know if I have any questions or concerns."

The perfect shop became available a month later on Crosby Street, five storefronts south of Houston and one block east of Broadway. The side street location was close to the popular Houston Market, in an area filled with a variety of bakeries and houseware shops, and within walking distance of Broome Street, but less crowded and slightly more gentile.

Two months later, on Monday, August 2, 1926, with money in the bank, her rent paid in advance through December, and three employees on the payroll, the doors to *A Touch of Cinnamon Dress Shop* opened with considerable celebration. Dozens of potential customers responded to the advertisement in the newspaper and to the printed flyers left with every agreeable vendor. For hours during that first day, women filed through the shop to meet Cinnamon and examine the different dresses she had on display, which she'd made in a variety of sizes in case someone wanted to make a purchase on the spot. The atmosphere on Broome Street several blocks away was like a carnival, with everyone bragging about her being a product of the *fine community* where she'd been raised. A group of twenty women ranging in age from grandmothers to teenage girls even walked up to Crosby Street to get a firsthand look at the achievement.

Velita was officially counted as one of the three employees, but she was actually the shop manager. Believing in this endeavor enough to quit her job at the tailor shop, with Alberto's blessing, she devoted herself full time to her daughter-in-law's venture. Her primary responsibility was supervising the other two employees, young women from Broome Street who'd been students of Cinnamon's when she'd first begun using Sophie's original correspondence course as a teaching aid. Reporting to work on opening day, the girls could not believe their good fortune at having been hired for the new business enterprise. Maggie was offered one of these positions in the beginning, but said she'd prefer to focus on her paintings. Velita kept her relief at this response to herself, having struggled over the years to make a seamstress out of Cinnamon's sister. Worrying about that impossible task again would have been dreadful, with all the new work to be done to get the shop business off the ground.

Her duties were extensive. Every morning she reexamined the status of each in-house order, many of which had already been contracted months ahead of the shop's opening through Mrs. Stafford or her referrals. Velita prioritized those orders by the dates the finished garments were required, and then broke each outfit or item of clothing into remaining tasks, which she assigned to her two employees.

Both she and Cinnamon monitored their protégées and continued helping them improve their techniques. But Cinnamon's primary jobs included the tracking of expenses, on-going as well as projected, when measured against sales. She also wrote detailed daily journal entries on every aspect of the shop's operation, which she usually penned at night after all of her domestic chores were complete. Sometimes those chores spilled over into the shop's activities when she found it necessary to bring Claudine to work with her. But the neighbors soon realized the importance of her concentrating on the start-up operation, especially in the early months. In response, they organized a schedule for different families to take care of the child, enabling Cinnamon and Velita to pour all of their strength into the new business.

Vincente made a contribution, as well, through his periodic dress designs, which he sketched exclusively for the shop's customers. He would create them after hearing Cinnamon's physical descriptions of the woman placing the orders and the occasions for which the dresses or gowns would be worn. *A Touch of Cinnamon*'s incarnations of his designs were frequently seen in photos on the City's society pages, and Cinnamon wanted to boast about her husband every time she was asked to provide information on the designer of one gown or another. But Vincente insisted that his wife and mother not reveal him as the source.

"Just take the credit yourselves," he said repeatedly to them. "After all, if not for your ability to bring my designs to life, these sketches would have no value whatsoever. Besides, if the men on the dock ever saw me with one of my gowns, I'd never be able to go back and do real work again."

In spite of their pride in his talent, they kept their word to him and honored his request, even when the time came that their silence wasn't important anymore.

The relationship between Velita and Cinnamon had always been one of respect and admiration, but their alliance with this dress shop brought them to a new level. Each woman had skills that complemented the other. Each protected the other and worked quietly to correct any errors made by the other, whether in judgment or garment assembly. But the most powerful bond between them was their love for Vincente and their appreciation of his pure character and gentle heart.

Neither woman understood the many emerging parallels in their relationship when compared to that of Amelia and Mimi. But Joseph and his brothers were quick to see the similarities after arriving with their families to help celebrate the shop's inaugural week. Joseph elected not to dwell on the phenomenon, however, and he counseled his brothers not to mention the connections either. He feared that any comments they might make would tempt fate into creating an equally unhappy ending. In the end, there's no way Joseph or anyone else could have known that the relationship between Cinnamon and Velita was not the one in peril.

Chapter 13

Late at night on June 8, 1929
Now that everyone is asleep...

My dearest Angela—

Today we had the seventh annual Broome Street Graduation Festival for everyone in the neighborhood with a new high school diploma. (Can you believe that six years have gone by since our own graduations?) This time we had twenty-three honorees. When Maggie finished three years ago, there were only fourteen (still much better than the first year when we only had seven). So, not only is the event a great celebration for everyone, but it does seem to serve as a bit of incentive for youngsters to complete their studies, which was a hope when Vincente initially came up with the idea. At any rate, we were all exhausted, especially those of us who also had to work several hours at the shop. But my body was so restless that I was unable to be still or close my eyes when I went to bed. Do you ever get that way after an exceptionally long day? Rather than just lie there staring up at the ceiling, I thought I'd use the time to write a catch-up note to you, because when I'm supposed to be awake, there isn't a minute to spare.

How are you, my dear friend? And what is Jay up to these days? Are you still so desperately in love with each other (silly question, I know)—and when, pray tell, are the two of you finally going to marry? I realize that you've been waiting for the age difference to completely disappear. But my brother is twenty now, and I think that's close enough, don't you? Or has Papa convinced him to wait until he's finished with college? I suppose that would make sense, much as I hate to admit it, since he only has two years left. Or has he whittled it down to one with his irritatingly amazing mind? Whatever the case, do fill me in about your conversations on the subject at your first opportunity, so I don't start imagining things.

Our progress at the dress shop has been nothing short of astonishing. Last March (forgive the repeat if I already told you this in my last letter), I made the *final payment on the original loan to Mr. Stafford. Now that was a day, after three years of working to build our customers and our reputation! For once, I didn't shoo-shoo away the compliments either. This time, I'm very proud of what we've been able to do. I still owe Mr. Stafford $100—the ten percent of the first $1000 profit, which was part of our contract—but then my obligation to him will be over. I must say, however, that I will probably always feel in debt to him for the doors he has opened and the dreams he's helped us realize.*

Have you given any thought to the best time for your next trip to visit me? I do wish this didn't have to be such a one-way thing, with you always coming down here. But I'm not ready to face Papa yet, even all these years later. Maybe, I keep thinking, if he would just reach out to apologize, or make even the slightest effort to accept Vincente, then I would be willing to meet him part way. Do you see any signs of a thaw from your perspective? Anyway, regarding your next visit, how about coming for Claudine's fifth birthday on October 6? Hopefully, my brother will come with you as usual, and I will plan a fun agenda for all of us. When you have a minute, drop me a line and let me know how that sounds.

Meanwhile, I can't tell you how many times I've wished you were here beside me, so we could talk on through the night as we used to do. I love you, Angela. Give kisses to Jay.

Always,
Cinn

P.S. I don't suppose David ever mentions me, but if he should, please tell him I said hello. I'm finally able to think of him without shrinking from embarrassment. But I'm not at all certain how to begin communicating with him again, after we've each had so much happen in our lives that has gone unshared. Any suggestions you might offer as to how we could repair the situation would be deeply appreciated. One of my many regrets is that Claudine doesn't really know who he is, and she has missed out on her cousins as well, even though David only seems to sire boys. But DJ is just three months older than she (with his unbelievably ironic birthday of July 4th), and I imagine they would be great friends, if we were all close the way we used to be. Now that little Ryan is nearly three, do you think Lucille will be ready to have another? Of course, none of this is my business. Do give David my best, though, if you find an appropriate moment.

M.E.M.♥

"The nation is marching along a permanently high plateau of prosperity."

—Irving Fisher, Ph.D., Economics
Yale University
October 24, 1929

Stock Prices Slump $15,000,000,000
In Nation-Wide Stampede to Unload!

—The New York Times
October 29, 1929

"Vincente, what does this latest news actually mean for us?"

Cinnamon normally read the newspaper at the fish market in the mornings before the proprietor began using the pages to wrap his customer's purchases. But today, October 30, she bought her own copy, which was one of the few left by the time she arrived at the corner newsstand just after dawn. Although the last week had been filled with daily reports of market crashes, recoveries, and rumors of impending financial doom, Tuesday, October 29 was when the wealthy man's panic became equal to the common man's throughout cities across America.

The changes in fortunes over a few days were difficult to grasp, given the extraordinary opulence of the 1920's, particularly after President Coolidge took office. Even the residents of Broome Street had prospered. Between 1921 and 1929, the gross national product increased from $69.6 billion to $103.1 billion, and the phenomenal growth in demand for products and services led to falling prices, as production increased even faster. Jobs were plentiful on the waterfront and in the garment business, as well as in most major industries, and the street shops flourished as the boom's reach began extending into the most impoverished neighborhoods. This progress coincided with dramatic reductions in taxes from the excessive levels boosted a decade earlier to pay for World War I. Although wages for most uneducated trade workers remained low, they were higher than ever before, enabling many to begin saving and investing. Their cash was deposited in the bank accounts that they'd been persuaded to open as an alternative to their hiding places in boxes or under beds in their apartments. Many of them had also become investors, because stocks had become accessible to all socio-economic levels. These were often purchased *on margin*, however, otherwise known as *credit*—a wide-spread practice endorsed by the federal government, as well as by the financial community, during the euphoric boom of the 1920's.

People buying on margin would purchase shares from a broker for a small percentage of the stock's value, effectively receiving a loan for the rest. The buyers would not be required to repay the balance until they sold the stock. The benefit was that a small increase in the stock's price would result in immense profits for the investor, otherwise known as the *speculator*. But the danger was that, if the price of the stock declined more than the percentage they had put down, they would have to immediately cover the difference. On what became known as Black Thursday—October 24, 1929—the price of stocks fell so dramatically that many of these speculators discovered their entire investments had been entirely depleted. When the New York Stock Exchange closed the following Tuesday, October 29, the Dow Jones stood at 230, a forty percent drop from an all-time high of 381 less than eight weeks earlier.

Investing by the average man had been encouraged by President Coolidge, almost to the point where failure to do so was perceived as unpatriotic. In a speech to the National Republican Club in February 1924, Coolidge said, "An expanding prosperity requires that the largest possible amount of surplus income should be invested in productive enterprise under the direction of the best personal ability…" He pushed for even lower taxes to free up income for this purpose, and once his tax bill was passed, the stock market began its extraordinary climb.

After Coolidge decided not to seek reelection in 1928, Herbert Hoover won the Republican Party's nomination and was ultimately elected president that fall. When he took office on March 4, 1929, he could not have known that his administration would usher in the Great Depression. Following nearly ten years of unparalleled economic expansion, October 29, 1929 brought an end to the merrymaking. But when the Dow Jones dropped to 230 that day, the country was only seeing the *beginning*. The stock market's slide continued for three additional years, reaching the ultimate low of *41* on July 8, 1932. Hoover's inability to bring an end to the nightmare led to his loss of the presidency in the 1932 election, and brought Franklin Delano Roosevelt to the first of what would turn out to be four terms in office.

The far-reaching ramifications of those events in the fall of 1929 could not have been imagined, however, as Cinnamon read her newspaper on the morning of October 30, once again putting the question to her husband.

"How does this latest news affect us? I mean *us*, right here in this family."

"Not as badly as some, Cinn. And I'll gradually withdraw the rest of your shop money over the next few days, so at least we'll still have *that*, in case the situation gets worse. When things settle down, we'll put the money back in the bank. For now, though, I'll feel safer with it in our hands."

Vincente and Alberto had been watching along with everyone else since the previous Thursday, when the initial market downturn began raising alarms. Neither of them had speculated with stocks, believing that if they did not have the money to pay for the shares in full, they should not buy them, no matter how unpatriotic that might sound. Instead they had two accounts in the World Exchange Bank at 174 Second Street, about twelve blocks from Broome Street on Vincente's way to and from the waterfront. One account was Bradley's savings and now included anything left over from the combined family earnings each week. But there wasn't always money left over to deposit from their regular jobs, and the balance in that account never seemed to grow more than a few dollars each month. The second account, however, held proceeds from Cinnamon's dress shop, and on October 23 the balance was just under $3000.

What worried Vincente was the fact that the banks themselves had been investing on margin, and if stock prices fell far enough—if panic prevented a rebound—the banks might be forced to utilize all of their deposits to cover their losses. On Friday October 25, he bartered for a large steel strongbox in a metal-work's shop near the docks, and on Saturday the 26th, he began withdrawing cash from the dress shop account, in small amounts, to avoid attracting attention. Ultimately, his instincts would be proven correct. By the end of that November, investors had lost $100 billion in assets, and by the end of 1932, all of the banks in thirty-eight states had been forced to close.

President Roosevelt's administration would eventually produce historic social programs that not only helped ease the suffering from the Depression, but reopen the banks and guard against future despair. Among these was the Federal Deposit Insurance Corporation (FDIC) established by Congress in 1933, which insured individual accounts for $100,000 in banks that were covered. But in advance of all this, in 1929 when people everywhere were being completely wiped out of their savings, their jobs and their homes, Vincente's perception and calculated actions enabled his family to endure the cataclysm, to be of help to their neighbors, and also to keep the doors of the dress shop open.

The late autumn sun was setting earlier each day and caused lights to go on in the Broome Street windows by five o'clock on the evening of Friday, November 8, 1929. Vincente had just finished locking another $200 in the strongbox, and Cinnamon sat at the kitchen table, watching him put the box under the floorboards. Then he unrolled the braided rug on top of the hiding place and handed her the small brass jailer's key threaded through a long silver chain, which he insisted she wear around her neck beneath her undergarments.

"I hope you've been keeping your promise, Cinn, and not telling a living soul about this money or the key."

"Of course I have."

"You're certain that you haven't even told my mother?"

"That's right, although I can't imagine why you don't trust her."

"That's not the point. It's everyone *else* I don't trust. These are horrible times, and I don't want to take any chances. Only $300 remains in your shop account, which I'll withdraw in another few days. There's no telling what might happen, if word got out that we have the rest hidden in here. After the losses people have taken, your $2600 would tempt even normally upright citizens."

"But I thought you said things were going to stabilize. It's been almost two weeks since the crisis began."

"I'm afraid I underestimated the problem, just as thousands of others did. You can't believe the hysteria I see every day going to and from the docks. I can only imagine what must be happening in the rest of the city, and the *country*, for that matter. Everyone's tempers are quick to flare, and the panic makes them do and say things impulsively that they wouldn't do or say otherwise. The situation is actually very dangerous, in my opinion, and the contrast is shocking compared with a few weeks ago, when everything seemed so rosy."

"Do you think it will all be over by Thanksgiving?"

"No, Cinn, I certainly do not. Why?"

"Well, when Angela answered my last letter saying that she and Jay wouldn't be able to visit for Claudine's birthday, she suggested Thanksgiving as an alternative. I assumed you wouldn't mind, so I wrote back telling her that would be wonderful."

He moved behind the chair where she was sitting and began to gently massage her shoulders.

"I see. I suppose I'll forgive you for not consulting me, because I know how hard you've been working—and, yes, having them here for the holiday *will* be wonderful. Even if the trouble persists, there shouldn't be any reason why they can't come."

"Oh, thank you! You are so unbelievably good to me, and I'll never understand why God decided to bless me with the gift of you."

"Don't read too much into my forgiveness, love. I'm just hopeful that with both Jay and Angela here for the holiday, there's a slight chance we might finally have a turkey that doesn't look and taste like it's been thrown off the top of a building."

On the morning of Tuesday, November 12, Velita and Cinnamon left their apartments at nine o'clock and walked together to the shop. Several women were scheduled to come in for fittings throughout the day, so Claudine stayed home with the neighbors. The weather was finally feeling seasonal, a cool drizzle making the streets slick and shiny beneath the continuous flow of motorcars that rumbled past them.

"I'm going to look a fright by the time we get there," Cinnamon said, pulling the rim of her hat down close to her eyebrows to shield her face from the rain. "Do you suppose we'll ever be able to afford a motorcar ourselves, so we can arrive wherever we're going without our hair and clothes being completely messed up?"

"It's only water, Cinn. You'll dry out before our first customer comes in."

"That's not the point, nor is it an answer to my question."

"All right. No, I do *not* think we'll ever own a motorcar, especially not now. We're just fortunate that we still have our work! And instead of a motorcar, I think we should be praying that our customers' husbands don't lose their jobs either, although I believe a few already have."

Cinnamon looked sheepishly at her mother-in-law, as potential ramifications of the economic downturn began unfolding in her mind.

"No matter what happens, Velita, we simply cannot lose the shop! I swear to heaven that I'll be willing to live the rest of my life without a motorcar, if the door to our little business is still open after all of this is over."

Vincente left the dock when his shift ended at noon, first taking the subway and then walking the rest of the distance to the bank on 2nd Street. The morning drizzle had given way to a steady downpour by eleven o'clock, and water was pooling along the curbsides of nearly every street. As he reached his destination, he jumped a stream that was running through the intersection and up over the sidewalk, almost to the front door of the bank. Through the window, he could see the long lines of people standing at each teller station, just as they'd been doing every day since October 26, when he'd made his first withdrawal. Today the lines appeared even longer, though, and when he pulled the door open, he heard the loud pitch of voices as patrons talked with each other and with the tellers. Everyone was expressing dissatisfaction over matters he could not discern, and even the bank employees appeared to be more agitated than they'd previously been.

It's a good thing we only have $300 left in here, he was thinking, trying not to feel guilty about the other $2600 under his kitchen floor. He was in line for half an hour before he reached the front with his withdrawal voucher for $290, an amount that would leave just enough in the account to keep it open. When the teller glanced up at him, with eyes that understood his objective, he looked right back at her with a confidence he wasn't really feeling, as if to indicate this was a perfectly normal financial move for him.

"Too bad I didn't bring my boat with me," he quipped, trying to change the unspoken subject and gesturing outside toward the rain, which was now blowing sideways.

"What?" she asked, clearly incredulous that he was making any attempt at humor.

"This must be how Noah felt," he added with a grin, hoping to provoke a smile from the woman while he watched her count out $290 in bills on the marble counter.

When she handed him his money and withdrawal receipt, she finally responded to him, her small blue eyes filling with tears.

"The captain of the Titanic would be a more appropriate reference than Noah, *sir*, if you're intent on making an analogy."

"Right," he said through the catch in his voice, wishing he could start the conversation over again. "I'm sorry."

After tucking the money down his inside jacket pocket, he moved out of line. Making his way toward the door, he was sobered beyond even his worst expectations by the fearful faces of the men and women he passed on his way outside. Suddenly, he felt very fortunate—and then he felt guilty for feeling that way, as he thought about the teller again.

Distracted by what had just happened to him, he stood in the deluge, on the corner in front of the bank, for at least a minute. Then he shook himself free of that poor woman's face when he realized how drenched he was becoming. Having forgotten to wear his hat when he left the apartment that morning, he brought his left arm up to his forehead to shelter his eyes from the driving rain. The closest subway was only a block away, so he used his other hand to pull his coat collar up around his neck and then began wading into the stream overflowing the sidewalk from the street. As he was sloshing through the ankle-deep water, he heard a screeching sound and the shrieks of several voices coming from his left side. But his arm was over his face, and he couldn't see—not for a few seconds anyway, not until the swerving, sliding black motorcar slammed into another vehicle in the intersection and then careened out of control, grill first, through the flooding rain water, directly in front of the bank.

Velita had fallen asleep on Cinnamon's sofa. Maggie and Claudine had been quiet in their room for more than hour, and Alberto had gone with the twins back to their own apartment. The crush of neighbors had receded once the family's need for privacy and rest became apparent. But there was comfort in knowing that so many caring people were close by, as Cinnamon sat on her kitchen floor with the open strongbox in her lap. The $290, which the doctor had handed to her just before they left the hospital, now rested on top of the other money. Yet instead of relief, she felt anger. If Vincente had not gone to the bank, this would not have happened.

Apparently, he'd described his view of the accident to the medical staff in the ambulance, which had navigated through the torrents from Bellevue Hospital at 1st Avenue and 27th Street to retrieve the injured. The driver of the motorcar had been thrown into his front windshield when the car came to a stop against the bank's stone wall. Cinnamon wasn't certain of the man's fate, but she'd heard a rumor that he'd died on the scene. One other pedestrian had also been hit, but he was ambulatory and appeared to have only minor abrasions. Vincente remained conscious most of the time while waiting for medical assistance, a fact that astonished all of the witnesses. Aside from being thrown in the air by the collision's force, he'd landed face down in the flooded curb water and would have drowned if passersby hadn't pulled him out. The problem now, as the doctor had explained to the family, was the extent of injuries to his chest and abdomen, made worse by the lifesaving pulls and jerks that removed him from the water and carried him inside the bank. They would know more about the severity of Vincente's condition after he woke up again, which the doctor said was probably going to happen over the next twenty-four hours. He'd lost consciousness once the ambulance reached the hospital, but not before he'd made the doctor promise to give Cinnamon the $290 inside his jacket pocket.

After turning the small brass jailer's key to relock the strongbox, she slipped the silver chain around her neck and dropped the box into its place beneath the floorboards. Standing up, she replaced the rug, then walked softly into the living room and past the sofa, where a heartbroken Velita had finally been pulled into sleep. Blowing rain was still splattering against the window panes next to her, as she sat down on Amelia's side of the library desk. Little difference existed, she thought, between the dark, ominous night out there and the cold blackness inside this room. Leaning back into the soft folds of her grandmother's old leather chair, she let her arms fall over the sides, leaving the whole center of herself open and susceptible. Swiveling slightly to face the window, she stared defiantly at the raging rain on the other side.

"Come il diavolo è entrato nella casa mia?" she whispered, not even realizing that she was speaking Italian. "How *did* the devil get into my house?"

She tried to imagine her husband's strong gentle arms wrapped around her and his deep voice assuring her that all would be well. But despite the clarity of that vision, on Thursday, November 15, 1929, just three days after the accident, Vincente was gone.

December 18, 1929

Dear Cinn—

Your letter arrived just after Thanksgiving and a few days before Angela returned home from her stay with you. Although I'm certain this holiday season is dreadful for you, I know you drew strength from having your dearest friend close at hand during those first difficult two weeks. (I'm sorry that Jay could only stay a few days, but we needed him back here at the mill.) While it seems a lifetime ago that I lost my father and then Mother in San Francisco, memories of those early moments without them still sting. Thus, you and Claudine, and the rest of your family, are in my prayers. But I'm afraid that is the most I can give you right now.

In your letter, you spoke of times past, and of the original, comfortable security of our relationship, which I agree we shared. You were always very amusing and endearing to me, as beautiful children can generally be. I hope I was able to reinforce the strength of character I believe resides within you, and that I trust you will rediscover and use to your benefit in this time of sorrow. That strength, Cinn, should serve as both your rock and your compass now. *I* cannot serve as *either*. There is no major part for me to play in your healing or your future, and there is no possibility that I'll come visit you in order to, as you said in your letter, help reestablish a much-needed connection to your Albany family.

Details about what actually happened between you and your father over your marriage to Vincente vary with the storyteller, but the ensuing division has always been clear. Until you find a way to mend things with him, I cannot put myself in the middle. Even if that particular situation did not exist, my life otherwise is full enough with trials and responsibilities. The growth of our lumber business would amaze you, as would the accompanying mill expansions. My civic and community involvement has also increased in parallel. My two boys take whatever time is left after my work, a part of being a parent that I suspect we do share in common, since your Claudine is only a few months younger than my DJ. Children at age five are in a constant stream of motion. Ryan is even worse at age three, not yet having developed any fear of my discipline.

But the most troubling issue, which I tell you in confidence out of respect and as a means of explanation, is Lucy and her health. Ryan's birth was not an easy one for her, and she still suffers many effects. Those would be considerable on their own, but adding to her distress is the doctor's advice that she not bear any more children. This, of course, doesn't blend with our plans and hopes, and we are not yet adjusted to the change.

So, you see why I cannot be of any assistance to you, despite your grief and your genuine need. The courage of your request is noted and appreciated, however. I will keep you in my thoughts.

Always,
David

She'd been so proud of herself—so strong. Through the worst of the arrangements, the wake and the funeral, she'd been steady and dependable, concentrating on taking care of the others, particularly Claudine and Velita. Her daughter knew her daddy was missing, but the child had no grasp of the words *he's not coming back* and was thus spared the agony of that particular truth. But Velita was not as fortunate. The loss of her son had pushed her deep within herself, and Cinnamon was determined to pull her back. She was not going to stand by and watch Vincente's mother disintegrate the way Mimi had been lost.

Alberto was suffering, too, although few witnessed the depth of his anguish, other than his daughters, and occasionally Maggie and Cinnamon, who saw his swollen face in the mornings. Yet, he seemed to be gathering strength from some unknown place, all of which he gave to his children. At the same time, he and Cinnamon shared an implicit admiration for one another's ability to hold everything together. Joseph and his brothers added solace when they came to Broome Street for the funeral, although they only stayed the one day. Olivia and Helena had remained in Albany with the girls, sending their love and sympathy in letters carried by Joseph. The fact was that the Magglios could not bear the weight of this particular good-bye. Alberto and Cinnamon couldn't either, but they were not given the option of staying away. Nonetheless, they were gracious and understanding of each family member's need to manage this inconceivable loss independently.

When all the fuss was finally over, when Vincente had been buried and everyone retreated to their own homes and towns, Cinnamon forced Velita to go back to work with her. Several shop customers still needed gowns for occasions that weren't going to stop just because Cinnamon's husband had been killed. When they returned to the shop on the Monday after Thanksgiving, they discovered that their vendors and the majority of their clientele were treading gently around their heartache and extending deadlines whenever possible. But the women—particularly Velita—soon realized that fulfilling their original commitments helped ground them. They began to find harmony in the fact that they did not have to wonder what to do with themselves when they woke up every morning. There was always something important to accomplish each day that lured them into seeking purpose and value in the long empty hours that followed breakfast. Unfortunately, they did not have a remedy for their nights, which seemed to be much worse for Cinnamon than for her mother-in-law. *Her* bed was lonely one. *Her* husband was the one dead.

Nonetheless, the healing had started. Velita was rescued through her faith—that merciful God again—and thus her recovery had a sustaining power. Cinnamon thought she was infusing herself with the same antidote by chronicling the tragedy's stages in her journal. But although she was true to the facts, every word was too carefully chosen, every phrase too methodically constructed, all with the thought that her heirs—or maybe even strangers—might one day read what she was writing after she, herself, was gone. Afraid that she'd sound maudlin or full of self-pity, she never wrote down to the core of her feelings, never cleansed what was festering in the place where she was hiding the dreams she'd shared with Vincente.

As a result, while everyone else in the family was purging themselves of their sorrow and working through their grief, Cinnamon's scars were closing in over open wounds. In the letter she'd written to David during the Thanksgiving weekend, she had unknowingly increased the pressure beneath her heart's surface by exposing her vulnerability and inviting him to come visit her, thinking that even a few hours of conversation with him would be healthy for both of them. Instead, she'd received his return letter, which she'd opened with hopeful expectations after retrieving it from the post office earlier that day, only to find that the razor's edge of his words had ripped her decaying wounds wide open.

…So, you see why I cannot be of any assistance to you, despite your grief and your genuine need. The courage of your request is noted and appreciated, however. I will keep you in my thoughts…

"*Please*, David, I hope you don't over-exert yourself with your concern," she said sarcastically, sitting at the library desk and directing the comment to the paper in her hands as her voice gathered intensity from deep within her chest.

Then, slowly, she began to rupture. First she crumpled the letter into a small ball, but just as quickly opened up the ball again and tore the pages into tiny pieces, throwing them in the air. Standing up from her grandmother's chair, she took wide sweeps with her arms and began shoving everything on the desktop onto the floor. Opening the drawers, she grabbed spools of thread, sewing machine bobbins and cardboard pattern guides, frantically lobbing them across the room.

"You ***bastard***!" she screamed, picturing David's smug face. "Oh, that's *right*! ***I'm*** the *bastard*! Our merciful God at work once again!"

Thread spools were bouncing back toward her after hitting the walls, so she picked them up and threw them again, not caring how loud she was, or who might hear her.

"An almighty and powerful presence decided to annul me and my poor mother out of our home," she cried, "tricking me into believing that my father was a decent person. But he's really a ***fraud***—and I'm a ***bastard***!" She intentionally screamed that particular word louder than the others. "A ***bastard!*** And then there was *Bradley*. Hello, God? Are you there? Are you *ever* there? *No*! Because if you were, you would not have stolen him, too! He was such a *good man*, and his leaving ***killed*** my mother! ***You murdered her*** when you took him away!"

A small candy dish left her hand, scattering in porcelain pieces on the floor, along with chunks of plaster from the impact of the dish against the wall.

"And ***now***," she said, her voice hoarse from screaming, her tone lower and broken, "you've taken my Vincente. If I didn't deserve him," she continued, dropping to her knees on the rug in front of the desk, her arms stretching up toward the ceiling, "***then why did...you...give...him...to...me***? Why didn't you just leave me alone? Why did you let me have such a gentle man—and let me trust in being safe—and then ***rip him from my life***?"

Lying down on the rug, she rolled onto her side and pulled herself into a fetal position. With her arms pressed against her chest and her fists knotted beneath her chin, her words descended into an agonizing, hollow moan.

"*Voi dio merciful*, are you through with me? My house is almost empty. *Siete finiti con me*? *Are you through with me*? ***Are...you...through...with...me...now***?" she repeated over and over, until her voice faded and a kind, unseen spirit eased her breathing and closed her eyes.

Alberto found her there several hours later, after coming in search of her when she didn't arrive next door for dinner. Looking around at the chaotic broken mess in the normally fastidious room, he thought he understood what must have happened. Rather than disturbing her, once he was certain she was all right, he quietly picked up the broken glass, leaving the harmless bobbins and spools of thread for later. Then he covered her with the crocheted throw from the sofa and left her to rest, hoping she would feel better upon awakening—which she did. But several years would go by before an answer would come to the question she'd repeated over and over that night.

Are you through with me? *Are you through with me*? *Siete finiti con me?*

The answer was *no*.

Chapter 14

September 23, 1931
Three o'clock in the morning

Honestly, if I don't stop reminiscing, I'll put myself so far into the doldrums that I'll never find my way out. It's difficult not to look backwards, however, when I'm preparing to end another chapter in my life and start a new one. All the people who aren't here any longer line up for a mental review, and the consequences of my previous actions cry out for editing.

I think it's interesting that when we're actually living through the events of our existence one-by-one, we're so close to the moment that we can't see how a particular event is setting us up for another down the road, or is possibly the result of one in the past. But in fact, each episode is inexorably linked in the chain that becomes the life we lead. Sometimes (even though the exercise threatens to drive me batty) I try to imagine what the impact would be on my life in its totality if I had the power to lift even one link out of the chain and either do it over—or more sensibly, throw it away…

M.E.M.

Sitting on her mother's side of the desk, Cinnamon closed the cover to her journal and leaned back into the chair that had become sculpted to her body through the years. She was tired. There had been a throbbing at her temples for days now, and just below her apparent enthusiasm and cheery disposition were tears she knew would pour out at the slightest provocation. The struggle to pry her past from her present had been gathering strength, as the ghosts of those who'd died competed for her attention. She knew she had to get up early in the morning to finish altering a customer's jacket, but she'd been unable to sleep—and even writing in her journal hadn't helped. Chances were good that she would see the sunrise from this chair unless she could stop herself from wondering where she would be right now, if certain links in the chain had never been connected in the first place.

The first year after Vincente's death had been fuzzy. An emotional haze covered the people on Broome Street, although everyone kept to their routines, courageously proceeding with the things that needed to be done in their lives from day to day. Sometimes they talked about him, or commented that *Vincente would have enjoyed this*—or *would have **loved** this*—but not very often, because the sound of his name was still too raw for them to hear. During this time, his surviving family was never left alone, always surrounded by nurturing neighbors whose hearts were broken, too. Occasionally laughter would surprise them by creeping into their conversations, letting them know that healing was possible—just not quite yet.

Gradually, however, as the recovery process began to work, the Mentinis started to realign and redefine themselves, rerouting the pathways of their daily and nightly activities around the places where Vincente used to be. Visions of him were still there, but they were sealed away more and more as the months passed. This gave his loved ones the option of looking or remembering when they wished to do so, rather than being slapped in the face at will by the bleak empty spaces that once held his voice, his body, his strength.

This stabilization also made apparent the need to focus on a few practical matters, primarily the fact that their loss of Vincente's income meant they could no longer afford two apartments. Since the flat originally occupied by Bradley and Mimi was the largest, a collective decision was made that Alberto and Velita should move in with Cinnamon. Upon her insistence, her in-laws took the bedroom that she'd shared with Vincente, while Claudine and Maggie continued to occupy the second bedroom. Cinnamon slept on the sofa, declaring that the living room was quite fine with her.

"Honestly," she'd said to Alberto and Velita when they wouldn't stop objecting to the arrangement, "I'm very comfortable in that space. And I spend so much time at the desk anyway, sewing on one side or writing on the other, that I'm often sitting in that room in the middle of the night anyway. Please don't worry about me. As long as I can stay with my familiar belongings, I'll be perfectly all right."

Rosa and Maria each took a room in separate neighbors' apartments in Velita's building, where they'd already been providing childcare and assisting with the housework. Thus, all of the Mentinis were still clustered close to one another, just in slightly reconfigured home places. As a result, Alberto was able to negotiate storage space in the basements of both buildings for most of their furniture. Everything else was transferred to Cinnamon's flat.

Alberto also withdrew the balance of Bradley's savings within a month of his son's death, using the money to cover Cinnamon's immediate living expenses, in addition to the funeral and burial. From that point forward, his earnings from the tailor shop and the proceeds from *A Touch of Cinnamon* would need to take care of the reconstructed Mentini family, for which he was now completely responsible. While he worried about the vulnerability of these circumstances, Cinnamon did *not*. Every night just before she fell asleep on the sofa, she had a quiet, private conversation with the spirit of her husband, telling him again how much she loved and missed him, and thanking him for the security of the $2890 hidden beneath her kitchen floor—a secret she had still not shared with anyone, in keeping with her promise.

Frequently during that first monochromatic year, a little color would drop into the neighborhood or the dress shop in the form of Mr. Gregory Stafford. His appearance never failed to lighten Cinnamon's mood and inject a little excitement into her life. He was also quite pleasant to look at, always well turned out in one of his exquisite suits of clothes. The garments were constructed with fabric and detail appreciated by Cinnamon's trained eye, and had generally been sewn under Alberto's supervision at the tailor shop. A point of further admiration was Mr. Stafford's motorcar, which could *nearly accommodate a dinner party for eight in the back seat,* Cinnamon wrote in a letter to Angela.

...He's rather charming, for an older man, and quite solicitous of Velita and me. At least once a week or more, he comes to pick us up and drive us to his amazing home on East 67th Street, so we can fit garments on his mother (who lives there with him), or take new orders from her (which she places with us nearly every time we see her).

My family and neighbors have asked me why he isn't married at his age. (Velita and I have decided he's well into his thirties, most likely.) Of course, I have no earthly idea how he could still be managing without a wife, or why he would have elected to be without companionship. He must be very particular, because he certainly would not have any difficulty finding a woman who wished to be with him. Aside from the fact that he apparently has an abundance of personal resources, he's reasonably attractive and comes equipped with a refreshing sense of humor as well.

We are extraordinarily blessed that he's taken an interest in the dress shop, and that he seems to trust us with the investment he made. I'm working very hard not to disappoint him, in view of his kindnesses to us...

Gregory Stafford was a second-generation American of English descent. His grandfather had immigrated as a boy with his parents, and the family originally settled in Boston. They arrived in the United States with considerable wealth, and when his father was a young man in 1890, he was drawn to New York City, where he married a socialite and began investing in the real estate development of lower Manhattan. Gregory remembered his father taking him downtown to see the buildings they owned. Some were under construction. Others had been there awhile, including the one housing Alberto's tailor shop. As a result, he was familiar with Cinnamon's streets and those of the surrounding neighborhoods. But apart from collecting rent with his father, and later by himself after his father died, he had little personal contact with the economics of that area. Until he was in his late twenties, he had even less knowledge of the people who actually lived and worked in his buildings, since the activities of his social circle never took him much further south than 34th Street.

As his business and fortune continued to expand, he maintained the Stafford family residence with his mother on East 67th Street, where the two of them entertained and lived a relatively unpretentious lifestyle, by their neighborhood standards. Gregory had watched his father work very hard, despite his affluence, and he'd inherited a similar work ethic. He also saw his mother remain an active member of civic and charity organizations, frequently hosting events in their townhouse to benefit a library branch in a disadvantaged community, or some other equally worthy cause.

Whenever he visited any of his buildings downtown, he made a point of being approachable, extending himself and asking his tenants about their families. This was another tactic he'd learned from his father, who believed that most people, regardless of their station, were honest and pure of intentions.

"If they are treated with respect," he would say, "they will work hard and do everything in their power to meet their commitments to you. Their motivation will come not only from their need to maintain their dignity, but from their desire not to disillusion you."

Gregory found this lesson to be true in nearly every circumstance, even when tenants were having personal difficulties that interfered with timely rent payments. He discovered that if he granted them a little leeway, blending compassion with the rules, they almost always managed to steer themselves back on course and repay past due amounts, per their agreements with him.

What he could not abide was deceit, even in small measures. Tucked away beneath his calm, distinguished manner was a short emotional trigger, which was rarely fired but could be guaranteed if someone lied to him. Most of his tenants had no occasion to witness this volatility. But those who did were eager to spread the stories about him throughout lower Manhattan. One such narrative told of a man who'd garnered Gregory's sympathy over the fellow's wife and her failing health. Her extended hospitalizations and the need to care for his three children had left the man unable to work at his factory job. Gregory not only instructed the building's superintendent to let the family slide for two months without paying their rent, but he also delivered a few dollars in cash to help them with their food purchases.

One summer evening in the third month of this arrangement, the superintendent observed a noisy fire escape altercation between the man and his wife, who looked anything but ill at the time. She was flailing away at him, screaming that he was a lazy, good-for-nothing excuse for a husband and lobbing verbal insults regarding the extent of his manhood, while making certain the neighbors could hear her.

The next day, when the superintendent began asking questions of the other tenants about the family, he learned that the man had been less than honest. There were, indeed, three children, the eldest of whom was a twelve-year-old boy. But for the past three months, that boy had been sent to work in his father's place in the factory. Effective federal child labor laws would not be in place for several more years yet, and though Americans had gradually become outraged at the prevalence and conditions of child labor in various industries throughout the country, the absence of legislation allowed abuses to continue. In New York factories, the employment of children as young as ten was not uncommon.

After the superintendent reported this situation to Gregory, a few more weeks passed without event, and without any appearance by Gregory in the neighborhood. Then unexpectedly, city authorities showed up at the building one morning and took custody of all three children, removing them temporarily to an orphanage operated by Dominican nuns. The superintendent was present as well and gave the man and his wife twenty-four hours to vacate their apartment for failure to pay rent. Gregory's physical presence was not needed for everyone within the community to understand that he had orchestrated the retribution. They'd witnessed scenarios like this before when someone else had tried to deceive Mr. Stafford, only to find that the person's living arrangements had been reorganized by a swift and commanding invisible hand.

Rumors circulated later in the year, indicating that Gregory had monitored this most recent man and his wife as they'd moved in with another family and tried to stabilize their affairs. Eventually, the children were returned to their parents, after the man found work again as a factory laborer. Had he not made this effort, no one doubted what the ultimate outcome would have been. Thus, while people in and around Broome Street expressed outward appreciation for Gregory's friendly manner, they were daunted by the wide reach of his influence and the associated power that enabled him to mete out such extreme penalties. Fortunately, for all sides, this silent intimidation held most of them to a high standard of integrity in their dealings with him.

Cinnamon preferred to focus on his more endearing qualities, which she believed were the more dominant aspects of his character. This conviction was based on her personal experiences with him, beginning with the day in 1923 when he volunteered to chauffeur her and the Mentinis to the train for her ill-fated journey to Albany. By the time the year of mourning for Vincente ended in January of 1931, she had still never seen for herself the legendary hammer-hand linked to so many stories about Gregory Stafford.

"I honestly don't think he played any part in their eviction," she said to Velita one afternoon when they were working alone in the shop, discussing the latest rumors about another family's misfortune. "In fact, I wouldn't be surprised if all these tales took their original root in someone's imagination."

"You're just defending him because you know he's smitten with you."

Velita was keeping a steady hand on the silver satin fabric, as she guided the ball gown's bodice seams between the needle plate and the sewing foot. She intentionally did not look up at her daughter-in-law.

"What did you say?" Cinnamon asked.

"You heard me."

"I absolutely cannot believe you'd think he's the *least bit* smitten with me, or that I would even notice, if he were."

Velita released the foot pedal pressure and straightened her shoulders as she leaned back against her chair. Now she *was* looking at Cinnamon, a gentle smile softening her face. She'd always maintained a youthful appearance, seeming more like a sister than a mother to Rosa and Maria, who were now twenty, and to Cinnamon as well. Since Vincente's death, however, her skin had aged a decade, her fawn-colored complexion drained of its blush, the fine lines around her eyes and mouth now deeply etched. But when she spoke of her son, some of her former glow reappeared, and Cinnamon could always tell by her smile when this was about to happen.

"I *do* believe that Mr. Stafford is quite taken with you, Cinn, and that he *has* been for a long time. Under any other circumstances, I suspect he would have made his feelings known by now. But he is such a gentleman that he's remained very subtle over the last year, and he would probably be horrified to hear me speaking like this. Nonetheless, I'm glad you brought it up."

"I beg your pardon? *I* certainly did *not.*"

"Really? Who's your witness?"

"Velita!" Cinnamon looked up from the cutting table, her scissors pausing mid-snip, with a section of pattern and fabric wedged between the blades.

"I'm *playing* with you, my dear, trying to lighten our collective burden, as it were. You see, I've been thinking lately that you are still so young, with so much of your life ahead, that I hope you don't have to spend very much of it alone. Vincente wouldn't want that either, nor would he want Claudine to grow up without a father figure. So, this is something I've been hoping to say to you for awhile now. Whether you find yourself with Mr. Stafford or someone else, I want you to know that you have my blessing to move on and to marry again."

Cinnamon could not believe she was hearing this, knowing how painful it must be for Vincente's mother to consider such a parting. Rolling a chair across the room, she sat down beside Velita and held her hands.

"You're so sweet to try and release me—to let me feel as if I'm free—and I'm sure your words will give me peace of mind one day. But I don't think I could ever love anyone else. After watching Vincente—and Bradley with my mother—I'm afraid such a high mark has been set for measuring romance that I doubt I'll venture near the game of love again."

"I don't recall mentioning anything about *love*," Velita answered, lifting Cinnamon's long curls over her shoulder the way Mimi used to do, and then smoothing them down the young woman's back with the palm of her hand. "I was referring to *marriage*. The security of being with someone like Mr. Stafford would make romance and love seem like small details easily done without."

"Right. And I'm certain that Mr. Stafford would be overjoyed to hear us putting his name in the same sentence with possible marriage to *me,* the little seamstress from Broome Street. You're a dear and wonderful lady, Velita, and I deeply appreciate your kind notions about my future. But I think our energies would be better applied to serious matters, such as Mrs. Vanderline's ball gown, for instance."

Despite Cinnamon's dismissive response, Velita's intuition was correct. Gregory Stafford *was* smitten with her, and he was getting very close to telling her how he felt.

The first step in his plan was a small dinner party for six people on East 67th Street, in early April of 1931. Gregory's mother had purposefully configured the group to include another couple approximately Cinnamon's age, also in the courting stage of their relationship. She invited an elderly woman from her bridge club, as well, to even out the number.

"This could possibly be a very uncomfortable situation for her, "Mrs. Stafford said to her son a few days in advance of the date. "After all, this will be the first time she's ever been in our home in a capacity other than an employee, and I don't want to overwhelm the poor girl."

She was not concerned, however, with Cinnamon's social skills or her ability to comport herself appropriately. After Gregory confessed his interest in the Mentini woman, which she could not understand at first, in light of his lifelong exposure to families of his own station, she investigated Cinnamon's background. Fortunately, the McClintys of Albany had their own pedigree, which was not quite at the Stafford level, but certainly respectable. Furthermore, Mrs. Stafford learned that the McClinty Mill had supplied lumber for the construction of several buildings now in the Stafford arsenal, some of the transactions dating back to a time when Nathaniel was still alive and Gregory's father was overseeing the lower Manhattan construction sites.

Once she was familiar with the history of Cinnamon's bloodlines, and after observing years of Velita's refined influence on the girl, Mrs. Stafford elected not to stand in the way of her son's romantic interest. But she did work to maintain some control over the manner in which the courtship unfolded.

Gregory arrived at Broome Street in his motorcar at six o'clock on the evening of April 11, and he was surprised to see the block uncharacteristically deserted. He did not know that Cinnamon had asked Velita to spread the word that she preferred not to have an audience gathered in the street for her departure this time.

"I'm nervous enough as it is," she said again, while Velita helped her fasten a few more hairpins in her Gibson Girl hairdo. She still preferred this elegant style over the short curly bobs that had become more fashionable, even though the upsweep had taken nearly an hour to secure. But the effect was well-worth the effort, as the two women admired their work in Velita's oval vanity mirror.

"A cheering crowd will make me feel even more conspicuous than I already do with this odd match-up. How are *you* feeling about it, Velita? Do you believe I'm moving in a healthy direction by accepting this invitation?"

"You will have to answer that question yourself," Velita replied, gently kneading the back of Cinnamon's neck as she stood behind her, both women still facing the mirror. "I suspect you'll have more information to help you after this evening is over."

"All right. But please, *please* keep everyone off the street when he gets here."

The neighbors did cooperate, but she could see a half-dozen faces in nearly every window on the block, as Gregory held the motorcar door open for her. What she couldn't hear was their buzzing about how regal she looked. She and Velita had used one of Vincente's designs for the simple evening suit cut from a sea-green, silk shantung fabric. The slightly flared straight skirt dropped just below her knees, and the fitted waist-length jacket was the latest style. A white satin blouse and ruffled collar added a flair of formality, with the line of ruffles continuing down the bodice and ending at the skirt's waistband. Her pearl stud earrings and the combs adorning her hair coordinated with the pearls on her square-heeled pumps. A shoemaker two blocks away had traded tailoring work for the pair of shoes, which he'd covered in a pale grey matted silk. Velita had then selected two dozen pearls from the shop's wedding notions and hand-stitched a cluster of twelve on each toe.

As the motorcar drove away that evening, everyone watching from the windows—especially Velita, Alberto, Maggie, Rosa and Maria, who were crowded around the double-sided desk—could sense that something was changing. *Cinnamon* was changing. She even carried herself with a new grace, and she looked perfectly proper, as if she belonged on the seat beside him. They all recognized the scene before them as the fulfillment of a dream, although the principals were different than in the original vision. This had been Bradley's dream for Mimi, his *someday* that didn't arrive in time.

"Perhaps Bradley and Mimi can see her, too," Velita whispered to Alberto, who stood behind her at the window, with his arms around her.

"Yes, I'm sure they can," he said, leaning down to kiss the edge of her ear, "and I pray that what she's about to discover around that uptown corner will be everything Bradley believed he'd find there."

By 1931, the Depression had caused conditions throughout the City to be far different than they would have been for Bradley in the early 1920's. The contrast between the classes was the most disturbing element for Cinnamon, as she traveled back and forth from one end of the scale to the other. People stood in line waiting for food vouchers or free coffee and donuts in every community. But the lines in lower Manhattan wrapped around block after block, while those in the northern neighborhoods were shorter and on far fewer streets.

Cinnamon came to understand that the disparities were often grounded in history. Old Upper East Side money had roots sufficiently deep and vital, in most cases, to survive the Depression's financial drought. True, the Staffords and their associates had incurred losses themselves. But few in their circle were wiped out and reduced to standing in line for their dinner. In fact, in the very worst of times, most of Gregory's friends and their families had a greater individual net worth than the residents of a neighborhood like Broome Street would see in a lifetime if they put all their assets into a single account.

These were the two worlds Cinnamon straddled for three years, beginning with the small dinner party on April 11, 1931. She did so with amazing agility, once her frustrations about inequality and injustice became tempered by her realization that she was now in a position where she could extend help to her downtown people. Gregory and his mother were exceptionally generous in that regard, finding work for as many as possible at their construction sites, funneling referrals to Alberto's tailor shop and *A Touch of Cinnamon*, and extending loans to families who were on the verge of becoming homeless.

Each gesture was made as a business arrangement rather than a charity handout, enabling people to maintain as much of their dignity as possible. But Cinnamon struggled with guilt every time she entered the East 67th Street townhouse for another party or a private visit with Gregory's mother, who summoned her with increasing frequency for afternoons of tea and conversation. During those sessions, the women began to learn about each other while they planned fundraising events or hand-addressed another batch of invitations, and while Cinnamon was unknowingly being schooled in matters of importance to life north of 59th Street.

In her own neighborhood, a building the size of the 67th Street townhouse was configured to house between four and six different families. But on the Upper East Side, the four-story structure was considered a relatively modest single-family residence. Only twenty-five feet wide, Gregory's home was pressed so close to those on either side of it that, from the street, one could not tell they were separate buildings. But the facades of the homes in this area defined their differences, as did the unseen depths of the individual properties and the varying degrees of opulence contained within those rectangular boundaries.

The facade of the Stafford home was red brick. Each of the four stories had three tall, narrow windows in even lines from the first floor to the fourth, except on the ground floor, where the front door was in place of the far left window. The door was painted black, and black shutters framed the windowpanes, producing an understated symmetrical look from the street. An entrance yard was the full twenty-five feet wide but only eight feet deep, and was separated from the two adjacent properties and the sidewalk by a black wrought iron fence, with a gate in the middle. The short eight-foot walkway that led from the gate to the front door was paved in the same red brick as the house. On both sides of the walkway were identical arrangements of shrubbery, a border of seasonal garden colors, and flowering plum trees meticulously pruned to a slender ten-foot height.

Captivating as that entranceway might have been, opening the gate was but a preview of the magic awaiting on the other side of the front door. The house itself was fifty feet deep, and the rear yard extended another forty feet beyond the back wall, creating a complete property measuring twenty-five feet wide by ninety feet deep. Entering the front door, one stepped onto a black and white marble floor tiled in a diamond pattern. The narrow staircase leading up to the second level was on the right near the arched doorway into what Gregory and his mother called the Welcoming Parlor. A white fireplace with gold detailing was on the far wall of that room, its chimney traveling up through the other three stories, where fireplaces opened into those rooms as well.

The Welcoming Parlor was decorated in an almost Spartan manner, from the solid black marble flooring to the six white upholstered armchairs arranged in a semi-circle and facing the fireplace. A French Provincial sideboard, topped with a pair of crystal-drop lamps, was positioned along the staircase wall. At the back of the room, an identical sideboard, with another pair of lamps, was next to a doorway that led to a maid's bedroom and bath at the rear of the house. Through the parlor's two front windows, waiting visitors looked out onto the landscaped entry courtyard and the deep purple leaves of the flowering plum trees, unable to see East 67th Street a mere fifteen feet away.

Returning to the black and white foyer, one saw to the left of the front door a steel elevator cage, which stood ready to transport the Staffords and their visitors to the other three floors, as an alternative to the stairs. The cage was the most modern available, equipped with a manual pulley and door release, as well as a folding steel ladder that dropped from the elevator floor in case of an emergency.

Moving toward the back of the house, beyond the elevator and the staircase, the foyer narrowed into a hallway, at the end of which was the door to the kitchen. On the right, just inside this seat of culinary creativity, was another door connecting the maid's room and bath to a short corridor leading into the Welcoming Parlor again. Further right, at the far end of the kitchen, was the opening to the dumb waiter, which was built into the wall with a pulley system used to transport food and dishes upstairs to the dining room and the breakfast room located on the floor directly above. Next to the dumb waiter was another fireplace, this one finished in a dark red brick, with a chimney extending up through the other levels, where a second fireplace opened onto each floor in the rear half of the house.

The back door of the kitchen led to the yard, which was enclosed on all three sides by a twenty-foot high stone wall. From this ground level, there was no sense whatsoever that other houses and gardens bumped right up to the property from every direction, especially since the area had been landscaped and sculpted into a miniature park. Among the trees and flower beds, white iron benches and concrete bird baths dotted the ground, and at the far end, a thick wisteria arbor spread shade across the twenty-five-foot width, from one stone side wall to the other.

With the exception of her visit five years earlier, when Gregory reviewed her business plan for the dress shop, this first floor was the only part of the house Cinnamon had seen, prior to the dinner party on April 11, 1931. Even on the business plan day, she could not recall looking up from her shoes while walking the two flights of stairs behind Vincente and Alberto to Gregory's office on the third level. Generally, when she came to East 67th Street, she and Velita were there to deliver a garment or to double-check a fitting for Mrs. Stafford, and she never felt any curiosity about what might be on the three floors above her. The ground level with the Welcoming Parlor was sufficiently impressive. At the end of each visit, she and Velita were routinely escorted back into the kitchen for a traditional glass of lemonade. There the view of the rear gardens was captivating, and beyond this, she had no desire to explore further. But after April 11, she grew very familiar with the rest of the house, which was filled with Victorian and French Provincial hardwood furniture, sofas, chairs, loveseats, and chaises upholstered in velvet, chintz and tapestry fabrics, hand-knotted Oriental room carpets, crystal lights and chandeliers—and someone who was not only paid a salary, but given room and board, as well, to keep it all spotless.

In addition to the tall windows on the front of the house, each of the upper levels had the two fireplaces, a powder room, commode and lavatory, and either an enclosed porch or open terrace overlooking the rear yard and gardens. Facing 67th Street on the second level was the formal living room, one corner of which had been configured into a music area complete with a white baby grand piano. On the back half of the second floor was the banquet-sized dining room and a small English breakfast room, both of which opened onto a smoking porch framed with sash windows that looked down on the rear gardens. This level was where the Staffords did most of their entertaining.

On the third floor, which was Gregory's space, the library windows opened onto East 67th Street, the rich mahogany shelves, leather chairs and books reminding Cinnamon of the Madison house. A horizontal hallway separated the library from Gregory's bedroom and office, both of which opened onto the hallway and also onto a rear terrace through French doors. From this vantage point, one caught the first glimpse of houses standing on the properties beyond the Stafford's rear stone walls.

Gregory's mother occupied the entire fourth floor of the townhouse, which she called her *perch*. The rest of her home could be filled with people moving around and overflowing from the Welcoming Parlor up to the living and dining rooms, or perhaps up and down from the living room to the library on the third floor. But nestled on her top level, she could be alone, private and free from intrusions.

A combination parlor and reading room on this upper floor faced East 67th, and was furnished with three Victorian loveseats, two chaise lounges and four wingback chairs with ottomans. Clearly the only place in the house where a woman could stretch out and truly be comfortable, there was also plenty of light—both oil and electric—balanced throughout the space, with rich textures of tapestries and velvet adding further to the room's serenity. Creating a feminine refuge had obviously been the primary intent behind Mrs. Stafford's original design for the space.

Her bedroom and dressing area were on the back half of that level and were furnished with soft, neutral French Provincial designs and colors. Double French doors opened onto an enclosed porch with large sash windows just like Gregory's smoking porch on the floor below. But Mrs. Stafford's porch was all in white—the walls, the ceiling, the window frames, the wood plank flooring, and the wicker furniture—with a rainbow of color bursting from the bright chintz cushions on the chairs and loveseat. Looking down three stories to the rear garden, Mrs. Stafford always felt as if she could find springtime on her porch, even in the winter when the sky was dreary and the yard below was stripped of all greenery and fanciful colors. Cinnamon was generally escorted to this place in the house when Gregory's mother wanted to spend time with her. Later on, when the courtship became serious enough to occasionally include Claudine, the child sat there with Mrs. Stafford as well.

This idyllic townhome in this surreal world, on a street she'd walked long ago with her mother and Bradley, was where the focus of Cinnamon's life slowly began to shift as the months of 1931 progressed. She wasn't aware of the subtle but deliberate process of mentoring and grooming taking place with each of her visits to East 67th, although the progression was quite evident to Velita. Every time Cinnamon returned from a day with Mrs. Stafford, she stood a little taller, walked with a little more poise, and spoke with a little more clarity about a much wider range of subjects than before. Velita never heard her daughter-in-law mention being in love with Gregory, and a tiny part of her heart hoped she never would. But whether there was love or not, she suspected that one day soon the role of mother-in-law would belong to someone else. When that happened, despite her happiness about the secure and favored life that would cradle her granddaughter and her dead son's wife, she wondered how she was ever going to find the strength to let them go.

Everyone in the apartment was asleep when the new telephone on the wall of the floor's common hallway began ringing just before midnight on September 22, 1931. Sleeping on the living room sofa, Cinnamon was the closest to the door. She was also the first person from any of the other apartments to reach the phone. But a crowd of representatives from families on several floors had congregated around her by the time she recognized Angela's voice on the other end of the line. All of a sudden her heart felt as if it would leap from her chest. There was no possible way for this call to be good news, especially at this hour.

"Cinn, is that you? Are you there?"

"Yes, Angela, it's me. What's wrong?" she asked, looking around at the dozen neighbors who were now watching her with concern.

"Oh, it's so awful that I can barely speak," Angela said, her words difficult to understand through the obvious congestion of her tears. "It's Lucille—and David is inconsolable."

"What? What about Lucille?"

"She *died* tonight, Cinn. She actually *died*—and I still cannot believe it's true."

Cinnamon scanned all the faces watching her, looking for *what* she didn't know, while Angela's words flew around her head. ***What?*** She thought she was speaking, but she was just standing there, staring at her neighbors.

"Cinn? Are you still on the line?"

"Yes, I'm here, and I'm hoping I heard you incorrectly. You said something happened to Lucille?"

"I *said* she *died*—about eight hours ago."

"But *how*? Was she sick? I can't understand this."

"No one thought she was *that* sick. The doctor told her not to have any more babies, but then Teddy arrived last January. Lucille had a very hard time with him, but we thought she was going to be all right."

"I didn't know anything about this, Angela. Why didn't someone tell me?"

"David said he didn't want to disturb you, and Jay made me promise. Then, by the time winter was over, she seemed to be so much better. People from her family practically lived at the Madison house, taking care of DJ and Ryan and helping with the baby. I thought that everything was fine."

"Well, why *wasn't* it? What happened to her?"

"Apparently, things never healed, only she didn't tell anyone how badly she was actually feeling. She always looked tired when I saw her, but I'd be tired too if

I cared for two little boys, a baby, and David. She was very sick, though, and something must have been torn inside of her, because this morning it broke. Oh, Cinn, I wish you weren't so far away."

"I do, too, Angela. Where's David?"

"He's at Fox Run with your father and Sophie. The boys are there with him, too, including baby Teddy. Jay said that Irene is doing everything she can to help, but I can't even think about those three children growing up without a mother. This is *so sad*!"

"Yes, it is, and I'm still stunned," Cinnamon said, motioning for the crowd of neighbors to return to their apartments and indicating with a series of hand gestures that she could handle the rest of the conversation by herself.

"Do you think you could come up here, Cinn?"

She hadn't been expecting *that* question, however.

"I don't know, Angela. I really can't be away from the shop right now. Besides, I never knew Lucille, and I doubt very much that David wants to see me."

"Well, *I* want to see you, and this is too awful for words! We should all put our problems with each other away when something like this happens, so we can be together and help those who are suffering."

Cinnamon stiffened.

"I agree with you," she said. "That's precisely how *I* felt when my Vincente died. I know *you* were there with me, but I'm afraid I can't say the same for anyone else."

Even through the crackling phone connection, Angela could not mistake the sharp edge in her friend's voice.

"I'm sorry, Cinn. I wasn't thinking."

"I know, but don't worry about it. I still love you. I'm *not* coming up to Albany, though—at least not now. Tell David I'm very sad about his terrible loss. This truly is an unspeakable tragedy, and my heart breaks for the children. Thankfully, they have plenty of family close by to help them. Believe me," she said, as she thought about Velita and Alberto, "that support will save their lives."

"All right, I'll tell him, and please forgive me again for not thinking this call through more carefully."

"Stop with the apologies, Angela! You did what you thought was best. Now, go give my brother a kiss for me, and let everyone know they're in my prayers."

"I will. 'Bye."

Tuesday, November 3,
1931—1:08 A.M.

Dear Cinnamon—

You have every right not to even open this letter, much less read beyond the date, after my callous response to you when your Vincente passed away. But if you have, by some miracle, reached this point in my words, I beg you to continue.

As you know, I lost Lucille in September. Until that hellish moment, I had no concept of the pain you were suffering when you wrote to me asking for my help and attention in your own time of grief. You were right to turn to me, and I was so very wrong to deny your simple requests.

In my search of late for a reason why I acted in such a dishonorable manner, I'm only able to come up with my selfish preoccupations, and, perhaps, a small amount of concern that you might have needed more from me than I could give you. I learned about the full extent of your feelings for me shortly after you went back to New York that summer just before I married Lucille. Apparently, Angela confided in Jay, and he (as you know) has never been very good at keeping secrets.

Please don't be upset with either of them. They both love you very much and, I believe, were only trying to clear up my confusion about why you decided to leave Albany again. I do wish you could have trusted me enough to tell me yourself, Cinn. You were always such a special light in my life, one that I missed dreadfully when it went out. Had I known what you were dreaming, we could have talked things through, and I certainly would have handled the announcement of my engagement in a different manner. Then your misunderstood behavior would never have become an issue.

This clumsy attempt to explain is actually a plea for mercy. I'm so sorry that I turned you away when you were sad and lonely, and I hope life is easier for you now. I've been thinking that perhaps you might like to bring Claudine up here for a visit. DJ is just her age, and he could use a friend right now. A beautiful little cousin would be good medicine for him. As my oldest son, he understands that his mother won't be coming home, unlike his brother Ryan, who still believes she will be walking through the door any minute (something I imagine myself at times, I must admit). Teddy, of course, is too young at ten months to know that conditions have changed. When I look at him, I see Lucille more in his features than I do in the other two, and I try very hard to avoid thinking about the fact that his being here with us is the reason his mother is not.

At any rate, your father and I have been speaking about the merits of a visit from you, and I believe the time may have finally come for reconciliation on all fronts. I understand that your days are full of commitments with your dress shop. (We are all very proud of your achievement, by the way.) But I'm wondering if you might also be ready for some companionship to balance out your hard work.

My prayer, in my own desperate time of need, is that I will have the opportunity to belatedly offer you the support you deserve—the support you should have had from me unconditionally a long time ago. If you can find your way to pardon me, maybe we can begin to put this family back together.

Your reply will be anxiously awaited, and then we'll make your travel arrangements for the earliest possible date. Meanwhile, please know that we love you.

Always,
David

Sitting in the Broome Street apartment on her mother's side of the library desk, Cinnamon read the letter three times. At each pass, she hoped that when she arrived at his signature she would feel something other than affronted by this first communication from him in almost two years. *At least I'm not angry*, she thought, smiling at the recollection of thread spools and bobbins flying around the room. She knew only too well how he was hurting, and the love she would always have for him made her deeply sad about his distress. Her heart was also heavy for his three little boys. She imagined that Lucille had probably been the one who had administered most of their care, and that arrangement must have left a frightening vacuum in the boys' lives, not to mention leaving David sorely unprepared for his new role.

But while she empathized with their situation, she was appalled at David's arrogant suggestion that he might still have anything she needed, or that Angela's inability to keep a secret was unveiled exclusively to him. Her friend had confessed years earlier to her that she'd told Jay about her crush and the subsequent mortification over David's engagement. So, these revelations in his letter had absolutely no power over her, something she was rather relieved to discover. Opening the center drawer of the desk, she removed her pen and journal, deciding to jot down a thought while the words were fresh.

November 12, 1931

The problem with prolonged separations and remote residential distances between family members and loved ones is that we think of them as being the same people they were the last time we saw them. We have no understanding of the changes brought upon them by the experiences they encounter every day—experiences that have completely excluded us by default.

It's a bit like a vacation resort hotel that we visit routinely each year. We become familiar with the layout. We are comfortable with the consistency of the room décor and the rockers lining the front porch. We look forward to the fun and laughter that we remember from previous years and that we fully expect to find there again the next time.

But one year, while we're back in our homes, a terrible fire strikes the resort hotel, burning one wing—our wing—to the ground and leaving both smoke and water damage in much of the rest. Two people also die in the blaze. After the tragedy's shock begins to subside, the hotel's owners set themselves to the task of rebuilding and recreating the original detail in every corner. When we return for our customary visit the following year, we hear the story and say "how awful that must have been." But when we see our room, we see the same room—with new furniture, draperies, lamps and sheets—yet still the same room, with the same view and the same appearance from the outside.

We don't stop to consider that, in reality, nothing is the same. Everything has been rebuilt from the ashes, and the two lives lost in the fire leveled an unseen impact on the familiar staff still working there. They all look the same, too. But they are forever changed as well, and we don't understand any of that, because we weren't there to live through a single minute of it with them.

M.E.M.

Replacing the journal in the drawer, she removed several pieces of her stationery for the letter that would not be contained.

November 12, 1931
9:30 in the evening

Dear David—

Your correspondence arrived today, and your heartbreak is evident. As you indicated, I know how you are feeling, and my strongest prayers are for the well-being and eventual happiness of your three boys. The road will not be easy for them, or for you. But McClinty men have historically been survivors, and I trust that the four of you will find solace in that heritage.

To answer one of the points in your letter, I'm trying very hard to forgive everyone for everything—even you, and most particularly myself. But this requires a great deal of energy, and I'm not at all certain how effective my efforts will be. Thus, I'm not prepared yet to comment on your request for a pardon, other than to tell you that I appreciate your asking.

Addressing some of your other points, my life is indeed quite full with business at my shop, and with Claudine (who is well and growing up quickly). My sister Maggie and Vincente's family also occupy much of my time, as does my attention to the outside companionship you seem to think exists only in Albany. I do thank you for your invitation to visit and to help you, but unfortunately, such a trip will not be possible at this time.

Your letter was a nice addition to my day, however. Perhaps correspondence is a safer way to start over—or, as you said, to "put this family back together," given the complexity of our circumstances. Please tell my father hello. That's about as far as my reach will take me toward him, until the softening you describe in him is communicated directly to me, without you as the intermediary.

Tomorrow I will stop by my church and light candles for all of you—the brightest one for Lucille, who I'm certain watches over you still.

Always,
Cinn

November 13, 1931

The closer I look at my memories and past pages of these journals, the more I suspect that life has only so many events it can throw at us. Those situations might be wrapped in different colors or otherwise camouflaged to fool us, but careful inspection shows that circumstances do eventually begin to repeat themselves the longer we are here. I suppose the test is whether or not we've been paying attention, and whether we learned anything the first time around that will keep us from looking like complete idiots yet again. I further suspect that, no matter how confident I try to sound, I will continue to fail miserably at such assessments.

M.E.M

The economic and political climates in 1932 fed off one another in a frenzy as the Great Depression's impact deepened across the country. President Herbert Hoover believed that aid to the hungry and the "deserving unemployed" should come from local governments in the states and counties rather than from the federal government. Based upon his recommendation, the Congress established the Reconstruction Finance Corporation in January of 1932, with the intent of providing indirect relief to the unemployed by lending money to insurance companies, banks, farm organizations, railroads, and state and local governments. The theory was that, if the federal government aided big business at the top of the nation's financial structure, business would then create more jobs and relieve unemployment at the bottom. This policy was not working, however. By 1932, nearly 14 million people remained unemployed across the country—and banks had closed in thirty-eight states.

Meanwhile, Cinnamon followed with great interest the activities of Franklin Delano Roosevelt, who'd been elected governor of New York in the fall of 1928 and who'd been battling with a Republican legislature for many progressive measures. These included state-supported old-age pensions, unemployment insurance, public development of electric power, and laws that regulated the working hours for women and children. As the Depression became increasingly serious, Governor Roosevelt enlisted help from a group of Columbia University professors, which he dubbed a "brains trust," to devise social programs that would combat hard times, stressing the need to assist what he referred to as "the forgotten man." In 1931, Roosevelt became the first governor to set up an effective state relief administration, and by 1932, Cinnamon could actually see the programs helping her neighbors on Broome Street.

That spring, she began attending functions with Gregory and Mrs. Stafford, where she overheard men discussing Roosevelt as a possible Democratic presidential candidate to run against Herbert Hoover in the next national election. Capitalizing on the new medium of radio, which could now be heard in the majority of American homes, Governor Roosevelt broadcast a series of what he called his "fireside chats," where he spoke frankly and directly to the people about difficult issues. After listening to these broadcasts on different occasions at the East 67th Street townhouse and at the Broome Street apartment, Cinnamon began to understand the man's popularity. She was not surprised when he was nominated as the Democratic Party's candidate for the presidency at their Chicago national convention in June of 1932, and she was careful to stay abreast of his campaign's progress, so she could speak intelligently about the issues whenever she was with Gregory.

The balance of that summer became a whirlwind of excitement and activity for her on both the upper and lower east sides of Manhattan. While business at the dress shop wasn't exactly booming, orders from Mrs. Stafford and her friends were steady, and new customers also came in from time to time. Claudine, now eight years old, suddenly expressed an interest in helping Velita at the shop after school let out, and Cinnamon encouraged her daughter's developing interest in the craft of dressmaking. The skill had proven to be a life-saving economic tool for the Mentini family, and Velita's mentoring was an immeasurable gift as Claudine began learning the trade.

At age 22, Maggie preferred to stay on Broome Street, where she'd begun to teach the neighborhood children how to paint. Looking eerily like Mimi, with her thick dark hair, brown eyes with green flecks and milky freckled skin, she found that she had little trouble persuading vendors and shop owners who'd known her all her life to assist her with this endeavor. They contributed supplies of brushes, paints and palettes; and they helped her assemble a half-dozen makeshift easels, to which she attached defective paper being discarded from the print shop. Every afternoon, weather permitting, she set up the easels and supplies on the sidewalk outside her apartment, and every afternoon the next generation of Broome Street children gathered to learn.

Cinnamon was witness to this on occasion when she returned early from either the dress shop or East 67th Street. Although she was pleased to see her sister's talent being used so productively, she worried about the economic viability of such a skill and tried to enlist Maggie's help with the shop's operation. But these efforts only served to aggravate the tension that had always hovered just beneath the surface of their relationship. Consequently, Maggie remained nested on Broome Street, providing childcare and housekeeping assistance to the neighborhood women when she wasn't losing herself in her art.

Following the Democratic convention in June, Cinnamon regularly accompanied Gregory and Mrs. Stafford to political meetings organized in support of Roosevelt. They also began including her as their guest when they attended social events in the homes and apartments of other Upper East Side residents. They even took her along one time when they were invited to a twenty-fifth wedding anniversary party north of the City at a spellbinding estate on the Hudson River. In spite of her exposure to the Madison houses, Fox Run and East 67th Street, she was wholly unprepared for the grandeur of this private home. Upon first sight, as Gregory's motorcar chugged up the mile-long driveway, she thought the size of the house more in keeping with a branch of the New York library. She could not fathom that one family of six people lived there by themselves, with servants to help them, no less. She also wondered how these supporters of Roosevelt could pretend to speak from a position of authority in their discussions about the governor's social programs and their intended beneficiaries, when they lived in houses like this one without a single need unmet or a luxury lacking. But she kept her observations and opinions to herself, unwittingly striking an impressive stance on Gregory's arm as he introduced her around the room, and while she practiced Mrs. Stafford's well-rehearsed techniques to remember everyone's names.

"He's getting ready to propose to you," Velita said to her the night following this latest soiree on the Hudson, when the women were having tea together in their apartment. "He and his mother are making certain that people know who you are, and then he's going to ask you. I can just feel it."

"I think you might be reading too much into all of this. But dear heavenly days, what in the world will I do if you're right?"

Velita smiled across the kitchen table at the young woman who'd stolen her son's heart so many years ago, and whose strength and ingenuity had blessed the lives of everyone in this family.

"*Here's* what you will do, Cinn," she said, reaching across the table and gently squeezing her daughter-in-law's cheeks. "Now, repeat after me—*I*."

"You are *so* silly," Cinnamon replied, trying not to laugh as she talked through her lips scrunched in Velita's hand. "Oh, all right—*I*."

"*Will.*"

"Will."

"*Be happy.*"

"Be happy."

"*To.*"

"To."

"*Marry you!*"

"Velita! You are too funny—and I love you so much."

The proposal took place in the formal living area on the second level of East 67th Street, shortly before guests began arriving for Mrs. Stafford's 60th birthday party on August 6, 1932. Gregory chose a moment when he and Cinnamon were alone, while his mother finished dressing upstairs. He'd just given her a porcelain music box that played a waltz by Chopin, and as she was admiring the sound and the workmanship, he startled her by going down on one knee. In a humorous, thundering voice, he announced that he loved her and then produced from his pocket a small blue box from Tiffany's. As he opened the lid, a narrow platinum band topped with a two-carat diamond solitaire came into view.

"Will you please honor me by becoming my wife?"

Before she could react or say a word, he slipped the ring on her finger. He looked so sweet, and decidedly younger, from his position on the floor. Looking down at him as he continued to hold her hand in his, she actually felt a tingle of desire for the first time.

"I…will…be happy…to…marry you," she said, smiling as the words came out in Velita's precise rhythm.

Standing again on both feet, he leaned in to kiss her where the corner of her lips met her cheek. He had never kissed her there before, or anywhere other than on her forehead or fingers.

"Thank you, Cinnamon. You've made me a very happy man."

Their engagement was announced at the party that night, and the wedding was set for Saturday, October 29—a date already agreed upon by Mrs. Stafford and her son.

"We want you and Claudine to be living with us in the townhouse as soon as possible," Gregory said to Cinnamon several days later, after she'd echoed Velita's question about why the wedding had to happen so quickly. "Mother and I think it's important that we're married prior to the election in November. After Roosevelt's certain victory, I will want you to travel with me to Washington for a number of affairs that will be scheduled in advance of the inauguration. Also, you'll need to be busy redecorating my bedroom—excuse me, *our* bedroom," he added, blushing more than she was at the thought. "I promise that you'll have free reign to do whatever you like with the room, as long as you don't make it pink." He smiled, but she could tell he was serious on this point. "Mother's already refashioning the sitting room on her floor to accommodate a bedroom for Claudine. So you see, my darling, there is much to be done in short order, and all of these activities require that you be my wife."

"But what about my dress shop? That involves a great deal of my time, too. As my original benefactor, you should know better than anyone else that I cannot simply abandon the enterprise."

"No, of course you can't. As a matter of fact, I've been thinking that we should try to sell your shop, in order to relieve you of those obligations."

What? The last thing she was prepared to do was defend her need to keep her business, and his very suggestion was alarming. Was the security he offered her going to cost her everything she'd built on her own?

"Excuse me, Gregory. I don't mean to be disrespectful, but why on earth would I even consider selling? My financial obligation to you has been fully repaid, and that shop helps provide a livelihood and dignity for Velita and our two employees. As long as I'm properly tending to the operations, any conversations regarding my business should, if I may be so bold, begin and end with me."

He had not anticipated this reaction from her, assuming that she'd prefer a more leisurely life after marrying him. All of the other women he'd courted had been more than anxious to abandon any pretense of independence. Of course, not a single one of those women had even *been* to a neighborhood like Cinnamon's, or lived through a fraction of what she'd survived. Their dialogue was making him realize that his predisposed assumptions about women needed to be reassessed with his fiancé in mind.

"Please forgive me, my dear," he said, pausing long enough to make certain he was choosing his words carefully. "Other than Mother, there have not been many self-directed women in my life. You are right, and I will make more of an effort in the future to include you in discussions and to consider your point of view. In the meantime, out of deference to your wishes, we will discard any notion about selling the shop, for the time being at least. Of course, marrying me will fill up your agenda with new projects and responsibilities that you'll somehow have to incorporate with your business duties. We'll also be traveling on frequent holidays, which I hope will make you happy, but which will necessitate your making arrangements at the shop to accommodate your absences. Given these complexities, are you still certain that you want to take all of this on?" he asked, smiling and obviously not seriously posing the question to her.

But she thought the question *was* a serious one, and no, she *wasn't* certain. She didn't have enough courage to be *that* honest with him, though, or to risk losing him with some regrettable, ill-considered response.

"Yes, Gregory. My world to date has been filled with the challenge of wedging a small amount of recreation into a large measure of work and obligation. With you I'll be blessed to have a reversal of those proportions. Nonetheless, I can promise you that whatever the blend, I will not let you down."

"Good. I'm glad that's settled. Now, where were we?"

"We were discussing the plans you and your mother have made for our wedding."

Her conversation with Gregory had settled the shop issue for the moment. But the same discussion had also increased her reservations about the path she was taking with him. Until now, she'd been moving back and forth between two worlds—working and taking care of her family in one, and playing dress-up in the other. Yet very soon, there would be just *one* world. Mulling over Gregory's comments to her—and thinking about the control his mother tucked inside her loving demeanor—she not only prayed that her choice was the right one, but hoped with all her heart that she would have the strength to actually walk away from the other option. After all, no one was forcing her to leave Broome Street.

Details for the October 29 wedding began unfolding with noteworthy speed, and after an initial spate of aggravation at her continuing exclusion from the Stafford planning sessions, she decided not to make a fuss. She really did not care where the ceremony was set, which chef they chose, what food was going to be served, or whose names were on or off the invitation list, as long as her Broome Street family was included. She *did* inject herself, however, into the subject of what dress she was going to wear.

"After all, Gregory, gowns are my specialty, and they've been my means of support all these years. Surely," she continued, turning on the coy smile she'd learned to use so effectively, "your mother can't expect me to find my wedding dress elsewhere, when she won't have her *own* gowns made any place other than at my shop."

Meeting with no further argument on this particular issue, she appreciated the small victory. But she suspected the topic of her dress must not have been that important to Gregory and his mother or they wouldn't have given up so easily. After several minutes of feeling annoyed, she told herself that the benefits of her relationship with this man far outweighed these small irritations, and she pushed any lingering reservations to the back of her mind while moving forward with her hectic calendar.

"What's tickling you so much?" Cinnamon asked when she heard Velita giggling. The women were closing up the shop together following one of the few full days Cinnamon was able to devote to the business during the month of August, and they were both so tired that they'd been acting a little silly for the past hour.

"Oh, I was just trying to visualize Vincente—picturing what must be going through his head right now. He's probably feeling a frustrated sense of irony at the moment."

"Why? What makes you say that?"

"Well, he's watching from heaven while his mother scours his sketches in search of the perfect wedding dress for his widowed wife to wear when she marries another man. Don't you imagine that he might be slightly perturbed, and perhaps wishing that his talent had been in something like woodworking instead?"

Cinnamon smiled as she lowered the shade on the shop's front door, then pulled the door shut and turned the key in the lock.

"I suppose you're right. That *is* quite a vision. Do you think his spirit is leading us to select the ugliest design in his collection?"

"Actually, no," Velita answered, her face glowing. "He still has his reputation to protect, and his most exquisite sketches seem to float right up to the top. What a dilemma for him!"

"Maybe he'll wait until everyone has seen the finished garment on me, and then he'll arrange for one of the wedding guests to bump into me with a full plate of pasta or something."

Both women laughed out loud as they began their walk home to Broome Street, enjoying the private irreverence that they knew Vincente would also find amusing. All the same, while they navigated the crowded sidewalks on that steamy summer evening, Cinnamon honestly did not think *any* of this was very funny.

By seven o'clock on Monday morning, September 12, 1932, Velita had already been in the kitchen for an hour. Cinnamon pretended to be asleep on the sofa, but the coffee's irresistible aroma was urging her to get up against her will. Gregory had driven her home late the night before, following another social gathering in the Hudson River countryside over the weekend, and she hadn't slept more than a few hours per night since last Thursday.

This latest event had originally been scheduled as a political rally for Roosevelt. Even the wealthy had become conscious about conserving their resources, however, as the Depression worsened. In the final stages of preparation, two birthday parties and an engagement celebration for the homeowner's daughter had been combined with the rally. The series of festivities began with a reception on Friday afternoon and concluded with a brunch on Sunday. The drive back to Broome Street had then taken another three hours. By the time she finally stretched out on the sofa after brushing her hair and changing into her nightgown, she could not have kept her eyes open another minute, if someone had paid her to do so. Now, at the dawning of this new day, she would have stayed in bed until noon had she been free to choose. But the smell of sausage cooking was lifting her into a sitting position.

"Buona giorno," Velita said when she saw the mane of red hair rise above the back of the sofa.

"Good morning to you, too," Cinnamon answered sleepily, thinking to herself how much more comfortable this sofa was than the huge overstuffed bed she'd shared with Gregory's mother during both weekend nights. Looking around the room at the crowded, neatly organized clutter in every corner and on every shelf, she also began to realize how much she was going to miss this place. *Where on East 67th am I going to have any private space to put my things?* Suddenly, the clanging ring of the telephone in the hallway jarred the moment.

"I *told* Alberto this was going to start happening," Velita said, walking out of the kitchen and wiping her hands on a towel. "As soon as people stop being afraid of that box, I said to him, they'll start ringing each other up at the least whim. Let one of the neighbors answer it," she added, as Cinnamon stood up and pulled on her robe.

But the ringing continued and continued, while everyone on the floor apparently waited for someone else to answer the telephone. Eventually the noise stopped, followed by the sound of old Mr. Gianno yelling into the receiver, as if the faraway person on the other end of the line wouldn't be able to hear him unless he shouted.

"Ciao? Chi sta facendo questa telefonata?"

Pause.

"Chi? Perdoni il mio inglese. English...no so good. Who?"

Pause.

"Sì, capisco. Cannella. Sì—*Cinnamon*. Prego aspett un momento. Stay!"

She could hear the telephone's earpiece bumping against the wall, as it swung from the end of its cord after Mr. Gianno dropped it, and she pulled the apartment door open just as he was getting ready to knock on the other side.

"Thank you," she said, patting his musty bathrobe on the back, and then walking over to the box on the wall.

"Hello?"

"Cinn, is that you?"

It was *David's* voice! ***Excuse me***?

"Yes," she said cautiously. "Why are you calling?"

"This is David, Cinn."

"I *know* who you are. Why are you calling? Can you hear me?"

"I can hear you, Cinn, and I am *so* sorry."

She thought he was referring to her letter. But she'd written to him so many months ago. Why was he only now responding? And at seven o'clock in the morning, by telephone? Then she heard him answer her unspoken questions with the words that would lead to her meeting with destiny—the one for which she'd been setting herself up her entire life.

"Cinn, it's your father. He passed away shortly after midnight."

The information circled around her as she stood still, and as she was feeling none of the things she thought she should be feeling. Velita and Mr. Gianno were watching her from their respective apartment doors, waiting to learn the who's and what's of this call. But Cinnamon was neither moving nor speaking.

"Cinn?"

"Yes, David?"

"Are you all right?"

"Yes."

Wasn't she supposed to have some questions? Wasn't her heart supposed to be breaking?

"I know you're probably in shock, Cinn. We are, too. But the time has come for all of us to put away our differences with each other, because now we really *do* need you to come home."

Three more years would pass before *coming home* had anything to do with Albany in a permanent sense. But David was right. There was no way she could escape returning for her father's funeral. The journey back to her birthplace for that solemn experience made her understand how deeply the roots of her family extended into the core of who she'd become, despite the wide divisions that separated her from her beginnings. Quite unexpectedly, however, the same trip also made clear to her that burying her father would be the least of her difficulties in the fall of 1932.

CHAPTER 15

Jonathon McClinty Dead at Age 51
—The Albany Times Union
September 13, 1932

The headline had been screaming in Cinnamon's head since she walked past the newsstand in Albany's Union Station. She had arrived with Claudine and Maggie the morning after David's call, following a rush of arrangements and changed plans. Velita was the one who suggested that Maggie go along, uncertain what circumstances might be awaiting Cinnamon after her long absence and estrangement from key people in her family, not the least of which was her now deceased father. She also understood that David's three young boys might require special attention, in light of all the adult distractions, and she knew there would be no better interim caretaker than Cinnamon's sister. Oddly enough, Maggie voiced no objection to the idea. Neither did Cinnamon, who was nervous about returning to her home place under these depressing circumstances, and who took comfort in Maggie's company. The two of them might not have the closest of relationships, but at least Cinnamon felt she could trust her sister.

Gregory also wanted to be a part of the trip, expressing his desire to support his betrothed through the ordeal. But she anticipated enough tension as it was, without adding Gregory's presence to the thorny mix.

"You are such a dear," she'd said to him when he drove down to Broome Street, after she'd called him with the news. "It's just that I haven't been home for nine years, and to be completely honest with you, there wasn't much tenderness exchanged between my father and me during that time. Fortunately, my brother and I managed to stay close, and his new wife and I have been the best of friends since we were children. But there are other—well, for lack of a better term, *misunderstandings* that were never straightened out, and that I suspect will be forced to a resolution one way or another while I'm there. Despite your concern, you needn't be burdened with my muddle."

"All right," he said, his arm loosely draped across her shoulders as they sat in his topless motorcar outside her apartment. "I respect your wishes, although I'll travel up in a minute if you discover you need me."

"Thank you. I appreciate your understanding so very much."

"How are you doing otherwise? I know this has come as an enormous shock to you."

"Yes, it has, and yet I'm not feeling what I think I should be feeling. He was my father, and I really did love him. But the issues that developed between us drove us so far apart that we couldn't reach each other any more—not that either of us tried very hard. And then, because all the life I've been living *here* has had no connection whatsoever to life up *there*, the *reasons* for us to keep trying sort of withered away. I'm embarrassed to tell you this, Gregory, but I haven't cried a single tear since David called this morning. It's almost as if—for *me*, anyway—my Papa already died nine years ago. Does that make me sound like a terrible person?"

He could not imagine, from his own experience, how anyone could arrive at such an empty ending with a parent. But he admired her for being so candid with him. There was, he began to realize, a great deal about his fiancé that he did not know. Furthermore, he'd been so tied to his full agenda of late that, even when she'd been on his arm, he hadn't stopped to actually *look* at her or to explore any aspects of her heart, mind and history outside the realm of her pedigree.

"No, you don't sound like a terrible person, my dear, and based on what you've just told me, there is ample justification for your mixed feelings. I'm certain this trip will be very trying for you."

As he continued, he was oblivious to the many faces clustered in the apartment windows above him, looking down inquisitively while the two of them talked in the open motorcar. Her endearment to the people in this neighborhood was one of the many things about her that he did not fully comprehend, and even she didn't appreciate how much they were all going to miss her after she married him and moved away.

"You're the most determined woman I've ever known, aside from Mother, and I have no doubt that you will manage your way through whatever you encounter. How long do you anticipate you'll be gone?"

"I can't say for sure—a week, possibly. We'll leave for Albany tomorrow morning. David said the wake will be on Wednesday and the funeral on Thursday. Then, if arrangements can be made in time, we'll all gather for the reading of Papa's will on Friday. However, in view of my apparent disfavor," she added with a weak smile, "there may be no reason for me to wait around for that meeting. But I suspect things will become clear shortly after I get up there."

Jay and Angela met the train the next day. When Cinnamon first saw them through the passenger window she was pulled back into memories of arrivals and departures in this station. Now she wished that she'd made an effort to come back for at least one happy visit while the family was still intact. Across the aisle from her, Maggie had been watching the scenery with childlike curiosity since they began approaching Albany's city limits half an hour earlier. Cinnamon had never considered that her sister probably had no memories of her own birthplace. She was only two when Bradley moved them to Broome Street, and there'd been no reason for her to come back for the last twenty years. She was approaching this town as a total stranger, with no mental pictures of the Madison house, or the cottage, or The Corbett Place—and she'd never seen Fox Run. Cinnamon's family up here did not actually belong to her sister. *How strange is <u>that</u>? I hope she's not going to be uncomfortable.*

But there wasn't time to ponder this any further. The porter had taken their bags down the railcar's steps and placed them on the platform, where her brother waited with her best friend. In spite of the grim circumstances, their greetings were warm, their embraces long and strong, which came as a great relief to all of them.

Jay was behind the wheel, and Angela was beside him in the front passenger seat. Maggie sat with Cinnamon in the back, with Claudine in between them.

"Mama has not left her room since we brought her home from the hospital yesterday morning," Jay summarized, after explaining for half an hour the chronology of events to his sister, while looking at her through the rearview mirror as he drove. "She's very fragile, and she has all of us terribly worried."

"There always seems to be *one* whose soul becomes paralyzed," Cinnamon responded, thinking of Mimi and absently looking out the window.

"What? I couldn't hear you," he said.

"Never mind. It was nothing."

Just then, the roofline of Fox Run's main house came into view, as Jay drove past the ice cream shop on New Scotland Road.

"Look, Claudine," Cinnamon said, pointing at the familiar landscape. "There's your grandfather's house."

"But you told me he's not there any more, Mommy."

The words sounded raw in the voice of a child, and everyone remained silent for several moments.

"Yes, that's right," Jay replied. "Your grandfather's in heaven."

"Is he there with Daddy?"

The question provoked a spontaneous and somewhat irreverent wave of laughter that circled through the car, as the adults conjured their own visions of Jonathon meeting up with Vincente in the hereafter.

"Maybe they're in the same neighborhood," Jay answered at length, grinning at his sister through the rearview mirror again, "but probably not on the same block."

When the motorcar turned into Fox Run's driveway, several men and women who Cinnamon did not recognize came out of the side door and stood waiting for them.

"That's part of Lucille's family," Angela said, as if reading the question in Cinnamon's mind. "She had two sisters and a brother, and they've been rotating the care of David's children all these months. I'm not sure what he would have done without their help."

As if on cue, two little boys ran around from the back of the house. Another woman followed close behind them and held a toddler in her arms.

"Claudine, those are your cousins," Angela said to the child, who was now leaning forward into the front seat. "That's DJ on the left, in the blue shirt. He's almost exactly your age. Ryan is next to him. He's a couple of years younger than you. And that's baby Teddy in his aunt's arms. He's not even two years old, poor little fellow."

"Why is he poor?" Claudine asked.

"He's not poor from money," Cinnamon interjected, realizing that Angela could not possibly know how many times her daughter had heard the word *poor* on Broome Street. "She means that it's sad because Teddy's mommy went to heaven right after he was born, so he never really got a chance to meet her."

"Oh," Claudine said, staring at the little boy and trying to process the information. "A *lot* of our people went to heaven, didn't they?"

Angela turned around to check the emotion on her friend's face just as Jay brought the motorcar to a stop under the side portico. But Cinnamon looked away from her when, out of the corner of her eye, she saw someone coming down the steps and heading toward the car—someone whose broad, imposing silhouette moved along the ground. Then the car door on her side was pulled open and a large, familiar hand—darkened by sun and age, but wholly recognizable—reached in, palm up and open, waiting for hers. Keeping her focus down, she placed her hand on top of his and let him guide her out of the car. When her feet were on the ground, she raised her head to see him.

After more than nine years of absence and alienation, David stood in front of her. The deep blue shadows of his eyes were hollow. His face seemed thinner, older, and filled with pain. But he was trying to smile, hesitantly, almost in a flinch, as if he were expecting her to lob an unkind remark at him. But nothing could have been further from her mind as she walked into his embrace. Instinctively and without a word, she put her arms around him, locked her wrists behind his head and buried her face in the curve of his neck. Then he lifted her off the ground, *but not as far off as he used to be able to lift me when I was skinny,* she thought, imagining that he was probably thinking the same thing. Feeling herself sway as he held her and turned around in slow motion, she was surrounded by the warmth, the strength and the smell of him—and the walls she'd constructed around her heart began falling away.

Drake and Irene unloaded the luggage and carried the bags upstairs, placing Cinnamon's in her old bedroom, which was remarkably unchanged, right down to the porcelain bric-a-brac on the bureau. Maggie and Claudine were taken to the room next to hers, which they would be sharing, and everyone was urged to be especially quiet while settling in, since Sophie was in seclusion across the hall. Then Irene offered to finish unpacking for them. Maggie and Claudine found this so astonishing that they both wanted to stay and watch, until the expression on Cinnamon's face told them that would not be an appropriate thing to do.

When the visitors returned to the parlor downstairs, the awkward confluence of fresh grief and the end of such a long separation made the introductions to Lucille's family a bit forced. Adding to this discomfort was Cinnamon's realization that she'd never been in this house as an adult, much less as a parent. *I'm the grownup now. There's no father or mother to guide me here. Instead, others are looking to me*. Recalling her journal entry about the vacation resort hotel, she smiled to herself, understanding that this adjustment was going to take time for each person in the room.

Plans had been made for the evening meal to be served at four o'clock that afternoon, enabling everyone to return early to their respective homes and prepare for the two long days ahead of them. While Irene worked in the kitchen, the men all went out on the front porch to smoke their cigarettes, and the women remained in the parlor to become further acquainted. There was no acceptable way for Cinnamon to avoid this exchange. But Maggie had nothing in common with any of these people, and she'd grown tired of pretending interest in their strained attempts at conversation. Capitalizing on the fact that she'd been brought along to help with the children, she graciously excused herself and made her way to the kitchen, where David had sent his boys. Claudine had gone with them, too, having discovered that DJ was every bit as interesting as her mother and Angela had told her he would be.

When Maggie walked through the kitchen's swinging door, Irene turned around from her place at the stove, staring in wonder as she had earlier at the young woman's resemblance to Mimi. Fleeting visions sped through her mind of a steamy Madison kitchen, a pregnant Mimi with her feet propped up on an upturned flower pot and Amelia fussing around her.

"Hello, my dear. Please come in and join us," she said, gesturing toward the table in the bay window, where the four children sat watching her. "I know this is a very sad time for everyone, but I must tell you that I'm very happy to see you. I knew you when you were a baby, and I was very fond of your mother and grandmother."

"That's what I understand, and I'm delighted to meet you—or should I say *see* you—again."

The two women exchanged smiles as Maggie gravitated toward the children. Ryan was next to Teddy, who was balanced on a stack of books piled on the curved bench in the window. DJ and Claudine sat beside each other, across from the two boys. Tin cups of hot chocolate were on each of their placemats, and they were dipping their pudgy fingers into the huge bin filled with crayons, which Irene had positioned in the middle of the table. The multiple sets of eight different colors presented an intriguing range of options for the children to use with the brand new coloring books they'd just been given.

Ryan had requested blank paper rather than the book, and before Maggie entered the kitchen he'd been deeply focused on his original drawing of David's black motorcar as it looked parked on top of cotton clouds in a pale blue sky. His concentration had been so intense that he'd been gripping the black crayon by its tip, his face hovering a couple of inches off his paper, while his tongue pushed out from the inside of his right cheek. As Maggie began moving toward the table, he rotated his eyes upward in her direction, without moving his head. The other children turned to look at her as well.

"Who are *you*?" Ryan asked suspiciously. "Do you work here?"

"No, I don't. But I…"

"Then why are you here?"

"Well, I came from New York with Claudine and her mommy."

"Why?" Ryan pressed, confidently serving as spokesman for his brothers, whose attention shifted back and forth from Maggie to their coloring books.

"Because…"

"Because she's part of the family," Irene interjected, hoping to shorten what she knew could become a catechismal litany.

"She's *my* Aunt Maggie," Claudine piped in.

"Are you *our* Aunt Maggie, too?"

"Actually, Ryan, I'm…"

"Yes," Irene interrupted again, for the sake of simplicity. "Her name is Aunt Maggie for all of you."

Maggie walked around to the window side of the table.

"Would you mind if I join you for a little while?"

He stared up at her apprehensively, and then over at Irene.

"Ryan, say 'no, I won't mind at all'," Irene prompted.

"No, I won't mind at all," he answered obediently, while blocking Maggie's view of his drawing with his arms and hands.

"So, tell me," she said, sidling onto the bench next to him, "who exactly are *you*? And who are these other two handsome gentlemen?"

Obviously appreciating the fact that she was addressing him as an authority, he placed his suspicions aside, sat up straight, and launched into his reply with a charming dramatic flair.

"My name is Ryan McClinty, and I'm five years old. My father is David McClinty, and he is *very* old. My Mama went to heaven, so she's not here today—but she is *not* old. That boy over there is my brother DJ. He's six years old, which is not very older than me. And *he*," Ryan said, pointing to the amazingly quiet child sitting on the stack of books next to him, "is my baby brother Teddy. He's still one years old, but he'll be two someday soon, my father says. He needs lots of help with everything. See those books? We all live on Madison Avenue in Albany, New York," he continued, gesturing around the table, "except for *her*," he said, pointing across at Claudine. "I don't know where *she* lives. Where *do* you live?" he asked, momentarily curious about her.

"On Broome Street," she answered politely. But Ryan didn't seem to care as his attention snapped back to his drawing.

"I'm very happy to meet you," Maggie proffered, although none of the children seemed to be listening now. "You know what? I enjoy making pictures more than anything else in the world. Would you mind if I draw with you?"

Her request was handled expeditiously by Ryan, who silently pushed his unused coloring book in front of her, without so much as an upward glance.

"Oh, thank you very much. This is a lovely new book. But I was really hoping you might let me use some of your blank paper.

This aroused Ryan's interest.

"You can draw from scratch?" he inquired in a skeptical tone of voice.

"Yes, I can—a little bit."

"Let me see you do something," he demanded, handing her a single piece of his paper.

With dexterity and speed—and no small measure of amusement—she began sketching a portrait of the four children just as they looked sitting there at the table. Ryan scooted closer to her, his eyes fixed on the sharp points of the crayons as she spun them across the page. When she was finished, she signed her name on the bottom, along with the day's date, and presented the page to Ryan as a gift.

DJ, Teddy and Claudine were now alert to the proceedings and enviously eyed the completed drawing.

"May I please have one, too?" DJ asked.

"Of course. I'll make one for each of you."

Spellbound by this development, Ryan handed her more paper and remained mesmerized until the fourth copy was finished. Then, after realizing that he *loved* this new Aunt Maggie, he quickly completed the picture he'd been working on when she came in, and handed it to her as he edged up against her.

"Here. This is a present for you, too."

"Why, thank you, Ryan. It's beautiful!"

"I know," he answered, taking a clean sheet of paper from the pile to start a new drawing.

Irene had been observing the scene, and when Maggie looked over at her, there was a sense of balance in the room that both women acknowledged. For Irene, the ambiance was reminiscent of times past. For Maggie, the feeling was one of reprieve now that she knew this trip wouldn't be totally unbearable.

Over the next two days, emotions ran thick as the wake and funeral pushed the reality of Jonathon's death into everyone's faces. Sophie was so distraught that she was taken back to Fox Run by Lucille's family after only an hour at the viewing. Cinnamon couldn't blame her for this frailty, finding the vision of her father laid out in the open casket impossible to look at for more than few minutes. But the stream of people from Albany's business, social and civic arenas kept filing through the funeral home. She didn't know most of them, and she felt self-conscious when so many of them who seemed to know *her* acted stilted around her, frequently whispering among themselves, while eyeing her from another part of the room.

Not understanding these subtle waves of condescension, she stayed close to Jay and Angela. She also kept an eye on David as he wound his way through the solemn crowd, and as the guests paid their respects to the deceased, while, at the same time, seeking favor from Jonathon's business heir-apparent. *This is almost like eavesdropping on a dance or a courtship*, she thought, *and very close to disrespectful.* But she couldn't stop herself from watching, nor could she avoid the uncomfortable realization that, even though she was Jonathon's daughter, she was nearly as much of an outsider as Maggie. She had not grown up in her father's house and thus had not been exposed to whatever it was that all these people represented.

Maggie stayed at Fox Run with Irene and the children the next day and observed as the line of motorcars turn left out of the driveway en route to the funeral Mass. Cinnamon rode in David's car, beside him on the front seat. Jay and Angela sat in the back, with Sophie between them. The rest of the family, primarily Lucille's relatives, followed in automobiles behind them. As they made their way to the Cathedral in silence, Cinnamon stared out the window, recognizing the same roads she and David had taken when they went to see the Magglios together during a long-ago summer. Thinking about Lark Street for the first time this trip, she wondered if she would have a chance to see Joseph and the others before she went back to New York. *I doubt that David would be interested in taking me again. He's scarcely said a word to me—and I was beginning to think we'd be all right with one another.*

Mass seemed interminable. Beneath the Indian summer sun, the packed Cathedral became hotter by the minute. Even when the service had concluded and the pallbearers had placed Jonathon's casket in the hearse, the crowds continued to mingle in the heat, talking with one another and saying private words to Sophie, Jay and David. No one offered any personal condolences to Cinnamon, however, other than a polite smile, and she was relieved when the procession of cars finally began snaking its way to the memorial park.

Thank God this is almost over, she thought after they passed through the cemetery gates and pulled over to the side. Moments later, as she walked the path behind David, Angela, Jay and Sophie, through the grave markers and up the grassy slope to the tent waiting for them at the top of the hill, she found herself whispering, "I am *so* ready to go home."

This sentiment became even stronger when she neared the crest of the hill, because she was completely unprepared for what she was about to see. Her father's casket was on a wooden platform beneath the tent. Under the platform was a deep, dark hole, and as she realized that her father would soon be lowered into that hole, her heart began racing and the gruesome vision overwhelmed her. Jay and David were supporting Sophie, helping her to a front chair near the edge of the grave. Angela was in the row behind them, and the crowd began to assemble in a circle around the tent.

But Cinnamon stayed back, letting people pass her and form a wall of bodies that obstructed her view of the scene. Within minutes, no one was filing by her any longer, and she heard the priest's voice under the canopy as he began his delivery of final prayers and blessings. Drawn toward two gravestones to the left of the burial site, she walked in that direction. Alone and unnoticed, she then met unpredictably with the rest of her heritage—the names rising up and reaching out to her from the neatly groomed lawn.

NATHANIEL McCLINTY

NOVEMBER 5, 1857—JUNE 12, 1904

THE FINEST MAN THEY WILL EVER KNOW
WILL BE MISSED BY
AMELIA—BELOVED WIFE
PETER AND JONATHON—BELOVED SONS

and then,

MY PRAYER AND GREATEST WISH IS THAT NOT ONLY WILL I BE GRANTED THE POWER TO FORGIVE ALL THINGS, BUT THAT THE SAME POWER WILL BE GIVEN TO THOSE I LOVE.

AMELIA ELIZABETH McCLINTY
FEBRUARY 2, 1858—APRIL 23, 1906

Looking over at her father's burial tent, the demise of her family began to assault her, as she dropped to the ground on the same spot where Mimi sat before leaving Albany in 1913. *Forgiving is part of the point*, her mother had said to her that night on Broome Street. *I know you love him...It's all right to love your father, but don't grant that love any power over you...After the words, you must find a way to let go. If you fail to do that, you will never be free...*Finally recognizing the origin of Mimi's message, she also understood that her mother had been trying to leave instructions for her. Lifting her head, she saw the backs of the people gathered close around her father's grave. Disheartening as that casket looked over the hole, the reality was that *he* wasn't in that box—and her ability to grasp the significance of Mimi's directive had come too late.

"I'm so sorry, Papa," she said softly. "I should have listened to Mother. I should have let you back in. No matter what happened between us, I wouldn't be here if not for you—and we should have had the chance to say good-bye to each other."

Still without a tear on her cheek, she brushed her fingers across the lettering on her grandmother's marker, rose to her feet and walked down the hill. Waiting alone in David's motorcar while the interment service continued, she put her head down in the back seat and thought about everything and nothing, wondering in the hush if the forgiveness that had been so important to her mother and grandmother was something she'd ever find a way to confer upon herself.

Later that day at Fox Run, when the funeral reception guests had all departed and the food had been cleared away, a subdued and weary family gathered together in the parlor to share stories about the man they had just buried. But once they started, they realized that no one felt like talking. Besides, they needed to be up early the next morning to meet at the law offices of the McClinty family attorney for the reading of Jonathon's will. Sophie was already in bed, having been given additional medication by Dr. Coomey. After checking on her one more time, Jay and Angela left for their home in Albany, deciding not to spend the night at Fox Run, as everyone else was doing.

"We'll see you tomorrow at nine o'clock," Jay said, looking drawn as he kissed his sister good-bye.

When they'd gone, Cinnamon helped Maggie and Irene prepare the children for bed. Once they were tucked in, David came upstairs to tell the boys good-night, and then he retired to the guest cottage. Irene offered fresh tea in the kitchen to Mimi's daughters, hoping to share a few moments alone with them. Cinnamon gratefully accepted, following Irene downstairs and sitting down by the window, where she propped her legs up on the bench.

But Maggie declined, saying she could barely keep her eyes open and excusing herself to join Claudine, who was fast asleep in the room they were sharing. She wasn't really tired, however, just restless and ready to go home. But she *was* looking forward to spending one more day with David's boys, particularly Ryan. She thought that if she ever had any children of her own, someone just like him would be perfect for her—bright, artistically gifted, and innately skeptical of all people and things. They could share the exploration of their creative passions and keep each other out of trouble. How fulfilling life would be with someone she could care for, someone who valued the same pursuits as she did, who needed her and truly wanted to spend time with her. Of course, nowhere in this vision was a father for her mythical boy. Smiling to herself as she slipped beneath the covers next to her little niece, she recalled a conversation she'd overheard not too long ago on Broome Street.

"You only know what you're brought up with," Alberto had answered when Velita asked him if he thought Maggie remembered Bradley. "She probably has vague memories of him, but through no fault of his own, he wasn't there. She knows he was her father, but what does that really mean to her? The truth is that she grew up watching her mother, and then her sister, raise children without fathers to help them. *That's* what she remembers—that's the model she was brought up with. If she ever finds a husband, she won't even know what to do with him."

"But she's been lucky enough to have *you,*" Velita said, squeezing her arms around him. "And you've been able to fill in some of those missing pieces for her."

Yes, Maggie thought, returning from the recollection and pulling the handmade patch quilt up over her body to her chin. *I have been very lucky about that.* Then she closed her eyes and attempted to fall asleep by thinking about Ryan and trying to imagine some sort of future for herself. This trip had given her a taste of the world outside of her experience, and she suddenly felt completely unprepared for anything other than Broome Street. She had her painting and her high school diploma. Yet she wasn't interested in marriage, and she had no meaningful skills—unlike her sister who had somehow figured out how to be successful in several different worlds at the same time. *Maybe Cinnamon was right. I probably should have learned how to sew.*

Worried that her restlessness would awaken Claudine beside her, she carefully slipped out from beneath the quilt, wrapped her robe around her shoulders and sat down in the window seat. Parting the lace curtain panels, she looked down on the yard behind the house. The night sky was slipping from deep blue to black, as slivers of light from an Indian summer full moon filtered through the tree branches onto the grass. She saw the shade pulled on the front window of the guest cottage, although it looked as if a lamp was still lit inside. She also saw the heavy door to the barn pulled slightly open. But everything else was dark, and she didn't hear anyone moving around downstairs or in the other bedrooms. Assuming that Irene and Cinnamon had finished their tea and that she was the only one still awake, Maggie remained seated in the window, glad that no one was around to interrupt her or to see the unrestrained streams of tears flowing down her cheeks.

In the room next door, Cinnamon also wrestled with sleep. But staying inside was not a solution for her. She needed a little Fox Run air to help sedate her. So, she put a light sweater on over her nightgown, pushed her feet into her slippers and made her way downstairs. Then she tiptoed through the hall and kitchen, and out the back door. The baking heat of the day had given way to a pleasant warmth, with just a hint of a breeze and a touch of humidity, as she headed through the darkness in the direction of the pond. She was certain that a few minutes of breathing deeply on the stone bench beside the water would be all she needed to make her sleepy.

But as she was passing the barn, she heard something through the partially open door. It sounded like someone was crying—a man. Slightly fearful about exploring further, she peered into the opening, nonetheless. Through the barn's rear windows, the high moon over the field out back threw enough light inside for her to see someone sitting on the stacked bales. The person's legs were pulled up to his chest, his head and arms resting on his knees, and he was, indeed, crying. As her eyes began to adjust, she could just barely distinguish his features. It was David.

Not wanting to startle him, she moved slowly through the doorway and whispered his name. When he heard her, he looked up, and, after realizing who she was, turned his head away from her.

"Go back to bed, Cinn," he managed to say through a gravelly voice.

"David, are you all right?"

"Yes. Now go back to the house."

"No, I won't," she said, sitting down behind him and putting her hands on his shoulders. "Not until I'm sure you're all right."

Remaining in his folded position and continuing to look away from her, he removed a handkerchief from his pants pocket and blew his nose.

"What are you doing out here anyway, Cinn? I thought you were in bed long ago."

"I couldn't sleep. Too many things running around my head after a day like this. I was on my way to the pond to clear my thoughts."

Finally stretching his legs out, he put his feet on the ground and turned to face her. Even in the dim moonlight, she could see how swollen his eyes were, and he appeared to be in the same shirt and pants that he'd worn to the cemetery.

"Cinn, I'm so very sorry," he said, after sitting there looking at her for uncounted minutes.

"Sorry for what, David?"

"For all the years of misunderstanding between us."

"Please, let's not dwell on that. It's in the past anyway."

"But it's my fault that your father never made things right with you. I should have done something to help, so you could have been together more—so he could have spent time with his granddaughter, who he never even had the chance to meet."

"No," she declared softly, placing her hands on either side of his face, as she watched his eyes fill with tears again. "It was *me*, David. When I found out what he did to my mother, I shut him out completely. And I wasn't exactly selfless in the rest of my relationships, either, during those years. I didn't really start thinking about other people until after Mother died. I wish now that I'd been more compassionate toward my father while he was still here. But there certainly wasn't anything *you* could have done about it."

"Yes, I think there was," he answered, leaning in closer to her. "But now he's gone, and when we were at the cemetery today, I…thought…I don't…know if I can…"

He was breaking down, and suddenly his arms were around her, pressing her into him as he sought comfort. Without thinking, she maneuvered her face into that spot in the curve of his neck, while his heart accelerated against her chest—and while neither of them moved or said another word. Then she felt his warm breath on her ear, his lips skimming softly along her cheek, under her jaw, and forward to the front of her neck, up over her chin and slowly, gently to her mouth. At the same time, his hands were underneath her sweater, moving down the silky fabric of her nightgown toward her waist and around to the front of her.

"David," she whispered, knowing she should get up and run as soon as he began leaning her backwards onto the straw. But her arms were around his neck, and his body was strong and warm on top of her. *Just a few more minutes*, she thought, as she was pulled into the deep velvet sensation of his touch. *Just a few more minutes.* But after two decades of fate calculating this moment, *a few more minutes* could not be restrained—and although she knew this was the very worst of ideas, she forgot to remember to stop.

The moon had risen even higher in the sky by the time David and Cinnamon stood near the barn's doorway, looking at each other in silence. They had already said everything in the darkness, as they nestled side-by-side on the hay, agreeing that the passion building between them had been inevitable, and that they had just made a terrible mistake. But they also agreed that the sin they now shared had taken control of them because they hadn't been thinking clearly in this time of emotional weakness. Although they could not undo the last hour, they each promised to take the sin to Confession, repent, and then never speak of it again.

Yet even in the midst of this rational, over-simplified analysis of the situation, they knew that the line they had crossed would forever complicate their relationship—*and just when things had begun to clear up*, Cinnamon found herself reflecting. Still, they were both fascinated by the irony—by the realization that the love so forsaken between them for the last nine years suddenly felt full and protective again, strengthened by this new secret that they would take to their own graves with them. Somehow, they weren't afraid, either, as they walked out of the barn, the moonlight shining down on them through the trees. What could be the ultimate harm if no one knew, and if it never happened again?

"Good night, Cinn," David said, lifting her up and kissing her lightly on the forehead. "Everything will be all right."

"I know," she answered, kissing him back on his cheek. When he set her down, she pulled her sweater close around her chest to keep the breeze from opening her nightgown, then she reached up to touch his face one more time. "Sleep well now."

"You, too."

As he walked over to the guest cottage, she made her way to the back door of the house, each of them glancing over their shoulders to wave at the other. Neither of them noticed the lace curtain panels fluttering closed on an upstairs bedroom window.

There were few surprises when Jonathon's will was read the next morning. The precise size of his estate was not disclosed in full, but the individual bequests indicated that he had amassed quite an extraordinary sum. The deed to Fox Run passed, as expected, to Jay, with the stipulation that Sophie maintain possession and live there in comfort and safety for the balance of her lifetime. All furnishings, decorations and household items were also left to Jay. As long as his mother lived, however, none of those items was to be touched. A further stipulation stated that Fox Run could not be sold without the written consent of David, Cinnamon and Jay, or any surviving combination of the three while at least two of them remained alive. Jonathon had already signed over the Madison deed to David years earlier, so that took care of the residences.

Controlling ownership of the mill was placed in David's name, while Jay maintained a minority partnership. Jonathon's personal effects—his clothing, jewelry and other assorted belongings—were left to David and Jay as well, to be divided between them as they saw fit. His motorcar was also given to the men, to be kept or sold at their discretion, the use or proceeds to be divided equally. There was a handful of stocks to be transferred, but few in the portfolio had any value remaining at this point in the Depression. Apparently, there was a substantial amount of cash, however, the larger share of which went to David. This included what was left of the money from his mother Lily's estate, which Jonathon had invested and then had done his best to salvage after the crash in 1929.

Finally, nearly an hour into the reading, the attorney reached the point in the will that addressed "the only female child." Cinnamon had been bequeathed a trust fund that she could begin collecting immediately, having past the required age of twenty-one by more than five years. Her eyes widened in disbelief when she heard that these funds would flow to her whether she married again or not, and that they would pay her, on a quarterly basis, in the approximate amount of $3000, to be readjusted annually. Although she had not been given any property rights, and despite Jonathon's avowed displeasure with his daughter, he'd made certain that she would remain comfortable throughout her life. This assumed, of course, that she would use the money judiciously, and that *someone with both a brain and a heart is elected president, so we can bring an end to this damn economic famine*, as the attorney paraphrased Jonathon's remarks to him.

Cinnamon looked across the wide mahogany table at David, working hard to ignore the guilt that had awakened her that morning. She hoped he could see that she was steady, and she wondered if he was thinking—as *she* was—that this trust fund might have been her father's own way of trying to make amends. While reflecting, she overheard the attorney read something else that contained her name.

"…further bequeathed to the female offspring, Margaret Elizabeth, items contained in a roped-off section of Fox Run's attic…"

But those words were lost in the miasma of her distractions. As if last night and David weren't enough, the $3000 per quarter was just beginning to sink in.

Cinnamon traveled to New York as scheduled the next day, with Maggie and Claudine. Her father had been buried. All the necessary papers had been signed, and promises had been made for Jay and Angela to visit as soon as Sophie stabilized. The balance of events from that week in Albany seemed, almost, to have never happened—except that, clearly, they *had*. David retreated to the Madison house with his three sons and the rotating assistance of women from Lucille's family, while operations and management of the mill consumed most of his schedule. Orders for lumber were down, and although he was forced to reduce hours for his laborers, he did not let anyone go who wished to continue working there at the lower wage. When he wasn't focused on business, he spent some of his time with the boys. But otherwise, he seemed to prefer being alone, appearing stronger by himself, somehow, than he'd been before Jonathon died.

The day after she arrived back on Broome Street, Cinnamon began cleansing her soul in the confessional with Father Panito, followed by hours spent in the lengthy acts of penance he gave her. In her heart, she wondered if she would ever be completely freed from the clutches of her indiscretion. But she was determined to devote the rest of her spiritual life toward that objective, if God was going to require as much of her. Otherwise, the evolution of daily events was thankfully keeping her too busy for idle worry.

On October 29, 1932, slightly more than a month after she returned from Albany, she married Gregory, as planned, in the rear chapel of St. Patrick's Cathedral. Notwithstanding the weight of her transgression, which she could not seem to shake, she looked nothing short of stunning that day. Her dress was made from one of Vincente's sleek, simple designs, with an off-the-shoulder bodice and a long, straight skirt that opened into a short rounded train on the floor behind her. Alberto found an ivory silk fabric for the dress that was woven with silver threads and embroidered with tiny beads, all of which transformed the rather plain pattern into a gown of shimmering elegance. Her hair was swept up and back in a combination of braids and soft curls, through which Velita had laced rows of tiny silk flowers fashioned from the same fabric as the dress. As she stood admiring the undeserved vision of herself in the chapel dressing room just prior to the ceremony, she wished that her mother and Bradley could be here to witness this. *Papa, too,* she thought. But they were undoubtedly together in a celestial gallery somewhere—probably in a setting orchestrated by Amelia—and she hoped that as they watched her, they all still loved her, in spite of her failings. She couldn't bear to think about Vincente being with them, however, or what *he* might be feeling. As his face and smile flashed through her mind, she could only hope that he was forgiving her, since *none* of this would be happening, if he were still here.

The guest list for the exchange of vows had been kept intentionally short, but did include Alberto, Velita, Maria, Rosa and Claudine on Cinnamon's side. Maggie had been invited as well, of course, although she'd claimed at the last minute that she was feeling ill and insisted that she would surely end up ruining things if she tried to attend. Recognizing the trick, and exasperated with her sister's dark moods, Cinnamon expended no effort trying to make her change her mind. *If she can't stop pouting long enough to come to my wedding, then I give up.*

There was a much larger attendance at the reception, which was held at a swank, midtown restaurant that had been reserved in its entirety for the party. Other than Alberto and Velita, everyone there was from Gregory's circle. She'd met most of them previously at one event or another, and they were visibly impressed by her elegance and the fact that she remembered all of their names. While she was appropriately gracious in her receipt of their compliments, she refrained from any unnecessary conversation with them, feeling a decided absence of sincerity in their tone. In truth, she didn't really trust them, knowing that her value to them would evaporate, in an instant, without Gregory.

Understandable as this may be, I'm more convinced than ever that I need to hang on to my dress shop at all costs. No one can take <u>that</u> identity away from me. Oh my, what awful thoughts to be having on my wedding day!

Following a week-long honeymoon at the Long Island beach estate of a Stafford family friend, Gregory's new wife officially moved with Claudine into the house on East 67th Street, while Maggie continued to live with Alberto and Velita. Two months after the wedding, Cinnamon's trust fund began to flow, and Gregory agreed that she was free to use the money however she chose. He asked only that she review her ideas with him beforehand to help prevent any unnecessary losses. This precaution was only until the Depression's hold began to moderate, he'd told her, which everyone predicted would be soon, now that Franklin Roosevelt had been elected president.

The first thing she hoped to do with her inheritance was to move her former in-laws and sister away from Broome Street. But none of them wanted to leave the neighborhood, and no amount of charm or temptation was persuading them otherwise. So, she gave them money every quarter, instead, to cover the majority of their living expenses, and then she used most of the rest to sustain *A Touch of Cinnamon* through the increasingly difficult economy. She still visited the shop whenever possible and returned to Broome Street one Sunday every month for Mass at St. Paul's, followed by a meal and conversation with Alberto and Velita in the soothing familiarity of their apartment. But the primary focus of her life, and the new people contained therein, shifted rapidly to the Upper East Side, especially when her swift and much-heralded pregnancy became obvious, confining her once again to the inside of a house.

...Being imprisoned in this residence, she wrote to Angela, *is definitely less monotonous than the Broome Street apartment was with Claudine. At least there's a variety of rooms to alter my moods, and plenty of stairs to help me stay active. In addition, Mrs. Stafford (I don't know what else to call her yet, and I can't bring myself to call her Mother, as she's been encouraging me to do)—anyway, she's very kindly agreed to let me set up my sewing machine on her enclosed porch (the one with all of the lovely wicker furniture), so I can make things for the baby and feel useful in some small way. This whole business of needing to hide my body for the better part of nine months is truly prehistoric...*

Gregory's mother agreed with her on that point. Furthermore, Mrs. Stafford was amazingly contemporary and sympathetic to the plight of *all* women in this condition. She even assisted Cinnamon with her new round of editorial letters to several New York newspapers on the subject. The heroically shocking lines written by her new mother-in-law were not only exciting, but they served to draw Cinnamon closer to the woman. These letters were also copied word-for-word, on occasion, into Cinnamon's journal—for posterity.

March 18, 1933

"To my knowledge," *Mrs. Stafford wrote in her letter today to the New York Times, "**there has not been drawn any biological connection between a woman's reproductive system and the operation of her brain. Thus, when she is with child, she should have no difficulty continuing to function in a most productive manner, or walking without falling down, or refreshing herself outside in the clear air, where contact with other people is healthy and invigorating. Given these facts, the continuation of such archaic confinements only highlights the unwillingness of men to share equally in the consequences of their own behavior, the acting out of which requires the use of a few of their own body parts that are clearly not connected to their brains either."***

Yes, Angela, she actually took this one to the post office this afternoon! How surprisingly delightful she is!

M.E.M.S.

Naturally, the letters were signed with fictitious names, and in the early 1930's, their advocacy had limited public support. But the letter-writing campaign helped pass the time, as did Angela's visit in April of 1933. Jay stayed behind in Albany to remain close to Sophie, who never rebounded from Jonathon's death. Although Cinnamon missed seeing her brother, she was happy to have her dearest friend close by, even if only for a short time. During their three weeks together, she and Angela shared in preparations for the baby, in the never-ending intrigue of the East 67th Street house and its gardens—which were extraordinarily beautiful in the spring—and in the confession Cinnamon made to her lifelong ally, after much agonizing.

"There are some things I simply could not put down in writing to you," she said one afternoon, when the two of them were having tea beneath the wisteria arbor, far enough away from the house to protect their whispers.

"Yes, I can see why that would be true," Angela said an hour later, when Cinnamon repeated the understatement after finishing her revelations. "Well, I'm grateful that you still trust me sufficiently to tell me, Cinn. You know how much I'll always love you, no matter what trouble you get yourself into. *This* one wins the prize, though, I must say."

The intimacy of their companionship might not have done anything to help repave Cinnamon's way back into God's good graces. But Angela had a knack for making her friend feel immeasurably better about herself than she did after spending hours in the confessional. Thus, by the time this important visit was over during the first week of May, Cinnamon's self-confidence and sense of worth had been reinforced, and she believed herself to be fully prepared for the next life-altering event.

Slightly more than a month later, amidst the reserved enthusiasm of the 67th Street neighborhood, Gregory Brian Stafford Junior was born into the family, on June 21, 1933—four weeks earlier than expected. He was perfect, and nearly seven pounds, despite his prematurity. Of course, his arrival followed what Cinnamon was convinced had been the longest and most painful birthing experience in the history of mankind.

Ora siete finiti con me? Now are you through with me?

Almost.

CHAPTER 16

Wednesday, September 12, 1934
Nine o'clock in the evening

My dearest Angela—

Your letter arrived this afternoon, and I cannot begin to express my happiness over your news! I know that you had begun to believe you and my brother would never be blessed with a child, but in my heart I always trusted otherwise. A merciful God could not possibly leave two people as wonderful and devoted as you without the joy of recreating yourselves into a perfect, beautiful bundle. He also must have been thinking that sending a new life to you would be the best way to ease the sadness of Sophie's passing. As I understand from your last few letters, her death so soon after Papa's has caused Jay to search for a new definition of himself without parents. I experienced the same thing, but having my children close helped me accept that I am now the oldest of the line. At least I'm able to look at them and know for certain that life does, indeed, go on. Something else I found of value is the rather humorous vision—and please forgive me if this sounds a bit wicked—of my father now having to contend with both Sophie and my mother at the same heavenly time (on the off-chance that he ended up in the same place where they are).

At any rate, I pray this news of a child on the way has eased my brother's sadness and brought back the cheerful confidence we're accustomed to seeing in him. Now that your (and my) prayers have been answered, I am so very happy for you! I'm also doubly happy for me, knowing that I will be there to see my niece or nephew introduced to the world, to watch the little tyke go through all the phases you and I have gone through together (well, not all of them, I hope), and to share the rest of the journey with you. Furthermore, the fact that you and Jay have decided to purchase the old Corbett Place as your new home is the sweetest frosting on all the rest. What an extraordinary intersection of miracles!

Speaking of miracles, preparations are nearly complete for my move up there. I'm afraid my expectations were far afield from reality with respect to the amount of work involved, not to mention the emotions. Claudine has been particularly difficult, although I cannot really hold her at fault. When **I** *was nine years old, if I remember correctly, I wasn't much of a gem myself. Last night, she became Sara Bernhardt reincarnated as she begged me to postpone our departure until after her tenth birthday, which I can hardly believe is less than a month away.*

When she is sad, she looks even more like Vincente than she does otherwise, and, as you know, she was carved in his image as if I played no part whatsoever in her creation. This resemblance has given me great comfort, though, over the last five years, and has kept an important part of him alive with me (where the rest of him should have been). In any case, I was able to calm her down temporarily with descriptions of life at Fox Run. She claims not to remember much from her only trip there after Papa died, except for her time with DJ, of course. There are moments when I wish I didn't remember either. But I suppose the endless penance of recollection is a relatively light sentence, considering what happened there that week. Fortunately, little Greg has no allegiance to any residence, and thus I have one less thing to fret about as I chase him from one corner (or floor) of this house to another. When he began walking two months ago, he went straight from a crawl to a full sprint—laughing every step of the way, I might add, as I pursued him.

I'm so anxious for you to meet him, although I still have a hard time believing that you haven't yet. At least you saw him "under development," for lack of a better term. Wasn't I such a mess then? I hadn't grown that big with Claudine by the day she was born. But when you saw me incubating Greg, I was only—well, what was I? Six months? Yes, let's use the number six. At least your visit that April enabled you to see our home on East 67th Street. Even though Gregory Senior wants us to travel back here to New York on holidays as frequently as possible, who knows when the occasion will arise for you to come with me? On the contrary, you will probably be ready for me to go away now and then, since you and I will finally have the long-awaited joy of seeing each other as often as we please—every single day, if we choose—now that I'll be living at Fox Run. Nonetheless, I'm glad you could share briefly in the grandeur of this uptown house. Bradley comes to mind over and over again when I look out the window. He would have loved this place so very much. Mother even more.

Well, we will have plenty of time to examine history together after I get there. Meanwhile, prudence would suggest that I redirect my focus toward the future. I do hope my father isn't stomping around heaven with displeasure at Jay's decision to transfer Fox Run's ownership to me. Even if we'd been able to mend our estrangement before he died, the fact that I'm a woman instead of a man would still have kept my name off the deed in his last bequests. I do hope my brother isn't inviting lightning strikes by taking this action. Nonetheless, as Papa continues to monitor us from wherever he is, I trust he will be pleased with the love and attention the estate will receive from me, without regard to my gender. Gregory has assured me that all necessary resources will be made available to maintain the property in a manner in keeping with the McClinty heritage. But I also hope Papa can see that the dress shop has provided me with ample means of my own, independent of Gregory's. I know my father was convinced I'd never amount to anything after I married Vincente, and yet it was because of Vincente that I found my way. Oh, there I go again. Sorry.

My goodness, I just looked at the time. Gregory will be home from his club any minute, and I must get myself ready for bed. Thankfully, the need for long letters will be a thing of the past before we can blink. Please take care of yourself, dear friend, and the precious little life growing inside your tummy. Your nine-month confinement might still have a way to go, but the loneliness and isolation you expressed in your latest letter are nearly over. I'm almost there to be with you, to laugh with you, and to thank you endlessly for your friendship.

Meanwhile, give the biggest hug and kiss you can manage to my brother, and tell him we'll be arriving on the three o'clock train, Thursday afternoon, next week. Also, please tell David that I said hello. I do hope his grief over Lucille and Papa has come to an end. Now that he and I will be living in the same town again, I also hope that "everything else" will settle naturally, over time, without too many awkward moments. Thank God you'll be close at hand, Angela.

'Bye for now.

Love,
Cinn

P.S. I forgot to mention that Maggie told me last week she has decided not to come with us—and after all the arrangements had been made! I simply will never understand her, nor do I think I should be expected to try any more. Ever since she came to Albany with me when Papa died, she's been behaving strangely, and I think I've finally reached my wit's end with her. Enough is enough, don't you think?

M.E.M.S.♥

September 18, 1934

For my son, as our return to Albany nears. May God please hear my prayer and bestow upon this boy only the best of what his mother and father had to contribute. He doesn't deserve any of the worst—and Lord knows he has inherited the potential for both, in larger quantities than would normally have been advisable.

Dream on, little child—little child of mine.
Close your eyes and imagine that the world is fine.
While your heart's pure as gold,
Life cannot be oversold,
And it's all right to dream on—so, dream on.

Make plans, little child—little child of mine.
Learn to try, and to fail, and to stand in line.
You can be what you choose.
You have nothing to lose,
And you're free to dream on—so, dream on.

I can open all the doors for you.
Selecting one is yours to do.
My love will be here, even when you're gone.
I'll know I've done my very best,
When you emerge from every test
Determined to continue dreaming on.

As you grow, as you learn, little child of mine,
Every day will add more tarnish to your youthful shine.
But I'll teach you to be strong,
And to learn to say, "I'm wrong,"
And enrich you with the power of dreaming on.

M.E.M.S.

September 20, 1934
Aboard the train to Albany

This entry is being written as I begin the journey back to the place where I began. We pulled out of the station a few minutes ago, and I am struck by the fact that when I last traveled anywhere by train, it was just after we buried Papa, and also right after the other "problem." Despite everything I'd been through before that trip, I was still so young in many ways, and so very foolish, I need not add. Now as I head back there—even though, chronologically, it's only been two years—I'm clearly not young any more. I suppose we'll find out about the foolish part soon enough.

Gregory has been very kind to support this move. At first I worried about the extended separations, which will certainly alter the rhythm of our life. But now I'm comfortable with the arrangement. This marriage has never involved the same level of emotional investment that I shared with Vincente, and fate must have set that up by design. What I do not have, I cannot miss.

I've been watching my children, who are happily (for the moment at least) situated across the aisle from me. Claudine looks so grown up for a not-quite-ten-year-old young lady, and she's such a little mother to Greg. I can't believe how patient she is with him. Of course, he's paying attention to her now because of the chocolate candy she's been feeding him by the nibble. We'll see how she does when he decides he wants to practice his new walking ability and dodge her grasp from one end of this car to the other. That should test me, as well, over the next few hours of this trip. Fortunately, he no longer needs the bottle. If he will just decide to abandon the diapers as quickly, I will be in heaven.

Ever since I wrote my most recent letter to Angela last week, I've been consumed with thoughts of Vincente and the time we had together. While I have never stopped missing him, I have not been this preoccupied with thoughts of him for a long while. I guess I shouldn't be surprised, though, given the fact that I'm leaving behind the only world he ever knew, the same one I so amazingly learned to cherish along with him. Yesterday I took the children to the cemetery to say goodbye to him, and to Mother and Bradley also. I'm very glad I made the effort to go, but I must say that I've had quite enough of graveyards these last few years. I hope there's no need to visit one again for a long time.

Thankfully, Velita, Alberto and the twins are happy and reasonably content, due in large part to the shop, which turned out to be such a salvation for all of us. Oddly, I have not a single worry, knowing that the operation is now in Velita's hands. Once I've become settled at Fox Run—and during one of Gregory's stays at East 67th—I'd like to buy a ticket for her to visit me (Alberto and the girls, too, if they're willing). I want to share the trees, and the animals, and the peace with them, to give them the gift of a vacation from the concrete and endless racket. They deserve that, and so much more.

Perhaps Maggie will then decide to accept my invitation, if she knows they're all coming, too. Last night I was so angry with her, as I tried to figure out, again, why she's developed such an aversion to me. I realize that the road between Vincente's death and this train ride home to Albany today has been complicated for all of us. But my sister has suffered the least of anyone, and I can't fathom her behavior for the life of me.

Well, I see that little Greg has taken his short legs on a run up the aisle, with Claudine close on his heels. So, I suppose I should shift into my mother mode. When I write my next entry, I'll be at Fox Run—home, at last, where everything will have come full-circle.

M.E.M.S.

The circle would remain securely closed—and the rhythm of life steady—for almost twenty years thereafter, as Fox Run became the rightful center of Cinnamon's existence and the source of her family's stability. Gregory traveled north to spend one week each month with his wife and the children, sometimes bringing his mother with him, who became enamored with the property's serenity. As Mrs. Stafford's health began to fail in the 1940's, she seemed to draw strength from the land, and her company was always a cheerful addition to the house. Holidays were alternated between the residences, with Thanksgivings generally spent in New York and Christmases inside Fox Run's winter magic. Every summer, Cinnamon and the children spent July and half of August on East 67th Street, and thus, all of the seasons had order, few of them presenting any new catastrophes.

Claudine and Greg lived the rest of their childhoods and early adulthoods in the idyllic setting of Albany's countryside, enriched by their relationships with David's boys, as they spent time back and forth between Fox Run and the Madison house. In the process, their alliances became as strong as the blood that bound them together. Claudine grew up to be a striking young woman, in whose every feature Vincente could be seen breathing. Velita and Alberto became more astonished at this reflection with every one of their visits, which took place several times a year whenever Gregory was in New York. Sometimes Maria and Rosa accompanied them, but not very often once they married and began having their own families. When Claudine finished college and married as well, Velita and Alberto gradually stopped traveling north. But Cinnamon never failed to visit Broome Street each time she was in the City. She also maintained partial ownership of the dress shop, although management and a controlling interest were transferred to Velita and Alberto in 1939, after the permanence of Cinnamon's new living arrangement became clear.

Young Greg allowed himself to be taken on these junkets to New York until he was old enough to do otherwise. Having left the City before he had any memories of living there, he never acquired a taste for the crowds and frenzied pace. He preferred the open land and country air of Fox Run, where his inclination toward being a loner was more easily accommodated. His Grandmother Stafford teased him about this, saying she worried that his excessive exposure to trees and greenery would cause him to have an allergic reaction to the concrete and stone in her neighborhood.

"Wouldn't that be awful," she'd said, "for you to be covered in red blotches every time you come to my house for a party?" As much as he loved his grandmother, he didn't seem to find her supposition very amusing.

Despite his limited sense of humor and dearth of social pleasantries, Greg presented himself as a likeable fellow more often than not, to most people. To his mother's delight, he also developed an early interest in the McClinty lumber business, accompanying David or Jay to the mill whenever his school schedule permitted. His eagerness to learn about the industry pleased both men, and they were delighted to begin mentoring him, in the event that his interest survived adolescence. His cousin Teddy shared in this fascination and was a frequent companion of his at the mill, as well as at the Madison house and Fox Run. Teddy was older by more than two years. But because Greg's personality was the more dominant, the age difference seemed to evaporate, and they readily became friends. Eventually, neither of them would be able to remember a time when the other wasn't there.

Given all this domestic balance, Cinnamon once again invited Maggie to come live with the reconfigured family at Fox Run after they'd been back in Albany for six months.

"There's plenty of space here, as you know," she'd said to her sister in a letter, "and you could have the guest cottage as your own apartment. I even think there's enough light available through the southwestern windows for you to set up a studio, if you'd like to do so."

Ideal as this arrangement may have sounded, Maggie obstinately declined—much to everyone's consternation—and she elected, instead, to remain on Broome Street. Tempted to wash her hands of the girl once and for all, Cinnamon gathered her self-control and pretended respect for this independent decision.

"I know I should let her see that I'm livid," she confided to Angela. "But I don't want to completely alienate her. Someday, I hope she'll take advantage of the opportunities being placed in front of her. If I inform her that I think she's an idiot, she might never come to her senses."

"This has to be very frustrating for you, Cinn. I wish I could help."

"Me, too. At the very least, I wish someone could tell me why she seems to hate me so much. Why *do* you suppose that is?"

"I couldn't say, although I think you tend to build the problem up in your mind, making it seem bigger than it actually is."

"Really? Well, I hope you're right. Since she won't let me help her by bringing her up here, I'm planning to give her a little money so she can pursue her education. If she turns *that* down, though, even *you'll* have to admit there's something we don't understand."

But this new offer was one Maggie *thought she could live with,* she'd said in a telephone conversation following her receipt of Cinnamon's letter highlighting the financial details. In spite of her little sister's monotone on the other end of the line, Cinnamon was certain she'd heard words of appreciation and sincerity. Attempting to reassure herself of this, she repeated the conversation over and over again to Angela, until Angela begged her to stop.

"Of *course* she's grateful, Cinn. Why *wouldn't* she be? You've been extraordinarily generous with her. Some people have a harder time expressing themselves, that's all."

"I suppose you're right. Sorry. I guess this is something else that I should *just let go.*"

"Please do! You're making me crazy with your fretting."

The gift from her sister's trust fund ultimately enabled Maggie to take advanced courses in art history, and to study the lives of classic painters such as Cézanne, Giotto, Delacroix and Vermeer, in addition to the more commonly recognized names of Rembrandt, Michelangelo and Leonardo da Vinci. She was beguiled by the dissection of their works and techniques, which were placed in the context of real human beings, complete with frailties and weaknesses that coexisted with their genius. Her fascination with the details led her to excel in every course. She also demonstrated an unanticipated flair for incorporating this new knowledge into her sidewalk art classes. Soon she developed a reputation throughout the neighborhood for bringing the study and practice of painting to life, in a literal sense.

The only way to accommodate the number of students who wished to learn from her was to become a *real* teacher, which she did after two years. Hired by her local public schools, she taught art classes in every grade from first through twelfth, and her insightful rapport with children helped her tailor the material and associated storytelling to each level. She also offered private tutoring whenever time allowed. Before long, she was earning a respectable income, in spite of the Depression, particularly as a woman who had not married. Her accomplishments were remarkable, and although her successes may have been confined to a small area of lower Manhattan, those students who were fortunate enough to have her for a teacher never forgot her.

This path would not have been Cinnamon's choice for her sister, if she'd been the one in control. But, eventually, she was forced to admit that Maggie had done quite well for herself—despite her confounding stubborn streak—except, of course, for her social development. Lovely as she was, with Mimi's slender height and dark beauty, Maggie had never expressed any interest in being courted. On the contrary, she'd rebuffed men who'd stepped beyond a casual interest in her or in her paintings, and she was seldom seen with the same gentleman more than once. Instead, she continued to live in the second bedroom of the Broome Street apartment, insisting as soon as she started teaching, however, that she be allowed to pay rent. Occasionally, she traveled to Albany with Alberto and Velita, after giving in to Velita's coercion. But when she did, she preferred spending time at the Madison house with David's sons, especially with Ryan, who often visited her in New York, as well, when he grew older. While she loved her niece Claudine very much, and tolerated being around Cinnamon for short periods, Maggie could not abide her nephew Greg. Offering no explanation for this, especially in view of her normal affinity for children, she went out of her way to avoid Fox Run, something which further tested her relationship with her sister. Yet, staying at David's house did seem to minimize the tension as much as possible, while the next twenty years unfolded in a relatively quiet fashion.

Those twenty years also blessed the ever-deepening friendship between Cinnamon and Angela, who gave birth to her only child when she was nearly thirty years old. Starting a family at such a late age was very unusual in the first half of the twentieth century, and when Preston McClinty was born in April of 1935, Angela had such a difficult time that she and Jay went to great lengths thereafter to prevent further pregnancies. Painful memories of losing Lucille through Teddy's birth were easily rekindled, and Jay had no intention of taking any chances with Angela's life. Even if more children had been an option, Angela loved to tell people that she saw no need to improve upon perfection.

"Preston has spoiled me for all other babies. He is so well-behaved and so sweet, as if he came out of me fully installed and ready for tea."

He was a very handsome little boy, with hair and eyebrows so blonde that they were almost white. His eyes were a mysterious grey, sometimes looking blue, sometimes green, and always curious and intent, and his perpetual smile illuminated his entire face. Since Angela had been given the chance to raise only one child, everyone agreed that Preston was, indeed, the ultimate synthesis of everything she deserved.

Three or four times a week, the women brought their children together in one house or another, never losing their hunger for each other's company, after spending so many years of their lives apart.

"I can't imagine what I would be doing," Angela said to Cinnamon in the parlor at Fox Run, when Preston was eight months old, "if you were still in New York all the time."

"Then don't think about it and cause yourself unnecessary distress. The point is that I am here for you now, and you for me. God obviously set this up—the move back to Albany, I mean—knowing that Preston was on the way."

"Right. All of this was just for *me*, Cinn. You are too funny."

"Well, who *else* would it be for? I doubt very highly that the good Lord intended to do anything special on *my* behalf."

"Do you know what I think?"

"What?"

"I think you need to stop tormenting yourself."

"Easy for you to say, Angela. The worst thing *you've* ever done is keep my secrets."

David and Cinnamon saw each other only at family gatherings for the first few months that she was back in Albany. But one day, he and Jay were at Fox Run to discuss some details about Jonathon's estate that required her involvement. When those discussions were over, David accepted her invitation to stay for dinner, after Jay left for home. Irene, whose advancing age and swollen joints were only slowing her down slightly at that point, was happy to see the two of them engaged in a friendly conversation with one another. She'd witnessed the tension between them on more than one occasion, and on this particular night, she offered to cook David his favorite baked chicken, in hopes of prolonging the conciliatory moment.

Her efforts were successful. David and Cinnamon sat at the table together for three hours. As their dialogue lingered on over liqueur following their meal, the topics of conversation touched upon their children, politics, Roosevelt's first-term accomplishments, and then Cinnamon's feelings about her life, now that she was home. Carefully choosing her words, she painted a positive picture, for the most part, but finally did mention her one frustration to him.

"You realize, don't you, that I never learned how to drive? Of course, I didn't have any reason for the skill in Manhattan. But now I'm all the way out here, with two children—and even though Papa's motorcar is still parked right outside the door, I'm always dependent on someone to take me everywhere. Not only would I love the freedom of transporting Claudine and Greg on my own, or going to see

Angela without assistance. But I'd really like to begin visiting the Magglios on a consistent basis. I've only been to see them once since I returned, and Joseph is not well these days. They did so much for my mother and Bradley—and for me, too—and they are blood family to Claudine. She and I should be spending more time with them. But I have no way to get there, without bothering someone else."

In a spontaneous gesture, David offered to teach Cinnamon how to drive, using Jonathon's car. Their lessons began the following weekend on the grounds of Fox Run, and the experience soon had them laughing together, or shouting at one another—sometimes both at once. Periodically, Irene could barely bring herself to watch through the kitchen window as the big black motorcar, with Cinnamon behind the wheel, barreled forward toward the cottage or some other immoveable object. Fortunately, the car never hit anything—at least nothing of any value—and the associated stories became more comical with every telling. Ultimately, these sessions became less about her learning how to drive and more about David and Cinnamon reconstructing a nourishing relationship, with certain doors forever closed securely behind them. While her lessons continued, David began taking her downtown to visit with the Magglios once a month, and even after she'd become a licensed, independent driver, he still escorted her to the Lark Street apartment for many years.

March 4, 1950

Nearly two decades of peaceful predictability have gone by, marked only by a few very sad, but inescapable, losses. After all of those horrible things that seemed to happen one right on top of the other so many years ago, I would say that I have been blessed with far greater serenity and abundance than I ever deserved to be.

Today, however, is one of those sad moments. Gregory's mother was quite an extraordinary woman and was only a few months away from her seventieth birthday, for which she had grand plans. We are discussing the possibility of following through with that celebration, in her honor, even though she's no longer with us. East 67th Street hasn't seen a good party in a long while, and I do believe this would make her very happy.

Through everything, she never failed to be kind and generous to me, and to Claudine—and to Greg Junior, of course, which goes without saying. I'm certain I'll miss her less than Gregory will, but I think not by very much. I'm glad she's at peace, yet so sorry she's gone.

M.E.M.S.

In addition to Gregory's mother, the nearly two decades had taken a few others as well. Joseph Magglio was perhaps the most heartbreaking in 1939. He'd lived his entire life for the sole purpose of caring for his brothers, his sister, and their families. He also made Cinnamon feel a part of his family, and through the stories he'd told her during her later visits to Lark Street, she'd come to understand the depth of his relationship with her mother and grandmother. Those two women had opened the first door for him, which he'd gratefully entered in pursuit of his art. That quest eventually became ***Magglio Originals***—his own tiny piece of the American dream—but from the beginning, his efforts had never been for himself.

As she grew to appreciate his noble devotion to the best interests of everyone else, her admiration for him expanded in kind, along with her respect for her mother and grandmother and their ability to detect those qualities in him in the first place. By the time of Joseph's death, she had come to think of him more as a grandfather than a friend. Therefore, the loss of his life-force was not easy to accept. She continued to visit Lark Street for more than a year after he died. But without his leadership and control, the rest of his family began to scatter. The last time she stopped by, the shop windows were darkened, and Helena was the only one home. Thereafter, she never returned to the apartment, unable to endure a Lark Street without Joseph's lovable, booming presence.

The next crucial passing came in 1944 when Irene left, closing out one of the last remaining connections to Cinnamon's childhood. Since shortly after the start of World War II, the housekeeper's worsening arthritis and subsequent weight gain had rendered her unable to perform her job responsibilities for more than a few hours each week. Cinnamon continued to pay her salary as a pension benefit for all the years of unbroken service, urging the woman to relax and enjoy herself, for once. But even with her obvious physical limitations, Irene fought desperately against this new reality.

"Coming to work is the only thing standing between me and the Great Beyond," she'd asserted to Jay one day, after he'd been enlisted to convince her that retirement was a *good* thing.

When Cinnamon heard about this comment, she stopped pressing the issue and began bringing Irene to the estate every weekday morning so she could *make herself useful*. After two additional employees were added to the household staff—only as a *supplement*, Cinnamon assured her—Irene took great delight in sharing with the new-hires her collection of McClinty Favorite Recipes, and probably more inner-circle McClinty stories than Cinnamon would have preferred. In light of her forty devoted years with the family, however, Irene was allowed the freedom to leave her mark. In the end, the Great Beyond was held at bay for less than two years. Many months would then pass before the absence of her familiar, comforting voice would stop echoing throughout the rooms of Fox Run.

Events ranging from the theatrical to the horrific took place across the country and the globe between the years of 1934 and 1953. Under the administration of Franklin Roosevelt, America began to recover from the Great Depression, in large part due to Roosevelt's sweeping slate of social programs. But prosperity's return was also fueled by heavy defense spending before World War II.

Roosevelt had been slow to publicly acknowledge the growing menace of fascism on the European continent during the 1930's. Not wishing to jeopardize his domestic agenda, he did not challenge the congressional neutrality acts intended to keep the country out of war. But Germany's aggression increased in 1939. When Hitler overran Poland in September of that year, the action formally marked the beginning of World War II, and Roosevelt began to question the wisdom of America's isolationism. His requests for major increases in defense expenditures as a precaution finally brought economic recovery. But the attack on Pearl Harbor on December 7, 1941 made clear the fact that Japan also had aggressive intentions, and by December 11, the United States was at war on several continents.

Although the Depression was over, World War II brought a new economic crisis and, from 1941 to 1945, took millions of American soldiers away from home to fight or die overseas. Ironically, this period was part of Cinnamon's *peaceful two decades*, during which time the members of her family were not only spared, but they prospered. Their men were either too young or too old, or already dead, and thus were not sacrificed for the war. Furthermore, the demand for lumber was so great that the increased business at the mill resulted in enough hiring to almost double the size of the payroll.

July 5, 1944

We are all very lucky to be so comfortable and not losing anyone we love. My guilt at our good fortune has drawn me to the needy downtown, who don't seem to require a Depression or a world war in order to find despair. I've been taking Claudine and Greg with me, too, so they will come to understand how blessed this family has been. I'm also hoping they might grow to appreciate the admirable, altruistic qualities of their grandmother and great-grandmother much sooner than their mother did.

M.E.M.S.

By the fall of 1945, the war was over. Roosevelt just missed seeing the victory, dying on April 12 of that same year, after serving three full terms in office and few months of his fourth. His vice president, Harry S. Truman, succeeded him and began to preside over the post-war recovery, the onset of the Cold War, and the early phases of the Korean conflict, beginning in 1951.

When Dwight D. Eisenhower was elected president in 1952, Cinnamon's nearly two decades of peaceful coexistence with fate were about to expire. The beginning of that end had arrived when Greg Junior eloped with his high school sweetheart as soon as he turned eighteen, in June of 1951. In April of 1952, his wife Victoria gave birth to Cinnamon's first grandchild, Kenneth James Stafford. Greg then enlisted in the Army that following July, without discussing his decision in advance with anyone in the family. Victoria was already pregnant again, with William, although no one knew yet, not even Victoria.

By early May in 1953, Greg had been stationed in South Korea for eight months, and in a rare telephone call home to Cinnamon, he'd mentioned to his mother that he had a furlough scheduled in Hawaii, over the weekend of May 23. Subsequently, the family arranged to fly Teddy to Hawaii as a surprise. That Sunday—May 24—both men were killed in an explosion outside the restaurant where they'd had dinner. They each left behind a widow and two small children, not to mention David and Cinnamon, who were both immobilized physically and emotionally by the unfathomable disaster.

In seemingly unrelated and implausible incidents, two more members of the family were lost shortly thereafter. Within a month of Greg and Teddy's burials, Cinnamon received a phone call from New York with the staggering news that Maggie had taken an overdose of sleeping pills in her Broome Street bedroom and had never awakened. Inundated with grief over her son's death and that of Teddy, Cinnamon forced herself on the train to Manhattan, able to do so only because Angela was there to help and accompany her. They were still in New York a week later when David's middle son Ryan drove his car into a tree on a dark country road south of Fox Run. The police said he'd been traveling at an extremely high rate of speed, and that there had been no skid marks. Maggie was buried beside Mimi and Bradley in St. Paul's cemetery near Broome Street. Ryan was interred in the McClinty family plot two miles from Albany's Immaculate Conception Cathedral. But nothing even remotely resembling an explanation for the tragedies existed in either city.

During the next two years, all noticeable signs of life vanished from both Fox Run and the Madison house. Shattered surviving members of the family struggled to pull themselves through the paralyzing series of events, and they worked desperately to keep Cinnamon and David alive. She had lost her son and her sister, and he'd lost two of his three boys, all in less than two month's time—almost as if they'd been sent to war after all. At first, none of the others left behind believed that a complete healing and recovery would ever be possible, given the depth of the macabre circumstances. But *they* hadn't grown up on Broome Street—and blessedly, they were proven wrong.

July 4, 1955

It's a bit like your favorite sock—strong, reliable and warm, but worn a little thin. Then, after an extraordinarily difficult day inside rough shoes, you discover that a hole the size of a half dollar has caused more of your foot to be out of the sock than in. At first you think the sock must go—that the end has truly come at last. But then someone shows you the trick of darning. Although the process takes a long time—weaving thread back and forth, in and out, from one side of the hole to the other, and then up and down the same way—eventually the technique gathers the fabric together again, and, in the fullness of time, the hole is mended. That part of the sock looks a little different from the rest, because what had basically been open air before you started your darning has now been reconstructed into new cloth. But the sock is strong, reliable and warm again—against all odds, no less—just as we will be, now that the darning of time has begun to repair the wreckage inside our hearts. Siete rifiniti con me? Are you through with me now?

M.E.M.S.

Yes—except for the truth.

July 13, 1988
10:30 in the morning

Dearest Megan—

While you and Kenneth are out today discovering the reunion I arranged, in spite of all of you, I want to write a few things down that we might not have a chance to discuss in detail, as I'd originally hoped. (This is the "paperwork" I told you I needed to do. How silly am I?) Anyway, I remember in the moments right before my mother died, Velita spoke of the way she believed our bodies begin to disappear inside our skin when "we're getting ready to leave," as she put it. Although I realize that my slim figure is most likely due to the God-awful diet Heidi's been feeding me for the past several weeks, there's a small chance that the face I just looked at in the mirror is, in fact, well on its way to its shrinking exit.

Oddly enough, I'm all right with this thought, now that my story is in your hands. I know you will finally uncover the truth about what really happened to Greg and Teddy, which is my final request of you, in case you're wondering. I have always had my suspicions. But everyone else thought I was psychotic when I refused to buy the official explanation about the accident. Deep inside, I now see that much of my problem stemmed from my being afraid to find out that I was right.

You might not think that discovering the answer is important, but I'm asking you to do this for me. Besides, the challenge will give you an opportunity to get beyond surface greetings with people in your family that you've never spent any time getting to know. Talk to your cousins. I think many of them will have pieces of information that will be helpful when consolidated in one place. You also have a great deal of insight into this family's history now, and into the personalities who helped make me the person I am—and the person you are, too, by the way. There just isn't sufficient time left for me to tell you everything myself, which was my plan when we originally started this whole thing. Sorry.

But a more accurate version of the McClinty Family Chart, than the one you currently have, is in the bottom drawer of my bureau. That will be enlightening for you, to say the least, and will give you a fairly good start—but you'll have to find your way through the rest of the stuff on your own. Soon enough, you'll learn that I've made provisions for you to do this with the smallest possible impact on your life, and I'm hoping you will come to view the assignment as something other than drudgery, once you get going. Besides, the exploration won't last forever.

One of the toughest certainties for me to accept, as I've made this journey through more than eight decades, has been that nothing good, or pure, or joyful ever does last forever, or even anywhere near long enough. But I've also come to understand that, in return for those disappointments, life blesses us with a wealth of consistencies that give us ample reasons to have a party. Just think, Megan. Every year, no matter who we are or what our stations might be, we have something special to anticipate. Fresh flowers. Easter. Summer's steam. Fireworks. The colors of Fall, Thanksgiving, and Christmas. Snow. These are the foundations of grand memories. They are always there, and they exist for each of us, inviting us to have fun. After we've blended those with the inevitable litany of birthdays, weddings and new babies, we somehow find time for the rest of our lives, much of which falls substantially short of a carnival, often leaving us weak and fearful.

But toward the end, we start looking through the rearview mirror at the patchwork of our life's experiences, trying to find the purpose in—well, in everything. Events fall into categories—those that make us proud, and those we botched all to hell. Ultimately, though, when the full picture has come into focus, we begin to appreciate that none of it would have been worth a damn if it hadn't been for all of our celebrations. So, whenever you're feeling glum, call everyone up and invite them over, or out!

When you get home this afternoon, I'd like to spend a few minutes with David. He's really been wonderful for me, especially these last twenty-five years, since I shared with him the news I'd been keeping locked inside. What was it that my mother said? "The words you hold prisoner will first diminish you and then consume you, becoming stronger than the good things you want to do and be." That came so close to being a prophesy fulfilled for me. Please be on guard for similar inclinations in yourself, which you could very easily have inherited through my line. If you're ever tempted to hold a treacherous secret captive in your heart, Megan, don't!

David has been making certain I never do that again. I think he and I have helped each other round out these last years of our lives with a healthy serving of contentment. Not bad, all things considered. Please be sure he knows that I'm grateful for him—and that I love him—in case there's not an opportunity for me to tell him myself.

I love you, too, and I love Kenneth and William just as much. No one could ask for finer grandchildren. Thank you for being so patient with me these last few years. I hope I've told all of you how I feel about you as many times as I should have.

Always,
Gram ♥

MEGAN

CHAPTER 17

Megan opened her eyes to a combination of sounds she didn't recognize. Lying on her side on the edge of the chaise lounge, she had no idea how long she'd been asleep. But she knew where she was this time, and the light stealing in through her grandmother's lace curtains appeared to be from morning sun. *We must have gone through another night. And what is that noise?* The slow hum of the ceiling fan above her was part of what she was hearing. Yet there was more—a soft whirr punctuated by a barely distinguishable flap-flap-flapping sound, coming from behind her on her grandmother's bed.

"Must be the tape recorder," she mumbled, pulling herself into a sitting position. Then she looked to her left and saw her grandmother's body stretched out beneath the lightweight blanket embroidered with rose petals. She could also see the length of silver hair spread across the pillow. But she couldn't see her face, which she had half-expected to discover staring back at her, as usual.

"Gram? Are you awake?"

When there wasn't any answer, she got up and walked around to the side of the bed. The right reel of the tape recorder was turning slowly, the paper end of the tape slapping against the take-up rod—and Cinnamon's arm was resting on top of the control buttons.

"Gram?" she said again, reaching down to lift the blanket covering her grandmother's cheek. "Oh my **God**!" Her heart began racing as she looked upon gray, lifeless skin. "**Gram!**" she repeated, shaking Cinnamon's shoulders. "No, no, no, no, **no**!"

Racing around to the opposite side of the bed, she grabbed the blue princess telephone and dialed the operator, who answered after three rings.

"Please, **please**! I need an ambulance!...10 New Scotland Road. Hurry, **hurry**! It's my grandmother!...I don't **know**! She's not moving—and she's been sick...She's **eighty-two**, for God's sake! What difference does it make? Just **send** someone—please!"

After hearing the operator's assurance that help would be there shortly, Megan ran out to the staircase landing.

"**Kenny**! Wake up! **Kenny**!" she screamed.

"He slept in the cottage last night. What's wrong?"

David was standing at the bottom of the stairs in his pajamas and bare feet.

How will I tell him? Then Heidi walked into the front hallway from the kitchen, her robe pulled loosely around her nightgown and her hair flattened against her head under her sleeping net.

"Miss Megan, is everything all right?"

Unable to find her voice, Megan just stood there looking down at them. But her silence seemed to be explanation enough.

"Good Lord almighty!" Heidi exclaimed, her eyes widening with awareness. "I'll run and get Kenneth," she said, already on her way out the door.

"David," Megan finally whispered, watching the tears begin to roll down his cheeks. "I'm so sorry."

"I want to come up there."

"All right," she said, moving to meet him as he gripped the banister. She wrapped her arms around his waist, as he lifted one foot and then the other onto each step, his shaking body at odds with his determination.

"Maybe she's just sound asleep," he said. "She's always been hard to rouse, you know. Do you think..."

Before he could finish, Kenneth exploded through the front door and flew past the two of them, leaping multiple stairs at a time.

"An ambulance is on the way, Kenny," Megan said to him as he zipped by and disappeared into Cinnamon's room.

"Holy crap! What's all this?" she heard him say a moment later.

Dismal as the scene was, she couldn't help but smile as she imagined that he must have thrown back the blanket and discovered the collection of journals and papers that their grandmother had been referencing during the last two days—and that she'd insisted on keeping with her under the covers. Next she heard books being thrown to the floor, and when she and David entered the room, they saw Kenneth kneeling on the mattress, feverishly delivering CPR.

David inhaled sharply at the sight, and even though he was out of breath from the climb, he would not sit down. Instead, he walked over to the bed and reached out to take Cinnamon's hand while Kenneth worked on her. Megan stood by the chaise lounge at the footboard, and was joined by Heidi whose palms were pressed tightly against the sides of her face.

After a few more minutes, they heard the sirens in the driveway and then the footsteps coming through the open front door and up the stairs. In what seemed like a movie being screened in the room, the four of them watched the paramedics take over the CPR, strap an oxygen mask to Cinnamons' mouth and nose, and give her some sort of injection. Then they loaded her onto a stretcher and carried her outside, still unable to elicit any response from her.

Within seconds, the ambulance sped down the driveway and turned left on New Scotland Road en route to the Albany Medical Center's emergency room. Megan, Kenneth, David and Heidi were left behind, standing in silence on the porch and looking at one another. There had been such noise and commotion all happening so quickly, but now everything was quiet, the stillness of Fox Run settling around them and pretending nothing out of the ordinary. Yet, each of them knew what they saw in the others' eyes and understood the finality of what they'd just witnessed.

Regrouping and catching their breath inside the house, they agreed that Kenneth would be the one to follow the ambulance to the hospital.

"I'll call you when I get there," he said, kissing Megan on the cheek and embracing David, who felt limp in his arms.

After he drove away, Heidi disappeared into the kitchen to brew a pot of coffee, and Megan helped David into the parlor, where he finally agreed to sit down. All of them were unexpectedly calm, as if they were awaiting further instructions before they allowed their emotions to be freed. David actually put his head down on the sofa and closed his eyes. When Megan realized that he'd fallen asleep, she tiptoed into the hall and made her way back upstairs.

What a shipwreck, she thought, reflecting on the chaos in her grandmother's room. She also noted that her mind seemed to be controlling her heart by leading her into an orderly, productive activity, such as straightening up the mess. Sheets and blankets had been tossed in every direction, and a half-dozen journals that had been kicked and stepped on were strewn across the floor, along with a smattering of loose papers. Deciding that the bedding should be washed, she removed the bottom sheet and the pillow cases, placing them with the rest of the linens in the dirty clothes hamper. Then she fluffed the pillows and smoothed the puffy comforter over the mattress, tucking in the bottom corners the way her grandmother always did.

Turning her attention to the floor, she gathered the journals and stacked them neatly on the desk. The loose pieces of paper were of varying sizes, and some of them looked as if they'd been wadded into balls then smoothed out again. As she picked them up one-by-one and assembled them in a flat pile next to the journals, she did not read what they said, believing she already knew more than she wanted to know at this point. Then she noticed what appeared to be a letter, folded neatly in thirds, sticking out from beneath the nightstand. At first, she wasn't going to read it, either. But she decided to peek at the top section, to see what part of the story was being referenced.

July 13, 1988
10:30 in the morning

Dearest Megan—...

What? July 13? "That was just *yesterday*," she said out loud. Sitting down on the chaise, she unfolded the rest of the letter, noticing the pace of her pulse beginning to compete with the methodical order of her mind, as certain sentences stood out more than others.

While you and Kenneth are out today discovering the reunion I arranged,in spite of all of you, I want to write a few things down that we might not have a chance to discuss in detail, as I'd originally hoped. (This is the "paperwork" I told you I needed to do. How silly am I?)...there's a small chance that the face I just looked at in the mirror is, in fact, well on its way to its shrinking exit.

Oddly enough, I'm all right with this thought, now that my story is in your hands. I know you will finally uncover the truth about what really happened to Greg and Teddy, which is my final request of you...

You might not think that discovering the answer is important, but I'm asking you to do this for me...Talk to your cousins. I think many of them will have pieces of information that will be helpful when consolidated in one place...

A more accurate version of the McClinty Family Chart, than the one you currently have, is in the bottom drawer of my bureau. That will be enlightening for you, to say the least, and will give you a fairly good start—but you'll have to find your way through the rest of the stuff on your own. Soon enough,you'll learn that I've made provisions for you to do this with the smallest possible impact...

...Thank you for being so patient with me these last few years. I hope I've told all of you how I feel about you as many times as I should have...

The tears began rising in Megan's eyes for the first time since she woke up that morning.

"Oh, Gram, this is too horrible for words. Please don't let this be true. Please don't be gone." *Maybe Kenny will call us with a miracle*, she thought. Then she blinked to clear her vision, as her focus jogged back up a few paragraphs in the letter.

...A more accurate version of the McClinty Family Chart than the one you currently have, is in the bottom drawer of my bureau. That will be enlightening for you, to say the least...

She looked over at the bureau on the far wall and stared at the bottom drawer.

"Do you always have to be so dramatic, Gram?" she asked, continuing her monologue as she got up and walked across the room. Leaning over, she pulled the bottom drawer open and saw, in plain view, a copy of the chart.

That doesn't look any different than mine. But then a flash of color caught her eye. Taking the chart in her hand, she brought the paper to within a foot of her face, her eyes fixed incredulously on the markings.

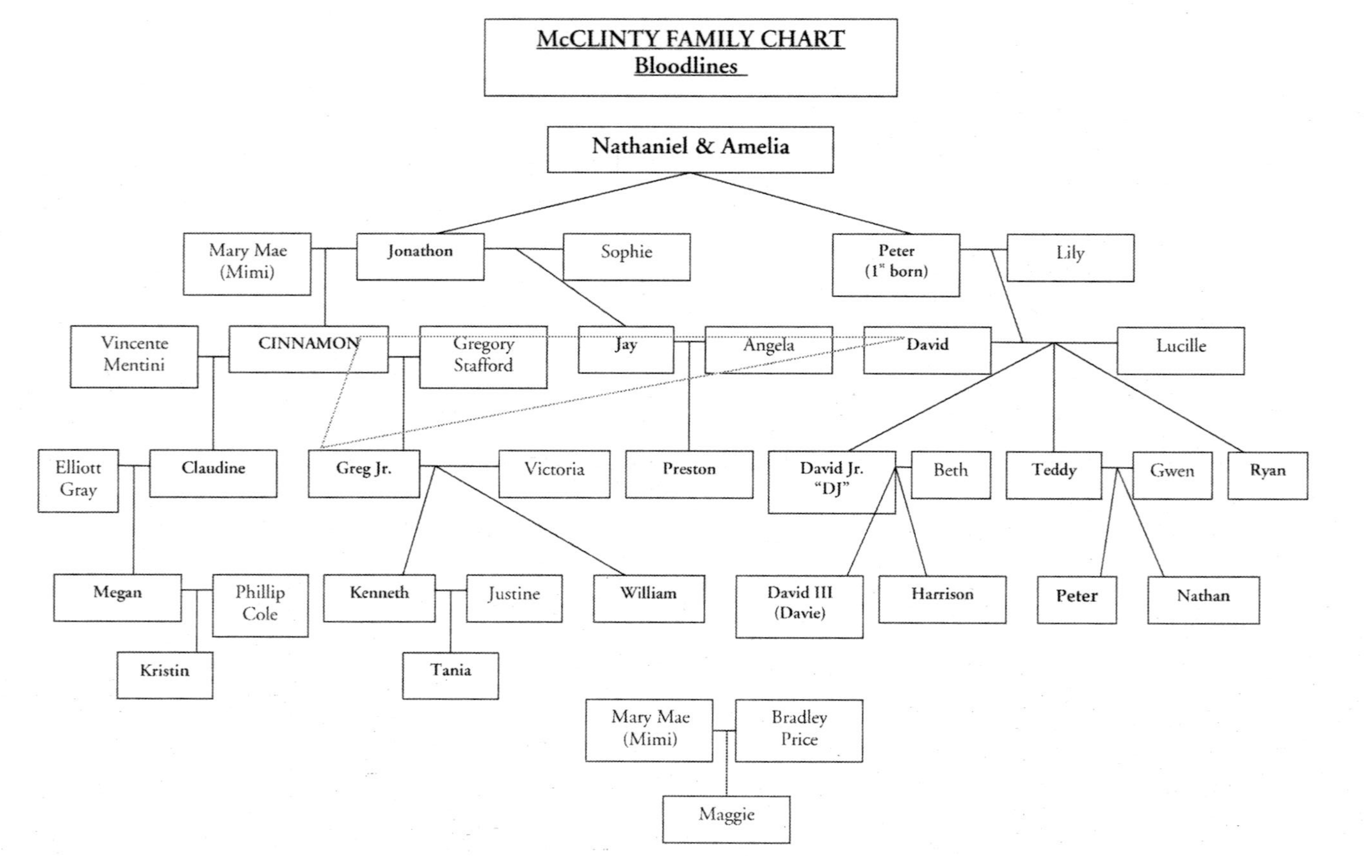

McCLINTY FAMILY CHART
Bloodlines
Nathaniel & Amelia
Mary Mae (Mimi)
Jonathon
Sophie
Peter (1st born)
Lily
Vincente Mentini
CINNAMON
Gregory Stafford
Jay
Angela
David
Lucille
Elliott Gray
Claudine
Greg Jr.
Victoria
Preston
David Jr. "DJ"
Beth
Teddy
Gwen
Ryan
Megan
Phillip Cole
Kenneth
Justine
William
David III (Davie)
Harrison
Peter
Nathan
Kristin
Tania
Mary Mae (Mimi)
Bradley Price
Maggie

"Excuse me, Miss Megan."

The sudden insertion of Heidi's voice caused her to jump backwards and drop the chart.

"I am *sorry*, ma'am! I did *not* mean to scare you."

"That's okay," Megan answered, her hand reflexively pressing against her chest as if to slow her heartbeat. "I was a little preoccupied," she added, picking up the chart from the floor, folding it over and over again, and then slipping it into the front pocket of her jeans.

"I'm only interrupting you because Kenneth is on the phone," Heidi explained. "And he was worried when you didn't answer."

"What? I didn't even hear it ring."

Looking over at the princess phone, she saw the cord unhooked from the wall. After walking to the bedside and snapping the plug back into its socket, she lifted the receiver to check the connection.

"Hello? Kenny?"

"Hi."

When she heard his voice, she sat down on the bed, with Heidi continuing to watch from the doorway.

"Meg, I wish I could tell you something different, but…"

"Is she…?"

"Yes. As we thought, she was gone before we even discovered her this morning. But they tried their damndest to push life back into her. If there'd been any chance at all, they sure would have found it, and I told them how much we appreciate their efforts. How are *you* doing? And how's David?"

Oh my God! David! If the chart is true…Kenny is his grandson! William, too.

…If you're ever tempted to hold a treacherous secret captive in your heart, Megan, don't!…

"Megan?"

"I'm here. Okay."

"Okay *what*?"

"Uh, well…okay, what are we supposed to do now?"

"I gave the folks at the hospital the name of the mortuary, and they said the transfer will be handled later this morning. So, I guess we need to start making calls to let people know. And the arrangements need to be scheduled and publicized. How are you holding up? You don't sound very good."

"No, I probably don't. But I'll be all right once…once things settle in. Are you coming back here now?"

"Actually, I thought I'd go over to the Albion Inn. Since most of our people are there by now, the news can be delivered to them all together, unless you'd rather do this some other way."

"Your idea is probably the best. I need to be the one to tell my mother, though. I'll try to reach her when we hang up. But call me when you get there to make sure I found her, before you say anything to anyone else. Have you told Justine yet?"

"No. I'll see her as soon as I get to the Inn."

"And I'll call Phillip."

"Good. After I make the announcement to the family, I'll bring Justine and Tania with me to Fox Run. We can talk about the other details then."

"Okay."

"Are you sure you'll be all right until then?"

"Yes, I'm sure. See you later."

As she placed the receiver in the cradle, she looked up and saw that Heidi wasn't standing in the doorway any longer. *She obviously got the message. Now I need to go explain things to David. Oh Lord, I can't stop thinking about that chart!*

But when she went back down to the parlor, David wasn't there.

"Mr. McClinty asked me to tell you that he doesn't want you to be concerned about him," Heidi said, when Megan entered the kitchen. "He also mentioned that he'd like to be by himself for awhile."

"I should let him know about Kenny's call, though."

"I'm afraid he heard already, Miss Megan. He was listening the whole time. I guess he must have picked up the phone in the parlor when I came upstairs."

"Really? Well, maybe it's better that way, hearing it from his…from Kenny. How did he seem to you?"

"Sort of a mess, to be honest. But he said he was going to call Barnes to let him know about Mrs. Stafford. That seemed to give him a mission. Otherwise, he looked about as bad as *you* do, please forgive me for saying so. Come to think of it, *I* don't feel so good, either."

Megan walked around the counter and took the woman into her arms.

"We've all been through quite an experience this morning. Would you like to take the rest of today off?"

"Oh, no, ma'am," the maid replied, gently pushing herself from Megan's embrace and lifting the skirt of her apron to wipe her eyes. "If you don't mind, I'd like to fix a little breakfast for you. Maybe Mr. McClinty would also eat something. I've been through this kind of thing before, you know, and I've learned that staying busy is what keeps me from getting too far down in the dumps."

…when the full picture has come into focus, we begin to understand that none of it would have been worth a damn if it hadn't been for all of our celebrations. So, whenever you're feeling glum, call everyone up and invite them over, or out!

"Perhaps you have a point, Heidi. Breakfast sounds good. And while we're on the subject of food, do you happen to know the name of the last caterer my grandmother used? I think she's probably expecting us to throw a party."

"Good morning. This is the Albion Inn. How may I help you?"

"Could you please connect me with Mrs. Claudine Gray?" Megan asked as she sat curled in the corner of the parlor sofa. "I don't know her room number."

"Certainly. One moment, please."

Megan waited through two rings, then three, wondering why her mother wasn't picking up. As lengthy as this day seemed to her already, the fact was that it was only 9:15, and Claudine was a notoriously late riser. But then she heard the unmistakable sound of a hand fumbling to get a grip on the telephone receiver, followed by the low growl of the just-awakened.

"Hello?"

"Hi, Mom."

"Good grief, Megan. Why must you be such a watchdog? I asked Justine to let you know I was planning to call your grandmother at 9:30 to set up a visit for later today. Couldn't you have waited another fifteen minutes?"

"I didn't get the message, Mom, but…"

"You don't trust me, do you? Well, for your information, Lyle isn't even staying at this hotel. He has friends that…"

"Mom, please be quiet."

"What?"

"I'm sorry. It's just that we have some news—some not very *good* news."

Megan squeezed her eyes shut, wishing she and her mother were together—wishing there were some other way to do this.

"Mom, it's Gram. I'm afraid she's gone."

"What? No! What did you say?" Claudine's voice was punctured by her attempts to catch her breath.

"This time she wasn't kidding."

"But this can't *be,* Megan. I was going to see her this morning. I had so much…so many things I wanted to say to her. She…she can't go…not before…before I tell her…that I…"

The last time Megan had heard her mother's heart break was six years earlier when Elliott died. Megan's heart was broken then, too. But the lessons learned from the emotional vacuum created by her father's sudden departure were still vivid, and Megan wasn't going to allow a repeat of that scenario.

"Mom, I know how sad this is for you, and I wish you'd had a chance to see Gram. But she knew you were home, and that made her very happy."

"Oh dear God," Claudine groaned, almost choking on her grief. "I simply cannot believe this. How…how are *you*?"

"I'm all right, and thank you for asking," Megan answered, smiling at the invisible hand she saw at work here.

"When did…this happen?"

"I found her when I woke up this morning."

"She was peaceful?"

"Yes. Very peaceful?"

"Well, that's a blessing, at least," Claudine continued, her voice beginning to regain strength. "Does the rest of the family know yet?"

"Kenny's on his way to the Inn now. He said he'd take care of making the announcement to everyone."

"Then I'll call Lyle and have him drive me out to Fox Run, so I can help you—unless you have other plans, of course."

"That would be wonderful, Mom. I could use you here, and I *really* need one of your hugs."

"I need one of yours, too, so very much. We should be there in a couple of hours."

"'Bye."

Megan's call to Phillip was easier because he was out of the office at a breakfast meeting and could not be reached. So she left a message with his secretary that simply said, "Emergency has happened," assuming he would understand. Then, not knowing what to do with herself while she waited for Kenneth and her mother to arrive, she thought about taking a walk around the grounds and was headed toward the front porch when the telephone rang.

"I'll get it, Heidi…Hello?"

"Good morning. My name is Anthony Parnell, and I'm looking for Megan Cole."

"This is she speaking."

"Megan, you don't know me, but I'm your grandmother's attorney…Hello?"

"Yes, sir. I'm sorry, but my grandmother…"

"I know. That's why I'm calling."

"You *know?*"

"That's correct. I received a phone call from the medical center about an hour ago."

"But how…?"

"Your grandmother was very thorough, which I'm sure comes as no surprise to you. She instructed Dr. Coomey, as well as the Chief of Emergency at the hospital, to notify me immediately in the event that something happened to her."

"I see. She seems to have left messages all over the place."

"Pardon me?"

"What? Oh. I was just thinking out loud. So, Mr. Parnell, how can I help you?"

"Actually, I'm here to help *you*. Were you aware that she named you executor of her estate?"

"No, I wasn't," Megan answered, hesitating as she considered what this might entail, and wondering why this piece of information had to be delivered at such a sensitive moment.

"I understand how you must be feeling," Mr. Parnell continued, as if reading her mind. "But your grandmother was quite insistent that I contact you as soon as I received a call about…about her status."

"Forgive me. It's just that a whole stream of things seem to be happening all at once around here."

"I'm sure that's true, and my role is to be of assistance—not only for the next few days, but afterwards, too. I think you and I will be spending some time together for awhile."

"But I live in Atlanta, and as soon as everything is over, I'll need to go home."

"Don't worry. As I said, your grandmother was very thorough. If you wouldn't mind, I'd like to stop by later this afternoon, before you begin making the arrangements. Mrs. Stafford gave me a list of things that she wanted to have incorporated into the next few days."

In spite of her overloaded senses, Megan couldn't keep herself from laughing. She also discovered, to her pleasure, that she didn't need to explain her reaction to this man.

"Of course," she said, speaking through her smile. "What time would you like to come by the house?"

"How about three?"

"That will be fine. See you then."

For some reason, her conversation with Mr. Parnell made her think about her work. Since this day's complications were almost at capacity already, she decided to get one more call over with, while there was still room. While first refilling her coffee cup in the kitchen, she suggested to Heidi that she take a break from cooking and put something on other than her nightgown. Then she reluctantly returned to the parlor. Sitting back down on the sofa, with the telephone in her lap, she dialed the main switchboard number in Atlanta and waited for the familiar voice.

"Good morning. Strategic Data. How may I direct your call?"

"Hi, Glenda. This is Megan."

"*Megan*! How *are* you?"

"I'm fine, thanks. But it looks like I'm going to be gone a few more days. My grandmother died this morning."

"Oh, no. I am *so* sorry for your loss. Is there something I can do?"

"Just put me through to Jerry, if he's there. You and I can talk more when I get home."

"Jerry's not here. He's at some off-site meeting with the other execs. Strange vibes around here, Megan. Do you know what's going on?"

"Not really. I..."

"Hold on a sec. There's a bunch of other calls coming in."

"That's okay, Glenda. Just give Jerry my message."

"Will do. Talk to you soon. 'Bye."

Now she *did* need that walk. As she passed through the kitchen, she announced her intention at the door to Heidi's small rear apartment, where she could hear the maid rustling around as she changed her clothes. Then she stepped outside into the yard. A light drizzle was falling, but the temperature was comfortable. *First I'd better check on David*, she thought, walking to the cottage. When there wasn't any answer to her knock, she entered quietly and discovered he was sleeping peacefully on top of his bedcovers. A blanket was bunched around his shoulders and neck, and when she looked closely, she saw that it was identical to Cinnamon's—white, with embroidered rose petals. Noting her grandmother's subtle symmetry, she forced back a rush of tears that threatened her. Then she turned and tiptoed through the living room and back outside again. To her left, through the grey, wet air, the old barn seemed to beckon. She'd been inside that place hundreds of times during her life. But new images were teasing her now as she pulled the massive wood door open and stepped into the hazy light.

Once her eyes adjusted, she felt a smirk on her face.

"Oh, stop it!" she said to herself. "This isn't supposed to be amusing."

Yet, somehow it *was*, as she thought about her grandmother creeping around out here so long ago. Sitting down on the chair-shaped bales of hay nearest the loft ladder, she imagined that she might be in the precise place where *it* happened.

"This is ridiculous, Gram. What in the world were you thinking when you decided to leave me with this bombshell? Do you think I'm some sort of private investigator in my spare time? And what about Kenny and William? It shouldn't be *my* place to tell them about David. The two of you should have stepped up to that plate a long time ago. And remember, I haven't made any commitments to you about *any* of this. If I didn't love you so much, I'd..."

Just then she heard Heidi's voice trumpeting across the yard.

"Miss Megan! Miss Megan!"

It is nice in here, though—sort of like a cocoon set aside from the rest of the world. I can see why it was your favorite place.

"Yes, Heidi?" she answered, peering around the barn door.

"What in heaven's name are you doing in *there*?"

"Stealing a little quiet time, to think."

"That's exactly what Mrs. Stafford used to say whenever we found *her* in there. Seems to me, in this beautiful place, that there are a lot nicer spots for someone to think than in a dirty old barn."

"Heidi?"

"Yes, ma'am?"

"Were you calling me for a particular reason?"

"Oh, yes. I'm sorry. Your husband's on the phone."

"Hi, Meg. How are you holding up?"

"All right, I guess. It's so good to hear your voice."

"You can hear me all you want in a few hours. Kristin and I are booked on the five o'clock flight to Albany tonight, so we'll be arriving shortly after seven."

"That's wonderful, Phillip. You have no idea how much I need you, and miss you. I'll have Barnes meet you at the airport."

"I was just going to rent a car."

"That really won't be necessary, honey. We have the limo, and both Kenny and Justine have their cars, too."

"If you say so. Hey, you—I want you to know how very sad I am about this. I guess we all knew it was coming. But honestly, if anyone could have figured out an alternative, it would have been your grandmother. I was beginning to think she'd be around forever."

"Me, too. Somehow, though, I believe she was ready—finally. And, of course, the rest of the family was already scheduled to arrive at the Inn by noon today. So, we don't even need to make a lot of calls. Kenny will gather the group together and tell them all at the same time. She really had this planned perfectly."

Phillip chuckled to himself, recalling how often he'd poked fun at the last ten years of rehearsals.

"All along she was preparing you, making sure your reactions would be instinctive when the time came for you to deal with it. In hindsight, despite my cynicism, that's pretty amazing."

"Yeah? Well, she didn't exactly prepare me for *everything*."

"No? What did she leave out?"

"I'll tell you tonight, and *show* you, too. This one will blow you away."

"Should I take an earlier flight?"

"No, silly. By the way, before I forget, please make sure Kristin packs the navy blue dress she wore to your birthday party at the Club, and also have her throw in a couple of her sundresses and a sweater. Double-check that she puts appropriate shoes in her bag, too. We haven't scheduled any of the arrangements yet, but I don't want her showing up here with just a pair of jeans and sneakers."

"Okay. Got it. We will both be suitably prepared for all potential occasions."

"I think you can leave your tux at home, though."

"Oh, darn."

"I do love you, Phillip, and I can't wait for you to get here."

"Me, too. See you tonight."

Megan had barely hung up the telephone when it rang again. *And so it begins.*

"Stafford residence," she said, having no idea why she was suddenly sounding so formal.

"Hello. I'm looking for either Kenneth or Megan?"

She didn't recognize the woman's voice.

"May I say who's calling?"

"Excuse me. I should have identified myself first. My name is Katrina Wallace, but they would recognize me by my family name—Magglio. Are either Megan or Kenneth there?"

"Yes, this is Megan," she said, struggling to reorder her thoughts.

"Megan, how do you do? Please forgive me for calling to introduce myself at such an awful time. I had planned to phone later in the week. But when I heard the news, I felt the need to speak with you. I'm so very sorry for your loss."

"If you're referring to my grandmother, how did you find out so quickly? She only passed away a few hours ago."

"My husband is a resident at the Medical Center. Aside from my family's connections to Mrs. Stafford, your grandmother was quite well-known at the hospital. Her admissions and stays there were more like *events,* and Paul—my husband—said that word spread throughout the entire complex shortly after she was brought in this morning."

"Well, I can't say that I'm surprised. She was truly a character."

"So I'm told, Megan. I've heard stories about her all of my life."

"By any chance, are you and your husband the owners of ***Magglio Originals*** on Lark Street?"

"Yes, we are. The shoemaker two doors down from the shop called us with your name and number shortly after you left yesterday, and I was thrilled to get the message. My parents and grandparents were great storytellers, but they didn't always write everything down. It wasn't until my mother died that I learned I would need to find you, and of course, I didn't even have your married name."

"Did you ever try calling here? I'm sure Gram would have been happy to tell you how to contact me, or Kenny, who lives right here in Albany."

"Her instructions were very clear. I was only to contact her grandchildren."

"Her instructions?"

"They were included with my mother's will. Actually, they were in my *father's* will, but he died first and Mother apparently consolidated all of his papers with hers."

"Katrina—it *is* Katrina?"

"Yes."

"I apologize if I sound a little dense, but I seem to be running into a new set of my grandmother's instructions every time I turn around. And now I'm even more confused. Who exactly was your father?"

"Yes, I suppose I did get ahead of myself. My father was Charles, the son—the only child, actually—of Christina Magglio. Christina was my grandmother. Joseph and Anthony Magglio were my great-great-uncles, and their sister Velita was my great-great-aunt. Joseph never married, and Anthony and Olivia never had any children. Christina's sister Rebecca had lots of health problems, apparently, and died in her twenties. As a result, my grandmother was the only one to continue the Magglio line. Then, of course, her only child was my father—and my parents only had me. So the responsibility for the stories and all the things in storage was left in my hands. I know I keep repeating this, but I was *so* happy to find out about you!"

"Wow. I'm not sure I'm up for all of this today."

"Please forgive my intrusion, Megan. We can talk another time."

"No, that's not what I meant. It's hard to explain. There's just a lot of information coming at me all at once. But your calling is perfectly all right. In fact, you and I are some sort of cousins, aren't we?"

"Yes, we are. I think we're *third* cousins. Your grandfather Vincente and my grandmother Christina were *first* cousins."

"This is very weird."

"I know—and I don't want to further complicate things for you right now. But if you have time after the next few days are behind you, my husband and I would like to invite you up to our home in Clifton Park for dinner. We've been keeping everything in a self-storage unit not too far from the house."

"Everything?"

"Yes. Oh, my. She didn't tell you, did she?"

Why on earth would she tell me? And mess up her scavenger hunt?

"Well, I haven't been through any of her papers yet, Katrina, but at the moment I'm afraid I'm in the dark."

"I can show you her letters when you come for dinner, but the gist of it is that she asked Uncle Joseph to watch over quite a collection of her things. One truckload was delivered to the Lark Street shop in the late '30's, and another delivery was made in 1953, shortly after her son was killed. There's furniture, knickknacks, lamps—all sorts of things. If you decide you don't want some of it, my husband and I attend auctions all the time and would be happy to sell it for you."

...further bequeathed to the female offspring, Margaret Elizabeth, items contained in a roped-off section of Fox Run's attic...

"Thanks. Now I think I know what some of those *things* might be. When we meet, I'll tell you the story, as I understand it anyway."

"I can't wait, Megan! How should we do this? Do you just want to call me when you have a better idea what your week's going to look like?"

"Yes, that's probably the best plan."

"Once again," Katrina said, after leaving her home and work phone numbers, "please accept my deepest sympathy. I wish we'd been able to meet before things turned so sad."

"I feel the same, but I'm very glad we've made the connection."

When the women had exchanged their good-byes, Megan carried her coffee cup back into the kitchen.

"Hello, again, Heidi. You look very nice."

"Thank you, ma'am. I *feel* better."

"I'm glad one of us does. Frankly, I'm a bit saturated. Before too much longer, Kenny and Justine will be here with Tania. My mother's also coming, accompanied by her—well, I guess you could call him her *boyfriend*, for lack of further detail. Then Gram's attorney is going to stop by to unveil God-knows-what instructions that she left with *him*. Plus, my husband and daughter are flying up from Atlanta—and...a...par-tri...idge...in...a...pear...tree-ee..."

Heidi looked up from the sink, the silliness escaping her.

"Are you hungry?"

"No, but I'm sleepy, and I'm going to take a nap in Gram's room for about an hour. I'll unplug the telephone again and close the door, so just take messages if anyone calls. In case you don't hear me moving around by one o'clock, though, please come get me."

"Will do. I'll also have some lunch ready for you."

"Here's a better idea. Why don't you just call the New Scotland Deli and have them fix a bunch of trays for us? You know, cold cuts, cheeses, fruits, the usual.

I'm sure the other folks will be ready to eat by the time they get here, and the last thing I want to worry about right now is what we're going to feed everyone!"

Family and friends at the Albion Inn were visibly shaken when Kenneth delivered the news to them in a private meeting room. Despite the years of rehearsals, their bleached expressions indicated that they were pitifully unprepared to hear that she had really died. At first they thought he was kidding and that Cinnamon had added a new morbid slant to her ritualistic grieving parties. But realizing he was serious, they acted as if they'd never considered what they would do in the event of her actual demise, and the previously festive atmosphere grew abruptly subdued.

After Kenneth finished his announcement and left for the estate with his wife and daughter, the other guests broke up into small, quiet groups clustered in the bar or in their individual suites. Most of them ate their meals that night in their private quarters, while they awaited information about the arrangements, which Kenneth had promised would be relayed as soon as details were confirmed. Jay and Angela's son, Preston, who had arrived at the Inn a few hours earlier, agreed to be the intermediary. Later that afternoon at Fox Run, when Anthony Parnell had concluded his review of Cinnamon's final wishes, Megan called Preston and told him that the group should assemble at seven the following morning, in the banquet hall at the Inn.

"I'm sorry we have to get everyone up so early, Preston, but I'm afraid Gram left quite a list for us."

"Don't worry about it, Megan. No one's going to be surprised at any plans she might have put in place. Now, go do whatever you need to do. I'll take care of all the people on this end, including Dad. See you soon."

She had no doubt that Preston would handle things masterfully, and this gave her considerable peace of mind as the rest of the day and night evolved into a blur. By the time Barnes drove in from the airport with Phillip and Kristin, it was almost nine o'clock, and Megan could not keep her eyes open for more than an hour after she embraced them both with an almost slap-happy reception. David, who'd been talking through his tears since Kenneth brought him over from the cottage around 2:00 that afternoon, seemed to brighten as more and more family arrived. But by 9:30 that evening, he felt so drained that he let Heidi make up the sofa bed for him in the library. Even a walk across the yard to the cottage was more than he could manage, and the thought of being alone had grown more frightening to him as the day wore on.

Claudine and Lyle drove back to the Inn around 10:00 that night, but Kenneth and Justine decided to stay at Fox Run. They slept in one of the three guest bedrooms upstairs, and Kristin shared another room with Tania. Finally, when all the lights were out, Megan fell asleep in Cinnamon's bed, wrapped in Phillip's arms. Feeling sedated by her husband's touch, she wondered, as she drifted off, if the last seventeen hours might have just been a long awful dream after all.

At six-thirty the following morning, a cavalcade of sluggish, bleary-eyed people made their way through the corridors of the Albion Inn, down the elevators, across the courtyard and into the banquet hall. There they were met by aromas from three urns of coffee, several bowls of freshly cut fruit, and baskets filled with warm croissants. Conversation was limited to pleasantries as they milled around, waiting for *what* they could only imagine.

At precisely seven o'clock, Megan entered the banquet hall with the others from Fox Run. She'd been selected as spokesperson during the drive from the estate, and after circulating around the room for fifteen minutes, she walked to the far end where a microphone had been set up. Behind her, the crowd tightened in a gesture of unity. Then all eyes were suddenly focused upon her. Looking back at them, her heart was stung by their crestfallen faces and by the number of people so intimately affected by her grandmother's death, as well as her life. Feeling a bit shaky, she turned toward Kenneth, William and Claudine, the most direct descendents besides herself, who were huddled together in front of her. They gave her a collective thumbs-up for strength, as Phillip, Kristin, Justine and Tania pressed close to them, with David supported in their midst.

"Good morning, everybody."

"Good morning," came an uneven chorus in response.

"I'm sorry we had to call this gathering so early. But we have a great deal to accomplish over the next few days, and we wanted to let you know what's happening, before we're all swept up in the commotion."

She was relieved to feel her emotions holding steady, as she watched them nod empathetically.

"You know, by now, that yesterday we lost Margaret Elizabeth McClinty Mentini Stafford, a woman whose life was nearly as long and full as her name."

This brought a smile to a few faces, although most of the audience wasn't certain if humor was appropriate yet.

"All of us are aware that nothing will ever be quite the same—quite as wondrous or nearly as much fun—without her. But I think you'll agree that she would not be happy to see us looking glum, especially not after giving us so many opportunities over the years to practice our partying skills."

A few more faces were brightening across the room.

"In fact, you'll probably be amused to learn that she anticipated we might behave this way, and she made rather extensive plans to counteract our gloom."

Megan was pleased to see them loosening up, but she was unprepared for the heartening round of applause. *Gram, you are amazing.*

"Her directives, which her attorney shared with us yesterday afternoon, include provisions for a round-the-clock banquet right here in this room, beginning now and lasting through the funeral reception. Different buffets will be rotated, depending on the time of day or night, and all manner of beverages will also be available. If you're tired or wish to have some privacy, just request that your selections be brought to your suites.

"Some of the details for the next several days are not finalized yet. But the wake will be tomorrow and Sunday. Her funeral Mass and burial will be on Monday the 18th. Specific times will be forthcoming. Preston has agreed to help pass messages along to you, and he will communicate any additional information as soon as we can get it to him. Meanwhile, we'll post the locations of the funeral home and the cathedral on the board over there by the door before we leave this morning. However, a car service has been engaged to provide all transportation for you, unless you absolutely want to drive yourselves.

"We've all been together many times before, right here in this Inn—under false pretenses, of course. But Gram was only trying to get us ready for this. Let's not disappoint her. She's at peace now, and she would want us to rejoice in her safe passage. Think of her. Talk about her, and remember her laughter. We'll find, I believe, that she'll stay alive right here with us, which I'm sure is what she had in mind. Thanks so much. It's very comforting to have you here."

When they realized she was finished, another round of applause erupted.

"I'm so proud of you," Phillip whispered in her ear as he took her hand. Holding on tight, he then allowed himself to be swept up in the unique magic that only his wife's grandmother could create, while he and Megan socialized for the next hour surrounded by everyone still living who'd been special to her.

Doctor Preston McClinty was 53, only a couple of years older than Phillip. But the two men seemed to have little else in common, although Phillip had never spent any time verifying this supposition. As he watched from the opposite side of the banquet hall, he admitted to himself that Preston made him feel inadequate. Aside from his professional accomplishments, the good doctor seemed to grow more dashing with age. His full head of hair was now an eye-catching snow white, and the smooth Irish skin on his face had scarcely given way to a noticeable line or wrinkle. From this angle, he didn't appear to have added any girth to his midsection, either. A bit embarrassed by this sense of inferiority, Phillip decided to make an effort over the next several days to learn a little more about the man he'd met when he married Megan twenty years ago and had only seen a handful of times since.

Part of the reason for this infrequent contact was that Preston rarely showed up for Cinnamon's annual emergency reunions. His rationale was simple. He routinely spent a great deal of his time in Albany anyway—crisis or not—and he was fully in tune with the old woman's charade. Furthermore, he would not allow anyone to dictate his use of even a single day, no matter how much he loved his Aunt Cinnamon.

A respected cardiologist in the Boston medical community, Preston had never married, much to the chagrin of many eager debutantes. The issue, once again, was control.

"I can orchestrate my time, if I'm dating," he'd told his mother once. "But I suspect I would no longer be in charge if I were married." Given this approach, his bachelorhood seemed safe, although a truckload of women was still trying, even though he was well into his fifties.

He'd always been extraordinarily close to his parents—as well as to his aunt, despite his kidding to the contrary—and after his mother Angela died in the fall of 1977, he began driving from Boston nearly every weekend to check on his father. Within a year of Angela's death, Preston had convinced Jay to sell the house on Madison Avenue, still referred to by the family as The Corbett Place, although Jay and Angela had lived there for more than forty years. With Cinnamon's assistance, Preston had then located an upscale retirement village about fifteen miles from Fox Run, where Jay had been comfortably settled for the last decade.

At age 79, Cinnamon's brother was finally beginning to slow down, but not by much. Preston had recently persuaded his father to relinquish his car keys, but otherwise, Jay's bright wit and keen mind kept him far more youthful than most of his contemporaries. Of course, his sister had a great deal to do with his sustained energy and cheerful outlook, including him in activities at Fox Run at least once a week, where he and David enjoyed bantering with one another. Barnes had also become a good friend, chauffeuring the old man him to and from the estate, as well as to doctor's appointments whenever Preston couldn't get away from Boston. In addition, the limousine could be seen parked outside Albany's Opera House one Saturday night each month, while Jay attended the performance. He was usually by himself, in the box seats he'd shared with Angela, since he refused to give up his season tickets. But the best times for him were on Sunday afternoons when Barnes would pick him up at his retirement villa and drive him to Fox Run for dinner. Preston was usually waiting there to greet him, along with David and Cinnamon, and sometimes the McClinty grandchildren, who always made him feel like a celebrity.

This family solidarity had been painstakingly reconstituted after Cinnamon's relocation to Fox Run in 1934 and had been fiercely protected ever since. The multiple tragedies befalling the McClinty's in the 1950's had threatened to dismember their renovated unity. But through some inexplicable triage, separate pieces of the family were restored to health one-by-one, and by 1960 they'd become whole again. Megan knew at least *that* much even before hearing her grandmother's parable, although she'd never been curious about any of the associated details. But now, as she observed Preston hovering over his father across the room, she was thinking about the changes that would be forced upon the family's symmetry once again, this time by Cinnamon's death.

She turned out to be such a cornerstone. How is Jay going to cope without his sister? Preston must be very worried about his dad, but Uncle Jay looks to be in remarkably good spirits. Of course, Gram probably planned on this, too, and made some sort of secret provisions for her brother that will be unveiled to us through another one of her abracadabras.

Megan's mind continued to meander, moving from Jay back into her grandmother's story and the inseparable connection with Angela. *I never appreciated the depth of their friendship,* she thought, feeling an unexpected rush of guilt at not having attended Angela's funeral eleven years earlier. *But Kristin was only five at the time, and leaving work was so difficult. Besides, I never really knew Angela, and Gram said she understood. She told me she wasn't upset with me.*

But no matter what she said to herself, the guilt was resurfacing, along with the ricochet of Cinnamon's voice on the phone in 1977 asking, "Are you going to be with me, Megan, when Jay and I bury Angela? Your mother and Elliott are over in Europe, I think." The memory of her answering, "I'm sorry, but I can't get away, either, Gram," made her feel uncomfortable, even to this day. *I've never had a friendship like that myself, though. There's been no time. So, even if I'd known her story then, I probably wouldn't have understood how important a role Angela played, or how awful the loss of her must have been for Gram.* Feeling Phillip's hand still closed around hers, she wondered how many other moments of consequence she'd missed—or ignored—over the years. Then seeing Claudine walking toward her, with her arms linked in Lyle's and DJ's, Megan pushed her self-reproach aside, to be dealt with later.

"My dear daughter."

"Yes, Mom?"

Megan noted that Claudine had cried through yet another application of makeup, but was putting on an impressively cheerful front.

"I was just telling DJ that I thought Mr. Parnell mentioned something to us yesterday about a brunch tomorrow. Am I remembering correctly?"

"Yes, but it's not for everyone—just the grandchildren. That's one of the things I need to work on after we get back from the funeral home this morning."

"*We*?"

"Don't play selective memory with me, Mother. I know you don't want to go, but Gram's list specifically requested that you be involved in the selection of her casket. Remember? *I'm* supposed to take care of the headstone and the message on it, and *you're* supposed to do the casket."

"Right. Good God," Claudine asked, looking back and forth between her companion on her left and her cousin on her right, "can you imagine how strange my mother had to be to come up with something like that? By the way, Megan, did she leave you with any suggestions about what she wanted the headstone to say?"

"Her note just said that I should come up with whatever I think fits her."

"Well, I guess I drew the easiest straw with the casket! Seriously, though, do you honestly believe she's going to have any clue whether or not either of us follows every single line of her orders?"

All eyes, including Phillip's, turned toward Claudine with an unspoken *you bet your life we do*!

"I hope heaven is ready for her," Megan's mother said, shaking her head and laughing along with everyone else.

Three hours later, the immediate family had selected a bronze casket with crème-colored satin *bedding*, as Claudine called it, and signed the final papers for the service package Cinnamon had pre-selected at the funeral home. They'd also been to the cemetery's business office, where they ordered the headstone and paid an extra $350 to expedite the engraved plaque. When they returned to Fox Run to concentrate on the remainder of Cinnamon's to-do list, none of them could believe it was only noon.

"Time seems to be expanding to accommodate all of her wishes," Megan observed, while the family sat around the dining room table eating Heidi's chicken sandwiches.

They nodded at her in agreement, as the list of those wishes stared back at them from the pages stacked next to Megan's plate.

Brunch the following day was arranged exclusively for all of the McClinty grandchildren, in a private dining room reserved at the Inn. Cinnamon had already prepared handwritten invitations, in her distinctive penmanship, with blank lines left for the date, place and time. Megan and her mother filled in those missing details shortly after they arrived back at the estate from the cemetery's office, and they put the completed invitations in a zippered portfolio, along with personalized place cards for each attendee. The place cards had also been prepared in advance and were to be positioned around the brunch table in an order outlined on the list from Mr. Parnell. On one side of the table would be Cinnamon's grandchildren—Megan Elizabeth Cole, Kenneth James Stafford, and William Theodore Stafford. On the opposite side, David's grandson's would face them—Davie and Harrison McClinty, DJ's sons, and Peter and Nathan McClinty, Teddy's boys.

Very funny, Gram, Megan thought, as soon as she understood the arrangement. *And just how are you planning to make this lineup blend with reality? I hope you're not expecting* <u>*me*</u> *to do it, because I don't think there's enough courage in America.*

Later that afternoon, Barnes delivered the zippered portfolio to Preston, who took care of distributing the invitations to the appropriate suites. He also posted two fliers in the banquet hall—one specifying information-only particulars about the brunch for those *not* attending, and another listing times for the wake, funeral Mass and burial. Once Preston had called Fox Run to let them know that all items had been expeditiously handled, Megan ignored the pile of messages on the sideboard in the front hall and excused herself before dinner.

"Honestly, I couldn't eat a thing. Right now my body needs rest more than it needs food."

Neither knowing nor caring what the others were thinking, or what they were planning to do for the balance of that evening, she took a shower and slipped into the pair of clean cotton pajamas Phillip had thoughtfully tucked in his suitcase. She remembered brushing out her hair and putting her feet under the covers on her grandmother's bed, but she did not recall her head reaching the pillow before she fell asleep.

Shortly before noon the next day, the Fox Run Limo, as everyone at the Inn had dubbed the vehicle, arrived at the hotel. Megan and Kenneth climbed out and walked inside, where William met them in the lobby.

"Everyone's already waiting for us," he said.

Good grief, Megan thought, as they entered the small private dining room through double doors. Colorful floral arrangements filled every corner, and a man was playing classical selections on an upright piano in front of the picture windows that looked out onto the courtyard. Each of the seven place settings at the table included the finest linens, silver, china and crystal, all glistening beneath the deflected light of the enormous chandelier hanging directly above—and each setting was marked by Cinnamon's personalized place cards. An eighth place was prepared at the head of the table, that place card reading Anthony Bennett Parnell, Esq. When this addition was spotted, a few rude jokes began spilling forth from David's grandsons regarding the potential for early retirement funded by Cinnamon's anticipated bequests.

"I didn't even know we were in her will, did you?" Peter asked his brother.

"I heard she was sort of goofy," Nathan answered. "Maybe she got confused."

"Good," Harrison added. "I think she's the only one in the family who ended up with any money."

"Excuse me, guys," Kenneth said, just as Megan was about to speak up. "That's not funny. What's the matter with you? Where's your respect? And none of this is about money, anyway. So, cut it out!"

"Sorry," three of the young men said in unison, although Nathan still seemed to think the whole thing was quite humorous, until Megan shot him a look that also erased the smile from his face.

"Frankly, Megan," Kenneth whispered to her, after William started a diversionary debate with the men about the viability of the New York Yankees' pitching staff, "I can understand their confusion. Why *did* Gram do this? They're her cousins three times removed—just like we are to David—and they never even came to visit her. I thought this was supposed to be a brunch for *her* grandchildren, not *the* grandchildren."

"Her instructions said *McClinty grandchildren,*" she whispered back, not at all ready to deal with the crux of the issue. Then she shrugged her shoulders and scrunched her face into an *other-than-that-I-have-no-idea* expression. She suspected that this pre-ordained breakfast meeting might have something to do with the *little project* Cinnamon left in her hands, *but this was obviously not the appropriate time to inform Kenny that he and William were David's grandchildren as well as Gram's.*

Just then, the head waiter came in and asked them to take their assigned seats. "Mr. Parnell is running a few minutes late, and he requested that we begin the meal service for you."

Halfway through the first course of fruit and cream, the dapper legal counsel for Margaret Stafford swooped into the room and arrived huffing at his assigned place. All seven cousins rose, in unison, to their feet.

"Please," he instructed in a voice that sounded particularly commanding in the small room. "Sit down and continue eating. I'm the tardy one, and I hope you'll accept my apology."

They sat down in perfect timing with him, as if the movement had been choreographed. Once he'd swallowed his first bite of fruit, however, he glanced up and realized that no one else was eating. Instead, seven pairs of eyes were fixed on him, waiting.

"Oh, I see. Apparently, food is not your priority this morning. Well, I suppose I can't blame you. Perhaps we should get right to the point. Then maybe your appetites will return."

After folding his napkin neatly beside his fruit bowl, he sat up straight, put his elbows on the table and pressed the fingers of both hands together in a steeple just below his chin.

"First, let's pause and reflect for a minute on the reason we're here. We've gathered to pay our loving respects to a fine woman, who will be deeply missed. The late Margaret Elizabeth McClinty Mentini Stafford earned her own way, and cherished her family as the center of her life. She made her share of mistakes, as most of us do. But she remained a grand and special lady, whose legacy will live on, through each of you."

He lowered his hands and took a drink of orange juice.

"She asked that you all be assembled in this manner, in order that I might convey to you a note she penned in anticipation of this event. I'm as much in the dark about what it says as you are."

Oh, Gram, Megan thought, afraid to look up, *what are you doing*?

Mr. Parnell removed an envelope from his inside jacket pocket and broke a wax seal on the flap. Then sliding his chair back, he stood up, cleared his throat, and in that same commanding voice, began to read aloud.

July 11, 1988

To my grandchildren and to David McClinty's grandchildren—

All of you should be enjoying breakfast as you hear this greeting. Sadly, I cannot join you, but I promise that I'm watching from someplace nearby. So be careful what you say.

My last request of you is that you spend time getting to know each other. Begin sharing experiences. Bring your own children together, and keep the McClinty heritage intact. We are a strong family, but not as united as we used to be, due to our busy, separate worlds.

Make time for each other. Tell one another your family secrets. Keep the heredity of events moving forward. Schedule occasions—and make them first-class, multiple-day affairs, like the one you're experiencing now. And schedule them in honor of me, to perpetuate knowledge and love within our family.

Contrary to what you might be thinking, I have not taken leave of my senses as I write this. Well, maybe just a little bit. But I'm sane enough to know precisely what I want to do with my money. Therefore, in order to facilitate your reunions, a portion of my estate has been used to establish a trust fund for them. Mr. Anthony Parnell will administer the fund and will also oversee the orchestration of your events.

There are sufficient monies to support two trips per year for all of you, plus your spouses and children, to any location in the world. I would ask that you also invite DJ, Claudine and Preston to be your guests, if their calendars permit. They are the only surviving cousins from the generation that preceded you, and they should not be forgotten, despite their advancing age (no disrespect intended...). Speaking of advancing age, please take Jay and David along with you, as well, assuming they are healthy enough to travel safely.

There are only a few restrictions attached to this plan:

- ❖ *You must all arrive and depart within twenty-four hours of each other, spending a minimum of three full days and nights together in the same hotel or resort.*
- ❖ *Each of you, your spouses and your children, must be in attendance—except in case of a medical emergency—or the entire excursion will be canceled. Excuses about your needing to be at work or in some sort of meeting or seminar will not be acceptable. Mr. Parnell has the authority, however, to review individual situations, making occasional exceptions at his discretion.*
- ❖ *Those of you without spouses may invite one guest to join you.*
- ❖ *Mr. Parnell will organize and make the arrangements for these trips, coordinating to the best of his ability a convenient time for all of you. Depending upon your choice of location, he will also plan any tours or special junkets that might be of interest to you.*

These reunions will continue indefinitely, as long as you want them to happen, and as long as you follow my guidelines. I want you to see the world, on my nickel, as the saying goes. Think of me while you're there. Talk to each other. Confide in one another—and teach your children to do the same. Remember—in the end, it's all about family, because when the rest is stripped away, families are the only things that stick. Even when people are dead, you can't get rid of them. You'll see.

Now, enjoy your breakfast and be reverent when you officially say good-bye to me day after tomorrow. I love all of you very much.

Always,
Gram/Cinnamon

Everyone at the table was frozen in place, as Megan found the courage to lift her eyes for the first time. *Oh, this is real cute, Gram. If this is your way of organizing a few opportunities for me to talk with my cousins, I'm grateful. But I'm sure I could have figured out something slightly less elaborate on my own.* Still, she couldn't help but be tickled by her grandmother's continuing propensity for extremes.

Eventually, the four courses of breakfast were served and consumed, although very little conversation took place in the process. The words of Cinnamon's letter seemed to hang around the room, leaving the cousins guarded about what they might say in the unseen presence of this odd woman's spirit. By lunchtime, however, as the group dispersed, the French Riviera and several Caribbean Islands were topping the list of choices for the first excursion, which most of them were proposing should take place as soon as possible. But Megan excused herself from this dialogue, suddenly having something of more immediate importance on her mind. Using the telephone in the banquet hall, she dialed the number for the cemetery's administration office.

"Hello, this is Megan Cole. You are handling the arrangements for the burial of my grandmother on Monday...Margaret Elizabeth Stafford...Right. Actually, I'd like to speak with someone about making a change to the plaque on her headstone...Yes, I realize the stone won't be in place, but I was assured that the plaque would be there on Monday for everyone to see...I appreciate your checking...Yes?...Wonderful! Are you sure there's time to make this change?...Oh, thank you *so* much. Here are the details..."

Megan kept waiting for the okay-let's-get-serious part of this ordeal, but nothing of the sort seemed forthcoming. Demonstrating her aversion to what she called *canned music,* Cinnamon had arranged for a series of men with violins to rotate their easy-listening shifts at the funeral home throughout the two-day wake. The funeral director's initial objection to this unorthodox entertainment was quieted by an envelope handed to him by Mr. Parnell. A second envelope was required when ten round tables, each with eight chairs, arrived complete with white linen tablecloths and floral centerpieces.

...There is never any place to sit down at those things, she'd written in her instructions to the attorney. *There are always chapel pews or chairs up close to the casket. But in the adjacent room where people gather to talk, if you can't sit down, you don't stay very long. That's not what I want. I'd like my friends and family to be comfortable and to have a place where they can talk to each other. Make sure there's a table for refreshments, too...*

By the time the two days were over, Megan wasn't sure how many envelopes had been given to the funeral director. But as people lingered for hours in and around Cinnamon's bier, the steady stream of comments about the unusually beautiful setting and the considerate social accommodations made yet another powerful statement about her grandmother's instincts, and about her steel-jawed determination to make the impossible happen. Even in her death, she was creating unique memories that everyone would talk about for years to come—and this was never more in evidence than on Monday.

A chartered fleet of white stretch limousines was at the disposal of family and guests staying at the Inn, the fleet leading an attention-grabbing procession behind the hearse. The route followed the Thruway from the funeral home to the Cathedral, where each person entering the church received a professionally printed **Program of Service** listing the sequence of events, the music being played at each point, and the names of surviving family members—all in gold lettering. The flower arrangements blanketing the altar were completely white, in accordance with guidelines that had been distributed to Albany's florists. Finally, five white gilded bird cages were positioned along the kneeling rail, each cage housing a dove of unspecified gender. The **Program of Service** explained that these were symbolic representations of Cinnamon's two children and three grandchildren, thereby answering one of the many questions rolling through the dumfounded congregation, as they gaped at the reverential hoopla. By the time Megan walked forward to the altar and up the steps of the lectern for her portion of the eulogy, she could hardly keep a straight face.

"Hello, dear family and friends," she began, a bit startled when she first heard her voice amplified throughout the sanctuary. "As I was preparing for today, I was worried that my emotions might make it difficult for me to get through this part. But I'm sure you'll understand what I mean when I tell you that I'm finding it impossible to feel tearful amidst all of *this*," she said, gesturing toward the display of flowers and birds just below her, as a soft wave of laughter bounced off the cathedral's stone arches and pillars.

"Making things even worse," she continued, "most of what I'm planning to say to you actually comes from *her*—her own words—in something she wrote and read to me only a couple of days before she died."

Unfolding the piece of paper beneath the reading light, she struggled against the onslaught of giggles that threatened to derail any remaining thread of solemnity.

"The title of her short essay is ***Ordinary.***"

As anticipated, she had to wait more than a minute until the hilarity subsided.

"Anyway, as I was saying, Gram left us plenty of proof that she was special. Some would dare say a bit over-the-top. But I think it's clear that her memory will always remain highlighted in the minds and hearts of everyone here today.

That's why this piece of writing seems particularly significant. Here's what she said."

And then Megan began reading from the paper, suddenly feeling her grandmother's presence when she looked at the unmistakable handwriting, her voice catching on the tears that were taking her by surprise.

Ordinary. Such is the baseline of all human life—the place where everyone starts. Accidents of birth bring an infant into the merits and shortcomings of a family, or group, or town. Genetic contributions and twists provide individual ingredients and complications. From that point on, however, each person moves under his or her own power, back and forth, above and below the baseline of ordinary, eventually arriving at a mark on someone's statistical graph. That mark coldly represents the value of a person's entire existence, and the final position is what gets all the attention. But a person's ending doesn't always correlate with where he or she has been. A life that began as ordinary might have circulated through times of grandeur, or poverty, or perhaps a respectable, unremarkable point in between. The only thing we know for sure about endings is that a unique story lies behind every journey just completed—and there's certainly nothing ***ordinary*** *about that!*

Refolding the paper, Megan made no attempt to wipe her face as she looked up at the people filling every pew.

"There's no question that a unique story lies behind her journey, but I doubt very seriously that she qualified as *ordinary* for even one moment of her long and fascinating life. As a result, she gave all of us a great deal of joy. But I've learned that when there's an extraordinary amount of something wonderful in our lives, there's also an extraordinarily large empty space when that *something* is no longer there. I'm afraid I'm starting to feel that emptiness, and yet I also think it's safe to say that she won't let me, or *any* of us, remain gloomy for very long. That, in essence, is the resilient spirit she left us as her gift. Whenever we remember her, that gift will be given to us again, over and over, forever."

The rest of the Mass, the Communion service, the funeral procession and burial ceremony lasted for two more hours. Then, as the mourners began making their way from the cemetery back to the Inn for the reception, Megan stayed seated in her chair at the gravesite, with her grandmother's casket suspended a few feet in front of her. The thick sprays of white roses looked beautiful atop the gleaming bronze metal, and she felt a serenity that she was hesitant to disturb.

"Are you coming, Meg?" Phillip asked, standing shoulder-to-shoulder with Kenneth and William, the three of them waiting for her while the rest of the family walked down the grassy slope toward their limousines.

"Yes, but could you give me just a few more minutes—alone?"

"Sure," he said, then turned and silently followed the others.

Megan's focus shifted to the burnished plaque, which had been propped up on a pedestal after being successfully rushed through the engraving process and delivered in time for everyone to appreciate. Within two weeks, she was told, the headstone would be in place, and the plaque would be mounted in the recessed area carved to the precise dimensions of the framed message.

This is perfect, Gram, Megan reflected, secure in her conviction that only the hardest of hearts would ever be able to visit this grave without experiencing an improvement in their states of mind.

MARGARET ELIZABETH MCCLINTY MENTINI STAFFORD
JANUARY 26, 1906–JULY 14, 1988

"IN THE END, IT'S ALL ABOUT FAMILY.
EVEN WHEN PEOPLE ARE DEAD,
YOU CAN'T GET RID OF THEM.
YOU'LL SEE."

M.E.M.S.
JULY 11, 1988

Leaving the shelter of the white canopy that stretched over the burial plot, Megan walked toward the cluster of headstones a few yards away. Amazingly, she'd never been here before, and yet somehow the spot felt familiar. On the marker closest to her grandmother's grave, the message was short, but seemed to speak volumes—about a lot of things.

JONATHON ALLISTER MCCLINTY
MAY 4, 1881–SEPTEMBER 12, 1932

A SOLID MAN

The gravestone next to Jonathon's was appropriately powerful.

NATHANIEL MCCLINTY

NOVEMBER 5, 1857—JUNE 12, 1904

THE FINEST MAN THEY WILL EVER KNOW
WILL BE MISSED BY
AMELIA—BELOVED WIFE
PETER AND JONATHON—BELOVED SONS

Finally, to the left of Nathaniel, Megan stood facing, for the first time, the resting place of the woman whose legacy would not be stilled.

> MY PRAYER AND GREATEST WISH IS THAT NOT ONLY WILL I BE GRANTED THE POWER TO FORGIVE ALL THINGS, BUT THAT THE SAME POWER WILL BE GIVEN TO THOSE I LOVE.
>
> **AMELIA ELIZABETH MCCLINTY**
> FEBRUARY 2, 1858—APRIL 23, 1906

"Thank you, Gram," Megan said aloud, "for going out of your way to make these people come to life for me."

Then she brushed her fingers across the lettering on Amelia's headstone, and made her way to the family waiting for her at the bottom of the hill. As she walked with her eyes looking straight ahead at nothing, she did not notice the three unobtrusive plaques, level with the ground, that marked the gravesites of Ryan and Teddy McClinty, and Greg Stafford Junior.

The Coles had reservations on a flight to Atlanta the next day, giving Megan only forty-eight hours before she needed to return to Albany for the reading of Cinnamon's will.

"Are you sure you want to make the added trip?" Phillip asked, concerned that she was pushing herself to the point of exhaustion. "You could just stay up here through the weekend."

"Yes, honey, I'm sure. I really need to get an infusion of our regular life, even if it's only for a couple of days. The last week has been a bit bizarre."

"Really? I hadn't noticed."

She jabbed him in his ribs with her elbow, then slipped into his arms as they laughed together.

"Seriously," she said, rocking back and forth against his chest, "I just want to get things back on an even playing field, before the next round starts."

"All right," he said reassuringly. "Let's go home."

She called Jerry Rogers from her own kitchen the next morning while Kristin was still sleeping and after Phillip left to have breakfast at his club.

"I'll be in the office on Monday, Jerry—back in the saddle and ready to do battle at your side. I hope this comes as good news to you, and that you even remember who I am."

Clearly relieved to hear a lilt in her voice and to learn that her absence was nearly over, he began itemizing the issues that she was going find on her desk.

"Please, Jerry. Do we really have to do this now?" Her voice had a plaintive tone that he was unaccustomed to hearing from her. "I'm pretty saturated already with things to worry about. If this can wait until I get there on Monday, I'd really appreciate it. Tomorrow night I have to fly to Albany again for some legal matters, and I need to find my sea legs first."

"Sure. I was just trying to soften the blow," he answered, uncomfortable that she didn't seem the least bit curious about what had transpired since they last spoke.

"Thanks. I knew you'd understand."

In fact, he *didn't* understand, but he elected not to press the issue. After their conversation ended, a stabilizing respite continued to elude her as her grandmother's story kept reverberating in her head. Much as she tried to think about other things—or about nothing at all—she could not stop herself from re-reading Cinnamon's last letter over and over again, with certain portions becoming more troubling each time.

...now that my story is in your hands. I know you will finally uncover the truth about what really happened to Greg and Teddy, which is my final request of you...

I refused to buy the official explanation about the accident. Deep inside, I now see that much of my problem stemmed from my being afraid to find out that I was right...afraid to find out that I was right...afraid to find out that I was right...

"Gram, I don't think I can do this," she said to herself. "Some things are better left buried, and this looks like one of them. Besides, I'm going to have enough trouble introducing Kenny and William to the truth about David. Thanks again for *that* headache, by the way."

Attempting to clear her mind, she decided to make an omelet. After removing the eggs, tomatoes, cheese, onions and sausage from the refrigerator bins, she began chopping and grating. But the same thoughts kept returning. She switched on the countertop television to watch the morning news broadcast, but that didn't help either. After twenty minutes, she wiped her hands on her apron and went upstairs to her bedroom, where she opened her top dresser drawer and stood looking down at the stacks of audio cassettes.

I don't need to hear any more of this, she kept repeating to herself. But she was powerless against the forces pulling at her. Taking the tapes numbered 1 through 4 back downstairs to the kitchen, she popped number 1 into the cassette player on the kitchen bookshelf. Then she pressed the PLAY button and began to listen hypnotically while she finished making her omelet.

""I was born Margaret Elizabeth McClinty on January 26, 1906 in Albany, New York to Jonathon and Mary Mae McClinty…"

CHAPTER 18

"I forgot to call Katrina!" Megan exclaimed, sitting bolt upright in bed.

Startled out of a deep sleep, Phillip sat up, too, squinting to see the digital clock on his nightstand.

"It's 3:30 in the morning, Megan! And who the hell is Katrina?"

"She's one of the Magglios, and I promised I'd call her. She's been holding onto a lot of Gram's things—for years, apparently."

Noting the empty look on her husband's face, she felt embarrassed.

"I'm sorry, honey. You have no idea what I'm talking about, do you?"

"No, but thanks for asking."

"Things have been moving so fast that I haven't had a chance to really *talk* with you about everything, other than the part about the family chart, of course."

"Frankly, I thought that was plenty. You mean there's more?"

Heaving a long sigh, she reached out and touched his face.

"When I get back from Albany on Sunday, I'll be able to focus a little better. Let's plan a night for just the two of us next week—say, Friday—so I can fill in all the pieces for you. Maybe we could go to your club."

"I don't believe what I'm hearing. *You* want to go to my club?"

"Well, it is a lovely place, despite some of the founding principles. And I'd like us to have some privacy where we won't be rushed—where we can linger for hours, if need be. I'm open for other suggestions, though."

"No, I like *your* idea, and this will be something to see. In fact, I'll notify my favorite reporter at the Journal. He's always looking for a scoop."

Smiling at him, she put her head back down on the pillow.

"Good. I'll leave the arrangements up to you."

"Okay," he said, assuming that, by next week, she would deny any memory of this conversation. "What time does your flight leave this afternoon?" he asked, pulling the sheet up over his shoulders.

"Five. It's the same one you and Kristin took."

"Then I'll come home around two-thirty. We'll need to leave for the airport by three."

"Sounds like a plan," she said, her voice fading as sleep overtook her once again.

Phillip, on the other hand, lay wide awake, staring into the darkness lurking between him and the ceiling, as that unwelcome feeling of apprehension began jabbing at him one more time.

Megan tried to reach Katrina when Phillip left for his office shortly after eight o'clock that morning. But she was greeted by answering machines at the home and work numbers, so she left the same message in both places.

"Katrina, this is Megan Cole—Margaret Stafford's granddaughter. Please forgive me for not calling you sooner. The last several days sort of ran away with me. I'm back in Atlanta at the moment, but I'll be flying up to Albany again tonight to take care of a few loose ends. I'll be there until Sunday evening. Tomorrow is pretty full, but if you and your husband are going to be free sometime Saturday, or on Sunday before four o'clock, please let me know. You can leave a message for me at Fox Run. Thanks, Katrina. I'll talk with you soon."

Refilling her coffee cup, she dropped two slices of bread into the toaster and dialed Kenneth's house. Justine answered on the second ring.

"Hey, Justine. Megan here."

"Hi, lady. What's up?"

"I was looking for Kenny. But if he's not there, it can wait until I get in."

"No, he's right here. By the way, I know we talked about your coming over to our house after you guys finish at the attorney's office tomorrow. But we just found out that Mr. Parnell has something else planned. Not sure what, though."

"More of Gram's instructions, probably. Will it ever end?"

"We can only hope. See you soon, Meg. Here's Kenny."

"Hello, stranger," he said in a gentle voice. "Feel better now that you've had a couple nights in your own bed?"

"A little, I guess. But I'm still in a bit of a time warp. Once I get back to Atlanta again on Sunday and reclaim my normal routine, I'm sure I'll be fine. How's David?"

"He's doing quite well, actually. I've gone by every afternoon to see him, and his spirits seem to improve each time, although he tends to talk about her as if she's still in the house."

"With all the instructions she left, who can tell that she's *not*."

"Agreed. I am glad, though, that Barnes has sort of been camping there. He's not leaving for his own house each night until he's sure David's asleep, and then he's back before the roosters crow. It's a temporary arrangement, but I'm more comfortable knowing that someone other than Heidi is on duty over there. It's also good for David to have Barnes as company. I think Heidi's starting to grate on him."

"I noticed. Have you given any thought to what we're going to do with David on a more permanent basis?"

"Not really. Why?"

"Well, I'm not sure that he should stay there by himself. It might become very lonely for him. Maybe we should think about moving him to Jay's retirement villa."

"I'm assuming you're volunteering to run this by him? The idea would not appeal to him, to put it mildly, and I'll turn into a total wimp if we have to convince him that leaving Fox Run would be good for him."

"I guess we could leave it alone, for now," she said, her stomach suddenly churning as she thought about the news her cousin would have to digest before much longer, assuming she could find enough courage for *that* conversation. "Oh, by the way, in all the commotion up there, I forgot to tell you about a call I received from the owner of **Magglio Originals**."

"Really?"

"Yes, on the day Gram died. That's actually the reason I telephoned just now. I'm afraid it will slip my mind again in the middle of everything else we'll have to deal with, once I get there."

She then proceeded to summarize her conversation with Katrina, highlighting the part about the storage unit.

"She wants us to come up to Clifton Park for dinner so she can show us. We'll need to figure out what to do with all the stuff, since it's really not their responsibility to keep it any more. Anyway, I'm not sure what their weekend looks like, but I think we should stay flexible until we hear back from her. Also, Kenny, if there's time, I…there's something else I need to tell…to talk with you about."

"Like what?"

"Like more of what Gram left behind for us."

"Just tell me now. I don't have to leave for the store for another hour."

"No. I'd rather we carve out some time in person."

"Then why did you bring it up, Meg? That drives me nuts!"

"Sorry. You're right. Never mind."

"Lord! Why do you women *do* that?"

"I'll try to think of an answer on the plane."

"By the way, what time are you coming in?"

"Around seven-thirty, I think."

"Want me to pick you up?"

"Thanks, but Barnes is already planning to be there."

"Okay. I guess I'll see you at Parnell's office then?"

"Right. We're supposed to be there at nine?"

"Yup. Have a good flight, Meg—oh, and one more thing."

"What?"

"Take a valium."

A familiar, dramatic energy was noticeable the next morning when the collection of family and friends met in Anthony Parnell's office, as Cinnamon's counsel began discussing her estate. While she'd never divulged even the barest of facts regarding her personal resources, everyone who knew her had always assumed that her financial status did not require her to clip coupons. She had, they'd assumed, inherited a substantial sum from her father, and from Gregory as well. In addition, they thought she'd probably received a respectable amount from the sale of her dress shop in New York City. But the group sitting in front of Mr. Parnell looked like a cluster of deer facing on-coming traffic when he announced the full value of her fortune to be in excess of six million dollars.

"A trust fund for annual family excursions has been established at five hundred thousand. She has indicated, however," the attorney continued, clearing his throat and pretending not to notice that no one in the room was breathing, "that if the family elects, by a majority vote, not to pursue the excursions, these monies shall become part of the foundation she has established to benefit Albany's homeless population."

He glanced up briefly, over the rim of his glasses, to survey their stupefied faces. But even though he was tempted to make some sort of joke, he decided to proceed without any extemporaneous comments. As he did, no one was more astonished than Megan when his words revealed that she was the major beneficiary. Her holdings now included Fox Run, which carried an updated appraised value of more than one million dollars, plus two million in cash, stock, jewelry and other assets. She smiled weakly at the others in the room—particularly her mother and Kenneth—hoping their dazed looks would soon be tempered by whatever Mr. Parnell was going to say next. Much to her relief, her name wasn't mentioned again, although the remaining bequests were hardly in line with hers. *I thought you were going to make this easy for me, Gram.*

Kenneth and William were each left $500,000, through a combination of cash and securities. William, who'd never been as close to his grandmother as his brother, felt as if he'd just won the lottery. Kenneth, on the other hand, had zealously watched over both Cinnamon and David for the last several years, and his disappointment was impossible for him to mask. *I'll give him part of mine*, Megan thought, irritated that her grandmother was making her feel so uncomfortable and knowing her cousin was too much of a gentleman to address this puzzling disparity on his own. She also decided to question Mr. Parnell privately, to see if he'd been given any explanation for the disproportional splits.

For the moment, however, she tried not to look self-conscious as the attorney continued to reveal the will's contents. Claudine's name was next on the list, and she was handed a sealed letter plus a cashier's check for $250,000.

"Your mother also left you a trust fund in the approximate amount of $750,000," he added, touched by Claudine's genuine surprise.

"Oh, my," she exclaimed. "I didn't expect her to be so generous with me."

As she dabbed her eyes with the crisp linen handkerchief Cinnamon gave her one Christmas when Elliott was still alive—and which was being used for the first time today—she also found some humor in the bequest's structure. Since most of her new money was in a trust fund, Claudine quickly understood her mother's intent—to guard against potential gigolos and protect her daughter from her own propensity for injudicious behavior. Noticing that the muscles in her body were finally beginning to relax inside the wide leather arm chair, she briefly closed her eyes to whisper *thank you*, feeling closer to her mother at that moment than she had in years.

From a shelf beneath his desk, Mr. Parnell then produced a small, wooden container—about the size of a shoebox—which had been hand-painted with bright red and yellow roses.

"This is for you," he said to David, standing up and walking around his desk.

"Thank you." David's voice was barely audible as he accepted the box, placed it in his lap and brushed his fingers back and forth across the top.

"Aren't you going to open it?" Kenneth asked, expressing the collective curiosity of those around him.

"No. Not now," the old man answered, far more impressed with his box than with Mr. Parnell's next announcement.

"Cash assets in the approximate amount of $300,000 each have been deposited into two separate investment accounts, for the sole purpose of providing David McClinty Senior and Jay McClinty with health and comfort for the balance of their lives. Mrs. Stafford named me as trustee. Funds of $150,000 each have also been established for the educations of Kristin Cole and Tania Stafford, the only two great-grandchildren. While I've been named trustee of these funds as well, control will revert to Kristin and Tania when they reach the age of twenty-five."

Two final bequests were for Barnes and Heidi. The loyal chauffeur received title to the limousine and was given the promise of continued employment, if he wished to stay. Barnes had no family of his own and lived in a duplex not more than five minutes from Fox Run. He'd been married once, but his wife died in 1965, the year before he was hired by Cinnamon and David. Without any outside commitments or ties to compete for his time, he had gradually begun to feel as if he were more a member of the McClinty family than an employee, and the family treated him as such. He could not imagine what he would do if he lost the need to report to Fox Run each day. Clearly, he would stay on.

Heidi was also offered the opportunity to continue working, and she was given $5000 worth of savings bonds, which she could keep regardless of her decision. She'd only been on the payroll for a year, and she'd been worried about her job security since Cinnamon's death. Originally from Massachusetts, she'd been divorced *ever since the Eisenhower era.* On her own, with no education and limited skills, she began supporting herself and her young son by cleaning houses. Initially unhappy with her menial status, she discovered that if she treated each house as a craft project, she felt better about her accomplishments at the end of each day. Over time, this approach helped her build a respectable reputation and an adequate income. But after twelve years, she'd been looking for a change. While visiting friends in Albany, she'd seen an advertisement for a *domestic management* position and mailed her application to Fox Run.

During her first interview, she met with Kenneth, David, Barnes and, of course, Cinnamon, and was impressed with the working conditions, the idyllic surroundings, and the snug convenience of the apartment behind the kitchen. She was also intrigued at the prospect of becoming part of the inner circle for such an interesting family. At the end of her second interview a week later, she was offered the job, and within a few days had settled into her new lodgings and place of employment. Since then, she returned to Massachusetts every two or three months for a short visit with her grown son and his family. But much like Barnes, she had begun to think of Fox Run as her home—and now there was no question in her mind. She would stay on, as well.

When Mr. Parnell had turned over the last page of the will, he congratulated everyone and thanked them for coming.

"I'll notify each of you when the various papers have been prepared for your signatures, which should be within the next week. Otherwise, there's nothing for you to do, or to worry about any more. Now, I'd like to invite all of you to join me for a lunch reception, which has been prepared at Fox Run while we've been taking care of this business."

They rose from their chairs as he did, each of them shaking his hand and telling him they appreciated his professional attention. Then they began shaking each other's hands, although the atmosphere was slightly more staid than Mr. Parnell had anticipated, considering everyone's new wealth. Keenly aware of the same chemistry, Megan felt increasingly awkward about the comparative size of her inheritance, as she made her way to Kenneth's side.

"Hey, can I talk to you for a minute?"

"Sure," he said with a reassuring lilt in his voice. "But I already know what you're going to say."

"You do? How?"

"Exceptionally rich women wear a certain look on their faces."

"Kenny, please. I have no idea why she set things up this way."

"I know. I'm only teasing you, and I still love you. Besides, she always did things for a reason, even though normal people could never figure out what those reasons were."

"You can have part of my money to even things up."

"Oh, stop," he scolded playfully, putting his arms around her and making her feel immeasurably better with one of his bear hugs. "Are you going with Barnes back to Fox Run, or do you want a ride?"

"Thanks," she said, responding to his first comment with a kiss on his cheek. "Well," she said, moving on to his question, "since I rode in with Barnes, David and Heidi, I guess I should go back with them, too."

"Okay. William has his own car, and Lyle is waiting outside for your mother in their rental. So, Justine and I will follow along with them, and we'll see you there."

David positioned himself as far away from Heidi as possible, once inside the limousine. The two of them refrained from their usual banter, while Barnes navigated the long black car along a maze of surface streets. Nestled into the rear corner of the limo's cabin, Megan welcomed the quiet. *Three million dollars,* she thought, the words just beginning to bear down on her. *Gram, you were such a sneak! How did you keep this secret? And why?* Then she thought about Phillip. *What will he say? He'll probably think I'm joking,* knowing how suspicious her husband was about Cinnamon's theatrics. Looking at David, whose eyes were closed, and at Heidi sitting across from her, she also marveled at her grandmother's inclusive nature, not having forgotten a single soul who'd been of help to her.

Then Megan noticed the gnawing edge of a headache, as she remembered the McClinty Family Chart, the storage unit in Clifton Park, and the mission her grandmother left for her. By the time Barnes steered through the narrow village streets and arrived at the estate, her mind was completely scrambled again, the weight of her thoughts pressing outward and pounding at her temples. *Gram, I sure hope you know what you're doing, because I think I'm turning into a real mess, thank you very much.*

The day's luncheon was modest by Cinnamon's customary standards, because this one had been Mr. Parnell's idea. He had personally arranged for the catered buffet and the bartender stationed in the library, and he received a resounding welcome when he arrived at Fox Run an hour behind everyone else.

"Your tribute is appreciated," he said, holding his champagne glass high, along with everyone else's. "But the day belongs to you and to Mrs. Stafford. "In keeping with her affinity for the elaborate, I wanted you to have an appropriate setting to toast your new good fortune. May your lives be blessed with dreams fulfilled, and journeys well-traveled."

"Here-here!" they all responded in hearty unison.

"That was lovely, Mr. Parnell," Megan told him a short while later in the foyer. "You're not leaving so soon, are you?"

"Yes, I'm afraid I have another commitment. But I'll be in touch. How long will you be in Albany this trip?"

"Only until Sunday afternoon."

"All right. I'll find you. Meanwhile, call me if you discover some way I can be of assistance."

She said she would, but as she watched him drive off the property, she couldn't imagine how he could help her with what she had to do. In need of someone to listen to her, even when she wasn't making any sense, her first thought was of Phillip. Slipping upstairs to Cinnamon's bedroom, she stretched the phone cord over to the chaise lounge, then sat down and dialed her home number.

"*He*-llo."

"Good evening, sir. I'm looking for a handsome, charming man who's married to a very silly, but extraordinarily wealthy woman."

"Hmm. Can't say as I know anyone who meets that description."

"Wrong verb tense, sir."

"Excuse me?"

"The correct verbiage should be, *can't say I knew anyone,* blah-blah-blah."

"Oh, I see. Does this mean you're no longer silly?"

"Guess again."

"All right. Just exactly how wealthy *are* you? I mean, are *we*?"

"Repeat after me, honey—**three.**"

"Three."

"**Mill.**"

"Mill. *What*?"

"I-o-n—sounds like **yun.** Mill-yun!"

"*What*?"

"You already said that, Phillip."

"Are you serious?"

"Totally. So, what do you think?"

Frankly, he wasn't *sure* what he thought. In his business, he'd handled investments for many an overnight millionaire. With few exceptions, they'd all run amuck.

"I don't know what to say yet, Meg. My best estimate was off by several zeroes. Didn't she leave anything to anyone else?"

"Well, here's the news flash. Her estate is valued at over *six* million."

"You're kidding! That nice little old lady?"

"Yup. Mom, Kenny, William—even Barnes and Heidi—all got something. My share was the largest single block, though, which makes me a little uncomfortable. But guess what? Kristin now has a college trust fund worth $150,000. Tania has one, too. Makes you hope they want to *go*, doesn't it? We can afford to send our girl anywhere in the world!"

And so the screws of control begin to turn, he thought.

"Honey?"

"I'm here," he said. "Just trying to take it all in."

"Well, there's more. She's also created a trust fund for family excursions that I'll tell you about when I get home."

"Can't wait."

"You don't sound very happy about this, Phillip. I thought you'd be more excited."

"I am, Megan. It just caught me a bit off guard."

She recognized his verbal dance, and she could hear the insincerity in his voice, all of which made her bristle.

"Whatever," she said, her lighthearted tone suddenly brusque. "I'll call you again tomorrow."

"Wait, Meg."

"No. I should have saved this until we were together. My fault."

"I'm sorry. Let's..."

"Really, it's all right. I love you. 'Bye."

Still hanging on to the phone after she pressed the button to disconnect, she felt a rush of isolation. There in the very spot where her grandmother had died eight days earlier, her world seemed rudely off balance. But she quickly gathered her composure and went back downstairs, only to be summoned by her mother, who was leaning against the library door at the end of the hall and chatting with the bartender.

"Where in the world have you been, dear? Kenny was looking for you. He and Justine had to go pick up Tania, but he said he'd call you tonight. Something about going to Clifton Park tomorrow. Does that sound right? Who do you know in Clifton Park?"

"It's a long story, Mom."

"I see. Well, you look as if you could use a lift. How about another glass of champagne?"

"Fine." Megan's mind was still detached, as she thought about Phillip, about Kenneth, David—the *chart*.

"Bob, this is my daughter." Claudine gestured toward the bartender and forged ahead, as though there'd be some sort of penalty if she stopped talking. "Megan," she continued, passing the champagne flute, "this is Bob Crafton. Do you know that his grandfather and I went to school together? Now, isn't that one of the most unbelievable things you've heard today? That somebody's *grandfather* could have been a classmate of mine?"

Megan smiled weakly at her mother and then at Bob.

"Yes, it certainly is," she said patronizingly.

"I suppose we'd better go socialize," Claudine continued. "We'll be back to see you soon, though," she added, raising her glass in a salute to Bob.

Linking her free arm in Megan's, she pulled her daughter down the hall to the parlor, where they found David asleep. He'd been relatively animated most of the afternoon, sitting in Cinnamon's favorite wing chair and letting people fuss over him, valiant in his efforts to appear cheerful. But the deep circles under his eyes gave him away. He also drifted in and out of conversations more than usual, occasionally directing a dazed stare over the head of whomever was speaking to him. Despite his irregular expressions, however, he'd been consistently evading questions regarding his colorful wooden box, which he'd immediately carried to the guest cottage upon returning to Fox Run.

"I should go find Barnes," Megan said, softly touching the top of David's head, "so he can help us get our old friend here into bed. What are *your* plans, Mom? Will you and Lyle be leaving for Boston this weekend?"

"Actually, no. I thought I'd stay in town for a few days. Maybe drive out here tomorrow and help you go through some of your grandmother's things. What do you think?"

"I'm in *shock*," Megan answered, her voice almost haughty. "You've never stayed in town *before*!" As soon as the words were out, she saw her mother's fallen face and wished to heaven that she'd kept her mouth shut. "Mom, I'm sorry," she added quickly, wrapping her arms around Claudine. "I'm just really on edge for some reason. Please forgive me."

"Of course I do. But you're right, you know. And I may never forgive myself for that."

"No, Mom," Megan said, gently backing out of the embrace. "It was wrong and cruel of me to say what I did, and I do apologize. Gram loved you, but more importantly, she understood you. And she would not want you to hold on to any remorse. Believe me, if she were here," *and I honestly think she is*, Megan thought, "she would tell you that you must find a way to let go of any bad feelings, especially about yourself."

"That's funny," Claudine said, looking intently at Megan's eyes. "You almost *sounded* like her just then. In the letter from her that Mr. Parnell gave me in his office this morning, she said those precise words. *Find a way to let go.* Well, this has been a stressful week for all of us, and letting ourselves go—go to *bed*—would probably be the best advice. I'm serious about helping you with her things, though. It might be nice for us to share at least that much, so give it some thought. I'll call you in the morning."

"Okay, Mom."

Then the women put their arms around each other again, drawing strength from one another in this rare moment, as they wept together for the first time in memory.

Thirty minutes later, everyone was gone. Barnes had taken David to the cottage, and Heidi was busy clearing away the dishes, when Megan discovered that Bob left a full mixed pitcher of Bloody Mary's chilling inside the library bar's refrigerator. After pouring herself a glass, she sat down in a recliner beside the fireplace, her thoughts shifting to her new circumstances.

All of this is mine. Good God, that sounds awful! But it was true, and it was going to take some time to sink in. As she listened to Heidi rustling around, humming off-key to Albany's only country music station, she realized that this was her home now. *Careful. Second home. Vacation home.* But *home* nonetheless. She also became aware of a refreshing clarity in her head—a clear-cut direction, and a rush of bravery to take her there. *All right, Gram. I'll do it. I don't know how, yet. But I'll get it done.*

Awakening before dawn the next morning, she felt inspired by a sense of renewal. Knowing that neither Heidi nor Barnes would be working yet at this early hour, she dressed and went downstairs to the kitchen. There she drank a glass of apple juice with her vitamins, and then ground a fresh batch of Columbian beans, filling the coffee pot from the jug of spring water. While she waited for the brewing light to go off, she walked around the main floor with a grin on her face, opening curtains, lifting shades, and repositioning an occasional knick-knack on a table or straightening a painting on the wall. When the coffee aroma began following her from room to room, she returned to the kitchen, poured herself a cup, and went out the back door. *I still can't believe this is all mine*, she thought again as she inhaled Fox Run air and walked to the stone bench by the pond. When she sat down, she noticed the sunrise beginning to turn the cloudless sky a pale red over the treetops, and she recalled sitting in this same spot ten days earlier, surveying the land, kidding around with Kenneth, before the two of them located Nathaniel's plaque in the ivy.

That seems a lifetime ago, "which I suppose it was, technically," she said, finishing her thought out loud. "It was *Gram's* lifetime, and I didn't know *anything* then."

Glancing over at the barn, she tried to envision David and her grandmother strolling out through the massive door that night, their complicated situation fully illuminated by the moonlight.

Didn't Gram say she thought someone might have been watching them? "I need to find that part on the tapes again," she said, making a mental note as she saw Barnes turn off the road and pilot his new limousine down the driveway. Stepping out from behind the wheel, he spotted her waving at him, her long hair falling loose and backlit by the mounting daylight. Taking off his cap, he waved it at her over his head.

"Good mornin'!" he shouted across the lawn.

Returning his greeting, she walked to the house and went into the kitchen with him. Heidi emerged from her apartment shortly thereafter to join them. Their spirits were reassuringly high as they teased back and forth, exchanging small talk for nearly half an hour. But then Megan began to feel as if she were keeping them from something.

"Well, I guess you folks would like me to leave you alone, so you can get to work."

"Yes, Miss Megan," Heidi answered. "We have our regular chores to do around here, and since none of that is going to change, thankfully, we need to get busy. My first job is cooking breakfast, so you just go do whatever you want to for awhile. I'll call you when things are ready."

"Sounds good to me," Megan replied, refilling her coffee cup one more time. "What's *your* first job, Barnes?"

"Drinkin' coffee and watchin' Heidi."

Megan laughed, but Heidi did not.

"Oh, you do think you're so funny, don't you, Mr. Barnes Osgood! Well, you just hustle yourself over to the cottage and make sure Mr. McClinty's up and about. Here. Speaking of coffee, don't forget to take his with you."

'Y'know," he said. "You're just like havin' a wife, a mama and an *ex*-wife all in the same person."

"Hush!" Heidi commanded, laughing in spite of herself and relieved that Megan was laughing, too. "Go make yourself useful."

Apparently, Barnes' first job each morning was David, and Megan took comfort in that continuity. Her grandmother wasn't there, but everyone was carrying on as if she'd never left. The transition was simple and peaceful. Feeling gratified, Megan went upstairs to Cinnamon's room, opened the shades and windows, then sat down on the bed for a brief moment of reflection.

It's not the same, and yet it is. She's gone, and yet she's not. "Okay!" she said. "Out with the maudlin, in with the search. Time to dive into the haystack, pardon the pun."

Beginning with the bedroom desk, she arranged clusters of documents and scraps that looked as if they might have something in common. Then she moved on to the bureau, the end table drawers, the closet, in her search for—for *what*? While she was fascinated by the clothing and jewelry she encountered, what she really needed was information. But she found nothing of consequence, just some unpaid bills and an accumulation of third class mail.

Filing through the mounds of paper, she realized that a few practical aspects of this inherited state of affairs required immediate attention. Yesterday's notification of her change in financial status had been accepted rather matter-of-factly. Now the lengthening list of associated questions was beginning to bother her, particularly those concerning Fox Run's day-to-day operations. Using a sheet of stationery from the desk, she began making a list.

(1) Parnell re: details, i.e., Fox Run ops mgmt.

(2) Access to funds and when.

(3) Unpaid bills.

(4) Fox Run payroll?

(5) David.

After folding the list and adding it to her jeans pocket, she proceeded with her exploration. Drawn to the journals and loose papers that she'd organized the day before, she noticed the edge of something protruding from the pages of a journal about midway down in the stack. Opening the book in question, she discovered a newspaper clipping in an advanced state of decay, bearing no date other than the one referenced in the short article.

Mrs. Mimi Price, widow of New York World senior editor Bradley Price, passed away in her home on December 13, 1923, of natural causes. Mrs. Price was born, raised and educated in the Boston, Massachusetts area, and was a teacher

> **prior to her marriage. She is survived by two daughters, Margaret Elizabeth Mentini and Maggie Marie Price, both of whom were with their mother at the time of her death. Funeral Mass and burial will be held at St. Paul's Roman Catholic Church and Cemetery in lower Manhattan on December 17. Please consult with the parish rectory for details.**

In the margins, a clearly identifiable hand had written *absence of any reference to McClinty connection was intentional*, and, *Maggie not really there, but embarrassed to print.*

"Mimi. My great-grandmother," Megan whispered. "What a tragedy she turned out to be, and yet so much of what Gram ultimately became, herself, was imprinted by that sad creature. I wonder why Gram pulled this article out of wherever she was keeping it, and why she wrote the margin notes? Was she writing them to *me*?"

Flipping through the journal, she came upon the entry corresponding with the article, which she now remembered her grandmother reading to her.

...We buried Mother today. Now she's resting now, right next to Bradley, and I hope, at last, that she is happy again...

Feeling chills break out on her arms, she had a sense that this history could potentially become difficult to separate from present-day reality, if she wasn't careful.

"I need to go visit all of those graves sometime, to put everything in perspective," she said, placing the article back in the journal and closing the cover. "In the meantime, I need to stop dwelling on things I can't do anything about. I should also start keeping this stuff in a safer place," she added, gathering the six books and the collection of papers and dropping them into her travel tote beside the chaise. *Come to think of it, there have to be more journals than this*, she thought, noting that none of those in her possession contained entries beyond 1935.

Still waiting for Heidi to call her for breakfast, she began to seek out possible hiding places. Her first stop was the attic, remembering that *items contained in a roped-off section of Fox Run's attic* had been left to her grandmother when Jonathon died. But nothing was up there—not a chair, table or dish, not even any debris on the floor. Thinking that this attic had to be cleaner than most people's houses, she made her way back downstairs to the main floor. As far as she could recall, the only other source of amassed clutter was the antique secretary desk in the parlor.

During her visits to Fox Run as a child, her grandmother would prop her up on a chair piled high with needlepoint pillows so she could reach, and then scoot her up close to the desk. There she would find the paper and colored pencils that had been neatly laid out for her, and the magic would begin. She also recalled her fascination with the array of tiny drawers and cubbyholes inside the desk's cavity. Glass doors on the attached bookcase above were always locked, but the little drawers were *right there*, an arm's reach away, directly at eye level, while she drew her pictures. She was absolutely certain, at the time, that the grandest of secret treasures must be hidden in those drawers, which were strictly off-limits to her, and she obediently refrained from touching.

Occasionally, their spring and summer vacations brought all six of her male cousins to the estate when she was there, too. William was usually in the kitchen eating, so he seldom got into much trouble. But Kenneth and the others were generally not far away from some minor disaster, and more often than not, she was right in the middle of everything with them. Standing just slightly taller than the writing surface of their grandmother's desk, they would hover together, peering impishly into the cavern of drawers that teased them to open. Their little fingers loved to reach out and caress the array of shiny brass knobs, and every now and then one of them would actually dare to pull out a drawer. Of course, no one ever stayed around long enough to see what was inside. Instead, their short legs would hurriedly scamper in various directions, putting as much distance as possible between them and the desk.

The corners of Megan's mouth turned up slightly as she sat down at the desk, with those memories close by.

"I can't believe I still feel like I'm going to get in trouble," she mumbled, gripping the first knob and inching the drawer toward her.

To her astonishment, it was empty. So was the next one, and the next. Other than a few old stamps, pens, a ruler and some paper clips, she was both amused and disappointed to find nothing at all in any of them. *I must remember to tell the fellas about this.* Narrow cubicles beneath the drawers stored stationery in a rainbow of pastel shades, along with matching envelopes and a small box containing a collection of fountain pens and writing nibs. Several journal binders were there as well, but they were new and still unopened in their original wrappers. Otherwise, there was nothing of interest to be found.

Pushing the writing surface up and closed, she pressed several times before the latch was secure. Only then did she focus on the *bottom* section of the desk. Two solid doors enclosed a cupboard of some kind. *I guess I never paid any attention to this part before.* The doors wouldn't open, however. At first she thought they might be warped. But after tugging repeatedly, she realized they were locked, and she saw no evidence of a key.

"Rats!" she declared in frustration. "I've just spent the last hour getting nowhere."

Marching down the hall, she ran into Heidi, who was creating a flurry of movement between the kitchen and the dining room.

"I was just coming to get you, Miss Megan. Breakfast is cooked and warming in the oven, and I'm all set to serve you the very minute Mr. McClinty gets here."

"Is there a certain time when he comes over?"

"Yes. And it's called way-before-now. It's not his fault, though. It's Barnes. That man is always off schedule and out of step. Mrs. Stafford used to get so irritated. The two of them are worse than teenagers."

"I see," Megan responded, delighted with the unfolding blend of personalities. "Well, why don't I run over and check on them? At least that will give you a minute to relax. You wear me out just watching you."

"You're very kind. But I only have two speeds—fast and asleep. So, you needn't worry your head about me. Dropping in on them does sound like a good idea, though. No telling what they might be up to."

Megan went out the back door and ambled across the lawn to the cottage. There she found David awake and dressed, and playing checkers with Barnes on the ornate game table in his small living room.

"How delightful to see your pretty face in the morning!" David announced, nearly shouting and quickly losing interest in his three men who'd just been jumped by Barnes' king. "Now, if I could only figure out how to see you before I see *this* guy, everything would be perfect. He cheats, you know," David kidded, lobbing a wadded napkin at the chauffeur. "I hope you'll be staying with us a long time, my dear."

She averted his eyes, deciding this wasn't the right time to tell him she was leaving again tomorrow.

"Well, the most important thing, at the moment, is breakfast. Heidi is ready and waiting for us, and I've been sent to retrieve you gentlemen."

"That woman is *always* ready and waiting," David said, his tone of voice playful, despite his sharp words. "She really gets on my nerves!"

"You're just upset because she's funnier than you are."

"You can say that again, Miss Megan," Barnes interjected. "She's funny, all right."

"Funny *looking*, you mean," David added, his eyes laughing.

"All right. That's enough from both of you," Megan chided gently, heartened by their repartee. "You're being very unkind. Heidi is a nice lady, and you're going to hurt her feelings, if you're not careful."

"I guess Megan has a point," David said, giving Barnes a conspiratorial glance. "Especially since it seems that Heidi is the only woman left who'll have anything to do with either one of us."

"Now *that*, my man," Barnes replied, patting David on the back, "is depressing as hell!"

Megan saw them wink at each other and stifle their smiles.

When they were back in the main house, Barnes ushered David and Megan to the dining room, and then took his leave, announcing that he had a full day's work ahead of him.

"You wouldn't know a full day's work, if one climbed into bed with you," Heidi called after him, as she placed the serving dishes on the table. Trying not to look at David, Megan had a hard time keeping a straight face.

What began as a routine breakfast lasted for more than two hours, once David began opening up to her. She could tell that his need to talk was therapeutic, and she tried not to take advantage of the situation. Nonetheless, his firsthand knowledge of so many things was irresistible. Beginning with lighthearted comments about what a *pain in the neck* Cinnamon had become, his reflection gradually became more serious as he willingly answered the questions Megan introduced.

After Gregory died in 1960, the living arrangement at Fox Run had taken shape. David had been spending most of his time there anyway, staying in the guest cottage, since Gregory rarely traveled to Albany after the tragedy in Hawaii.

"And the Madison house had turned into a dismal hole for me," he said. "There wasn't even very much furniture left there, and it was way too big for me anyway. My boys had been trying to get me to move for years, but when there was only DJ left—well, I…"

He took a moment to compose himself.

"The memories in that house kept me awake all the time," he continued, "and your grandmother told me I looked so bad that I reminded her of a cement block. She always did have a way with words. Anyway, after Gregory passed away, she came up with the idea for me to live in the cottage. It was intended as a temporary situation, until the Madison house sold and I decided where I wanted to go. All of this was supposed to be for the betterment of my health. That's funny, because after I got here, she nearly gave me a heart attack by sharing her *special news* with me, as she called it."

He looked immediately at Megan to see what her eyes were saying, and when she reached for his hands in acknowledgment, he seemed immeasurably relieved that she knew.

"Hiding things all the time can make you so tired," he told her. "Years fell off her face the minute she told me, and I never understood why she thought she had to wait so long. It would have been so nice to know, while Greg was still—well, you know," he added, amazingly in control of his emotions. "There's a master plan for each of us, though, which you finally get to see when you're as old as I am. We had so many tragedies, she and I. But we had a lot of joy, too—all part of a plan. That plan is finished, though, and I must tell you, Megan, that I'm not sure how long I can stand it here without her."

Okay. That's enough. "I don't mean to change the subject," she said, folding her napkin on the table and pushing her chair back, "but we've been sitting here far too long. Why don't I help you back to the cottage? Maybe you can answer a few logistical questions about Fox Run on the way."

"Yes, I think I would like to lie down," he said, as she helped him up from his chair. "What is it that you want to know?"

"I found several unpaid bills on the desk in her room, and I presume those are now my responsibility. But I didn't see her checkbook anywhere."

"That's because she hasn't paid a bill in twenty-five years. Anthony Parnell took care of everything, for both of us. We'd either mail things to him, or he'd stop by."

"That sounds simple enough. I'll call him later. By the way," she said, as she guided him through the hall and past the parlor, "the bottom section of that desk over there is locked, and I couldn't find a key for it. Would you know where she kept it? Or what's inside?"

"I'm almost afraid to think about what she could have put in there. But a key? I couldn't say. The only one I've seen that's big enough is the one in the box."

"The box? *What* box?"

"The wooden one with the red and yellow roses, the one Anthony gave me in his office yesterday," he answered, his arm linked in hers while they walked down the front steps and across the yard to the cottage. "She painted those flowers herself, you know. I saw her, but she wouldn't tell me why she was doing it. Made me guess, like on a game show, if you can believe it. Of course, I never got the right answer out of her. She *was* such a pain. Anyway, she put a few little things in it for me. Would you like to see them?"

She put a few little things in it? Standing next to him in his living room, she couldn't stop her pulse from accelerating.

"No, David, I don't want to pry."

"You're not. Besides, I offered, and you already know the story anyway. So, we don't need to keep secrets. Actually, this is good. That key is the only thing I didn't understand. If you hadn't mentioned it, I probably would have made myself nuts wondering what it was for. It might not work, but you're welcome to try it."

She followed behind him as he shuffled to the rear of the cottage and into his bedroom. After opening the closet door, he removed the box from the top shelf, sat down on the bed, and leaned back against the headboard.

"Here, Megan. Sit beside me. I need to rest."

"Then let's do this after your nap. It's not that important."

"Nonsense. Sit. Come to think of it, I have something else that might be of interest to you. On the same closet shelf over there is a big tin container. It's where I keep a lot of the letters she wrote to me. Most of them started showing up after I moved into this place. Never could understand her. I used to tell her she was a crazy woman, always complaining about not having enough time to do this or that, but spending hours writing to me. She could just as easily have said what was on her mind right to my face. We only lived a hundred feet from each other, for God's sake, and we spent every day together. But, as usual, she never heard a word I said. I found letters stuffed in my clothes, in the medicine cabinet, in my food. Nearly drove me out of my mind. Anyway, if you want to take a look at them, please help yourself."

Stay calm. There's plenty of time. Take a deep breath. "Thank you, David. I just might do that."

He raised the lid of the wooden box, which he was balancing on his lap.

"Here," he said, nonchalantly handing her a large silver key. "That's the one I was talking about. She also left another note for me. Then, of course, she gave me *this*."

He held out an envelope for her to take, his eyes suddenly growing cloudy.

"Do you want me to open it now?"

"Yes," he said.

As she removed and unfolded the contents, Megan realized that she was holding the birth certificate for **Gregory Brian Stafford Junior**. Struggling not to hyperventilate, she focused on the printed responses to the form's routine questions.

...**DATE OF BIRTH:** June 21, 1933...**SEX OF CHILD:** Male...**LEGITIMATE?** Yes...**CONGENITAL DEFORMITIES:** None...**BIRTHMARKS:** One. Triangular-shaped, 5 inches in length, right side of body just above waist... **BLOOD TYPE:** O...

When she lifted her eyes, David tilted his head slightly and shrugged his shoulders, a narrow stream of tears sliding down his cheeks.

"It's like looking at a ghost, isn't it? I wonder, Megan, if I'll learn to stop reacting this way before I die."

"Listen. You don't have to learn how to stop *anything*."

"Oh, so you think," he said, the mischievous look reappearing on his face, despite the tears. "For your information, I had to learn how to stop having sex. No one seems to have the time. Even Heidi won't consider it."

"You are completely impossible, you know!" she said, relieved that the disquieting moment seemed to have ended.

"Well, it's your grandmother's fault. Okay, where were we? Oh, yes. There's one more thing in my box—a poem. I'd like to read it to you, if you wouldn't mind."

His voice was strong, his emotions steady. As he verbally lifted each line from the page, his eyes remained clear, his breathing calm.

She's with him, Megan thought. *As sure as I'm sitting here, she is with him.*

A Magic Like December

When I see you for the last time,
It will be just as we've planned.
Simply take my hand
And say hello.

When I love you for the last time,
You will feel my body quake.
Perhaps my heart will break.
I don't yet know.

But we'll give ourselves a magic
Like December
That we'll call upon some night
When we are cold—

And we'll build a time that only
We'll remember,
That will make us smile some day
When we've grown old.

When I know you for the last time,
There'll be laughter all around,
And the sweet and gentle sound
Of us at play.

When I kiss you for the last time,
If a tear should brush your cheek,
Please don't try to speak.
Just walk away.

For you have been a magic
Like December
That I'll call upon some night
When I am cold—

And you are in a time that only
I'll remember,
That will make me smile some day
When I've grown old.

M.E.M.S.
July 11, 1988

"I want to sleep now, Megan."

"All right," she said, amazed that she could speak at all while she unfolded the blue crocheted afghan from the foot of his bed and pulled it over him.

How could a love that powerful have gone unnoticed all these years?

On her way out of his room, she held the key tightly in one hand and went to the closet, where she removed the tin container from the top shelf. It was at least a foot long and about five inches deep, and quite heavy. As she switched off the light, she turned to look at David again. His eyes were closed, his respiration deep and slow. Cinnamon's poem was pressed firmly between his hands and his chest.

After walking directly from the cottage to the parlor, she slipped David's key in the desk lock and was delighted to feel it turn easily, the doors swinging open on the first try. The only item inside was a metal strongbox, measuring two feet square by eight inches deep, which was secured by a padlock and inserted vertically into the desk's filing section. After removing the box and relocking the desk, she carried her discovery upstairs to her grandmother's room and shut the door behind her. She then began prying and hammering at the padlock with every object she could find—nail files, hangers, shoes—all to no avail. The strongbox was on the floor, and she was pounding on it with a bookend, when she heard Heidi knocking.

"Miss Megan, excuse me for bothering you. Are you awake?"

"Does it *sound* like I'm sleeping in here?"

"No, ma'am, it does not. That's why I thought it would be okay to knock."

"Well, what on earth do you need?"

"Oh, I don't need a thing. It's just that you have a visitor."

Megan concentrated for a moment to make certain she hadn't overlooked an appointment.

"I'm not expecting anyone. Who is it?" But Heidi had already gone.

Moving quickly from frustrated to irritable, she left the still unopened box on the floor and stomped downstairs, prepared to deliver a statement on common courtesy to whomever had dropped in unannounced. But as she spun around the corner into the parlor, she saw Preston McClinty standing in front of the desk, admiring the collection of leather-bound books behind the glass.

"Hi," he said, moving toward her, his arms outstretched. "I hope I'm not interrupting anything."

"Good heavens, no," she insisted, her mood moderating instantly from deep within his embrace. "How wonderful to see you. What brings you to Fox Run?"

"I flew in from Boston yesterday to check on Dad. He's been confused by all the people who've been calling him, because, through some self-defense mechanism, he seems to have forgotten that his sister is dead."

"Oh, no."

"I've been trying to bring him back to reality, but he just keeps nodding at me and asking me what time she wants us over here for dinner."

"What are you going to do?"

"I don't know yet. I did buy an answering machine for him, though, and I programmed it to pick up on the first ring. The messages are recorded internally, so he won't hear them. Someone on the staff there will transcribe them for me several times a day, and there's also a remote feature I can use from Boston. I'm hoping that fewer calls from well-meaning friends will help reduce his confusion. Other than that, I'm not sure what I'll do. But I really didn't come by to talk about Dad. I heard you were staying through the weekend, and I wanted to make sure you were okay."

"You're very sweet to be concerned. But I'm fine, just suddenly busy putting her things in order. You know how it is."

"Yes. That's why I've been worried about you. Are you sure there isn't any way I can help you out while I'm here?"

"Honestly, I'm sure. Thank you, though, for..."

*...Talk to your cousins. I think many of them will have pieces of information that will be helpful when consolidated in one place...*The words surged at her unexpectedly.

"Actually, now that you mention it, Preston, maybe there *is* something you can do. Do you have time to stay and visit for a few minutes?"

Megan had just poured a glass of wine for each of them, and they were seated at the bar in the library when the telephone rang.

"Maybe I should have you install one of those silent answering machines here, too," she said to him lightly, as she picked up the receiver. The caller was Katrina Wallace inviting Megan to brunch in Clifton Park in the morning.

"I know you're leaving for Atlanta tomorrow night, so if this is pushing you too much, I'll understand."

"No, that's fine, Katrina. I'm very anxious for us to meet. Does your invitation also include my cousin Kenneth? He was with me when we left the note for you on Lark Street."

"Of course. I should have been more specific. We are definitely hoping to see both of you."

Megan then wrote the directions on the back of a bar napkin, after a fruitless search for a message pad.

"Wonderful. We'll see you tomorrow at nine-thirty."

Apologizing to Preston and thanking him for his patience, she then dialed Kenneth's house and left all the brunch information on his voice recorder when no one answered.

"Call me if there's any problem with this," she said in her message. "Otherwise, I'll be at your house about 8:15 in the morning. That will give me time to say hi to Justine and Tania, and then we can drive up to Clifton Park together. 'Bye."

"Everything okay?" Preston asked, as she sat back down on the barstool next to him and took a sip of wine.

"Yes. Just a little unfinished Gram-business."

"Uh-oh. Sounds dangerous," he said with a smile. "Now, a few minutes ago you mentioned that there might be something I could do for you?"

"Well, it's really not a *do*. Frankly, I'm looking for a chance to bend your ear on sort of an offbeat subject. It might take a little while, though. So, if you're short on time, we can get together again on my next trip up here."

"I'm at your disposal, Megan. The wine is good, and the company is better. I don't have to be back in Boston until day after tomorrow, and Dad's villa complex is having a combination lunch and bingo game for the next several hours. That makes me all yours."

Megan excused herself for a minute and went to the kitchen where she asked Heidi to prepare a tray of cold cuts, cheese, crackers, fruit and an assortment of condiments. When she returned to the library, Preston was refilling his wine glass and had opened a second bottle of Chardonnay, which was chilling in the bar sink.

"I think everything is in order now, so we can concentrate," she said, sitting down next to him again.

"All right, my friend," he queried softly. "What's the problem?"

She summarized highlights from her recording sessions with Cinnamon, reciting verbatim the instructions in her grandmother's final letter about solving the mystery behind Greg's death. At the last minute, however, she decided not to mention the delicate matter of David's paternal connection to Cinnamon's dead son. *Maybe later.* Amazingly, Preston appeared to be completely absorbed in what she was saying.

"You realize," he said, when she came to a stopping point, "that I think you're crazy. But if you want to spend your time on this wild goose chase, I'll help if I can. I'm not sure what I can do, though."

"Share your memories with me, Preston. Anything you can remember about Greg, the family, their lives back then."

"My world was pretty narrow, Meg, and my perspective will be fairly limited."

"I don't care. It's still important."

"How far back do you want me to go?"

"I'll leave that up to you."

His exploration of the early years was clumsy at first. But the wine made him feel more at ease, as he recalled the remarkable friendship between his mother and Cinnamon.

"Once I was old enough to look at them with some measure of objectivity, I was impressed that their relationship had been so durable. To this day, I've never known two people more different from one another. Why they ever got along is the *real* mystery."

"Not really. Not if you study them. They filled each other's empty spaces."

"What a lovely thing to say, Megan. Rather lyrical. Have you been a poet in hiding all this time?"

"No, I can promise you I haven't," she answered, amused at the thought. "My lack of talent in that area strained the patience of many an English teacher. My grandmother was the poet."

"Indeed? I didn't know. And thus we uncover another facet of an already intriguing personality."

"You have no idea how many layers there were to her. But she was a very prolific writer—something I think she inherited from her mother and grandmother. Maybe someday there'll be a chance for me to show you pieces of her work."

"I'd like that very much."

Their eyes fastened together for an instant, and Megan felt a wave of—what *was* that?—pass through her body.

"I just lost my train of thought," he said, his coy smile awakening all of her senses. "Oh, yes. I was talking about Mother and Aunt Cinnamon. Despite their differences, they shared an uncompromising dedication to their three children, which included me, naturally."

The grin on his face revealed subtle dimples that she'd never noticed until now, as he continued describing his parents' heartwarming marriage, the constant visits back and forth between Fox Run and The Corbett Place where he'd lived—and *his feelings about his cousins!*

"Even though DJ was the oldest, your mother was always the one in charge, Meg. No matter what activity, or trouble, we found ourselves in, the origins could generally be traced back to Claudine. Most of us went along with her, because her ideas were terrific, frankly, even if she *was* a girl. She'd have us digging underground passages to the Orient—usually in some neighbor's prize garden—or searching for abandoned treasures, with maps she claimed had been drawn by pirates. As you might suspect, she made sure she was directing our operations, while the rest of us were stuck with the digging. I think she picked up her leadership skills on the streets of New York City before they moved back to Fox Run. Supposedly, that was a pretty tough neighborhood."

Broome Street, Megan thought. *I wish I had time to tell you.*

"Most of us didn't complain about her bossy ways, though," Preston continued. "Ryan was the only exception. He was sort of an odd bird. Talked to himself more than he did to the rest of us. I remember being sad about him at first, thinking he might be lonesome. Mother explained that artists often have difficulty expressing themselves, other than through their work, and some of them don't have many friends. *That* I understood. But as Ryan got older, he turned mean, and none of us felt comfortable around him any more."

"What happened?"

"He beat up a boy at school, who'd called him a sissy. And he didn't just punch the kid in the nose. He beat him senseless. Unfortunately, Lucille was dead, and David wasn't much of a disciplinarian, although he did come down on Ryan pretty hard after that incident. But Ryan felt no remorse. He even laughed about it to us. From then on, we all kept our distance from him—and believe me, no one ever called him a sissy again. Weird guy!

"What about Teddy?"

"Ah, yes. Teddy. I idolized him. He was four years older than me, handsome, funny and a gentle, caring soul. But he had a bit of a cross to bear, because even though no one would talk about it, Lucille died giving birth to him. When he was old enough to understand, I think it was very hard for him to deal with that piece of information. Over the years, though, it seemed to add to his sensitivity. You would have loved him, Meg. Anyway, when your grandmother moved back to Albany, Greg was added to our play group. His age was right in the middle between Teddy and me, and the three of us hung around together quite a bit when we were younger. Greg started pitching off on his own when we got into our teens. But Teddy and I stayed close. C'est la vie. In the end, I lost them both."

And so we have arrived. "What about that, Preston? I mean, what about losing them? What do you remember?"

"Everything. Sort of like the Kennedy assassination. Some events are just frozen in space and time, each second instantly and vividly recalled."

He took a bite of cheese and cracker from the tray Heidi had brought in a few minutes earlier, followed by a sip of wine—then another sip.

"I was eighteen, finishing my senior year in high school. *You*, by the way, were only six or seven, and very spoiled, if there's enough of my memory left to serve me correctly."

"I was not spoiled."

"Yes, you were. But you got over it. At any rate, Dad came to my school to pick me up. He was a mess, and I could hardly understand him. When I finally did, I couldn't believe what I was hearing—both Greg and Teddy dead! Even now, it doesn't sound real."

Preston then reviewed that first infamous week of family history using words like *numb, hysteria, nightmare, bizarre.*

"But the one image etched most clearly in my mind," he said, his voice growing quiet, "was the night I went to the airfield with Dad to meet the plane from Hawaii. I watched those caskets being unloaded, as if the scene were part of a newsreel in a theater. Dad stood straight as a statue. I looked over at him once and saw his face. He was crying. I'd never seen him cry before. His body stood tall and strong, his head high. But his face…I'll never forget it, Megan."

Still sitting side-by-side on the barstools, they leaned into one another. She brushed her fingers across the top of his hand. His left shoulder and arm were pressed against her right. Their faces were inches apart.

"What an awful memory to carry with you."

"It was. But as a physician I can tell you that even the most ghastly visions eventually begin to fade, and we lost Greg and Teddy a very, *very* long time ago. Besides, that incident was just the start of two turbulent years for the family, as I'm sure you're well aware."

"From what I understand, Gram was in pretty bad shape and not part of the real world during that whole period, starting from the moment when she heard about Greg's death."

"Actually, that's not quite accurate. Mother and I talked about this once, and she finally told me I'd be better off if I left it alone. So I did. But I remember how sturdy your grandmother was in those first few days. She was obviously, and understandably, distraught and in shock. We *all* were. Yet Aunt Cinnamon was lucid, very involved with the funeral arrangements, and personally handling phone calls and visits from people who were extending their sympathy. She was also determined to learn, and more importantly *accept*, any details of what had happened. I remember sitting in the parlor of this very house, with my mother beside me, as a completely rational Aunt Cinnamon said that the only way to survive such an unimaginable atrocity was to find out the facts, no matter how unbearable the truth might be. *From knowledge comes healing,* she said to us."

"But Preston, Gram told me that she was in seclusion and in really bad shape for two years after Greg died."

"Well, that's partially true. Some people in our family believe she never *did* come out of it. I swear to you, though, that her suffering was under control, until the day after the burials. And now that I'm thinking about it, the changes didn't start showing up in her until after the big blowout argument."

"What argument was that?"

"The one between Aunt Cinnamon and Uncle Gregory, after the funeral service. They were right here in this library that night, with the door closed. I was in the parlor with Mother and Dad, so we couldn't really understand what was being said. But the pitch of their voices was shaking the china in the cabinets. Cinnamon finally came running down the hall, sobbing uncontrollably. She headed straight upstairs and shut herself in her bedroom. *That's* when Aunt Cinnamon's breakdown started, in my opinion. The years have mixed up the chronology for a lot of people, but your grandmother was just fine until that moment."

"What happened after that?"

"Well, it wasn't over, you know. In fact, it was only beginning, although none of us would have believed that it could get worse. But a few weeks later, Aunt Cinnamon's sister committed suicide, and within days of Maggie's death, Ryan also killed himself."

"*What*? I thought Ryan died in an automobile accident."

"He did die in an automobile, but it wasn't an accident. All the evidence indicated that his foot was on the accelerator when he rammed into the only tree near that section of road—a very straight road, I might add, with no complicating weather, and no evidence of alcohol or drugs."

"How horrifying! But *why*?"

"That's an answer I don't have for you. Aunt Cinnamon was in Manhattan taking care of her sister's funeral arrangements when she heard about Ryan. Fortunately, Mother was already there with her to help her get home. After that, no one in the family thought that she *or* David would live through the ordeal."

"What about Gregory? Where was *he* during all of this?"

"He just sort of faded away. Never once came back to Albany after Greg and Teddy's funerals. Dad couldn't understand it, and he even went to New York to talk to him. He knew Gregory was also grieving over his son's loss, but leaving his wife alone with her suffering was something none of us could imagine. When Dad got back from New York, though, he said that talking with Gregory was like having a conversation with the side of a building—a *frozen* building. The man did send money several times a month, through Dad, but other than that, he was totally useless. So, my mother started going out to Fox Run every single day, since she was the only person your grandmother would let inside, other than the household staff. Mother said that sometimes she'd just sit and read, or crochet, or write letters, not even seeing Aunt Cinnamon. Other times, she said her dearest friend in the world had reverted to being a child and was in complete denial about everything. I went away to college in the fall of that first year, and whenever I came home on vacation, I was more worried about my mother than the time before. She looked so drained, and her spirit was gone. Dad was really concerned, too. But no amount of talking could keep her away from Fox Run. As it turned out, though, she probably helped save Aunt Cinnamon's life. My dad, DJ and I share the credit for keeping David going. It was a pretty brutal couple of years."

"I can't even imagine! How were they finally able to put it behind them?"

"I was completing my undergraduate studies, so I can't report firsthand. But Dad said that, when Mother came back from Fox Run one day, Aunt Cinnamon was in the car with her. He said she looked incredibly thin and the color of chalk, but her strength of mind was alive and well, along with her sense of humor. Dad called me that night, and the relief in his voice took a real load off my mind. Having both his sister—and his wife, too, in a sense—among the living again was nothing short of a miracle. The next day, I think, they all went to see David at the Madison house, and they managed to bring him out, too. I was only home for short vacations after that, once I started med school. But things seemed about as normal as possible, except, of course, for your grandmother's conspiracy theory, which we all wrote off as a minor side-effect of the nightmare. Eventually, thank God, she stopped harping on it."

He finished the last of his wine and set the glass back down on the bar with a light thud, as if placing a period at the end of his sentence.

"There you have it, Meg. You ask a simple question and get War and Peace in response. Sorry. Was any of that soliloquy the least bit useful to you?"

"Whew! I'm afraid I'll have to let it all sink in before I can answer that. But thanks so much for sharing what you remember with me. The story would be fascinating enough, even if I didn't *know* any of the people. You must think I have a few buttons missing, though, and I do appreciate your indulging me, especially with your busy schedule. Can I get you something else? More food? Another drink?"

"No, thanks. I've had more than enough already, and I really should be on my way. Dad's bingo game is probably over by now, and it doesn't take him very long to find trouble. But I'll be staying with him until tomorrow night, you know, in case you need me. Meanwhile," he added, kissing her lightly on her cheek and stroking her hair, "please try to get a little rest. You've been through a lot, and that old Superwoman Syndrome can knock the wind out of you, if you're not careful. Take it from the old doc here."

Then, as quickly as he'd appeared, he was gone. Megan was watching through the parlor window as he drove away, shaking herself free from the lingering influence of his touch, when she remembered the wealth of material awaiting her upstairs. Despite the slight buzz from three glasses of wine, she felt the first clear plan of attack since her grandmother's death. *I need to find the journals from 1953,* she thought, as she returned to Cinnamon's bedroom and flipped again through the six books she'd placed in her travel tote. *Maybe I missed something.* But that collection of writing only represented, as she'd seen earlier, a portion of time through the mid-1930's.

Lying down on the plush carpeting, on her back, she put her hands behind her head and stared up at the ceiling fan, trying to slow the swell of aggravation. *They've got to be here somewhere.* Rolling over on her side, she was starting to push herself to her feet when she caught a glimpse of something underneath the bed—a box.

"Eureka!" she said out loud, pulling the box toward her and seeing journals piled nearly to the top. Lifting her discovery onto the chaise lounge, she began thumbing through each book. After a dozen or more, her fingers suddenly came to rest on one of the yellowed pages, as an eerie tremor swept through her.

May 24, 1953

Tonight when I go to sleep, if I'm even able to sleep, my prayer will be that a merciful God will allow me to awaken and find that this is all a frightfully horrid mistake. Morning will bring us word that they were wrong—that my son was not taken from me, after all. Please, let there be no truth to this nightmare.

May 25

The torture will not end. Two men from the Army came to the house this morning. They were very polite and tried to be comforting. But they said that Greg and Teddy will be coming home tomorrow, so how could they expect me to be comforted? My mind knows now that this has happened, but my heart will not yet accept what I've been told. Perhaps when Greg has returned—perhaps when I can see him—I will find that breathing my next breath will have become easier. Maurice gave me some pills to help me sleep. I have just taken two.

May 26

Greg and Teddy did not come home today as promised. There is some sort of procedural delay in Hawaii, while they attempt to clarify the details behind the accident. We are now told that the boys will be here tomorrow. The pain is nearly too much for everyone. It's the waiting more than anything. DJ brought David to see me this morning. He looked far worse than I expected he would, and I'm so glad now that I never told him. Twice the pain would surely be fatal to him. Gregory has not yet traveled to Albany, and there was no sign of life in his voice on the phone last night. I'm very worried about him, but he's assured me that he'll arrive before Greg does. Thank God for Angela. She has scarcely left my side.

May 27

No one will let me see him! He is sealed away from me, and all I can touch is the steel box that holds him. How will I ever be able to live with this, if I cannot see my boy one more time?

May 29

Yesterday I was with Greg all day, while people came to pay their respects. Today I said goodbye to him. I'm told the ceremony was lovely, but I have no memory of it. Tonight I feel nothing. Perhaps tomorrow, after I visit the cemetery again, I will begin to find some connection to life without my son, although I suppose I'll need to find my heart again before that can happen.

May 30

<u>God took my son and crushed my soul, then asked me to be strong and go forward</u>. This I was prepared to do. But there is no possible way for me to bear the vile stench that spews forth from the man I call my husband! Life, for all meaningful purposes, has now come to an end. Come il diavolo è entrato nella casa mia? How did the devil get into my house?

August 11, 1953

Truth has the power to enrich, to change, or to ruin lives—sometimes in the telling, sometimes in the withholding. I fear that I'm guilty of both, and enrichment is the consequence I've been denied. Instead, change and ruination are consuming me. I cannot imagine when I will next marvel at the miracle of a sunrise, if, indeed, the new insidious truth I read about today proves itself valid. However indirect my culpability may be, the loss of Maggie and Ryan is fully on my conscience—and all the light in my soul appears to have been extinguished.

The next entry, on a clean page, was written almost two years later.

Endings and Beginnings
April 14, 1955

Angela took me home with her today, so I could see my brother. She always has such good ideas. The sight of Jay made me realize how very much I have missed him—missed everyone, actually. Then, as I thought further, I realized the most remarkable thing. I'm finally feeling again. I also lifted the shades on my bedroom windows when we returned to Fox Run this afternoon, to let in the sunshine. I think, maybe, it's time to begin anew.

The remaining pages of that particular journal were filled with commentary about her re-entry into the world of her family and her daily life, the entries spanning more than a year. As she read, Megan felt the revitalized essence of her grandmother in every line.

...Everyone thinks I'm a raving lunatic...Went downtown to do some overdue shopping this afternoon. Thought I could use one or two new outfits. Can't believe how fashions have changed in these few short years. Vincente would be horrified!...They were all talking about me. I could tell by the way they turned away...The subject came up again today in a conversation with Jay and Angela. But I don't care what they say. From knowledge comes healing, and in order for me to stay well, I must never stop searching for the true explanation. Never!...

The final entry in this particular journal was written on July 4, 1956.

This is your life, of which you speak.
These are the loves you sought to earn.
Write it down, so they'll remember.
Write it down, that they might learn.

And thus, I will continue.
M.E.M.S.

Megan closed the journal cover. Behind her, on the bed, was David's unopened tin of letters. The strongbox was on the floor, still unlocked.

"Dear Lord," she whispered, "what the hell am I getting myself into?"

She had only one more day left to deal with this, before her life returned to normal. As she stared at the unfinished business inside her grandmother's inventive boxes, she realized that no matter how much she wanted to pursue the search, there was no realistic way for her to get it all done—not on *this* trip. *I should focus on a single piece of the project, and then put the rest away,* she decided, pushing the box of journals, including the six from her travel tote, back under the bed, along with David's letter collection.

"I guess it's you and me," she said, lifting the strongbox from the floor and setting it on the chaise. "Then, that's *it*—absolutely, positively *it*!"

But there wasn't much strength of conviction to accompany her words. Suddenly wishing for the reassuring sound of Phillip's voice, she walked over to the princess phone on the end table and dialed her house in Atlanta. But no one answered, and she decided not to leave a message.

It's Saturday, and he's probably out with Kristin doing something fun, like I should be. "Oh, well, I don't know what I'd say to him anyway. Besides, tomorrow night I'll be home." *And then I'm sure I'll be okay.*

Chapter 19

Megan found Barnes on the opposite side of the pond, pontificating about some obscure political issue to a landscape maintenance man who was spraying the lawn. *See, this is the kind of thing I need to know about,* she thought, as she approached them. *For instance, who scheduled this man? And why? How does he get paid? Etcetera, etcetera, etcetera.*

"Hi, Barnes. And hello to you, too," she said, nodding at the landscape man. "I'm Megan Cole, the owner's granddaughter." *Not quite accurate any more. Strange.* "Is this some sort of regular lawn maintenance you're performing?"

"No, ma'am. I'm spraying for crabgrass. Mrs. Stafford ordered this done about a month ago, but we've just been able to get to it now."

"Oh, I see," Megan said, deciding not to press the point, since this fellow was just doing his job. "Well, thank you very much." Turning her attention back to Barnes, she continued. "Could you help me out with something?"

"Sure," he answered, gesturing goodbye to the landscape man. "What's up?"

She led him to the front porch where she'd carried the strongbox.

"We need to figure out a way to break this lock. I've tried every girl-tool I could find," she added, smiling at him as he ran his hand over the dent she'd made with the bookend. After examining all sides of the box, he invited her to follow him to his tool shed behind the barn, where he spent fifteen minutes using a crowbar, pliers, and a vice, all to no avail.

"Miss Megan, I'm afraid to hammer on this much more. If anythin' of value's in there, it's gonna be a mess. And I'd hate to be the one you remember ruinin' whatever it is. My wife used to have a padlock like this on a thing she called her treasure box. It was really old, somethin' bought durin' the Depression—and she had a key for it, like a jailer's key, only smaller. Betcha the locksmith in Delmar could open this in a jiff. Want me to run it over there?"

Discouraged but wondering if this might be a subtle message telling her to leave the whole thing alone, she smiled and took the box from him.

"Thanks, Barnes. But I don't think I'm going to worry about it after all. It's probably not that important. I appreciate your trying, though."

"Okay," he said behind her, as she made her way across the yard. "Let me know if you change your mind."

...My wife used to have a padlock like this one...she had a key for it, like a jailer's key, only smaller...

...Vincente had just finished locking another $200 in the strongbox, and Cinnamon sat at the kitchen table, watching him put the box under the floorboards. Then he unrolled the braided rug on top of the hiding place and handed her the small brass jailer's key threaded through a long silver chain, which he insisted she wear around her neck beneath her undergarments...

"What?" Megan's pace quickened, until she was sprinting toward the kitchen door. "Could it be possible?"

Upstairs in Cinnamon's room, she returned to the jewelry chest on top of the bureau, which she'd so hastily discounted earlier in the day. Carefully re-examining the contents of each miniature drawer, she sifted through dozens of pins, necklaces, earrings, bracelets and charms, untangling each piece to make certain she hadn't missed anything. Then, in a back corner of the bottom drawer, she saw it. Curled under a strand of pearls was a long silver chain, and hanging from the chain was a small brass key.

"Very funny, Gram. Did you overlook this little detail in your volumes of instructions and clever clues, or are you trying to have me committed on purpose?"

Seated on the bed, her heart and head both pounding, she turned the key in the padlock. It sprang open without resistance. But the box was severely dented, thanks to her own use of force and that of Barnes, so she had to use the letter opener from the desk to pry the lid open. After that, a slight breeze could have blown her over, as she stared inside.

Tied with a long piece of white lace ribbon was a stack of currency. When she picked up the money and studied it, she discovered that she was holding twenty-eight $100 bills, four $20's and one $10, each bearing a Series date of 1929. They were still crisp and looked as if they'd never been removed from the box.

"Oh my God! This must be the money from her dress shop. And she never used any of it? I can't believe this."

But there was more. Underneath the money was a folder that filled the entire space inside the box and looked like a large envelope made out of poster board. The folder was wedged down along the sides and corners, so Megan used the letter opener again to ease it up. After gently opening the flap, she found herself inhaling deeply while she pulled out a one-inch thick collection of fashion sketches, all signed at the bottom by Vincente Mentini.

…"Imagine the power," he'd said, during one of their recent fire escape dialogues, "if wealthy, influential women from the uptown neighborhoods depended upon me for the designs that would make them look more beautiful and elegant than their contemporaries—or better yet, than their rivals." He was the only person she knew, now that Bradley was gone, who had living dreams and who spoke about them with passion…

"Vincente," Megan whispered. "Grandpa." She could almost feel the presence of this distinctive man she never knew, as she was fixated by each page of his designs—the lines, the detail and beauty. "These could be made into garments *today*, and no one would be able to tell they were created…oh my gosh! It's been almost *fifty years*! Gram, this gift is beyond imagination. You must have loved him so very much."

Afraid to handle the fragile drawings any longer, she was sliding them back into the folder when something else caught her eye inside the strongbox—a weathered parchment envelope, secured with a brittle wax seal that broke easily with a nudge from the letter opener. *I'm not sure I can take much more of this*, she thought, afraid of what might be coming next. The folded correspondence was written on plain stationery, which had probably been white in the beginning, but was now yellow with age.

September 19, 1938

Margaret, rather than use the telephone, I have decided to write all of this down for you and bring it with me when I am out in your neighborhood later this week. I trust you will be pleased with this surprise addition to your collection of McClinty family history.

As I suspected when you brought little Greg into my office, I can now tell you with certainty that his rash is from the measles. Fear not. He will recover, my dear, although he will be rather uncomfortable for the next week or ten days. Do continue to keep him as quiet as possible, and in low light, until the rash has disappeared. Also, please trim his nails, to minimize any scratches he might inflict upon himself.

While I was examining him, I discovered something else that I thought you might find of interest, which I did not have time to discuss with you that day. As I'm certain you are aware, Greg has a birthmark about five inches in length, on the right side of his body, with a distinct shape like an arrow or a triangle. Having delivered many of this family's children, and ministered to most of the adults, I have grown acquainted with this unusual physical trait, unique in my experience to the McClinty family. I do not know for certain if your father and his brother Peter were also born with the mark (even though you may <u>think</u> I'm

old enough to have been there), but there are vague references to a "blemish" on each of them, in the files of record that were passed on to me when I took over this practice. The mark is clearly present, however, on Jay, David, David's boys, and now Greg. While the birthmark seems to show up predominantly on McClinty males, it is now obvious that McClinty women are also carriers, since it has passed through you to your son.

Knowing what an effort you make to keep detailed data on your family, I hope you will find this of as much interest as I do.

Sincerely,
MC
Maurice Coomey, M.D.

P.S. During your husband's next visit to Albany, perhaps he would have some time to call me and come down to my office. As you are aware, he was kind enough to give blood at the hospital during his last trip up from New York. But there seems to have been some sort of mix-up with his donation, and I want to be certain our records are correct. Please mention this to him the next time you speak with him. Thank you, Margaret. See you soon.

Megan could almost feel how her grandmother's heart must have been racing.

"She was probably panic stricken! The journals…Would she have written about this?"

Dragging the box out from under the bed, she spent nearly half an hour, before she found the book containing entry dates that corresponded with Dr. Coomey's letter.

September 19, 1938

This afternoon Maurice came to call. He said he had a surprise for me. Little did the man know of the power behind his announcement. It appears that Greg's birthmark, which I have always found so fascinating, is one he shares in common with other McClinty men, specifically David and his boys. Funny. When I first learned the news, I wondered how I could possibly have been blind to this fact. But memories have such free spirits. On the night that led to this predicament, we were surrounded by darkness—and the truth is that I have never, to this day, actually seen David unclothed.

At any rate, Maurice was certain I'd echo his enthusiasm about this phenomenon, and he prepared a special letter for me on the subject, for which I expressed the proper appreciation. We then had tea and spoke of other things. He had thankfully taken his leave when the enormous sense of alarm began to choke me.

Guarding against the resurrection of this topic will be no small challenge, in light of the further complication raised by Gregory's generous contribution of blood at the hospital during his last trip up here. Ever watchful, Maurice apparently uncovered what he called a "mix-up" on the official record of Gregory's donation. Never imagining that anyone would have occasion to compare the blood of my husband and son (and me, too, I suppose, since Maurice has all of my medical files as well), I have never given any thought to how I might handle the question of compatibility.

Before I can think clearly, I must find a way to quiet my heart. Tomorrow I shall decide what to do with the good doctor's letter. Prudence would suggest that I set it on fire, but Maurice is right. Data about my family is very important to me, and one day when I'm dead (and therefore cannot be murdered), this piece of information might be interesting to a McClinty heir. So I will need to consider very carefully the letter's disposition. One thing is already plain to me, however. It must completely slip my mind to tell Gregory that Maurice wishes to speak with him. I must also pray that Maurice forgets about it as well. Otherwise, the part about my being dead might become a reality far sooner than anticipated.

Leafing through successive pages of the journal, Megan could find no further references to the Coomey letter or any subsequent difficulties arising on the subject. *I can't believe the whole thing just went away, nor can I believe she was joking around about it!* Tempted as she was to continue traveling through the living intensity of Cinnamon's journal entries, she forced herself to stop. According to her watch, it was almost five o'clock. She needed to go check on David, and Heidi said that dinner would be ready about six. Tomorrow she had to get up early for the brunch in Clifton Park, and she would have to pack tonight, so she could take her bags with her to Kenneth's in the morning. *Time's up.*

"Sorry, Gram. I can't deal with another minute of this. Besides, I need to digest everything that's happened today. I don't care about your instructions. You're not the boss anymore."

Feeling freed by this declaration, she zipped Vincente's money inside the pocket of her travel tote, deciding to mention it to David later. *I'm not even sure what to do with it. Can you just deposit something like this in a checking account? Is it really still money after sixty years?* Then she replaced Dr. Coomey's letter in the strongbox and eased the design folder down on top of the envelope, pressing the folder tightly along the edges, *just as Gram must have done when she created the hiding place.* Once all the journals were back in the box she'd found under the bed, she decided to store a few things in the attic. First carrying David's unopened tin of letters, and then the journal box, she walked up the narrow flight of attic stairs. When her eyes adjusted, she selected a spot in a far, dark corner, where she tried to imagine an area roped off and filled with family treasures more than half a century ago. When she was finished, she turned around at the top of the stairs and was reassured to see that the items she'd just tucked away up there were completely invisible in the shadows. *And this floor has been empty so long, anyway, that no one would think to look for stuff up here now. Good God, do I ever have a headache!*

"What in tarnation is *this*?" David asked, when he and Megan were sitting in the cottage living room after dinner. Looking closer, he counted the currency and noted the Series date on each of the bills. "Where did this come from?"

"From Gram."

"What?"

"The key you gave me opened the desk in the parlor, where I found a strongbox. Long story, but another key opened the box, and the money was inside."

"But why the hell didn't she put it in the bank?"

"You're asking me? I don't know, David. Maybe she was afraid to, and I think there might have been some sentimental value as well. According to what she told me, when the stock market crashed in 1929, Vincente withdrew the money from her dress shop's savings account. He hid it under the kitchen floor of their apartment, in a strongbox."

"Oh, brother."

"Anyway, the accident that killed my grandfather happened when he was on his way home from the bank with the last withdrawal. I could be wrong, but she told me there'd been $2890 in savings—and you're holding $2890 in your hands."

"Well, let's see. Fifty-nine years later, she *still* didn't put it back in the bank? That's not sentimental. It's flat out stupid! Can you imagine how much it would be worth by now, if she'd invested it after the Depression was over? What was she *thinking*?"

"Your guess is as good as mine, but she apparently intended *you* to have it, because the key she left for you ultimately led to the money."

"Right," he said, chuckling softly and shaking his head. "Like it wouldn't have been easier to just leave a note that said *there's some money in a strongbox in my parlor desk*? And why would she want *me* to have Vincente's money?"

"It wasn't *his*. It was from her dress shop."

"Whatever, Megan. You take it. It's better off with you anyway."

"Are you sure?"

"Yes. Trust me. Want to play some Scrabble?" he asked, abruptly changing the subject and tossing the money on the coffee table.

Knowing that she still had to pack, she asked for a rain check.

"We'll do a best-of-five series on my next trip."

"What? You're leaving?"

"Yes, I'm afraid so, David. I've been away from my family and work a long time. But I'll be here regularly from now on, probably once a month, at least."

"Oh. I didn't know. I thought you'd be staying longer, and I was looking forward to seeing you in the mornings. You have a way about you that reminds me of your grandmother. What will I do all day?" he asked, a look of fear suddenly spreading across his face. "Who will I talk to?"

She hadn't really prepared herself for this.

"Please don't worry. Kenny will come by every afternoon, like he always does…*I hope*…and Barnes and Heidi will be here all the time, of course. Plus, I'll call you each day—more than once, if you'd like."

"Okay," he said, the sparkle in his eyes growing dim.

Watching him consider the loneliness, a rush of guilt began pressing against her conscience. Then an idea came to her.

"Don't move, David. Just sit right here. I have something for you."

When she returned, she carried in her arms the box of Cinnamon's journals.

"What in the world is this?" he asked, the curiosity brightening his face again.

"It's Gram's life, actually. In addition to being a letter writer—as you told me you discovered—she was also an avid journal-keeper. When you read her entries, you can almost hear her voice. I'm sure she'd want you to have these, and maybe she won't seem so far away to you. This might also help keep you company while I'm gone."

"That's very thoughtful, Megan," he said, picking up one of the books at random and thumbing through the pages. Then something Cinnamon had written caught his eye, and he began to laugh. But when he looked up, rows of tears were streaming down both of his cheeks.

"I can't begin to tell you how much I'm missing her, and I can't promise you how long I'll last without her."

That's the second time he's said that, she thought, more alarmed than she'd been before. "Well, I'm not sure heaven's quite ready for both of you," she said, trying to pull him up with humor, which usually worked. "Plus, I want that game of Scrabble with you…*and Kenny and William don't know who you are yet*…so you don't have permission to go anywhere. All right?"

"You're awfully pushy, Megan," he answered after a short pause, his smile slowly returning. "All right. Take care of your family, and try not to get fired. But come back as soon as you can."

"I will," she said, moving beside him on the sofa, putting her arms around his neck, and kissing him on the forehead. Then she pointed to the money again. "Are you positive you don't want to keep this and have Mr. Parnell put it in a safe place for you?"

"You mean like *she* did? In a box shoved in a desk?"

"Be kind, David."

"Sorry. It was just so dumb of her. Really, Megan. Take it and use it for something fun. Now, go pack or whatever you need to do tonight. It's past my bedtime."

After her bags were organized, she took a shower and washed her hair, so she wouldn't have to worry about it in the morning. But it was still only nine o'clock, and the thought occurred to her that she hadn't received a call from her mother that day. Deciding to use the telephone in the library, she went downstairs and noted that Heidi had turned off most of the lights, as was her custom, before retiring to her apartment behind the kitchen. Megan couldn't remember the house ever being this still. Every noise was magnified—the hum of ceiling fans, the creaking floorboards, and the pendulum in the foyer's grandfather clock—while she made her way to the library. She also had a strange feeling, as the dim lighting combined with the earth colors and dark wood to cast an eerie effect across the old Victoria house. Of course, there'd always been other people around when she visited, so she would need to adjust to the sights and sounds of being alone here.

...I'm too young for so much to have changed...

"Where did *that* come from?" she asked the empty room, after pouring a chilled glass of Chardonnay from the library bar's refrigerator. Then dismissing the peculiar sensations, she sat down in the leather wing chair and dialed the Albion Inn. Her mother must have been reading in bed beside the phone, as she often did at night, because she answered before the first ring was finished.

"Hi, Mom."

"Well, hello, Megan. This is a surprise."

"I thought you were going to call me today."

"I was. But then I figured you were probably busy, since you're only here for the weekend. We can always get together another time."

"I hope so—and soon, Mom. How long are you planning to stay in town before going back to Boston?"

"Oh, probably another week or so. I've been looking at some property."

"Really? For what?"

"For *me*. I'm considering the purchase of a place not too far from your grandmother's house. Excuse me, *your* house. It's really quite enchanting, on five acres tucked back in the hills."

"I cannot believe what I'm hearing! You sound as if buying a house is the most natural thing in the world for you to be doing. When did all of this come up?"

"Actually, Megan, I've been looking into the possibility for quite some time. I thought it would make your grandmother happy, but unfortunately...Anyway, nothing is final yet."

"But you told me that napping on a plane was the closest you ever wanted to come to settling down again."

"Yes, I did say that, once. Now I feel differently. Do I need your permission?"

"Of course not, Mom. I'm sorry. You just caught me off guard."

"Well, I'll be sure to keep you informed in the future, dear. Now, you were asking how long I'd be here. Is there something you need me to do?"

"No. I just wanted to talk."

"I see. *My* turn to be caught off guard."

"Guess we're both out of practice. But I really would like to sit down with you sometime and attempt a normal, peaceful conversation. Do you think that's possible?"

Claudine paused, touched by the answered prayer and relieved that her daughter had made the first move.

"Yes I do, and I'd like that very much. How often do you plan to fly up?"

"At least once a month, for awhile. I'm really worried about David, and there are lots of Fox Run details to put in order. So, my attention will be needed here on a fairly regular basis."

"Don't overload yourself, Megan. You have a tendency to want everything wrapped up in neat packages all at once, and I suspect there are a couple of people in Atlanta who need your attention, too—not that it's any of my business, of course."

"You're right, though. That's why I'm going home tomorrow night."

"Good. Follow those instincts. And let's stay in touch with each other more frequently. Maybe we could have our normal, peaceful conversation the next time you're here. Let me know in advance, and I'll make a point of being in town, assuming I don't live in my new house down the road from Fox Run by then—in which case, I'll already *be* here."

"Sounds like a plan, Mom. Take care."

Megan held a meeting with Heidi and Barnes the next morning at seven o'clock, as soon as she heard them both puttering around in the kitchen.

"While I'm shoring up my life and family back in Atlanta, I'll be relying on the two of you to manage things around this place. Kenneth will basically be in charge in my absence, and he'll come by as much as possible. But you'll be our eyes and ears here. Naturally, we expect that you'll continue the routines you've already established, making sure things are running smoothly. But above all else, I'm telling you now that you both have one main job—caring for David. Nothing else should ever take priority, under any circumstances. Pamper him and spoil him shamelessly. I know," she said, noting their raised eyebrows and Heidi's pursed lips, "but humor me. Most importantly, please do everything in your power to see that he's not spending his days alone."

They gave her their promises, as she handed them a list of phone numbers and addresses that covered all possible places she could be reached in an emergency.

"Day or night. I want to be called immediately, if anything should happen."

By 7:45, Barnes had loaded her luggage in the limousine trunk, and Heidi had prepared a thermal mug of coffee for her to drink on the way.

"Are you sure you don't want to take a muffin or something, Miss Megan?"

"I'm sure, Heidi. We're going to a brunch. But, thank you," she added, giving the woman a firm hug, just as the telephone started to ring. Debating whether or not to answer it, she went into the parlor and picked up the receiver, in case it was Kenneth or Katrina.

"Megan, good morning. This is Preston."

"Well, hi, there!"

"I know it's early, but I was hoping to catch you before you left."

"You just made it. I'm ready to walk out the door. Is everything all right?"

"Absolutely. I only wanted to wish you a good trip and to tell you not to worry about anything up here. Whenever I'm in town visiting Dad, I'll be sure we include David in our activities. I'll also call Fox Run from Boston periodically, if you'd like. You'll have more guardian angels around that place than you can count."

"Preston, you are such a dear person. Thank you so much."

"I haven't done anything yet."

"Yes, you have, more than you know. Yesterday was very important to me."

"Actually, I discovered it was for me, too, Meg. Now, please give my best to Phillip and Kristin. I hope…I'm looking forward to seeing you again very soon."

"Give my love to Jay as well, and do be careful. Watch over yourself the same way you take care of everyone else."

"Have a safe trip. 'Bye."

"Who was that?" David asked, entering the parlor as she was hanging up the phone. He held a cup of coffee in one hand and a piece of toast in the other.

"Preston. He was just checking in."

"Hmm. He's such a nice boy."

He's fifty-three! Why do you and Gram do that? "He's going to come visit you whenever he's in town to see Jay."

"The way he always does."

"Yes. The same as always," she said, taking his coffee cup and linking her arm in his, while she walked with him outside to the limousine. "I love you, David."

"I love you, too, Megan."

Then he took another bite of toast, doing a much better job with his emotions than she was with hers.

As Barnes guided the limousine down the driveway and out onto the street, Megan watched David and Heidi waving goodbye to her. Their images grew smaller and smaller through the rear window, until a wall of pine trees eliminated them from view all together. Turning around in the seat so the view was behind her, she tried to push the crushing impressions out of her heart, but they wouldn't fade. Fumbling in her purse for a Kleenex, she didn't feel like she was going home today. Instead, she felt as if her home—her family—were being left *here. Gram, what is this? Cut it out, please!*

The stopover at Kenneth's house was just long enough for Megan to say a quick hello to Justine and Tania, and for Barnes to transfer her luggage to Kenneth's car. Then she sent Barnes on his way back to the estate, giving him a long hug and thanking him again for being such a good friend to David. While she blew kisses to Justine and Tania, her cousin started the car and began the drive to Clifton Park. The ride lasted nearly half an hour, but they scarcely said a word, both of them a little apprehensive about what might be waiting for them.

Katrina and Paul Wallace, who seemed genuinely excited about this meeting, greeted them on the sidewalk outside their modest tri-level home, in a tract neighborhood with well-groomed lawns and neatly bordered gardens. As the foursome introduced themselves and made their way inside the house, Megan became increasingly intrigued by this new tie to a remote branch of her family, in the midsection of her life. She could tell that Kenneth was interested, too, even though Katrina was Megan's cousin, not his.

But the link here is Gram, and Kenny doesn't realize yet how much closer he's tied to all of this than he thinks. I absolutely must find a way to tell him.

The two Wallace children, ages 8 and 10, joined the group for a light brunch with simple conversation. Their dialogue centered on getting-to-know you questions and answers, an exercise that served as a welcome bridge between the new-found relatives. They felt as if they were supposed to have something in common, and yet they were total strangers, bringing their independent histories to the table. Megan made the most noteworthy contribution when she told them about her discovery of Vincente's designs the previous day. That led to a more in-depth discussion of the Magglio connection, which turned out to be a perfect segue to the morning's finale, the reason for the visit in the first place—the trip to the storage unit.

Paul Wallace drove the mile and a half with everyone in his minivan. When they arrived at the cluster of long white buildings, fronted by dozens of closed garage doors, Megan's throat began to feel dry. Her heart started racing, too, as she looked at Kenneth's flushed face.

"This way," Katrina said, as they all got out of the van. "There's a twin building that runs parallel behind this one, where the units open onto a gated alley instead of the street. We thought things would be more secure back there."

Katrina unlocked the gate, and they walked about a third of the way down the alley to Unit 241. Then Paul reached into his pocket and pulled out a separate key ring, inserted the lone key into the deadbolt, turned the handle and pushed the white steel door up and open.

"Give us a minute to get the lights on," Katrina said, "and to remove all the blankets."

Kenneth and Megan held hands while they waited in the alley, peering into the twenty-by-forty foot storage space filled almost to capacity. Then, as they stepped into the room, their grandmother might just as well have been standing there beside them. Megan's breathing grew shallow when she recognized the first five pieces grouped together on the right. A ten-foot high expanse of mahogany bookshelves was against the wall, and in front of the bookcase was a double armoire, also in mahogany. A sofa covered in a faded rose-colored velvet was next to the armoire, along with a leather ottoman and a high-back wooden rocking chair.

"These are all from Broome Street," Megan said, completely sure of herself and amazed that she had any voice.

"What's a Broome Street?" the Wallace's ten-year-old son asked.

"It's a place in New York City," Katrina answered, smiling at Megan, "where your great Aunt Velita and your Uncle Vincente lived a long time ago. Megan's grandmother and Vincente were husband and wife.

"Oh," the little boy responded, doing his best to process what his mother was saying.

"That's right," Megan added, taking comfort in the familial bond she felt surrounding her, "and your great-grandfather Matthew, along with his brothers Joseph and Anthony and some of their friends, made everything in this room, with their bare hands."

As the little boy began looking at the furniture with a new level of appreciation, Megan turned to Kenneth.

"Believe it or not, this grouping was just about all that would fit in the Broome Street living room. But there are a couple of pieces that I don't see, Katrina."

"I think you'll find them toward the back. Aunt Cinnamon took a few things with her from lower Manhattan when she married Gregory, and she brought those items with her when she moved back to Fox Run in 1934."

Prying herself away from the Broome Street pieces and the visions of fire escapes and street vendors that kept replaying in her mind, Megan moved slowly down the narrow center aisle of the storage unit. More awestruck with every step, she saw the three round mahogany reading tables from the Madison house library, plus the two end tables, the tea table, and the burgundy floral chintz sofa.

"According to Uncle Joseph's records," Katrina said, as if reading Megan's thoughts, "all of the original library pieces are here, except the actual book shelves, of course, which must have been magnificent. What was the name of the man who built them?"

"Emanuel," Megan answered. "Emanuel Smith, and yes, those shelves were supposed to have been exquisite, going all the way up to the ceiling, so you needed a ladder to get to the books on the top. Emanuel built that ladder, too."

"I guess there was some fear for awhile," Katrina continued, "that the library furniture had been lost. But Aunt Cinnamon found it in the attic at Fox Run, roped off with a bunch of other things. Mother said that Joseph cried with joy when he was able to fill in those blanks spaces in his notes."

"Where's the desk, though?" Megan asked, a note of concern in her voice.

"In the back. It was one of the last pieces Aunt Cinnamon sent to us. She took it with her to East 67th Street, but then she returned it to Aunt Velita's apartment before she moved back up here. It was part of the shipment delivered to my mother after Cinnamon's sister Maggie died."

Megan continued moving down the aisle, mesmerized by the items arranged on wire shelving along the left wall. Six brass table lamps of varying sizes, with different patterns of the same colorful stained glass shades trimmed with beaded crystals, all looked as if they might have been made yesterday. Next to the lamps were two needlepoint footstools, a yellow knitted blanket wrapped in plastic, and a stack of folded white lace.

"In Uncle Joseph's documentation," Katrina said, as Megan moved in for a closer look at the lace, "it says that those are the curtains from the original Madison nursery. The footstools and afghan were all part of a coordinated theme in the living room and parlor."

"Yes. The seasons."

"That's right."

"Katrina," Megan asked, daring to hope, "do you, by chance, have any of the paintings?"

"We do," she answered, a broad smile spreading over her face. "We have *all* of them. You'll see them at the end."

"Oh my God, Kenny," Megan squealed, gripping his arm. "This is unbelievable!"

Struggling to contain herself, she moved her fingers across the headboard of Emanuel's cherry wood crib, which had been disassembled and was leaning against the wall. Beside the headboard stood the mirrored dresser, and resting on top was the shade from the stained glass floor lamp, all of which had decorated the nursery once upon a time. She also saw a braided rug in blues, yellows and pinks that was rolled up and standing on end.

"This whole group," she said to Kenneth, "was in Gram's bedroom when she was born."

She was about to amplify her description when she stopped moving. Perpendicular to the back wall was a double-sided desk—the place where Amelia and Mimi sat facing each other while they worked or visited, and where Cinnamon later started her dress shop business and did most of her writing. The burgundy leather top had been freshly polished, and so had the two matching high-backed leather chairs on opposite sides of the desk.

"I must confess." Katrina said. "I cleaned those pieces and arranged them in that manner, knowing you were coming today."

"Thank you," Megan replied, squeezing Kenneth's hand and feeling the hair rising up on her arms. "I can almost see the women in our family—all the way back to our great-great grandmother—sitting right there in front of us."

Katrina turned and faced her guests.

"Since we've reached the end of the room, and before you start wondering, the artwork is *this* way." Gesturing toward a door on the wall behind the desk, she continued. "We had special temperature controls installed in here to regulate the cooling and humidity."

With that, she opened the door and flipped on the dim recessed lighting, at which point Megan felt as if she were walking backwards in time. Her initial line of vision was drawn to the left wall, where four canvases were hanging—two of them side-by-side, the other two directly underneath. All four paintings had brass plaques mounted on the lower shelves of their frames. The top two were engraved with the words Spring and Summer, and other two said Fall and Winter.

Her eyes still fastened on that wall, Megan began speaking in a whisper, as if she were in a gallery.

"Spring, Summer and Fall were painted for the Madison house, Kenny. Spring was in the parlor, Winter in the living room and Fall in the foyer. But Winter came later, when Gram and Vincente were married. At the time the wedding gift arrived, Gram didn't even know the other three paintings existed."

"Mother said that Uncle Joseph was afraid they'd been destroyed," Katrina interjected. "Apparently he wasn't very fond of Cinnamon's father, believing Jonathon could actually have been capable of putting these beautiful things in a fireplace or something."

When Kenneth made no sound in response, Megan looked up at him and realized he hadn't been listening. Following the direction of his eyes, she, too, was silenced. At the far end of the room, illuminated beneath individual lamps that cast a soft, low light, were two more canvases. Hanging beside each other, a few inches apart, were the portraits of Mimi and Amelia.

…their faces were strong, yet soft—one still dripping with youthful beauty, one aging with extraordinary grace. Their eyes, different blends of Irish green, saw not just each other, but everyone in the room, everyone they met, with the same clarity and absence of bias. Joseph loved these women beyond his powers of verbal expression, and by painting their portraits, he had, in a quietly selfish way, hoped to somehow preserve that love beyond the inevitable ending of this bittersweet day…

The cousins stood motionless for more than a minute, unable to stop looking at the two women staring back at them, half expecting them to float off their canvases and begin speaking.

"Well, I don't know about you, Meg," Kenneth said at length, "but I need to sit down."

"Me, too."

She backed out of the art room and took the chair on what had originally been Mimi's side of the desk. Kenneth sat across from her, on Amelia's side, while the Wallaces gathered close with their children.

"You guys have done a masterful job preserving all of this," Megan said, her words staggered in between breaths, as she looked up at Katrina.

"I've just been following Uncle Joseph's directives, which were religiously passed down to my mother, and then to me. But now *you're* finally here, and I feel like I've reached the end of a treasure hunt."

Megan and Kenneth both laughed at the same time.

"You took the words right out of our mouths," Megan said. "And we need to talk with you about taking this responsibility off your hands, so you won't have to worry about it any more. We also need to discuss what we're going to do with everything. Some of the things should be *yours*, you know," she added, curiously pulling the center desk drawer open a few inches as she was speaking. "After all, if not for Joseph and your family, who knows where this history might have ended up?"

"Well, we can have those conversations at your leisure," Katrina replied. "The lease is paid here for another year, so there's no rush."

"Okay. On my next trip, we'll take you out to dinner. Meanwhile, why don't you start thinking about which things you'd like to keep. We're in this together. Right, Kenny?"

"Right," he answered, still unable to shake the faces of Mimi and Amelia from his head.

"This drawer," Megan said, unexpectedly shifting the subject, "is where Gram used to keep her writing materials and journals. The side where you're sitting, Kenny, is where she did her sewing. I think the way Emanuel built the desk is so fascinating, especially now that I'm seeing it in person." She pulled the center drawer toward her a little further. "Since it's broad enough for two people, the drawers are exceptionally deep, creating a huge amount of storage space, which Gram must have loved in that tiny apartment. Look. I keep pulling this open, and the drawer just keeps coming and coming."

At that moment, the edge of what looked like an ivory-colored piece of paper became evident in what turned out to be the back corner of the drawer.

"What's this?" she asked, reaching her hand way in.

"I don't know," Katrina said. "I thought the desk was completely empty," she added, her eyes widening along with everyone else's when Megan's hand came out of the drawer holding a sealed, letter-size envelope, addressed simply to **Cinn**.

"Katrina, when did you say this desk was delivered to your family?" Megan asked, wondering if her hands were shaking as much as she thought they were.

"In 1953. Velita had it in the Broome Street apartment. But after Maggie died there, Velita and Alberto couldn't bear to live in the place. So, they rented another apartment and shipped all the things that originally belonged to Mimi and Bradley up to Aunt Cinnamon, at Fox Run."

"But did Gram ever unpack them, or did she just have them sent directly to your family?"

"I don't know. Why?"

"Because this letter is addressed to her, but it doesn't look like it's ever been opened. Do you suppose she even knew it was in here?"

"Who's it from?" Kenneth asked.

Megan removed her nail file from the cosmetic bag in her purse and gently sliced through the envelope's seal. Then she pulled the multiple-page letter out and unfolded it, her eyes diving immediately to the signature at the bottom of the first page.

"It's from Velita. But you know what?" she asked rhetorically, refolding the letter and slipping it back inside the envelope. "I have a funny feeling about reading this right now. Frankly, I've run across a few surprises in her personal things, and I'm a little nervous about what the letter might say."

"Of course. We understand," Katrina responded empathetically. "I'm just sorry now that I didn't examine the desk more thoroughly, so we could have found it for her while she was still here. I feel terrible."

"Don't be silly, Katrina. How could you possibly have known something might be stuck way back in there?"

"Do you suppose there's anything else in the other drawers?" Kenny asked, reaching for the knobs on his side.

Megan pushed the letter into her purse and stood up.

"Well, if there is," she said, "it will have to wait. I'm full-up on family finds and disclosures for one day. You've given us such an unbelievable experience, though," she added, putting her arms around Katrina. "And we are so grateful for the love and care spent on the maintenance of these beautiful treasures."

For the next several minutes, they all pitched in to replace the protective blankets over the furniture and shelves. Then Paul double-checked the temperature settings in the painting room, turned off the lights, and pulled the storage door shut, locking the deadbolt. The quick ride back to the Wallace home took place in near silence, except for the tentative agreement to have their first dinner together in August. Shortly thereafter, a round of grateful goodbyes had been exchanged, and Megan and Kenneth were in his car, heading back to Albany.

"I don't need to be at the airport for another four hours, so why don't we stop and have a bite of lunch somewhere?"

"Okay," he said. "I'm not very hungry, though."

"Me neither. But I want to read this letter, and I'd like to have you with me when I do."

"Sounds intriguing. Oh, by the way, Meg, what did you mean when you said you've run across a few surprises in Gram's personal things?"

"Later. Long story."

The diner was nearly empty.

"Everybody must still be in church," Kenneth said, looking at his watch.

They both asked for coffee and scanned the menu, while the waitress was filling their cups. Kenneth ended up ordering a grilled cheese sandwich and fries, his appetite stimulated by the aroma of saturated fats cooking on the grill. But Megan could not even think about eating, as she removed the letter from her purse, slipped it out of the envelope and unfolded the pages. Shooting a quick glance at her cousin as he slurped his coffee, she lowered her eyes to the paper and silently began to read.

June 27, 1953

My dearest Cinnamon—

I cannot help but believe that our pain would be easier to bear if we were together. Yet you have lost so much more than I have, and I appreciate how desperately you are torn from one place to the other. We will simply have to pray that God keeps us close in spirit, while we find our way through these unspeakable happenings.

Many hours have been spent making the decision to send you the attached letter, which I found on the nightstand beside her. While you were here, I had it in my hand to give to you several times. Sadly, you were called away to your latest tragedy before my courage was full enough. The option exists for me to destroy it and never let you see it at all, and yet I know I'd never forgive myself for withholding it from you. No one will ever comprehend why she did this to herself, but if her words to you offer any explanation, I believe you would want to see them. I hope this helps you, although I can make no sense of what she's saying. Please remember the love that Alberto and I will always have for you. We are here if you need us, so do not hesitate to come home whenever you wish.

Velita

Megan took a drink of water and looked up at Kenneth again.

"So, what does it say?" he asked.

"I haven't finished it yet," she said, "but I don't think it's going to be very pretty."

Then she placed Velita's letter face down on the table, took a deep breath, and began reading the second page.

June 24, 1953

Cinn—

You will never believe me. I didn't know this would happen. If I say I'm sorry a million times, it cannot help or make them come back. All I see is black. No more color. No more paint. I was always so angry with you, even when I tried not to be. Then I saw you a long time ago, at Fox Run, and I kept feeling worse when you married Gregory. It wasn't fair! When I told him, though, I was just being mean. Yes—I TOLD HIM. Are you satisfied? But I never imagined that he could do something like this! I only wanted to get you in trouble—not to really hurt anybody. You can't forgive me, Cinn. I know that. But I am sorry. I'll say it a million times—a million, million times. But there's no way to make it better now, and I can't bear it.

Maggie

"Are you all right, Meg?"

"No."

Kenneth picked up the page from the table and took the other one out of her hand.

"Can you please translate these for me?" he asked, after reading them both.

"No."

"Megan, come on. I thought we were buddies in this?"

"We are," she said, a dull ache seeping in behind her eyes. "First I need to think."

"About what? Please! Let me help you."

"I will. But not yet. I need to go make a couple of phone calls."

While she was at the pay phone, he read the two pages over and over, no less bewildered when she returned than he'd been before she left.

"Can I help you *now*, Meg?"

"Yes. But let me apologize in advance, Kenny, if what I'm going to do and say seems strange or cryptic to you."

"Excuse-é-moí?"

Laughing at him in spite of herself, she lifted the letters from his hands and replaced them in her purse.

"I'm taking a little detour on my way home to Atlanta."

"Oh?"

"That's right, and I would be deeply grateful if you could drive me to the train depot in Albany."

"Okay. So far, *strange* is appropriate. At the risk of sounding pushy, where the hell are you going?"

"To New York. I want to visit the cemetery where my grandfather and the others are buried. Gram's got me tied up in knots, and little things like these letters aren't helping. I think that, if I can just close the loop, I'll be able to let it all go. I *have* to find a way to let it go. Then I promise that you and I will sit down together when I come back up in August, and I'll tell you the whole thing. But I'm not ready to do it now. Can you understand?"

"No, but I'm not mad or anything, in case you were going to ask. And are you sure it's a good idea for you to be by yourself in New York? And how are you getting home to Atlanta, by the way?"

"I'll fly out from LaGuardia tomorrow. Tonight I'll stay in a hotel. I already left a message for Phillip. And yes, Kenny, I'll be fine."

"I guess it's settled then. What time do we have to be at Union Station?"

"Yesterday."

Her train pulled into Grand Central Terminal shortly after five o'clock, leaving her several hours of summer daylight to accomplish her objective. The porter in the lounge car had given her a few suggestions about safe places she might stay that night, and when she arrived at the station in New York, she only needed to make two phone calls before she found a room available nearby. Unfamiliar with the City, however, she caught a taxi outside the terminal, a little embarrassed a few short minutes later when the cab came to a stop three blocks away, in front of her hotel. By the time she'd checked in and freshened up in her room, it wasn't even six o'clock yet.

Following the directions of a native New York gentleman, who'd bought her a drink on the train, she walked west on 46th Street to 5th Avenue, and then found a subway entrance for the line heading south to lower Manhattan. Self-consciously feeling like a tourist, she figured out what to do and where to go once inside the subway station's cavity, and within two minutes of purchasing her token, she was onboard. Forty-five blocks later, a fellow passenger was kind enough to help her identify the stop she was looking for, just north of Houston. When she emerged from the subway, she took a minute to get her bearings on the street level, and then walked two blocks east to Mott, where she turned right. Once she crossed Houston, a peacefulness began to settle over her, and she seemed to know exactly where she was going.

...For all of the crowded conditions and economic struggles, there was something uplifting about the durability—the certainty—of these streets, of the sidewalk displays and kiosks, even the fire escapes. But what she had not anticipated was the recognition...Walking south on Mott Street, she crossed Spring, and then Kenmare. With Broome Street next...

Rounding the corner at Mott and Broome, she walked another half-block, until she was standing in front of the apartment building where Bradley had originally moved his family, where Cinnamon and Vincente had then lived after they were married—and where Maggie had died. The building next door on the right was where Alberto and Velita's original apartment had been located, where Mimi first met the Mentini family and ultimately lost the battle with her demons. Stepping out to the curb, Megan leaned back and looked up at the web of fire escapes attached to the seven stories rising above her, still in place, just as they'd been for nearly a hundred years. Trying to imagine which landing had been outside her grandmother's flat, she was oblivious to the locals on the street, who were eyeing her with apprehension. Drawn hypnotically into the visions Cinnamon had painted for her, she did not realize how conspicuous she was in her fashionable pantsuit, with the long curls of her copper-colored hair falling loose over her shoulders and down her back.

"Scusi, signora. Posso aiutarla trovare qualcosa?"

Suddenly back in the moment, Megan realized that a man was standing beside her, and for the first time, she was nervous about being there alone. *What the heck am I doing? I don't even know what kind of neighborhood this is anymore*!

"Pardon me?" she asked, doing her best to be polite—and to not appear terrified.

"You are lost?" The man had a welcome look of kindness in his eyes, which was a relief, since his eyes were only inches away from hers.

"Oh, hello. No, I'm not lost. My family used to live here a long time ago, and I just came to see the neighborhood."

"No English too good. Are you lost?"

"Thank you," she said, smiling as she imagined Mimi and her grandmother working their way through this sort of language barrier every single day. "St. Paul's church?" she asked, deciding that any extra nouns and verbs would be senseless.

"Catholic church of the St. Paul?" he replied, looking intently at her for verification.

"Yes. Sí." *Is that Italian or Spanish?* "And the cemetery, too? Where dead people are buried?" she asked, realizing as soon as the words were out of her mouth how ridiculous that must have sounded.

"La gente ***morto***?" His eyes widened and a shocked look spread across his face.

Having no idea what he'd said, and seeing that this exchange was going nowhere, she mentioned the name of St. Paul's again, this time with a question mark in her voice. Then she pointed in one direction up the street, and the other direction down the street, shrugging her shoulders, in hopes of signifying confusion.

"Oh!" he replied, a look of comprehension on his face. "Cammini al angolo e faccia una giusta girata. Arriverete alla chiesa del paulo santo in *due blocchi.*"

Am I still in the United States? Fortunately, as he spoke, he also stretched his arm out toward the corner *up* the street, curving his hand to indicate that she should turn right, and finally, holding up two fingers. "Due blocchi," he said again. "One, two. *Due* blocchi."

"Muchas gracias," she said, hoping that *due blocchi*, which he'd repeated three times, meant *two blocks* rather than *you'll be mugged shortly.* Then she extended her hand to him and bent forward in a slight bow of gratitude.

"*Grazie*," he said with emphasis, smiling back at her. "Siete benvenuti. Goodbye, signora graziosa."

As she walked away from him, a warm sensation rushed over her, and she could almost feel Mimi, Velita and her grandmother moving along beside her. She no longer feared for her safety, either.

St. Paul's was precisely where the man said it would be, and like the rest of the neighborhood, appeared to have been frozen in time. Adjacent to the church, and filling the balance of land in the square-block property, was a cemetery surrounded by a six-foot high wrought iron fence. Trying to ignore the surge of adrenalin pumping through her body, Megan walked all the way around the block, looking for a gate. When she didn't find one, she opened the front door to the church, hoping there would be someone inside who could help her. A few worshipers, who lingered from the five o'clock Mass, were clustered in the pews nearest the altar. As she headed down the center aisle toward them, she noticed another door at the rear of the church, on the wall to her right, and through the window on top of the door, she could see outside light coming through. Cutting across a middle row of pews, she followed the side aisle, and then peered out the window, directly into the cemetery.

Opening the door, she left the low-lit sanctuary, with its enduring scent of incense, and moved across a surreal historical line, into a setting of patchy green grass and a thick ceiling of tree branches. She was certain there must be at least a thousand headstones and grave markers spread out in front of her. Astonished that this place was so matter-of-factly situated in the midst of lower Manhattan, she began to consider how she was ever going to find her family in here. *Maybe I should wait until tomorrow and see if the rectory has some sort of map for the graves,* she mused.

A few narrow brick pathways curved through the cemetery, leading eventually to all corners. But most of the graves could only be reached by walking across the grass, which she began to do. The first few markers indicated those lives ended in the 1800's and early 1900's, and she noted that, with an occasional exception, the further she walked from the church, the more recent were the graves. By the time she reached burial sites ranging from 1915-1920, the early evening sunlight was fading, and she worried that she wasn't going to have enough time. *They probably would have secured a family plot near the first person who died, and that was Bradley, in 1921.*

As the dates starting moving consistently into the 1920's, two of the brick paths intersected and then forked in a forty-five degree angle. She selected one direction and followed it until the dates had shifted into the late 1930's. Then she turned around and retraced her steps back to the fork. The second path led toward the rear of the church, and she wove in and out of the graves on both sides of the walkway, until she saw the name **Mentini** etched on a four-foot tall concrete stone several yards away.

After taking a moment to slow her breathing, she moved—on tiptoe for some reason—up to the grave that she saw belonged to Alberto. *He died in 1954 at the age of 71, the year after Maggie.* Other than the dates, the stone offered no information or message. To the right of Alberto was a carved marble headstone, far more elaborate than his and bearing more writing. *Gram was obviously involved with this one.*

VELITA MENTINI
Born February 26, 1887—Died October 4, 1966
Perfect Mother and Wife
Eternal Friend

She outlived Alberto by twelve years, Megan was thinking, when her attention turned to the marker on Velita's right. **VINCENTE MENTINI—April 6, 1904—November 15, 1929—In God's Hands Far Too Soon.**

"Grandpa," Megan whispered, unexpectedly feeling tears swell in her eyes. Running her fingers across his name, she tried to picture how handsome he must have been and what fun they would have had together. "I'm so sorry I missed you," she said, taking a Kleenex from her purse and blotting her face, which was now streaked with mascara.

After pausing in that spot for quite a few minutes, she moved on to the grave next to Vincente, which was located several feet away. But it turned out to be someone she didn't know. So she walked back past Alberto, to the site on his left. **BRADLEY PRICE** was buried there, having died on May 28, 1921, at the age of

41—and Megan was both surprised and disappointed that nothing else was carved on the marker.

"He had such dreams and strength of character," she said out loud. "It seems so unfair that he..."

Her sentence trailed off when her line of sight shifted to her left, toward the two remaining graves in what she could now see was a distinctly defined section for these six people.

MARY MAE "MIMI" PRICE
Beginning on May 19, 1883
Ending on December 13, 1923
In the Safety of Her Husband's Arms, Again

The words were so simple and yet spoke to Megan about her beautiful, gifted great-grandmother, whose fatal flaw had been letting herself be defined by the other people in her life. When those who'd influenced her had either abandoned her or died, Mimi had no sense of *herself* to help her survive.

"*Gram's* strength must have been inherited from Jonathon's steel-jawed nastiness," Megan said, unaware that a man in a long black robe had spotted her from the side door of the church and was walking in her direction.

"And *you,*" she continued, looking at the sixth grave, "are the saddest of them all."

MAGGIE MARIE PRICE

Born on Valentine's Day
February 14, 1910
Left Us on June 18, 1953

May the Angels Be with You
So You Will Never Feel Alone Any More

"I don't know what you did, Maggie, but I'm here to tell you that I don't *want* to know. There's an entry in one of your journals, Gram, that talks about truth having the power to affect people's lives—sometimes in the telling, I think you said, and sometimes in the withholding. Well, I'll make sure I tell Kenny and William about David, but the rest is going to stay buried with *you,* Maggie. I'm very grateful for what I've learned, but I'm..."

"Excuse me, miss." The voice came from behind her and startled her, since she hadn't seen anyone else in the cemetery. Spinning around, she discovered a priest standing there.

"I'm sorry if I frightened you," he added.

"That's all right, Father. I guess I was in my own world."

"Unfortunately, you will have to leave now. We lock the access to our cemetery at sunset each night. But you're welcome to return tomorrow, if you'd like. I open everything up before the seven o'clock Mass each morning."

"Thank you, but I'll be going home to Atlanta tomorrow. It's okay, though. I found what I was looking for."

The two of them began walking together back toward the church.

"Do you have family buried here?" the priest asked her.

"Yes, I do. That group of six, with the names Mentini and Price."

"Well, rest assured, my dear, that we love and guard all those who've been left in our care."

"I can see that, and I feel much better knowing where they are."

"Good night, and God bless you."

"Same to you, Father."

While riding the subway back up to midtown, the thought occurred to Megan that Vincente's sisters Rosa and Marie were not in the family plot. But she knew they'd both married and assumed they must have moved away, maybe to another borough, and were buried there, perhaps with their husbands. *I'll track them down some other day. For now, my circle is complete and my conscience is clear. By tomorrow, I'll be rested and back to normal. Thanks, Gram, for the tour.*

At eight o'clock the next morning, before leaving her hotel room to check out, she called Phillip to confirm with him that her flight would be arriving in Atlanta shortly after noon. He was remarkably cheerful, and relieved that she was almost home. Buoyed by this conversation, she hoped the positive tone would help carry her through the second call she needed to make.

"Strategic Data. Hello? How can I connect you? To which extension? I mean, *with*?"

What? Who the heck is this answering the phone? And where is Glenda?"

"I'd like to speak with Jerry Rogers, please."

"Who? Oh, okay. Hang on a sec."

Appalled at the absence of professionalism, and half expecting to be disconnected, Megan was relieved to hear Jerry's voice more than a minute later.

"Hi, Jerry. This is Megan."

"Good morning! What time are you coming into the office?"

"Actually, that's why I'm calling. But first, who *is* that on the switchboard?"

"It's part of the update. I'll fill you in when you get here—which will be *when*?"

"Well, something came up, and I won't be in until tomorrow. I'm still in New York. But I'll be in the office at eight o'clock sharp. That will give us time to talk before the day descends."

The pause was longer than she'd anticipated it would be.

"Jerry? Are you still there?"

"Yes, but I wish you hadn't just said that you're still in New York."

"I know. But I really needed to wrap things up before I come back. I don't want any loose ends distracting me, and I promise that my nose will be securely fixed to the grindstone when I get there."

"I sure hope so. Our favorite vice president is gunning for you."

"Curtis?"

"Yup. He's not a great believer in personal crises under *normal* circumstances, but especially not in the middle of a corporate restructuring. Of course, we all know that he's *genetically* unpleasant, but he's especially riled up about *you* at the moment. I'll try and cover for you for one more day, Meg. But given the fact that continued employment is an uncertainty for all of us, you need to get here as soon as possible to protect your turf—and your job. Can you imagine yourself without any money?" he added, his voice returning to a more playful tone. "I mean, how would you pay for all your shoes?"

She decided this wasn't the time to tell him that she'd just inherited three million dollars, particularly since she knew that getting back to work was critical for her state of mind.

"I can't bear the thought," she answered with a chuckle. "I promise I'll be there with bells on in the morning. And, Jerry?"

"What?"

"Thanks—for your honesty and your friendship. I really appreciate you very much."

"You're welcome. But don't worry. I'm keeping score."

CHAPTER 20

"I gave all the journals to David. The memories are more his than mine anyway."

Megan and Phillip were sharing a glass of wine together in the gazebo before dinner that night, both of them grateful in their own private ways that she was safely home. After hearing the rest of Cinnamon's story, Phillip was particularly thankful that his wife had decided not to pursue her grandmother's *project,* as Megan called it. He also hoped, as he listened to her chatter incessantly, that his nagging sense of apprehension would disappear after she'd been home for a few days.

"I'm not sure yet what I'll do with all the tapes," she said, pulling her knees up to her chin, as she floated on the custom-made swing suspended from the gazebo's twelve-foot ceiling. "Maybe I'll put them in a safe deposit box. And when I'm in Albany next month, Kenny and I will have dinner with Katrina and Paul, so we can agree on how to divvy up the stuff in the storage unit. After seeing the way they've cared for everything all these years, it doesn't really matter to me who gets what. At least I'll know it's in the best of hands, and still in the family. Oh! I also found a stack of fashion designs that Vincente sketched. They're incredible, and each one has his signature at the bottom. But I put them back in the strongbox and took them up to the attic. And there's a container of her letters that David gave me. But I didn't even look at them—just put them in the attic, too. I guess I should save them, for posterity. What do *you* think?"

"I'm sure you'll come up with the answer, honey," Phillip said, when she finally took a breath. "Give it a rest for awhile, though."

"I will. By the way, Preston came by Fox Run the other day, and he said to tell you hello. He was very gracious—spending time with me and answering all of my silly questions. He also gave me a fresh historical perspective on the family. But he didn't like Gram's project any more than you do. I'm sure he thought I was nuts for even considering it. He was right. You are, too, sweetheart. Gram is probably eavesdropping on us right now, furious with me for messing up her plans. But, she'll get over it. Oh, I almost forgot," she said, putting her wine glass on the wrought iron coffee table and jumping to her feet. "There is one small item I need to take care of tomorrow. Wait 'till you see *this*," she added, walking inside the house to get her purse.

When she reappeared, she opened her bag and handed him the stack of bills totaling $2890, still tied with Cinnamon's lace.

"What in the world?"

"That was in the same strongbox with Vincente's designs. I'm pretty sure it's the money from Gram's dress shop. She had it in a savings account, but when the stock market crashed in 1929, Vincente withdrew it and put it under the floor of their apartment's kitchen. Can you even imagine that?"

"No," he said, examining each bill as he counted. "I *cannot* imagine."

"The sad thing is, though, that Vincente had just left the bank after making the last withdrawal when he was hit by that car. Doesn't it just break your heart to think about it?"

"Was this listed in her will?" he asked, apparently not paying any attention to her.

"Nope. Not even a hint. Why?"

"What are you planning to do with it?"

"Invest it. What's with all the questions?"

"Is there any documentation at all to prove this is part of her estate?"

"No, Phillip. I told you I *found* it. What is your problem?"

"Well, for starters, you can't stroll into a bank with this. The Federal Reserve is probably the only institution that would honor these old bills. The pictures, the layout, have all changed completely since this printing. For all we know, they could even be counterfeit. They still look brand new, after sixty years! Frankly, I think we should take them to a professional, who can validate them for us. If they are real, their redeemable value could be substantially higher than their face. So, of course, there's also the tax issue, and you have no proof that this money is part of your grandmother's estate. No, I think we need to carefully consider the right way to handle this."

Looking up, he saw her staring at him with the most peculiar expression.

"Excuse me, Phillip, but who's being overly dramatic *now*? And *we* aren't going to do *anything*," she announced, snatching the bills out of his hand and stuffing them back in her purse. "I'll take care of it."

"Whatever, Meg," he said, growing more troubled by the minute and finishing his wine with one upturn of his glass. "What time is the roast supposed to be ready?"

When Megan entered the lofty marble lobby of Strategic Data's corporate headquarters the following morning, she was disconcerted not to see Glenda in her rightful place on the receptionist's platform. Instead, a sloppy cluster of three unknown women was visible above the switchboard console, and their frenzied, disordered activity made her blood pressure rise. The ambiance of this lobby and entrance had been meticulously designed to invoke first impressions of professionalism and pride. But the crude scenario unfolding in front of her was an embarrassment. Knowing she wouldn't be recognized, she conducted a short experiment to help her understand the extent of damages.

"Good morning!" she said, greeting the workers with all the conviviality she could muster. Casually timing their response, she was appalled that more than a minute had passed before anyone even looked down to acknowledge her presence. Further distress was forthcoming.

"Sorry!" one of the women finally exclaimed, sucking an errant wad of chewing gum back into her mouth. "These phones are impossible. In all the jobs I've ever had, I've never seen such a ridiculous system. So, who do *you* need to see?"

"I'm not sure of the name," Megan answered, finding the scene so disastrous that it was almost funny. "But I believe the person's title is Director of Administrative Services."

"Well, if you don't have a *name*, then it's going to take a minute to find him."

"I didn't say it was a *man*. In fact, I recall someone mentioning that my appointment was going to be with a woman."

"Nope. Not a chance. Around here, if someone is that high up, it will definitely be a man. Trust me! Now, have a seat over there while I check the files."

"Can't you just pull up the department or the title on that computer?"

"Beats me. I've only been here since Monday, and the training in this place stinks."

"Are you from a temporary service?"

"Yeah. All three of us are. Anyway, I'll need your name so I can tell somebody you're here."

"My name is Megan Cole, and *I'm* the Director of Administrative Services," she said, walking around the platform and heading toward the bank of elevators.

"Wait, ma'am! I'm supposed to let someone know you're coming."

"It'll be okay. *Trust me*," Megan replied, mimicking the woman and smiling, hoping she'd only have to see the trio one more time when she fired them later that day.

Arriving on the twelfth floor, Megan went straight to Jerry's office, which was a few doors down from her own. As she walked, she was heartened by the warm reception she received from everyone she ran into on the way. Jerry seemed glad to see her as well, and following an appropriately professional embrace, the two of them took the elevator down to the cafeteria for a ceremonial cup of coffee.

"I knew that would be your reaction to them," he said, after learning about her experience in the lobby. "See why we need you so much around here, Megan? No one else has the foggiest notion how to staff and manage your area."

"Well, it doesn't look like anyone gave the arrangement any thought at all. I've seen fruit flies with more intelligence and class than those pinheads downstairs. Whose idea *was* that?"

"Uh, the executive team?"

"Yeah, right. Good answer. Now that I'm back, do I still have the power to reconfigure the lobby circus act?

"Yes, Ms. Cole, you definitely do."

"Great. Where's Glenda?"

"I'm afraid she has another job, Meg."

"I know! But *where*? Oh, never mind. I'll find out."

They carried a second cup of coffee back with them to Jerry's office and closed the door. By noon, his summary and analysis of current company events was complete. Although she wasn't happy about the status of things, she felt up to date and was grateful to still be employed. As she piled her notes into her briefcase, she assumed she'd spend the balance of the day in her own office with her managers and the remnants of their staffs. But as she got up to leave, Jerry's phone buzzed from the outer office.

"Yes?" he said. "Fine. Please bring it in now."

His office door was then immediately thrown open from the outside, introducing a parade of surviving employees—including Megan's three managers—all of whom were blowing noise makers. The beaming young woman who led the group was carrying a cake, and Megan's eyes widened as she flashed a knowing smile at Jerry. The woman with the cake was Glenda!

"She's our assistant now!" Jerry responded, in a gallant answer to Megan's unspoken question. "Yours and mine—that is, if you don't mind sharing. Well," he added, as Megan reached out to shake his hand, really wanting to hug him instead, "I had to do *something.*"

"Do you suppose," she asked him in a confidential whisper at one point in the merrymaking, "that we might negotiate a little time for our new assistant to set up a training program for receptionists?"

What was left of the afternoon seemed to evaporate. Even the brusque appearance of Curtis—a man who carried the art of brevity to extremes—could not interrupt the free-flowing rejuvenation that coursed through her mind.

"Megan?" Curtis always said her name as if he were taking roll. "Your return is both welcome and fortunate. I won't keep you any longer from what I'm sure is a challenging load."

"Curtis, before you go, I'd like to schedule some time with you. I'm compiling a list of requirements for manpower and funding, based on the new directives Jerry reviewed with me this morning. If you wouldn't mind, I'd really appreciate your playing devil's advocate, once I've put the numbers together. I might be overlooking something that happened while I was away."

"Yes. Good. See me tomorrow morning at seven-thirty."

By the time Megan arrived at home that night after preparing for her meeting, her family had already eaten.

"Well, *that* didn't take very long," Phillip declared good-naturedly.

"*What* didn't?" she asked, setting a place for herself at the table.

"Getting our lives back to normal."

"I guess you're right, but I don't plan to make this a habit anymore. New priorities."

"Right," he said, trying to remember how many times he'd heard that statement before. "By the way, Anthony Parnell called."

"Really?" She was surprised how quickly the whole Albany thing had become a million miles away. "What did he want?"

"He said he needs your signature on a number of documents, in order to begin releasing funds to you, and he wanted to know if he could fly down one day this week."

"Sure. I don't see why not. But he'll have to meet with us at night, because I'm not taking one more minute off work."

"Funny. That's what I told him. He's coming on Friday, and I made reservations for dinner at my club." Noting the look on her face, he continued. "Well, you *said* you wanted to go there."

"I did?" she asked, trying unsuccessfully to look serious. "Oh, all right. I suppose just this once. After all, it *will* be something of a celebration. I mean, how often do we come into three million dollars?"

"Should we take Kristin with us?"

"Hmmm," Megan hummed. "I don't know, honey. What do you think?"

"Maybe we should wait awhile, until we can say the words without stuttering."

"Good point. Besides, weren't you and I were scheduled for a date together Friday night?"

"So we were. And our daughter's already planning on a slumber party at Gina's house."

"I guess it's settled then. A hot time awaits us, dear man."

"I'll alert the media. During your thirty hours at work today, did you tell anyone there about your inheritance?"

"Are you kidding? They'd lay me off for sure, thinking I didn't need the job anymore. But ironically, I realize that I need it more than ever, just for different reasons than I used to. So, mum's the word."

Three days later, in the privacy of the Brigade Towne and Country Club's conference room, Megan signed the necessary papers, and Mr. Parnell handed her an impressive check.

"I assume you have a good financial adviser," he joked, knowing that was Phillip's profession. "This is the first of many such receipts," he said, sipping his brandy and watching as both Megan and Phillip sat transfixed at the hefty six digits. "Manage them well."

During dinner, it occurred to Phillip that Mr. Parnell might be an appropriate person to hear about the money from Cinnamon's strongbox. But he caught himself just as he started to say something, deciding, instead, that Megan might think he was interfering. Besides, staying away from the whole story for awhile was probably advisable. As he watched his wife having such a good time, laughing and getting a bit silly after three glasses of champagne, he wasn't even mildly convinced that this thing was anywhere close to being over yet.

Megan's phone calls to Albany were excessive, but she needed the conversations to keep her concern about David in check. Although she didn't speak with him directly on every occasion, she did talk to Heidi, who reassured her that all was going well. Kenneth was also conscientious about keeping her updated, and his assessments about David's state of mind echoed the other positive things she'd been hearing.

"Yes, Miss Megan," Heidi reported one night, "Mr. McClinty keeps busy, doing his reading or working out in the garden. He brings the loveliest fresh flowers into the house, just like *she* used to do, and he seems to take great pleasure in that. His appetite is healthy as well, and he's always making some kind of joke. You know how he can be! Lately, he's been trying to convince me that I should start dating him. Can you even imagine such a thing? And he plays Scrabble with

Barnes *all* the time. Sometimes I complain because Barnes forgets to do his chores or watch over the yard workmen like he's supposed to. But then I remember what you said, and I figure we can always grow new grass. So, I've stopped hounding them."

"I'm glad, Heidi. David certainly comes before the yard. And I'll be bringing in a manager before too much longer to help out with things. Meanwhile, just keep me informed. That's all I ask."

For the first week she was home, Megan tried repeatedly to reach her mother at the Inn, leaving half a dozen messages for her. When Claudine finally returned the calls, she began by hastily apologizing for taking so long to respond, and then announced that she'd made her decision.

"I suddenly feel the need for something permanent, and I've been negotiating for three days now with the sellers of the property I mentioned to you. The house has been vacant for months, and their expectations on price were way out of line. But I think they're finally going to accept my last offer. I'm sure you find this all very peculiar, dear, but I'm wildly excited and I can't wait for you to come visit me."

"Actually, I like hearing you sound so happy. I also like the idea of your living someplace where I *can* visit you. You know, Gram is probably watching us from wherever she is, and she's got to be speechless over this development!"

"Your grandmother was many things, but *speechless* is hardly a word that leaps to mind. At any rate, I do enjoy feeling grounded again."

"Me, too, Mom. Maybe when you're settled in your new place, I could bring the whole family up."

"That would be lovely."

Megan had been home for almost two weeks, and even though she'd never missed a nightly call to Fox Run, she hadn't actually spoken with David for several days. With her concern heightened, she tried to reach him during the day from her office on Friday, August 12.

"I'm sorry, Miss Megan," Heidi said, "but he's sleeping again. Do you want me to go wake him up?"

"No, that's okay. But could you please have him call me when he feels up to it? Tell him I really need to hear his voice. Oh, before I forget, does he know about Lake George and Saratoga yet?"

"No, ma'am. Kenneth was pretty insistent that we shouldn't say anything."

"Okay. Thanks, Heidi. I'll talk to you again soon. Tell David I love him."

"Don't you fret, Miss Megan."

Kenneth had mentioned during their last conversation that Preston would be in Albany the weekend of August 20. He'd apparently made elaborate arrangements to take both Jay and David on an excursion to Lake George. They had reservations at the Sagamore Hotel, an extraordinarily beautiful historic structure on the water's edge, which had been fully restored and renovated in 1985. As if this surprise weren't enough, Preston also planned to treat the men to a day of thoroughbred racing at Saratoga Springs, the center of Upstate New York society during the month of August every year.

"Preston is so excited about this, Meg," Kenneth said, sounding like a kid himself, "and he's invited me to go along, too. I think he's afraid the old guys will poop out on him. After he twisted my arm, I accepted his invitation. I did tell him, though, that chances are *we'll* be the ones ready to come home long before those two characters even start to slow down."

Megan wished she could be there to see the look on David's face when he found out about the weekend plans. He used to love going to Saratoga in August, but hadn't been there for many years. Sharing vicariously in the excitement being orchestrated by Kenneth and Preston, she was already looking forward to hearing every little detail from David. *I'll call him right after they get back, when he'll be fresh off the experience.*

On Monday, August 15, she left the office at an amazingly early five o'clock and was home preparing spaghetti sauce by six. Phillip came home early, too, a few minutes ahead of Megan, and mixed a martini for each of them. She was sipping hers while chopping onion and fresh tomatoes and watching the evening news on the countertop television. He was sitting at the breakfast bar, nursing his drink and reading the Wall Street Journal. When the telephone rang, Phillip answered it.

"Hello?" After a few motionless moments of listening to the caller, his eyes touched Megan's from across the room. His face was grim, his voice sober.

"Honey, it's for you. It's Kenneth."

She felt light-headed—nauseous—as she studied her husband. Then the air became heavy, its leaden weight closing in around her.

"No! Don't look at me like that. Oh, *please*, Phillip. Please don't tell me something has happened to David."

"He's had a stroke." Kenneth's voice was solemn and barely audible. "I'm afraid he's in pretty bad shape."

She couldn't speak, and she was crushed by an overwhelming sense of helplessness. Kenneth continued, in sympathy with her silence.

"Meg, I know how you feel. I've been in a fog for the last hour. Irrational as it may sound, I had this feeling that he'd always be around."

Choked with tears, she struggled to put a few words together.

"Where's DJ?"

"I can't find him. He's on vacation or something. I asked Mr. Parnell if he could track him down for me."

"What about William?"

"I left a message for him on his machine. Told him to get in touch with me here at the hospital. How soon can you fly up?"

"There's no way I can make it tonight. But I'll see you as early as possible tomorrow morning. I'll call Barnes when I've made the arrangements. And Kenny, promise me you'll talk to David. Whisper to him, hold his hand, and let him know you're there. Tell him I'm coming, too. Tell him to hang on. Maybe he can hear you."

"Megan, I don't think…"

"Kenny, please. Just stay beside him. Promise?"

"Okay. I promise. 'Bye."

She dropped the phone onto the cradle without a goodbye in return, letting Phillip hold her as she wept. Given his ongoing concern about his wife's state of mind, he could not have imagined a worse turn of events.

"I'll never forgive myself if I don't go, honey."

"I understand, but what about your work? You've only been back for two weeks."

"I know. But this is *David* we're talking about. I couldn't begin to put my job ahead of him right now, and I can't believe anyone would ask me to."

"You don't have to explain this to *me*, Meg. I'm well aware of the unusual circumstances. But he's a distant cousin to you, and I'm afraid people like Curtis will have a hard time reconciling David's illness with your being gone again."

"Well, that's *his* problem." Grabbing the box of Kleenex from the counter, she broke free from his embrace and headed toward the study. "Excuse me, sweetheart. I have a few calls to make."

But Jerry Rogers didn't like the idea either when she reached him at home.

"As your friend, Meg, I'm warning you that you're inviting trouble."

"Why? Because a person very dear in my life has had a stroke, and I want to be with him?"

"No. *Because* things are still extremely unstable around here! There isn't a single secure position in our entire building, as you well know. And when you're not present-and-accounted-for, you become more and more vulnerable. I'm just worried about your *job*, for God's sake!"

"Look, Jerry," she answered, steeled by the sudden clarity of it all. "My five senses have been consumed by that company for fifteen years. I've never allowed *anything* to come between me and the almighty corporate priorities, not even my husband or daughter. Would you like to know how much accrued vacation time I have? Fourteen weeks! But I've been lucky to scrape together a *long weekend* off during the past year! Well, I'm beginning to think I've made an enormous error in judgment. Lately I've been discovering that there are actually important people in my life who have absolutely nothing to do with Strategic Data. How's *that* for a concept, Jerry? Wonderful, interesting people! *Family*! And oddly enough, they're not only coming alive for me, but they're dying, too. And like a brick falling on my head, I can see now that the game of Scrabble I postponed will be hard to play with him, if he's dead! Pardon the obscure analogy, but the *point* is that I'm tired of waiting until the *end* to show up."

"Megan, I…"

"No. Please listen to me, Jerry. I'll call Curtis myself in the morning, and you can keep your distance from my situation, if you want to. I'll understand. But over the last two weeks, you and I have managed to rebuild a semblance of order in that place, despite the depressing atmosphere. Departments have been consolidated. I've realigned what's left of the support staffs and organized new training programs for each of the functional units. Not a bad day's work, if you ask me. And thanks to your genius, we also managed to keep Glenda. As a result of our efforts, life on earth, as we know it, should endure without me for a few more days. If Curtis has a problem with this, then maybe I should reconsider just exactly what it is that I've been working sixty hours a week to build!"

"Meg…"

"Jerry, let me get the rest of this out. I'm almost through. You know how much I love my job, and how appreciative I am of the opportunities given to me over the years. That's not the issue. It's just that I've been looking at a whole lot of grave markers lately, and I've decided that I don't want a carving of a computer terminal or a desk on *mine*. I want my epitaph to say something about what kind of *person* I was—what sort of mother, or wife, or friend—not how devoted I was to a corporate monolith, or how many unbroken days and nights I sacrificed in pursuit of the bottom line, leaving me too late, or too tired, or too not-there-at-all to share dinner and conversation and *time* with my family. So I *am* going to Albany. If there's no job for me when I get back, well, so be it. I'm not going to miss out on the important stuff *any more*!"

"Megan?" Jerry spoke, after a pause indicated that she might be finished. "Is it my turn yet?"

"Yes," she said, trying to send him a smile through the tears of release that suddenly clouded her vision. "Sorry," she added, surprised at how much lighter she felt.

"Now, don't go apologizing and ruin your great speech. You made some excellent points, you know, even if you are—forgive me for saying so—incredibly long-winded."

Glad to hear her push out a laugh as she blew her nose, Jerry continued, his voice taking on a compassionate tone.

"And frankly, the same things have been bothering me, too. When you get back, maybe we can work on rebalancing things together. Okay?"

"Okay," she whispered, feeling completely drained.

"I do think it would be wise, though, for you to call Curtis in the morning. I'll talk with him, too."

"Jerry, thank you. And no matter what happens, I'll never forget the friendship and loyalty you've given me—especially tonight."

Barnes met Megan at the Albany airport shortly before ten o'clock the next morning and drove her directly to the medical center. Kenneth was waiting for her in the lobby. They took the elevator to the Intensive Care Unit without exchanging a word, running into Dr. Coomey as he was leaving David's room. They were both deeply moved by the old man's appearance when he paused briefly to greet them, his expression telling them a story of someone beaten down by the prospect of yet another goodbye. Even older than David, Dr. Coomey had somehow survived, while still managing to look years younger than the few of his contemporaries who were still alive. He was the physician who'd delivered both Megan and Kenneth into the world, and there'd always been an aura of immortality about him. But all of that seemed to be ending.

Life's fragile fabric is unraveling, and I don't know how to make it stop, Megan thought solemnly, as she put her arms around the doctor and then watched him shuffle slowly down the hospital corridor. Afterwards, she and Kenneth spent a quiet hour with David, each taking turns whispering their thoughts of love and family to him. His vital signs were weak, and the prognosis offered little hope of improvement. But the two cousins remained vigilant, clinging to fading expectations, and to each other.

At one point, when Kenneth left the room to call Justine, Megan gently smoothed David's covers around him, then leaned over and kissed him on the cheek.

"I'm sorry," she said, sitting beside him on the bed. "I haven't told Kenny yet. I've been putting it off, and now I am *so* angry with myself. But I promise I'll do it this afternoon. He'll be so proud, once he knows, and I'm praying you'll be able to see that. I love you so much, David. We *all* love you, and we don't want you to go. Can you hear me? *Please* don't go."

When Kenneth returned, she convinced him to walk with her to the cafeteria for a sandwich, but only after making the nursing staff swear to send word downstairs immediately if anything should happen. A few minutes later, they were seated at one of the dining tables, the food on their trays remaining untouched.

"He really looks awful, doesn't he, Meg?"

"Peaceful, though," she said, indirectly answering his question, as she sipped steaming black coffee from a Styrofoam cup. "He seems very peaceful," she repeated, trying to bolster her resolve. "Kenny, there's something I need to tell you, one of those surprises I learned from Gram. You should know—and William should, too—before David…Damn it! This is horrible!"

"Spit it out, Megan. I want to get back upstairs."

His impatience was overriding his usual curiosity, and she could tell she had a very small window of time before he would get up and walk away from her.

"Kenny, listen to me. David…he's not your cousin."

"What? What are you talking about?"

"He's…*please God, help me with this*…he's your grandfather."

She saw his jaw tighten.

"I beg your pardon?"

"I know this is going to be a shock, and hard to believe, and I wish to heaven that you weren't hearing about this under these circumstances. But Gram and David had a…a relationship. The actual *relationship* part ended very quickly, and they sort of buried it in their friendship later on. But the truth is that their love resulted in your father being conceived. Gram married Gregory a month later, and David didn't even know your dad was his son until way after Hawaii—until after Gregory Senior died, actually. That's when David moved to the cottage."

Kenneth sat frozen in his chair, staring straight through Megan, as his mind tried to process her stunning disclosure. Then, slowly, his anger began escalating.

"*Excuse* me?" he asked, his back becoming rigid, as he placed his hands palms down on the table. "*Dad* was David's *son*?"

"Yes. I'm sorry, Kenny. I…"

"*Sorry*? You're *sorry*? No *shit*!" His voice had grown loud, and other diners in the cafeteria were looking over at them. "Megan, why didn't anyone *tell* us? Why didn't *you* tell us? Tell *me?*"

She was even less prepared for this than she thought.

"Kenny, forgive me. I only found out myself the day Gram died. She left me a letter, asking me to...But I was trying to wait for the..."

"For the *what*? For the perfect moment? For the ideal setting? For David's *funeral*?"

"Please, Kenny, let me explain!"

"Oh, give it up, Meg. This is just beautiful! I've loved that man beyond my understanding for almost forty years. He inspired me. He played ball with me. He stepped in so many times, came to my games at school, helped me over the rough spots when other kids had their fathers with them. He was even waiting for me in the hospital when Tania was born. In fact, both he *and* Gram were there. And now, when he's lying upstairs in a coma—when I can't talk to him or tell him how much he's meant to me—*now* I find out that he's my *grandfather*!"

He rose to his feet in the midst of his outburst, oblivious to the attention he was drawing. But then he gradually lowered himself back into his chair, and his voice began to moderate.

"Damn it, Megan. Why in God's name didn't we *know*?"

"That's one of so many unanswered questions, Kenny. And since the responsibility suddenly became mine, I've been struggling to find the words. I honestly *did* plan to tell you, when I came up in August. Absurd as it might seem, I didn't want to just blurt it out. But I also believed I had more time than this. I really didn't think something would happen to him so soon. Why he and Gram never said anything to you, themselves, is something we may never know. Maybe they thought the truth would hurt you."

She could see the intensity of his reaction beginning to subside, but she could barely hear him when he spoke.

"I think I'd better make a serious effort to find William. If there's any way for him to get here tonight...Please excuse me."

"Kenny," she said, grabbing his hand as he stood up, "are you angry with me?'

"No, Meg. I'm fine. Really."

Reassuringly squeezing her fingers, he left to find a telephone. When he returned, they took the elevator back upstairs. During the next four hours, they sat side-by-side near David, while she answered as many of Kenny's questions as she could about Cinnamon's story. Folded inside this retrospection, the two of them were unaware of the activities going on around them. Members of the nursing staff darted in and out periodically, and Justine stopped by to take her husband and Megan out to dinner. But she changed her mind after seeing them imbedded in their private dialogue, and respectfully left without telling them she was there.

William arrived from Buffalo at seven that evening. Then he and his brother stayed alone in David's room, emerging briefly to make a phone call, or buy a cup of coffee, or speak with Megan, who held vigil in the Intensive Care lounge. But outside of the small private corner in Albany's Medical Center, nothing else in the world mattered to any of them.

At the end, David's secret grandsons were standing on opposite sides of his bed, each of them holding one of his enormous hands, when he died shortly after dawn. They stayed there for the longest time, looking at him, touching him, and trying to reconcile their unique bond with him. Just before they said goodbye, Kenneth and William prayed aloud with a single voice, hoping through some miracle that their grandfather knew they had finally found their rightful place in his life.

DJ was vacationing with his wife Beth, in an obscure cottage on the Cape. Locating them had thus taken many hours of valuable time. Once Mr. Parnell notified them of the emergency situation, they endured a jostling commuter flight to Boston's Logan Airport, followed by a persistent weather delay. Desperate and frustrated, they ultimately rented a car and made the exhausting four-hour drive to Albany, in the middle of the night. By the time they arrived, however, David was gone.

"I can't seem to put any of it in place! How can he be dead? I didn't even know he was sick! Why didn't someone *tell* me he was sick?"

"It was all very sudden, DJ," Kenneth answered, making a futile attempt to console this man he now knew to be his uncle. "He didn't suffer, though, and he wasn't alone."

"But I should have been here with him," DJ replied in a broken voice. "I was the only one he had left."

In sharp contrast to Cinnamon's final extravaganza, David's funeral that Friday was an unassuming event. Phillip and Kristin flew up to Albany and were anticipating that Megan would return with them to Atlanta the following morning. But that was before Mr. Parnell informed her that she'd been named as a beneficiary in David's will.

"It will all be said and done on Monday," she told her husband, dismissing his concern about her being alone at Fox Run over the weekend. "Kenny said that William is staying in town, too, so I'll have plenty of company, if I need it. Then I'll come home Monday night."

Right, he thought. *There must be an echo in here!*

A small group of family and friends gathered at Fox Run after the service, including Preston, who was there without Jay. He explained to the group that he'd decided not to tell his father about David's death, fearing the news would further confuse him and jeopardize his health.

"He's all that remains now of their generation," Preston said. "So I appreciate your support in helping me keep this from him, until I figure out the best way to handle it. Of course, he'll probably end up outliving me, and then there'll be hell to pay when he finds out I've been going to parties without him."

The light moment seemed to be appreciated by everyone, except Phillip. He was deeply sorry for the tragedies experienced by this family of late. But his priority was Megan, and until she was home with him—in mind, as well as body—he was not going to rest easily. Meanwhile, neither his patience not his sense of humor were very accessible. After pouring himself a brandy in the library bar, he made his way back into the front hall, where he lingered for a few minutes, leaning against the sideboard and sipping his drink. Feeling fortified, he decided to rejoin the group. Just as he rounded the corner from the foyer into the parlor, he saw his wife lift herself up on her tiptoes, on the far side of the room, and gently press her lips against Preston's cheek.

The next morning, after taking Phillip and Kristin to the airport, Megan sat at the table in the kitchen's sunny bay window for more than an hour. Given the depressing circumstances of this last week—of the last *month*—the weather seemed inappropriately bright and airy.

"Why isn't it foggy and raining like it *should* be, without Gram and David here."

"Now, now, Miss Megan." Heidi was doing her best to sound cheerful, despite the fact that she'd been awake crying half the night. "Mr. McClinty loved these beautiful days. And even though we're having an awful time, he's probably getting his share of sunshine somewhere, right alongside Mrs. Stafford. Neither of them would be pleased, you know, to see you sitting here, pushing your food all over your plate. You really should be eating something."

Megan felt sorry for Heidi, but she had no energy for even the most innocent debate.

"Thanks just the same, but I'm really not hungry. If anyone calls," she said, getting up and moving toward the back door, "I'll be over in the cottage. You can either take a message or come get me."

Regrettably, the housekeeper persisted.

"Are you sure you want to do that so soon? Maybe it would be better if you waited awhile longer."

"Look, Heidi!" Megan couldn't stop herself from blurting out the words. "I realize you're dealing with your own grief. But I want to be left alone, and I'm going to the cottage, whether you like it or not."

The two women stared at each other for a moment, before Heidi completely broke down, lifting the skirt of her apron and burying her face in it as she sobbed.

"I'm so sorry, ma'am, for overstepping my bounds. It's just that we were all starting to be happy again, learning how to get along without Mrs. Stafford. But now that Mr. McClinty's gone, too, I'm having real trouble. It's so sad, and I miss them both so much."

Feeling like a chump, Megan took the woman in her arms.

"Oh, Heidi. I'm sorry, too. This has all been very hard for me, but I certainly don't mean to take anything out on you. Please forgive me."

"Yes, of course I do. Thank you," Heidi said, wiping her eyes and returning her attention, without further comment, to the fresh flowers she'd been trimming and arranging at the sink.

Megan walked out the back door and across the yard. David's cottage was immaculate, although stuffy after being closed up for five days. She opened all the windows, drew back the curtains and switched on the ceiling fan in the living room. Vases containing fresh cut flowers were everywhere, but the water had evaporated leaving the flowers to crumble in the heat. She found a plastic trash bag in the cupboard, emptied the decayed blossoms and rinsed out the vases. When she was finished puttering, she began wandering around, feeling his presence everywhere.

In his bedroom, she opened the closet door and brushed her fingertips across the sleeves of his shirts. Inhaling his scent, she smiled. Each item of clothing was neatly placed on fabric hangers, all of his trousers grouped together, then his shirts, and finally the jackets and sweaters. Allowing her tears to fall freely, she returned to the kitchen and prepared a pot of tea. Then she went into the small study next to David's bedroom and switched on the radio, leaving the dial set at his favorite classical station. The music and the herbal fragrance from her china cup calmed her, as she leaned back in the leather desk chair and swiveled slowly. But then a pair of louvered doors on another closet caught her eye. Walking across the room, she pulled the doors open. On the floor inside was the box of journals—and on top of the box was David's tin of letters.

What? Didn't I leave that up in the attic?

Before she had time to further consider the question, she saw an envelope taped to the tin—and written on the envelope were the words **FOR MEGAN**. Feeling her whole body begin to shake, she peeled off the tape and removed the envelope's contents. After unfolding the pages, she recognized David's handwriting.

Sunday, August 14, 1988

Dearest Megan—

"Oh, my God! That was the day before his stroke!"

Sitting down on the floor, she rested against the wall and began to read. As she did, she could almost feel him there in the room with her.

I wish you were here so I could talk to you. Heidi told me you called, but I prefer to write this down instead of trying to explain over the phone. (Must be all those years of your grandmother's influence.) Today I don't feel very well, but if I'm better tomorrow, maybe I'll change my mind and call you after supper.

Anyway, Megan, I've been reading her journals—the ones you left with me. I also went back over the letters she wrote to me. (By the way, thanks for sending me all over creation trying to find the tin. I knew you didn't take it home with you, and something told me you might have stuck it up in the attic. Don't worry. I had Barnes get it down for me.) But you see, after reading all this stuff, my heart is very heavy, because now I believe your grandmother was *right*! I really believe now that he *did* know. *The bastard knew*! I used to think she was crazy, going on and on about it the way she did. But now I feel bad about making fun of her. I'm also sick to my stomach, thinking about what must have really happened over there.

The good thing is that you've read everything, too. Plus, you actually heard her tell you. At least I know that you've got the whole story. But I think that's where we should leave it, even though my heart is torn in pieces by the mental images. No one can be helped by digging things up now, so I want you to bury the truth—with *me*—and let the ordeal finally end. Whatever she told you, don't listen to her. Just let it go, Megan. *Make it be over*.

I missed you when you went home, but, of course, that's where you belong. I've already had my turn, and I think soon it will be time for me to go. So, I wanted to write this down, while I still can. Be happy, and have a very wonderful life. I love you, and I love the boys, too—*all* of them.

Always,
David

P.S. I know about the secret trip to the races planned for this weekend, and I'm going to try to live until then. I'll place a couple of bets for you while I'm there.

Unaware of how close she'd been to unraveling, Megan was helplessly pushed over the edge by this letter. Her emotional state was so stretched that she wasn't even producing any tears. But the mixtures of loss and grief—and fear—had so completely filled her heart that she was unable to focus on anything in the room. Instead, David's haunting words were overpowering her.

"*No*! She did *not* tell me the whole story! And I don't know what you're talking about. Who is *he*? What do you *mean*?"

Curled up on the floor in the corner, her clenched fists were pounding against the carpet as she cried out loud in a lonely, empty appeal.

"You can't leave me with this, David! *Please*! Take it *away*!"

All at once, someone gripped the tops of her arms and began shaking her, and then she heard a strong voice in contention with her own.

"Megan! *Megan*! Look at me!"

As the room came back into a hazy focus, she blinked to clear her eyes.

"Preston! What are *you* doing here?"

Prior to leaving for Boston, he'd stopped by Fox Run, compelled by an odd sensation that all might not be right. When his intuition was confirmed after Heidi directed him to the cottage, he became alarmed about Megan's physical and mental health and offered to give her a prescription to help ease her anxiety. But she'd politely declined, insisting that she was just tired. She'd also persuaded him not to contact Phillip, which his instincts were telling him he should do immediately, no matter what she said.

"Frankly," she confessed while sitting on the living room sofa in the cottage, "I'm more embarrassed than anything else, and I'm afraid I haven't been completely honest with you about what's going on here."

She then proceeded to summarize the rest of the story for him about David's actual relationship to Greg.

"Making things worse, I've uncovered a few other tidbits since that day when I was asking you all those questions. Now things are even more confusing."

"Megan, what do you have to gain by pursuing this? Your grandmother's gone. David's gone. What's the point in making yourself nuts?"

"If she hadn't been so specific in her last request of me, it might be easier. Besides, it's not just the part about Greg and Teddy, either. It's her whole story. She's managed to make all of my ancestors feel very real to me. I even went to a little cemetery in New York on my way home last month so I could visit some of their graves. It's almost like I've been pulled back into her life—*their* lives. Maybe that's her way of helping me get to the answers."

"Well, whatever her original intentions might have been, I can't believe she would have asked you to pursue this, if she'd known what it was going to do to you. She loved you too much—and frankly, you're a mess."

"I really wish you wouldn't mince words like that," she said, smiling at him and blowing her nose for the tenth time. "But seriously, I suppose you're right. And I'm sure I do look and sound completely ridiculous to you. But I'll only be here for a couple more days anyway, and I'll do my best to put this all away before I leave. Once I'm back home, I'll be fine."

Moving to the sofa, he sat down beside her and stroked her hair.

"You're really quite pathetic, you know. I'm driving to Boston today, but I'm not going to stop worrying about you. So, you need to promise me you'll call, if you need to talk. Here's my home, office and pager numbers," he added, taking a business card from his wallet.

"Thanks, Preston. Hopefully, I can get past this without needing to bother you—or without being locked in a rubber room."

Heidi's knock at the cottage door broke up their laughter.

"Please excuse me for interrupting, but will you be staying for dinner, Dr. McClinty?"

"No, Heidi, but thanks for the invitation. Next time."

"All right, then. Miss Megan, while I'm here, you had two messages. Your mother telephoned and asked me to say that she's moving into her new house today, and she'll call you again, as soon as the phone is working. Then, Mr. Parnell called, too. He said he wants you to stay at his office for awhile on Monday, after the will is read. But he wasn't sure what time your flight is leaving for Atlanta."

"Thanks, Heidi," Megan said, pushing aside her irritation at the housekeeper's intrusion, as she watched the woman turn and head back across the yard.

Preston then put the box of journals and the tin of letters back in the study closet, while Megan closed the windows and switched off the lights. After pulling the cottage door shut behind them, they walked around to the front of the house toward his car, which was parked in the driveway.

"It's very sad," Megan said, "that David never made it to his weekend with you at Lake George and Saratoga. I know he would have loved that very much."

"I was actually looking forward to it, too. Well, at least we were keeping it a surprise, so no one had to be disappointed."

"Be careful on your way home," she said, squeezing his arm and deciding not to tell him how excited David had been. *That might make him feel even worse.*

"I will," he replied, leaning down to kiss her on the forehead. "See you soon."

Megan sat paralyzed, along with the eight other beneficiaries in Mr. Parnell's office on Monday morning, as the attorney began to explain and disburse in excess of $21 million dollars. A banner-sized *What?* kept flashing across all of their faces, as a brief explanation unfolded. Jonathon had apparently invested the money Lily left for David, and he was able to salvage most of the accumulated balance before the bottom completely fell out of the market at the onset of the Depression. When Jonathon died, he willed all of that money, and more, to David, who'd parlayed those funds into a fortune secreted away, even from David's only surviving son.

"Prudence, wisdom, sound advice, the eventual sale of the McClinty Mill, and an occasional speculative venture into start-up companies such as IBM are the ingredients he blended toward this end," continued Mr. Parnell. "He wanted his wealth to remain private until after his death, since he was basically a very simple man, who enjoyed *counting* his assets more than he did *using* them."

The diversification of David's portfolio increased the will's complexity, but the sum totals behind each bequest were easily comprehended by everyone. DJ's share came to $6 million, and another $2.5 million each was left to DJ's two sons as well as Teddy's two boys. Thus far, the disposition made sense. But anxious looks were exchanged between David's son and grandsons when they calculated that only $16 million had been distributed. Mr. Parnell proceeded, however, as if he sensed no friction in the air.

"An additional $2.5 million each is bequeathed to Kenneth Stafford and William Stafford. Megan Cole inherits $250,000," he continued, afraid to look up from the legal document, "and Barnes Osgood is to receive $50,000. Mr. Osgood and Megan, I also have envelopes here for both of you."

Mr. Parnell concluded by reading a brief note out loud, "which David asked me to share with all of you."

Whatever accumulation of worldly possessions I am leaving behind is being given to those I love and to those who have loved and cared for me in return. Please bear in mind that any legal challenge will be viewed as a callous disregard for my final requests, and shall result in the full disinheritance of the party or parties who would raise such a challenge. Now remember how much I love each and every one of you, and how full you've made my life. That's what real wealth is all about! Live well but prudently, and don't forget me.

Always,
David McClinty

Mr. Parnell placed the will on the table and folded his hands, clearly signaling the end to what he had to say.

Oh, great, Megan thought, wishing she had a knife to cut the air in the room. *I can't believe David didn't include some explanation, so DJ would at least have a clue what's going on here. Well, I did my part. I guess it's Kenny's turn now.* She did consider mentioning the situation to the attorney, however, in case he had any suggestions. *Surely David must have told his own lawyer!*

When no one had moved or spoken in the room for several raw moments, Mr. Parnell arose and began shaking everyone's hands, which graciously served to bridge the awkward silence. But despite the polite, congratulatory remarks being exchanged, there was a distinct tension that only seemed to grow stronger as the group began to disburse. DJ appeared to be particularly shaken, confused by the introduction and allocation of such unknown riches, not to mention the inclusion of the Stafford boys at the same level as his father's grandsons.

No one had scheduled any sort of official party this time, which now seemed fortunate, as everyone began heading out in different directions. Since Barnes was planning to drive Megan to the airport, however, she said her goodbyes to Kenneth and William while still in the attorney's office.

"You might want to give DJ a call and invite him out for a drink," she whispered to Kenneth, after planting a kiss on his cheek.

"Right," he replied, shaking his head. "I can't believe Mr. Parnell didn't help me out with this!"

"He wants to talk to me before I go, so I'll mention it to him, if you'd like."

"Thanks, Meg. I really would. Meanwhile, call me and let me know when you've arrived safely home in Atlanta."

After he and William left, Megan wandered out into the corridor while she was waiting for Mr. Parnell to finish talking with his secretary. There she saw Barnes sitting on a wooden bench and leaning against the wall. The manila envelope on his lap was open, and he smiled when he saw her approach.

"Oh, Miss Megan! Look at this, will you?"

He handed her a paperback book entitled My Favorite Jokes, and a collection of restaurant coupons with a note attached.

Barnes—Use these to take Heidi out to dinner, if you can stand it! Ha!

—David

The chauffeur bravely struggled to retain his composure, as Megan sat down beside him and held his hand.

"I can't believe how much I miss him already, Miss Megan. My life'll be so empty and unhappy without him."

"I know. But think how dreary our lives would have been if he hadn't been here at all. His existence was a rare and special gift, and we are very lucky to have been blessed with him."

He nodded and wiped his face with the handkerchief he'd been holding for the last hour, then placed the book and coupons back inside the envelope.

"I'll wait for you down in the car," he said.

"Of course. I shouldn't be too long."

When he'd gone, she lifted the loosely sealed flap of her own envelope and removed the undated letter.

Megan dear—

Use the money I'm leaving you to buy something personal for yourself for a change, like maybe a new dress or two. I know yours is a small amount compared to the others, but you received your share from your grandmother. She and I did not mean to trick any of you, but we planned our estates very carefully. We wanted everything to be fair and to come out even. We figured you'd all work through any misunderstandings. She said it would be one way to get you talking with each other. I told her it might also be a way to make you kill each other, but she didn't think that was very funny. She never did have a sense of humor.

You might need to help DJ and his boys with the Kenny and William thing. I hope you don't mind, and I hope it's not too bad. Take care of yourself.

—David

Back in Mr. Parnell's office, the attorney made the suggestion that, in view of the recent turmoil weathered by the family, this might be a fitting juncture for the first of Cinnamon's subsidized vacations.

"Nowhere in any of her instructions did she say we had to wait for a specific amount of time to pass, before scheduling the first trip."

He continued by informing her that he had connections with the management of a large resort on the Caribbean Island of St. Croix.

"If we start planning right away, we could avoid any major conflicts with school. Tania and Kristin might have to miss a day or two, though, unless you don't think that's wise."

She needed only a moment to consider.

"On the contrary, I think you have a perfect idea! We *have* been through a lot, and if the girls need to bring along some homework, that can be worked out. I say let's *do* it!"

They tentatively decided upon the dates of September 23 through September 27, thus using a weekend for part of the trip. Mr. Parnell said he'd take care of polling the family and, if there was consensus, he would also send out the letters of confirmation once the reservations had been assured.

"All *you* have to do, my dear," he said, giving her a paternal hug, "is show up!"

Somehow, mentioning the issue of David's actual relationship to Kenny and William didn't seem appropriate at that moment.

Phillip pressed his fingers against his temples to slow the advancing headache. He and Kristin had taken Megan out to dinner after picking her up at the Atlanta airport, and now he was sharing a nightcap with his wife in the gazebo. Unfortunately, she'd just finished telling him about the potential excursion to St. Croix, not wanting to mention it in front of Kristin until the trip had been confirmed.

"But what about your work, Meg?"

"Oh, honestly! Why does everyone keep asking me that same question?"

"Well, because it's the first one that comes to mind when you mention spending a week in the Caribbean, after you've already been away for the better part of a month. Am I wrong, or didn't your career used to be important to you—you know, the one you've worked at so hard for the last fifteen years?"

"No, honey, you're not wrong. It *was* important to me. Maybe it still *will* be. I just don't know right now. Anyway, it's more than a month until the excursion, assuming those dates are good for everyone else. By then, I might not even *have* a job anymore, considering the state of affairs there when I left last week. But I'll give it everything I've got between now and then. Assuming I'm still employed, if my being away for what will only be three business days turns out to be a problem, I guess I'll have to make a decision. After all, I have *fourteen weeks* of accrued vacation—if you can even believe it—which I never used, because I was in the office all the time. Maybe I'll request a leave of absence. Better yet, maybe I'll just resign."

"I hope you're kidding."

"I am, at the moment. Not sure if I will be by September 23, though. Anyway, it will certainly be interesting to see how this all plays out, particularly since no one at work knows yet that I have $3 million worth of options I didn't have before. Excuse me, $3 million plus $250,000."

Phillip forced a strained laugh, in response to her infectious smile.

"God help us," he said, taking a long sip of his drink, "now that your bull-headed determination has been paired with an obscene amount of money."

Yes, indeed, he thought, inhaling deeply. *God help us!*

Chapter 21

"Kristin and I have been making lists to go with our lists," Megan said to Kenneth, after calling him a week before the scheduled departure to St. Croix, "and I was just curious if we're the only ones too excited to sit still."

"No, I think it's happening to everyone—even William. He called last night to say he's coming to Albany this weekend to do some shopping."

"Don't they have stores in Buffalo?"

"Careful. The Chamber of Commerce might be listening. Seriously, he and I have been spending quite a bit of time together during the past two weeks. Actually, I'm enjoying the hell out of my little brother, and I think it's mutual."

"What a nice thing to hear, Kenny."

"It's an interesting transformation. Who could have predicted it? Anyway, William's closets aren't exactly full of summer clothes. The Buffalo thing again. I really don't think he even owns a pair of shorts. So, the two of us will be menacing the mall together. He also says he's ready to buy an honest-to-goodness set of luggage. Apparently, he's decided that his collection of duffel bags advertising everything from gas stations to pizza parlors would not be appropriate for this trip. Funny, isn't it?"

"Yes, although *I've* been buying lots of new things, too—things I never knew existed that I suddenly can't live without."

"There's something addictive, Meg, about the combination of going on a vacation and being able to afford not only the trip, but all the accessories, too. With a little practice, I think I could get used to this."

"I know what you mean. And seeing each other more often, under pleasant circumstances, for a change, is the crème de la crème, don't you think?"

"I do. Gram and David—excuse me, Gram and *my grandfather*—put quite a plan together. The two of them grow more amazing to me every day."

"Sometimes I don't feel like they're really gone."

"Right. Well, they *are*," he said rather sharply, feeling uncomfortable whenever she took that spooky turn. "So, what are you going to do about your work this trip?"

"Gosh," she declared, deciding not to comment on his abrupt change of subject. "It's been at least an hour since someone asked me that question. As it stands right now, I've been given the nod to take four vacation days, but not a single moment longer. I'm assuming there'll still be a job for me when I get back, but I'm not going to worry about it. Now that I'm volunteering three times a week at one of the homeless shelters downtown, I'm beginning to see that there are lots of ways I can use my experience and background to help make a difference for folks who've run into hard times. And, of course, with the money and everything, I have some flexibility to move in that direction, if I want to. We'll see what happens. But today, the only thing on my mind is the thought of basking in the Caribbean sunshine!"

"Same here, although I'll admit that the first few minutes with DJ might be a little unnerving."

"That must mean you haven't had your little chat with him yet?"

"No, but I'm anxious to clear the air. And I'm hoping it will be easier to talk about who's related to whom, while sipping heavily on a rum punch."

"If you want me to help you—or to *be* with you—just let me know."

"Thanks, Meg. But I'm not going to pre-arrange anything. Once we're all there on Fantasy Island, the right timing and setting will just happen, I hope. Meanwhile, more incredible things are taking place up here. For example, Justine and Tania are out spending money this entire day—dawn until dark—and I'm not even terrified! There's definitely a new wind blowing!"

"Feels great, doesn't it? Sort of fresh and free."

"And rich!"

"Yes, Kenny—and rich. Uh-oh," she said, looking at her watch, "I have a meeting in a few minutes. Guess I'd better run. Could you ask Justine to call me tonight so we can compare our travel notes?"

"Sure. Don't work too hard. See you soon!"

As Phillip loaded the car, he was positive there could not be a single piece of unsold luggage remaining in the entire city of Atlanta.

"I thought you said we'd only be gone for five days!"

But Megan had already returned to the house, where she and Kristin were making a final review of their checklists. Assuming that the family's bizarre behavior would pass, Buck the dog did his best to become invisible beneath the kitchen table. He was unaware, as Megan locked the last door, that a neighbor would be his only cook and companion for the next few days. Sitting up, his ears at attention, he listened without great concern as he heard the car descend the driveway. Forty-five minutes later, the Coles were standing in line at their departure gate in Atlanta's Hartsfield International Airport.

The two-hour flight to Miami was followed by a layover there, then another two-hour flight to San Juan, another layover *there*, and a final experience in a ten-seat paperweight.

"Mom," Kristin asked, "why are those men putting our suitcases inside the *wings* of the airplane?"

"There are some things God doesn't want us to know," Megan answered nervously, as she watched the unsettling maneuvers taking place outside the window. "Maybe they just have different procedures in Puerto Rico."

She thought her weak attempt at humor had gone unheard. But, in spite of his mounting frustration with the length of this journey, Phillip was feeling playful.

"Wait until Kristin finds out," he whispered to his wife, "that our seat assignments are determined by how much we weigh!"

"What? Why would they do something like that?" she asked, trying to sound conversational.

"I thought you knew, honey. Balance is extremely important on those planes. Just a pound or two off, and, well…"

"Okay," she said, her voice suddenly squeaking. "But at least we have reserved window seats."

"*Every* seat is a window seat," he replied, trying desperately not to laugh. "One on each side of the aisle, in each of the *five* rows. Come on. Let's get going."

She wished she were unconscious, as the boarding began. But much to her relief, the scene soon grew comical. The pilot and copilot, both of whom wore colossal headphones and stiff green jackets adorned with braids and medallions, were clearly visible in the cockpit behind a short, open curtain. They looked ridiculous, like overgrown boys playing airplane in a pickup truck. And the faded blue jeans, which served as the bottom half of their uniforms, further confirmed the disturbing image. Rather than dwell on the fact that these two men had been placed in charge and would soon attempt to lift this tin can out over the ocean, Megan closed her eyes and tried to pretend she was on a bus.

The *crew* began executing their official routines, while the vehicle inched toward the runway. Panicked as she was, she had to smother a laugh when the copilot—easily identified as such by the sign bearing his title, printed by hand in three languages and then scotch-taped to his side of the cockpit wall—spun around in his swivel chair—*is that a good idea in a cockpit?*—to face the passengers.

"The seat pocket in front of you," he began, "contains a card which outlines the safety features of the AO1911 aircraft..."

They can't seriously believe this qualifies as an aircraft, she thought.

A gentleman across the aisle from her inquired facetiously if there would be a beverage service. But the copilot never broke his verbal stride. This absence of humor was even more disconcerting than the rest of the absurd picture, as they dangled in the air, supposedly aimed at their destination, for forty-five minutes. After landing uneventfully at the St. Croix airport, Megan wondered how complicated it might be for them to return home via a cruise ship.

Mr. Parnell greeted them in the hotel, where they discovered that Caribbean time was already ten o'clock at night.

"Mom, can I order something from room service? I'm starving!"

"Unfortunately, the kitchen is closed until morning," Mr. Parnell intervened. "But I had a feeling you might be hungry, so I arranged a small buffet on the terrace. Go unwind and freshen up in your rooms first. Take as long as you need. There's no rush."

"Is anyone else here?" Megan asked him.

"Not yet. The others are scheduled to arrive at various times tomorrow, beginning early in the morning through late afternoon. Some of them are spending an extra day or two, in Miami or Puerto Rico, on their way here."

"That's what we might have done," Phillip groaned, "if I'd known this place was halfway around the world! Where the hell *are* we, anyway?"

"We're late for dinner, you old grump," Megan answered, linking arms with her husband and daughter. "We'll see you in a few minutes, Mr. Parnell."

The three of them breathed deeply of the tropical atmosphere as they followed the bellman out the lobby door and down a long path toward a cluster of cottages on the beach.

"Are you *kidding?*" Kristin shrieked, when she realized that the bungalow she'd be sharing with Tania was only yards away from the breaking waves.

"This is just like a movie!"

"Before you get carried away," Phillip said, still grumbling, "keep in mind that your mother and I are right next door to you."

"Well, I'm inclined to agree with Kristin," Megan hummed. "This setting is beautiful, and I'm sure it will look even better in the sunlight, after a good night's sleep. But right now, I want to wash my face and join Mr. Parnell for dinner. You two can do whatever you'd like."

A short while later, the rhythmic sound of the surf was being carried by a breeze through the open dining terrace. Combined with his rum cooler, the tropical air lifted Phillip's mood, as well as his fatigue.

"This is actually quite interesting," he said with a smirk. "An hour ago, I was wishing I'd never met Megan, and now I feel more relaxed than I have in months."

"Helplessly at the mercy of the Caribbean Sea," Mr. Parnell responded. "They tell me it happens to everyone, and some victims become so powerless that they never find their home again."

"You made an excellent choice, Mr. Parnell," Megan said, smiling at both men. "Even in the dark, I can tell the location will be perfect. Thank you for bringing us together here."

"You're very kind, Megan. But your grandmother is responsible for this, not me—as if any of us could ever forget that!"

Childlike anticipation awakened Megan after less than five hours of sleep. Without disturbing Phillip, she donned shorts and a tee-shirt, brushed her teeth and wound her hair in a twist on top of her head. Holding her sandals in one hand, she opened the bungalow door and stepped out onto the tiny porch. The shimmering sea was at eye level, and the sunrise was casting a brilliant rose-colored reflection across the sky. She thought she'd never seen anything quite as splendid as she walked alone, hearing not a sound except the soft splashing of the waves against the sand.

"This really *is* like a movie," she whispered, moving barefoot into the water and letting the swirls wash up around her ankles.

Tracing the shoreline's edge for nearly a mile, she found herself seduced by the virginal beauty of the island and the massive expanse of hotel rising like a fortress up the side of the hill. She saw the open brick archways of the dining terrace several stories above her and was surprised at the elevation. Last night at dinner, she would have guessed the surf was breaking only a few yards away from them.

Feeling her stomach starting to growl, she retraced her steps, moving in and out of the water, each time letting the satiny swells climb higher on her legs.

"Hey, you!" Phillip's voice was being carried by the wind, as he stood some distance down the beach near their cottages.

"Good morning, honey," she called back to him, speeding up her pace.

"I didn't mean to hurry you," he said. "Just wanted you to know that I'm going up to the terrace."

"Is Kristin awake yet?"

"She left for breakfast an hour ago."

"Now *that's* amazing. We'd have to pay her to get out of bed this early at home."

"Well, let's appreciate it while we can. Do you feel like having a bite to eat?"

"As a matter of fact, I do, my dear man. That's why I was coming back."

"Good. Let's go together. I wonder how early they start serving rum around here."

Thanks, Gram, Megan was thinking, as her husband took her hand and led her up the path. *This is going to be a wonderful adventure, and just exactly what I've been needing.*

Mr. Parnell was seated by himself at a large round table when Phillip and Megan arrived in the dining terrace.

"Good morning, sir," Phillip said, extending his hand.

"Yes, it does seem to be," the attorney replied, standing up and offering his hand in return. "And Megan, you look very refreshed."

"Thanks. I feel wonderful," she said, looking around for her daughter. "Have you seen Kristin, by any chance?"

"Actually, I have," he answered in a cheery tone, as he sat down again. "She's playing hostess. Kenneth arrived a short while ago with Justine, Tania and William, and she volunteered to make use of her vast experience on the island by giving them an orientation tour. Ken said to tell you he'd meet up with you later—at the reception, if not sooner."

"What reception?" Megan inquired casually, sipping the frothy fruit juice that had just been poured for her by a waiter in black pants and a short white jacket.

Mr. Parnell gestured toward a printed agenda, fashioned after a wedding invitation, which he'd propped against the table's floral centerpiece.

"Each person will receive one of these when they arrive," he added. "I meant to give you yours last night, but I'm afraid it slipped my mind."

"I had no idea you were going to such lengths," Megan said, taking the agenda in her hands. "This adds such a special touch, and it could turn out to be something of a collector's item as the years go by—a memento of the first semi-annual whatever we're going to call these things."

"Once again, your appreciation is gratifying. But there's not a trace of original thought in any of the details you'll see here. Your grandmother left nothing to chance."

Megan leaned back into her chair, fixing her sight beyond the terrace archways and out over the sea.

"I don't know why I'm surprised. Gram is everywhere."

Phillip watched her face take on that vacant expression he'd noticed a few weeks earlier, and he was irritated by the renewed sense of alarm messing up his peaceful morning. But as she read the printed agenda out loud to him, her spirits seemed high, and he tried not to think about the shadows still stalking her.

In Accordance with the Final Requests of
Mrs. Margaret Elizabeth Stafford

Mr. Anthony Parnell
Welcomes You to the First Official
McClinty Family Reunion
September 23–27, 1988
St. Croix, U.S. Virgin Islands

<u>September 23</u>
Arrival
Reception: 6:00–8:00 Terrace Dining Room

<u>September 24</u>
Activities of Choice (See Attached Selection)
Breakfast Buffet: 7:00–9:00 Terrace Dining Room
Luncheon Buffet: 11:00–1:00 Terrace Dining Room
Casual Family Beach Picnic: 7:30–9:30 (Pick Up Reserved Picnic Baskets in Lobby)

<u>September 25</u>
Activities of Choice
Breakfast & Luncheon Buffets as Above
Dinner at Restaurant of Choice (List of Options Available at Front Desk)

<u>September 26</u>
Activities of Choice
Breakfast & Luncheon Buffets as Above
Formal Banquet & Dance: 7:30 Seaside Room

<u>September 27</u>
Breakfast Buffet: 6:30–8:30
Departure for Airport: 9:00

The Activities of Choice included something for everyone, from the most avid sports enthusiasts to the beach-huggers. There was, of course, the requisite swimming, tennis, and golf, in addition to scuba and snorkeling lessons. But there was also a six-hour round trip excursion to Buck Island's underwater national park, and a Rum Punch Cruise around the bay and harbor every afternoon from 4:00–6:00. Finally, there was unlimited access to lavish, duty-free stores, in both Christiansted and Fredricksted, the only two towns on the island. A special resort van was prepared, on a moment's notice, to take members of the McClinty family shopping or to any of the fine restaurants in the villages.

"Oh, my gosh!" Megan exclaimed, after reviewing the agenda. "How will we ever get all of this done?"

"I propose that the three of us in our little part of this family do whatever we want to do, whenever we feel like doing it," Phillip answered. "After all, this is supposed to be a vacation."

"Okay. That's a deal, honey. At the very least, though, we need to be together for the reception tonight, the picnic tomorrow night and the formal banquet on Monday. Otherwise, if you specifically want me to do something with you, you'll have to come find me."

"You're on, Meg, and I'm a very happy man!"

"Well, since that's settled, I'm not going to waste another minute," she added, finishing the last bite of her croissant and taking another sip of coffee. "If you gentleman will please excuse me, I'm going to find Kristin and get this day started."

Phillip and Mr. Parnell rose to their feet as she departed, then eased back down into the cushioned wicker chairs. Feeling no pressure to speak with one another, they let the soothing sea breezes pull them into their own thoughts—and Phillip tried his best to stop worrying.

By the time the reception began that evening, everyone had arrived. A rainbow of colors began decorating the dining terrace shortly after 6:00, as the family members gathered in their tropical shirts and sundresses, each person already sporting a healthy glow from the few hours they'd had in the sun after their arrivals. Preston was the last one to present himself, having flown in only two hours earlier, and he entered the room with a tall, perfectly-formed female creature attached to his right arm. After lifting two champagne flutes from a waiter's silver tray, he slowly began making his rounds, introducing his companion to his inquisitive relatives. Her first name was Marcella, but she was so beautiful that no one heard her last name, or cared.

"Wow," Phillip said. "What a trip *he's* going to have!"

"Can you believe how gorgeous she is, Mom?" Kristin whispered.

"No, I cannot. Nor can I believe the way you're all gawking. Would you like me to get you a bib?"

But even Megan was intrigued, having no idea that Preston had a girlfriend. Seizing an opportunity to speak with him, after watching Marcella glide toward the ladies' lounge, she tried not to sound like she was prying.

"Hi, Meg," he said, kissing her on the forehead. "Good to see you again."

"Same here, Preston. I hope you had a nice flight."

"It was okay. Too long, though."

"That's for sure. I didn't know you were bringing a date to the reunion." *Oh great. That wasn't too blunt or anything.*

"Neither did I, until Mr. Parnell called and reminded me that I was welcome to do so."

"Right. So, have you known Marcella very long?"

Preston grinned at her, flashing those dimples again.

"*Megan*? Are you the reunion's designated social columnist?"

"Goodness, no. I'm sorry. I was just…interested. Please forgive me for getting personal."

"I'm teasing you. And Marcella is a friend of mine—a new resident at the hospital."

Wonderful. Doctor Marcella.

"How nice. Well, I know you two will have a wonderful time. Oops, I should get back to Phillip," she added quickly, spotting Marcella coming across the room. "I'll talk to you later, Preston."

Feeling a bit like a bag lady compared to the tall, leggy creature who also practiced medicine, Megan was embarrassed at her uncharacteristic insecurity. *What in the world has gotten into me?*

The following morning, she met her mother on the dining terrace for breakfast.

"How's the new house, Mom?"

"It's fabulous, dear. I can't wait for you to come up and see me. I haven't felt so content since—well, frankly, since before your father died."

Considering this was the first time Megan had heard her mother refer to Elliott since his death, she was more convinced than ever that a strange chemistry was at work here. But she decided to respond as if this were a perfectly normal dialogue, electing to press deeper into their caged emotions at another time.

"I can't tell you how happy that makes me, Mom. So, where's Lyle?"

"Lyle who?" Claudine answered, smiling over the top of her Bloody Mary. "Oh, *him*. He didn't match my new house."

Megan laughed, truly appreciating the light in her mother's eyes.

"Okay. Next question, Mom. What fun things on the agenda are you planning to experience today?"

"I signed up for the excursion to Buck Island. The fellows driving the boat are really adorable."

"I noticed," Megan replied, playfully shaking her head. "But you *do* realize that the trip lasts for six hours."

"I do, and it sounds marvelous."

"Are you also aware that it's a *snorkeling* trip?"

"Yes, dear. I saw the sign."

"Do you know *how* to snorkel?"

"No, but I hardly think that matters. The other people are perfectly welcome to jump off the side of a boat, in the middle of the Atlantic Ocean, to look at fish and whatever. But those two skippers said it would be all right for me to stay onboard and work on my tan, while I finish the great novel I'm reading. I thought that would be a lot more interesting than just sitting on the beach. Now, tell me what *you're* going to do."

"Justine and I are taking the girls shopping in Christiansted."

"How nice. I think I'll do that tomorrow."

"That's when I'm planning to take the Buck Island cruise with Kenny and the other fellows, so I'll be anxious to hear all about it when you get back today."

Reveling in the natural, normal dialogue, and in the agenda so totally free from sadness or loss, Megan and her mother stayed on the dining terrace until almost ten o'clock when Claudine had to leave for the Buck Island trip. The shopping van departed for Christiansted an hour later, and a remarkable equilibrium began settling over the family.

That night at the picnic, a semi-circle of umbrella tables was cordoned off from the other hotel guests by an array of tropical plants and trees in portable containers. The chairs had been arranged to face out toward the sea, on a secluded stretch of beach just beyond the cottages. On the landward side of the tables were a peach-colored canopy and a tent that housed the grills and steamers needed to prepare clams, oysters, softshell crabs, and the two-pound lobsters flown in from Maine. A variety pak, including a mix of salads, fresh vegetables and fruits, was available for each person in the picnic baskets lined up in the hotel lobby, all of which were claimed by 7:45. Mr. Parnell worried that he should have arranged for some sort of band or calypso ensemble, but as everyone gathered in the picnic area, there didn't seem to be a need for music, with the waves crashing over the sand dunes only a hundred feet away.

Although everyone was dragging a bit from their sun and rum punch-filled day, there was an affable synergy evident as they hovered together, delighting in the mess they were making with their lobster shells, all of them looking far more like rags than riches. Later, after the sweet sorbet had been served, they watched together as a spectacular cranberry sunset illuminate the bay. Sailboats and flags and ancient buildings became brilliant with color, then white, then bright, and finally dim to dark, as the sun slipped down past the far edge of the sea.

When the amazing show of nature was over, incandescent gas lanterns cast a glow across the picnic area, encouraging everyone to stay a little longer. Then a few diehards went back to the terrace lounge, where a band was playing and a crowd was dancing. But most members of the family were half asleep by then, and they gravitated to their cottages after saying their warm, unhurried good-nights. Kristin and Tania tried desperately to stay awake, savoring every second of this non-stop slumber party. But even they only lasted a few minutes. Next door to them, Phillip was in a deep sleep long before Megan climbed into bed. Lying beside him, as exhausted as she was, her eyes simply would not close.

I have to stop analyzing everything. This trip is a fabulous experience, and it's having an incredible affect on all of us. I just need to let myself relax. Right, Gram?

...These reunions will continue indefinitely, as long as you want them to happen, and as long as you follow my guidelines. I want you to see the world, on my nickel, as the saying goes. Think of me while you're there. Talk to each other. Confide in one another—and teach your children to do the same. Remember—in the end, it's all about family, because when the rest is stripped away, families are the only things that stick. Even when people are dead, you can't get rid of them. You'll see...

Megan was on the hotel dock at nine o'clock the next morning, for the departure of the Buck Island cruise, with her cousins and two dozen other resort guests. The fifty-seat trimaran arrived at the small island's blinding white beach two hours later, shortly before eleven. Everyone disembarked there for lunch and snorkeling practice along the shore, before the craft set sail again, this time destined for the underwater nature preserve. When the anchor was dropped forty-five minutes later, they were clearly out in the open sea, an unobstructed 360 degrees of water and horizon offering the only view.

Not realizing, until this point, what his brother had talked him into, William began expressing himself.

"If you assume, for one minute, that I'm going to jump off the side of this boat into the mouth of a shark, all of you people are nuts!"

"William, there aren't any sharks out here," Kenneth kidded. "This is a national park!"

"Show me a tree, and I'll show you a park," William responded, trying to sound calm. "Take a look around! We must be half way to England! I should have know better than to listen to someone who cleans clothes for a living."

The repartee continued, and by the time all five of his male cousins had ganged up on him, William decided he'd never hear the end of the tale, if he didn't jump in with them. Once he'd passed the panic point of actually entering the water, he genuinely enjoyed the experience, astonished at the complex paths, hills and ravines, all below the sea's surface, and all populated with the most stunning living creatures he could imagine. But when his tour group returned to the boat, after their maximum twenty minutes in the frigid water, he discovered that Megan had opted for her mother's plan, remaining dry and warm beneath her wide-brimmed hat and sipping on her third rum punch.

"What's the matter, Meg?" he asked, shaking his head of wet hair all over her. "Chicken?"

"Well, aren't *you* the brave one all of a sudden?" she teased.

"You're damn right I am," he announced, as his tour companions broke into a round of applause on his behalf. "And I was the *best*."

When all the swimmers had returned, the trimaran picked up speed and headed back to the resort. Megan remained in her cushioned corner with her book and her drink, loving the sea spray as it whipped over the railing onto her face. On the opposite side of the boat, she saw Kenneth and William huddled together with the McClinty boys, each of them taking turns saying things she couldn't hear. Then Kenneth began speaking, with William standing by his side, as DJ's and Teddy's sons listened closely. Megan studied their faces and tried to read their lips, hoping she knew what was being said. Mellowed by the scene and the sun, she closed her eyes and let herself be rocked to sleep by the vessel's undulating movement. She did not awaken until they docked, just after 3:30.

As the passengers filed across the gangplank and onto solid ground, she noticed that all of her men were quieter, no longer joking around. But they didn't appear to be upset, as they helped each other with their snorkeling gear and walked close to one another up the beach toward their cottages. Even though she was following right behind them, they seemed to have completely forgotten she was there. *Okay, Gram. So far, so good.*

Monday night's black tie banquet was the pièce de résistance and was held in the candlelit Seaside Room. The private dining hall was adjacent to the terrace and was framed by a columned loggia that opened to the sea. In contrast with the picnic two nights earlier, the McClinty family members and their guests arrived at this final reunion event looking like the glamorous, sunbathed jetsetters they now believed themselves to be. The men preened in crisply tailored tuxedos, while the women made one grand entrance after another in brilliant beaded gowns sewn from colorful imported fabrics. As Megan admired the collage of designer dresses, she found herself thinking about Vincente, a little smug in the knowledge of his sketches hidden away in Fox Run's attic. *Someday, I'm going to do something important with those, in honor of him.*

Meanwhile, she had a duty to perform at the opening of the banquet, as everyone stood around the sparkling tables, holding their champagne glasses.

"Mr. Anthony Parnell," she began, addressing the room with her back to the sea, "has done a superb job of organizing this inaugural event for us. No detail has been neglected, and despite his modesty, we have finally managed to corner him."

He was by her side, as she turned to look at him.

"I'm sorry, Mr. Parnell, but you've been giving Gram all the credit for this, and we've decided not to listen to you any more. This has been a full-time project for you, and we want you to know how grateful we are for your efforts," she continued, handing him a gift box containing a Waterford crystal decanter and four wine goblets.

"Megan, this is very thoughtful of you—*all* of you," he said sheepishly when the applause had subsided. "But this is my job, and I'll be doing the same thing twice each year, as long as you agree to continue. Believe me, your grandmother compensated me quite liberally for my efforts—in advance, of course," he added with a grin.

"Maybe so," she said. "But this is from *us*, not her. And we can be just as stubborn as she was. It runs in the family, you know."

Subsequently, the five-course meal, the vintage wines, the live music and the Caribbean breezes weaving through the dining hall transformed the elegant atmosphere into a long and joyful finale. Everyone gradually lost sight of how much champagne and liqueur had been consumed, as they reminisced about Margaret Stafford and the legends passed down about her. But the band kept on playing as the hours clicked by, and the musicians promised to stay until the last person fell over in exhaustion.

Shortly after 1:00 in the morning, Kristin, Tania and Justine surrendered and left for their respective cottages. Soon thereafter, Phillip kissed Megan on the cheek and announced that he, too, was finished. But Preston, Marcella, Claudine and a Latin gentleman friend she'd found on the beach somewhere could not be pried from the dance floor. Still seated at one of the tables, Kenneth and William were clustered again with David's other grandsons. Surveying the assorted groupings, Anthony Parnell leaned back in his jumbo rattan throne chair and sipped a cognac. He was, indeed, quite pleased with himself, and he raised his glass in a solitary salute to an industrious, invisible partner.

Megan watched DJ pat his wife Beth affectionately, as she departed for bed. He was trim and healthy, still handsome and looking so much like his father. He also appeared a decade younger than his sixty years. This was especially true at this late hour, with his formal, starched white shirt unbuttoned halfway down his chest and his black bow tie unfastened and sticking out of the pocket on the front of his tuxedo jacket. Standing outside on the breezeway, he stared into the darkness over the bay and seemed a little unsteady on his feet. Yet he continued to drink from a newly filled glass of wine, as Megan walked up beside him and tapped him on the shoulder.

"Feel like taking a stroll on the beach?"

"Sure, Meg," he said, working hard to focus on her. "You might have to carry me, though."

They laughed and headed cautiously down the steps of the terrace, guided and beckoned by the sound of the surf. Megan held a black satin shoe in each of her hands as she and David's son walked, in silence at first, on the cool, wet sand. Then, after he lit a cigarette, he abruptly began to speak.

"Well, Meg, I know about my father and your grandmother. Yup," he added, when she looked up at him in surprise. "My boys, and Teddy's, too, apparently heard the story from Ken and William yesterday, and they were kind enough to share the finer points with me while we were getting dressed for dinner tonight. Quite an appetizer, receiving confirmation that Greg was my brother—*half* brother, technically. I must admit that I've had my suspicions for quite some time, but none of the boys had a clue. Beth *still* doesn't know," he sighed, taking a deep drag on his cigarette.

"DJ, I..."

"Please, Meg. Since the subject's come up, I have a story of my own. This tropical air has been loosening my courage, and I'd like to get this out, before I sober up. You'll do me a great favor, if you'll just walk alongside me and listen."

"Okay," she whispered, tossing her shoes toward the dry dunes and hoping she'd remember them on the way back.

"The good news," he began, "is that my beautiful mother Lucille was long gone before her sons started getting killed—or killing *themselves*. The bad news is that I think, if she'd been here while Ryan and Teddy were growing up, we might still have one or both of them among us. She wouldn't have been happy about Teddy going over to see Greg in Hawaii—because she probably wouldn't have liked young Mr. Stafford any more than I did—but I'm not sure if she could have stopped Teddy from making the trip. I *do* think she could have kept Ryan from going off the deep end, though, and I don't mean *after* the accident. I mean way before, when he was a kid being influenced by—well, let's just call them people without the purest of hearts."

Megan had been walking and listening, almost afraid to breathe, for fear he would stop talking. *Where in the world is this coming from? Gram? Is that you?*

"At any rate," he went on, "I was the oldest, Ryan was the genius, and Teddy was the lovable baby, and that's pretty much the way we were categorized by everybody all of our lives. But even though Dad arranged for Mother's family to watch over us as much as possible after she died, no one paid a lot of attention to the special needs we each had *because* of our differences. Teddy and I turned out okay—I keep trying to convince myself—because the oldest child and the baby in a family are supposed to have built-in survival instincts. Teddy had a *little* problem with the fact that Mother died as a result of his birth, but he really handled it quite well. Ryan, on the other hand—well, you can't ignore genius, or else the same elements that create the brilliance can turn putrid. And that was certainly true with my brother!"

When he paused for a minute to finish the last drops of his wine, she worried that she was going to lose him and the rest of his story. So she took a chance and spoke.

"I'm so sorry about all of that, DJ. Hard as I try, I cannot imagine the toll taken on so many good people close to you. But I've always wondered. What exactly *did* happen to Ryan?"

This big, burly, gentle man, to whom she'd probably never said more than two dozen sentences in her entire life, now stopped and looked at her as if she were his best friend. Then he sat down on the sand and patted the ground beside him, asking her to join him.

"Ryan, as you probably know," he said, picking right up where her question left off, "was a gifted artist, whose talent began seeking out the dark side of life. His paintings seemed to follow his mood swings, and both became very depressing. He started lashing out physically, too. Even beat some kid up pretty badly at school. Eventually, Dad was persuaded to take him in for a checkup, and afterwards, the boy was on some sort of anxiety medicine, which he took every day, until the end…Anyway, please don't be offended at what I'm going to say next, but I'm convinced it's part of what happened to him. Through an odd series of circumstances, Ryan met your grandmother's sister, Maggie, who was practically old enough to be his mother. She was an artist, too, and unfortunately, she was the only one who could speak his language. While he was still young, he saw her fairly infrequently when she came to Albany to visit Cinnamon. Funny thing. She never stayed at Fox Run. She was always with *us,* in our house on Madison Avenue. I thought it was weird, since she was no relation to us whatsoever. Don't get me wrong. She seemed nice enough on the surface, and she was really good with kids. But her influence on Ryan, in my opinion, was never healthy. As I said, though, there wasn't anyone paying very much attention."

He paused again and pulled out a silver flask from his tuxedo jacket. Then he twisted off the lid and poured the dark contents into his wine glass.

"It's Merlot," he said, flashing a boyish smile. "I asked the bartender to fill this up for me when no one was looking. "Anyway," he continued, after taking a big swallow, "when Ryan graduated from high school, he started going to New York all the time to visit Maggie on his own. I really don't remember her coming to visit *us* any more after that, so my family wasn't in tune with what was going on with the two of them. But I guess they sort of became soul mates, painting together and sharing their deepest, darkest secrets, which ultimately proved fatal."

"Why?" Megan asked, fully immersed in his story and no longer afraid to ask questions. "What did they do?"

"They *talked*, Meg. I didn't know anything about it, until after Greg and Teddy were killed, and even then I didn't believe it. Ryan came to me really upset, looking like he hadn't slept for weeks. He said something was eating him up inside. Maggie had apparently come up with this idea that Dad and your grandmother had an affair, and that Greg wasn't really a Stafford, but a McClinty—our *brother*, in other words. Having just buried Teddy and Greg, I didn't think this was an appropriate conversation to be having, but Ryan insisted on it. He said that, in some sort of fit, Maggie had gone to visit Gregory Senior and told him about her suspicions, intending to cause some distress for her sister. Then, a few months later, of course, Greg and Teddy were dead. Ryan was convinced there was some connection, and that's when he came to me. But I kept telling him that the Army ruled the deaths accidental, caused by a freaky gas main explosion. He wouldn't listen, though, and I guess Maggie wouldn't either. They both had this notion that Maggie's conversation with Gregory had led directly to the disaster—and a month later, she overdosed on pills. Then, of course, the worst…" he said, his voice beginning to catch. "A few days after he heard about Maggie, Ryan drove himself into a tree. I'm not sure what tormented him more—the loss of his soul mate, or the possibility that she might have contributed to our brother Teddy's death."

DJ put his head down on his knees and began sobbing like a child. Megan wrapped her arms around him, until he stopped. Pulling a bar napkin from another jacket pocket, he wiped his face and took a deep breath.

"I'm sorry, Meg. That's been building up for thirty years."

"Please don't apologize. I'm just glad you could finally say it all, and that I could be here with you."

"Me, too."

"So, you're telling me that Gregory *knew* about Gram and your dad? And he also knew that Greg wasn't his son?"

"No. That's what Ryan told me he heard *Maggie* say. Believe me, that's a long way from being proof positive. Unfortunately, I think it *is* very possible, however, that two young and talented people gave up their lives for what was probably a product of their wild paranoia."

"But we know the part about Gram, your Dad and Greg *is* true."

"Right. But I can't believe Maggie put on a sweater and rode the bus or something all the way from her little downtown apartment up to the ritzy East Side of Manhattan, just so she could make this announcement to Gregory. It doesn't make any sense to me, and I tried so hard to help Ryan see that."

"Do you know if Ryan ever told his story about Maggie to anyone else? Or did *you*?"

"Well, *I* certainly did *not*. Are you kidding? But I couldn't say for sure about my brother. He really didn't have any friends, though, so I'm not sure who he would have been talking to. He also still lived in the Madison house with Dad. In fact, toward the end, about the only time he went out was for his medical appointments to have his prescriptions renewed. I think he was addicted to whatever drugs he was taking."

"Where did he have to go for *those* appointments?"

"Dr. Coomey's office. Why?"

She was totally silent.

"Meg?"

"Dr. Coomey," she whispered. "Oh my God!" *The letter in the strongbox, the birthmarks, the blood…*"DJ, I can't believe this!"

"Neither can I, Megan."

Rather than try to explain what she meant, she suggested that they head back and get some sleep.

"I might be wrong," she said, helping him get to his feet, "but I have a hunch it's almost time for breakfast."

Feeling unsteady, he put his arms around her and leaned on her for support.

"Thanks, Meg. I'm guessing this is all going to seem very silly in the morning, but you've allowed me get something off my chest that I've been carrying around way too long. Promise me, though, that this conversation will stay our secret."

"I promise. And believe it or not, you've been a big help to me, too."

They walked to the cottages holding hands, and then, without speaking another word, they disappeared behind their separate doors. Megan didn't discover until a number of days later that she'd forgotten to recover her black satin shoes from the beach.

The tanned and bleary-eyed McClinty's straggled into the terrace dining room a few hours later, while their luggage was being loaded in the back of the shuttle van, all of them feeling glum about this trip ending so soon. By the time they arrived at the airport, however, they were discussing potential dates and locations for the next reunion, the majority favoring a Swiss Ski Lodge during the month of February. With these new images in their heads, they boarded two ten-passenger mini-planes for Puerto Rico. In San Juan, everyone disbursed in different directions, still talking as they waved goodbye to each other. Margaret Elizabeth McClinty Mentini Stafford had, indeed, accomplished one of her key objectives. Her magic lived on without her.

Megan waited until the 747 bound for Atlanta was airborne before reaching across the center seat separating her from Phillip. Then she lightly touched his arm and smiled at him, with all the courage she could muster.

"Sweetheart, you're not going to like this, but I have to tell you something."

"Can't this wait until we get home?" he asked, leaning back against the headrest and squeezing his eyes shut.

"No, honey, it cannot. When we arrive in Atlanta, I'll be gathering my bags and catching the first available plane to Albany. It's time to put an end to Gram's project, and now I finally know what to do."

After Megan made her connection in Philadelphia and completed the last segment of her flight to Albany, the hour was nearly midnight. Barnes waited for her at the airport, as she'd requested when she telephoned from Atlanta. The next morning, she overslept, awakening shortly before nine o'clock to the enticing aromas of freshly brewed coffee and sausage on the grill. But there wasn't time to savor the beginning of this Fox Run day. Instead, she took a quick shower, pulled her hair into a ponytail, and dashed downstairs to the kitchen in her jeans and a tee-shirt.

"Good morning, Heidi. Sorry I don't have time to chat or eat right now," she clipped, pouring a large mug of coffee. "I'll catch up with you later." Then she hurried down the hall to the parlor, where she dialed the number she'd committed to memory on the plane.

"Dr. Maurice Coomey's exchange," announced the hollow voice.

"Hello. I'm trying to locate the doctor. Do you know if he's at his home? That's actually the number I dialed."

"Yes, ma'am. He has all of his calls forwarded here to his answering service. Is this an emergency?"

"Not exactly. But I do need to speak with him as soon as possible."

She requested that her message be marked *urgent* and then hung up, remaining curled in the corner of the sofa. Just as she was starting to fidget and consider what productive project she might undertake while she was waiting, the telephone rang.

"Megan, this is Dr. Coomey. My service paged me and said you called. What a surprise! I thought you'd still be down in the Caribbean."

Her quickening pulse and dry mouth were disconcerting, but she managed to hold her voice steady.

"No. We all flew home yesterday."

"Well, what in the world brought you back up *here* so soon?"

"*You* did."

"Me? I don't understand."

Any lingering compassion she might have felt for him was neutralized by her determination to get this done, and her words began to sound brittle.

"Would you have time to meet with me today? As soon as possible? I'd really prefer to address this with you in person."

"What's bothering you, Megan? Are you all right?"

"Dr. Coomey, please don't press me. I don't want to discuss this over the phone. The note of mystery is unintentional. I simply do not want to begin the conversation until we're together—until I can see your face."

His prolonged pause was telling, and when he spoke again, the timbre of his voice had changed.

"I see. Can you meet me at my old office at noon?"

"I'll be there."

She arrived early, and Dr. Coomey was late, making the cumulative wait seem interminable, as she sat on the upholstered bench across from the fourth floor elevator. His office door was locked, leaving her nowhere else to go until he arrived. He'd long ago ceased holding any regular hours, and Megan had no idea why he still rented space in this archaic building. She did admire him, though. After practicing medicine for over fifty years, he was still trying to maintain some sort of routine. *I really shouldn't be confronting him like this.* But then a contrary thought pushed forward from some alien, uncaring fragment of her mind. *No! You must finish this, regardless of what it takes.*

Shortly before twelve-thirty, the elevator door opened and the old man stepped out. She felt her resolve start to buckle at the sight of his weathered face and the sound of his shallow breathing, but she forced herself to continue.

"I apologize for keeping you waiting."

"No problem," she replied crisply, following him down the corridor and then standing behind him while he fumbled with the lock.

Inside the reception area, he switched on the lights and proceeded through another door into his private office, where he turned on his desk lamp and the air conditioning unit mounted in the window.

"Sorry it's a bit stuffy. I don't come here too often any more. Would you like some coffee? I could make us a small pot."

"Thank you, but there's no need to bother. Hopefully, I won't take up very much of your time."

He sat down behind his desk and motioned for her to use one of the decaying wingback chairs facing him.

"All right. What is it, Megan? Does this have something to do with your grandmother?"

"Yes, I think you know that."

"No, I'm not sure I do."

"Dr. Coomey, before Gram died, she spent many long hours recording her life story on tape, in my presence. She told me her most carefully guarded secrets, and, more importantly, her greatest fears, which she carried with her for the last thirty-five years of her life."

Her pulse quickened as she saw clear signs of understanding spreading over his face.

"In a letter she wrote to me the day before she left us, she asked me to bring closure to those fears by uncovering the real story behind Hawaii."

"Megan," he said, his voice beginning to break, "that was an *accident.* Everyone else seemed to understand that. But your grandmother became so obsessed for awhile that she lost her grip on…"

"*No*!" Megan was balanced on the edge of her chair, both of her hands pressed against the desk. "I am *sick* of listening to people talk about her like that! She might have been upset, and for good reason. But she didn't lose her grip on *anything*!"

The last traces of color were draining from the doctor's cheeks as she continued.

"I also need to tell you that, in addition to the tapes, I've been through her journals and papers. And you know better than most people how diligent she was about writing things down. She kept things that *others* wrote to her, too. One letter in particular was from *you*, Dr. Coomey. She locked it away inside a strongbox! That's how important it was to her. Do you know which one I'm talking about?"

"No, Megan, I don't. I can't think of…there's a…no, I…"

"*Yes*! Yes you do! You wrote everything down for her, so she could keep the information with her family records. Remember *now*? The one about Greg? The birthmark? The blood? You even delivered the letter to her in person. And you know what? That night she wrote about your visit in her journal. She was a little bit nervous about what you'd given her. Do you know *why* she was nervous, Dr. Coomey?"

"No, I don't. I *didn't*. She never said anything to me, and I really didn't understand what I'd walked into, until the day I…"

The last few threads of his composure dissolved. Huddled in his chair, he covered his face with his hands and wept. She didn't move, or speak, or offer him any consolation. She simply stared at him and braced herself for what was to come. At length, he removed a handkerchief from his pocket, using it to dry his cheeks and blot the perspiration from his forehead. Then he looked directly at her, with an expression that begged for understanding.

"I swear in front of God, Megan, that I did not realize the truth about Greg and David. I loved them all so much."

Fleeting memories of his old friends were pummeled by the resurrection of this nightmare, as his eyes began to lose their focus. He leaned forward and rested his elbows on the desk. Although his breathing was becoming more labored, he persisted, speaking in a low steady tone.

"All right. I'll tell you. Margaret was in New York, and Gregory took the train up to spend a few days at Fox Run while she was gone. Usually, it was the other way around—him in the City and her up here—but I didn't think anything about it, when he called me."

Their eyes met. *Oh, no*!

"He'd received the message I left for him at his Manhattan office. I'd tried to reach him when I didn't hear from him, after I gave my letter to Margaret. I was very worried about the donor records, convinced that the lab had made a mistake when he gave blood. Those records needed to be corrected. He was typed as AB when he came into the clinic, but that wasn't possible. Your grandmother was B, and there's no way Greg's type O could come from that combination. So I was certain someone at the lab had made an error. Gregory asked me to bring all the records to the estate, so he could review them and help straighten things out. That's what he said—*straighten things out*. But..."

He began weeping again, and this upsurge caused his voice to grow extraordinarily loud, as the strength behind his words overrode his irregular breathing. He was virtually shouting at her, and nothing could have stopped him from pushing forward into the entombed detail. Megan felt her heart beating in her temples, as she sat motionless, afraid to move.

"Gregory was sitting behind his desk in the library at Fox Run, and I was watching him turn the pages of my files. I remember telling him that I came prepared to draw another blood sample, for his convenience, so he wouldn't have to make a special trip anywhere. But after a few minutes, he just looked up at me and said that wouldn't be necessary. He told me there'd been no mistake—that he *was* type AB. And then he just sat there, staring at me. Right in front of me, his face turned to stone, and that's the moment I *knew*. The odd coincidence of the McClinty birthmark showing up on Greg, the blood, and a few other things about David and your grandmother that seemed strange to me over the years—they all came together, and I was horrified! But I was also frightened—frightened for Margaret, because the expression on Gregory's face was telling me this wasn't the first time he'd come across this information. He'd invited me out to Fox Run to *confirm* something he already knew! I was trying to think of something to say to him, when he very deliberately picked up the telephone and dialed the operator, never taking his eyes off me, making *sure* I knew what he was doing. He told the operator he wanted to make a long distance call—to *Hawaii*."

Megan was on her feet, leaning forward across the desk, her fingers clutching at the flat leather surface.

"*What*? Who did he call over there?"

"I don't know, Megan," the old man answered, cowering in the corner of his chair. "He just asked if the person was there and said *this is Mr. Stafford*. Then they must have put him on hold, and he sat looking right through me the whole time. After a minute, he asked me to go away. He said he wanted some privacy. I couldn't wait to get out of there, but as I was leaving, the person he was calling must have come on the line. Gregory seemed to know him, and I remember that he hesitated. I'll never forget that part, Megan. He *did hesitate*—and when I was closing the door, I saw him holding his head in his hands. Then...then he said..."

The physician's entire body was shaking as he looked up at Megan, his face twisting against the spasms brought on by the memories.

"*What* did Gregory say?" she shouted, crashing her hands down on top of the desk. "Goddamn it! Tell me what he *said*!"

More than three decades of torment poured out of the old man, in an excruciatingly powerful moment.

"He…he said *Greg's name*! He said *plans had changed*, and he said *he didn't want any mistakes this time*! His voice was shaking, and I couldn't bear to listen any more. I just closed the door and ran out of the house. Oh dear *God*," he cried, "a month later Greg was *dead*! And Teddy, too. I couldn't believe it…How could he…"

Megan felt as if she'd been hurled against the wall.

"…What he could not abide was deceit, even in small measures. Tucked away beneath his calm, distinguished manner was a short emotional trigger, which was rarely fired but could be guaranteed if someone lied to him…Thus, while people in and around Broome Street expressed outward appreciation for Gregory's friendly manner, they were daunted by the wide reach of his influence and the associated power that enabled him to mete out such extreme penalties…"

"…the changes didn't start showing up in her until after the big blowout argument…between Aunt Cinnamon and Uncle Gregory after the funeral service. They were right here in this library that night, with the door closed…years have mixed up the chronology for a lot of people, but your grandmother was just fine until that moment…"

"…It wasn't fair! When I told him, though, I was just being mean. Yes—I TOLD HIM. Are you satisfied? But I never imagined that he could do something like this. I only wanted to get you in trouble—not to really hurt anybody…"

"…Ryan was convinced there was some connection, and that's when he came to me. But I kept telling him that the Army ruled the deaths accidental—caused by a freaky gas main explosion. He wouldn't listen…and then…a few days later…Ryan drove himself into a tree."

Gram's husband had her son killed? Megan was blinded by the thought. All she could see was Cinnamon's body locked away in her bedroom, trying to deny—or escape—this hell. *She did know! But she died hoping to be proven wrong!*

Dazed and sickened, Megan ran from Dr. Coomey's office, along the corridor, past the elevator and down the three flights of stairs.

"Megan, wait! Please wait!" he cried after her. Then he picked up the telephone and slowly dialed 911.

Megan found a pay phone in the lobby and frenetically ordered the operator to charge the call to her credit card. Within a few moments, someone said, "Dr. Preston McClinty's exchange."

"Please! This is an emergency! I need to speak with Preston...Dr. McClinty!"

"I'm sorry, ma'am, but Dr. McClinty is out of town. Several of his associates are handling his..."

"*No*! He should be home by now! You have to find him! This is Megan. Tell him...tell him that *I know*. And tell him..."

She dropped the receiver and left it dangling. Somehow, she found her way to the car Barnes had rented for her and proceeded to drive erratically through the city, miraculously avoiding the State Patrol. Speeding back to Fox Run, she ran up to the attic, brought the strongbox back down to Cinnamon's room and dropped it on the floor. Then she went to the jewelry box on the dresser, removed the chain with the jailer's key and unlatched the padlock. After pulling Vincente's designs out of the strongbox and tossing them on the bed, she grabbed Dr. Coomey's letter, scrambled down the stairs and out the front door, running around the side of the house to the cottage. Startled by the ruckus, Heidi came through the kitchen's swinging door into the foyer, just in time to see Megan dashing down the porch steps.

Inside the cottage, she threw open the closet door in the study and dragged out the box of journals and the tin of letters, dropping the Coomey letter into the box. The she pulled the box and tin onto the front stoop of the cottage and ran to find Barnes.

"Don't ask me any questions! Just go down to the hardware store and buy a large steel trash can."

"Okay, Miss Megan. But why? Are you all right?"

"I *said* no questions!"

"Yes, ma'am."

"If you must know, Barnes, we're going to have a fire! A *big fire*!

Overhearing the commotion and Megan's frightening words, Heidi looked through the parlor window as Barnes was driving away. When she saw Megan running back to the cottage, the housekeeper started to panic. Picking up the phone on the table beside her, she dialed Kenneth's home number, which she knew by heart. But no one answered, and when she tried his office, the lady said he was still in the Caribbean with his family.

"Oh, dear," Heidi said in a whimper, standing in the parlor by herself. "What am I supposed to do now?"

Back in the cottage, Megan's face had taken on a crazed look as she paced from room to room, and then in a circle around the small dining table.

"God took my son and crushed my soul, then asked me to be strong and go forward. This I was prepared to do. But there is no possible way for me to bear the vile stench that spews forth from the man I call my husband. Life, for all meaningful purposes, has now come to an end. Come il diavolo è entrato nella mia casa? How did the devil get into my house?"

Heidi responded to an urgent knocking on the front door thirty minutes later.

"Dr. McClinty, sir! I can't believe it! I've been trying to find someone to help me, and, may the saints and angels be praised, here you are!"

Preston walked around her and into the front hall.

"I've been at my father's house since last night. My exchange called me a little while ago and said that some hysterical woman named Megan left a completely incoherent message this morning. Is she *here*?"

"Yes, sir. That's what I mean. Miss Megan came home about an hour ago, and she's been acting like a crazy person."

"Where is she now?" he asked, squeezing the tops of Heidi's arms.

"I saw her go inside the big barn a few minutes ago. I don't know why…"

Without another word, Preston bolted through the front door and hurdled the porch railing.

Life, for all meaningful purposes, has now come to an end. Come il diavolo è entrato nella mia casa? How did the devil get into my house?…Come il diavolo è entrato nella mia casa?…Come il diavolo è entrato nella mia casa?

Brilliant sunlight suddenly cascaded along the timbers as the enormous door screeched open. Through her blurred vision, the outline of his face was unsettling. He looked…different. And now…*No*! He was prying her arms away from his neck, struggling against her, pushing her away from him, throwing her to the ground, holding her down and pressing her wrists against the rough surface of the floor.

"*No*!" she screamed again, the sound crashing and reverberating inside her head. "I have to tell you! Let me *tell* you, David! It was Gregory! He killed our son!"

Without any warning, something slammed against the side of her face, and the light went out.

The afternoon shift had just finished changing at the Albany Medical Center, as Phillip and Preston sat quietly in the cafeteria. There'd been little sleep for either of them since the previous day. After securing Megan's emergency admittance more than twelve hours earlier, Preston had remained in the hospital complex while waiting for Phillip to arrive. Concurrently, Phillip traveled throughout the night, on a circuitous series of connections from Atlanta, before landing in Albany late that morning. Both men had lost count of how much coffee they'd consumed.

"I'm really sorry, Phillip. I swear to you that striking her was a last resort, and I feel awful about it. But she was completely crazy, and I couldn't restrain her. Trying to subdue that puny little body of hers was like putting your arms around an exploding bomb. I can't believe how strong she is."

"You don't need to explain, Preston. I'm just thankful you were there. Her face is a little red, in more ways than one. But if that's the worst of it, I'll consider us lucky."

They smiled weakly at each other and sipped mindlessly from their Styrofoam cups.

"What do you think caused this?"

"I wish I had an answer, Phillip. Maybe an emotional buildup from the last couple of months. I just don't know. The tests I ordered have largely been inconclusive, and frankly, I don't expect to find anything noteworthy in the rest of the results. I'd like to believe that whatever pushed her over the edge is dead and buried—history."

"Yes, let's hope that's true. But did she *say* anything that might help us understand?"

Preston finished his coffee and stood up.

"I don't think so. Besides, does it really matter? It's *over*. Right?"

The two men looked knowingly at each other and shook hands. Then Angela's son left for the airport. *He's not such a bad guy after all*, Phillip thought, as he rode the elevator up to the sixth floor. Megan was propped up in bed in her private room, finishing the last few bites of her lunch, when he entered. She smiled, her eyes bright and clear, her face rested and happy, except for the red welt along her left cheek.

"Preston's gone, and he sends his love, again. How are you feeling?"

"Like I could eat fiberglass. Actually, I'm not sure this *isn't* fiberglass. So, does he think I should be carted off to a padded cell or something?"

"No. He suggests we forego the padding. Seriously, we're officially chalking this up to fatigue, even though a few us know that you actually *are* bonkers."

"Kenny's probably in *that* group. He phoned while you were downstairs, and apparently, he and Justine have been getting calls from all sorts of folks, who've been inquiring about my forthcoming commitment. How on earth did word spread so fast? Anyway, he claims he's worried about me and said he'll come to visit later."

"Are you going to tell him what happened?"

"No! I'm not telling anyone anything, *ever again*. When Dr. Coomey was here last night, I finally felt all the doors close. That poor man! After he managed to live all these years carrying that stuff around with him, *I* could have given him a heart attack. I never would have been able to forgive myself."

"As it turned out, honey, his condition wasn't that bad. I spoke with one of the paramedics who treated him, and they said his hyperventilating really scared him. The more frightened he became, the harder it was for him to breathe. But they assured me he'll be just fine."

"He'll probably end up outliving *me*," she said. "And that would be okay. He's earned it. Oh, speaking of earning things, I called Curtis and suggested that the company might be better off without me right now. He agreed," she added with a laugh, "but gave me the option of trying to do some of my work from home for awhile. Guess I must have earned a few brownie points over the last fifteen years that I didn't know about. Anyway, he was surprisingly sensitive, and told me to take the rest of the week off."

They both chuckled, since it was Friday. Then they talked together about normal, simple things—about Kristin spending the next few days with the neighbor, about Buck needing to go to the vet. Phillip also mentioned that he'd put the cash from Cinnamon's dress shop in their safe deposit box, until Megan decided what she wanted to do with it. This was a relief to her, because she hadn't been able to remember where she'd last left the money, and she was afraid to tell him. She *did* remember tossing Vincente's designs on the bed, however, and asked Phillip to put them someplace safe when he got back to the estate later that night.

As the next hour passed, he could see that his wife was stabilizing, and he was reassured by her objective observations about what had happened to her. He was also relieved to hear her talking rationally about the slow steps she'd need to take as she moved forward. That was the most important thing to him—seeing her rational again. *Now is probably the appropriate time*, he thought, feeling the paper through his jacket pocket, *while she's already working on closure—and while she's still in the hospital.*

"Your grandmother would be very proud of you, Megan."

"You think so? Because I'm as loopy as she was?"

"No. Because you didn't let her down."

"Yeah. But look where it got me. Talk about overdoing things! By the way, sweetheart, thanks for hanging in there with me. I know I've been a mess."

"Yes, you have. But it's all over now—all except one more little thing."

"Excuse me?" she asked anxiously.

"Don't worry, honey. This is a *good* thing," he said, removing the envelope from his jacket. "This came to my office, via certified mail, on the day your grandmother's will was read up here last July."

Seeing her body stiffen, he took her hand.

"Relax. I read it first, and believe me, I wouldn't give it to you if I thought it would cause more problems."

Slowly taking the letter from him, she slipped on her reading glasses and leaned her head back against the pillows.

July 13, 1988

Dear Phillip—

Please put this in a drawer or something, until everything is over. Then give it to Megan. You will know when the right time has come. Thank you.

By the way, I realize that you and I never became the closest of friends after you married my granddaughter. But I'm grateful for the way you have loved her—and I've been meaning to tell you that I think you're a very nice boy.

M.E.M.S.

Megan looked up at her husband. She could see how pleased this note had made him, and she squeezed his hand before moving on to the second page.

July 11, 1988

My dearest Megan—

You are the sum of those who've lived before you, the women and the men, the good and the bad (not always categorized in that relative sequence, but usually). Your unique sense of self is purely "Megan," though, and I'm very proud of what you've accomplished—of the woman, wife and mother that you've become.

But in order for you to fully appreciate what breathes inside of you, and in order to make the best use of the gifts you've been given, you must grow to understand the minds, hearts and souls of those who came first, knowing them to the point where you can almost hear their voices. As I close my eyes in readiness for the long night ahead, I hope I've been able to give you that sense of intimacy. When you revisit the stories I've told you, maybe you'll recognize the pieces of you that were passed on from all of us.

Please take your new discoveries and continue building a rich and happy life with your wonderful little family. One day, before too long, your very own grandchildren will be added to that life. They will be immeasurably blessed to have you as their grandmother, and I will rest peacefully in the knowledge that you now understand what to do with that awesome responsibility.

I love you, Megan.

Always,
Gram

Phillip was watching her closely, looking for signs of distress. But her eyes were clear and dry. She did feel a slight tug at her heart, but nothing that would threaten the contentment and sense of resolution flowing through her body.

"Honey," she said, taking his hand again, "in the midst of everything, I think I left all of Gram's journals and letters in a big box on the cottage porch. Do you know what happened to them?"

"Yeah, I do. Preston said that Barnes…"

No!

"…carried everything up to the attic in the main house."

"Oh. Well, that was nice. I suppose that's as good a place as any, at least for the time being."

EPILOGUE

November 14, 1988

The Army lieutenant in charge of the archive transfer section at Hawaii's Schofield Barracks wandered lethargically through the heat in the cavernous storage area. This routine operation had been underway for two weeks, and, in the process, he and his men had purged thousands of aging documents from hundreds of dust-laden filing cabinets. Procedures required that all of the folders marked "classified" be examined individually, in case there were portions that needed to be removed and saved prior to shredding. These judgment calls were the lieutenant's, and a small stack of such discoveries awaited his review on his desk. But he felt no great sense of urgency. One more week had been allocated for the storage center to be fully emptied, so there was plenty of time.

A corporal assigned to the archive detail approached the lieutenant from the opposite side of the building. The enlisted man carried a large envelope in one hand.

"Sir! Excuse me, sir. Here's another one."

The officer accepted the envelope, which had been repeatedly stamped in red ink with the word **CLASSIFIED** on both the front and back sides.

"How's everything going over there, Corporal?"

"Steady, sir. Slow, but steady."

"Well, you're doing a fine job, and I appreciate your enthusiasm. There's a slim chance that this assignment won't appear on any Army Recruitment Poster in the near future."

"Yes, sir. Thank you, sir," the enlisted man replied, not sure if he was expected to smile in response.

As the corporal walked away, the lieutenant slipped the envelope under his arm, lit a cigarette and ambled across the warehouse floor toward the massive thirty-foot wall of windows facing the sea. Looking out through the grimy glass panes, his thoughts turned to visions of combat and patriotic heroism—scenes he now mournfully believed would never include him. Peacetime brought many blessings, and he was thankful for all of them. But the soul of a soldier longs for battle, and somehow, cleaning out filing cabinets in a building slated for demolition left the lieutenant's soul notably unfulfilled.

Turning his back to the huge windows, he leaned against the sill and removed the envelope from under his arm.

"I might as well pass judgment on this one while I'm standing here," he mumbled, not yet ready to return to the stifling confines of his office.

Carefully sliding his thumb beneath the envelope's seal, he lifted the flap and pulled nearly fifty pages of bound data out into the light. On top was the summary memo.

MEMORANDUM

September 8, 1953

TO: **Colonel Randolph Nather**
United States Army
Divisional Headquarters

FROM: **Captain Charles Lindenthol**
United States Army
Criminal Investigation Detachment (CID)

SUBJECT: **Final Report:** **Deaths of Private Gregory Stafford, Jr., and**
Theodore McClinty (civilian),
Honolulu, Hawaii—May 20, 1953

We have determined from our undercover contacts within the Honolulu Police Department that Private Stafford was involved with illegal activities, working as a liaison for members of the Li Sao crime organization. Private Stafford was indebted to this criminal enterprise in the approximate amount of $35,000, due to losses he incurred at the Waikiki Palms Club during his furloughs in October and December of 1952, as well as in January 1953.

His unlawful undertakings classified him as a security risk, but his arrest was postponed in cooperation with the HPD, while they were using him as a shill. Their target was the commanding tier of Li Sao. The MP had also been asked to delay taking Private Stafford into custody, until conversations with Stafford's father could be resolved. The senior Mr. Stafford, a wealthy New York businessman, was attempting to intervene and had contacted his senator in an effort to negotiate leniency. There was also some effort in process to make restitution for the debt Private Stafford had incurred.

On May 20, 1953, however, through an improbable accident, a gas main exploded outside the Waikiki Palms, as Private Stafford was leaving the club. Stafford was killed instantly. Theodore McClinty, Stafford's cousin, was also killed. Internal Affairs has concluded that McClinty, a civilian, was innocent of any wrongdoing and was instead an unfortunate victim of circumstance.

In summary, the United States Army and the Honolulu Police Department hereby rule that the incident was a verifiable accident, with no association whatsoever to Private Stafford's illicit dealings, or to his father's stateside attempts to help his son.

THIS CASE IS NOW OFFICIALLY CLOSED.

The lieutenant impassively re-read the memorandum, as he finished his cigarette. He'd seen hundreds of dossiers similar to this one—some worse, some not quite so bad—and he was unmoved by such cavalier approaches to life, death and duty. He revered soldiers who died honorably, while defending their freedom. But men like Private Stafford were killed as a consequence of dishonorable deeds. Regardless of what the report said, the soldier was not where he should have been, and the lieutenant had little sympathy for deaths occurring as a result of stupidity. He did feel some compassion for the McClinty victim. But collateral damage was inevitable in any conflict.

"Well," he said, thinking out loud, "at least this case kept a few people busy for awhile. And the families were notified of the general resolution, I presume."

He could not locate verification in the file that a copy of Captain Lindenthol's official summary had been forwarded to New York. But after double-checking the attached documentation, he saw that there hadn't been any inquiries or correspondence from the family for more than thirty years.

"Anyone who might have wanted this detail," he added, still speaking to himself, "is certainly long gone by now."

Turning again to look out the massive windows facing the sea, his mind began drifting toward thoughts of his next leave and to fantasies about where his next assignment might take him. After a few minutes, he pressed his spent cigarette into a foil ashtray on the window sill and walked to his office on the opposite side of the warehouse. Pouring himself a cup of lukewarm coffee the same color as tar, he sat down at his desk and opened the folder again. Sipping the coffee slowly to anesthetize his taste buds, he gradually began inserting the entire report, page by page, into the shredder beside his credenza.

Ordinary. Such is the baseline of all human life—the place where everyone starts. Accidents of birth bring an infant into the merits and shortcomings of a family, or group, or town. Genetic contributions and twists provide individual ingredients and complications. From that point on, however, each person moves under his or her own power, back and forth, above and below the baseline of ordinary, eventually arriving at a mark on someone's statistical graph. That mark coldly represents the value of a person's entire existence, and the final position is what gets all the attention. But a person's ending doesn't always correlate with where he or she has been. A life that began as ordinary might have circulated through times of grandeur, or poverty, or perhaps a respectable, unremarkable point in between. The only thing we know for sure about endings is that a unique story lies behind every journey just completed—and there's certainly nothing ***ordinary*** *about that!*